Sexton Blake Wins

JACK ADRIAN wrote his first book, a Sexton Blake thriller, in his early twenties. After seven years on the editorial side of IPC Magazines, he went freelance in 1975. He has written comic strip scripts, science fiction, and war, horror and mystery stories under a variety of pseudonyms and is an authority on twentieth-century popular and genre fiction. He is the editor of *'Sapper': The Best Short Stories, Edgar Wallace: 'The Sooper' and Others* and has written introductions for Leslie Charteris's *The Saint in New York*, and Edgar Wallace's *The Four Just Men* (all published by J.M. Dent).

D0321317

SEXTON BLAKE WINS

Selected and introduced by
Jack Adrian

J.M. Dent & Sons Ltd
London   Melbourne

This selection first published in Great Britain by
J.M. Dent & Sons Ltd, 1986
Selection, Introduction and Select Bibliography ©Jack Adrian, 1986
Text ©IPC Magazines Ltd, 1986

This book is set 10/11½ in Plantin by PRG Graphics, Redhill
Printed in Great Britain by Cox & Wyman Ltd, Reading
for J. M. Dent & Sons Ltd
Aldine House, 33 Welbeck Street, London W1M 8LX

British Library Cataloguing in Publication Data

Sexton Blake wins. — (Classic thrillers)
 1. Detective and mystery stories, English
 I. Adrian, Jack II. Series
 823′.0872 [FS]   PR1309.D4

 ISBN 0–460–02482–5

CONTENTS

INTRODUCTION

Jack Adrian

Over the years Sexton Blake has had a bad critical press: 'the office-boy's Sherlock Holmes', 'Holmes on the cheap', 'the sleuth of the second-rate', you name it. Certainly he made his debut hard on the heels of Holmes' much publicised dive (or non-dive) over the Reichenbach Falls, as did scores of detectives hurriedly concocted to appease an avid market. It is also true that later he somewhat provocatively took up residence in Baker Street and then had a less than subtle nose-, brows-, chin- and hairline-job which transformed him into a far more striking Holmes, pictorially, than Holmes himself. But there the similarity ends. In sheer longevity Blake wins hands down, having outlasted Holmes by upwards of forty years, and in feats of physical prowess there is really no comparison. While Sherlock pondered, Sexton rolled up his sleeves.

Holmes was of course no stranger to the fistic or defensive arts (he'd boxed at college and had even mastered 'baritsu' before it had been invented), but his adventures were on the whole physically undemanding. During the course of an investigation rarely was it the case, for instance, that a skilfully wielded blackjack caused a Stygian pit of black unconsciousness to rear up and engulf him till he knew no more. Blake on the other hand, in case after case, went through the mill. He was slugged, clubbed, chloroformed, gassed, knifed, dynamited, run down, gunned down, injected with poison, ejected from planes, hurled over cliffs, pushed in front of trains, almost devoured by man-eating plants, virtually sucked dry of his 'life essence', nearly shot to the Moon in a rocket—and the number of times the floor suddenly dropped from beneath him must run into four figures.

Holmes may have careered around London and the Home Counties, and on the odd occasion somewhat further afield. But did he ever tramp through Papua New Guinea pursued by head-hungry cannibals? How many times was he stuck in the skin-blistering heat of the Gobi Desert with a bullet-holed water bottle and no help within a ten-day march? When was the last occasion he slugged it out with a crazed, sabre-wielding aristo atop a plunging Alpine cable-car with a thousand feet of nothing below and the cables fraying? And while it's all very fine to trail along behind Holmes on one of his brilliant ratiocinatory treks through a complex maze of deceit and chicanery, where's the fun in ending up feeling like that blockhead Watson every time? Where's the fun in having to put up with, even at second hand, all those bouts of bad temper, arrogance, downright rudeness?

My preferences in this matter of Blake v. Holmes must by now be clear to the most purblind. But then I'm biased. Perhaps it's time for a declaration of interest. Or possibly a confession. I wrote a Sexton Blake. I was paid half the going rate because the story had to be 'cleaned up and cut down by half', although when it finally appeared in the bookshops, under a house-name that seemed more suited to an undertaker or a bent solicitor, not a word had been changed, not a comma snipped. As an experience to put steel into the beginner-writer's soul, it is to be recommended. Even so, the sum I got, to one not too long out of blazer and straw boater, was staggering. And it was gratifying to have become a member of a fairly exclusive and slightly raffish club that had opened its doors in the November of 1893, when a 41-year old Scot living in Peckham Rye wrote a 20,000-word detective story entitled 'The Missing Millionaire' for a new weekly paper called the *Halfpenny Marvel*. The Scot was Harry Blyth and he called the hero of his tale Frank Blake. By the second week in December, when the story was published, Blyth had become Hal Meredith, his detective—by someone's happy inspiration—Sexton Blake.

The *Halfpenny Marvel*, along with *Chips*, *Comic Cuts*, the *Halfpenny Wonder* and the adult weekly *Answers* (launched as a direct challenge to George Newnes' hugely successful *Tit-Bits*), was the solid bedrock upon which that Fleet Street tyrant and eccentric genius Alfred Harmsworth (later Lord Northcliffe) built an empire dedicated to popular journalism and lowbrow fiction, the Amalgamated Press. (The AP later took in the *Daily Mail*, the *Times*, women's weeklies and monthlies, children's comics and story-papers, trade journals, fiction magazines, shop-girl romances, knitting-pattern weeklies and tales for tiny tots.)

Unlike the Fleet Street and Salisbury Square entrepreneurs of an earlier age (the penny-dreadful merchants), who went out of their way to smother their fiction-factory origins once wealth and respectability had been achieved, Harmsworth was no snob and could get very tetchy with the upper echelons of the AP who sneered at the monthly libraries and weekly story-papers that poured from the firm's Farringdon Street premises. Harmsworth became a power in the land through the *Daily Mail*, but his personal fortune and the key to that power was due in no small part to the millions of pennies and halfpennies plunked down on newsagents' counters every week for the story-papers and comics he'd launched at the start of his career. (In the mid-1890s *Comic Cuts* alone was said to have a weekly readership of two and a half million.)

Harmsworth was no sentimentalist, however. For the majority of his contributors there was none of that royalties nonsense. He paid, in 1893, nine guineas for 'The Missing Millionaire' and on accepting the cheque Harry Blyth effectively signed away all rights to the story, the name, the character. Not even the far-sighted Alfred Harmsworth guessed that it was one of the bargains of the decade.

Blyth's Blake stories (he only wrote about half a dozen before other pens took over) are virtually unreadable today and were unusual then only in that Blake tended to solve his cases by dashing around on a bicycle. Yet during the Golden Age of the 1920s and 1930s, when his adventures appeared weekly in the *Union Jack*, monthly in the *Sexton Blake Library*, on the screen in both silent films and talkies, on the radio and on stage, Blake became quite literally a household name. And perhaps it was the name that saved him from oblivion: that 'Sexton' really was a stroke of genius on someone's part.* Even so, he could still have faded out like all the rest. Stories about him surfaced from time to time in different AP papers written by a variety of AP hacks: all more or less forgettable, the character characterless. For a couple of years in the early-1900s he didn't surface at all. It was left to a bright and bustling young AP editor, W.H. Back, to recognise that there was potential in that name, if nothing else.

* Oddly enough, Conan Doyle too had had second thoughts. For Holmes' Christian name he'd originally doodled 'Sherrinford'.

Back, casting around in 1904 for a series-character he could run in the *Union Jack* as a regular feature every fortnight, pulled Blake out of cold storage and proceeded to inject blood into his veins. He called in the better writers of the day and demanded from them strong plots, vivid backgrounds, character-development and -continuity; above all, readability. Back cheekily installed Blake in Baker Street then gave him as an assistant, instead of a dough-witted plodder, the sparky street Arab Tinker; a plump and talkative housekeeper, Mrs Bardell (a source of rich comedy in the hands of later writers); and the sagacious bloodhound Pedro. For good measure a souped-up Rolls was substituted for the bicycle.

Back had started as he meant to go on. A new century meant new ideas, a fresh approach, a sweeping-away of fusty old values and the snail's-pace of Victorian life in favour of the marvels of the new technology: electric lights, instant communication, rapid transportation. While other sleuths were still ordering their mushers to 'follow that hansom!'—and Conan Doyle (in 1905) was refusing point-blank to have Holmes chase villains on a motor cycle, even though he was using one himself—Blake was ploughing through road-blocks at 20 mph, and taking to the air long before Bleriot juddered across the Channel.

The results were more than satisfactory. Within a year the *Union Jack* was entirely devoted to his exploits and its circulation was climbing. Success bred success. Other AP papers began to feature him in long serials, including one that ran for over a year and chronicled his school and Varsity days: a sure sign a character had made it. Specially-written 80,000-word novels, as well as serial reprints, were published in the *Boys' Friend Library* at regular intervals. Two adult weeklies, *Answers* and the *Penny Pictorial*, both ran a series of short stories featuring his 'early' cases (that is, before Tinker arrived on the scene). From 1907 Sexton Blake plays, mostly adapted from *UJ* stories by that tireless melodramatist John M. East, went on tour in the provinces; Russell Boque's *Sexton Blake on the East Coast*, a spy drama, was a hit in the London suburbs in the latter part of the First War. From 1914 to 1919 at least eight silent films were made, of which two, *The Clue of the Wax Vesta* and *The Mystery of the Diamond Belt*, had a great success.

Willie Back later became an Editorial Director at the AP but never lost his affection for the character he'd re-created. In the middle of the First War—at a time when the idea was thought half-witted—he launched the *Sexton Blake Library*. At first this was a 3*d* paperback, one issue a month. In less than a year the *SBL* became two issues a month, proving that Back had all his wits about him. In 1919 the number of monthly issues was raised for four at 4*d* each and, apart from a heady period in 1922 when it became five issues, stayed that way for over twenty years. At the same time the *Union Jack* (later transformed into the *Detective Weekly*) was reaching a readership of well over half a million a week.

Blake was remarkably lucky with his editors. During the 1920s and 1930s, his Golden Age, he owed most of his immense popularity to just two men, Leonard Pratt and Harold Twyman.

Pratt, who became editor of the *SBL* in 1921, was the archetypal company man, from tea-boy through sub to chief sub and then editor. He was not a great editor, but then he didn't need to be. Once the *SBL* had achieved a certain momentum—and a certain style, a recognisable format and presentation—he demanded only that his writers deliver the goods. He had four 60,000-word thrillers to send to the printers every month and it didn't much matter to him whether what his writers delivered was lacklustre hackwork or high-profile prose that was cunningly plotted and grippingly written—just as long as the stuff flowed in. Masterpieces will always appear (as they did; fairly frequently from certain writers), but you can't muck about waiting for them when the printers have a machine idle. This businesslike attitude is one of the chief attributes of the good pulp editor. Quantity is what matters; quality can look after itself.

Pratt's major contribution to the Blake saga was that he recognised, very early on (indeed, long before the majority of mainstream publishers and editors: but then pulp fiction is often ahead of the game), that it was the highly distinctive Edgar Wallace brand of mystery and detective fiction—not so much deduction as thrill upon thrill and a startling denouement—that would have a profound influence on cheap fiction for a long time to come, rather than the stodgy effusions of William le Queux, say, or even the slicker, more glamorised High Society thrillers of E. Phillips Oppenheim. Accordingly he prodded his own writers into developing the peculiarly Wallacean world of mysterious cowled figures sporting long-barrelled Browning automatics and ruined abbeys with secret super-science labs beneath (in short, sheer old-fashioned melodrama but with a hi-tech gloss), as well as breathless action and the-villain-as-least-likely-suspect into the Blake mythos. The *SBL* thrived.

If Pratt was a workaday editor with one great idea—an idea he later (1929) took to its logical conclusion when he created the *Thriller*, a weekly non-Blake paper that was wholly Wallacean in character—Harold Twyman, who took over the *Union Jack* also in 1921, was a great editor with ideas galore. Younger than Pratt by a decade or more, he was a genuine innovator who edited with dash and flair, a feverishly energetic creator in feverish and exciting times. Planes were crossing the Atlantic, trains seemed continually to be cracking speed records; archaeologists were digging up the astonishing past; scientists were creating an even more breath-taking future; wireless had destroyed distance, bringing far-off great events literally into the suburban living-room at the twist of a dial. All was reflected in the weekly *UJ*.

Twyman forced his writers to snatch their plots from the here-and-now. Was there an earthquake in Japan? Within days a 25,000-word yarn featuring it would be on his desk, within weeks on newsagents' counters. The Motor Show? Plans for a revolution-ary new fuel would inevitably disappear and readers would learn of it the week it 'happened'. A total eclipse of the sun in the offing? Perfect setting for a story about a loony cult led by an arch con-man, with an impossible murder for good measure. That last, incidentally, may well be the very first time (1927) infra-red was used as an aid to murder. It was certainly not the last time, especially during Twyman's reign, that scientific breakthroughs were plundered for the benefit of the increasingly sophisticated Blake readership.

The *UJ* was a terrific paper. It was busy, lively, bang up to the minute, constantly changing and improving. Twyman beefed up Blake's character and kept circulation rising with high-prize com-petitions, with the *UJ* 'Detective Supplement', which treated all aspects of criminology in a readable though largely unsensational manner, and then with a middle-page spread called 'Tinker's Notebook', a colourful mix of true crime and police court gossip mainly written by Peter Cheyney. It was Twyman who, more than any other writer or editor connected with the saga, created the Blake of the Golden Age: the lean, limber manhunter, by turns implacable and compassionate, by no means humourless, capable at one moment of lightning-fast and ferocious action, the next displays of dazzling deductive pyrotechnics. It was Twyman, too, who sorted out the Blake image by talent-spotting a young artist, Eric Parker, in the early-1920s, whose Blake (tall, spare, high-browed, lantern-jawed, with the eyes of a hawk, the profile of an eagle) so triumphantly out-Holmesed Holmes that Parker grew old with the character, contributing in the end hundreds of *UJ* covers and illustrations as well as nearly 900 *SBL* covers over a quarter of a century.

The culmination of Twyman's reign was the *Detective Weekly* ('Starring Sexton Blake') which, launched in 1933, deliberately targeted not only the vast juvenile audience but those adults who took the *Thriller* and such general interest papers as *Tit-Bits, Answers, Ideas, Pearson's Weekly*. In fact, an adult readership had been aimed at as far back as the late-1900s. It's significant that Tinker, who began life as a larky urchin, swiftly became a tough and wise-cracking 20-or-so who could drive a car, pilot a plane, pull an automatic and fire it with as much flair as Blake himself. Certainly from the time of the First War a far higher proportion of adults bought and read the *UJ* and *SBL* than the multitude of papers issued by the AP's juveniles department.

It was unfortunate that, only a year after the *DW* was launched, Twyman left the firm after a disagreement over editorial policy. The paper went into a long decline under a number of editors who had nothing like the enthusiasm—indeed, genius—for the job, and died at the first bite of the Second War paper shortage. The *SBL* continued through the War and into the 1950s, although in a rather more low-key fashion than before. Blake's opponents tended to be black-market moguls and wide-boys, seedy spivs and racecourse racketeers. It wasn't quite the same as those glorious days of the detective's Golden Age, when those who'd tried conclusions with him had mainly been drawn from the super-criminal class, out to steal the Crown Jewels at least, or hold London to ransom, or even loot the entire country. There's no getting away from the fact that the Blake of the early-1950s was a shadow of his former self.

His last editor, the remarkable Bill Howard Baker, changed all that. In 1956 Baker took over the *SBL* and heaved Blake into not only the Nuclear Age but also the brutal and hard-bitten world of Raymond Chandler and Dashiell Hammett. Cowled figures were out, mean streets were definitely in. Even Pedro the bloodhound seemed somehow more vicious. Suddenly Blake had a bevy of new writers, an office-block HQ in Berkeley Square, a svelte and swishy secretary, Paula Dane, and an organisation with investigative stringers in Rome, Paris, Berlin, New York, Los Angeles. This did not, however, mean that the detective had lost his compassion for the little man in dire straits through no fault of his own, or for the friendless widow facing eviction.

Over 60 years earlier Harry Blyth had laid down Blake's ground rules: 'If there is a wrong to be righted, an evil to be redressed, or a rescue of the weak and suffering from the powerful, our hearty assistance can be readily obtained'. Baker's Blake still held to these principles, perhaps more fiercely than ever before; certainly his assistance to those in trouble was rendered in a considerably more muscular fashion. There was still the cosy pre-War atmosphere of Baker Street for off-duty periods, and Tinker was still his good right hand; but the prose was clipped and punchy, the villains more sadistic, the girls (both good and bad) more knowing, and Blake himself, in his pursuit of evil, had become utterly ruthless. Bill Baker performed drastic but necessary surgery on the character (just as Willie Back had done 50 years before) and ensured another 15 years of incident-packed shelf-life in a series of paperbacks and hardbacks that stand comparison with the best of the scores of mainstream thrillers published through the 1960s. Blake only retired (in 1969) when Baker's urge to reprint the entire Greyfriars saga in *The Magnet*, from 1908 to 1940, became too pressing.*

If Blake was lucky with his editors, he was even more fortunate in his writers, who were an extraordinary and, like most pulp writers, pretty rackety crowd. George Teed had been a plantation owner, sheep farmer, rubber planter and had generally knocked around the hot spots of the world before he settled down to write

---

* Actually the very last original Blake story, *Sexton Blake and the Demon God*, was published in 1978, the novelisation of Simon Raven's television serial, which could have been a delightful pastiche but turned out to be a monstrous parody.

some of the finest Blake stories of the Golden Age, bringing his wide rolling-stone experience and immense descriptive powers to the saga. Gwyn Evans had been a newspaperman in Palestine during the early-'20s troubles. Rex Hardinge travelled solo across Africa, from the bottom of the Sahara through to Kenya. Gilbert Chester (Clifford Gibbons) built and drove racing cars at Brooklands, drew astrological charts, and was writing about gutsy, hard-boiled dames a decade before the term was coined. Cecil Hayter yachted with Northcliffe, shot bears with Teddy Roosevelt. Stanley Gordon Shaw lived with Red Indians, tramping the Canadian backwoods as a trapper, lumberjack and farm-hand.

Others led more sedentary lives, but only just. Most brought hard experience to the Blake saga: not a few could add that extra touch of authenticity to scenes of prison life, from first-hand experience. As one Blake editor bitterly remarked, 'Some of those buggers were bigger crooks than the villains they wrote about'.

And what about the villains they wrote about? Well, there was Dr Satira, for instance, with 'the eyes of a snake, the head of a vulture, the face of a fiend, and the voice of a cooing dove', whose pets were a bunch of murderous Missing Links; the mysterious Miss Death, whose mask was a silken skull and whose life-expectancy was about six months (which was why she went crook in the first place); Waldo the Wonderman, who could heave over trolley-buses with his bare hands; Mr Mist, whose discovery of the secrets of invisibility caused no end of problems for West End jewellers and wealthy patrons of the arts; Leon Kestrel, the Master Mummer, whose genius at impersonation was so comprehensive he could even pass himself off as Blake himself; Prince Menes, reincarnation of the High Priest of the Ancient Order of Supreme Ra, out to dominate the world—not to mention corner the white slave market so he could pack off young girls to Egypt and force them to perform unspeakable rites in his 10,000-years old temple beneath the Sahara; the abominable Dr Cagliostro, whose mighty underground Colosseum was the scene of ghastly acts of torture and inhuman savagery, put on for the amusement of millionaire sensation-seekers; the hideously vulpine Max Lupus, whose scheme for getting rid of Blake was so diabolical that even . . .

Sheer pulp, of course. No denying that. Indeed, a good deal of the stuff hammered out by so many writers (nearly 200 over a

70-year span) was flawed, trashy and often downright silly. Yet the pace, colour and immense vigour of so many of the stories, especially during Blake's heyday of the 1920s and 1930s, cannot be denied either. The best writers could have transferred their talents to the hardback market, banging out thrillers for the numerous publishers who specialised in providing suspense fodder for the lending library chains. Certainly a good many of the Blake crowd could show Sapper, say, or Sax Rohmer a thing or two when it came to pace, plotting, dialogue, or characterisation. A handful could even have broken into the 'literary' field; but novel-writing, as one of the best Blake writers of the inter-War years, Anthony Skene, once gloomily pointed out, is an expensive hobby. For a goodish mainstream novel that would take six months or so to write and might (but only might) gain favourable reviews, the average author could expect, at most, £50 during the 1920s. In 1929 Skene himself dictated (his favourite method of composition) four 60,000-word *SBL*s and nine 25,000-word *UJ*s, earning for himself the sum of £492. At a time when the average income over the UK was £180 a year this was pretty good going (although in the same year Charles Hamilton—Frank Richards, creator of Billy Bunter, etc—was racking up a staggering £1,500 for his weekly *Magnet* stories alone).

Most saw writing Blakes as a job which paid the bills and ensured a rather better standard of living for themselves and their dependants than, say, clerking it in an office. And you got a good deal more fun out of it. That the best Blake writers had fun writing Blakes (far more than Conan Doyle ever did from writing about Holmes) is evident from the stories themselves. There was the fun of dreaming up some new and bizarre problem for Blake to solve, of creating some new and ultra-malevolent villain to defy him, of dropping him into some new and wildly improbable fix—and then pulling him out of it without fatally damaging the reader's willing suspension of disbelief.

Dorothy L. Sayers, in a perceptive essay, praised the Blake stories and argued that 'their significance in popular literature . . . would richly repay scientific investigation'. True, although one must not take them too seriously; solemn critiques of cheap fiction seldom achieve their purpose. 'The best specimens', wrote Sayers, 'display extreme ingenuity, and an immense vigour and fertility of plot and incident'. Here, in this volume, are gathered together just a few of the best specimens from Sexton Blake's Golden Age: long stories and short stories, packed with incident, colour, thrills, over-written in the best possible sense and offering hours of pure entertainment and pure nostalgia.

This anthology is dedicated to
four editors, without whom there would
have been no Sexton Blake

W.H. Back
(1904–1915)

Leonard Pratt
(1921–1954)

Harold Twyman
(1921–1934)
and

Bill Howard Baker
(1956–1969)

SEXTON BLAKE WINS

THE HOUSE OF THE HANGING SWORD
Gwyn Evans

Gwyn Evans (1899–1938) was an irreverent soul, mercurial in temperament, careless in his writing, carefree in his habits and outlook on life. Irrepressible and utterly irresponsible, he was the best-loved of all the 200-odd writers who contributed to the Sexton Blake saga over a period of 75 years. His style was a rich mix of Edgar Wallace, Dickens and the King James Bible (he was a pronounced atheist but his upbringing was Chapel), and his talent was prodigious. But so was his inability to profit from it. Although his plots were often inspired—his opening sequences rich in eerie atmosphere and sometimes wonderfully bizarre— time and again the exigencies of his rackety life-style and the ever-present need for money effectively sabotaged his initial ingenuity. A dazzling plot-premise frequently collapses in ruins long before the final chapter. Rarely did he have the time (possibly even the inclination) carefully to pace out his stories, and in many of his novel-length Blakes, especially, there are often enough loose ends hanging around to knit an Arran sweater. And yet, one can forgive him much for his sheer gusto, his breakneck pace and his moments of high comedy. (It was Evans who transformed Blake's housekeeper, Mrs Bardell, into a gloriously comic character whose fractured English and monstrous Malapropisms are a lasting delight). In particular, he will be remembered for all those outrageously Dickensian Christmas issues of the Union Jack *during the 1920s, in which nostalgia and festive good cheer dripped like fat off the goose under which Blake's table invariably groaned once the chase was over.*

'It will not be a very long run now, Mr Zeed.'

John Gadsley, the solicitor, turned with a smile to the other occupant of the big, black limousine that was speeding along in the dusk of a winter's evening, through a winding country roadway.

1

Mr Ephra Zeed, the solicitor's companion, was a spare, angular man, dressed in dark clothes of a slightly old-fashioned cut.

He coughed in a deprecatory fashion, and in a prim voice answered.

'I am—er—not in the least fatigued, Mr Gadsley,' he said. 'In fact—er—this automobile journey is quite a refreshing change of routine.'

Ephra Zeed's face, however, did not look as if he was enjoying it. He sat against the luxuriously appointed tonneau seat in lank awkwardness, unlike his companion, a rotund, red-faced little man with twinkling eyes and a brisk, bird-like manner.

Ephra Zeed, lately actuary to that distinguished firm of chartered accountants, Messrs Ledbury, Rollaston & Slack, had recently resigned his position in the firm, but his was a nature that did not settle down easily to retirement. He had no hobbies and no vices.

For forty-five years his life had been one long routine plan, bound down by the parallel lines that ruled alike his life and his ledgers.

This motor journey into the heart of the Chiltern Hills was indeed an exception to the ordered routine of the accountant's life. His thin blood felt an unaccustomed glow of adventure.

It was a phrase 'something to your advantage' which he had seen two days previously in 'The Daily Radio' that was responsible for his meeting with John Gadsley, the solicitor.

That Puck-like man pressed a switch, and a glow of yellow light illumined the tonneau.

'You will find my client, Lord Blaynton, a charming host, Mr Zeed,' he commented. 'Marlesden Manor, though off the beaten track, is one of the finest Tudor mansions in Bucks.'

Mr Zeed pressed the tips of his long, bony fingers together and nodded non-committally.

'Ah, yes!' he observed. 'I had the pleasure of doing some confidential estate work for his lordship some years ago, but I have not had the honour of his personal acquaintance.'

'You'll find him a charming man, Mr Zeed,' responded the solicitor. 'I don't know the precise details of the work he requires, but in a general way I believe it is something of the same nature that you did for him before. I am afraid his lordship is rather eccentric in business matters,' he added, 'but he evidently remembers your work, and it seems to have given him satisfaction, for he insisted on our finding you. It is fortunate that you saw my advertisement in "The Daily Radio".'

Ephra Zeed gave a prim smile.

Like all men of his type, he was at heart a snob, and the fact that his prospective client had a title helped to stifle any misgivings he may have experienced about altering his accustomed routine.

He glanced through the window of the car. Mist blanketed the hollows of the valley, and over the Chiltern Hills only a faint red gleam against the western skyline now remained of daylight.

The chauffeur switched on his headlights as the car went forward along the winding road that had led for so long through the mist-laden valleys.

A turn to the right, and at length they approached a stretch of woods. The graceful, silver-barked birch-trees looked bare and desolate and almost ghostly in the glare of the headlamps.

Here, up a side road, the car drew up at length before a pair of wrought-iron gates.

There was a tiny lodge to the right of the entrance-gates behind the leaded windows of which a yellow lamp gleamed.

The chauffeur blew his horn, and a moment or two later an ancient man clad in corduroys and leggings shuffled towards the gates and swung them open.

Mr Zeed stared forward eagerly into the gloom. Ahead of him he saw a long, three-quarters timbered building with quaint, twisted Tudor chimneys.

It lay rather long and vague in the filmy light. Only here and there a light burned behind leaded casements. But for the faint sound of wind in the leafless branches of the thick wood, all was silent.

'I'm afraid you are not seeing the manor at its best,' observed the lawyer apologetically. 'In the daytime, however, you will find much to interest you.'

They drew up a few moments later at the door of the ancient manor.

The solicitor alighted, and, accompanied by Mr Zeed, who gripped a small attaché-case, they mounted the steps of the terrace and rang the front door bell.

3

A white-haired butler appeared in the doorway, and the lawyer smiled.

'Ah, Carver, is his lordship at home? We are expected, I think.'

The manservant nodded.

'Yes, sir. For the moment Lord Blaynton is engaged,' he answered. 'He asks you to wait.'

The butler flung open the door, and the three stepped into a large square hall.

There was a queer, stuffy atmosphere about the place that struck a chill into Mr Zeed's thin blood. A dim light revealed mullion-leaded windows, ancient oak beams and massive panelling.

'If you'll step in here, sir?' said the butler, and he led the way to the left of the hallway down a long corridor where portraits lined the wall. Old oil-paintings of the past.

A long line of Blaynton ancestors, with dark and brooding eyes, seemed to stare banefully down at the solicitor and his companion.

The queer, all-pervading odour of must and decay was now more pronounced as they neared the end of the passageway.

'Would you be so good as to step in here, sir?' queried the manservant, with a bow.

A moment later he opened a door and stood aside.

Mr Zeed blinked as he entered a long, oak-panelled room. He was dazzled for a while by the blaze of light which emanated from a huge alabaster bowl in the ceiling.

It had a peculiar blue-white radiance that was startling after the subdued lighting of the hallway.

A half-involuntary cry rose to the accountant's lips as, save for a long oaken table and a few chairs, the room was utterly devoid of furniture.

A fire burned in the huge wide grate, and it was the only note of warmth and comfort in that vast and cheerless room.

Mr Zeed turned towards the lawyer, and then he gave a gasp, for behind him the door had clicked, and the suave Mr Gadsley and Carver, the butler, had gone.

A flush darkened Zeed's sallow cheeks.

'What's the meaning of this?' he began.

From the other side of the buttressed fireplace there came a low, soundless chuckle.

A tall, black figure emerged, and Mr Zeed's eyes goggled in terror.

The figure was garbed in a long, monkish robe. A heavy cowl was drawn over his head, and through the slits of his mask his eyes gleamed at the accountant.

'Welcome, Ephra Zeed, to the House of the Hanging Sword!' he said, in a harsh, metallic voice. 'You'll find some friends of yours here.'

He turned, and Zeed saw that there were others in the room half-hidden by the solid bastion of the fireplace.

He made a half-step forward, and found that he was covered by an automatic gripped unwaveringly in the other's fingers.

'What—what does this mean?' stuttered Zeed.

'You had better ask your friends,' said the cowled man grimly.

A moment later he stepped backwards and pressed a hidden switch in the panelled wall. There was a click, and part of the panelling swung backwards like a door.

Then there came the clang of steel, and Zeed stood there, his scalp tingling with terror in that fantastic room.

'The black scum!' rasped a harsh voice.

As in a daze, Mr Zeed saw a burly, red-headed man, dressed in an ill-fitting, ready-made suit, who emerged from the window corner. Next to him, straddling a chair, sat a bald-headed old man with a straggling white beard.

'What sort of tricks are they playing at? That's what I want to know!' snarled the first man.

Ephra Zeed experienced a queer feeling in the pit of his stomach.

He turned to the door and rattled at the knob.

'Mr Gadsley, Mr Gadsley!' he shouted.

There was no response, but from somewhere he seemed to hear the hollow echo of a mocking laugh.

He turned to the other two men in the apartment. Somehow or other, their faces were vaguely familiar, but where he had seen them before he could not conjecture.

'This is extraordinary conduct, gentlemen,' he said. 'How long have you two been here?'

'About an hour,' grunted the red-haired man, 'and what I says is there's going to be trouble unless I gets my dues.

'It's no use you banging at the door or at the window, dad,' he said, turning to the white-whiskered old gentleman. 'They've got steel shutters half an inch thick.'

His bony legs trembling slightly, Mr Zeed sank into a chair and mopped his wet forehead.

'But this is an outrage!' he stammered.

The accountant glanced suspiciously at the red-headed man. He looked rather like a labourer, and Mr Zeed was again conscious of that queer feeling that he had seen both the men before, but where and in what connection he could not remember.

The old man looked dubiously at Ephra Zeed.

'Excuse me, sir,' he began doubtfully. 'Haven't I seen you before at some place, some time? Funny sort of name, if I remember rightly. My name is Nissim. I'm a retired oil and colour merchant from Chelsea.'

'And mine,' said the accountant primly, 'is Zeed, Ephra Zeed.'

'And my moniker is James 'Acker, and I'm a good worker—when I can get it. So now we all know each other.'

A tap sounded at the door of the room, and the three rose to their feet simultaneously.

There came the sudden grate of a key in the lock.

'Wait in here, please,' came the suave voice of Carver, the butler.

'Right,' said a crisp, incisive voice, and a soldier, dressed in a long, khaki greatcoat, entered the room, removing his cap as he did so. He glanced curiously at the other occupants.

'Look here, Carver,' began Zeed truculently, 'I insist on knowing the meaning of this outrage. I protest—'

'You'll know soon enough,' said the butler, and, with a quick movement for one of his apparent age, he turned and once more the key grated in the lock.

The soldier stared in perplexity at the three other men.

He was a tall young man, with a weatherbeaten face and corporal's stripes on his arm.

'This is a rum business, and no mistake!' he said. 'What's the big idea?'

'Look here, this nonsense's got to stop!' said Zeed, and a dull spot of colour again flamed in his sallow cheeks.

'What's that?' gasped the red-haired man, Hacker.

Zeed did not answer.

Something turned his blood to water. It was a low moan of anguish, a sobbing sound that began on a high note and wailed down the scale until it was inaudible.

The four men looked at each other, and the face of Nissim was ashen with the colour of death!

* * *

With a fat cigar in his pudgy fingers, Mr Otto Krimm glanced at the clock on the mantelpiece of his roomy flat in Jermyn Street.

He wore evening dress of an extravagant cut, too much jewellery, and a frown of irritation.

Mr Krimm had had a tiring day in the City. His red, protuberant lips pursed in a tuneless whistle, and then, with a grunt, he bent forward and pressed an ivory bell-push.

Almost immediately a wooden-faced Japanese manservant entered the apartment.

'Is everything fixed, Ito?' he demanded.

The Jap drew in the breath between his large white teeth in a sibilant and acquiescent hiss.

'Yes, sir,' he replied.

'Remember, as soon as the lady arrives I am not to be disturbed on any pretext,' ordered his master.

There came a faint whir from the passageway.

Mr Krimm's pulses leapt a little at the sound.

'See who that is,' he ordered, and as the manservant withdrew he flung his sodden cigar-butt into the ornate black-and-chromium grate.

Ito returned a moment or two later, accompanied by an exceedingly pretty girl.

At a glance there was something ethereally beautiful in her appearance. She was clad in a wispy dress of powder blue. The faint hint of rouge on lips and cheeks, and the touch of dark blue on her eyelids gave a sparkle to her features, but on close observation one would have noticed a certain faded hardness about the eyes and resolution in the mutinously tilted chin.

'Ah, my dear, you're looking radiant!' said Mr Krimm.

Terry Lee smiled and blew him a kiss.

In the mellow glow of light from the pendant electrolier, she looked scarcely more than a girl, though sophisticated Mr Krimm knew that she was thirty-five, and had remained at that age for more years than one.

He took her wrap, and they passed into the dining-room where Ito was giving a final touch of artistry to the cut-glass and napery of the table.

There was an atmosphere of quiet festivity about the scene, and as the Jap deftly shook a cocktail, Krimm squeezed the girl's arm.

Mr Krimm admired Terry Lee and enjoyed her cynical wit, also her capacity for pleasure. He knew women well, and Terry Lee, late of the Hilarity Theatre, suited his mood that evening.

'Happy, kid?' he inquired, as he patted her slim, long, scarlet-nailed fingers as they rested on his sleeve.

'Quite, Otto,' replied the girl.

'I thought we'd have a quiet meal here and go on to the club later,' commented her host.

Terry Lee gave a sigh as she fingered the latest gift of the infatuated financier, a pearl necklace, about her neck. The girl seemed to be in high spirits this evening. Her dark-lashed eyes were dancing as she sat down at the table and raised a brimming glass of champagne to Mr Krimm's rather thick lips.

'It suits me, my dear,' she said.

There was no expression at all on the Jap's yellow face, as he ministered like some priestly acolyte to their wants.

The dinner was perfectly cooked, and when the liqueur stage had arrived, the Oriental bowed and withdrew from the room.

'And now, what about that little trip to Paris, my dear?' said Krimm.

He broke off suddenly, for the girl's face had turned ghastly.

'Look!' she gasped. 'Look!'

She pointed a shaking finger at the large ornate mirror above the mantelpiece.

'That face!'

The financier followed her pointing finger, and snarled out an oath.

For the fraction of a second in the mirror he glimpsed a pale, ethereal face. It was the face of a girl, with a queer, bluish pallor, almost phosphorescent, surrounding it like an unearthly aureole.

The eyes were wide open and seemed to stare into the room with a strange, hypnotic glare.

Krimm rose to his feet, and the glass dropped from his nerveless fingers with a crash.

'Nonsense,' he cried. 'Nonsense.'

The large, luminous eyes of the face in the mirror turned and seemed to rest with a glance of ineffable scorn at the pair.

Terry Lee gave a scream.

Krimm mouthed incoherently, and a thrill of superstitious horror shook his whole frame. Where had he seen that face before? Those dark, brooding eyes—

Then, suddenly, he remembered, and the cold fingers of fear swept icily down his spine.

'Great heavens, not that,' he murmured. 'Not—'

His voice broke, and, as he lurched forward, the face in the mirror vanished as quickly as it had appeared.

Shaking with fear, Otto Krimm reached for the decanter, while a sob broke from the painted lips of the girl.

*   *   *

'She's gone, Mr Blake. Vanished! Where is she?'

'Well, that's rather a difficult question to answer offhand, madam,' said the Baker Street detective quietly.

The celebrated Baker Street criminologist ushered his visitor into the consulting-room, and, at the same time, covertly studied her face from his lowered lids.

She was a tall, buxom, rather hard-featured woman of indeterminate age, and, at the moment, rather agitated in her manner. She was, in fact, palpably nervous. Her hands fiddled with the silver top of her handbag, and she tapped restlessly on the floor with her foot.

'Would you mind beginning at the beginning, and telling me everything in detail, Miss—'

'My name is Hornby, Mr Blake. Annabel Hornby. I am secretary of the League of Sex Equality, about which you have doubtless heard. I am a near neighbour of yours, in Orchard Street, and the disappearance of our organiser, Mrs Skeffington Smythe, is naturally a matter of grave concern to me.'

The woman smiled nervously.

'I am sorry,' she apologised, 'for being so vague, but Mrs Skeffington Smythe's disappearance is a most serious thing for the League.'

'Disappearance?' Blake raised his eyebrows.

He had heard of the militant Mrs Skeffington Smythe, who, as chief organiser of the League of Sex Equality, had recently headed a Monster Meeting of Protest at the Albert Hall, attacking the opposing forces that refused them to the right to earn on equal terms with men.

Blake bent forward, a gleam of interest in his shrewd grey eyes.

'A remarkable woman, if I might say so, Miss Hornby.'

That lady nodded.

'Yes, Mr Blake, and that's what makes her disappearance so strange.'

Blake settled back in his saddle-bag chair.

'Please let me have the details,' he said.

'Well, as you may imagine, Mrs Skeffington Smythe is an extremely independent woman,' continued his caller. 'Two nights ago, Tuesday night, to be exact, she left her flat in Orchard Street, and has not returned. I had an appointment with her for an important committee meeting yesterday. I called at the flat, rang the bell, and got no answer. A porter on duty in the hallway—they are a block of service flats—stated that he last saw her at five o'clock on the Tuesday. Since then she has not returned.'

Blake shrugged his shoulders.

'Unusual, perhaps, but not remarkable,' he commented. 'As you say, Mrs Smythe is a lady of extremely independent action. Her absence for two days is not significant?'

Miss Hornby shook her head decisively.

'But it is most unusual, Mr Blake,' she insisted. 'I have known her for nearly ten years; in fact, all the time she has occupied the flat. To my knowledge, save when she has been away on holiday, she has never stayed a night away from the flat. What is more, the meeting which was arranged for yesterday was a most important one, certainly one she would not willingly miss.'

Sexton Blake nodded thoughtfully.

'Mrs Smythe may be ill, you know,' he said. 'She might have been knocked down by a motorcar and taken to a hospital. There are a score of explanations for her absence.'

Miss Hornby shook her head again, and set her thin lips firmly.

'I have rung up the flat a dozen times and have obtained no reply, Mr Blake,' she said. 'Furthermore, I have made inquiries of all the London hospitals, but no person answering her description has been found.

'What is more,' she added, and her short, sharp sentences were

10

rapped out breathlessly, 'I have just left her flat. I persuaded the porter to allow me to use his pass-key. The flat was empty. There was no sign of foul play nor anything unusual.'

Blake slowly filled his briar pipe.

'I think, madam,' he suggested, 'that it is early yet to become needlessly alarmed about Mrs Skeffington-Smythe's disappearance.'

He raised his eyebrows slightly, and there was a quirk of amusement at their corners. Even middle-aged ladies of conventional habits had been known to go off on a spree on occasions.

'My advice to you is to go to the police,' he said.

'The police, pah!' said Miss Hornby. 'Mrs Skeffington Smythe doesn't like the police, Mr Blake. As you doubtless know, she has had trouble with them many times. Nothing criminal, you understand, but her militant tactics naturally bring her up in conflict with the law.'

Blake nodded.

'I still think you are worrying yourself needlessly, Miss Hornby,' he observed. 'If I were you I would give her until a reasonable time this evening to communicate with you. If she does not, then I will look into the matter on your behalf.'

Miss Hornby rose to her feet and closed the mouth of her bag with a click.

She thanked him profusely, and the famous detective, with his quiet courtesy, ushered his visitor out of the room.

Blake did not trouble much about the matter for an hour or two, but shortly after tea Tinker returned from a visit to the cinema with an evening paper under his arm.

'Funny thing about these disappearances, guv'nor,' said the youngster. 'There's another of them reported in tonight's newspaper. That makes four in less than a week!'

Blake raised his eyebrows slightly as the youngster pointed to the headings in the 'Evening Globe':

MYSTERY MAN MISSING

LOCKED DOORS IN DESERTED HOUSE

NEIGHBOURS NERVOUS.

'A house in Norland Terrace, Mitcham, has stood with locked doors and drawn blinds for over a week. It is the residence of a wealthy widower, Mr Vaughan Sandford, sixty-five years of age. A week-long procession of callers have knocked at the front door and have been unable to obtain an answer. The fear that something was wrong led the neighbours to call in the police, who made search of his home last night. They were accompanied by Mr John Robson, a next-door neighbour, and a friend of Mr Sandford. The police gained entrance to the house through a window in the basement. Inside, however, they found nothing which answered the question asked by the neighbours ever since their anxiety was aroused: "Where was Mr Sandford?" What the police discovered was that several rooms were securely locked. By the light of flashlamps they examined every door, window, and open room, but without obtaining any clue as to what had happened, or where Mr Sandford is.

'Mr Sandford had the reputation among his neighbours of being a recluse. This is the fourth mysterious disappearance this week, and Scotland Yard appears to be temporarily baffled. Mr Sandford, it is understood, was slightly eccentric in his habits, and hardly ever left the house since the death of his wife some years ago.'

'What do you think of it, guv'nor?' inquired Tinker.

Blake shrugged his shoulders.

'There seems to be very little to go on,' he said. 'As a matter of fact, I have just had a visitor this afternoon who has reported a fifth disappearance. Sounds rather like an epidemic, but I can't see any tangible connection in the affairs.'

A thunderous rat-tat sounded at the front door.

Tinker grinned across at his chief.

'I'll bet that's old Coutts!' he said, with a chuckle, as he turned to answer the knock.

Blake smiled, and made a gesture of half-humorous resignation as he heard the gruff voice of the Yard man greeting Tinker on the stairs.

A moment later Coutts entered, his red face slightly more florid than usual, and his blue Melton overcoat muffled tightly about his neck, for the night was raw and foggy.

'Hallo, Blake!' he greeted his colleague gruffly. 'Sorry to trouble you, but there's a devil of a row on at headquarters. My ears are still tingling from the Commissioner's bawling-out!'

12

'Sit down, old chap,' said Blake hospitably. 'The cigars are at your elbow. Give the inspector a drink, young 'un,' he added.

Coutts stretched out his red, ham-like hands towards the cheerful blaze in the consulting-room grate.

'The Commissioner certainly has a habit of getting under one's skin,' he said ruefully, 'and, as usual, I get the rough end of his tongue. I suppose you've seen the newspapers tonight?'

Blake nodded.

'You're referring, I suppose, to the Mitcham affair?'

'That's right,' said Coutts gloomily. 'And not only the Mitcham affair, but the Chelsea business, the Barracks business, and the Surbiton case, to say nothing of the man Hacker.'

'Well, let's get them in chronological order,' said Blake, with a smile. 'What's troubling you, Coutts?'

For answer, the Yard inspector groped in the capacious pocket of his coat and unearthed his notebook.

'You're a good fellow, Blake,' he said. 'I wish you'd give these depositions the once-over. I'm telling you frankly I'm up a gum-tree. Here's a list of the missing, with sundry comments.'

He handed over his notebook to the famous detective.

Blake puffed at his briar and sank back into his armchair as he studied the brief but highly significant depositions of the Yard man.

Inspector Coutts was no author, and his descriptions of the missing people were shorn of much of the picturesque verbiage employed in the newspaper reports.

Stark and brief though the descriptions were, however, Sexton Blake mentally filled in the details.

'Well, Coutts,' he commented at length, 'they certainly seem to be a motley assortment of people. Diverse, not only in occupation but in age and locality. Here's James Hacker of Stepney, for instance.'

He tapped his notebook with his finger.

'He appears to be a general labourer, a hard-working man with a clean record and apparently no earthly reason for disappearing. Then there's John Nissim, a retired oil-and-colour merchant who has hitherto led a blameless existence in Oakley Crescent, Chelsea.'

'I know, Blake,' broke in Coutts. 'That's the queer part of it. I've looked into the private lives of all these people, and I can't find a single reason for their disappearance. They're all highly respect-able, and all appeared to be in good spirits on the day of their disappearance. The Commissioner has a wild theory that all these five cases are linked together somehow, but that's absurd on the face of it.'

Sexton Blake frowned thoughtfully.

'There certainly does not appear to be any point of contact,' he remarked. 'Let's look at the others. Here's Corporal James Stanger of the Loamshire Regiment. He's missing from Wellington Barracks, and then there's the peculiarly named Ephra Zeed, a retired chartered accountant from Surbiton. About the only tan-gible link that I can possibly see is the fact that two of them—Zeed and Nissim—are about the same age and are both retired from business; but that, of course, is no link at all.'

'I know,' exploded Coutts. 'That's the baffling part of the whole business, Blake. Believe me, I've made the closest inquiries about each single man. There seem to be utterly no reason why they should have vanished. Apart from James Hacker, who had been on the dole for the last fortnight, there was not one who was even financially embarrassed. No bodies have been discovered that remotely resemble any of the missing men, and there is no reason for thinking any of them had suicidal tendencies. Take this chap Zeed, for example. His life has been as regular as clockwork. I interviewed his housekeeper, a dry little stick of a woman!'

'Indeed,' replied Blake. 'And what had she to say?'

Coutts shrugged his shoulders.

'Nothing whatsoever. She said he was a good employer, inclined to be fussy over trifles, but she added that when she last saw him he seemed to be in exceptionally good spirits. All he told her was that he would not be back to lunch, but as he often lunched out, that was not unusual. Hallo!'

The phone bell shrilled suddenly, and Tinker crossed over to the instrument and lifted the receiver.

'Hallo! Yes,' he answered, and listened for a moment or two to the harsh voice at the other end of the wire.

He then clapped his hand over the mouthpiece, and turned to Coutts.

'It's Harker of the Yard speaking, Couttsy! He's all excited, and wants to talk to you at once!'

14

Coutts grunted.

'I'll talk to him!' he snapped. 'I told him to ring me here if anything new cropped up.'

Tinker handed the receiver to the inspector.

Sexton Blake slowly refilled his briar pipe, and once more scanned the depositions in the Yard man's notebook, while Coutts barked gruffly into the telephone receiver.

'Yes, what is it?' he demanded.

'There's another of 'em gone,' twanged the voice of his colleague, Harker, over the wires.

'Another of them!' echoed Coutts blankly. 'Who is it this time, for the Land's sake?'

'Otto Krimm,' came the reply. 'You know Krimm, the financier. Last seen two nights ago. The Commissioner's raising Cain. Not a darned clue to go on.'

Coutts stifled an oath.

'OK, Harker!' he snapped. 'I'll look into it. Goodbye!'

He hung up the receiver and turned to Blake.

'If this sort of thing happens much oftener, I'll be the next on the disappearing list,' he remarked.

Blake rose to his feet, and his eyes shone with suppressed excitement. He was thinking of the visit paid to him that afternoon by Miss Hornby.

'I think you had better add the name of Mrs Skeffington Smythe to your list, Coutts,' he said. 'That makes seven people in all. Seven in less than seven days.'

'But it's preposterous,' said the inspector. 'It's not an ordinary case, but a blooming epidemic.'

Tinker gave a chuckle from the corner.

'As Splash would say, chief, there's not even a decent corpse in the story.'

Blake's lean face was very grave.

'Not yet, perhaps,' he said, 'but I'm afraid that omission will be rectified very shortly.'

He clasped Coutts' burly shoulder.

'You can count me in on this,' he remarked. 'This looks like being a super case.'

*   *   *

15

'And that is really all I know, Mr Blake.'

The speaker was a hatchet-faced, bespectacled little man with a manner that was a quaint blend of suavity and pomposity.

Sexton Blake frowned as he turned to face Mr Binnett, the confidential secretary to that influential financier, Otto Krimm.

He and Coutts had motored round to the Jermyn Street flat of the City magnate immediately after the telephone call from Harker of the Yard.

Coutts sniffed with disfavour as he sank down into the luxurious embrace of a silken orange divan in the millionaire's drawing-room.

There was something exotic about the room which repelled the inspector, but Blake, who knew a little of Mr Krimm's luxurious habits, was not surprised at his surroundings.

'Send that Jap here again, Mr Binnett,' said Coutts. 'I'm not satisfied about his evidence.'

The secretary gave a stiff bow and left the boudoir.

Coutts gloomily surveyed his notebook.

'There you are, Blake,' he said. 'Up against a blank wall again. Krimm was due at his office two days ago for an important board meeting. According to that chap Binnett, it was essential that his employer should be there, and yet no one has seen or heard of him for the past forty-eight hours.'

He groped into his pocket and unearthed one of the vicious-looking black cheroots which he affected.

Blake deftly forestalled the effects of his smoking it by proffering one of his own Calixto Lopez cigars, which succeeded in mollifying some of the Yard's man disgruntlement.

A tap sounded at the door of the room, and Binnet entered, accompanied by the Japanese manservant.

Blake's gaze rested speculatively on the man's lemon-hued, impassive features.

'You say, Ito, that you do not know the name of the lady who was dining with Mr Krimm the night before last?'

The Jap drew in his breath sibilantly like the hiss of a snake.

'No, sir,' he answered. 'She was a very pretty lady. She has been in the flat before. I hear Mr Krimm call her "Terry". She is an actress woman, I think.'

'About what time did Mr Krimm and his visitor depart?' Blake demanded.

16

'About 8.30, sir,' replied the manservant.

'Did he appear agitated in any way?'

For the fraction of a second Ito hesitated.

'Well, sir,' he answered, 'my master seemed as if he had too much drink taken, and the young lady looked very pale.'

'Did he leave any instructions?' queried Blake.

The manservant shrugged his shoulders.

'No, except that I was to have his breakfast ready at the usual time in the morning and to see that his hot-water bottle was filled.'

'How did he leave the flat? Did he walk, or—'

'By taxi, sir. I phoned up for one from the rank at the corner.'

'Ah,' said Coutts, 'something to go on at last.'

He closed his black official notebook with a snap.

'I'll get busy right away on that, Blake,' he announced decisively.

Blake turned and faced Binnett, who was hovering uncertainly on the tips of his patent-leather shoes.

'Do you know if Mr Krimm has any enemies, or if he has been threatened lately by anyone?' he demanded.

The secretary shook his head.

'No, sir,' he answered. 'Of course, as a business man, he has many rivals, and like most rich men, he incurred a good deal of jealousy amongst his associates.'

'I see,' answered Blake quietly.

He turned once more to the Japanese.

'You say your master appeared agitated. Have you any idea for what reason?'

A faint quirk of a smile played round Ito's thin lips.

'Well, sir,' he answered, 'myself I do not like to say, but it seemed as if he and the young lady had had a quarrel.'

'And where was the dinner served?' queried the detective.

Ito opened the door and pointed to the adjacent dining-room.

'In here, sir,' he said.

Blake sprung to his feet and crossed over to the room indicated.

The florid decoration of the place was even more exaggerated than that of the boudoir which had excited the disgust of Inspector Coutts.

Blake swept the room in one swift photographic, comprehensive glance, then suddenly his lips tightened.

On the oval mirror above the mantelpiece he saw the image of a

17

shining sword, double-bladed with a heavy ornate hilt.

He turned round to Ito and gripped him by the shoulder.

'What is that?' he demanded crisply.

The Oriental stared at the strange symbol, and a frightened look crept into his almond eyes.

'I don't know, sir!' he gasped. 'It was not there this morning, I will swear.'

Blake crossed over to the mirror, and as he did so the image of the hanging sword seemed to fade into a vague blur.

It looked like some trick of the light, but the detective was not satisfied. From his vest pocket he whipped out a small but powerful lens, and through it he scrutinised the shining surface of the mirror.

'What have you found there, old man?' asked Coutts.

Sexton Blake smiled enigmatically.

'It looks,' he said, 'like the Sword of Damocles. However, we will soon make certain.'

He turned to Ito.

'Go down to the car and tell my assistant to bring up my research case,' he said.

Ito bowed and withdrew as noiselessly as a shadow.

Blake turned to Coutts.

'You check up on that taxi,' he said. 'I shall emulate Alice and start through the Looking Glass.'

Coutts grunted.

'And I shall be as mad as the Hatter,' he remarked, 'if I don't get to the bottom of all these disappearances.'

He nodded, and bade a curt goodnight to the obsequious Mr Binnett, and took his deaprture.

'Here's the case, guv'nor!' announced Tinker, bringing up the neat leather valise, without which Blake never embarked on an investigation.

'A little job for you, Tinker,' said the detective. 'Photograph this mirror, and use one of those duplex infra-red plates. Then chase back to Baker Street as soon as you can. Take a taxi. I'll go back in the Panther.'

Tinker unlocked the attaché-case and got busy.

Blake turned to Mr Binnett.

'I'm afraid, Mr Binnet, that I cannot enlighten you much at the present juncture regarding Mr Krimm's disappearance. Keep in touch with me by telephone, and let me know immediately if you get any communication from him.'

'But what do you think could have happened to him, Mr Blake?' queried the little man. 'The business is all at sixes and sevens. How am I to explain to the Board of Directors his vanishing like this without a word or a line of explanation?'

Sexton Blake shrugged his shoulders.

'You'll have to mollify them to the best of your ability, I'm afraid,' he said. 'Mr Krimm's disappearance will, in my opinion, possibly have some startling results.'

But not even Sexton Blake realised how baffling the mystery of the disappearance of Mr Krimm was to prove, nor of how vast and far-reaching the consequences were to be.

*   *   *

With a feeling that his throat was encircled by a red-hot wire, and that a sledgehammer was beating his already dazed brain to pulp, Mr Otto Krimm gradually recovered consciousness after a time.

It was a feeling that in his chequered career he had experienced before, mostly due to over-indulgence in alcohol.

His first reaction was to lie back and groan, and the second to raise himself painfully to a sitting position and blink blearily around for something to ease his parched throat.

He rubbed his eyes, and was conscious of a queer sense of isolation.

'What the devil—' he began in a harsh, rasping voice, as he glanced about him.

He discovered that he was lying on a hard truckle-bed in a cold, small room, that he instantly recognised as a prison cell.

On a shelf in the corner were three or four tin utensils, and hanging by the side of the bed was a record card.

Mr Krimm shuddered violently, and closed his eyes.

'I must be dreaming,' he murmured.

He gave another violent shudder, and tentatively opened his eyes again. He scratched his stubby chin in bewilderment, and noticed that he was wearing a blue suit of unfamiliar cut.

Fearfully he glanced at the steel grille set up high in the door of his cell, and saw with a sense of creeping discomfort that an eye was watching him through the Judas hole in the steel door.

He licked his dry and parched lips nervously, and with trembling hands he reached for the metal mug on the shelf.

There was a tin water-bottle near it, and with trembling hands filled the cup, spilling a surplus on the floor.

He gulped and guzzled the water down his throat, making unseemly noises. Then shakily he dabbed some of the water into his hand and clapped his palm to his aching forehead and tried to think.

At last, in fragments and snatches of vague memory, it came back to him.

That face—that ghastly dead face in the mirror!

Of course, it was all imagination. That's all it was.

He and Terry had laughed it off. And then what had happened?

Again he pressed his throbbing temples.

They had taken a taxi; that was it. Terry wanted to dance at the Milan Club.

And then, what? Again he groaned. Here his dizzy brain failed him. There was nothing after that. Just blank darkness.

And here he was. He had not been drunk, anyway, and yet here he was in a prison cell.

A convulsive shudder shook him. Reminded of his surroundings, he rolled unsteadily to his feet and looked fearfully at the steel grille and the iron door of the cell.

He was now conscious of body aches and pains.

His eye fell on the record card beside his bed, and his heart was suddenly gripped in the icy clutch of fear.

He read his own name, followed by a number, and after it was the single, simple and terrible word, 'murder'.

The wretched man felt his flesh creep with a queer, unnameable horror. He beat his fists against his temples.

This was surely some hideous nightmare, from which he would wake up.

He tottered back to the truckle-bed again, and sank down, hunching his head on his breast in a despairing gesture.

Then to his ears came the sound of measured footsteps. The Judas hole in the door was opened, and a grim face peered in at the cowering Krimm. Then it was shut again and the door of his cell was flung open.

A grave-faced, grey-haired warder entered the cell with a tin plate of porridge and a hunk of bread.

Krimm rose to his feet with a strangled scream.

'What's the meaning of all this?' he demanded harshly. 'Who are you? What am I doing here?'

'Now then, none of that stuff!' snapped the warder. 'You'll know in due time what's happened to you.'

Otto Krimm's brain reeled.

'For Mercy's sake tell me!' he pleaded. 'What am I here for?'

'You'll know soon enough,' came the grim reply. 'Brace yourself up, man.'

Krimm stretched out a groping hand. He felt physically sick. Pain—actual pain—gnawed at the pit of his stomach.

'It's a mistake—a dreadful mistake!' he shrilled. 'I demand to see a solicitor. You've no right to keep me in here.'

'Eat your breakfast, mate!' said the warder, with gruff kindliness.

With a clang like the knell of doom he shut the cell door. Otto Krimm put his throbbing head in his hands.

What did it all mean? His brain seemed to be bursting with questions.

* * *

The inexplicable disappearance of the missing seven was destined to have many far-reaching results and to add a memorable chapter to the Case-Book of Sexton Blake.

To the detective, who was always interested in the bizarre and unusual, the apparent incongruity in the status of the missing people presented just those unusual features which appealed to his shrewd, analytical brain.

On the morning after his visit to Mr Krimm's flat in Jermyn Street, he was lounging apparently indolently before the fire in the consulting-room. On his knee was a bulky volume, and between his teeth he gripped his favourite briar.

Blake suddenly looked up from the volume he was reading.

'I mentioned "Alice in Wonderland" last night, young 'un,' he said to Tinker, 'and I can say with Alice that the case grows "curiouser and curiouser".'

Tinker nodded.

'The baffling part of it is, guv'nor, that we don't know where to begin. Do you think there is any link at all between these seven people?'

Sexton Blake shook his head, and tapped the open volume on his knee with the stem of his pipe.

'The details of the egregious Mr Krimm's career in the index are brief but illuminating, young 'un,' he said. 'He's a particularly loathsome specimen of his type. His financial deals have been shady for years. He's only just managed to steer clear of convictions for fraud. Actually, I doubt if Society would be any the worse if people of Mr Krimm's kidney disappeared for good.'

Tinker nodded.

'Yes, I guessed there was something fishy about him,' he commented. 'Wasn't there some unsavoury scandal over a company that went bust?'

'There was,' replied the detective. 'Well, I shall not lose much sleep about Mr Krimm's disappearance,' he added. 'The thing that interests me, however, is why this sudden epidemic? Poor Miss Hornby is at her wits' end. Mrs Skeffington Smythe is still missing.'

'She's a tartar, all right,' chuckled Tinker. 'One of the good old pre-War suffragettes, wasn't she?'

Blake smiled.

'All I can say, Tinker, is that if by any chance Mrs Smythe has been kidnapped, Heaven help the kidnappers.'

Tinker grinned.

'Why in the name of Mike should anybody want to tackle a woman like that?' he said. 'She's not particularly rich, but for that matter, none of the people who have vanished are particularly rich. It baffles me, guv'nor.'

Blake puffed slowly at his pipe.

'There are three methods of approach to this case,' he said. 'One is to treat each disappearance as distinct from the others, and to tackle one only on its independent merits or demerits. The second is to assume that all, or nearly all, of the disappearances are connected in some way, and connected by a criminal reason. The third method is to regard the whole seven cases as being a coincidence. After all, there is no law against a man disappearing, or a woman, for that matter. The odds against the latter hypothesis are too great, however.'

'But which theory do you favour most?' inquired Tinker.

Sexton Blake shrugged his shoulders.

'A combination of one and two,' he remarked. 'Let us assume, just for the sake of argument, that these seven disappearances are interrelated in some way. We have actually only tackled one of the disappearances. That is the case of Otto Krimm. Coutts has made exhaustive inquiries into the other cases without any tangible results whatsoever. Let us, therefore, concentrate on Krimm.'

'What about Mrs Skeffington Smythe?' broke in Tinker. 'Did she know Krimm? Perhaps they've eloped together,' he added flippantly.

Blake frowned.

'I could discover from Miss Hornby if the two were acquainted,' he said, 'but that won't help us much at the moment. What exactly have we got to go on?'

He ticked off the facts on his lean, muscular fingers.

'Krimm left the flat two nights ago with the full intention of returning. Note the instructions regarding the hot-water bottle and for his breakfast.'

'Yes, that's assuming that Ito, the Jap, is telling the truth,' interposed his young assistant.

'Somehow or other, I don't trust that fellow much.'

'Neither do I,' said Blake. 'However, we have a much more valuable clue on which to work than vague statements of the manservant. Hand me over a print of that photo again.'

Tinker crossed over to the laboratory and returned a moment later with an enlarged photographic print of the mirror in Krimm's dining-room.

The photograph had been taken with infra-red plates, and showed with startling clarity two images that had been so faint as to be almost invisible on the glass itself.

'There's a good deal of significance in that hanging sword, Tinker.'

'Yes, and what about the girl to the right of it?'

He pointed to the image of a girl with wide-open, almost hypnotic eyes. The expression was one of infinite sadness and reproach. The face itself was surrounded by an aureole of clustering curls, giving it an almost child-like appearance.

The infra-red rays had produced a woolly effect about the picture, resembling the cottonwool-like spirit photographs at seances.

'It's a rum business altogether, guv'nor,' he said. 'Was Krimm a dabbler in Spiritualism or anything of that sort?'

Sexton Blake shrugged his shoulders.

'Goodness knows. His type are generally interested in the occult. The main question is whether this sword and picture relate in any way to Krimm's disappearance. The sword might be a warning from someone who bore him a grudge. On the other hand, it might be some bizarre scheme of decoration of Krimm's own devising. Anyway, there are plenty of fingerprints on this mirror, which, fortunately, the infra-red rays have brought out very well. I have asked Coutts to give them the once-over, and we may or may not find something material.'

Tinker groaned.

'It's all such a tangle,' he said. 'There doesn't seem to be a single thing, as you say, to go on. Just take a list of the seven missing people in alphabetical order. There's James Hacker, a labourer; then there's Krimm, practically a millionaire; then there's old Nissim, the oil-man; and then this recluse, Sandford, from Mitcham; and Mrs Skeffington Smythe; the soldier, whose name I don't know, and last, the amiable Mr Ephra Zeed. Dash it all, guv'nor, there doesn't seem to be any point of contact between them at all,' added Tinker, a little querulously.

A double knock sounded at the front door, and Blake smiled.

'This is Coutts, I expect,' he observed. 'I wonder if he's any news for us.'

A few moments later, the burly Yard man breezed into the consulting-room.

'This is too much, Blake,' he exploded, without even the preliminary of a morning greeting.

'What's happened now?' queried Sexton Blake, with a twinkle.

Coutts removed his hard bowler hat and flung it on the couch.

'There's another of 'em gone!' he said. 'We got the information this morning. I've a darned good mind to tell the next anxious inquirer to apply to the Lost Property Office.'

Sexton Blake closed the volume of the Index, and rubbed his hands together with a little gesture of satisfaction.

'Who's the latest disappearance?' he queried.

'A girl name Henrietta Rushworth, a maid in a stockbroker's house at Notting Hill Gate,' answered Coutts. 'She went out to post a letter at 7.30 last night and hasn't been seen since.'

'Two women and six men in less than a week,' said Sexton Blake reflectively. 'Any further information?'

Coutts helped himself to one of Blake's cigars before replying, and having lit up, hoisted one leg over the other.

'Harker's dealing with the latest,' he said. 'I've traced the taxi in which Krimm and his girl left Jermyn Street, but I got precious little information out of the driver. Krimm, it appears, was a bit intoxicated. The cabman deposited them at about ten minutes to nine outside the Milan Club in Shaftesbury Avenue, and that's all the information he can give me.'

'H'm!' said Blake thoughtfully. 'Not very illuminating. Anything else?'

Coutts grunted.

'Well, I compared the photograph you sent me with the files in the Criminal Records Office, and I discovered one peculiar thing. Two of the fingerprints tally with those of an old "lag".'

Sexton Blake's eyes sparkled.

'Ah, something tangible at last,' he said crisply. 'Who is he?'

'A man of the name of Just,' answered Coutts. 'He served four years at Maidstone for manslaughter. That was some ten years ago, and we've lost all trace of him since then.'

'Just!' echoed Sexton Blake. 'Let's have the J. volume of the Index, young 'un.'

He turned to Tinker, who crossed over to the bookcase containing the Index.

'I seem to recall the name,' continued Blake. 'Wasn't he a doctor? He killed one of his patients through criminal negligence?'

'That's right,' commented Coutts. 'He gave a girl named Jill Bryant the wrong medicine and killed her. There was some doubt about the case, if I recall correctly. At first, the charge was one of murder, but it was reduced to manslaughter.'

Blake's keen grey eyes narrowed as Tinker handed over the Index volume. Swiftly he turned over the leaves of that unique criminological record.

'Ah, here we are!' he said, pausing and scanning the neatly and tersely written biography to which was appended some news cuttings.

'Julian Just, accused of the manslaughter of Jill Bryant. Tried at the Old Bailey in 1919.

'He was accused of criminal negligence with intent to do

grievous bodily harm. Jarrett, KC, was defending.'

Rapidly Blake read through the account of the trial, and then closed the volume.

'Very interesting,' he observed. 'The question remains, why should Just's fingerprints be found on the mirror in Krimm's dining-room?'

'H'm!' grunted Coutts. 'That's what's baffling me. No one can find any trace of him after his release from Maidstone. There may be a dozen explanations of it,' he added gloomily.

Suddenly Blake pounded his fist into the palm of his hand.

'By Jove, Coutts, there is a connection,' he exclaimed, 'and a distinct connection at that! I mentioned the Sword of Damocles a little while ago. There is also a Sword of Justice. That image was produced on the mirror by artificial means deliberately. The solution of chlorate of mercury is a common method used by conjurers for causing writing to appear and disappear at will through the application of heat. You can see by this photo. The infra-red plates have brought out the whole thing in detail. Just's fingerprints were on that mirror—obviously he is connected with the disappearance of Krimm.'

Blake picked up the photograph again and examined it intently.

His eyes sparkled with excitement, and an unwonted flush of colour crept into his cheeks.

'Look at that!' he said to Coutts, pointing to the impression of a girl's head which had appeared to the side of the sword.

He pounced once more on the Index volume and turned up the newspaper cuttings again.

'See?' he said. 'With her hair worn in ringlets and without a hat, the two faces are identical.'

Coutts craned over Blake's shoulders as he pointed to the photograph—old and faded now—of the dead girl, Jill Bryant.

'Great Scott, Blake!' he exclaimed enthusiastically. 'We've got something real at last! I'll send the wires buzzing with an AS message with Just's description right away.'

Sexton Blake slowly refilled his briar.

'You can use my phone,' he remarked.

And then, to Tinker:

'I want you to go to all the theatrical agencies and find out any information you can about a girl whose name is Terry. Find out

26

where she lives and as much as you can about her. Bring it straight back here.'

Tinker nodded, and hurried out on his mission.

Blake puffed for a while in thoughtful silence as Coutts hurriedly called up his colleague, Inspector Harker, at the Yard and issued his instructions.

The CID man replaced the receiver with a satisfied grunt.

'At last, Blake,' he commented, 'we can get moving. I've been running around in circles this week, but once we get hold of Just, then I reckon we'll learn a lot about Mr Krimm's disappearance.'

Sexton Blake nodded.

'Remember that Just is fourteen years older than he was when you had the last description of him,' he observed. 'He might have grown a beard, and most certainly have changed his name; and then, again, he might be well outside the country by this time.'

Coutts' face fell.

'Yes, that's true enough,' he admitted grudgingly. 'But, hang it all, what else can we start on?'

A tap sounded at the door of the consulting-room, and Mrs Bardell entered.

'Which there's a Miss Hornby to see you, sir,' she announced.

Blake gave a half-imperceptible sigh.

'Very good, Mrs Bardell. Please show her in,' he instructed.

A moment later the plump, squat figure of Mrs Skeffington Smythe's secretary appeared.

Coutts and Blake rose to their feet as she entered the room.

'Ah, good-morning, Miss Hornby,' said Blake quietly. 'You have good news, I trust? Will you sit down?'

His visitor dropped into the proffered chair with an expression of thanks.

'Yes, Mr Blake, I have indeed news,' she replied, 'but it is far from satisfactory. I received this letter this morning from Mrs Skeffington Smythe.'

She withdrew an envelope from her bag and handed it over to Blake.

The detective opened it and took out a piece of blue, linen-grained notepaper. There was no address on the letter, which ran as follows:

Dear Miss Hornby,—This is just to state that I shall be away for an indefinite period. Circumstances over which I have no control compel me to keep my whereabouts secret. I am in good health and am well looked after. I shall not communicate with you again until I see you in person.

Sincerely yours,

AMELIA SKEFFINGTON SMYTHE

'Strange!' said Blake. 'Do you mind if I show this to my colleague, Inspector Coutts?'

Miss Hornby shook her head, and Coutts took the letter eagerly from Blake's fingers.

'It's a most extraordinary letter, Mr Blake,' said the secretary.

'You have no doubt at all that it is Mrs Skeffington Smythe's handwriting?' asked Blake.

His visitor gave a curt little laugh.

'Why, I have been her confidential secretary for years, Mr Blake,' she said. 'Mrs Skeffington Smythe wrote that letter right enough.'

Blake picked up the envelope, and taking out his pocket-lens, examined it minutely.

'H'm!' he commented. 'Posted at Hammersmith at 7.30 last night. Fairly expensive notepaper, but of fairly common make. I'm afraid we can't find out much from that.'

'Mr Blake, it's dreadful!' exclaimed Miss Hornby. 'All the work of our league is at a standstill. We're having a committee meeting this afternoon, and how on earth am I going to explain Mrs Smythe's continued absence? This letter is no explanation at all; it simply deepens the mystery and uncertainty.'

'That's right,' broke in Coutts gruffly. 'That letter seems to indicate, madam, that Mrs Smythe is kept a prisoner somewhere.'

He shot a significant glance at Blake, who replaced the letter in its envelope.

'Would you let me keep this for a little, Miss Hornby?' he said. 'I don't wish to appear too sanguine, but there are indications that I shall have some goods news for you shortly. I may say that Scotland Yard is straining every nerve on your behalf, and you can rest assured that we will let you know at once when anything transpires.'

Miss Hornby rose to her feet, and her cheeks were flushed a

little.

'Oh, thank you, thank you, Mr Blake!' she said. 'You can't tell what relief it is to know that you're helping in this affair.'

Blake smiled, and with a tactful courtesy escorted her from the consulting-room.

Coutts jammed his hard bowler hat at an aggressive angle on his bullet head as Blake returned.

'What's your next move, Blake?' he demanded. Sexton Blake shrugged his shoulders.

'You get the drag-net out, Coutts,' he said. 'I think I shall concentrate on the lady in the case, Mr Otto Krimm's mysterious Miss Terry.'

*   *   *

In the rambling old manor house sheltered away from the winding highway by a thick copse of fir-trees, three men sat around a heavy mahogany table in a room plainly furnished, whose colour motive was mahogany and a deep purple that was almost black.

The heavy plush curtains had been drawn across the windows excluding every ray of sunlight, and the sole illumination was an enormous pendant bowl of alabaster which shed a soft diffused radiance on the scene.

Three silent men they were that sat there in that quiet room.

They were clad in purple robes almost monkish in pattern. Their faces were shrouded with heavy hoods save for the slits in the cowls through which their eyes glittered luminously.

The table was set on a raised dais above which was suspended a naked steel sword. One of the hooded men, taller than the other two, rose to his feet with a soft swish of his robes.

'So you say that the prisoner is proving recalcitrant?' he said, in a soft, musical voice. 'What of the others, No. 2?'

The second man gave a mirthless chuckle.

'Oh, they find they have to make a virtue out of necessity. The man Hacker seems perfectly satisfied, but neither Zeed nor Sandford is inclined to be tractable.'

'Good!' said their leader. 'Have the man Zeed brought in. It is as well that he should realise that he is no longer his own master.'

The other bowed and crossed over to the great plush *portières*.

'What of the women?' inquired the chief, in his low, melodious tone to the remaining hooded man.

The other laughed.

'As comfortable as can be expected in the circumstances, Chief,' he said. 'Mrs Skeffington Smythe is still seething with indignation, but the girl Rushworth is finding a romantic glamour in the affair which one would expect from one of her mentality.'

'The man Zeed!' said the deep, booming voice of No. 2, and a moment later he reappeared, escorting the shambling figure of Mr Ephra Zeed.

Two days had elapsed since his arrival at that grim old manor. Two days in which the chartered accountant's clock-bound, well-ordered world had been brought toppling into ruin.

Zeed's face was an unhealthy yellow colour, and his watery eyes blinked nervously as he faced the cowled figures of his captors.

Gone was the slightly pompous assurance of his first arrival. He cringed now like a whipped cur as the stern eyes of the Chief regarded him speculatively through the slits in his cowl.

'I hear you are not satisfied with your treatment, Zeed,' said the Chief.

The unhappy accountant licked his dry lips nervously.

'I'm not well,' he said. 'The strain is telling on me. After all, it is an outrage—'

'A what?' snapped the Chief, and his voice cracked now like the lash of a whip. 'You know the alternative, my friend. At the appointed hour you shall earn your freedom. Until then you are under the Law of the Hanging Sword. Remember your promise, Ephra Zeed, and remember my words to you on your arrival. "They that oppose me shall be cast down to destruction, and they shalt be brought into desolation and be utterly consumed with terrors."'

His voice became vibrant as he chanted the words of the Psalmist, and Zeed wilted as if from a blow.

The Chief signalled to the shortest of the cowled figures, who disappeared behind the heavy curtains again.

'Stay here, Zeed, and perhaps you will realise why this has befallen you.'

Ephra Zeed looked round on the long, sombre room with the hopeless air of a rat in a trap.

Suddenly the heavy plush portieres parted, and, escorted by the grim figure of No. 2, a woman entered the room.

She was tall and massively built. Clad in brown-grey tweeds, with a mannish collar and her hair cropped short, she stood for a moment defiantly.

Ephra Zeed took one look at the woman's stern face with its beaky nose and square jaw. Her eyes behind her horn-rimmed spectacles seemed to hypnotise him.

'Do you know that woman?' demanded the Chief.

Zeed gulped and gave a hoarse cry.

No word, however, broke from his parched lips, but he nodded his head dumbly.

At last he knew the reason for the astounding nightmare of the past forty-eight hours, and the ordeal that was in store for him.

Never in his life had he wanted to see that woman again, and she was here in this great, gloomy house of terror.

His heart quailed at the thought of what was in store for him.

*   *   *

In his small but well-equipped laboratory, which Tinker irreverently referred to as the 'stink shop', Sexton Blake, clad in his familiar red dressing-gown, stooped intently over a test-tube held in his thin, muscular fingers.

Before him, on a zinc-topped bench, a Bunsen burner blazed and spluttered, and overhead a mercury lamp threw the shadow of his lean features on the white-tiled wall, where it hovered and flickered frantically.

Blake was a peculiar combination of a dreamer and a man of action.

He had the Napoleonic faculty of being able to take his mind off one aspect of a case and concentrating on another matter if there was no data available on which he could proceed.

Having established the fact that in some way there was a connection between the ex-convict Just and the missing millionaire, Blake had entrusted the routine work to Tinker, and was now relaxing in his favourite hobby of chemistry.

Suddenly he heard a quick step in the adjoining room, and Tinker's clear young voice calling:

'Are you in, guv'nor?'

Blake replaced the test-tube on the rack and opened the communicating door.

'Hallo, young 'un! You've been some time,' he said. 'Got the information?'

Tinker nodded and wrinkled his nostrils distastefully at the smell of the unpleasant brew that was boiling above the Bunsen burner.

'Phew, guv'nor! It was a tiresome business,' he said. 'I went round to at least half a dozen agents before I got what I wanted. I don't know why it is, but theatrical agents always choose the top floor of the highest buildings they can find that have no lift.'

Blake smiled and switched out the gas-jet.

Together they returned to the consulting-room.

'Well, what's happened?' he inquired.

'The first thing I learned was that there are about half a hundred Terrys connected with the Stage, guv'nor,' Tinker said, with a grin, 'and not one of them by any chance seemed to have the remotest connection with our friend Krimm. I gave up looking at it from that angle and inquired about Krimm himself.

Sexton Blake nodded approvingly.

'Yes, and what did you discover?'

'That the amiable Mr Krimm is about the most hated man within half a mile of Poverty Corner,' said Tinker. 'I learnt that he's really financing a lot of shady theatrical agents, who put shows on the road and leave the poor, wretched chorus-girls stranded. He's a nasty piece of work is Mr Krimm.'

Sexton Blake nodded.

'I thought as much, young 'un,' he remarked. 'Where did you pick up all this?'

'Well,' replied Tinker, 'it cost me about nine bob in beer at the Thespis Club. Those actor chaps seem to have a deuce of a thirst. I met one old boy who grew positively sulphuric when I mentioned the name of Krimm, and it was he that put me on the track of this girl named Terry. Terry Lee her name is. She's not so young, I'm told, but very attractive. It seems that lately old Krimm has been thinking of opening a new night club and of putting Terry Lee in charge as hostess.'

'Ah!' said Blake softly. 'Where does Miss Lee hang out?'

Tinker shook his head.

'That I couldn't find out. But I'm told she's a fairly frequent visitor to the Frou Frou Cabaret Club, in Shaftesbury Avenue. That doesn't open until seven at night, though, and I was thinking it wouldn't be a bad idea if I—'

'In other words,' broke in Sexton Blake, 'you wouldn't mind a night out, young 'un?'

Tinker grinned.

'Well, guv'nor, I shouldn't mind snooping around just on the offchance of picking up something,' he replied.

Sexton Blake smiled. He placed his hand in his pocket-wallet and withdrew a crisp banknote.

'To reimburse you for the necessary expenses, Tinker,' he commented. 'I know these actors' thirsts.'

A phone bell shrilled suddenly, and Blake lifted the receiver. He heard the voice of Coutts at the other end of the wire.

'I say, Blake,' said the Yard man excitedly, 'we've just heard from Zeed. He's written a letter to his housekeeper!'

Blake raised his eyebrows.

'What does he say?' he demanded.

He heard distinctly Inspector Coutts clear his throat before going on.

'It's practically word for word the same letter that Miss Hornby received from Mrs Skeffington Smythe:

Dear Mrs Salter,—I shall be away for an indefinite period. Please carry on as usual. I enclose five pounds for current expenses. I am in good health and am well looked after. Please do not worry.

Yours truly,

EPHRA ZEED

There was a slight pause.

'What do you make of that, Blake?' inquired Coutts. 'It looks to me as if the whole boiling of them have been kidnapped.'

'Yes,' answered Blake, 'but who has kidnapped them, and why is it still as baffling as ever? I'm following up the Terry clue,' he added. 'And, by the way, Coutts, just a tip. It would be as well if you were to put a man on to the trail of that fellow Ito. I'm not at all sure of him.'

'I've done that already, Blake, but the blighter has not stirred out of the house yet. Apart from Mr Binnett, no one has called at Krimm's flat.'

'I see,' responded Blake. 'Keep me informed of all the latest developments, won't you? Goodbye!'

He rang off, and his lean and clever face was very thoughtful.

*　　*　　*

Sexton Blake finished his dinner, and meditatively regarded the crimson depth of his port glass.

He had dined alone.

Tinker had elected to dine 'up West', and had departed half an hour before, a resplendent figure in evening dress. The youngster had been nothing loath to combine business with pleasure.

A tap sounded at the door of the dining-room, and Mrs Bardell made her appearance.

'An excellent dinner, Mrs Bardell,' Blake smiled at her. 'That entrée was an inspiration.'

His housekeeper beamed delightedly at the tribute.

'Which I'm sorry to disturb you, sir,' she announced, a trifle breathlessly, 'but there's a gentleman of the name of Missing wants to insult you.'

Blake found it hard to conceal a grin.

'Shall I show him into the insulting-room?' she added.

Blake's gaze became thoughtful. Mrs Bardell's use of the English language was peculiarly her own. She never conceivably announced persons by their right names. ('Denouncing' them, she called it.) But in view of the circumstances, the name 'Missing' seemed to the detective a peculiarly appropriate one.

'He's down in the hall,' proceeded Mrs Bardell, in a husky whisper.

'Very well, show him up,' said Blake.

He was still clad in his mantle of reflection, and his hand groped mechanically into his tattered pockets for his pipe as he re-entered his consulting-room.

A moment later Mrs Bardell ushered in the newcomer.

He was an imposing figure. He wore an old-fashioned, long black ulster and a broad-brimmed black hat, which threw his face, which was lean and cadaverous, into a sinister shadow.

He wore a high, old-fashioned collar and a saffron-coloured tie of startling vividness.

His voice was deep and sepulchral as he shambled into the room.

'Mr Sexton Blake, I presume?' he said, with a queer, stiff bow, and removed his hat.

The detective nodded.

'Pray be seated, Mr—'

'Nissim,' supplied the stranger. 'Walter James Nissim, Mr Blake, at your service.'

Blake's eyebrows arched interrogatively, and instantly his attitude grew alert.

'I've come to you about my brother, sir,' exclaimed his visitor.

'Ah, yes!' responded Blake. 'Mr John Nissim, of Oakley Crescent, Chelsea, I understand?'

The other bowed awkwardly again.

'Yes, sir. My brother, as you will doubtless recall, has been missing for some days, and it was on the advice of Scotland Yard that I called in to see you this evening.'

'So you met my colleague, Inspector Coutts?' remarked Blake, his eyes kindling with interest.

The man nodded.

'Yes, Mr Blake. This morning I received a most peculiar communication from my brother John.'

He groped in the capacious folds of his ulster and pulled out an envelope.

Blake leant back in his chair, and beneath lowered lids studied his quaint visitor.

His appearance was eccentric, and smacked more of the Latin Quarter of Paris in the nineties than of the present day.

'Are you in the same line of business as your brother, Mr Nissim?' he queried.

The visitor nodded.

'Yes, Mr Blake. We have two oil-and-colour shops between us; but my brother is older than myself, and he retired a year ago, leaving the management to me.'

Blake nodded.

'I see. Are both establishments in Chelsea?'

Nissim shook his head.

'No; we have a branch shop in Pottery Lane, Pimlico. I live over the main shop in Judge's Walk, Chelsea.'

Sexton Blake's eyes narrowed a trifle.

'Can you throw any light on the mystery of your brother's disappearance, Mr Nissim?' he inquired.

His caller again shook his head.

'No, sir; the whole thing is a complete mystery to me. My brother John had not an enemy in the world, and we were the best of friends and partners.'

Blake stretched out his hand.

'You had better let me have a look at that letter,' he said quietly.

The other handed over the envelope.

Blake noted that it was of the same type of blue, linen-grained paper as that which Miss Hornby had received, and it had been posted in Hammersmith the previous night.

He opened the envelope and took out its contents.

In a crabbed, spidery handwriting was written the following:

Dear Walter,—It has come at last, all that I feared and dreaded. I cannot write and tell you where I am, but I am in no immediate danger. If you do not hear further from me in forty-eight hours' time, I want you to close the shop and go to live in above the Pottery Lane branch. This is vitally important, and I beg of you to obey my wishes.

I cannot be too explicit in this letter, but would refer you to our conversation a month back about Ali Baba. "If you will seek diligently you will find the solution."

At the moment I am safe.

Your brother,

JOHN

Sexton Blake's eyes sparkled as he read the extraordinary epistle.

He glanced across shrewdly at his visitor, and tapped the paper with a lean forefinger.

'This is rather an amazing document, Mr Nissim,' he commented. 'Frankly, I can make very little of it. What is this reference to Ali Baba?'

His visitor shook his head gravely.

'Mr Blake,' he said, bending forward earnestly, 'I've never told a soul before, but some queer things have been happening lately in my shop in Judge's Walk. I'm not a fanciful man—in fact, I'm considered rather hard-headed—but for the past month I've been driven to the conclusion that my house is haunted!'

Blake elevated his eyebrows slightly.

'Haunted?' he repeated. 'What precisely do you mean, Mr Nissim?'

The other rubbed his lantern jaw uncertainly.

'Well, I can't express it exactly any other way, Mr Blake,' he said apologetically. 'I'm a bachelor and I live alone in the shop. My brother has got a nice little house in Oakley Crescent, and when he retired he thought he would cut himself loose from the business altogether. So he gave up his old rooms to me.'

Blake nodded encouragingly.

'Well, sir,' continued Nissim, 'about a month ago these queer things first started to happen. At first I took no notice of them, but lately the things have been growing worse and worse.'

'But what things?' demanded Blake sharply.

Mr Nissim shrugged his shoulders apologetically, and his voice sank into a whisper.

'The hauntings, Mr Blake,' he said. 'For instance, when I'm alone at night I've heard a sudden crash from the next room, and found a vase or an ornament in fragments. I've gone there at once and found nothing there to account for it. Not a soul in the room! That's happened dozens of times in the last fortnight, Mr Blake. I found a heavy overmantel clock smashed to bits only yesterday.

'Then I hear queer muffled screams late at night, and although I've searched the house from top to bottom I have been unable to find anything to account for the noises.'

'Have you a wireless set?' interposed the detective.

Nissim shook his head.

'No,' he replied. 'I can't bear the things.'

He bent forward, and his lean, cadaverous face was very grave.

'Two nights ago, Mr Blake, the strangest thing happened. An old painting of my brother, which was done of him some years ago by an artist in exchange for goods received, fell from the picture-rail into the fireplace. I'm not superstitious, Mr Blake, but that seemed an omen to me.'

The detective extended his lean hands and pressed the tips of his fingers together.

'Have you any theory of the supernatural to account for these manifestations?' Blake asked slowly.

Mr Nissim shook his head emphatically.

'No, Mr Blake, I haven't; but I tell you the events of the past month have shaken me up considerably. I can't sleep at night, and what with the worry of my brother's disappearance and now this letter, I'm at my wits' end.'

Sexton Blake lit his briar and smoked for a moment or two in silence.

'What does this reference to Ali Baba mean?' he asked again.

Nissim gave a self-conscious laugh.

'Well, I don't rightly know, unless it was the talk old John and I had some time ago about the jars above the shop.'

Blake glanced across inquiringly.

'You're referring, I presume, to the oilman's familiar trade-mark. Most ironmongers and colourmen have adopted it, and they are almost as familiar as the coloured glass bottles of the chemists.'

Nissim nodded.

'Yes, almost everyone of our trade has an earthenware jar above the shop. They're a recognised advertisement, like a barber's pole. Some are quite big, and others quite small, but I dare say that ninety per cent of ironmongers still use them.

'Well,' he continued, 'it was about these jars that my brother John and I were talking some weeks ago.'

He paused for a moment, and Blake, conscious of a slight feeling of strain in the atmosphere, crossed over to the sideboard and mixed two whiskies-and-soda.

He returned to his client and smiled.

'This will keep the cold out, Mr Nissim,' he said.

His visitor gave a grateful smile of thanks and raised his glass.

'Thanks,' he said. 'I'm glad I've come to you. I feel a lot better already.

'Well, I must tell you about my brother John. He was very popular with the artist crowd and other Bohemians down Chelsea way. They're a free-and-easy sort of crowd, and one night John and I were having a friendly confab in the Six Bells with Mr Mander, an artist and an old customer of ours. A great talker, Mr Mander,' he added reminiscently.

'I remember our talk turned to pub signs and the queer names some inns have, like the Goat and Boots, or the Who'd 'a Thought It?'

Sexton Blake nodded.

'An interesting subject,' he remarked.

'Well, then,' continued his visitor, 'Mr Mander pointed out to Old John that though some people considered ironmonger's shops the most unromantic and depressing places in the world with their tin cans and general atmosphere of back kitchens on washing-days, he didn't agree with them. This pleased my brother no end, Mr Blake, he having been in the trade forty years or more. Mr Mander, he laughed a good deal, and then said: "Why, Mr Nissim, you don't realise how romantic you are. Look at those jolly little red jars above the lintel of your shop. Do you know the secret of them?" '

Here Blake's visitor paused, and, stretching out a bony finger, pointed impressively at the detective.

'Believe it or not, Mr Blake, as Mr Mander said that my brother's face went as pale as death, and he dropped his tankard. He gave a queer choking sound, and then said: "What do you mean by the secret?" With that Mr Mander laughs again, and says: "Haven't you heard of Ali Baba and the Forty Thieves, Mr Nissim?" With that my brother looks relieved. "Why, yes," he said. "I've seen it as a pantomime many a time." "Don't you remember," says Mr Mander, with a chuckle, "when the captain of the robbers tried to get into Ali Baba's palace with his gang that he disguised himself as an oil merchant?"

' "So he did," said my brother. "And wasn't there a slave girl called Maudie or something that poured boiling water on the heads of the thieves before they could get out of the jar?" "That's right," said Mr Mander. "Well, the jars above your shop window haven't changed a bit in shape since the days of Ali Baba. Yours is a very old and honourable trade, Mr Nissim." '

Blake's visitor paused a moment, then continued:

'Well, we had a few more drinks, Mr Blake, and I thought no more about it; but on the way home with me my brother that night became very thoughtful and quiet.

' "Walter," he said—and I remember his exact words—"Walter, if anything should happen to me, remember what Mr Mander said about Ali Baba."

' "What do you mean by happen?" said I, joking like. He shook his head at that. "Nothing, Walter," he said. "Only a funny fancy has come into my head. All I can say is remember what I've said." '

Mr Nissim coughed, and drained his drink as he concluded his remarkable narrative.

'Very interesting indeed,' commented Sexton Blake. 'Evidently your brother was half expecting something to happen.'

'I've been thinking about it all day, Mr Blake,' replied the other. 'What with these weird things at home and those jars, I feel something terrible has happened to my brother!'

'Did you mention this to the police?' Blake inquired.

The other shook his head.

'No, sir, not in full. I thought they'd laugh at me!'

Blake rose to his feet.

'Your case interests me immensely, Mr Nissim,' he said. 'As a matter of fact, I have already formulated a theory, but more data is necessary. When do these ghostly manifestations occur usually?'

'Mostly after we close the shop at night,' he answered.

'Then,' said the detective briskly, 'I think, as a preliminary, it would be advisable to look over your premises. I don't believe in ghosts. I only believe in their inherent possibilities!'

A gratified look came into the face of his visitor.

'Oh, Mr Blake, if you could only help me,' he said earnestly, 'I'd be eternally grateful to you! I'm almost out of my mind with suspense. Could you come over some time and see if you could find an explanation for these weird happenings? I'm not usually a nervous man, Mr Blake, but I dread the thought of going back tonight!'

'Very good, then,' replied Blake crisply, with a glance at the clock. 'There is no time like the present. If you'll excuse me a moment while I change, we'll take a taxi to Chelsea.

'A spot more whisky before you go, Mr Nissim?' he added hospitably.

His visitor wiped his lips with the back of his bony hand.

'You're very kind, Mr Blake,' he commented, as the detective took up the tumbler, and crossing over to the sideboard, held it to the light while he mixed another whisky-and-soda.

Blake excused himself for a moment or two and entered his dressing-room, to emerge, soon after, clad in a warm tweed overcoat and a grey hat.

His visitor rose to his feet and fumbled uncertainly with his peculiar yellow tie.

'I feel relieved already, Mr Blake,' he said, as they descended the stairs.

Blake opened the door. It was a cold night, with a thin drizzle of rain falling. Blake turned up his coat collar, and, accompanied by his companion, walked sharply down Baker Street.

The singular narrative he had just heard was one that appealed immensely to the detective's love of the bizarre.

At last he had something material on which to work, but for the life of him, he could see no connection between the disappearance of a matter-of-fact Amazon, like Mrs Skeffington Smythe, and the oil jars of the obscure ironmonger in Chelsea. Still less could he discover any relation between the vanishing of Mr Krimm and the missing John Nissim.

It was, therefore, with a pleasurable sense of anticipation that he hailed a taxicab, and a moment later sank back in the seat with his companion, there to grapple with the problem.

* * *

Across the transformed ballroom of London's latest and liveliest night club, the Frou Frou, Tinker glanced with interest.

It was not yet eight o'clock, and the club did not warm up thoroughly for another two or three hours.

The place was ultra-modern in its furnishing. The floor was of smooth, polished black glass, and round the walls and alcoves of the place its designer had allowed his riotous fancy full rein. There were nymphs and dryads, dancing fawns, jovial-looking satyrs— all depicted with splashes of exotic colour.

Tinker had sampled the club dinner, and was pleasantly surprised to find that the cuisine was above the average in resorts of that description.

As he sipped his glass of claret his eyes roved over the throng of people present.

'Hallo, my young sleuth!' said a voice in Tinker's ears; and he simultaneously received a hearty smack on the back that made him wince.

Tinker spluttered into his glass and turned round half wrathfully to find the cheerful, grinning face of Bobby Hazeldine, the young racing motorist, beaming into his.

'Confound you, Bobby!' gasped Tinker. 'You've got hands like hams!'

That cheerful youth, quite unabashed, took a seat at Tinker's solitary table.

'Why this thusness, young fellow?' he queried.

'Why the ravelled frown and carping care? What are you doing all alone in these haunts of gilded vice?'

Tinker smoothed the silken lapel of his dinner-jacket. He knew and liked Bobby Hazeldine, who, despite his boisterousness, was a cool and brilliant motorist and a loyal, dependable friend.

He was a year or two older than Sexton Blake's young assistant, and inclined to stoutness.

'I'm having a night off, Bobby,' explained Tinker. 'Have some wine. What are you doing here?'

'Ha, ha!' laughed Bobby. 'I've come all over vegetarian—or is it fruitarian? I've got a date with a "peach".'

He glanced at his wrist-watch and frowned.

'Dash it all, she's twenty minutes late!' he added.

Tinker chuckled. He knew Bobby's fruitarian weaknesses.

'Do you come here often, Bobby?' he asked.

His companion shrugged.

'Oh, about twice a week. Not a bad spot,' he observed. 'The band is one of the best in London.'

Tinker gazed around the ballroom and abstractedly watched the dancers as they took the floor.

Half a dozen spot lights played on the moving throng of dancers, making a tone poem of colour.

'There's old Chipperdale,' commented Bobby. 'Tight as an owl, as usual.'

He jerked his head towards the adjoining alcove, where that scion of nobility was endeavouring to balance a salad bowl on his chin.

'Look here,' said Tinker. 'You seem to know most of the people here. Do you know a girl named Lee—Terry Lee?'

Bobby laughed outright.

'Why, sure. She sometimes does a song and dance turn when we have a cabaret night. Why, what's the matter; are you smitten?'

His companion shook his head. He was watching the crowd come in from the vestibule.

'Speak of angels,' said Bobby, nudging Tinker. 'You hear the rustling of their wings. There she goes.'

Tinker's pulses leaped a little as a girl stood for a moment at the entrance of the ballroom.

She was a shimmering vision in a sequinned, black evening dress. Her cheeks were flushed, and from her smoothly-shingled, honey-coloured hair, to the tips of her audaciously scarlet high-heeled shoes, she was the essence of feminine allurement.

A moment later she was joined by her companion. He was a medium sized, rather portly man, with iron-grey hair and piercing brown eyes, with an imperious nose and thin lips. He had one of those dark jaws that no amount of shaving robbed of a slightly blue tinge.

Tinker drew in his breath sharply as he recognised him.

'Gosh!' he exclaimed. 'That's Palfrey, KC.'

Bobby Hazeldine glanced carelessly in the direction of the pair.

'That's more in your line, old man,' he remarked. 'Isn't he the chap that defended the Barnstaple murderer?'

Tinker nodded.

From the tail of his eye he watched the eminent KC and his fair companion as they took a table in an alcove exactly opposite them in the ballroom.

Tinker frowned thoughtfully.

He had met Palfrey once with Blake, but he knew very little about the private life of the barrister, and it was rather surprising to find him in such frivolous surroundings as the Frou Frou, and in company with the elusive Miss Terry Lee.

'So that's Terry Lee,' he said. 'Know anything about her?'

Bobby's laughing face became grave for a moment or two.

'Are you interested professionally?' he inquired.

Tinker shrugged his shoulders.

'Not particularly, except that I heard that she was a friend of Mr Otto Krimm.' Tinker groped in his pocket for a cigarette case and proffered its contents to Bobby.

He did not think it advisable at that juncture to elaborate the subject, so he deftly switched the conversation on to Brooklands.

Bobby, however, was half-hearted in his answers, and his gaze kept straying towards the door. Suddenly his red face flushed a deep scarlet as a pretty girl in a long pink evening dress entered the ballroom.

'Excuse me, Tinker, old lad,' he apologised. 'I'll see you later.'

He rose to his feet and hurried in the direction of the new arrival. Bobby's fruitarian date had arrived.

Left alone, Tinker covertly studied Miss Terry Lee and her partner. Judging from her sparkling eyes and gay laughter, Terry Lee had not a care in the wide world. Her escort's usually saturnine face was now wreathed in a smile, so fond as to be almost foolish.

Tinker signalled to a hovering waiter and ordered a cup of Turkish coffee. When the man returned with his order Tinker unobtrusively slipped a folded note into the man's palm.

'The young lady on the table opposite,' he whispered. 'Do you happen to know where she lives?'

The man shot a swift glance in the direction of the couple.

'Ah! Mam'selle Lee,' he murmured. 'No, monsieur, but I'll ascertain for you.'

'Good!' said Tinker, as the waiter hurried away. Once he had obtained Terry Lee's address the rest was up to Blake.

As he sipped his coffee he turned over in his mind for the hundredth time the queer events of the past few days. To save his life he could trace no connection between the disappearances that had electrified Scotland Yard. The whole business seemed so utterly pointless, he reflected. If it had been an ordinary kidnapping, there would have been a corresponding demand for ransom, but who on earth would want to kidnap an out-of-work labourer or an ordinary housemaid?

On the other hand, he mused, if some homicidal maniac had been to work, surely the body of one or the other would have been found by now?

The more he thought of it the more unfathomable and baffling became the mystery.

He felt a touch on his sleeve, and the waiter whispered apologetically:

'I have made ze inquiries, sare, but no one knows Miss Lee's address. Maybe later I will find an opportunity to discover it for monsieur.'

Tinker glanced across the ballroom, which was now getting uncomfortably crowded. Palfrey, KC, was leaning over towards the girl, and their heads were close together, obviously in deep

44

conversation, but a few moments later they rose to their feet and made for the door.

Tinker paused for the fraction of a second, then hurried out after the pair as they left for the vestibule.

He grabbed his hat and coat, and while the girl waited for her escort in the vestibule, Tinker strolled nonchalantly in her direction.

He was about to speak when the barrister hurried towards the girl and took her arm possessively.

Tinker fell back a step.

There was nothing for it but to shadow them. He did not like the task, but in the circumstances, it was absolutely necessary.

Drawn up at the kerb outside was an array of limousines. One, a black, stream-lined Swallow, stood just in front of the low rakish MG Midget, which Tinker recognised as belonging to Bobby Hazeldine.

As the KC and the girl moved in the direction of the limousine a uniformed chauffeur held open the door.

Tinker was not near enough to catch the words of direction which the young lady spoke before she entered the car accompanied by her escort.

The chauffeur slammed the door to and took the wheel.

For a split second Tinker hesitated. Then from his vest pocket he took out a visiting-card and scribbled a few hurried words on the back of it.

'Give that to Mr Hazeldine with my compliments,' he said, pressing the card with a silver coin into the hand of the commissionaire.

The red tail light of the black Swallow was disappearing into the gloom ahead when Tinker sprang to the wheel of the little racing roadster.

'This,' he chuckled, as he felt the engine quiver to life, 'is where the fun starts.'

He little realised that the fun was to turn into grim tragedy.

*   *   *

'Here we are, Mr Blake,' said Walter Nissim, as about twenty minutes later the taxi swerved up from the Chelsea Embankment past the old church towards the King's Road.

Blake glanced at the ancient clock. It was nearly ten.

Judge's Walk, he discovered, was a long, narrow, straggling street leading up from the river. The houses were old, but had been built with the solidity and grace of the Queen Anne period.

The taxi drew up with a jerk before a small and unprepossessing ironmonger's shop. Blake alighted, and while his companion paid off the driver, the detective studied the exterior of the building.

Over the shop was the faded legend:

'Oil and Colour. J. Nissim. Ironmonger and Locksmith.'

Blake looked upwards instinctively.

On each side of the narrow lintel of the shop front he made out the familiar shape of the oil merchant's trade mark—two earthenware jars about two feet high, bulging at the top and tapering at the base.

By the light of an adjacent street lamp he saw that they had once been painted red, but the colour had faded and was now blistered and weather-worn.

Walter Nissim groped in his pockets, and presently unearthed a jingling bunch of keys.

The shop window, Blake noted, was filled with a characteristic impedimenta of an ironmonger's, a domestic assortment of tin pails, mops, scrubbing-brushes, etc.

Nissim inserted a key in the lock of the house door, and pushed it open. He fumbled on the left-hand wall for a moment, then switched on the light.

Blake found himself in a narrow passageway blocked somewhat by a tradesman's bicycle leaning against a decrepit-looking hat-stand. The atmosphere was permeated by a strong odour of paraffin and soft soap.

'I'm afraid I haven't very palatial quarters, Mr Blake,' apologised Nissim, 'but they're comfortable, I think you'll find. That is where the strange things happened.'

Blake smiled.

'I'm very interested,' he said. 'It's not often I have the opportunity of investigating psychic phenomena at first hand.'

His host led the way up a flight of stairs at the end of the passage, and Blake subconsciously noted that the carpet was worn and dusty.

On the first landing Mr Nissim paused.

'I have a woman that attends to my simple wants daily, Mr Blake,' he explained. 'I'm afraid both myself and my poor brother are confirmed bachelors.'

Nissim crossed the landing and opened a door to a room on the right. He pressed the switch and beckoned to Blake with a gesture.

The detective entered and found himself in a small, square, sparsely furnished apartment. The furniture, though shabby as to upholstery, had typical Victorian solidity.

There were two easy-chairs on either side of the fireplace, and Blake observed that the table had been laid for supper. There was a loaf of bread, a jar of pickles, a hunk of cheese, and a bottle of beer.

'Welcome, Mr Blake,' said the oil and colour merchant with a smile.

He bent down and seized a poker from the grate and stirred the sluggish fire into some semblance of a blaze.

Sexton Blake took one rapid glance round the room. The pictures on the wall were mostly of old sailing ships, and on the mantelpiece was a glass case containing two moth-eaten, stuffed seagulls.

There was a shabby bookshelf in the corner, and the volumes had dusty, mildewed leather covers, and many books were missing.

The sight faintly irritated Blake. The empty spaces were as unsightly as the gaps in a man's front teeth.

Blake also noted that a pair of communicating doors led to another room in the rear. It was evidently a bedroom.

Nissim gave a wry smile, and jerked his thumb towards the folding doors.

'That's where the ghost played his tricks last night, Mr Blake,' he remarked. 'The devil never does it in the room when I'm sitting in it. When I'm in the bedroom he seems to monkey about here. I was sitting reading last night when—'

Crash!

Even as Nissim spoke, there came the staccato sound of splintering glass from the next room.

Instantly the detective sprang towards the communicating doors and flung them open wide. As he did so, the room suddenly blazed with light.

47

Blake halted for a second on the threshold. He could not restrain a sharp cry of amazement that rose to his lips.

Facing him stood two men clad in loose black overalls, not unlike monkish robes. Their faces were hooded, and each one held a heavy black automatic which pointed unwaveringly at Blake's heart.

'Do not move or cry out, Mr Blake!' hissed the voice of Nissim from the rear. 'This gun has a hair trigger!'

Blake felt the scalp tingle as the sharp jab of metal pressed against his spine.

He was trapped, and resistance in the circumstances was useless.

It took a good deal to astonish the detective, but this unexpected denouement left him for a while literally speechless.

He squared his shoulders resolutely, and a fighting glint crept into his eyes.

The two cowled and sinister figures opposite him spoke no word, and their silence was even more menacing than the sardonic chuckle of the man with the yellow tie as he stepped into the apartment and closed the communicating doors. The room was empty but for a truckle-bed and a chair. The window was barred.

Nissim made a mocking little bow and waved his hands towards the sinister-looking figures.

'Meet the ghost, Mr Blake,' he remarked, with an evil leer.

Blake's eyes blazed with suppressed fury. Normally a brave man and used to tight corners, his first impulse was to make a fight for it; but the odds against him were overwhelming. For the moment he was helpless, and it was necessary to play for time.

'What's the meaning of this nonsense?' he demanded harshly.

Nissim grinned sardonically.

'You must admit, my dear Mr Blake, that the pretext on which I brought you here was both ingenious and artistic. I assure you it took me a considerable time to devise the story of Ali Baba and his jars.'

Blake made an impatient gesture. Inwardly he was seething with indignation for having fallen so ingenuously into the trap, but outwardly his face betrayed nothing of his feelings.

'It may interest you to know, Mr Nissim, that, ingenious though your story was, I suspected it from the beginning, and it was precisely because I suspected it that I accompanied you here. I will admit, however, that I scarcely expected meeting these melo-dramatic gentlemen.'

He bowed with a trace of mockery to the hooded pair.

'Excellent bluff, Blake,' Nissim countered, 'but it's easy enough to be wise after the event.'

A faint spot of colour appeared on Blake's cheekbones.

'My dear Nissim—if that is your name, which I doubt—you slipped up badly when you told me you had seen my colleague, Inspector Coutts, at the Yard tonight. As a matter of fact, I happen to know that the CID man is down at Reading. I received a phone call from him shortly before your arrival.'

Nissim bit his lip, and Blake smiled as the shaft went home.

'Furthermore,' continued Blake coolly, 'plausible though your story was, I am, I hope, sufficient of a psychologist to tell whether a man is genuine, and circumstantially your story did not ring true.'

'Huh!' sneered Nissim. 'Then if you were so almighty clever, why did you come here?'

Blake shrugged his shoulders. He was beginning to enjoy the other's discomfiture.

'The name of this street interested me, let us say,' he drawled. 'I was very anxious to meet Dr Just. Judge's Walk seemed to be an appropriate haunt of his.'

For a moment there was a tense and electric silence, and Blake saw Nissim's face change colour.

The guns in the masked men's hands wavered slightly, and Blake was quick to press home his advantage.

'That astonishes you, gentleman,' he said.

'Confound you, Blake,' snarled Nissim. 'You know too much.'

The detective shrugged his shoulders.

He did not deem it advisable to enlighten his captors regarding the trump card he held, but at the moment he was watching points, and the next move lay with the ingenious Mr Nissim.

That move was not long in coming.

'I'm glad that you've told me this,' commented the man with the yellow tie. 'It simplifies matters exceedingly. When I knew that you were interested in the disappearance of Mr Otto Krimm, I deemed it prudent to take precautions. These' he pointed once more to the silent, cowled men—'are my precautions.'

Blake smiled sarcastically.

'Highly melodramatic, no doubt Mr—er—Nissim, but I suppose you realise that you are liable to a minimum sentence of seven years' imprisonment for being in possession of firearms with intent to endanger life.'

'Tchah!' spat out Nissim. 'Don't quibble, Blake. Do you think I've not counted the cost of failure. It is because we must not fail that we have inveigled you here.'

' "Unconscious of their impending doom, the little victims play",' quoted Sexton Blake, with his faint, satirical smile.

Nissim's face was contorted by a paroxysm of fury.

'You won't find it so funny,' he growled. 'You have one chance alone of avoiding singularly unpleasant consequences. I have no personal quarrel with you; in fact, if you'll believe me, I have great faith, not only in your personal integrity, but in your intellectual capacity.'

Blake bowed mockingly.

'Really, Mr Nissim. You flatter me unnecessarily.'

'This is no moment for flippancy, Blake,' snapped the other. 'I assure you I am in deadly earnest. As I say, I bear you no personal animosity, and if you will give me your word of honour not to pursue any further inquiries into the disappearance of these eight people, I shall let you go unharmed. If you do not—' His finger trembled significantly on the trigger.

'That is indeed generous of you, Mr Nissim,' drawled the detective. 'May I point out, however, that were I to fall in with your suggestion I should lay myself open to a charge of connivance, and the penalties of being an accessory are as serious as for being an active instigator of a crime.'

'Now, don't be stubborn, Blake,' said Nissim.

His tone had changed, and his manner became almost ingratiating.

'I give you my word that no harm will happen to the missing persons. In a few days' time they will be returned to their homes. What is more, I very much doubt if any of them will prosecute for their temporary inconvenience.'

Sexton Blake glanced curiously at Nissim.

There was a queer, fanatical gleam in the man's deep-set eyes, and, despite himself, Blake felt that the man was utterly sincere in his statement.

His pulses throbbed a little. Strange as it seemed, the detective was exhilarated at this totally unforeseen turn of events.

At last the jig-saw puzzle of the eight missing people was beginning to fall into line. That there was a connection between each individual and this sinister trio was now obvious. What that connection was Blake was determined to discover.

'Well, Blake,' said Nissim. 'We are waiting. Give us your parole and you shall leave this house a free man. I'll admit frankly that we are not afraid of Scotland Yard, but you are different. You know too much.'

Again the detective bowed.

'My answer to your impudent suggestion, Nissim, is no!'

'You're a fool, Blake,' snarled the other; 'a stubborn fool. Nothing on earth will interfere with my plans—'

'Nor with mine,' said the detective.

Nissim's face grew ugly.

'All right,' he exclaimed. 'We've given you a chance, and you've refused it.'

If Blake had been an entirely cautious, prudent man, he would have temporised with his captors, but there are times when even the most prudent forget caution.

So far, Blake had worked almost entirely in the dark, but now he had come up against something really tangible.

Hitherto in this case he had operated almost entirely on deduction, and he possessed the theorist's eagerness for something practical. That is, he wanted to see and to make certain that his theories were correct.

Nissim misunderstood the detective's hesitation.

'Come now, Blake,' he said persuasively. 'Be sensible. Give us your word and we will keep ours. As a matter of fact, I can make you a further promise. If you give us your parole to say nothing about the matter, either now or in the future—'

'Don't be a fool, Nissim,' snapped Sexton Blake.

His mind was made up.

'I don't make bargains with crooks.'

'Good enough!' snarled the man with the yellow tie. 'Number One, Number Two!' His voice cracked as he turned to the two cowled men, who converged in on the helpless detective.

Instinctively, Blake braced himself for the attack.

'I'll give you ten seconds to decide, Blake,' growled Nissim.

The detective clenched his fists. He resolved to go under fighting.

The black-clad pair tautened their fingers on the triggers of their weapons as Nissim began to count.

'One, two, three—'

Blake raised his chin and glanced squarely at his assailants, but he did not speak.

Nissim finished counting.

'Seven, eight, nine, ten!'

Nissim turned to his men.

'All right, boys, give him the works!'

The two cowled monks raised their guns. Blake drew a deep breath. Whatever was coming to him he would not flinch.

Nissim gave a harsh cackle of laughter, and then it happened!

Straight into the face of the man from Baker Street the two cowled men fired.

A jet of intensely cold liquid squirted from the nozzles of their guns, and Blake's eyes streamed with tears. He choked and spluttered, almost nauseated by the sickly smell of the drug which had been squirted into his face.

His knees sagged under him as if they were made of wet cardboard, and a moment later he slumped to the floor in a heap.

Nissim peered down at the unconscious figure of the detective and rubbed his bony hands.

'He asked for it, the fool, and now he's got it!' he snapped.

*　　*　　*

The red beacon light at the cross-roads of the Watford by-pass winked and gleamed like a goblin's eye in the gloom of the winter night.

Tinker crouched over the wheel of his speedy little roadster and gritted his teeth. He had not bargained when he followed the black Swallow from Shaftesbury Avenue, for such a long run into the country.

Along the wide stretch of the Edgware Road the black limousine had almost eluded him, but the youngster held grimly to the trail. Far ahead of him on the smooth tarmac road he saw the red tail light of the Swallow.

The youngster could easily have overtaken the car, but there was no object in doing so.

He was frankly puzzled regarding Terry Lee's destination. He knew that the barrister lived in the Temple, and he could not make out the reason for this nocturnal excursion into Buckinghamshire.

Mile after mile the speedy little roadster ate up the straight new road. Tinker passed lumbering motor-lorries and an incessant stream of townward-going vehicles.

They roared through the sleepy town of Rickmansworth and on into the heart of Buckinghamshire. In the east Tinker made out the rolling mass of the Chiltern Hills.

The Swallow was making good speed; but Tinker jogged steadily along at about thirty miles an hour.

Suddenly, beyond Little Missenden, the car swerved to the left, and Tinker drew in his breath sharply.

The black Swallow twisted and turned in a by-road that seemed to have been laid out by a drunken man. The road was bordered by thick woods so that it was impossible to see beyond a corner.

'This is a new one on me!' murmured the lad as the big car ahead slackened speed.

Tinker braked into a mere crawl. He was nearly half a mile behind the Swallow now. Save for the hum of the engine, and the rustle of the wind, the night was very still.

The young man's sharp eyes, peering ahead through the gloom, saw that the black Swallow had stopped. Cautiously he jammed on his brake, and, parking the car in the shadow of a gnarled old elm, he hastened forward.

'And now what?' he murmured, tensing himself as he hurried silent as a shadow towards the black Swallow.

He heard the confused murmur of voices, and he flattened himself against a tree-trunk as the door of the limousine opened, and Terry Lee stepped out into the roadway. The chauffeur sprang down to assist her, and then Tinker drew in a deep breath.

Ahead of him appeared two weird apparitions clad in shapeless black robes and hooded after the manner of medieval inquisitors.

'Gosh!' ejaculated Tinker. 'What's happening?'

The two cowled figures spoke a few words in a muffled undertone to the girl, who gave a soft silvery laugh and pointed into the interior of the car.

A moment later the chauffeur entered the tonneau and emerged dragging the limp, inanimate figure of a man. In the pale rays of the moon Tinker saw the heavy, blue-jowled face of Palfrey, KC. Silently the cowled figures assisted the chauffeur to lift the unconscious barrister out of the car.

Tinker's pulses raced with excitement. Who were the mysterious masked men? What had happened to the unfortunate lawyer? These and a score of other questions surged through the puzzled brain of the youngster.

Between them they carried the limp figure into a tunnel-like opening amidst the trees. The chauffeur climbed back into the car, and Terry Lee followed the masked figures into the gloom ahead.

Tinker pressed himself back into the shadows. If the Swallow was returning to London, he must not be seen. He had half a mind to race back to the Midget and head her the other way.

The car ahead, however, continued on its way up the steep hill, and Tinker heaved a sigh of relief.

'What the devil does it all mean?' he muttered as he cautiously edged his way forward.

Against the skyline the lad saw the dark masses of the Chilterns looming awe-inspiring and mysterious. The youngster felt a queer, exultant thrill as he cautiously made his way forward. The chill night wind rustled through the branches of the trees and an owl hooted mournfully through the silent night as Tinker tiptoed forward and found himself before a massive pair of wrought-iron gates. On the right was a stone lodge, in the window of which a yellow light twinkled warmly.

The youngster hesitated as he stared up the long drive and saw in the distance the half-timbered bulk of Marlesden Manor.

'Gosh! It's a rum business!' he muttered.

He crouched in the shadows, and at that moment a black-hooded figure detached itself from the shadows behind the lodge and glided soundlessly over the grass in the direction of the Manor House.

Tinker stared.

Despite himself, a queer, superstitious tremor ran through him, for the figure was that of a man clad in a cowl that blended subtly with the shadows of the night.

'Gosh! Another of them!' said the youngster.

He felt the hair on the nape of his neck prickling as that silent figure continued to glide down the tree-girt avenue. The youngster jumped as the wind rattled the branches of an ancient beech, and, plucky though he undoubtedly was, Tinker felt as if someone had dropped a piece of ice down his waistcoat.

With a tremendous effort of will the youngster jerked himself into action. A twig snapped beneath his feet with the sudden loudness of a pistol-shot.

Tinker slid his hand into his hip pocket for his electric torch.

The gates of the Manor House drive were too lofty to scale, but he reflected that there was bound to be another way to enter. He hurried up the hill for the space of a hundred yards or so, and then noticed a stone wall about five feet in height.

It was an easy matter for the athletic youngster to scale this, and he dropped down on the other side with a little grunt of satisfaction.

'Well, we're in, anyway!' he muttered.

A thick shrubbery extended on either side of the driveway that led to the Manor. With infinite caution the lad made his way towards the house itself. He felt that he was on the threshold of stirring events, and his eyes kindled.

'Good old guv'nor! His hunch was right!'

He peered ahead and saw that the mullioned windows were ablaze with light.

Suddenly came a sharp cracking sound from the tangled shrubbery, and Tinker stopped dead in his tracks.

A vague, shadowy figure rose up before him and barred his pathway.

With a queer little thrill, Tinker saw that it wore the same black monkish garb as the others.

'Who the blazes are you?' snarled the voice.

The youngster clenched his fists and leapt for the shrouded stranger. His left slammed straight for that vague masked face, and his knuckles crashed into the man's jaw. They landed with a jolt that jarred every bone in his body.

Tinker gave an exultant yell, and the other man staggered backwards with a grunt of pain. The youngster bounded forward with a panther-like leap, and as he crashed through the under-brush, he heard a shrill peep of a whistle from the direction of the Manor House.

*　　*　　*

Sexton Blake came to himself with a cracking headache.

Some time must have elapsed since he had first lost his senses. He was cold. His head throbbed, and his wrists pained him abominably.

Those were his first dim impressions. Then his brain cleared, and he realised his position.

He groaned slightly. He was feeling surprisingly weak. Also, by the peculiar taste in his mouth he realised that he had been drugged. His gaze slid downwards, and he discovered that his ankles, legs, and wrists were securely trussed by wire flex.

Gradually his numbed brain began to clear and function.

Nissim had made good his threat.

Blake found himself lying on the truckle bed in the oil merchant's bedroom. There was no sign of the two cowled figures, nor of Nissim.

He laid his head back on the hard pillow to rest his aching limbs and to think.

He had been imprisoned times before by the desperate characters against whom he had waged perpetual warfare, and his prisons had been many and various.

He had no idea what time it was. He glanced across at the window, and saw that the shutters were of steel and securely locked.

How long he had been unconscious he had no idea.

Evidently the drug was a derivative of amil chloride, he reflected, and if that were the case his period of oblivion must have been brief.

He wriggled feebly, but the flex bit deeply into his wrists, and he had not enough slack with which to work.

Blake groaned again. The helplessness of his position was galling. The cold in that back room was intense, and his mouth felt parched and dry.

His captors had left on a light from an old-fashioned gas-jet that threw eerie and flickering shadows on the ceiling. The gas-jet was above the mantelpiece, and on a rickety washstand in the corner of the room Blake saw a water jug.

With a grunt he rose from the bed, and, trussed and hobbled though he was, managed to hop towards the jug.

It was infernally awkward to lift, but, to his delight, he found it full of water. With shaking hands he managed, despite his constricted arms, to lift it to his lips. Most of the water slopped over him in an icy douche.

The drink seemed to pull him together, and he gritted his teeth. Somehow or other he would have to get rid of his bonds, and that quickly. To cut through the tough wire was out of the question.

Suddenly Blake's eyes narrowed. It would be a painful process, he reflected, but it was the only way. His wrists were already raw from the friction of the flex, and the pain was agonising at every movement.

With an effort Blake flexed his muscles, and he half pushed and half buffeted one of the chairs into a position beneath the gas-bracket.

He then took a standing jump and stood up on the chair.

This brought the flickering flame of the gas-jet to a level with his breast. Swaying dizzily, and with clenched jaws, he held his wrists above the flame.

The agony was excruciating, and beads of perspiration trickled through his forehead.

His flesh was scorched and blistered, but he held on grimly. The sickening smell of burnt rubber was nauseating.

Gradually the wire became red-hot, and then, tensing his mighty muscles, Blake snapped the wire after a tremendous and sustained effort.

He almost fell to the floor, but with an exultant gasp he realised that his hands, at least, were free.

It was the work of a few moments to get rid of his fetters.

He strolled shakily over towards the communicating doors and found, as he anticipated, that they were locked.

'I shall be a mass of bruises by the time this is finished,' he said wryly, as he hurled his shoulders against the partition. The locks were old and stout, however, and after a while the detective desisted. If any of his captors were in the front room they would have taken action long before, he mused.

He took up a chair and crashed it against the panel of the door.

Time after time he rained a shower of blows on the panels, and, at last, one of them cracked beneath his onslaught.

Crash!

With a final titanic sweep, Blake sent the chair smashing through the panel.

He was free!

Perspiration poured down his face, and his wrists seemed to be aflame with agony. It was the work of a few seconds to scramble through the wrecked panel, and Blake found himself once more in the squalid front room which he had first entered earlier that evening.

He glanced at the clock on the mantelpiece, and found that it was 2 a.m.

His keen eyes roamed over the poorly-furnished room. Flung over a chair he saw a black cowled robe, and with a grunt of satisfaction, he folded it up and rolled it under his arm.

He made a thorough search of the apartment, but found no clue whatsoever to the activities of the mysterious Mr Nissim.

It was simply the room of an untidy and rather slovenly old bachelor. The sole correspondence dealt with bills and accounts, and there was no connection whatsoever to be traced between Nissim and Otto Krimm.

With his bundle under his arm Blake tiptoed down the stairs.

Not a sound disturbed the silence of the building, and Blake shrewdly suspected that the three men had no intention of returning.

He opened the front door and inhaled the crisp, frosty night air gratefully.

He hurried towards the Embankment, and at a coffee-stall at the corner of Battersea Bridge, refreshed himself with a cup of Bovril.

A taxi-driver eyed him curiously, for Blake's face was grimed with dust and sweat.

'Is your cab free?' asked Blake.

'Yuss, guv'nor!' came the reply.

'Well, have another cup, and then drive me to Baker Street,' said the detective crisply.

The taximan, nothing loath, accepted the offer, and within ten minutes Blake was bowling homeward. He tipped the man liberally, and, with a sigh of weariness, let himself into the house.

Tinker was in bed hours ago, he reflected, and he wondered

what news the young 'un had for him.

He opened the door of the consulting-room, and as he did so there came a startled gasp, and a weird apparition in a red flannel dressing-gown, her hair a cluster of curl-papers, started up at his entrance.

'Oh, Mr Blake, how you startled me!' gasped Mrs Bardell. 'Which the phone has been ringing half the night. Something dreadful has happened. Good gracious me, what have you done to your poor hands?' she added.

'Never mind my hands,' said Blake briskly. 'Tell me, what was the phone message?'

'I've wrote it down, sir,' said Mrs Bardell. 'Maybe I haven't spelt the names right, but that's how it sounded to me.'

From her bosom she plucked out a slip of paper and handed it to the detective. Blake's face grew grim as he read the message.

'My heaven!' he muttered. 'What time did you get this call?'

'About one o'clock, Mr Blake,' replied the housekeeper.

The significance of the message alarmed Blake.

Was he too late?

He bundled his anxious housekeeper off to bed, and then poured himself out a liberal dose of whisky, and as he did so his gaze fell on the tumbler on the occasional table by the side of the chair in which Mr Nissim had sat.

Blake smiled grimly. If his surmise was correct, that empty glass was his trump card.

Hurriedly he crossed over to the laboratory and switched on the light. He put a thin coating of black graphite on the exterior of the glass, and his eyes sparkled as he saw three unmistakable finger-prints.

He opened a drawer in the laboratory and took out an enlarged photograph of the mirror in Mr Krimm's dining-room.

One glance was sufficient for Blake's trained eye, and he gave a sigh of satisfaction.

The fingerprints were identical. The man in the yellow tie was undoubtedly the mysterious Dr Just.

*   *   *

Otto Krimm gave a hollow groan as he awoke from an uneasy slumber. A stubble of grey-black beard had grown on his usually slick, if flabby, chin. His eyes were bloodshot, and his hair hung in lank black wisps like rats' tails on either side of his head.

He blinked stupidly at the glazed tiled walls of his cell, and for the thousandth time he wondered what grim fate was in store for him.

That he was in prison there could be no shadow of a doubt. How he had got there, and what crime he was supposed to have committed, he had not the foggiest idea.

He began to pace restlessly up and down the stone-flagged floor of his prison. He was mentally and physically exhausted.

Suddenly, from the corridor outside, he heard the firm, steady footsteps of his gaoler.

He glanced up at the thickly barred window of his cell, and saw a pale and misty moon in the leaden sky. His eye fell on the record-card beside his bed, and again his flesh crawled.

There came the jingle of keys, and the door of his cell was flung open.

'Come on, you!' said the blue-uniformed warder.

Sweat started out on Krimm's forehead. He was gripping himself, fighting for control.

'Where are you taking me?' he stammered.

'You'll see,' said the warder grimly.

He gripped Krimm's sleeve, and together they marched down a long, vaulted, echoing corridor. A door opened suddenly at the end of the passage, and he heard the excited murmur of voices.

The warder tapped him on the shoulder.

'This way,' he said.

Dazedly Krimm stepped forward, and a gasp of horror rose from his lips.

He found himself in a spacious room. His eyes rested on a big open dock immediately in front of him. Before him on a dais sat a bewigged judge in his gorgeous crimson robes.

On the right was a jury-box with ten men and two women.

Krimm gripped at the dock-rail for support, and his brain reeled, for the judge's features were masked by a black domino.

Above the judge's head was suspended a great naked shining sword, and at each of the six doors of the great chamber stood a black-cowled figure. Grim, sinister, and menacing.

Krimm licked his dry lips nervously. He passed a shaky hand

through his lank black hair.

Amid tense silence one of the black-garbed figures stood up before the judge's dais.

'Otto Krimm, you are charged with the wilful murder of Jill Bryant on June 19th, 1919,' said the cowled figure in a stern voice. 'Do you plead "Guilty" or "Not Guilty"?'

His voice rang sonorously through the court. Through the slit in his mask his eyes rested on the prisoner in the dock.

Otto Krimm made no reply. His face was ghastly in its pallor. At length a strangled sob tore from his throat.

'I don't know what you're talking about,' he shrilled. 'I defy you, you devils! You can't touch me!'

'Silence!' thundered the judge.

Two black-cowled figures took their places unobtrusively at either side of the wretched man in the dock.

The members of the jury leaned back in their seats and glanced furtively at each other.

'Do you plead "Guilty" or "Not Guilty"?' went on the inexorable voice of the judge.

A groan rose from Krimm's ashen lips.

' "Not Guilty", curse you!' he snarled. ' "Not Guilty"!'

The judge scribbled a note on the pad before him, and motioned towards one of the cowled figures.

'Let the case proceed,' he said.

Krimm stared round the court like a trapped rat.

Suddenly he spied a familiar figure on the left of the judge's dais. It was Palfrey, KC.

His brain whirled as he recognised the eminent barrister who had defended him more than once when one of his shady financial deals had attracted the attention of the Public Prosecutor.

The famous advocate was a portly man with cold eyes and a silvery tongue. He was capable of magnificent flights of oratory, and was much in demand in criminal cases, but now a good deal of his assurance had gone from him. His eyes had a queer furtive look as he craned forward.

He turned to the jury-box.

'Members of the jury, the prisoner in the dock is charged with the deliberate and cruel murder of a young girl named Jill Bryant, and it is my task to unfold to you and to prove to you without the vestige of a doubt that he is guilty of the gravest crime in our calendar, an offence which the law enacts shall merit the extreme penalty, death!'

His voice sank to a whisper, and the wretched man in the dock shivered as if with ague.

For a moment or two there was a tense silence in that bizarre court, and then it was broken dramatically.

A cowled figure standing at the door through which Krimm had been ushered into the dock suddenly raised his arm.

'Stop!' said the voice. 'This farce must not proceed.'

The jury stared in amazement at one another, and the judge gripped the desk before him until his knuckles shone bone-white.

The tall figure at the door took a step forward. In his right hand he gripped a heavy revolver.

'Let no one move!' he said, in a voice of authority.

'Quick!' snapped the judge to the prosecuting counsel. 'Get him before—'

Bang!

A splash of flame spat from the cowled man's gun, and a bullet flattened against the sword above the judge's head until it clanged like a clarion.

A woman screamed, and the judge cowered back in his chair as the black-robed figure's cowl fell back, and he found himself staring into the implacable eyes of Sexton Blake.

From outside there came the shrill, pheep of police whistles. Blake strode forward, and his tall figure dominated the court-room.

'The game's up, Just!' he snapped. 'The house is surrounded. You'd better surrender!'

A moment later the four doors of the courtroom broke open simultaneously, and a wave of blue-clad figures headed by Detective-inspector Coutts and Tinker, hatless and flushed, poured into the room.

Otto Krimm felt the whole world rocking about his ears.

With a moan he slunk forward to the floor in a dead faint. He headed forward, and the whole world became a cataclysm of roaring darkness.

*   *   *

The fire had burned low in the grate of Blake's consulting-room at Baker Street.

Pedro dozed with his head between his paws, an occasional 'woof' showing that he seemed to be almost as keenly interested in the strange narrative which his master was unfolding to Tinker, as Detective-inspector Coutts himself.

It was two days after the dramatic raid at Marlesden Manor, two days of feverish activity on the part of the authorities at Scotland Yard.

Coutts was now leaning back in his favourite armchair, with one leg hoisted on his knee, a cigar at an angle of forty-five degrees in his mouth, and an expression of placid benevolence on his florid features.

'By thunder, Blake, you were magnificent!' he said. 'You and I have been in some curious adventures in our time, but I don't think I've ever seen anything quite like that confounded court at Marlesden Manor.'

Sexton Blake shrugged slightly. He was leaning against the mantelpiece, a favourite attitude of his when eludicating a problem.

'I think young Tinker deserves most of the credit,' he answered. 'If I had not had his phone message from Mrs Bardell, the case, I'm afraid, would have had a far more tragic ending. However'—and Blake's eyes twinkled—'I trust Tinker found himself sufficiently rewarded when Mrs Skeffington Smythe kissed him.'

'Stow it, guv'nor,' he said, his cheeks burning at the remembrance of the embrace with which that massive woman had enfolded him when she learned of his part in her rescue.

'Do you know even now, Blake, I'm hanged if I can see clearly what Just was driving at! He must be mad,' said Coutts.

Sexton Blake nodded as he filled his briar.

'He is certainly mentally unbalanced, poor devil,' he said, 'but you must not forget what he has suffered. For myself, I have a great deal of sympathy for him, and I'm glad that the information he gave us will undoubtedly land Otto Krimm into penal servitude.'

'Scaly blighter!' broke in Tinker. 'That's one good thing, anyway.'

'You see,' Blake continued, 'Just is one of those dangerous fanatics, an irresponsible idealist with enough money and determination to carry out his idealistic notions heedless of the law. As you know, for years he worked amongst the poor in Shoreditch mainly without a hope of a fee. In those days Otto Krimm had not risen to his present eminence. He was, however, a power in Shoreditch. He owned, and still owns, I believe, most of the slum property in that district, and he had literally grown fat and rich by exploiting the poor.'

Coutts nodded and rubbed a stubby finger against his bristly moustache.

'Jill Bryant,' continued Blake, 'was Krimm's wife. Her life with Krimm was a nightmare. After a few months, whatever affection he had for the girl had worn off, and he resorted to every form of brutality to break her spirit. In her despair the poor girl appealed to Dr Just.'

The Yard man again nodded.

'Yes, we've checked up on that, Blake,' he said. 'The poor creature had a terrible time.' Blake blew his smoke ceilingwards and nodded.

'Now, this is where Just behaved with incredible foolishness. As I said, he was a fanatical idealist. No one in his senses would have acted in the way he did, but I accept his statement as perfectly true. Quite impersonally he intended as an act of justice to kill Otto Krimm.

'Yes, having seen Just, I think I can believe his statement. He told the girl, didn't he, some specious story that if she wanted to escape from Krimm's clutches he would help her. The girl was terrified, but he allayed her fears by giving her a powder, telling her that it was a strong sleeping draught. He advised her to put it in Krimm's drink, and when he had taken it, to come to him, and he would shelter her.'

Sexton Blake smiled a trifle sardonically.

'Yes, that is where Just's action was utterly indefensible,' he commented. 'If Krimm had taken the powder he would have undoubtedly died, for it was a deadly poison. Suspicion would have at once pointed to Jill Bryant. Fate however, willed otherwise. She was a weak, wayward, foolish creature, Coutts. We can only conjecture that Krimm somehow or other learnt of her visit to Just. Anyway, the doctors at the inquest stated that the poor girl's body was black and blue with bruises. I can only surmise that Krimm had beaten her mercilessly, and to ease the pain, she, in despair, took what she believed to be a harmless sleeping draught.

Krimm, with his usual cunning, had two or three addresses so that his name never came into the case. The poison was traced to Just, and, as you know, he was struck off the medical register and sentenced to four years' penal servitude.'

'I'm not sure that he didn't deserve it,' commented Coutts, with a grunt.

'Well,' continued Blake, 'smarting under a sense of injustice, the doctor at first brooded, and in prison he hatched out a scheme of vengeance, first against Krimm, and as we know from his statement, against other enemies of society in the shape of other exploiters of the poor.'

'It's a good job, Blake, you stepped in when you did,' said the Yard man, with a grin.

'Then,' resumed Blake, 'an unexpected legacy made him comparatively independent, and he was thus able to buy the Manor House. Here he perfected his mad scheme of holding his own Courts of Justice to punish those whom the law could not touch. He had, however, the sense to realise that one man's judgment was fallible. I will grant him that for the purity of his motives. It would be against his humanitarian instincts to sentence his intended victims without a fair trial.

'Now,' continued Blake, as he slowly puffed his pipe, 'this is manifestly where he went off the rail. He was undoubtedly a megalomaniac, and nothing shows his madness more than in his decision to use as a jury the very same people that sentenced him to penal servitude.'

'Yes, utterly crazy,' observed Tinker. 'No wonder we were all baffled at the disappearance of those people. I can't help but admire the ingenious way he got them into his clutches, though.'

Blake smiled reminiscently.

'I suppose that Jap servant of Krimm's, Ito, was an accomplice of Just's, guv'nor,' said Tinker.

'Undoubtedly,' replied Blake. ' "Conscience doth make cowards of us", and melodramatic though the use of chloride of mercury on the mirror seems to be, it undoubtedly had a powerful effect, and, in fact, led to Just's undoing. The mercury reacts peculiarly to heat, and as the room gradually became warmer that night, the portrait of the dead girl grew more intense. The effect is transient, however, but it certainly frightened Krimm.

'Just is a clever psychologist. He almost persuaded me that his fantasy story of Ali Baba and the jars might have been true, and it was certainly a cute idea to pose as the brother of the unfortunate oil merchant, Nissim.'

'He must have told a different story to each one, guv'nor,' said Tinker.

'Of course,' replied Blake, 'different people, different methods. Zeed was decoyed ingeniously enough. The poor housemaid was decoyed there by the simple method of "pick up". One of Just's henchmen had been paying court to her in the role of a chauffeur; the rest was easy. As for Mrs Skeffington Smythe, he played on her known prejudice, and used the name of Lord Blaynton, a well-known sympathiser of women suffrage. He phoned her up, telling her that Fraulein Emma von Klein, the famous German feminist, was anxious to meet her at the manor.'

Coutts gave a laugh.

'I'd give a good deal to have seen that woman's face when she found herself a prisoner. Poor old Zeed was scared out of his wits at her. He had served before on the jury with her and knew the kind of woman she was.'

Blake gave a reminiscent chuckle.

'On the whole, they reacted very well,' he said. 'After all, he treated them kindly, and beyond their loss of liberty they're none the worse for their adventure.'

'How was the soldier decoyed there?' queried Tinker.

Blake smiled.

'Again, note the cleverness of Dr Just,' he observed. 'He had checked up on every member of the jury carefully months beforehand. He knew to a nicety their hobbies, foibles, and predilections. Our friend the corporal was a keen cross-word puzzle enthusiast. When, therefore, a young man purporting to come from the "Daily Radio" announced that the corporal had won a £500 prize, and asked if he could call at the office to accept his cheque, what was more natural than that the corporal should accompany the young man in his car.'

'Oh, yes. Just was clever,' said Inspector Coutts. 'The way he used that chorus-girl, Terry Lee, as a decoy for old Palfrey makes me laugh. He fell, hook, line, and sinker, for her.'

'Incidentally, how did Terry Lee get in with Just and his gang?' asked Tinker.

Blake smiled a little cryptically.

'Ah, there's the fact I only discovered by accident. Terry Lee's real name is Nellie Bryant. She was a sister of the unfortunate girl who died. Dr Just had been her unknown benefactor for years, and a sense of gratitude made her fall in with his schemes.'

'Well, Blake, I don't know what we should have done without you,' said Coutts. 'If you hadn't deliberately walked into Just's trap, the affair would have remained a mystery.'

Blake laughed.

'Did you know, Coutts, there are actually two reasons why Just wished to kidnap me. It shows the queer working of a maniac's mind. In the first place, he thought that I was liable to be dangerous, and, in the second, as he admitted frankly to me, he did not think it quite fair to act as judge, and, as he had great faith in my impartial judgement, his intention was to force me to act in that wholly illegal capacity.'

'The blooming cheek of it, guv'nor,' remarked Tinker. 'Gosh! You could have knocked me down with a feather. After I had outed that chap in the shrubbery, I kept quite still for a bit, then wormed my way to the back of the manor. When I peeped through the window and saw them preparing a courtroom, I thought I had gone off my head. However, it seemed to me the best thing to do was leg it back for the nearest telephone and ring you up.'

'You did splendidly, young 'un,' said Blake. 'I can always rely on you in any emergency, I'm glad to say.'

Tinker flushed at the tribute.

'By gosh, guv'nor, it seemed the only logical thing to do.'

'Yes,' replied his chief, 'but if the ingenious doctor had not overlooked that gas-jet, I'm afraid it would have been too late.'

He glanced ruefully at his bandaged wrists.

'Who were the other chaps in Just's gang? I didn't get all the names, guv'nor,' said Tinker.

Blake shrugged his shoulders.

'Protégés of his. Two were solicitors who had been struck off the rolls for non-professional conduct, including the unctuous Mr Gadsley, who fetched Zeed to the Manor House.

'Incidentally, four of the original jury that tried Dr Just were dead, so he was compelled to make-weight with some of his servants.'

Coutts bent forward and lifted his glass.

'Here's to you Blake, old man,' he said. 'Thanks to you, we've rounded up a pretty dangerous gang.'

Sexton Blake gave a regretful sigh.

'What's the matter, guv'nor?' said Tinker. 'You look a bit disappointed.'

Blake smiled wistfully.

'Yes,' he observed, 'enjoyable though many aspects of the case were, I only wish—'

'Wish what, guv'nor?' queried Tinker.

'That the story of the Haunted Jars of Ali Baba was true,' replied Blake, characteristically. 'It would have been a splendid problem to solve.'

THE TREASURE OF TORTOISE ISLAND
G. H. Teed

G. H. Teed (1878–1939) was a Canadian who, though university educated, caught the wanderlust bug at an early age and travelled the world, mostly steerage. In his own words, he 'wanted to see a palm tree'. He saw plenty of palm trees and a good deal more in a peripatetic career that took him through South America, across the Pacific to China, Japan and Malaya, down to Australia and later up to India. Teed's pre-writing days would perhaps not bear too close a scrutiny; at one time or another he was a rubber plantation manager, superintendent of commissaries in a fruit-packing company, coolie overseer and sheep farmer, but such bland titles cover a multitude of violent and hazardous occupations (he was certainly on hand when the negro outlaw Joe Gordon was shot dead in Costa Rica), some of which were by no means legal. All this hard experience was packed into just about every Blake story he wrote (in all, 196 novelettes and 80 full-length novels). He had a wonderful feel for place and immense descriptive powers; whether the scene was Shepheard's Hotel in Cairo or Dutch Joe's gin-shop in the East Indies, the reader never had to suspend his disbelief. Clearly, this man had been, and seen, and done. Too, his characters were thumpingly three-dimensional—full-blooded and red-blooded to a degree— especially his women; and while other writers were content with one or two lead-characters as a foil for Blake, Teed's cast-list ran to a score or more. His masterpiece was the predatory Dr Huxton Rymer, who sacrificed a career at the Franz Josef Hospital in Vienna to pursue the life of an outlaw, and whose monumental treatise on The Effects of Radium *was destined never to be finished so long as he lusted after other men's gold. Here he teams up with Marie Galante, the passionate octoroon with dreams of empire, in a typically tough and engrossing tale from Blake's Golden Age.*

Mr Sexton Blake had just opened the door of his house in Baker Street, and was about to descend the steps, when a large, black, closed car drew into the kerb and a footman got out to open the door of it.

There emerged a tall, handsome, well-preserved woman whom one would place in the early forties, dressed in a tailored costume of some plain black material and rich black furs. As he saw her, Sexton Blake took off his silk hat and ran down the steps with a smile of pleasure and hand out-stretched.

'Lady Richmond!' he exclaimed. 'This is indeed a pleasure! Am I right in thinking you were coming to see me?'

The woman gave him her hand in a friendly clasp.

'I have been fortunate to catch you, for I can see you were on the point of going out. I hope you can give me a little time, for I have motored up to London especially to see you.'

'Of course,' said Blake, already turning to lead the way back to the house. 'I was only going to the Venetia for tea. But it will be much nicer if you will have tea with me here and we talk at the same time. I trust Sir Herbert is well?'

A cloud seemed to descend upon the fair countenance of the woman, but she did not answer except in some inaudible murmur. Blake conducted her along to the consulting-room, where a cheerful fire was burning in the wide grate (for it was a cold day in early January), and, after assisting her to remove her furs, ensconced her in one of the comfortable low saddle-bag chairs in front of the fire. Then he walked across and rang for Mrs Bardell, telling her when she came to serve tea for two.

'And that dear lad, Tinker?' asked Lady Richmond when the housekeeper had departed. 'How is he?'

'He is in the country today,' answered Blake, drawing up another chair and reaching for a box of his choice A-Batschari cigarettes, which he held out to her. 'He took the car off early this morning and I do not expect him back before late tonight.' He held a match to her cigarette; then, when he had lighted one himself, he sat facing her across the fire. 'I trust nothing is wrong?' he went on. 'You say you motored up to Town especially to see me?'

She nodded.

'Yes. It is really about Sir Herbert that I have come. My husband does not know that I have done so, but I have never forgotten—

shall never forget, Mr Blake—what you did for me some years ago. You saved me from making a terrible mistake, and the happiness I have known since then has been entirely due to you.'

Lady Richmond was refering to a very delicate matter that Sexton Blake had taken in hand for her at a time when she had been subject to threatened blackmail in connection with a matter into which she had been innocently drawn through the speculations of a scapegrace brother.

'I am afraid you overestimate what I did,' murmured Blake. 'But if I was the means of helping you, then it gave me great pleasure to do so.' A sentiment which Blake meant sincerely, for he had always been a great admirer of the woman who was now seated in his consulting-room. 'Exactly what is the trouble, Lady Richmond? But wait! I hear Mrs Bardell coming. We can talk after I have given you tea.'

The housekeeper entered a few moments later with a daintily-laid tray, on which she had put Blake's very finest tea service; and when she had placed this on a small table between them and had seen that everything was all right, she once more took her departure.

'A perfect treasure, your Mrs Bardell, Mr Blake!' said Lady Richmond, as she poured out the tea. 'You are lucky in these days to have her.'

Blake laughed.

'She is a quaint soul, and a bit of a martinet at times,' he answered; 'but really I do not know what Tinker and I would do without her. She has threatened time and again to leave us when things have grown a little too strenuous for her liking; but, honestly, I do not think she could be driven away. She is too fond of Tinker for that.'

'And of you, too, I should say, judging from the way in which she looks after you. Let me see—it is two lumps, isn't it? You see, I have a good memory.'

Blake took his cup, and as he sipped it, waited. He could see that his visitor was trying to choose some point at which to begin what she had to tell him, and presently she withdrew her eyes from the fire and looked across at him.

'My husband does not know that I have come to see you,' she said at last. 'I suggested consulting you, but he did not seem to think the matter was quite in your line. But, knowing that nothing is entirely out of your profession, and being not at all satisfied with the present advice under which he is acting, I determined to motor up and have a talk with you. I shall be just as concise as I can, Mr Blake, and if you can help me I know you will. If not—well, my visit can do no harm.

'As I have already said, it is about my husband. You know, of course, that he retired from business about two years ago, and since then we have been living outside Ipswich. He still retains a certain interest in the business which he built up, but he takes no active part.

'Now, just after he retired he determined to take a trip to the East to visit the various branches of the business there, and it was while he was on that journey he contracted the trouble which is causing us so much anxiety today. I did not go with him. I was not well at the time and the doctors thought it unwise that I should attempt the East then.

'When Sir Herbert came home after an eight months' tour, he seemed about the same as ever in health, except for a certain disinclination to exert himself, which seemed natural enough, after the enervating climate in which he had been. We both put it down to this, and thought a few months in England would soon put him right again. But it did not do so. On the contrary. Since then he has grown worse—steadily worse, until now I am certain his condition is very grave.

'It was not until about seven months ago that he took the opinion of a specialist in London, and certain treatment was prescribed. This did him no good. Then he consulted another, and faithfully followed the new regime laid down by this man. The result was the same—negative. Then we tried a third, with the same failure on his part to respond, and at the present time he is under the care of a fourth—Dr H——.

'This man seems to be the only one who has even a suspicion of what is the trouble. He said frankly only last week that, in his opinion, my husband was suffering from some obscure form of Eastern disease, which he hoped would respond to the treatment he would try, but he did not hold out much encouragement. He has at least been honest.

'Now, I remembered that, not only had you spent a great deal of time in the East, but knew that you had once written a monograph on Eastern diseases and poisons. It was that thought which caused me to suggest to Sir Herbert that he should consult you and find out what you had to say. He seemed disinclined to do so, for he thought that you would not care to handle that type of case.

'I could not, as you know, tell him what you had done for me years ago, but I determined to come and see you on my own account. And I have done so. Now, Mr Blake, I can place in your hands all the information we have. I can ask Dr H——to tell you as much as he had told us of the disease, and it is possible that he would discuss the matter more fully with you in a professional way.

'I can only say that all he will commit himself to so far is to say that the condition of the heart and brain gives him some reason to suspect that my husband may be suffering from an obscure disease known as "goo-nah". It appears that this disease is known in China and some parts of Burma and India, but its treatment is quite unknown here. He says, further, that it is probably due to a germ which has never been isolated, and that until he can get some response to the various forms of treatment he must try, he can promise nothing.

'Now, before coming to you, I took the trouble to get a copy of the monograph you wrote, and in it I did find a brief mention of the same disease. That clinched my decision. So you see me here today.

'Can you tell me any more about that disease, Mr Blake? Have you made any further researches since you wrote that monograph? Or do you know any living medical authority who could help us? Might there be some man in Paris or Berlin or Vienna? I am told, and I have read it in your monograph as well, that some of the Viennese specialists have done more in Eastern research than our London men. I need not add that I have come to you as a last hope, and I am convinced that unless something radical can be done my—my husband will not survive for long.

'He grows more apathetic every day, and it is only because he has used every bit of a more than ordinary strength of will that he has fought the disease for so long. I—I shall be grateful to you from the bottom of my heart if you can hold out any ray of hope, and if you advise us we shall do anything—anything you say.'

And here, as her voice trailed off, Blake saw the beautiful eyes fill with sudden tears.

He reached out and laid his hand on hers.

'You know I will do anything in my power to help you and Sir Herbert,' he said quietly. 'Compose yourself, my dear lady, and we shall talk this matter over. But first excuse me while I just pick out that old monograph and see what I did say about goo-nah. I remember coming across the disease in my researches, but my recollection is not quite clear at this date as to just what I said.'

Blake rose and walked across to one of the bookcases, pulling up the leaded glass door. Then he ran his hand along the backs of several morocco-bound volumes until he found a slim, flexible book, which he took out. It was one of his own numerous monographs, and in this particular instance had been written some years before, just after a long period of concentrated research work on Eastern poisons and diseases.

He turned on a shaded light near the bookcase, and, opening, ran the pages of the little book over rapidly until he found what he wanted. Then, as his eye caught the reference, he paused and read what he had penned. As he went on the whole thing came back to him.

He had not written much about the mysterious disease known as 'goo-nah', merely stating that he had found traces of it in South China and Tonkin. He noticed, also, that he had added that cases which seemed to be of a similar nature had been reported from certain of the West Indies; but in that direction his research work at the time had not carried him far.

Then he noticed a footnote on the same page, in which he had mentioned the names of three authorities. As he read them he knew that there would be little comfort there for his visitor, for two of them had died in the meantime. The third was still alive, but——

Blake closed the volume and returned it to the shelf; then he lowered the leaded glass door and returned to his seat.

'You are quite right,' he said. 'I did refer to the disease known as goo-nah in my monograph, and now I recall perfectly in what circumstances I came upon it. I also gave a reference at the time to three authorities, but I am sorry to tell you that since the monograph was written two of those men have died.'

'But the third—is he still alive?' asked Lady Richmond eagerly. 'If so, can we not consult him? With your influence, Mr Blake—'

'He is alive,' put in Blake. 'At least, he was until very recently. And to be quite frank with you, Lady Richmond, if there is any man living who might be able to help you, he is that man. What knowledge there is of this obscure disease he possesses. To what extent that goes, however, I do not know. But there are certain difficulties—certain reasons why it is not going to be easy to do as you wish.

'This man is, as I have said, as much of an authority as any man living. He was one of the ablest surgeons living, and medical men flocked from all parts of the world to Vienna to hear him lecture and to see him demonstrate at the Franz Josef Hospital there. But since then he has fallen from grace, if I may use the expression. He is no longer a practising surgeon. He is something very different. And that is the difficulty.'

'But if he knows—if we can find him—what is he now, Mr Blake?'

'He is,' said Blake slowly, 'a notorious criminal adventurer whom I have been trying to get my hands on for several years. There have been occasions when I have done so, but there have also been times when I have allowed him to go under a truce. But a man who is now criminally adventurous—to place Sir Herbert in his care and his power—it is a risky thing to propose, Lady Richmond.'

'But you say he might be able to save my husband,' she pleaded. 'I—we will do anything—we will pay this man any fee he demands; and surely, under those circumstances, Mr Blake, he would consent. And you—you would leave him at liberty, would you not?'

Her eyes pleaded as did her voice.

'His name,' she said again. 'Let me go to him—let me advertise for him and see him! I am sure he would come if he knew you would not take advantage of your knowledge of his whereabouts.'

'His name,' said Blake, 'is Dr Huxton Rymer. As to his present whereabouts, I do not know them. But I have an idea that I could get track of him or get a message to him if I tried.'

He rose and paced up and down the room while the woman sat with bowed head resting on her hand. He looked at her from time to time, and his heart was sore, for she was one of the few women

75

who had ever really stirred Sexton Blake deeply. And whether it was the memory of that or not he at last came to a stop beside her and laid his hand on her shoulder.

'I will do what I can,' he said in a tone of gruff tenderness. 'I shall do my best to get in touch with this man, and then we shall see.'

For answer she caught his hand and pressed it against her wet cheek, and in that moment, somehow, Sexton Blake knew that he would do everything that lay in his power to help her.

But Huxton Rymer! To seek out that hawk on a matter of this nature—none knew better than Blake the danger it entailed.

* * *

'Peter's Restaurant, in Soho!'

Two figures stepped off the kerb of Oxford Street and advanced into the roadway as the taxi hailed by the taller of them drew up.

'Eh?' said the taxi-driver, looking deliberately up and down at the man who had spoken the words, and shooting a quick glance at his more youthful companion.

'Peter's Restaurant!' repeated the tall man, in a rough, domineering voice. 'You know it, I reckon? Don't make a tour o' London before you get to it!'

The taximan grunted and pulled down his flag. He was by no means eager to take these two individuals who thus accosted him at a quarter to twelve at night to such a rendezvous as Peter's Restaurant, which was, he knew, as notorious as his fares were unattractive. Nevertheless, he knew his legal position, and that he had no valid cause to refuse them.

So the cab, with a grinding of gears, swerved round in the wide roadway and headed about for Soho, with its two unwelcome passengers inside.

And, as he drove, the taximan could hear at intervals the low mutter of their conversation above the noise of his engine and the intermittent street-sounds which punctuated his progress at this late hour.

'Crooks!' he reflected. 'That's what they are, I bet! I know the type of bloke you see at Peter's all right!'

His two fares certainly justified that impression, both from their dress and from their destination; but in spite of appearances the taxi driver was wrong, a fact of which he would have been fully aware could he have heard their present conversation.

'And do you expect you'll see him without any trouble, guv'nor?' the younger was asking.

'I think so, Tinker,' replied the voice of Sexton Blake. 'XW 932 has always proved reliable in the past, and I think we can depend on the arrangements he has made this time. Rymer is a wily bird, though, and, in spite of the fact that he was willing to enter into a truce with us the last time we met him, he's still shy of us. In fact, he's shyer than ever just at present, for XW 932 tells me he has a rather big job on.'

'In other words, some swindle or other?' suggested Tinker.

Blake nodded, and a silence fell between them for a space as the detective gazed abstractedly at the deserted and darkened shops that bordered midnight Oxford Street.

The voice in which he had just spoken was startlingly different from that in which he had addressed the taxi driver. His normal, cultured tones had then given way to the harsh utterance of the typical East-Ender as an adjunct to their common disguise, of which the clothes they wore were only a part.

Blake was attired in a cheaply-cut blue suit and an overcoat with the same unenviable distinction, above which would have showed, if there had been light to see it, a grey flannel shirt, with a collar of the same material, and no tie. Almost two hours' work in his dressing-room at Baker Street had transformed him from his usual spruce self to an individual with a stubble-dark chin, an 'old' scar from eye to chin, and a thickness of neck and heaviness of cheeks that none would have identified with Sexton Blake, especially in conjunction with a limp which was apparent while he was on his feet, and which was artfully produced by the insertion of a small piece of wood in his left boot.

A dilapidated felt-hat crowned these efforts, and in his pockets he carried, among other things, a flashy cigar-case of imitation leather, filled with cigars of the same grade of flashiness, and a fully loaded automatic. This last was as much a part of the disguise as a weapon of offence or defence, for the *habitués* of the place whither they were bound would have regarded it without the least surprise.

As for Tinker, he looked just like any of a hundred young fellows of the cheap-jack, live-by-their-wits type which one can find in almost any part of London. Instead of a felt-hat, he was surmounted by a cap of large check pattern, and, in place of cigars, he was equipped for life's battle with a packet of cheap and popular 'fags'.

Any connection between Lady Richmond and the couple's present position, speeding disguised as cheap crooks to an obscure restaurant in Soho, was not immediately apparent. It was, however, as a direct result of that lady's appeal earlier in the day that Blake and Tinker were now on their way to Peter's Restaurant.

The detective had promised to find Dr Huxton Rymer, and to get into communication with him if it were humanly possible—and he had done so. But, as he himself had said, Huxton Rymer was a wily bird, and it had been no easy matter to arrange a meeting with a criminal who, in spite of Sexton Blake's recent truce with him at Christmas-time, still regarded anything in the shape of the law with swift suspicion.

The thing had been arranged through an intermediary, as had the previous meeting. XW 932, one of Blake's many agents in the London underworld, had, after negotiations that had lasted all the evening, at last telephoned to Baker Street the news that Rymer would consent to meet the detective, subject only to the condition that Blake's business was purely personal, and that no harm was intended.

'I shall be at Terry's at midnight, and shall wait till one.' That had been Huxton Rymer's reply, and Blake had accepted it.

'Terry's.'

That was the name which had given birth to the stubble-chinned individual with the cheap-cut clothes and the automatic, and to the tough-looking youth with the 'fags'.

Terry's joint, as it was known to its frequenters, was ostensibly a night club not far off the Tottenham Court Road. It was a place of bad repute with the police, and had been raided again and again, but without any success. Terry, the Irishman who ran the joint, had such a well-organised system of spies and look-outs that it was next to impossible to get inside without warning being given. And, though the police knew only too well that the law was being constantly broken, they could do nothing to stop it.

But that phase of Terry's was the mildest. In the so-called public rooms the law-breaking consisted mostly of the selling of drinks after hours; but the real business of the place was what went on in the numerous rabbit-warrens of rooms and passages below, above, and at the back of the main premises.

It was, for one thing, the main clearing-house of dope west of Aldgate. It was, too, the meeting-place of crooks of both sexes; and for anyone else to gain entry there was more than rare.

It had taken Sexton Blake a long time to get round that difficulty, but at last the detective's resourcefulness had surmounted it, and he knew that he and Tinker would be able to get into Terry's without much trouble. Incidentally, the means by which he had achieved this result would form almost a story in itself, and it would be injudicious to embark on an account of it in the present chronicle.

Their danger would come after they were in, for it was impossible to tell whether, in spite of their disguise, some fluke or other might not betray them. And among that inner circle of desperate crooks, such a discovery would mean that every snarling wolf in the pack would come down on them. What would be left of the pair if these wolves succeeded in getting their teeth in wouldn't interest anyone but the coroner.

The address he had given the taxi-driver was not, except to the initiates, connected in any way with Terry's.

Ostensibly, Peter's Restaurant was a dingy little restaurant run by a Greek known to his customers as Peter; but actually it formed the back way into the Irishman's place, and the greasy Greek was the doorkeeper of his back entrance.

The journey in the taxicab from where Blake had hailed it near Baker Street did not take very long, and it was just on the stroke of the hour when the cab jerked to a standstill outside the place.

Blake, who had spoken but little during the journey, resumed his harsh accents for the driver's benefit, and after a bit of rough badinage and the bestowal of a small tip, stood with Tinker on the kerb, and watched the man depart, expressing, as he drove off, his relief at seeing the last of two such 'ugly blighters'.

The couple entered leisurely, for Blake wanted to give the taxi-man time to get away before he spoke to 'Peter'. When he heard the cab grinding along down the street, he turned to the Greek, and uttered a certain password. The Greek who was alone in the place, rose at once, and waddled along to the back of the restaurant.

He led them into a kitchen at the rear, and at the back of this opened a window which opened into a court. They slid over the sill, and the window was shut behind them. Blake led the way across the court, and paused before a low door on the other side. He rapped there according to a code, and presently they heard the sound of footsteps inside.

The door swung open as if someone possessed of great caution was on the other side. Blake leant forward, and uttered another code signal, and this time the door swung wide. He and Tinker entered a narrow passage, in which a single light burned. They went along this until they came to a door at the far end, leaving the doorkeeper to close and bolt the courtyard door. Blake turned the handle of the second door, and stepped immediately into a small room, where half a dozen tables were laid, and at each of which three or four persons—a mixed company of men and women, whose appearance stamped them for what they were—sat eating supper. Detective-Inspector Thomas, of Scotland Yard, would have given quite a nice lump of his salary to have been admitted there at that moment.

There were two or three of the *habitués* whom both Blake and Tinker knew by sight, and to these they nodded. Blake cast a look round for signs of Huxton Rymer, but saw none, and kept on his way towards a door at the other end of the room. This, he knew, would lead him to the larger general room located above the main dance establishment, which was known as Terry's Night Club.

But before he could reach the door one of those incidents occurred that will come upon a man, no matter how carefully his plans have been laid.

At one of the tables in a corner near the door, which was their objective, sat a woman whose face was ravaged with deep lines of dissipation. Blake had seen her in the joint before, and had always observed her dressed the same—in a soiled pink evening-frock, much the worse for wear—and in the company of the same man, whom he knew to be a 'juice thrower', or safe breaker. But until that moment he had had no suspicion that the woman was other than just what she appeared to be. But before he reached the door he knew, to his cost, that she was either one of those treacherous creatures known as a 'nark', or else that in some way unknown to him, she had discovered his identity, on some previous visit.

At any rate, just as they were passing the table she gave a shrill, squealing laugh, and lurched to her feet, her face flushed, and her eyes blazing with the drink she had consumed. Then she gave a second squeal, that brought the attention of the whole room to them. And it was in this sudden, dead silence she screamed:

'Look at 'em, everyone—look at 'em, I say! It's that hound Sexton Blake, the 'tec, and his brat of an assistant!'

Down the room someone laughed. Then a chair crashed, and Blake and Tinker swung round, to find several men advancing upon them with the menace of murder in their attitude.

★ ★ ★

Blake brought his automatic out with a single twist of the wrist, and Tinker was only the fraction of a second behind him.

'Back towards the door,' said Blake, in a swift aside. 'We may be able to settle this without shooting.'

They backed up until they stood side by side against the door which led to the general room. At sight of the two heavy weapons held in such business-like manner, the advancing men gave pause. Blake eyed them from under the lowered brim of his hat with a menacing glare that was evil-looking enough for the worst criminal to possess.

'What's all this?' he snarled. 'Can't I come in this joint without some drunken moll shooting the roof like that? How do you get this way? This skirt here is soaked to the eyes with "snow". Anyone can see that, and I'll stand a lot from her for that reason. Sure she's got it in for me! Didn't I refuse to do a turn for her the last time I was in here? She's hop-head, that's all that's the matter with her; but if any of you guys want to start something—why, just go ahead. Before I finish there will be a lot of you go out of here on stretchers. Now, then, who's first?'

'What does she mean, then?' came a voice from the back. 'Why should she say you are Sexton Blake? Who are you, anyway? I've been round here for two years, and I've only seen you two or three times. Let someone who knows you tell us it's all right, and we'll be satisfied.'

'Who in blazes do you think you are, you cheap-jack porch scaler?' said Blake harshly. 'Who appointed you spokesman of Terry's? Find Terry himself, and he'll tell you who I am and what I am. I don't answer questions put by a pup like you. I'm here on business, and I'm going through with it. I am a dangerous guy to fool with, and you can mark me dynamite. So now if you want to go any farther, just come along and let me know which one is first. When I start things going, I won't need any visiting-cards to tell you who I am.'

The gang at the back—the toughest circle of the *habitués*, and, therefore, the most suspicious and most dangerous—seemed convinced by Blake's words and manner. They wavered. Even they might have settled down, had the harridan of a woman not taken a hand again.

Under calmer mood she would have said nothing, for to start anything like that in Terry's meant being barred, whether it was true or not, and she knew it. But now, with the flame of the drug and the drink in her mind, she was beyond all control. Before either Blake or Tinker could stop her, or even knew what she was up to, she had sprung across at Blake, had knocked his hat clean off his head, and then, with a vicious clawing motion, had brought her nails down the side of his cheek, bringing the blood in four jagged lines, and in the same act taking away part of the artificial scar he had placed there.

With a sharp movement Blake sent the wretched woman aside, and she staggered into the arms of the 'juice thrower' who was her escort. But the attack had brought the full attention of the roughs at the bottom of the room back to Blake and Tinker, and as the woman was whirled aside, one of them saw the lines across the fake scar, showing the unblemished skin beneath. With an oath he called the attention of the others to this. Half a dozen others sent their chairs crashing, and got to their feet.

'By heck,' yelled two or three at once, 'the woman is right. It is a fake scar on his face. Come on, men; we'll find out who he is, anyway!'

Blake saw that there was no hope for it now. In fact, the attack was already on, for the creature who had been with the woman pushed her aside, and, dragging out a wicked, double-edged, saw-tooth Italian knife, had made a leap for Blake. Tinker had seen him coming, and before he struck, the lad reversed his weapon and hit out with all his strength.

It was a perfectly aimed and perfectly placed blow. The butt of the heavy pistol caught the 'juice thrower' clean between the eyes. He went down with a crash among the plates. The woman started a chorus of screams in which the other women joined, and then from the back of the room a couple of guns crashed as two men shot. The bullets smashed into the door behind the pair, and at this Blake held his hand no longer.

He shot once, coolly. Scarcely had the crash of the heavy gun died away than Tinker also fired. There was a yell at the end of the room, and a man thudded to the floor. Blake said a quick word to Tinker. Then, stepping forward a little, he drove his heel back against the door.

It did not give. He had no chance to repeat the action, for the gang at the end of the room had decided on rush tactics. They came on as if they were going into a football scrum. Blake knew he and Tinker could probably pick off several before they went down; but he knew also that they could not get the whole bunch.

If he could only get the door behind them open, they might make a dash through that way, and get out by the front.

'One shot—right into them!' he rapped; and the two guns crashed out at one and the same moment. The heavy bullets thudded into the front of the mass of humanity, and two men went down, while those behind stumbled over them.

'Hold your fire, but keep them covered,' said Blake. 'I'll try the door again.'

He risked turning, but even as he did so a bullet ripped through the shoulder of his coat. He knew if they were to escape now they would have to do so within the next few seconds. The whole bunch would be shooting soon.

He kicked again and again at the door, and at last it gave signs of yielding. He drew back to hurl his whole weight against it, when Tinker's gun crashed out again.

'Turn, guv'nor—turn!' rapped out Tinker. 'There's some new move at the back.'

Blake whirled round just in time to see the door at the other end come crashing inwards, and then a bulky form stood on the threshold, gazing at the confusion before him. In the first glance Blake and Tinker recognised Huxton Rymer.

'Hey, you doc!' Blake called loudly. 'These fools have got it into their heads that we are a couple of narks. If you can do anything with them, put the muzzle on before more damage is done. If you don't I'll give them a worse dose of lead than they have had already.'

Now 'Doc' was the name by which Huxton Rymer was known throughout the length and breadth of the underworld, and while on any other occasion it would have suited his book to see Blake and Tinker annihilated, he did not want to have it happen just then. His reasons were purely selfish, it is true; but he had made the rendezvous with Blake, knowing that Blake would come to Terry's at considerable risk to himself, and he was sporting enough to stand on his appointment until he knew what it was about.

He had not known in what way Blake would be disguised; but as he heard Blake's voice, and saw the pair at bay at the upper end of the room, he took in the situation at once, and he plunged into the gang with arms flailing like a windmill.

'What do you mean, you fools?' he yelled, as he sent them flying. 'Friend of mine—appointment with me here! What crazy fool says they are narks? Get back, you fools! You there—into that chair, and you, and you, and you!'

He accompanied each word by fists and feet, and in two minutes had the gang scattered.

There was no question of gunplay against him, and Rymer knew there wouldn't be. The Doc was far too powerful and too useful a member of the crook world for any of that small fry to 'put out his light'. If any had done so he would have had such a vendetta against him that would have meant his death-warrant in twenty-four hours, and every man-jack knew it.

Rymer fought his way up the room to where Blake and Tinker stood. As he reached them, the harridan who had started the trouble tried to shriek something in his ear; but he turned on her with such a terrible snarl that she shrank back, and suddenly grew quiet. The effects of the drug were beginning to wear off, and she was beginning to realise just what she had let herself in for. And there were good reasons why she should cringe before the Doc.

At the same moment the door behind Blake opened, and the notorious Terry himself stood there. He stood gaping at the chaos of the supper-room, and at the three wounded men who still sprawled on the floor. He began to speak, but Rymer caught him by the shoulder.

'That hag of a creature started this!' he snarled. 'Get her out, and keep her out! Get those others out of the place, too, or you'll have the whole place pulled tonight. These two are friends of mine. Get us through and into the other street. I'll see you about this rumpus tomorrow.'

And because he had to obey, Terry the bold, Terry the snake of the night, turned meekly to obey. Blake and Tinker stumbled through the door and into the big general room beyond, where a score or more of other *habitués* were standing up, looking towards the door, curious, and yet glad that they had not been in the mix-up in the other room.

In five minutes Blake, Tinker, and Rymer were in a small side street. Tinker had snatched up Blake's hat, and this Blake now jammed on his head. Then he turned to Rymer.

'Well,' he said coolly, 'your friends gave us a warm reception while we were waiting for you. I suppose I may take it you had nothing to do with it?'

'You may,' said Rymer curtly. 'Personally it would have suited me well enough if they had "got" the pair of you; but I can't tell you how that fool woman knew you. When I made the appointment for Terry's I made it on the level. You wanted to see me. We can't talk in there now. Can you suggest a place?'

'Will you come on to Baker Street?'

'You will play fair?'

'You know that. I don't want to get you by such means. I have a matter to talk over with you, and possibly a definite offer to make you. I am only doing this because it is on behalf of very old friends of mine, and as far as I know you are the best man for the purpose.'

'Very well, I am willing to come.'

And five minutes later this strangely assorted trio were in a taxi, being driven to Baker Street—a place that Rymer ordinarily would have avoided as he would avoid a pest-house.

*   *   *

A little over a month after the events just recorded two men sat on the shaded veranda of the Myrtle Bank Hotel, in Kingston, Jamaica.

One, a man who might have been anything from forty-five to sixty-five, was reclining in a long deck-chair.

His pallid face and thin hands, which lay loosely across the knees, proclaimed that he either was, or had been, very ill. His skin had turned as yellow as old parchment, and there was not a particle of the clean-shaven countenance that did not show a maze of tiny wrinkles. His eyes were deeply sunken and dull: his whole attitude was listless in the extreme.

His companion was the direct antithesis so far as physical appearance went. He was deep of chest and broad of frame. His shoulders were built with a sweep of extraordinary power, and his limbs were as thick and strong as the trunks of small trees. In contrast to his companion his eyes were dark and full of fire, while his face showed deeply tanned above the neatly-trimmed, pointed beard and moustache.

His hands, too, lay across his legs, but there was nothing listless in them. On the contrary. They reflected as much strength as the face, and yet in the length of the fingers and in a 'something' in the flex of the wrist, they reminded one of the hands of the great painter, or musician, or surgeon.

And indeed that is what they were, for no more wonderful master of the knife had ever lived than he who possessed those hands. Years before, men had come from every quarter of the globe to see the famous surgeon, Dr Huxton Rymer, at work in the Franz Josef Hospital in Vienna.

He would have been there today, honoured as the greatest man in his profession, had it not been for the strange criminal kink within him that had caused him to throw everything to the winds— wealth and power and the adulation of his fellows, and go out into the world as a common criminal adventurer.

That was Dr Huxton Rymer today, or, rather, it had been a little over a month before, when Sexton Blake, the famous London criminologist, who had hounded him about the globe for years, had come to him at Terry's to put to him one of the strangest proposals he had ever listened to.

The man who sat in the long deck-chair beside him was Sir Herbert Richmond, the husband of the fair client who had visited Sexton Blake that day in early January to seek his help in a last desperate attempt to do something to save her husband from the strange malady which was threatening his life.

Blake had not been wrong in thinking that Huxton Rymer was

the only living European who might be able to read the riddle of the strange malady and conquer it. He knew that, years before, when he was in Vienna, Huxton Rymer had done a good deal of research work in rare Eastern diseases, and he knew that among these had been included that mysterious affliction known as 'goo-nah'.

It is known what happened when Blake and Tinker visited Terry's in disguise, and how, at the critical moment, Rymer put in appearance and got them away by means of another exit. They had gone on to Baker Street, and there Blake had made his proposal.

It is unnecessary here to dwell on all the preliminaries which attended the final settlement of the affair. Rymer had gone away that night promising to think things over, and, on his part, Blake had promised to get a definite offer out of Lady Richmond or her husband.

The following morning he had gone to see Lady Richmond at her hotel in Curzon Street, and from that things had moved swiftly. She had returned to Ipswich, where she had consulted her husband. Blake had gone with her, and the upshot of the matter was that Blake returned to London authorised to make any terms which might be necessary, but at all costs to make them.

The result was a firm offer to Rymer of a salary of five hundred pounds a month plus all his expenses of every description whatsoever if he would take charge of the case and devote his whole time to it. If he effected a cure he was to receive a lump sum of ten thousand pounds. If he failed; then, of course, the contract would terminate.

Rymer had asked for time to consider, and he had made good use of that interval. He had looked up the financial standing of Sir Herbert, finding that he was the retired senior partner of a well-known firm of East India importers, and rated as being worth between a hundred and fifty and two hundred thousand pounds. On this discovery Rymer had stipulated for a bonus of twenty thousand instead of ten, in case he effected a cure, and this was readily agreed to, although Blake demurred.

On that consideration Rymer agreed to take the case on condition that Sir Herbert should place himself entirely in his hands and under his orders for at least a year, and this, too, was entered in the contract. Then, when the papers were signed, he announced that it would be necessary for his patient to be taken to some mild climate for the treatment. After some discussion Rymer fixed on the West Indies as being most suitable for the purpose. It was agreed that Lady Richmond should not accompany them, and, in the event of his death, Sir Herbert, under Blake's advice, made a definite settlement on his wife. This was to the amount of a hundred thousand pounds, which was placed under her absolute control, while, of course, she would get the residue of the estate should he die.

Then arrangements were pressed forward, with the result that, just a little over a month after his interview with Blake, Huxton Rymer found himself at the Myrtle Bank with his patient.

He had not yet fixed on a place for their residence during the year which they would spend in the West Indies. On the voyage out Rymer had given this phase of the matter a good deal of thought, and when Huxton Rymer began thinking deeply, he usually arrived somewhere. The upshot of his cogitations in this particular instance was that he made up his mind to leave the matter in abeyance until they should reach Jamaica, and there to get in touch, if it were possible, with the mysterious and, among the blacks of the West Indies, all-powerful woman who was known as Marie Galante.

Those who have read the previous records of Sexton Blake's exploits among those islands will readily recall Marie Galante—the beautiful, exotic creature who had her lair far back in the hills of unknown Haiti, who was the mysterious head of the secret Empire of the Blacks which has today stretched its tentacles clear across the Atlantic to Liberia, and who, on more than one occasion had been assisted by Dr Huxton Rymer in her strange practices.

They will recall how Sexton Blake and Tinker penetrated into the hidden fastnesses of her retreat, arriving at a time when the snake and blood rites of the terrible voodoo practices were in full swing; and how, despite the jungle passion of the woman, they had dragged Rymer out of the devilish intrigue into which he had plunged, and in doing so had smashed one of the greatest plots ever conceived.

And now Huxton Rymer was back in the West Indies, trying to get in touch with the same flaming orchid woman. What that would mean even he did not try to answer. But something in the scented, balmy breezes of the Caribbean had seemed to whisper her name. Out of the purple night which had hung over Haiti as they passed, a voice had seemed to call to him—and it was on that night that Rymer made his decision.

As soon as they reached Kingston and had been installed in the Myrtle Bank he had taken pains to let it be known in certain quarters that he wished to get in touch with Marie Galante. That was a name that was only whispered among the blacks when it was spoken at all, but Huxton Rymer knew that scarcely had the word been dropped when the news was speeding away on the mysterious wings which would carry it with lightning speed from Kingston to Colon and from Barbados to Haiti. Sooner or later Marie Galante would know that he wished to see her, and he knew that she would either come or send for him.

In the meantime he began the treatment of the patient. In fact, he had already done so on the voyage out. His first care had been to take blood samples, and from these to try and isolate the germ which he had already succeeded in isolating in Vienna. Rymer knew for a fact what other men only suspected—that 'goo-nah' was due to a germ, and if that were the disease which was ravaging his patient, then he knew he had a fighting chance to conquer it if it had not gone too far.

Let it not be thought that Rymer was not playing the game on that point. He was. He was as conscientious in his handling of the case as any specialist could have been. Once they were installed in the hotel he had fitted up a small temporary laboratory, and, while keeping Sir Herbert under a simple regimen, had continued his experiments.

They had passed a week thus, and at the end of that time Rymer had triumphed. For the second time he succeeded in isolating the germ he sought, and now, on this day, while they sat together on the veranda waiting for tea to be served, he was able for the first time to give some definite news to the other.

It was this they were discussing when the white-clad negro 'boy' came along the veranda with a snowy tea-tray, against which was a great splash of dark crimson where the crystal bowl of guava was set.

'Yes, Sir Herbert,' Rymer was saying, as he poured the tea, 'I am able at last to tell you something definite. You know what I have suspected and what I was seeking? Well, sir, I have found it. It is already in the sugar culture, and in a few days I shall be ready to prepare vaccine and start injections. I do not wish to buoy you up with false hopes, but I have promised to be perfectly frank.

'If the disease has not run too far, we stand a fighting chance. But there is other treatment necessary in conjunction with the vaccine, and it will take some time to prepare it. This auxiliary treatment is just as important as the other, and it will be necessary for me to prepare my own medicine from certain herbs and spices which can be found here in the West Indies.

'That was one reason why I selected this part of the world. We could have gone to the Far East, where I could secure the same herbs and spices; but, in view of the fact that you contracted the disease there, I deemed it wiser to come here. Besides, the air of the Caribbean is much more tonic than that of the Chinese Coast or the East Indies, and I think, altogether, you will do better here. Here is your tea.'

The patient stretched out a thin hand and took the cup. But he was not giving it any attention just then. Instead, his eyes were fixed on the misty bulk of the lovely Blue Mountains which rose before them, and against the sides of which they could see dotted here and there the white hill bungalows of the Kingston residents.

He had already begun to feel a restfulness in the soft air and the benign sun, for there is no place in the world more lovely than those tropic British islands which stretch from the point of Cuba down through the beautiful Caribbean to the coast of the old Spanish Main.

He looked just about the same as when he had left England, but he was, to his own knowledge and to Rymer's critical eyes, a little brighter; and now, as he brought his eyes back from the lovely prospect of the Blue Mountains and looked at his companion, the dullness seemed lighted by a faint lustre.

'I—hope you are right,' he said, in a halting whisper. 'If you can drive this poison out of me you will be giving me back more than life. It is not that I am afraid to die. I am ready when my time comes, but I have work still to do, and I wish to live for that. But don't hold out false hopes. I will do everything you say. I am entirely in your hands, and I want the truth, and nothing but the truth, at all times. That is our bargain. If I am to die, you are to tell me, so that I can wind up my affairs. But if I am to live, then—be—very—sure—before—you—hold—out—that—blessed—hope—to—me.'

'You can trust me to do that, Sir Herbert,' said Rymer quietly. 'I have made my contract with you, and I shall keep it. And now, sir, sip a little of your tea. Afterwards I shall give you your medicine. But let me impress upon you that you must have hope. That is as essential as the will to live and to fight. If you keep those, then I can battle better, and with that vaccine and the other treatment—well, sir, we shall see what two months of it will do.'

The other nodded, and obediently began sipping his tea. Rymer sat with his gaze also fixed on the mountains which loomed so near at hand, seeming almost to lean out over the town. For the moment every thought but that of the medical problem in which he was interested had been banished from his mind.

And he was still pondering over certain phases of the experiments he intended making with the vaccine when he suddenly caught sight of a negro boy sliding along by the wall (which still showed traces of the terrible earthquake of seventeen years before) that shut the front garden of the hotel off from the road.

He had seen the same negro go by two or three times before, and now, as he fixed his eyes on the black, he saw his hand come up to his face and then sweep downward with a quick, sharp motion.

It was a voodoo sign, which Huxton Rymer had learned in the heart of Haiti, and as he saw it he knew that the man had some message for him.

After a few moments he picked up his topee and excused himself, saying he was going along to the nearby chemist's, and would be back in a few minutes. He walked down the path and out through the gate, and then, as he turned to the left, past the garden, he saw that the negro had turned and was following him.

Rymer kept on until he was out of sight of anyone sitting on the veranda of the hotel, then he crossed the hot, dusty road and entered the gardens. He strolled along more slowly when he was under the great nutmegs and pepper-trees, and it was not long before the black boy drew level with him. As he passed he drew close, and then, in the low, liquid tones of the island patois, Rymer caught the message:

'The old galleon at Spanish Town tonight at midnight.' And with that the boy disappeared into the tangle of the undergrowth.

*   *   *

Huxton Rymer had his patient tucked into bed by ten o'clock, and from then on he was free to dispose of his time as he wished. His first care was to arrange for a motor car to take him to Spanish Town, the old buccaneers' resort some miles out of Kingston, and as soon as he had closed the door of Sir Herbert's room he put on a panama hat and left the hotel.

It was bright moonlight outside, and as he walked along the dusty road, where the palm-leaves lay in feathery silhouette against the white, he presented a striking figure in his black trousers and white mess-jacket. He was a man to attract attention at any time, but never did he look more distinguished or imposing than in formal attire, and this was not altogether because of the devil-may-care manner which was such an integral part of him.

He walked as far as a public garage just near the Colonial Bank building, and there arranged for a dilapidated car to take him through to his destination. Then he returned to the hotel, and got a light duck coat and a heavy Service revolver. This latter he dropped into the hip-pocket of his trousers. He next filled his cigar-case with green 'Machados', which he had bought on his arrival in Kingston, and then, glancing at his watch, found that it was just half-past ten.

'Be time to start when I get back to the garage,' he thought. Throwing the duck coat over his arm, he started off again, one of the strong green cigars between his teeth.

Spanish Town, as has been said, was once famous as being the haunt of the buccaneers who plied their 'trade' up and down the Caribbean from Tortuga to the coast of Central America and along the whole stretch of the Spanish Main. It was along that coast that Drake harried the Spaniard and Morgan took toll of every ship that came his way. It was in those waters, too, that we fought the Frenchman, and there wasn't a ship that sailed under letters of marque or with the blatant skull and cross-bones at the masthead that didn't slip into Spanish Town harbour at some time or other.

Spanish Town today is a sleepy little place, and appears to have more attraction for the visitor to the island than for anyone else. The old square is much the same as it was, and half-way along the road to Kingston can still be seen the giant tree beneath which Morgan proclaimed his appointment as Governor of the island. Once out of the main square one gets almost immediately into the narrow streets of the blacks, who form almost the whole population. Beyond those twisting, puzzling thoroughfares are a few haunts into which it is rarely indeed that the ordinary visitor penetrates.

Now, it was to one of these places that Huxton Rymer was bound.

More than two hundred and fifty years ago a certain British privateer chased a richly laden Spanish galleon right up the Caribbean from off the coast of Costa Rica to Jamaica. She engaged her off Port Royal and drove her down the coast until she was just off Spanish Town. There the Spanish captain beached his ship before surrendering, and to this day the wreck still lies where she struck.

But since that time, owing to the numerous earthquakes which have changed the topography of the whole of the sea-bed about Jamaica, the sea is not where it was, and as she lies now the remains of the old galleon lie in a hidden spot with her nose jammed right into a certain narrow and little-known lane at the waterside of Spanish Town.

They built honest ships away back in those days, and the heavy oak of her timbers is as sound today as when she crossed the Atlantic laden with ingots of silver from the mines of Peru and the gold bullion from the heart of Colombia. She has served many purposes in her time, has that old hulk, but mostly she has been a waterside saloon where the sweepings of many countries have gathered in turn. For a time she fell into disuse, but not long ago she was rehabilitated as a saloon—and not one of the ordinary type. It was not a place that touted for business. There are a few persons only who have the entrée into its two rooms, or, rather, cabins. The outer one is for negroes, and the inner for certain mysterious visitors who come and go unheralded.

This was the spot where Rymer had his rendezvous.

He knew better than to attempt to take the car through any of the narrow streets leading to the galleon. In the first place, it would have been practically impossible to get the vehicle through; and in the second, he knew that there would be many mysterious incidents on the way which would make it out of the question to proceed. Therefore, he left it in the silent square or plaza, and, charging the negro driver to wait for him no matter how long he might be, he started ahead on foot.

He knew his way well enough. The last time he had been there had been to keep a rendezvous with the same Marie Galante, and it seemed an odd coincidence that on this second occasion the moon should be shining in just the same way. The lanes were deserted, but behind the whitewashed walls of the buildings Rymer knew that a teeming life was taking its way, and, indeed, as he went along he could catch the low murmur of voices through small, iron-barred windows set high up in the walls or the weird cadence of a fiddle coming from some hidden spot.

And he knew, too, that he took not a single step that was not observed.

But he went ahead as coolly as if he had been walking down Harbour Street in Kingston at broad midday. He took the turnings with the certainty born of knowledge, and at last he came to the narrow stretch of sandy lane that he knew would bring him to his destination.

Just as he reached it a strain of music broke out somewhere. It was in a quick, jerky tone that had a touch of the savage in it. It reminded him of the lilt of the modern tango that has come out of the Indian life of the Argentine. And it was playing a ditty that had been sung two or three hundred years ago by the buccaneers who sailed those waters.

But it was no casual outburst of music, as Rymer well knew. There was a signal and a message in it, and when at last he stumbled into the first or outer 'cabin' of the old galleon he was not a bit surprised to find it completely deserted.

He hadn't the slightest doubt that it had been well crowded even as he reached the top of the lane, nor did he doubt that he was even now being observed. But he went ahead as if he were ignorant of anything having happened.

He knew that Marie Galante would be at the rendezvous at midnight. He glanced at his watch under the smoky flame of an old oil-lamp that hung from one of the blackened beams overhead. The hands showed that it was already five minutes after the hour, and as he stood listening Rymer frowned with annoyance at himself for not having judged it better.

Was she in the inner 'cabin', or had she come and, not finding him there, had gone again? He advanced in the direction of the opposite bulkhead, where he knew a secret door gave into the inner 'cabin', when he thought he heard the murmur of voices on the other side.

He placed his ear against the bulk head and listened. This time he knew that he had not been mistaken. Someone was certainly on the other side, and they were talking—at least, one was talking, and it was the voice of a man. Still Rymer did not move. He had detected a touch of anger in the tones, and when a man runs up against that in the sort of place in which he was then he treads very warily indeed. There are too many traps about, hidden so that only the initiated can avoid them.

The man's voice seemed to break off. Then, after a short pause, another voice sounded. But this one belonged to no man. It was high and soft and low and liquid all at once, it seemed. It was a voice that Huxton Rymer knew only too well, for it was that of Marie Galante. As he heard it his white teeth showed against his beard as he smiled. For the moment he had forgotten everything but just that voice and that the untamed, exotic, beautiful creature was there within a few feet of him.

But now it broke off and again the man's voice sounded. This time it held a harsher timbre than before. As he listened, Rymer's smile passed and he frowned. He laid a hand lightly on his hip to feel his automatic, then his hand slid along the side of the bulkhead until his searching fingers found the secret catch whose position he had not forgotten. He pressed this with infinite caution, and at the same time, with his free hand, slid back the panel. It yielded, and a gap began to widen. An inch—two inches—three inches—and he could look into the inner 'cabin'.

There were two occupants of the place. Neither was looking in his direction. They were both standing on the other side of the old oak table that had been an original part of the galleon. The sides of their faces were towards Rymer. His eyes sought the woman first; and, as he once more drank in her exotic beauty, something that he thought had died suddenly stirred and the blood pounded to his temples. It receded, and he dragged his gaze away from the lithe, tigerish figure of the woman, who stood as regally as a queen, her whole form swathed in white silk mantilla which had been decorated with crimson splashes of silk. Then he looked at the man, and as he did so he gave an involuntary start. For he knew the man for one who had been knocking about the Caribbean for years.

Rymer had known him first as an inter-island trader who ran his own schooner—an American who had drifted down into those waters, no one knew exactly how. It now recurred to Rymer that somewhere, at some time, not long before, he had heard that this man Pearson was running a schooner for Marie Galante, but he had paid little attention at the time, and the gossip had entirely passed out of his mind until this moment, when he saw the girl in that old cabin.

There could be no doubt that things were not well between them. The girl's eyes were blazing, and her lips were curled in disdain as she looked at him. As for Pearson, it was plain that he had been drinking; but something told Rymer that the spirit he had taken had not intoxicated him as had the exotic allure of the girl.

Men had risen and fallen all through the brief career of Marie Galante. She had put her foot on the neck of every one who had fallen within the meshes of her web, and then had discarded them with as little thought as she would have flicked aside a guava seed. She had done this with all but two men—and one of those was Huxton Rymer. It had been Rymer who had wielded the whip, and it was just because he had done so that Marie Galante had crept to him in whimpering submission—had used the very altar of the voodoo ritual for his protection.

Now, as he listened, Rymer heard the man speaking again—and suddenly he discovered that it was he himself who was the cause of the altercation.

'You can talk and sneer and laugh!' snarled Pearson. 'But I know the truth. I gave up everything in my life for you! I came to you to serve you, and for three years I have carted your cursed blacks about this sea. I have turned renegade and I've soaked in the devilish rites which you practise in that hell-hole in Haiti. I have done this because I have been your maudlin slave, but I will stand your treatment no longer! I know why you have come here tonight. Do you think I don't know about that old business in Haiti when Huxton Rymer was there? Do you think I don't know it was this adventurer Rymer who killed General Alexis for you? Do you—'

'Wait, you cur!' She snapped the words out like a lash. 'You speak of the killing of General Alexis. Do you know why he was killed? I will tell you. He was killed because he dared to speak to me as you are speaking tonight! Because he dared to mouth my name as you have done! And if the man you speak of were here now he

96

would snap your neck like a twig of blackpalm for daring to do what you have dared tonight!

'You say you have served me! Well, you have been well paid! You were promised nothing. If you have any shreds of sense you would have seen that you are as nothing in my scheme of things! You have dared to threaten me and—another! I shall see that this is remembered! Now go—go back to the schooner and wait until I come! When I do your case shall be dealt with!'

'By Heaven! You speak to me like that!' he stormed. 'After what I have done, after the way in which I have served you, you throw me away like a squeezed orange! No, and no, and no! You will yield to my demands here and now, or I'll tear the false heart from you before I leave this cabin! I will give you one more chance, and then—'

Crash!

The panel slammed back the full way and Huxton Rymer stood in the opening.

'One more chance!' he drawled. 'One more chance! Yes, that is quite right, Pearson! You have one more chance to get out of here, quick, or—'

At the first sound Marie Galante had turned. Now she was standing, her lips parted and her breast heaving as she gazed upon Rymer. In the upsurging of her jungle passion for the man for whom she had been waiting she had utterly forgotten Pearson. And Pearson, poor besotted and benighted fool, was gazing at Rymer like a mad panther. And like a panther he sprang.

But Rymer had anticipated the attack. As Pearson came on he stepped quickly to one side. Pearson struck the bulkhead. Rymer drove his fist in, hard to a point just under the ear. The man shot slithering along the side of the bulkhead, but recovered. When he sprang again it was with a knife raised.

Rymer waited for him, the dare-devil smile showing still. He knew full well that Marie Galante was watching the battle, with the lust of the savage in her eyes.

Pearson rushed, more warily this time; but Rymer seemed to disdain him and appeared to take no precautions to defend himself. He moved ever so little as Pearson circled round him, watching for an opening, and then the attack came again.

Rymer came into action as if he had been released by a steel spring. He gave one lightning-like leap aside. The smile left his lips as he snarled and shot out his great arms.

He caught Pearson's wrist, and a second later there was a sharp crack and a scream of agony as the bone of the arm snapped like a bit of pipe-stem.

The knife dropped from his nerveless hand, and, deliberately, Rymer drew back his fist and drove it again and again full into the other's face.

Pearson was helpless to defend himself. He stumbled about the cabin while Rymer struck. The woman laughed aloud, and then at the last Rymer dragged him through the opening into the outer cabin, and threw him bodily into the dusty, moon-washed lane outside.

He walked back to the inner 'cabin' and deliberately closed the panel. He looked at Marie Galante where she stood under the swinging oil-lamp. Her lips and her eyes smiled at him, and the blood was hot in her face as she waited. Then suddenly Rymer held up his hand.

'Come here!' he said roughly.

And Marie Galante obeyed.

*   *   *

Some five months had passed since Lady Richmond had visited Sexton Blake in connection with the strange Eastern disease which her husband had contracted, and, in so far as Blake was concerned, a good deal of water had flowed under the bridges since then.

He and Tinker had handled a good many cases, some of a purely routine nature, and others which required all of Blake's skill and daring, and all the loyal assistance the lad could give him, before 'finis' was written to them in the famous 'Index'.

It was on a morning early in the month of May when, for a wonder, the breath of spring seemed actually to be over London, that a ring came at the front door, and a little later Mrs Bardell entered the consulting-room to announce that Lady Richmond had called.

In one moment Blake recalled the circumstances of her previous visit, and even while he waited for the housekeeper to show her in, he was recalling the facts in the case.

'Her last letter said that Sir Herbert was still improving under the treatment,' he reflected, 'and that there were good grounds for hoping that he would recover. That was, let me see, yes—um! about three weeks ago, or so. It has proved, after all, an experiment worth while. It has given Rymer a real chance, and apparently he has played the game. At any rate, Sir Herbert is on the road to recovery, and apart from the triumph of a cure in that particular case, the success of the whole thing will be, in itself, sufficient to rehabilitate Rymer, in the medical world—if he will only play straight.'

He got to his feet as the door opened, and Lady Richmond entered. Blake noticed that she was accompanied by someone, but not until he had greeted her and had drawn up a chair for her did he pay particular attention to the other individual. As he turned towards him, Lady Richmond said:

'This is Captain Pearson, Mr Blake. I have brought him along with me as he has something to tell you. He has already told his story to me, but I want you to listen to what he has to say, and then we can talk of it.'

Blake acknowledged the introduction and pushed forward another chair. Then he seated himself at his desk and looked inquiringly at Lady Richmond. She knew Blake well enough to interpret that look.

'Captain Pearson comes from the West Indies, Mr Blake,' she said. 'He arrived at Ipswich yesterday, and brought with him a letter from my husband. I have brought that letter with me, but before giving it to you, I want him to tell you just what he has told me. Will you do so, Captain Pearson?'

The lanky, clean-shaven man in ill-fitting blue, who had the stamp of the seafaring man all over him, shifted uneasily in his chair.

'I saw you once in Panama,' he blurted out, and with that grew dumb.

Blake eyed him carefully, and then was suddenly illumined.

'You are the Captain Pearson who used to run a trading schooner among the West Indies, aren't you?' he asked.

'Yes. The Helen B. Warr was my craft.'

'Quite so. I recall the schooner perfectly. You were in Colon while I was there. Wasn't there some difficulty with the authorities over some negro labour you had brought down to work off the canal?'

'That's right. I saw you in Major Goethal's office.'

'Yes, I remember,' said Blake, throwing back his mind to picture the incident. 'Well, Captain Pearson,' he went on, 'Lady Richmond says you brought a letter to England from Sir Herbert Richmond. She also says you have a tale to tell. What is it?'

The man shifted uneasily. It was plain that he was quite out of his element, and restrained by the presence of Lady Richmond. It was probably the first time in his life he had ever been on anything approaching speaking terms with a woman of her class, and he was baffled. Blake could see this, and knowing that the man must have something of value to say before he would come the whole way to England to say it, he decided that he had better talk with him when he was unhampered by the lady's presence.

'Perhaps you will excuse us,' he said, turning to Lady Richmond. 'If Captain Pearson will come along to the laboratory with me, I can hear his story there. After, we can discuss the letter of which you spoke.'

Lady Richmond could read in Blake's eyes what he meant, so she smiled her assent, and Blake carried the captain off with him. Once in the laboratory, where he found Tinker experimenting with some noisome 'stinks', and whom he promptly ejected, he opened a box of strong cigars.

'Now then, Captain Pearson, you have something to say,' he remarked when the other had his weed alight. 'You can speak here without fear of interference. What is it?'

'It is about Huxton Rymer,' answered the captain bluntly. 'I was knocking about the Caribbean when you were last there. I said in front of her ladyship that I had seen you in Colon, but I saw you in Kingston as well after you had smashed up that Haiti business that Marie Galante was running.'

At the mention of Marie Galante's name, Blake pricked up his ears, but said nothing. He wanted to know just what this stray traveller had in his mind before he committed himself.

'Yes, Marie Galante,' went on Pearson. 'And I'll tell you right here and now that it was just after that affair that I sold my schooner and took over command of hers. I have been with her for more than three years now, and I was satisfied until this man

Rymer came back on the job. I've got to ask you some questions as I go along, or I won't know if you know what I'm talking about.'

'All right; let me have the story your own way.'

'You are acting for Lady Richmond, aren't you?'

'Yes, of course.'

'And from what Sir Herbert Richmond told me, as well as her ladyship, I take it that it was through you this man Rymer was put in charge of Sir Herbert?'

'That is quite right.'

'Well, you made an awful mistake there, as I am going to prove to you. Now, Sir Herbert has made something of a confidant of me, and I know quite a lot about the business. I know, for instance, that he was suffering from some strange disease, and that the only man who could really help him was this man Rymer. I had heard him called "doctor", but I never knew he was a real medico. Since then I have found out quite a lot about him, and there is no doubt that he has found out what is the matter with Sir Herbert, and is curing him.'

'So I have understood,' said Blake coldly. 'And if that is so, what cause for complaint is there?'

'This much. He may be curing Sir Herbert of his bodily disease, but he has already swindled him out of every penny he had at his disposal, and he is also carrying on a much bigger swindle against him.'

'Explain yourself, please,' said Blake curtly.

'That's just what I am in England for,' rejoined Pearson. 'Now, then, Mr Blake, you are one of these persons who is supposed to be pretty near infallible. But you have made a big miss of it this time.'

'I shall be happy to listen to your criticism another time!' snapped Blake. 'Come to the point, please!'

'I have been talking to her ladyship, so I know that what Sir Herbert told me is so. It is true, isn't it, that before he left England he settled a certain amount of money on her?'

'I believe so. What of that?'

'And then he placed himself entirely in the hands of this man, Rymer, didn't he? At your advice, Mr Blake?'

'Yes.'

'Well, then, listen, sir. He went out to Kingston with Huxton Rymer. I am not saying that Rymer didn't treat him properly, because he did, and on that score Sir Herbert has no complaint. But almost at once, after their arrival in Kingston, Huxton Rymer got in touch with Marie Galante, and the pair of them cooked up what they thought was going to be one of the nicest and safest swindles in the world.

'The first thing Rymer did was to get a full power of attorney from Sir Herbert, so that he could handle all his affairs for him. Sir Herbert gave this without question. Now, in this treatment that Rymer was giving him—I don't know any of the technical details, only what Sir Herbert has told me—it seems that there are certain herbs and spices necessary, and they are not easy to find.

'Well, sir, what did Rymer and Marie Galante do but find a small key—coral island—where these things grew. It's only about forty miles off Jamaica, and they bought it for a song—about two thousand pounds for the freehold. Then Rymer went to Sir Herbert, and told him he had found a place where they could live for a year, and where he could procure the things he needed to prepare the medicine for the treatment.

'He also said that it was the only place of its kind in all the West Indies, and that they could not secure the drugs and herbs they needed unless they bought the place. To this Sir Herbert naturally agreed, and after a bluff at negotiations, Rymer came to say that the island was supposed to contain rich deposits of guano, and that the owner would only sell for a very high figure.

'Well, Sir Herbert told Rymer to do his best, and the upshot was that Rymer paid to a dummy—which was himself and Marie Galante—the sum of sixty thousand pounds for the island which he didn't think was worth more than two thousand. Then they moved across there—Marie Galante going as nurse—and settled down.

'A bungalow was built, and everything made shipshape, and until I got in touch with Sir Herbert, he thought that everything was on the level. There wasn't any guano on the island, of course. Any fool might have known that you don't get guano in commercial quantities in the West Indies.

'But I was still in Marie Galante's service, and I soon saw that where Rymer and that she-devil thought they had bought a worthless island, and had sold it at a profit, they discovered that they had stumbled on something worth more than any guano island, or any gold-mine, and the joke on them was that the title-deeds were in Sir

Herbert's name. Since that transaction the three months' general power of attorney which he had given Rymer had lapsed, and he had not renewed it.

'Since then Rymer and Marie Galante have started on a new tack. He is still treating Sir Herbert, but he has stripped him of every penny he has, and until he robs that island of all its wealth as well, Sir Herbert is practically a prisoner. As for myself, I have been running Marie Galante's schooner back and forth to Kingston with the cargo from the island, but when I had a chance to have a talk with Sir Herbert I did so, and the upshot is that he gave me a letter to bring to his wife, and told me to tell her all I knew. He hasn't had a letter from her for weeks, and she says she has only received the shortest of letters from him, which has been worrying her. But I know why.'

'You seem to know a lot, Captain Pearson,' said Blake drily, 'and it is not very difficult for me to make a guess why you are so eager to bring confusion upon Marie Galante and Huxton Rymer. But we shall deal with that presently. Firstly, however, tell me just what is this mysterious source of wealth which has been discovered on the key which was bought on Sir Herbert's behalf?'

'Tortoiseshell,' answered the other hoarsely—'tortoiseshell—the real amber-coloured shell. It is the biggest haunt of sea tortoise ever heard of, and that must be so, for Rymer said it. And tortoise-shell in the quantities they have discovered it is a bigger proposition that any gold-mine.'

And Sexton Blake nodded in assent. He knew that what Pearson said was a fact, which made it easy to understand some of the other things in the case.

* * *

Sexton Blake had already hinted that he had a shrewd suspicion why Pearson was so vindictive against Marie Galante and Rymer, and why he had gone to so much trouble to act as agent for Sir Herbert Richmond, who, if Pearson were to be believed, was practically cut off and a prisoner in the hands of Rymer and the woman.

Blake had seen Marie Galante on more than one occasion. He knew exactly what effect such a woman would have on men of Pearson's stamp, and he could visualise the inevitable upheaval when a man such as Rymer appeared on the scene and coolly appropriated the girl.

Blake had also seen something of Rymer's former relations with Marie Galante, and it wasn't very difficult for him to guess what the effect of his reappearance would be. But he wanted first of all to get all out of Pearson that there was to get. He didn't want the yarn of a jealous and disgruntled man; he wanted stone-cold fact if he were to be of any assistance to Lady Richmond and Sir Herbert. Also, if Huxton Rymer had played him false after the chance he had given him, then Blake wanted something solid to go on.

For these reasons he kept Pearson in the laboratory for a considerable time until he had pumped him dry of all he could tell him about the island which Rymer had bought.

Like a good many persons, Blake knew something of tortoiseshell in an academic way, and he knew that it was one of the most expensive items which go to the making of decorative articles. He also knew that at present it was in high favour on 'milady's' toilet table, which in itself was sufficient to bring the finer kinds up to a very high price commercially.

Therefore he could quite understand how it was that, if such a discovery had been made in connection with the island, the sight of so much potential wealth would be of tremendous temptation to Rymer. And while he could not help but feel a certain sort of contempt for Pearson, he had to confess that the man had his facts all right. And then there was the letter which he had smuggled out of the island to bring to Lady Richmond. After probing in first one direction and then the other, Blake suddenly said:

'Now, look here, Pearson, you have not done this out of simple regard for Sir Herbert Richmond. You have said enough to tell me that your primary motive is to have revenge on Marie Galante and Huxton Rymer. That means only one thing. So it will help matters along if you will tell me just how matters stand.'

Pearson, who had already had a sample of Blake's methods of getting at the truth, and who had, in a last resort, staked everything on the result of his trip to England, saw that it would serve no purpose to hedge. So, after some hesitation, he 'came across' with his version of what had happened that night in the cabin of the old galleon on the beach at Spanish Town. Blake heard him to the end without comment. He could sort the wheat from the chaff easily enough, and by the time Pearson had finished his tale Blake could visualise pretty well just what had taken place after Rymer arrived on the scene. When Pearson's voice died away he nodded his head slowly and said:

'The old galleon at Spanish Town. I know the old hulk you mean. I have been there, and have been in the inner cabin as well. So that is where it started! And that is the reason of your keen desire to be of service to Sir Herbert Richmond! Well, Pearson, your reasons are not of particular interest. In your way, you have motive enough, and if you keep on the level with us I can promise you that you shall have your chance of revenge. That is a matter of some four months ago. Since then you have still been in Marie Galante's service?'

'Until a month ago,' answered Pearson sullenly.

Blake could not restrain a slight curl of the lip. To be scorned by the woman, to take a beating from the man who had supplanted him, or, rather, to have been of absolutely no account while the other man was about, and then to remain in the service of the woman, was an exhibition of craven surrender such as Blake could not comprehend. But he realised that, after all, it takes all sorts of people to make up this old world of ours.

'What impelled you to clear out?' he asked, after a pause.

'The tortoiseshell business. I heard Rymer and the woman talking about things one night, and I knew they were swindling the old man. I waited my chance, and had a talk with him. He is a lot better now, and is impatient of the idle life he is leading. It was he who discovered the tortoises and saw the possibilities of the thing. Until I talked with him he thought that no shipments had actually gone through. He did not suspect that Rymer had been swindling him right along. When I told him several shipments had been made from Kingston to the English market, and that several remittances must have been received, he began to see the truth.

'It was another week before I saw him, but in that time he had tested the situation, and he asked me if I would get a letter out from the island for him. I agreed, and then, when we talked things over, he asked me if I would go through to England, give his letter to his wife, and wait until she laid plans. That's all.'

'Very well, Pearson. Where are you staying?'

'At the G—— Hotel, just off the Strand.'

'I shall communicate with you there. I shall go into matters this morning with Lady Richmond, and we shall decide on something. As I have said before, if we do take steps in the matter, or whatever steps we may take, you will not be forgotten. By the way, I take it that Rymer and Marie Galante must suspect you by now?'

'Yes. I wrote a letter to her from Kingston, telling her that I was going to get my own back.'

'You will excuse me, but that was about the worst thing you could have done,' said Blake sharply. 'You may have complicated matters of real importance through your childish desire to taunt her. Who has taken over command of the schooner?'

'The mulatto mate who was serving under me.'

'He is loyal to her, of course?'

'Yes. I sounded him, but there was nothing doing.'

'I'm willing to believe that,' said Blake dryly. 'But one thing is quite certain—if you wrote that letter from Kingston, then Huxton Rymer has had no difficulty in picking up your trail, and by this time he probably knows quite well that you have come to England on behalf of Sir Herbert. However, we shall have to deal with that complication later. And now, if you will return to your hotel, I shall, as I have said, go into matters with Lady Richmond and come to some decision.'

He let Pearson out of the house without taking him through the consulting-room, and when he returned to Lady Richmond he said little of the conversation he had had with the disgruntled captain. Almost at once he asked her if he might read the letter which Sir Herbert had sent through, and she readily produced it. Blake found that it consisted of several closely-written sheets of thin paper, and he read every word with the greatest care. It is not necessary to reproduce the letter in full, for some of it was purely private to Lady Richmond, but when he had finished it Blake was in possession of the following facts:

He knew, to begin with, that Sir Herbert had benefited tremendously from the vaccine and auxiliary treatment which Rymer was giving him. He knew, too, that Sir Herbert was now aware that he had been swindled on the purchase of the island to the tune of nearly sixty thousand pounds, and that in other ways Rymer and Marie Galante had stripped him of practically every penny he had been worth, exclusive of the money he had settled on Lady Richmond before leaving England.

From his letter one would not gather that he was particularly incensed over that. He was, above all, too full of gratitude to Huxton Rymer for what he had done to feel any deep anger. He was more sorrowful than anything else, but that the man's old spirit had returned was nevertheless plain. But it was where the old business instinct showed itself again active that Blake found his chief interest.

He gathered that Sir Herbert, finding himself more and more bored as his health improved, had cast about for some means to interest himself, and, quite by accident, through the medium of a negro fisherman had discovered that the island was a wonderful breeding-place of the rarest type of tortoise. The commercial possibilites of the thing had at once suggested themselves to him, and he had lost no time in organising the business. At that time, of course, he had had no suspicions of Rymer, and had talked freely with him about his discovery.

He had explained just what a wonderful discovery it was, and it was easy for Blake to see how Rymer and Marie Galante had promptly determined to turn the thing to their own advantage. It was not until the disgruntled Pearson had opened his eyes that Sir Herbert had realised the truth, and, while he expressed no anger against the pair, he showed in his letter that he was beginning to feel uneasy about his own personal fate.

To make matters worse, until he was definitely cured he was completely dependent on Rymer for the treatment, and for this reason he insisted most strongly that whatever was done must be done with the utmost regard for consequences, and that only after the most careful deliberation should any steps be taken.

That was a difficult proposition Blake had to face, and, apart from the fact that he knew he would do everything in his power to help the woman who leaned on him with such trust, he was filled with a deep anger against Huxton Rymer, and, through this, had an account of his own to settle.

It is not surprising, therefore, that within forty-eight hours of his conversation with Lady Richmond, he and Tinker, accompanied by Captain Pearson, were on their way to Kingston, Jamaica.

*   *   *

Blake would have been far better pleased had he had a man of different calibre to deal with than Captain Pearson.

To use Tinker's words, Pearson was a 'poor fish', and none knew it better than Blake. But the trader-captain was the one link connecting them with Sir Herbert, and until direct contact should be established Blake had no choice but to make use of him.

On the voyage out from Liverpool they had little association. To begin with, Blake and Tinker were at the captain's table, while Pearson was at another table at the far end of the saloon. On deck they exchanged a few words, but it was not until they were drawing near Jamaica—in fact, the evening of the day they first sighted Watling's Island (the little ragged spot which it is said was the first bit of the New World which Columbus saw)—that Blake reverted to the matter in which they were jointly interested.

Not that it had been out of his mind. On the contrary, he had thought of little else the whole of the voyage, and the more he considered the pros and cons, the more enraged he became at the foolish thing Pearson had done in writing a letter to Marie Galante after he had bolted from her service. He knew that Rymer would not take long to find out that Pearson had been talking with Sir Herbert, and the criminal adventurer was quite shrewd enough to anticipate what Pearson was up to. More than that, the whole of the West Indies was Marie Galante's territory, and if their arrival was looked for, then Blake knew the news would be on the wing within an hour of their setting foot in Jamaica.

He had considered the advisability of making the journey in disguise, and would have done so if it had not been that he knew this would be useless after the mistake Pearson had made. That handicapped him in every direction, for he knew it was an impossibility to hope that Pearson could return to the islands either in an ordinary way or in disguise without his return being known.

All he could do was to be on guard every moment himself, and to take care that Tinker did not under-estimate the danger they were running. After they reached Kingston—well, they must see what they could see. If Pearson proved of as little assistance there as he had been—or, rather, as big a handicap—they would have to shed him and work on their own. They had the location of the island where Sir Herbert was held prisoner, and that was about all they did have.

This was the state of things when they finally landed in Kingston and drove through to the Myrtle Bank Hotel. Pearson had gone to a smaller hotel at the other end of Harbour Street, and if he carried out Blake's instructions he would be kept busy for the next few hours, for Blake had charged him to lose no time in finding a schooner which they could charter. Of course, one thing that had to be observed above all was secrecy. Sir Herbert Richmond was a well-known man, and while it would have been possible to call upon the Governor of Jamaica for help, it was impossible to do this except as a last extremity, for the reason that, out of regard to his wife and his own name, it was inadvisable that the truth should leak out.

Nevertheless, Blake did call at Government House soon after landing, and there he had a guarded conversation with the governor that was sufficient to let him know that assistance would be forthcoming if he sought it. Sexton Blake's name and prestige were sufficient to guarantee that.

It was late afternoon when they landed, and from the moment they set foot in the Myrtle Bank both Blake and Tinker were on the qui vive. They knew that every single negro in the island was a possible suspect, for they knew the secret power wielded by Marie Galante. But they counted on some hours' grace at least, for it should take that length of time for the news to get to her that they had landed. It had been arranged that in some way they were to communicate with Pearson during the evening to find out what progress he had made, and, more to kill two birds with one stone, Blake had named the old galleon at Spanish Town to find the man he wished to see about a schooner.

They dined early, and immediately after dinner Tinker went off down the road to engage a car at the garage near the Colonial Rank. He came back in ten minutes, and to report that everything was all right, and about half an hour after that they set off together. It may have been coincidence, or it may not, but they were given the same car and driver used by Huxton Rymer some months before, although neither knew that. They did the journey through to Spanish Town in good enough time, and, like Rymer, they left the car in the plaza while they set off on foot to find the old hulk.

Now, it had been more than two years since they had been in that particular quarter, and on the last occasion their visit had been marked by a pretty strenuous passage. They went ahead with as much confidence as had Rymer on his visit, and, as on that occasion, there was a full moon sailing high in a cloudless sky.

Just beyond the whitewashed buildings between which they were walking they could hear the lazy wash of the surf, and it came the more distinctly to them as there was a light breeze inshore and their feet made practically no sound in the soft sand.

The lanes as usual appeared deserted, which was not strange in a Spanish type of town such as that old place, but now and then they caught the sound of low voices through one of the little barred windows high up above their heads.

And, as they reached the head of the lane leading to the old galleon, they heard, as Rymer had heard, the sudden wail of a violin playing an old buccaneering ditty. They had heard it before—and they knew the warning it conveyed.

But they kept doggedly on, only each dropped a hand to the side-pocket of his pongee coat to make sure that his weapon was handy for business, if necessary. No one molested them as they continued down the sandy lane, one half of which was moon-washed and the other deep in shadow. Yet not for a moment did that weird ditty cease.

Blake was just a few inches in advance of the lad, and it was his foot that first touched the old oak stanchion that made the threshold of the hulk. As he paused and gazed inside he saw that there was not the sign of a light. On the last occasion an old oil lamp had swung from a beam overhead, and by the bit of moonlight that filtered in he thought he could see a vague shape on the level of his head that might be the lamp. There was a smell in the air, too, of burnt oil, and as he sniffed it Blake turned to Tinker and whispered:

'Steady, my lad. I don't like the look of things. The lamp here has been alight up to a few minutes ago.'

Tinker whispered that he understood, and with infinite caution Blake advanced one foot over the sill. Then he brought the other forward, and Tinker followed suit. Another cautious advance took Blake inside, and, like a shadow, Tinker was beside him. Then they stood again listening. Slowly, ever so slowly, Blake turned his head first to the right, then to the left. But it was Tinker who caught sight of something that made him touch Blake's sleeve.

Blake bent his head, and Tinker breathed in his ear:

'Just ahead there, guv'nor, off to the left, isn't that a man crouching on the floor?'

Blake's eyes sought the direction Tinker indicated, and as he saw the blur to which the lad referred his gun hand came up swiftly.

'You there,' he whispered, 'get up, or I'll shoot!'

No answer. Again he repeated the threat, and when still there came no reply he took a step forward. He paused again, and whispered to the lad:

'Must be a bench or something. Let us investigate.'

They crept forward until they could almost reach out and touch the object which was now just beneath them. Blake bent over, his left hand outstretched and his right holding the revolver ready for instant action. His fingers went out and down until at last they encountered something, and he felt the contact. Still the object was motionless. Suddenly the truth flashed on Blake.

He muttered something to Tinker, and thrusting his weapon in his pocket, took hold of the object with both hands.

He began dragging it towards the door while Tinker kept pace, his automatic lying flat against his hip. At the door Blake pulled the burden so that a slanting moonbeam would fall on it, and as Tinker came beside him he gave a sharp gasp at what he saw.

And well he might!

It was the lifeless body of Captain Pearson, a knife buried to the hilt in his throat.

*   *   *

The next thing that Tinker was conscious of was the sudden grip of Blake's hand. Next instant he was dragged back into the cabin.

At the same moment something flashed in through the doorway and dropped with a clatter to the floor at the back.

Ten seconds before the lane outside had been as empty as a bottomless bag, now it was seething with a mass of black humanity which surged this way and that, almost filling the narrow space from side to side and extending along until it seemed to reach the very top where they had come in.

And, what made it all the more sinister, was that not a single word or cry was being uttered. In that weird, silent moonlight the invaders on which Blake and Tinker gazed looked like so many black marionettes prancing about. It was an exhibition of the old ju-ju that has followed the negro from the hidden jungles of Central Africa, and the truth came to Tinker as he heard Blake's tense whisper in the darkness.

'A trap!' he shot out. 'It means life and death to us, my lad! This is a full moon, a night for voodoo rites! That mob out there is drunk with the blood-lust of the rites. They have been deliberately turned on to us, and we shall have to fight our way out. Get your spare clips ready, and make every shot count. Here they come pressing along. They will be at the door in a couple of seconds. I'll give them a warning first; then we shall have to shoot our way through. This is the work of that devil Marie Galante!'

Blake jumped for the door and stood so that his tall figure could be plainly seen in the opening. Then he lifted his left hand, and at that the front rank of the mob seemed to hesitate.

'Back!' called Blake, in a resonant voice, 'Back, you dogs, or we will fill you full of lead!' Then he raised his voice still higher. 'Marie Galante!' he called into the white night. 'Marie Galante!' he repeated. 'You are there somewhere, I know. Stop this devil's work now while there is time, or take the consequences. Huxton Rymer will know what I mean.'

He broke off. In the sudden silence that followed a clear liquid laugh rang out. It seemed close at hand and yet far away. It seemed to fill the whole lane with its vibrant tone. It was the laugh of a Thing—not man or woman. It was the laugh of a devil, of a blood-pulsing creature of the evil jungle—and as he heard it Blake knew that their doom was upon them.

He called one more warning as that black mass, still silent, came on. Then he deliberately lifted his weapon and fired. The crash echoed and re-echoed up and down the lane, and as the sound died away the laugh of the unseen again rang out. This time it held a different timbre which seemed to alter the demeanour of the mob like magic.

From somewhere in the dense mass a shrill cry sounded, and this was immediately taken up, accompanied by a wild dancing movement that spread from one end of the crowd to the other. The frenzy was upon the crowd. Both Blake and Tinker knew that only a miracle could save them.

Blake shot once more, the heavy bullet bringing down a second victim. Then, as the front of the mob pressed towards him, he shot out his hand and felt desperately for a door. There was nothing, or, if there had been, it had been removed.

By then the confusion in the mob was terrible, and from every side knives began to come hurtling in through the open doorway. Blake and Tinker, one on each side of the jamb, shot coolly and carefully. They could not afford to waste a shot: that mob must be held back. Once the leaders gained the threshold it would be all up with them. A short, sharp fight inside, and then they must go down. Once they did it would be the end.

Black after black fell under the steady hail of lead, but still those behind pressed on, still screaming and dancing, and yet all the time sending in an apparently inexhaustible shower of well-aimed knives.

Blake knew the type of attack which Marie Galante had organised. He knew that the whole crowd of blacks had been through the awful rites of voodooism that evening, and now were mere hypnotised automata under the terrible power she wielded. If he had but remembered that this night was a night of voodoo rites, nothing would have brought him into that place of deadly peril. Nor would he have allowed Pearson to venture near Spanish Town.

But he had not thought of that, and now, as he slipped out an empty clip and inserted a fresh one, he made up his mind that the length of time they would live could be measured by the number of cartridges still remaining.

Tinker knew this as well as Blake, but the lad's courage was still high, and he was shooting like a veteran. He had held the mob back while Blake put in a fresh clip, and now Blake did the same for him. Just as Tinker finished they could hear the voice of Marie Galante, somewhere outside, haranguing the blacks in some jungle lingo which they did not understand.

But it had immediate effect, for now the mob surged forward as one man, and they knew that the last rush was upon them.

It was then, too, that a crash sounded behind them, and once more the voice of Marie Galante rose, it seemed all about them. Blake had just time to think that she must be underneath the place, when he heard Tinker give a cry, and he rushed back into the darkness from which it had come.

Tinker had spun round at the first sound of the crash, and had collided with two bulky figures which were coming upon them from the inner cabin. He could not see, but he knew that they must have come through the secret panel, and, despite the difficulty, he fired close to the body that was nearest. There was a grunt like that of some wild beast, and the body slumped to the floor. It was then he called out to his master, and as Blake dashed to his rescue Tinker shot again. His second bullet found its mark.

'They came from the inner cabin,' he panted, as Blake reached him. 'Can we make it, guv'nor?'

Before Blake had time to reply another rush was upon them, and in the same moment the little bit of light which had filtered into the cabin was blotted out. Blake had just time to see the front of the mob coming through the doorway, when suddenly the floor beneath them seemed to heave and rock as if the old galleon were again at sea.

Blake jumped back, his weapon ready, but not daring to shoot for fear of hitting Tinker. Then again a cry came in the lad's voice, and Blake felt a cold chill go down his spine as it died suddenly away, then rose in a muffled cry that was shot off as if powerful fingers had gripped his throat.

Something had happened to the lad while he had been standing almost beside him. What it was Blake could not guess. All he knew was that the lad had disappeared from the scene, and that the cabin was suddenly mephitic with the heavy stench of blacks.

He went clean berserk. He broke into a fury such as rarely seized him.

Somehow—Blake did not know how—he found himself near the door.

His eyes caught a glimpse of the mocking moonlight outside, and the sight drove him to a fresh access of fury. With him was the never-dying dominance of the white, but that alone was but a small portion of what carried him through that mob just then.

He was through, that was all, and suddenly he found himself outside the cabin—outside, cursing and screaming as wildly as any voodooed black.

His terrible fury drove the creatures away as he whirled about among them like a mad dervish until—he saw something.

He had rounded the corner of the hulk without knowing it, and then, as he came to a pause, his eyes fell on the figure of a bearded white man leaning back against the oaken timbers of the galleon.

Like the shriek of a hyena, his wild laugh cut through the night, and then, with a lightning-like twist of the wrist, he reversed his gun. On the very 'flip' of the action he pulled the trigger, and the man who lounged against the hulk suddenly staggered forward.

Against the pale silk of his coat a red stain began to widen. He clawed at the air and tried to get one hand to his hip. Then he went down, face first, into the sand, and as Blake lurched towards him, a wild, terror-laden scream rose with such vehemence that everything else was subordinated to it.

      ★   ★

Blake saw a flash of white, and before him stood Marie Galante, lithe and supple as a snake in her tightly wound scarf of white silk.

He saw, in her hand, the gleam of a nickelled revolver, and he knew she would kill him if she could. But with that shot which had laid Rymer low Blake's sanity had returned, and in one dive he was flat on the ground beside Rymer, his automatic pressed against the adventurer's temple.

'Drop that!' he snapped, his voice as cool as ever. 'Throw it on the ground, or I'll finish him!'

She glared at him with hate-inflamed eyes, but as he shifted his hand a trifle she allowed the pistol to fall at her feet.

'Now, then, listen to me, Marie Galante!' went on Blake, his voice suddenly dry from the reaction. 'This night's devil's work is going to finish now! Drive off that filthy crew of yours, and I'll talk! And make haste, for it doesn't need me to tell you that Huxton Rymer is near death!'

Indeed, the woman could not but see the great stain that was growing wider and darker every second, and all at once her face went white. Without a word she turned and ran to the corner of the hulk. She shouted some words that were unintelligible to Blake, and as if by magic the mob of blacks faded away.

All that was left were the bodies of those who had gone down under the fire which Blake and Tinker had poured into them.

Then Marie Galante returned, and stood looking down at Rymer. Blake took one glance at her, then he spoke harshly.

'If you want to save this man's life you will have to make haste,

Marie Galante!' he said. 'No subterfuge will serve you this night! Your devil's work has failed! Listen carefully, Marie Galante! *I know your secret!* No matter what you may wish tonight, your will is my servant. And again I say that every moment is taking the life-blood from the heart of the man you love! Will you obey me?'

She nodded dumbly, her eyes on Rymer.

'Then heed!' went on Blake inexorably. 'First bring back the lad who was trapped in that den. If he is not brought back unharmed, then Heaven help you!'

She turned and sped round to the front of the bulk. Blake sat waiting, the muzzle of his pistol still pressing against Rymer's temple, though, to tell the truth, he thought even then that Huxton Rymer was at last beyond any human aid. In a few moments Marie Galante reappeared, and behind her came two giant blacks, naked to the waist, supporting Tinker between them. He was dazed, but conscious, and as he slumped to the ground beside Blake, he muttered:

'Fell through a trap in the floor—be all right presently.'

And, to prove the truth of his words, he promptly fainted. But Blake's mind was relieved. He knew that Tinker was safe, and, putting his free hand on the lad's shoulder, he looked up at Marie Galante.

'How did you come here from the island?' he asked curtly.

'By motor boat,' she answered.

'Is it near at hand?'

'Yes; just there.'

And she swept her hand in the direction of the water.

'Then listen to me. You will return to the island at once. You will bring back here unharmed the man you and Rymer have been keeping prisoner there. You will also bring any papers which Rymer may have there. If Rymer dies, so much the worse for you! If he recovers consciousness I shall deal with him. But if you wish even his carcass, then make haste; for until I hear the sound of the motor boat on its way I shall do nothing to stop his life-blood from flowing away! Now begone, and do not question!'

For a moment the jungle woman's eyes blazed like those of a tigress, and she looked as if she would rend him tooth and claw. But then her eyes went again to Rymer, her breast heaved convulsively, and suddenly she was off like an arrow.

Blake sat just as he was until he heard the rapid phut-phut! of a motor boat, and only then he lowered his weapon. His first care was for Tinker, but as soon as the lad came round he set to work on Rymer. An examination showed him that his bullet had plunged into the body just above the heart and had passed out at the side.

It was a bad wound, and might prove fatal. That much he could see. But he did what he could to stanch the flow of blood, and when Tinker had recovered sufficiently they managed to carry Rymer inside the hulk. They laid him on the floor there, and settled down to keep vigil until Marie Galante should return. It was forty miles to the island and back, and Blake knew she could hardly do it under six hours, even if the boat were a particularly fast one. So when Blake had made the lad comfortable, he settled himself to wait.

The moon was low in the sky when once again he heard the sound of the motor boat. He got his weapon ready again, for he intended to be ready for any treachery. But Marie Galante's fear for Rymer had conquered everything else, and a few minutes later she entered the galleon accompanied by a tall, thin white man, dressed in white clothes. Blake greeted him from his squatting position, and in a few words found that Marie Galante had told him nothing, merely saying that he was to come along.

Blake explained what had happened, and then turned his attention back to the woman.

'You know what I want!' he said curtly. 'I want handed to me all the money, or its equivalent, out of which you and Rymer have swindled this gentleman; also, I want the full notes of the treatment which Rymer has been giving to Sir Herbert Richmond! When these demands are complied with you may take what is left of the man, and do what you will—until I reach Kingston. He has not regained consciousness since you left. You will know whether it is advisable to act quickly or not.'

'They are here—everything!' she cried, for the first time showing signs of breaking. 'Take them, and give him to me!'

Blake rose and took the steel case from her. She handed him the key, and then he asked for a light. A negro came at her call and lit the lamp. When he had opened the box Blake carefully checked the contents, and gave the details to Sir Herbert.

'Call that enough, Mr Blake,' said the rescued man. 'After all, the poor devil has done a lot for me, and I do not wish to be hard on

117

him. Let the woman take him if that is what she wants, though I do not think he will live long!'

So Blake nodded his head towards Marie Galante, and at that she sprang like a tigress in the direction of Rymer. But she drew up suddenly and gave a call. Her two gigantic negroes entered, and she spoke to them in the jungle lingo. They picked up Rymer and carried him out, and, walking to the door, Blake kept the little procession in sight until it had disappeared round the corner of the hulk.

Blake had won sooner than he had hoped; but the price had been a heavy one, for poor Pearson still lay in the hulk, where he must remain until Blake could inform the authorities at Kingston.

And Rymer? Blake could not answer that. He had obtained his demands, and he had given the unconscious man to Marie Galante as the price of them.

And if he could be brought back to life, she it would be who would do it—with her own heart's blood, if necessary.

But only the future could answer that.

UNDER SEXTON BLAKE'S ORDERS
John Hunter

By the time he wrote his first Sexton Blake Library *in 1936, John Hunter (1891–1961) had been a full-time writer for well over 20 years. Much admired by that literary maverick J. Maclaren Ross, Hunter was the nearest British equivalent to the high-production pulp-fictioneers who flourished in the States during the 1930s. Like them, he was not at all choosy about his markets, but wrote for just about any genre there was: historical, romance, western, fantasy, SF, thriller, detective, school-story, sport, straight adventure. The only kind of writing he didn't much indulge in was non-fiction. He worked under at least a dozen pseudonyms and probably clocked up around 20 million words in a writing career that lasted for over 40 years. He was somewhat addicted to the 'If only he/she had known' plot-device, but generally his writing was punchy, pacey, dramatic, often violent and always highly readable. He came to the* Sexton Blake Library *via the weekly* Thriller *(both publications shared the same editor), and went on to write nearly 50 Blake novels, only ten of which, unfortunately, featured his own character, the splendidly crooked Captain Dack. Skipper of the tramp-steamer* Mary Ann Trinder, *Dack's partnership with Blake was often an uneasy one, but his ham-hock fists nevertheless floored many a vile and vicious bilge-rat in the name of justice. Here, in a wartime tale of Nazis getting their just deserts, both Dack and Hunter— and Blake—are in fine form.*

Captain James Dack, owner and skipper of the *Mary Ann Trinder*, said to Sam Tench, his first officer: 'Sam, I'm going to smash Angelo Manetti into little bits.' He paused, then added: 'And I'm going to do it now.'

They were on the deck of the old *Mary Ann Trinder*, as she lay alongside the dilapidated wharf owned by Abe Gunson. Abe was away in the country, and Dack and Sam had the run of the wharf. Their ship had recently been damaged in a scrap with a Condor commerce raider, and she was awaiting repairs. Only magnificent seamanship had brought her into the London River.

Now the British Government, via various underwriters, were attending to the matter of the ship's repairs; but that took time. There were forms to be filled in and Departments to consult. Dack filled in the forms, and the Departments concerned at first thought that a child had been playing noughts and crosses all over them. There was a delay.

Delays might be considered rather comfortable for a while; but there were snags about this delay, and the biggest snag of all lay in the fact that Dack's tough crew had nothing to do and plenty of time in which to do it. Hence the entry of Angelo Manetti.

Manetti was born in Naples, but, through an error of official judgment, had managed to get himself naturalised British some time before the country of his birth thought it was on a good thing and sat in on a war beyond its capacity. Manetti, being legally British, remained free to conduct his affairs; and those affairs were mainly concerned with a joint or dump where honest seamen could get bad liquor and gamble at all hours. In effect, Manetti was a pest.

Dack's crew had been visiting his joint or dump, and there had been some trouble. Two of them were now in prison for resisting arrest: and though Dack was always largely willing to admit that his men were no angels, he knew that the root fault of all the happenings was in Manetti and his activities. Dack was quite right in thinking that the police should have shut Manetti up long since; but the police, zealous and efficient though they might be, can't be right all the time, because they're only human; so Manetti still flourished, until . . .

'Come on,' said Dack. 'You and me'll do, Sam.'

It was typical of him. Manetti's place was the roughest of rough houses. Manetti kept half a dozen bouncers, ex-pugilists of the lowest type, to deal with his unruly customers. But Captain Dack decided that he and Sam could, alone, clean up the plague-spot.

The time was evening, and dark. Manetti's place was in a waterside alley, and consisted of the whole lower floor of what was once a small warehouse. It had been sub-divided into rooms, and what went on in those rooms was nobody's business—save Manetti's.

Captain Dack rammed his peaked hat on his head, and, with Sam at his heels, strode in. The big room where all the drinking went on was two-thirds full, a place of bare floorboards and bare tables, with chairs around them. A half-caste lad was playing a piano. He looked ready to drop off the stool with fatigue. Manetti was a hard driver. Three or four husky-looking fellows were lounging about with just too much ostentation. They were the bodyguard. There was a high rumble of talk. No women were on view, which reassured Dack. He didn't like starting anything when women were present, even the sort of women Manetti welcomed to his place.

There was a bar across one end of the room, and behind it a weasel-faced fellow dished out drinks to hurrying and perspiring and brow-beaten waiters. Manetti happened to be behind the bar. He was a big pale man, dressed very well, and he always wore a smile. It was fixed, that smile, and it held no mirth.

Dack walked clean through the pathway between the banks of the tables, and as he did so he heard a babble of shouting. It came from beyond one of the doors leading out of the room. Somebody was quarrelling in the gaming room, though Dack did not then know it was the gaming room.

Manetti's eyes slid sideways. Two of his toughs drifted vaguely through the door. As the door opened the shouting lifted; then dropped as the door closed. Dack had reached the counter.

He asked: 'Are you Manetti?'

Manetti's teeth flashed as his smile broadened. 'Sure,' he said heartily. 'What can I do for you, shipmate?' He called seamen 'shipmate', though he had never been to sea. It sounded well.

Dack went on: 'I'm Cap'n Dack of the *Mary Ann Trinder*. You got two of my men jugged the day before yesterday.'

'I? Captain!' Manetti's voice was charged with reproach. 'There was a little trouble, but I assure—'

Dack broke in. 'This joint wants burning down.'

Manetti's smile vanished. His face was evil. He lifted his left hand. Captain Dack leaned over the bar, grabbed him by his bunched-up waistcoat and shirt and dragged him across it. Then he punched him twice clean in the face, and Manetti wasn't pale any more. He was scarlet. They heard the crack of his breaking nose at the far end of the room.

Manetti screamed. Two of his toughs barged in. Somewhere a whistle went, sounding the alarm. Sam Tench met the first of the toughs. The man had been a third-rate prizefighter, and he could kick as well. He never got a chance. He was drawing his right foot back when something hit him on the outside of the leg on which he was standing as his foot swung. It was a chair, and it hurt. It had been flailed with such force that it broke.

He shrieked, reeling. Sam walked in and punched. The man dropped. His companion hurled himself at Sam like a rugger-player in a flying tackle; and Sam laughed and brought his knee up.

It was fierce, rough fighting of a kind Sam and Dack had encountered all across the globe.

Dack still had hold of Manetti. The man was burbling horribly, terrified. Dack picked up another chair and threw it at the rows of bottles and lights behind the bar. The barman ducked, and stayed ducked. Some of the customers were leaving. Two more of Manetti's toughs came rushing in. Sam went to meet them. Dack went, too. He took Manetti. It was Manetti who stopped a kick intended for Dack. Then the two toughs ceased to take any interest in the matter at all. Manetti was sobbing his heart out, with agony.

And . . . a scream rent the air above the clamour of the fight.

The door of the gaming room opened. A man reeled through, fending himself with his hand. On his chest stood the black haft of a knife. He slid to his knees in the doorway.

Dack roared: 'Sam—hold this!'

He flung Manetti sideways. The man was broken and done for, his jaw sagging hideously. Dack reached the dying man in the doorway as yet another of Manetti's people came at him. The fellow brushed past the knifed man, and Dack stopped him with a right hook.

Silence came down on the whole place. A free-for-all was any-body's fight; but here was murder. Men nearest the door slipped out. Other men edged towards the door. Dack was leaning over the dying man.

He knew him by sight. He was a sea captain who had fallen on evil days entirely through his own fault. Drink had been his curse, and when he put a perfectly good ship on the beach he lost his ticket. He had gone down ever since—to this. His name was Trickett.

His glazed eyes looked into Dack's face. 'Dack . . . Dack . . .' He managed to breathe the name. 'I've got it. No chance. I know.' He struggled for words. 'Just when I was on a good thing, too. A packet of money.'

Dack said: 'Let me help you, Trickett. I'll lift you on that table. Sam's here. He'll fetch a doctor.'

'No. I'm making port, Dack. Listen. There's a ship. The *Hope of Asia*. Well found. Four thousand tons. I was to nav . . . navigate her . . . Big pay. You see Sturgess.' He added an address. 'Tell him I rec . . . recommend . . . you . . .' Trickett's face twisted into a ghastly grin. 'Kinda making a will, eh? Me, that never had anything. Leaving the job to you, Dack. Because . . . you tried . . . to help me.'

His head fell back.

It was just then that the police arrived. They rounded up everybody. They included Manetti. Curiously enough, nobody named the man who had killed Captain Trickett; save two people. That Trickett had been knifed over a gambling dispute was plain to anybody who knew the inside of the matter; but those who had been in the gaming room seemed to have been conveniently blind—for safety's sake.

Therefore, when Captain Dack, supported by Sam Tench, blandly stated that he and Sam, as innocent sailoring men, had walked into the joint without knowing its true nature, and had seen Manetti attack Trickett, themselves assaulting Manetti, but too late to save the captain, they were believed. For not a living soul denied it; all the said living souls being concentrated on keeping out of it.

Manetti was therefore doomed to meet his just deserts for something he had never done; but as the police strongly suspected him of at least two killings, without having any proof, nobody worried over-much; except, of course, Manetti; and he only worried until he took a short walk one morning at eight o'clock, a walk which finished the black career of as evil a creature as might be found anywhere.

There was one thing Captain Dack did not mention to the police, however; and that was what Captain Trickett had said to him.

As he pointed out to Sam, Trickett was getting a ship, and Trickett did not hold a master's ticket any longer. Trickett, too, had said he was getting big money.

Well . . . big money was always big money. Captain Dack went to see the man, Sturgess, whom Captain Trickett had named.

It was one of Captain Dack's Great Mistakes.

He would never have gone into the affair if it came, like his other jobs, through the agency of Gunson; for Gunson always knew a good deal about the matters he handled, and even Gunson would not have touched it. But Dack knew nothing. A dying man had put him on to it, telling him there was money in it; and Dack had nothing at all to do with his time.

*　　*　　*

Sexton Blake tossed the newspaper across to Tinker. They had just finished breakfast in their Baker Street rooms.

'Dack's on the side of Law and Order,' said Blake. 'So Law and Order have got to look out for themselves. He's given evidence that'll hang Angelo Manetti. Remember him? We ran up against him about six months ago.'

Tinker scanned the account in the newspaper and grinned.

'I like the idea of Dack and Sam Tench posing as little innocents,' he observed. 'I wish I'd been in court when counsel referred to Dack as the man whose ship fought a Condor and brought it down after sustaining heavy damage. I'll bet his chest shot out six inches.' Tinker laid the paper aside. 'How's the case going?' he added. 'Our case, I mean.'

Blake shrugged his shoulders. 'I can't get past that man Sturgess,' he admitted. 'When the Foreign Office called me in they gave me as much dope about him as they'd got. And I'm unable to learn anything more. Scotland Yard can't either. I'm no further than I was when I started.'

'Is it much ado about nothing?' suggested Tinker.

'Don't go all Shakespearean,' grinned Blake. 'It can't be. The FO told me they had certain sure information that this fellow Sturgess is up to something that's agin this country. They know he's chartered a ship, but what ship, and where she is, they haven't been able to find out. They only know this through a remark made to one of their agents in Lisbon by a man who was subsequently found murdered. They suspect the killing was a bit of mouth-shutting. Beyond these meagre facts they can tell me nothing; and I've discovered nothing. So I want you to keep an eye on Sturgess for me.'

'Surely the police are doing that, aren't they?' said Tinker.

'Yes. But I've got an idea. Sturgess rents an office in a court off Ludgate Hill. The police constantly watch it. I went round there yesterday and had a look-see. The buildings on either side of the office have been smashed by bombs. There's lot of rubble about, removal of wreckage, etc., going on. My view is this. Taking advantage of the wreckage and the cover it affords, Sturgess slips away from his office in some fashion or other, and keeps any appointments connected with this mysterious business, and then slips back. The result is that no suspicious people ever call on him. The police have tailed every visitor he's had, and all have proved to be innocent.'

'What is Sturgess?' asked Tinker.

'He calls himself a shipping agent,' said Blake. 'Though why he should have an office near Ludgate Circus instead of in the Leaden-hall Street district is something I can't guess. You'd better get down there today. Put on rough clothes. Look like a fellow who wants a job on demolition. And keep your eyes skinned and use your imagination.'

'Anything else?' asked Tinker. 'I'll carry you round for threepence.'

He departed half an hour later. His make-up was excellent. Over tousled hair he wore an old cap. A shabby and ill-fitting suit hung loosely on him. His boots were uncleaned and rough. A cigarette dangled from one corner of his mouth, and round his neck was a knotted handkerchief. He slipped out to the street, hurried for a short distance, made sure nobody was following him—a precau-tion he and Blake always took when on such a mission—and jumped on an 18 bus to Ludgate Circus, via the Marylebone Road. Such as he did not ride in taxis. It would be unwise to use one.

Blake went down to his club, first ringing up the Foreign Office to let them know where he could be found. He was feeling at a loss for one of the few times in his life. The man, Morgan Sturgess, went about openly. He lived in a nice London suburb in reasonable comfort. He was undoubtedly connected with shipping, even though in a comparatively small way. Scotland Yard had looked him up. Was it possible the Foreign Office people were wrong? Had M15 made a mistake? Was the agent in Lisbon misinformed? It was a pity the informant had subsequently been murdered in that melting-pot of Europe's refugees; though the fact of the murder seemed to indicate that the informant was a man who had to be silenced.

Blake walked into the bar of the club and ordered a beer. It was a famous club, and its membership was severely restricted to men who had achieved eminence in their own particular walks of life. Riches alone did not make for entry. The result was that influential and knowledgeable men could always be found there, and gossip-writers in the daily press would have given their ears to listen to some of the talk that went on.

A tall, hard-faced bronzed man was just draining one of the famous pewter tankards when Blake walked in, and Blake invited him to refill it. They strolled to a couple of chairs by the fire. Nobody else was in the bar at that time in the morning.

The tall man stretched his legs. Blake knew a good deal about him, knew him well as a friend. They had something in common, for the tall man was connected with the inside of certain Imperial matters which were never publicized and the cost of which never appeared in the estimates. Blake, looking back on the meeting, always afterwards counted this as one of his lucky days.

Blake said: 'Is it right you were on the last Commando raid, Mathers?'

Mathers looked at him from under his eyelids. 'Who told you?'

Blake was a little surprised at the question. Commando raids were no longer secrets—after the event.

He said: 'It was mentioned in my hearing. Sorry if I've put a foot wrong. I'll say nothing about it to anybody else.'

Mathers loaded an old burnt pipe. 'I wonder,' he said, slowly. 'Things get out, don't they? People will talk. Yes, I was on the raid that took place three weeks ago. What did you hear about it?' Again he gave Blake that look from under his eyelids.

Blake was remembering now. 'It was a very proud father who told me,' he said. 'But I don't want to get anybody into trouble by mentioning names. The father of a lad who was in it, of course.'

'Hm.' Mathers stubbed the tobacco down in his pipe. 'Ring him up, or see him, and tell him to keep his mouth shut, if you will, Blake.' Mathers hesitated. 'We were supposed to blow up an oil dump near Le Zoute on the Belgian coast. Perhaps you read the newspapers sometimes.'

'I've learnt to read,' smiled Blake; and Mathers permitted his hard face to crease into a grin. 'But you did blow the oil dump up, didn't you?' added Blake.

'Oh yes. They did that all right. And gun emplacements and heaven knows what else. They're amazing people, these Commandos. Er—know Le Zoute at all?'

'Fairly well. Very swagger. Full of charming and picturesquely coloured seaside villas, and all the rest of it. Why?'

'Nice place to live, if you have to be in Belgium, eh?' said Mathers. 'Especially,' he added, 'if you've got the pick of all those villas.'

'The pick?' said Blake. 'They can't all be empty. Why, only the other night Colonel Britton of the BBC named a quisling who's living in one of them.'

Mathers nodded, and looked round. 'I know I can trust you, Blake. I want your friend to shut his mouth about that raid. And I'm telling you why. Of course, I'm not a member of a Commando. I was there—specially. You see, I've lived in Le Zoute, and I know it backwards; and I talk German like a native. That was why I went. The newspaper accounts mentioned no prisoners, did they?'

'No. But look here, old man—'

'Oh, it's all right. I know you. I want to be sure you'll stop your friend talking. We did bring prisoners back. We brought six. My prisoners. I took them out of one of the finest villas in Le Zoute. I told you they had the pick. They would. They were von Graustein and his staff. We're keeping it dark for certain military reasons I need not go into; but when it breaks it'll be as big a sensation as the Hess job. The raid on Rommel's HQ in Libya before our offensive started had the same thing in mind; but the lads were cruelly unlucky that night.'

Blake sat back. 'Erich von Graustein,' he said slowly. 'He's Hitler's best pal. He was one of the old Munich beer-hall gang.' Blake paused. 'If all that's said of him is true . . .'

'It's true,' said Mathers quietly. 'Von Graustein is the incarnation of everything that's evil in Nazidom. I'm not given to highfalutin talk, but the man is a fiend. It was he who had the fifty Belgian women stripped and shot in the main street of Ghent because a woman, not arrested, and not among the fifty, had tried to kill a German soldier for attacking her daughter. It was he who . . . But why go on? The man's record stinks to high heaven. Well, we've got him, and his precious staff with him. And he knows that at the end of the war he'll be tried . . . by Belgians. The cur went on his knees to me and begged me to let him go. He knew me. I've met him often in the Adlon and the Eden cocktail bars in Berlin before this show started. General von Graustein and five of his staff, his inner clique, all as black as himself. Well— they'll hang, unless I'm mistaken; and, frankly, Blake, I wouldn't mind pulling on the rope that hangs them. Have another beer.'

Blake said: 'Hitler will be sick, won't he? The way things are in Germany. After his Russian adventure, I should imagine he and the army chiefs aren't just one big happy family.'

'I know. That was the real motive for taking Graustein. Not so much to bring him ultimately to justice as to rob Hitler of one of the few men he could rely on to stand by him in an internal crisis. Erich von Graustein is more valuable to Hitler as a friend than as a general. He's one of the men who put Hitler where he is, and who would do anything to keep him there.'

Blake sat back. A queer thought had flashed into his brain. He put it into words.

'Hitler would go to some lengths to get von Graustein back, wouldn't he?' he suggested.

Mathers smiled. 'I should say so. But he's got to find out where he is on this little island first. Graustein isn't in any camp or recognized prison, old man. You did say you'd have another beer, didn't you?'

They were brought, and the conversation changed; but Blake kept thinking about Erich von Graustein. He knew he could not ask Mathers where the man was imprisoned. Mathers had merely told him what would, ultimately, and probably quite shortly, be published in the newspapers; because such matters cannot be kept quiet for long.

Von Graustein's record would have made Caligula shudder. He was the blackest creature of all those perverted and abominable monsters spewed up by Nazidom. And, with Rudolf Hess, he had been Hitler's closest personal friend, one of the two men on whom Hitler could rely to the last inch.

Blake lunched at the club, and went back to Baker Street in the afternoon. Tinker came in. He was excited.

'You were right,' he said. 'Sturgess does slip away. And he does it cleverly. A box van drove up to the back of the building in which he has his office. A few parcels were unloaded, the van being backed right up to the doorway. The driver—a tough sort of fellow—then looked round to make sure nobody was watching. He didn't see me. I was behind a heap of rubble; and other heaps of rubble hid the workmen and casual watchers. Sturgess slipped into the back of the van, the driver shut the doors, and it drove off.'

'What did you do?' asked Blake.

'Some of the workmen came to their jobs on bikes. The bikes were standing near me. I hopped on one and followed the van till I met a taxi. I put the bike against a shop front and had the taxi trail the van. I had to tell the taxi-driver I was police, because he seemed to think I wouldn't be able to pay. I followed Sturgess, who went to a shop near St George's Circus. I reckon he perhaps rents a room over it. Just for convenience and secrecy. I had my cab standing by. I saw whom he met, but, of course, I couldn't get into the shop and listen to any talk. In fact, I came back. The bike was still where I left it. I paid the taxi off and rode the bike back. The working chap was going to knock my head off, but I gave him a quid note for his pains and told him a long sad story. The quid note calmed him down. It's in my expenses, by the way.'

'You'll get it,' said Blake. 'Whom did Sturgess meet?'

'Captain Dack,' said Tinker.

* * *

Tinker continued to watch Sturgess. Now he knew something of the man's methods he was able to carry on the watching with more certainty. This watching was tedious and productive of no further results for some time. Blake, meanwhile, had paid a surreptitious visit to Gunson's wharf, where he had found that the *Mary Ann Trinder* was so badly damaged about the superstructure that it was obviously impossible for her to put to sea.

This made him think. What were Dack and Sturgess up to? It was plain that Dack's own ship could not be used, so that the ship

Sturgess was supposed to have on hand was not the *Mary Ann Trinder*. Patient and persistent observation of Captain Dack revealed that he did not again see Sturgess, and that his movements were quite innocent, as were those of Sam Tench. Casual enquiry told Blake that Abe Gunson was still down in the country. He had apparently gone to visit a relative, and had been taken with influenza while there, with the result that he was in bed. Police enquiries in the district in question proved this to be true. Abe Gunson was obviously not connected with the Sturgess job, and that made Blake uneasy.

He liked Dack, in spite of the big seaman's viewpoint as to what was strictly honest and what was not. He knew that Gunson, though willing to handle all manner of questionable matters, always vetted those matters and would not touch them if they exceeded a certain limit; but whereas Gunson was shrewd as a weasel, Dack was not, and Dack might easily have dropped into something which overstepped the mark.

At last, after five days, Tinker's patient watching of Sturgess was again rewarded. He came back one evening with his report.

'Sturgess has seen another bloke at the shop by St George's Circus,' he announced. 'The same procedure as before. The box van and the secret get-away. I trailed the man who called on him. He runs a club—a man's club. Not one of those all-day drinking places which have sprung up everywhere; but what seems to be a decent little club for working men in a side street. His name is Lassiter, and it's called Lassiter's Club. It's run very well, I discovered, and anybody can't join it. I mean—you can't be taken in by a pal, pay five bob, and you're a member. They've actually turned down applicants.'

Blake reflected. He went to see Inspector Pike at Scotland Yard.

'Lassiter's Club,' said Pike. 'Wait a minute, I'll find out what the local station knows about it.' He telephoned. A few minutes later he got his answer, and he added, to Blake: 'It's given the OK by the divisional station. Well conducted. It's run in a private house. That's the curse of the club law in this country. Anybody can get together enough friends, let them all pay a nominal subscription, and he's got a club on the spot, with a club's drink licence thrown in. It's not fair to the licenced trade.'

'Is it old-fashioned? The club, I mean?' asked Blake.

Pike shook his head. 'No.' He added the exact date on which Lassiter's Club was opened.

A cog jolted over in Blake's memory. He sat up very straight.

The date was two days after the Commando raid which brought back General Erich von Graustein. Was it a coincidence?

He returned to Baker Street, changed his clothes, and, that night, sallied forth. He was ragged and looked dirty. When he was near Lassiter's Club he walked on the kerb and pretended to pick one or two things out of the gutter. He swooped on a fag-end a man in front of him threw away.

Outside Lassiter's Club he hung about, and as men went in he touted them for coppers. He did this with everyone, so that they had to talk to him, even if it were only to offer a curt refusal. He got back to Baker Street about midnight, to find Tinker sitting up, waiting for him.

'Unless I'm a bad guesser,' said Blake, 'practically all the members of Lassiter's Club are foreigners. Naturalized, I imagine, but definitely of foreign birth. Those I spoke to tonight had accents, some hardly discernible, some you could cut with a knife. But . . . there's something else.'

He paused. 'There was a big fellow, and he had had a drink or two. I asked him for a copper for a bed—the usual graft—and he was quite amiable. I then asked him if there were a chance to get a job in the club, handing out the usual honest-working-chap-down-on-his-luck stuff. He was too tight to realise that no able-bodied man need be out of work these days. He was almost maudlin sympathetic. He put his hand on my shoulder and assured me he'd give me a job tomorrow in the club if he could get it for me; but he couldn't. Strict rules. It was a club for sailormen, he said.'

'What?' Tinker stared. 'You mean that this Lassiter chap has got together, under the guise of a club, a bunch of foreign seamen, eh?'

'That's it,' said Blake. 'From what my amiable friend said, there were about thirty members. Well, that's just a nice-sized crew for a freighter. Their difficulty, of course—if they're on a crooked game—would be the master and the engineers. They could pick up foreign scum off wharfsides as deckhands and greasers of a kind; the sort of men who wouldn't be allowed on a decent ship. A man like Sturgess would know where to lay his hands on such riff-raff, being, as he is, on the fringe of the shipping business. I expect his sole connection with shipping has always been on the shady side, and maybe he's met Lassiter in this connection before. But crooks don't easily get masters' and chiefs' tickets. Hence Captain Dack; willing to turn a dishonest penny, provided it's not too dishonest.'

'I wonder if he knows how dishonest this job might be,' said Tinker seriously. 'After all, the fact that the Foreign Office is mixed up in it shows that it's something against the national interests, and not ordinary knavery, and I'm sure Dack wouldn't lend himself to anti-British operations.'

'He's proved that in the past,' agreed Blake. 'I'm going to start watching him. I'm leaving Sturgess to you, and you've got the address of Lassiter's Club, so that you can give it the once-over now and again. And directly we get anything concrete we'll set the Foreign Office moving and sit back.'

'Smothered in glory,' grinned Tinker.

But a number of things were to happen before the sitting-back and the glory accrued.

*   *   *

Watching Captain Dack was easy to a man of Blake's experience; for the large seaman took no precautions against being followed and, confidant, as usual, in his own immunity from all perils, he went widely on his daily round.

Sam Tench was disapproving of the whole matter. To start with, he was not in it.

Captain Dack said to him: 'They only want a master. That's me. Easy job, too.'

'What is it?' asked Sam.

'Secret and confidential,' replied Dack, and Sam Tench grunted derisively.

Yet Dack did not tell him any more, which made Sam wonder; for Dack always confided in him. It was not until afterwards that Sam learnt why Dack had failed to take him into his confidence.

Meanwhile, the old *Mary Ann Trinder* lay alongside Gunson's wharf and waited while the forms were passed from department to department, and surveyors looked her over, and officials wrangled, and a good ship which might have been carrying valuable cargoes was useless. And Abe Gunson, after a bout of influenza which led to congestion of the lungs and near-pneumonia, slowly convalesced at his relative's house in the country, and knew nothing of the whole affair; which was unfortunate for Captain Dack, for Gunson's cunning brain might have seen the snag in it.

Then, one night, the whole thing broke wide open.

Blake, finding how easy it was to trail Dack, had abandoned shabby clothing and was going about dressed as he did normally. It facilitated travel and service wherever he might need it. When on such jobs he always carried forty or fifty pounds in pound notes, against the emergencies of sudden travel, and he was glad he had money with him that night.

Captain Dack went to Waterloo and booked a rail ticket. Blake booked a rail ticket, too. It was easy. The big station was ill-lit under the black-out, and Dack, in his bull-voice, enquired the time of a train to a certain small coast town in the south. Blake was thus able to book through with certainty. He saw Dack get into a compartment in the front of the train, and he got into one in the next coach.

As the train made its way through the black countryside Blake wondered if the ship Sturgess had chartered might be lying in the little port Dack had asked for. He did not know its name. But he could reckon, with fair certainty, that Dack was to navigate it. Dack could navigate anything, from the *Queen Mary* down to a steam-tug.

There was a wind off the sea when Blake followed Dack down the winding road from the station to the little port. As usual, the railway ran about a mile back from the small town.

A ship was lying alongside the quay. Smoke was wisping from the funnel, and Blake, creeping near in the intense blackness, saw her name. *Hope of Asia*. Dack had gone on board her.

The pattern was fitting together. Here was the ship Sturgess had chartered, and here was Captain Dack. How long the ship had lain there, waiting for this night's work, Blake could not guess. Sturgess had been safe in keeping her lying there, so long as nobody knew she was under charter to him. All the Foreign Office had known was that, somewhere, he had secured a ship; but which ship they could not tell.

Blake stood in the shadow of a big old tarred wooden shed and watched. He heard voices. Two men had come up the aft companionway to the deck. The voice of one of them was that of Dack.

The two men moved to the gangplank, and Blake had a fleeting glimpse of the face of the second man, and felt glad he had gone down to Lassiter's Club instead of sending Tinker. For this second man was Lassiter himself. Blake had seen him that night, and now recognised him.

Dack appeared to be dubious about something.

'But where's the blamed crew?' he asked.

'Coming,' Lassiter assured him. 'Any minute now. You can get away directly they're aboard, can't you? The engineer's had steam up for several hours.'

'How do we clear?' asked Dack.

'I've seen to that,' replied Lassiter. 'The harbour-master's given us clearance this afternoon.'

Dack grunted. 'Right. Lemme see. It's about half past nine. I saw a nice little pub on my way down. I can do with a drink. I'll be there if you want me, or back here by just after ten if you haven't sent for me.'

He lumbered off, and Blake remained in the shadow of the shed, while Lassiter returned to the cabin. It occurred to Blake that while there was something mysterious about the absence of the crew, there was also something significant, and in a sinister fashion.

Somehow, Lassiter and Sturgess had managed to get hold of at least one ship's engineer who was as dishonest as Dack, and he, with such staff as he needed, was already on the ship, and had got steam up. Blake hadn't to guess far to realise he must be a 'member' of the club. The rest of the crew, however, might just as easily have been on board. So—where were they, and what were they doing? Why couldn't the ship have sailed at once? Why was Dack's arrival postponed until the last moment? Because that was plain to Blake. It might have been expected that Dack would have arrived in the morning and have seen to the general preparations for the ship's departure.

Blake slipped away and went up the narrow High Street. It was easy to pick out the inn Dack had noticed. It was the most comfortable-looking one in the street.

Blake edged open the door of its bar and peeped in. Captain Dack was standing by the bar counter. A little group of men were playing darts, and were engrossed in their game. The landlord, at that moment, picked up a tray on which were some filled glasses and went towards the bar parlour.

Sexton Blake went straight in and stepped to Dack's side.

'I want a word with you,' he said quietly.

The dart-players were at the end of their game and striving to get the necessary double; so they ignored Dack's exclamation, an exclamation he quickly smothered by emptying his beer-mug. He followed Blake into the dark street, and Blake led him up towards the railway station. It had a tiny waiting-room, where there was a fire. Nobody was in the waiting-room.

'Now,' said Blake, 'what's the game, Dack? And before you ask what I mean, let me tell you I've been watching you. Lassiter's been watched and so has Sturgess.' He paused. 'Do you know who commissioned me to do this? The Foreign Office.'

The statement had its effect. Dack, as usual, looked like a large schoolboy caught out in a prank. He stared, and rubbed his chin with a gigantic hand; then spoke.

'That means something . . .' He sought for a word and added: 'International.'

'Looks like it,' said Blake, gravely. 'And there's a war on, Dack. If a man's not careful he might find himself working against his own country.'

Dack drew a deep breath. He muttered: 'Are they having me on a bit of string? If they are . . .' He again stared at Blake, and asked: 'What do you know about it, Mr Blake?'

'You tell me what you know,' countered Blake. 'I'm asking for your own sake, Dack. This might be a sticky business. And you know you can trust me, when I tell you that.'

Dack nodded and told his story. It was very simple. He told it without reserve, for it must be admitted that he was feeling very anxious about the affair. He started with his visit to Manetti's place, suppressing, of course, the small matter of false evidence which had sent Manetti to a well-merited punishment; and he added: 'I saw this chap Sturgess over a shop near St George's Circus. Now, Mr Blake, I'm being straight with you. Usually, when I've gone into any game that—well, showed a biggish profit, I've known a bit about it, but this time I didn't. You see, the old ship's laid up, there's no money coming. I was sick to death of hanging about doing nothing. And this chap Sturgess, after asking me a few questions, told me to come back another time. Guess he looked my record up meanwhiles. I went back.'

Blake nodded. That must have been when Tinker saw Dack.

Dack proceeded. 'Sturgess said he had a ship. The *Hope of Asia*, same as Trickett told me. She's laying down at the quay here. He wanted this ship navigated to a certain point south of Land's End. A certain spot on the sea, mark you, Mr Blake. Only a navigator could do that. I asked why. He said she was to meet another ship that couldn't come into a British port. He left me to reckon that second ship was an enemy. I said I couldn't do a thing like that. Sturgess then said it was all right. The second ship was on the crook as far the enemy government was concerned. What she was bringing was smuggled goods, mainly liquor. It had to be transferred to a ship that could come into a British port. See? Sturgess said the stuff would be all right, because it was hidden cunningly in what seemed to be cases of canned meat. The stuff would be put into bottles over here. He said there was a hundred quid down for me, and a percentage on sales. Well, Mr Blake, I'm not against the sale of good whisky; so I said I'd do it. But then . . . I got uneasy. I was told to do nothing till I was tipped off where to go. I asked about the crew, but was told that was not my affair.'

Dack stopped. He was plainly relieved at having told his story to a responsible person.

Blake looked him over. 'Dack,' he said, 'you're a fool. I don't know what this job is—but it isn't smuggling—and you should know it. I don't know what ship you're to meet in the Atlantic, but she won't be loaded with stuff illictly brought to this country. You should know that, too. You're due to sail any moment, aren't you?'

'Yes. I've got the run of Gunson's office, you see, and they telephoned me this afternoon to turn up here tonight. I'd heard nothing from them up to then. They kept me in the dark.'

'Right. Then there's only one thing to do. I could get this ship stopped; but I'm afraid that if I did I should merely check a big game instead of completely scotching it. So I want you to take me on board with you. You can do that all right. Hide me up by the bridge somewhere.'

Dack did not argue. He was very contrite. His whole manner indicated that, all along, he had known there must be something outside ordinary trickery about this job, but that he had tried to persuade himself to the contrary.

He took Blake down to the ship and put him in the little chart-house abaft the bridge and on a level with it. He locked the door of the chart-house and put the key in his pocket. As the only navigator aboard, he could easily forbid anybody to enter it.

Blake had only been in there five minutes when he heard booted feet on the deck. A little later he heard Dack's voice issuing orders, strong and steady and easily. The ship began to throb. Blake, lying on a bunk kept in the chart-house for use when dirty weather made necessary the captain's constant attendance by the bridge, felt anxious. He and Dack were alone on the *Hope of Asia,* and though Dack was a host in himself, there must be about thirty potential enemies aboard her—and armed, if Blake was anything near right.

She must have cleared the piers, for she was lifting and rolling, when the chart-house door opened and Dack put his head in.

'The crew's aboard,' he said unnecessarily; then added: 'They brought six blokes with them. They came in lorries. Six passengers. You can come out here. It's a dark night, and I said I'd handle her alone.'

Blake came out with a rush. Six passengers! Was the incredible theory right?

Erich von Graustein and five of his staff!

Blake huddled behind one of the dodgers, his eyes just above the level of its edge, and looked downwards. He saw three men approaching the ladder to the bridge. One he discerned to be Lassiter. The other two walked with a fine stride, one of them being tall and erect. They began to climb the ladder. Blake slipped back into the chart-house, but before he went he hissed to Dack: 'Agree with everything.'

Through the chart-house window he could see them when they reached the bridge. Lassiter was with the taller one of the other two. The third man stood back a little.

Lassiter said: 'Captain Dack, this gentleman wishes to speak to you.'

Dack looked across his shoulder. 'What is it? I allow nobody on my bridge when I'm at sea, bar them I orders here. I'm a ship-master, not a guide to sea scenery. Tell me quick what you want, and get down out of it.'

The tall man stiffened. As his head moved, Blake saw the momentary gleam of a rimless monocle in his right eye-socket. He was dressed in civilian clothes, but that did not disguise the military set of his shoulders. His head was shaven, the back of it flattened.

He said curtly: 'You are talking to a general officer of the Reichswehr. Lassiter has omitted to introduce me. I am General von Graustein.'

'I don't care if you're General Post,' said Dack. 'I don't have anybody on my bridge.' He remembered Blake's hissed warning and allowed himself to be a little more friendly. Spinning the wheel idly under his immense hands, he glanced at the general.

'Look here,' he said. 'I'm doing this job for money, and now I'm doing it I'll see it through. If that's what you came to tell me, you don't have to worry. All I think about is money. Maybe you've thought I was sure to find out I'd been lied to about picking up a smuggled cargo, so you've come to explain and . . . perhaps . . . threaten. It's not necessary. I didn't believe the smuggling yarn from the first. And now. You're a general. I expect you fight battles, or send soldiers in to fight 'em for you. When you're doing it you don't have outsiders looking over your shoulder, do you? Well, I'm navigating this ship, and I don't want outsiders looking over my shoulder. I know where I've got to make for, and I'll make it at the time appointed. I'll give you good night, General Whatever-your-name-is. There's a warm cabin aft.'

Lassiter said quickly: 'Captain, I—'

Erich von Graustein checked him. The general spoke perfect, clipped English.

'All right. This man is a little abrupt, but he is correct. I wished to see him, and I have seen him. I approve of him. He attends to his duty. That is our good German way of doing things. We will go.'

His aide stood to one side as he went down the ladder. Lassiter lingered a moment.

'You're OK, Cap,' he breathed.

'You're telling me,' grinned Dack.

The *Hope of Asia* held on her way, and Blake slipped out and huddled down below the dodgers at Dack's side.

'It's plain what's happened,' he said. 'This gang have pulled off the biggest escape stunt ever. They went in fast lorries to wherever Graustein was imprisoned. Probably some country house. They were armed and there are about thirty of them. They must have rushed the guards, after first cutting telephone wires outside. Then they picked up the prisoners and came down to the coast. A clever job. Dack, can you use the radio?' He knew Dack never shipped a radio operator.

'Yes,' said Dack. 'But I couldn't get near the cabin without raising Cain. I heard Lassiter detail two blokes to guard it—with guns.' He paused. 'Mr Blake,' he added, 'through my folly we're ditched, and that murdering swine's going to get back to his accursed Fatherland. To have more women and kids shot . . .'

Blake was thinking. 'Perhaps not,' he said softly. 'Dack, have you heard of poetic justice?'

'No. Only justice,' said Dack simply. 'Where's the poetry come in?'

'It doesn't,' smiled Blake. (It should be recorded that the whole of this conversation, of course, took place in whispers, with Blake squatting behind the dodger, and Dack apparently looking ahead and attending to steering the ship.)

Blake went on. 'Do you keep your flags and pennants in the chart-house?'

'Sure to be there,' said Dack.

'Right. And this is an English ship. She'll have a Red Ensign, won't she?'

Dack said bitterly: 'Unless they've burnt it and put a Swastika in its place. I wish I'd never heard of—'

'Perhaps you won't when this job's finished,' said Blake. 'Perhaps you'll get a good laugh. What time have you to keep this appointment?'

Dack told him and added: 'We shall make it with three hours to spare. I insisted on a margin in case of dirty weather; but the weather's fine. So I shall run her a bit slow.'

'Don't,' said Blake. 'These people won't know where they are, or what they're doing, once they're out of sight of land. Belt her up, Dack. Get there three hours ahead of schedule, and cruise. Got that? Don't lie to. Cruise.' He paused. 'Run past the spot, and then turn back—heading for England. See? That's the scheme!' Blake sounded excited. 'Overrun the rendezvous, then swing her and head back to it. You'll be coming from the other way. A seaman would know it, but this gang on board here wouldn't.'

'Does that mean anything?' asked Dack. He sounded bewildered.

'It means everything,' said Blake, 'if I'm right in my theories.' He peeped over the dodger and pointed downwards. 'What's that big thing amidships—covered with canvas?'

'A launch,' said Dack. 'Never seen one like it on a freighter of this kind before. They said they had it put aboard special—to help shift cargo. Lying, of course; but there she is. I'm to have it ready and swung outboard just ahead of the meeting time.'

Dack's eyes narrowed.

'I see,' said Blake. 'Nice work. Right. You'll do that, Dack. Have her swung out half an hour ahead, so that you've finished that job with plenty of time in hand; because you and I have another job to do.'

'What is it?' asked Dack.

'This. We've got to get those two men guarding the radio cabin. We want their guns, to start with. Then I want you to send out an SOS giving your exact position. Keep sending it for several minutes. I want it picked up by two different people.'

'Who?' asked Dack.

'The British Navy and the ship we're meeting.'

'The ship we're meeting!' gasped Dack. 'But that'll blow the gaff.'

'No it won't. Not the gaff I've got in mind. It'll confirm the deception we're practising by overrunning the rendezvous and turning the ship back towards England. Do it, Dack, and don't argue, because I'm getting into that outswung launch then. You will have with you the Red Ensign, and right on the appointed time you'll show it. Oh—and before morning and daylight, find and hide a stout steel bar. It might be useful.'

Dack scratched his head.

'This beats me,' he said. 'Where's the poetic justice come in?'

'It comes in if the ship we're destined to meet is the sort of ship I think she is,' smiled Blake; and there it was left.

He crept back to the chart-house.

*　　*　　*

The *Hope of Asia* slogged through a grey sea, white-headed under a stiff breeze. Behind her, tugging and nosing and dipping, the launch towed. It had been put outboard at Dack's orders, and hitched astern. There was a driving drizzle of rain.

The ship had overrun the rendezvous with a good three hours in hand, had turned, and was heading back. The turning had been done very cleverly by Dack, by degrees at a time, and the people aboard did not realize it. No sun showed in the overcast sky to indicate to the deckhands which way the ship headed. Nobody could see the compass but Captain Dack. As for the passengers, they were as ignorant of sea matters as most passengers.

On Blake's advice, Dack had invited Lassiter to the bridge in daylight and had made a few enquiries, such enquiries sounding quite natural under the circumstances, and, therefore, being answered frankly by Lassiter.

The engine-room staff were in it as much as the rest of them. There was only one 'mug' on board, as Dack afterwards bitterly told Blake: the said mug being Captain Dack. It was what Blake wanted to know. That no other innocent person, or deluded fool, was on the ship.

Dack had routed in the chart house and found a Red Ensign. It lay at his feet on the bridge, ready for breaking, and with it was a long, thick steel crowbar.

And now it was zero hour.

Blake whispered: 'Come on, Dack. Tie your wheel. Over the top and best of luck.'

A little earlier Dack had told the one or two deck-hands on deck that they could get below forrard and that the cook should serve them with something hot from the galley. It was an order such slackers and undisciplined riff-raff were only too eager to obey. Now Dack hitched the wheel by lines passed through the bridge rails so that the ship held a steady course.

He and Blake dropped down to the deck. Dack, carrying the flag and the crowbar, went straight to the radio cabin. The operator was there—a sallow youth with lank black hair; obviously of Italian extraction. Two men were with him, tough-looking fellows, who lounged in chairs in the confined space.

The youth said: 'Anything wrong, Cap'n? Why have you come here?'

Dack said: 'OK.' He was talking to Blake, outside.

As he spoke he hit one of the big fellows under the jaw and knocked him and his chair backwards. Blake was in like lightning, and he had the other fellow before he could pull his gun. The youth screamed and tried to run out of the cabin. Dack slugged him a rabbit-punch as he ran, and he dropped as if hit over the head with lead.

They searched the two toughs and found their guns. Blake stood by the cabin door. Nothing moved on the wet deck. The ship held her course truly.

'Send,' hissed Blake; and Dack got down to the ticker.

Dot-dot-dot. Dash-dash-dash. Dot-dot-dot. Again and again he tapped it out.

Blake hissed: 'Don't give the right name of the ship. Any old name you can think of. And our position.'

Dack tapped out: 'British freighter *Walton Lass*. *Walton Lass* calling. SOS SOS. *Walton Lass*.' He added the position.

The radio was crackling away. The ship was holding on. There had been no reply to the signals.

'Keep sending,' ordered Blake. 'How are we for time?'

'Three minutes,' said Dack. 'What beats me is the other ship ain't in sight. She's late.'

'Maybe,' replied Blake grimly. 'Keep sending.'

Another minute went. Blake touched Dack's arm.

'The Red Ensign,' he said. 'We must leave the radio, and hope for the best.'

They raced aft along the deserted deck, and Dack, with sure and practised hands, broke the flag. He still carried the crowbar.

He said: 'The good old Red Duster.' He paused. 'Not that she's so dusty, either.'

On went the ship. Another minute had gone by. It was time.

Blake said: 'Into the launch, Dack. Help me haul her close.'

It was difficult, even with Dack helping. There was a big wake to contend with and a choppy sea, and the pull of the steamer. Suddenly Dack checked and pointed sideways.

'Look!' he gasped.

A long white line was running across the sea's face as if an invisible giant traced it—heading straight for the ship.

Blake laughed. 'Poetic justice, Dack! We're heading for England and we're showing the Red Ensign. We've sent out a call under a false name, a call that's been picked up by at least one of the ships I hoped would pick it up. The ship that fired that torpedo. That's the ship we came to meet! See her?'

A submarine was breaking surface some distance away. On its conning tower was a number with a great U over it.

The torpedo struck the *Hope of Asia* clean amid-ships.

Men came pouring up from below. They included those in the cabin. The launch was now under the stern, bucking and kicking like an unbroken horse.

Dack and Blake dropped into it; but two others dropped in too—deck-hands, panic-stricken.

The submarine had swung its gun round, and a shell crashed into the *Hope of Asia* as Dack cut the tow-rope of the launch and bent to its engine.

As he and Blake looked up they heard General Erich von Grau-stein shouting. There was anger in his voice, mad rage; but there was something else which warmed Blake's heart. Terror that bit deep, the terror of the cruel bully who has come to the end of the road.

The man was raving. One of his country's own submarines was trying to slay him; but in his insane wrath he did not appreciate the irony of the fact. He only appreciated the nearness of Death.

The gutter-scraped crew were trying to sling out the ship's boats. The submarine concentrated on them. One of them went sky-high, in splinters. Another was hit as it dropped. At that range, the gun crew could not miss.

'Head for the sub,' ordered Blake. 'We've got to stop her run-ning in close and finding out the truth before it's too late.'

On the submarine's narrow deck an officer had glasses clapped to his eyes. Quite suddenly the gunfire ceased. It was too late to leave any of the *Hope of Asia's* boats intact; but it did leave the ship still afloat, though sinking rapidly.

Blake snapped: 'He's read her name. Keep going, Dack.'

At that moment trouble started between the two deck-hands, and they commenced slugging each other. What the row was about there was no telling. It was likely that their antagonism had originated on board the *Hope of Asia*, and the quarrel had broken out anew on some score known only to themselves. What they snarled was so intermingled that it was quite unintelligible.

They sprang to their feet and fell into a clinch, struggling furiously and getting in short-arm jabs to the body as the chance offered. Breathing in heavy gasps, they staggered and reeled in the limited space, rocking the launch perilously.

Dack, steering with the utmost difficulty, turned, cursing as only the hardened skipper could. Blake edged nearer, seeking the right moment to step in and finish the fight. It was then that the real situation was made clear.

'Curse yer! Let go!' growled one of them. 'Chuck 'em over, would yer, and them got guns?'

The other man did not reply. He did not have the chance. The detective strode in and with a well-directed punch in the ribs dropped him senseless exactly on the spot where he stood.

'He wanted to drahn yer, guv'nor,' the man left standing gasped with difficulty, 'and get away in the launch. We hadn't an earthly, and I knew it. He meant to do the lot of us in and quit on his own, he did.'

Having recovered his wind the floored man sprang to his feet, and would have started the rumpus again, but Blake clipped him smartly under the chin. He staggered back, colliding with his companion, and the pair finished huddled up on the thwarts.

Blake showed his gun.

'Play safe, you two,' he snarled, and over his shoulder gave Dack the okay to keep going.

Nobody fired at the launch as it drove towards the submarine. The officer, having read the name of the ship, knowing it to be the ship he was to meet, was a frightened man. He awaited the arrival of the launch. He had been advised that von Graustein would put off in a launch, and his instructions—as Blake had shrewdly guessed—were that he was then to shepherd the valuable ship to a French port. He had lost the ship, but his highly placed passenger might be in the launch. The officer braced himself for the biggest dressing-down he had ever received, and at the same time felt very bewildered.

Why, he asked himself, had the Red Ensign been flying? Why had an SOS message in a false name been sent out? What had happened on the ship he had come to meet? He had imagined that ship overdue. He had seen, through his periscope, after picking up the SOS, a ship flying the English flag homeward bound—not coming from the direction which the *Hope of Asia* would use. Of course his periscope had not allowed him to read the ship's name. He could only do that through glasses. He had thought himself handed a sitting bird, and he would not have been a real U-boat commander if he had not taken advantage of it.

Whatever might be the outcome, Sexton Blake had neatly tricked him and everybody else, as Captain Dack was now admiringly understanding.

The launch ran alongside the U boat.

The officer began: 'Herr Kapitan . . .'

Blake was on the deck. He hit the officer as he spoke. It was a beautiful punch and it skittled the man into the sea.

'The bar, Dack!' shouted Blake.

Dack jammed the great iron bar into the shutting-hinges of the conning tower. The ship could not now submerge without swamping.

The gun crew tried to rush, but two automatics spat death. Two of their number dropped to the deck and slid outboard.

Blake leaned down the conning tower and shouted German at those below. He knew they were trying to shut down. He could hear the creak of the jammed machinery. He advised them that whoever tried to climb to the deck would be shot dead. One did try. Blake got him clean. The others did not try.

The *Hope of Asia* tilted, then took that long awful sliding dive which sinking ships take when the last moment has come. Heads showed on the water. Blake's face was set and grim. He hated to stand there and watch; but they were traitors to the country which had accepted them and given them the status of its nationals, the rights of its own free people, and they deserved their fate. As for Erich von Graustein . . . Blake felt glad. He honestly admitted it. There were dead women and children in Belgium to remember.

She was gone, and Dack spoke. He had no sentimentality about him.

'Good riddance,' he said. 'Well, we've got a submarine. What do we do with it? Raffle it?'

Blake pointed out and up.

'Your SOS was heard all right,' he said. 'Look!'

A great Sunderland flying-boat was coming downwards, into the wind. She was the second flying-boat to escort a captured submarine into a British port.

★   ★   ★

Captain Dack stretched himself and looked round the cabin of the *Mary Ann Trinder*. On the morrow he was to take her to a shipyard and soon she would be at sea again.

'Yes,' he said. 'Me and Mr Blake did it, Sam. Alone, mark you. Entirely on our own. That, of course,' he added offhandedly, 'was why I couldn't tell you anything about it. Captured a submarine, we did, and drowned the worst man in Germany bar one. An admiral came to see us when we got to port. He said it was splendid work. An admiral, mark you. He shook hands with me. Gold braid and all. I think I'll get a jacket like it.'

Sam sniffed. 'Is that what he called it? Splendid?'

'The admiral did,' said Dack complacently. 'But Mr Blake called it poetic justice. So did I.'

Sam looked at him darkly and almost asked him if he knew what that meant; but refrained. Dack seemed so sure of himself.

THE MAN I KILLED
Rex Hardinge

Rex Hardinge (1904–   ) was one of a small band (Gwyn Evans was another) to whom Sexton Blake was a childhood hero who became an adult taskmaster. Hardinge was born in Poona, son of an Indian Army officer, and most of his early days were spent travelling around the sub-continent. He joined the British Army in the early 1920s but was invalided out, took ship to Africa, worked on an orange plantation, then went back to India for a brief stint in Lahore on the Civil and Military Gazette *(Kipling's old stamping-ground). By then he'd already had a successful shot at writing Blakes and in 1929 he returned to England and settled down to hammer out fiction by the yard, mainly for the Amalgamated Press. Oddly, though most of his time away from England had been spent in India (a colourful enough backdrop, one would have thought, against which to spin any number of thrilling yarns), it was to Africa that he most frequently turned for his plots. In his case, however, it cannot be said that out of Africa came something new: frankly, Hardinge was a bit of a one-plot man. Nevertheless, his writing was always pacey, full of action and movement, and often vibrant with the harsh clamour of racketing automatics, which was exactly what a good many of his readers wanted. Occasionally, on one of those perfect days when all the creative gears seem to mesh, he would hit on a story, and a fresh approach, calculated to appeal to even the most jaded of editors—as here.*

A plea of insanity would never save me from the gallows, for I was never more sane than on the night when I killed Brandt.

Lying now in hospital, with the end very near, I want this statement I am dictating to my solicitor to be as true as I can make it. There must be no shirking behind such excuses as madness for what I have done.

I come of a family of clear-headed thinkers, and no taint of madness has touched us as far back as can be traced. Besides, there was nothing hot-headed about my actions that night. I was cool and deliberate over every move. I knew what I had to do; how it had to be done. All that remained was to do it. I killed Brandt much as a man would stamp out a cigarette-end on the floor. That man isn't mad when he does that; nor was I when I killed.

Only Sexton Blake ever formed a true estimate of this case, and he never talked a quantity of long-worded rubbish about paranoia. A great man, Blake!

I've known him for years. My father knew his, and there was all the old family connection that makes a firm foundation for a friendship. I watched Blake's career, rejoiced over his successes, and pitted my brain against his when he was at the summit of his powers.

It was turning dusk when I reached Hampstead on my way to destroy Brandt, and a very fine drizzle of rain gave me the excuse I needed to turn my coat collar up to conceal my chin, draw the brim of my hat down, and conceal my face. I was surprised at my own confidence that the evening's work would be crowned with success.

For months I had realised that I must kill this man; for weeks I had been perfecting my plans, fitting each little detail into its slot, bringing the margin of error as near to complete elimination as possible. To commit the perfect murder is a task that has been attempted by many men. Only the failures receive publicity, shortly before they pay the penalty for their carelessness.

I had not been careless, and could not afford to be a failure. Too much was at stake.

I had travelled to Hampstead by a roundabout route from my flat in Baker Street—within a stone's throw of Blake's chambers. My car was parked at Victoria, and I used more than one bus and underground train before walking the last stretch up the hill.

Brandt's house stood at the top, a magnificent mansion, built before the War, and decorated by one of the most famous firms in the country. It had cost him a fortune, but he could afford it. Out of a lucky charm, this extraordinary South African had made sufficient money to be ranked among the richest men in England. Brandt's 'Happidols' were to be found on almost every watch-chain, as mascots on every second car, as brooches on most coats, as mantelpiece ornaments. These comic little creatures with their large heads and happy smiles, made from every variety of metal, from lead to gold and platinum, had taken the fancy of the entire world.

Brandt and his Happidols! Brandt, small and plump, with the round, plump face of one of his own mascots, and a smile to match, the man who spread happiness with his Happidols—the man I killed!

I walked at a regulated pace, knowing to the last fraction how long it was taking me to cover each yard. Time is the essential factor of any perfect operation. Split-seconds spell the difference between success and failure, and I had every action timed. The triumphant outcome of my night's work depended largely on the watch on my wrist.

I reached the gate in the wall around Brandt's garden, and opened it with a key that I had cut myself. The thought occurred to me of what an interesting talk Blake and I could have on the trades that a man has to study when he dabbles in crime, but we would not be able to have that talk because we were operating now on different sides.

Before crossing the well-ordered garden towards the windows of Brandt's study, I concealed the case that I was carrying in the thickest patch of bush that I could find. Then I went forward more slowly. Far in the distance—or so it seemed to me—I could hear the hum of traffic. The world was moving about its business beyond this garden, but for me nothing else existed except my plans, and the man waiting for me behind those windows.

As I drew near, I could hear the faint, sweet strains of a violin, which told me that Brandt was spending the evening in his usual way. He flattered himself as a violinist, and certainly loved music. Each evening it was his habit to play piece after piece, with scarcely an interval between them, from 7 o'clock, when he finished his early evening meal, to 9.30, when his butler took him a glass of special invalid tonic. No engagement could get him out during that period, which he described as his offering to the gods that had brought him luck and wealth.

It was 7.14 exactly when I stood outside the open window, listening to the muffled strains of the violin coming through the thick curtains. My plans were reaching the climax-point. At that moment, I was a law-abiding citizen, except for the fact that I was committing the petty misdemeanour of trespassing in another man's garden. I was simply Matt King, chief sporting correspondent of the 'Telegram'; popular because I entertained well and loved sport; the trusted friend of men like Sexton Blake; understood to have no cares in the world, to be one of those lucky devils for whom everything goes right; young enough to have a great future before me, backed by a past of hard work and success—and, within thirty minutes, I would deliberately have placed myself outside the pale, become a murderer, and across my future would always be the shadow of the hangman's noose.

Brandt was playing Dvorak's 'Humoresque', seeming to my tautened nerves to draw out every plaintive note too long. I stepped through the window carefully, drawing the heavy curtain aside.

He was there, standing before his music-rest, his rubicund face made more ruddy by the red-shaded light, which alone lit the room. He was an affected player, swaying about the room in time to the music, seeming to wrestle with his violin and to twist himself into as many queer postures as a circus contortionist. The red light was also reflected in the shining shapes of countless Happidols, with which the room was decorated.

Perhaps my nerves were not as steady as I imagined, and my vision was distorted, but, to me in that light, the wide, grotesque grins took on a new significance, and the fat, ridiculous features seemed to leer gloatingly in a manner that was entirely evil.

Brandt finished the 'Humoresque' with an elaborate flourish, and lowered the violin to turn over the music. But I could not allow him to start the next piece. I had only seventy-five seconds, according to schedule.

I made a slight movement, and he turned and saw me. Surprise wrinkled his forehead, as his eyebrows went up.

'King! You here?'

'Yes, I'm here! I've come about the Happidols. You understand?'

I could not recognise my own voice, although I was automatically repeating a rehearsed statement.

He did understand; knowledge of the truth showed in his face, which puckered oddly, becoming white around the mouth, wrinkled in a myriad lines. The violin dropped from his hands, as he moved towards his desk. And then I stepped in close, and hit him.

There was no weapon to be disposed of after this killing—one of the most difficult problems in a job of this sort—for I used my fist. Brandt had not lived a healthy life, and I knew of the state of his heart. Before I entered the newspaper game, I fought for my living, both in England and America. Not polite first-class boxing, but old-fashioned bruising in the booths of travelling fairs. I am still powerful, and know where to hit. Perhaps the strangest fact about that night is that both Blake and I were taught that death-blow by the same man, only I doubt if Blake has ever had cause to use it.

Brandt uttered a cry; the surprise on his face was accentuated for a moment before the life went out of it. The Happidols on the walls leered down as he crumpled up on the carpet that they had provided the money for.

His stillness and pallor; his contorted attitude—the knowledge of what I had done in this quiet, comfortable room—filled me with sudden panic that made me want to run. But I knew that, if I did run, I could never run fast or far enough to forget the sight of him lying there, with wide-open, fixed eyes that accused me.

All was silence in the room, until I became conscious of the regular ticking of the clock. That reminded me of my schedule, and the all-importance of the time element. I had lost the slight margin that I had allowed myself, and had not a second to spare. I opened the window, the better to complete my arrangements there. Then I picked up the violin and bow, and put them back into Brandt's nerveless hands.

As I stepped back into the night, and hurried across the garden, the strains of the violin followed me, the wild, abandoned notes of one of Brahms' Hungarian Dances, beautifully played.

The time was 7.25.

*   *   *

As I went to Victoria to collect my car, I knew what a surgeon must feel like on his way from the hospital after the conclusion of a tricky operation. The strain has been terrific, but he feels that he has achieved something. His mind runs back over each phase of the job, reviewing it coldly and dispassionately, although he has just played with life and death; anticipating complications which might set in, and the measures to be taken to check these.

I felt exactly like that. I knew—as many a surgeon must—that I must only consider what I had done just as a job that had been forced upon me, and which was now concluded. I must not dwell too much on the personal element, or the possible outcome, else my nerve must break.

I took a roundabout route again, but hurried. The car was where I had left it, at a garage where it is the normal routine for cars to be parked for varying periods, and where mine had been left every evening at the same time for two weeks past, so that there was nothing abnormal in its being there tonight. I drove to the Imperial Sporting Club, where Young Jacobs was to meet Harry Bates for the world's middle-weight title, and where Dick Mason met me by appointment.

'Right on the dot, Matt!' he said cheerfully. 'Eight o'clock you said, and eight o'clock it is.'

I glanced at my watch, and breathed a sigh of relief, for I had a morbid dread of slipping up anywhere on my schedule.

'I've got some guests coming tonight, Dicky,' I told him, 'and I'm going to watch this show as a member of the public for a change, so this is your chance to do your stuff alone.'

'Gosh, we're getting big ideas!' was the impudent retort. 'Chief sporting reporter of the "Telegram" sits among the nobs, while aspiring junior does all the dirty work. Matt King fans need not despair, however, for the familiar signature will foot the account, as usual. Who are your guests? Am I allowed to come and kow-tow to them, or must I watch from the distance with envious eyes and a sense of awe?'

'You may come and wait at the entrance with me,' I told him, surprised at the grin that I managed to conjure up to match his. 'Perhaps one of them will pat you on the head as they pass by. If you've washed your hands today, you may even shake hands.'

'Words of gratitude fill my throat, and tears my eyes. Is there time for a drink and a sandwich to continue the filling process?'

'There is,' I replied, for I felt suddenly that I must have that drink, for my nerves gave warning that there was a breaking-point.

Later, as Mason and I stood at the entrance, I had overcome the absurd sense of reaction which had momentarily made my hand tremble. I felt again that I could see this job through to its ultimate end, and I concentrated my brain on exchanging with the young-ster by me what passes in Fleet Street as repartee. And yet a freakish thought made me wonder what the crowds thronging into the club would think, and do, if they knew that they were brushing against a murderer?

Cannan, managing editor of the 'Telegram', arrived and stopped by us for a moment.

'Who are your guests?' he asked.

Cannan spends his life asking questions on matters that seem no concern of his, but that frequently form the basis of the scoops that have put the 'Telegram' ahead of the front rank.

The arrival of Sexton Blake's long grey car saved me the trouble of answering. Tinker was driving, with Arnold Dane, one of the few men who can put a big fight across realistically in a novel, beside him. Blake and Lord Service, undoubtedly the best known and admired sportsman in England, stepped out from the back.

'Moving among the nobs!' sniggered Cannan coarsely, as he went forward to greet Blake.

I smiled, for I had chosen the company in which I was to spend the next hour with deliberate care. The word of any of these men was worth a dozen affidavits.

'Crime feeling the depression, Blake?' Cannan was asking the detective.

Blake smiled and shook his head, explaining that he was taking a night off. He looked tired, and as though he needed the break. I knew that both he and Tinker had been working at more than the usual high-pressure for some time past, and had used this knowledge when pressing them to be my guests.

'We've just come from a murder,' interposed Dane cheerfully. 'So get out your notebook, Brother Cannan—or are you one of those linen-defacers who use a shirt-cuff? Murder at Ratti's! Live lobster swallowed by young detective in disgusting manner at disgusting hour—'

'It wasn't alive!' protested Tinker.

'It would have been if you hadn't chosen it to make what you call an early supper,' retorted the novelist. 'Lobster at 7.30, before a fight—a double murder, Cannan—murder of a lobster before its time, and murder of a youthful digestion!'

'Must we talk of murders?' I put in, forcing a lightness into my voice which I did not feel.

It is part of the cussedness of life that one's friends must innocently select a topic that jarrs.

'At least you people only talk them,' interposed Blake. 'Not like some people I know, who never mention the subject in polite conversation, and become most embarrassed when they hear the word, but who unhesitatingly bump a bloke off when in the mood.'

'Bet there's a murder tonight, because we're taking the night off!' declared Tinker, who had already made the most outrageous wagers on the fight, and was ready to bet on anything.

'There will be,' agreed Dane gloomily. 'The last time I had a night out with Blake a man shot his wife and six children.'

'As your host, I'll see what I can provide for you,' some puckish whim forced me to promise.

My sensations during the preliminary bouts were the most extraordinary that I have ever experienced. I seemed to be two men. One of them was playing the perfect host, laughing gaily, criticising the fights, trying to cap Blake's jokes, as I had often tried in vain to cap them on festive occasions in the past, for when he throws aside the cold, restrained manner which his work forces him to assume, Blake can be the best companion imaginable, for he has a unique selection of amusing stories, which he tells in a dry, humorous way, and with superb mimicry.

But there was another me, unsmiling, and obsessed with chilling thoughts of Brandt's house on Hampstead Hill. Between me and the fighters in the ring, visions kept coming of that comfortably furnished study, the leering Happidols, and—Brandt, crumpled on the floor, with the violin and bow in his dead fingers.

It seemed incredible that he would not come in before the big fight, as was always his custom. Brandt had never missed a big show of this sort, although, on account of his habit of devoting the early part of the evening to his music, he was always late. People always turned to smile towards him, when they saw him coming, for he was the man who had spread happiness with his Happidols.

Time and again I had watched him from the Press seats, hating him, knowing even then that some day I must kill him.

During an interval between bouts, I made an excuse to go out to the cars. I managed to avoid the attendants and reach Blake's Grey Panther unnoticed. When I returned, the main fight was just starting, and the time was 9.20. Jacobs and Bates were already in the ring, and that peculiar hush filled the hall which immediately precedes the first exchange of blows. Bates was like a tiger, and we all knew that it was his avowed intention to 'eat' the quietly confident Young Jacobs in one round.

'Bet you he doesn't!' whispered Tinker, and arranged still another rash bet.

I felt myself stiffen in my chair as I saw Fred Smith, of the Sporting Club management, coming towards our seats. I scarcely recognised my own voice as I risked a quick comment about the boys in the ring. I guessed what Smith was coming for, and braced myself as he touched Blake on the shoulder.

'No holiday for you, old man!' he whispered unfeelingly. 'Detective-Inspector Coutts, of Scotland Yard, requires the presence of Mr Sexton Blake at one end of a telephone instrument. Jump to it! I've left the receiver off the hook in my office.'

Blake sighed wearily, and, after a hurried explanation to me, followed Smith towards the office. The minutes that passed seemed longer than hours. Bates had proved over-confident, and was down for a count of five. The referee's voice seemed to take an eternity over the counting of each second. Fortunately, my companions had their eyes riveted on the ring, for I know that I felt as pale as a ghost, and my hands were clenched so that the nails cut into the palms. It seemed that Blake would never come back, and yet I knew, and had counted on, his strict, old-fashioned courtesy, which would forbid him to leave without making an explanation to his host.

At last, when I felt that I could stand the strain no longer, he was back, bending over me to whisper:

'Sorry, Matt, but Coutts wants me. You're certainly a host who keeps his promises, and young Tinker has won one of his bets.'

'You mean,' interposed Dane, who was listening, 'that it's a murder?'

'I do,' replied Blake, smiling at me. 'Matt promised to do his best to provide one for us, didn't he?'

* * *

I rose quickly to my feet, and followed Blake and Tinker up the gangway. Blake remonstrated with me, but I insisted on going with them.

'You can't shake me off. Cannan was only two rows behind

where we were sitting,' I explained with a chuckle, 'and I felt his eyes boring holes in my back. I don't usually cover crime stuff, but he'd eat me alive if I let you out of my sight now.'

'A murder scene isn't a pleasant place for a man to visit who isn't accustomed to the job, Matt,' Blake pointed out. 'It's not in your line at all; you're too highly strung. You go back, and watch those lads trying to kill one another in a manner that you're accustomed to.'

'Not on your life! I've long wanted to have a hand in a murder,' I replied stubbornly. 'Who is it? Anyone interesting?'

'I'm not telling you, Matt,' he replied. 'And I'm not taking you with me. Murders are not in your line.'

I could have laughed at that. Murders not in my line! That was good to a man who had just committed the perfect murder! But I realised that I must not appear to be too eager. Blake is a dangerous man to bluff, and, even when backed by a friendly smile, his eyes were like gimlets that seem to bore down behind all pretence.

I shrugged my shoulders.

'Have your own way,' I surrendered; 'but, if I promise not to follow up in person, will you give me the name and address, so that I can phone to the office for one of the crime gang to go along? Give us the chance to get in early, Blake.'

He hesitated, his foot on the running-board of his car; but Tinker interrupted before he could reply.

'Blinking self-starter won't work, guv'nor!' grumbled the lad. 'I can't make it out. The old Panther was running like an antelope on the way here, and I know the battery's fully charged.'

'Better look in the bonnet and see if anyone's pinched the engine?' I suggested lightly.

Tinker did not smile, for it was his habit to fuss over the Grey Panther like a hen with one chick, staking his reputation on the car always being in tip-top condition, for Blake's instant use. His reputation was something to stake, what is more, for I seldom met a finer mechanic than this cheery, broad-shouldered youngster, who had acquired all Blake's thoroughness over every job he tackled.

'Golly!' he exclaimed, after lifting the bonnet. 'This is a bit thick! Someone's cut just about every cable in the ignition system!'

Blake's face set stonily as he also bent over the car, and I suggested calling for the attendant.

'Tinker can deal with him!' snapped the detective. 'I'll have to take a taxi.'

'You'll have to do nothing of the sort!' I put in, playing my next card. 'I've got a car. It looks as though I'm doomed to have a look at this murder. Let's go.'

He hesitated, and I recognised the ruthless machine that criminals feared, so different from the quiet friend I had known for years. But he followed me to the car, and climbed in beside me.

'Brandt's place at Hampstead, Matt!' he ordered quietly.

'What? But you don't mean—'

'I do. Do you know the way there?'

'Sure. I've interviewed him after he has made big donations to sporting charities,' I replied. 'But, Blake, why should anyone kill Brandt?'

'Why shouldn't they? He's rich, isn't he?'

'Robbery? Of course, I hadn't thought of that,' I confessed, biting my lip, for I had almost made a slip, and the watchful eyes were on me.

'I shall want you to stay around, Matt, as I haven't got Tinker with me,' he continued; and I rejoiced quietly, for every move in the game was coming my way so smoothly. It was imperative for my plans that I stay with Blake for as long as possible, and I felt that it would be just as well for me to be at Brandt's house during the preliminary investigations. Careful though I had been, there might be some detail that I had overlooked. By being on the spot, I would at least have a sporting chance of remedying any oversight. Also, I had to pay my visit to the garden, and I felt that I must get that over soon.

The house was ablaze with lights as we drove up, and Detective-Inspector Coutts met us in the hall.

'Sorry to get you away from the fight, Blake,' he declared. 'How was it going?'

I could not help an inward smile as these two—undoubtedly the strongest anti-criminal co-operation in England—delayed discussion of murder, while Blake gave a brief, clear account of the opening stages of the Jacobs-Bates fight.

'Matt King has turned crime reporter,' Blake continued, pointing at me. 'He insists on making a nuisance of himself around here.'

157

'He's late!' snorted Coutts. 'There's a mob of 'em camped out in the gardens, including Firth from the "Telegram". But I expect that—like all those newspaper tecs—he already knows the murderer!'

'You bet I do,' I replied, not liking the sneer, and winking deliberately. 'I knew before the murder was committed!'

But truth spoken in jest makes a poor joke. Coutts snorted, and led the way to Brandt's study. Staggered at my own coolness, I followed the detectives along the passage, but I realised that I must not let my sense of humour run away with me. Coutts was still talking.

'The case has many unusual points,' he explained heavily, 'but the main reason that I have asked you to come along is because we found five photographs in the top drawer of the desk. All are of the same man—identical snapshots—a type we know well, the cheap American crook. They were evidently taken at Coney Island Pleasure Beach, with one of the side-shows prominent in the background.

'Written on the back of each is a message—"I'll be seeing you!" and there is a note on one in a different handwriting, which says: "Refer to Sexton Blake".

'I decided to refer to you for two reasons,' went on Coutts. 'Not only because of the message, but because of your frequent visits to the States you have a fuller knowledge of the lesser American crooks than we have at the Yard. It is part of our job to know the big men, but it would be asking too much to expect us to have records of all the smaller fry. We have a big enough job trying to keep track of our own crooks.'

I followed them into the room, forcing my eyes not to seek immediately the spot where I had left Brandt's body. I looked deliberately towards the far wall, and a grotesque Happidol grinned back at me. The grotesque idol was welcoming me back, and reminding me that it had also witnessed what had happened during my last visit. It shook my nerve for a moment, and I must have shown my distress, for Blake's hand closed on my arm.

'I advised you not to come, Matt,' he reminded quietly. 'The first murder scene is capable of bowling out any man; though, let me tell you, this is a clean job compared to some!'

He was smiling at his friendliest, but I shook off his hand and turned away, because I knew that I could not face those probing eyes for a moment.

'I'm all right; just the sudden shock. After all, I used to know the man,' I explained. 'It's not so long ago that I saw him.'

I allowed myself to look towards where Brandt lay then, and saw that he was where I had left him, but had been turned on to his back. A doctor was bending over him, had opened his coat, and ripped away the shirt. But Brandt's fingers still held the violin and bow, straight down at his sides. His face was hideous, and I hated him so intensely that I forgot my repulsion at the thought of death. The wave of hatred that brought a red mist of rage to my brain restored my nerve to me; made me glory in what I had done, and the part that I still had to play.

Confound Blake, with his sharp eyes and acute, eager brain! I could, and would, beat him at his own game. My reasoning could be as cold as his; my methods as perfect. At that moment I hated Blake, because—at the back of my mind—I knew that I was afraid of him.

He stooped down by the doctor, and the two began to talk together in low tones. I drew nearer to them, determined to overhear what they said. Much of it was in scientific jargon, for Blake had a brilliant medical training behind him, and knew more than the average general practitioner. The doctor was describing the cause of death, and Blake was prompting him with shrewd questions.

'Very unusual,' muttered the doctor. 'The blow over the heart cannot have been a hard one, and yet—'

Blake looked puzzled as he examined the faint mark to which his companion pointed. I knew what he was thinking; it was one of the risks I had had to take. He knew how few men knew the secret of that death-blow. My salvation lay in the fact that he did not know that I was among them, a fact which he must never learn.

He turned towards me.

'This is in your line, after all, Matt,' he said slowly. 'How many men have you heard of being killed by a blow over the heart?'

'Very few,' I replied, 'although accidents do happen. But there's generally something wrong with the man's heart to begin with. Burgess, one of the best welters in England, went out that way during a title bout at Birmingham, but it was proved at the inquest that his heart had not been good for years.'

'You never heard of a blow which could always be counted on to kill a sound man if it hit him over the heart?'

'Good lord, no! That is, nothing short of a colossal slug, delivered with every ounce of force by a strong man. The muscles around the heart will withstand any ordinary blow.'

'This isn't an ordinary blow,' muttered Blake, 'and it's not a powerful one either—just a tap will do, but it needs long training and practice to administer that tap.'

He rose to his feet, and approached Coutts, who had produced the photographs that were found in the top drawer of the desk, and was waiting impatiently for Blake to finish with the doctor.

I drew close to study the photographs over Blake's shoulder. They represented a clean-shaven, hard-faced man, with hair brushed straight back from his forehead, and bulky figure forced into a light, double-breasted suit. The man was of a type made familiar in England by the films, the nucleus of every American gang, the 'coke'-filled thug employed as bodyguard by the Big Shot. The photograph was of the while-you-wait variety, with a Coney Island side-show as a background. Each of the prints was identical, and each carried the same message: 'I'll be seeing you!'

'Do you know him?' asked Coutts.

Blake nodded thoughtfully.

'I've come up against him somewhere,' he decided; 'but I've come up against so many during visits to America to help with the cleaning-up process over there that I can't just place him at the moment. As you said yourself, Coutts, it is almost impossible to remember all the foreign small fry that one comes up against. I'll take one of these prints along, if I may, and look through my records to see if I can match it. Who found Brandt?'

'The butler. But I've already got his story, and there's nothing about the case to interest you,' replied Coutts. 'If we find the original of that photograph, we find the murderer.'

'You've got it all worked out, then?' asked Blake; and I had to hide a smile at Coutts' confident reply, though Blake's persistence troubled me, for he had already done all that I wanted of him according to my schedule.

'Sure!' replied Coutts. 'The original of these snaps was out to get **Brandt** for some reason, so he sent him these photographs at intervals as a form of warning. We happen to know that Brandt travelled a great deal in America, and he sought the protection of the Chicago police on one occasion, because he had got mixed up in a row at a speakeasy during a visit there. He was rather a queer bird in that way, and frequently gave us trouble by poking his nose into unsavoury corners. I take it that he angered the original of those photographs, who decided to get him. We've had many similar cases, where the intending murderer sent threatening messages to frighten his victim until he had the opportunity to come and do the job. The original of those photographs came to England, and murdered Brandt at exactly 9.27 tonight.'

'Excellent!' exclaimed Blake. 'You know the time to the very minute!'

Coutts scowled, scenting the sarcasm. I no longer smiled, for I was watching Blake. Something in the close attention with which he was studying the photographs in his hand filled me with foreboding. Instinct warned me that I was up against an error, an error that it was going to be hard to remedy. I had never seen Blake look quite like that before. This was the man-hunter, cold and ruthless as a machine, and I realised that I had set a dangerous force working against myself.

I peered over his shoulder at the photograph. What could be wrong with it? Panic seized on me, so that I felt I must snatch it out of his hand; throw it, and the others, into the fire.

Blake turned to the telephone, and, with a nod to Coutts, gave his own Baker Street number. Tinker had returned home after repairing the car, and I heard Blake mention the name of Callaghan.

'Get together all the records of Bud Callaghan that we have, and bring them here quick!' he ordered.

Coutts asked a number of startled questions, but Blake's only reply was that he thought he had placed the original of the photograph. He took a seat by the desk, and sat there like a statue, staring at Brandt's body. I followed the direction of his gaze towards the violin that Brandt still held. I saw the left hand, which gripped the fiddle, and remembered—what I should have remembered before! My knowledge of failure increased. Two errors already in the perfect crime!

But I clenched my fists, and knew that I must fight. Blake gave no indication of having seen the second error. I might yet manage to remedy it. But I dreaded those sharp eyes of his that seemed to miss nothing. Would they observe the significance of the hand in which Brandt held the violin?

The door opened at last, after a ghastly interval of silence in that room of death, and Tinker entered. Once more, I looked over Blake's shoulder as he studied the folder that the lad had brought. There were three photographs of the man of the Coney Island snaps—two profiles and a full-face. Each was labelled 'Bud Callaghan.'

Blake turned to Coutts again.

'So this man came here tonight and killed Brandt, Coutts?' he repeated quietly.

'That's our present theory,' was the dogged reply. 'The evidence points to it.'

'I hope you believe in ghosts, Coutts,' continued Blake, and I hated his quiet voice; 'because, otherwise, your theory fails. Bud Callaghan, the original of those photographs, was shot dead by a Chicago detective on the 24th of January last—four months ago—and was given a swell funeral. Here's a photo of the funeral cortège!

'We've got to find a new theory and a new murderer,' continued Blake. 'May I question the butler?'

Coutts gave an order, and I studied the man who entered the room with concentrated interest, for on his testimony now rested much of the success of my plans. He conformed to the type still found in many houses, the old-fashioned style of servant, tall and pompous, with a plump, elderly face framed by neat side-whiskers, and thin white hair. He was evidently much upset over the tragedy, and his voice trembled when he told Blake that his name was Robert Adams, while he kept his troubled eyes averted from the body of his master.

'Tell your story in your own way,' prompted Blake. 'Right from the very beginning, Adams; and, remember, what seems an insignificant detail to you may bring your master's murderer to the punishment he deserves.'

'Every night it was the master's habit to play the violin from 7 to 9.30,' was the careful reply, the old man seating himself gratefully on the chair that Blake pushed forward. 'We have all grown so used to this habit, sir, that we would feel there was something wrong in the 'ouse if we was not to hear the music of the violin during this time. As he finishes each *morceau*, which is French for "piece", sir, there is only a short pause before he begins the next, so it's a regular concert we are treated to, sir. I have never known him stop before I knock at the door at 9.30 with the cup of Beefagen, which it is his custom to take at that hour. I was in the passage tonight some minutes before the 'alf-hour, sir.'

The old man paused, and rubbed his chin with long, nervous fingers.

'You see, sir, I'm a bit of a music-lover myself,' he went on. 'Always attend the Proms, when I 'as the opportunity; and it has been my 'abit to reach Mr Brandt's door some minutes before 9.30, so as to indulge myself in a few minutes of quiet listening to the music, if you understand me, sir?'

'And tonight?' prompted Blake.

'The master played better than ever before, sir—quite as good as many of the foreign gentlemen I've 'eard at the fashionable concerts. Beautiful, it was,' insisted Mr Adams. 'But he stopped playing at 9.27. It wasn't the end of the piece, sir. He just stopped short and abrupt—and he didn't play again.'

'What did you do?' pressed Blake.

'Well, I 'esitated, sir—not quite knowing what I ought to do, sir. Then I remembered that Mr Brandt had been 'aving trouble with his 'eart, so I knocked once at the door, and then went straight in.'

'The door wasn't locked?'

'No, sir. It never is. This door 'asn't got a lock, sir.'

'I see. And there was no one in the room except Mr Brandt? You're quite sure about that?' insisted Blake.

'Quite positive, sir. That window was open, as it is now, as it is always kept open by Mr Brandt, who is a believer in fresh air, sir,' explained the butler. 'But he lay on the floor, crumpled up, still holding the fiddle that he had just done playing. I didn't touch him, but sent at once for Dr Everett.'

'Did you touch the violin?' asked Blake, and the question sent a cold chill through me.

'No, sir,' replied the butler.

'Thank you, Adams. There is only one more question,' went on Blake. 'You say that Mr Brandt stopped playing abruptly. What actually do you mean by that? Did he play a false note, and then stop?'

'No, sir. He just stopped in the middle of a bar.'

'The note wasn't drawn out, rendered false, as you would expect if a man was hit while playing?'

'No, sir—I'm confident of that, sir. He just stopped abruptly. And I was in the room a minute afterwards.'

'Did you move that violin, doctor?'

Blake turned to the medical man now, who shook his head.

'There was no cause to,' was the reply. 'His hands were down at his sides, holding the fiddle and bow, and I was able to open coat and shirt without disturbing them.'

'Brandt died immediately? He wouldn't have had time to—shall we say—put the violin down and take it up again between the time that he finished playing and was found dead?'

'He most certainly would not.'

'What's it all about, Blake?' interposed Coutts. 'Where's all this taking us?'

'I'm just wondering,' replied Blake, 'how Brandt could have played that violin, when—as you will see for yourself—he has the middle finger missing from his left hand, the hand with the fingers of which a violinist makes his notes?'

I knew that I could do nothing as Blake crossed and took the instrument from Brandt's hand. He looked at it closely, and then placed it under his chin.

'According to evidence,' he went on, 'Brandt was playing this instrument up to the very moment that he died. He was found holding it in his *left* hand a minute after the music ceased. Do you play the violin, Coutts?'

'Not on your life!' replied the startled inspector. 'I did once have lessons on the piano when I was a kid, but—'

'I see what you're driving at, Blake,' I interposed desperately. 'But surely a man could train himself to finger his instrument, even if he was one finger short? The other fingers would have to do extra work.'

'Quite right, Matt,' he agreed quietly; 'but, listen! I am going to play the opening notes of Mendelssohn's "Spring Song" as a normal violinist would play it, holding the instrument in my left hand.'

The resulting sounds were hideous. Then he changed the violin to his right hand and bowed with his left.

'Because of his disability, Brandt played the violin in the opposite way to the normal, holding the instrument in his right hand,' he explained briefly. 'To do this, he had to reverse the strings. Normally the strings on a violin are G, D, A, E. Brandt had to have them the other way round. What caught my eye, after observing that missing finger, is the fact that the G-string is always a silver band-string, while the others are catgut. I noticed that the silver string on this violin was on the wrong side of the other three! Now, can you tell me, Coutts, how this man can have been playing this violin up to the very moment of his death, when we find him holding it in a way that makes it physically, and musically, impossible for him to have been playing?'

Blake's words put a new complexion on the entire case, and I realised that the evidence of the violin would go a long way towards destroying the alibi that I had built up with such elaborate care. The violin had been heard by the butler up to 9.27, and Brandt was found dead with it in his hand a moment later. This would seem to prove that Brandt had died at that moment, and my alibi was that at 9.27 I was with Blake, and had been with him for more than an hour. Perhaps I would not need an alibi, for no finger of suspicion pointed in my direction as yet, but the knowledge that I had so perfect a one had given me a sense of security that I now lacked.

Blake had just proved that Brandt could not have been playing the violin at the moment when he fell. The next step forward in his reasoning must include the possibility that Brandt had died before 9.27, and that would open up lines of investigation that might lead anywhere. I realised that I had started a force moving that I could not stop, and the knowledge threw my mind into a state of chaos. As I watched Blake, so quietly efficient and alert, I realised how it was that one murder so frequently led to others. I knew that I must stop at nothing to keep him from unearthing the truth. Crazy plans began to form in my head.

I made a murmured apology, and found my way back to the hall.

'Had enough, Matt?' Blake's voice called after me. 'You shouldn't have come, old chap. Find a drink—you need it!'

The butler heard the words, and appeared with a decanter and glass.

'A shocking business, sir,' he muttered. 'Shakes one up cruelly. Worse for me, if I may say so, sir, as Mr Brandt was a good master. A bit queer-like at times, perhaps—'

By the thickness in his voice, and the depleted state of the decanter, I was not the first one to need, and take, a drink that night, and I left Adams surreptitiously helping himself to another.

'My first murder,' I mumbled, once again finding a crazy thrill in the double meaning of the statement. The brandy had steadied me, given me fresh courage and confidence. What if I had stumbled twice in my plans, and made the further error of bringing Blake on to the scene, imagining that I could outwit him? There was still time to win out.

Other murderers had beaten Blake for a time, and they had not started with the advantage of having his confidence. They had only had the stern man-hunter to deal with, whereas—for the time being, at least—Blake was still the kindly friend where I was concerned. I must make my next move while he still had no suspicion of me.

My thoughts flew to the box that I had left in the garden. I had hidden it with extreme care in the bushes by the wall, but I had twice learnt already tonight how dangerous it was to feel satisfied with what I had done, and I feared that, at any moment, Blake's diabolical powers of reasoning would lead him across the lawn to the evidence that lay in the bushes.

As I stepped into the garden I almost cannoned into a figure lurking by the steps. Instinctively I clutched at it.

'What-ho!' exclaimed the familiar voice of Firth, who handles the big crime stuff for the 'Telegram', and a torch shone in my face. 'I thought I'd nabbed the murderer, and it's only little Matt King. What are you doing here, my lad? Since when were murders listed as sporting events?'

'They aren't,' I retorted. 'This is my first, and I'm leaving the rest to you!'

I drew him away from other shadowy figures that approached, and explained to him how I came to be at Hampstead, passing on as much information as I dared of what I had witnessed in Brandt's room with Blake.

'Cod in collars!' grumbled Firth, whose exclamations were entirely his own. 'Some fellows have all the luck! I come here after a story, and all I get is rheumatism from hovering around wet grass, while you walk in to a ringside seat as usual. And, boy, you don't seem to appreciate that you must've been born with a silver type-writer in your mouth, and a special pass to all exclusive gatherings in each hand. Listen! You trot along back and freeze on to Blake as though you were a Lancashire man "oop for t' Coop", whose pal is carrying the tickets. Blake's that pal with the tickets, so don't lose sight of him—'

'I was only coming to find you,' I excused myself glibly. 'This is your line, not mine, and I don't want to mess it up. I want you to stay around, so that I can get the stuff through to you before Coutts makes any official statement. Don't use a word of what I've just told you until we get Blake's okay, but I'll have plenty more for you. The trouble with you blokes is that you can't run your own shows. I have to leave a grand fight to do your dirty work for you.'

'Yeah?' retorted Firth. 'Well, if you want a good fight, you repeat those words to me tomorrow and I'll show you! Now jump to it, brother!'

I turned back towards the door. Every journalistic instinct wanted to go in and get the stuff for Firth, another gigantic scoop for the 'Telegram'. But the story was too personal—my whole future, my very life, was mixed up too deeply in what was to Firth merely a story.

I regained the hall and found Adams thoughtfully considering the empty decanter. I glanced at my watch. It would only take me a few minutes to set my mind at rest about the case; then Firth could have his story.

Adams led me erratically through the house to the back door, and bowed me out into the darkness of the garden again. I managed to skirt round the lawn, where the red pin-point lights of numerous cigarettes indicated the camp of the newspapermen, and reached the bushes. Looking back, I could see the detectives framed in the window of Brandt's room, and I knew that the journalists would have their attention fixed on that square of light.

I stooped down and felt among the bushes for the case.

A cold sweat of fear came out on my forehead as I rose to my feet again. I tried to persuade myself that I had mistaken the spot; searched the whole length of the wall; but—leaning against a tree at last, panting as though I had run a great distance—I had to face the indisputable fact that the case had gone!

How long it was that I continued to hunt about in those bushes, even after I had convinced myself that I was wasting time, I could not say. Then I let further precious minutes go by while I tried to reason out who might have moved the case. Its disappearance was incredible, for no one can have known of its existence. There was no one about when I put it there, unless—the thought seemed to take all the stiffening out of me—unless someone was hidden in the garden at the time of my previous visit!

But who could have been? And how long were they there? Did they follow me to the window? Were they watching while I was in the room with Brandt? The flood of questions and their terrrible import made me dizzy, and I had to hold to the tree for support. I realised how correct, as usual, Blake had been in his judgment, when he said that I was too highly strung to come into contact with murder.

I enjoy a good scrap; contact with fights has been the whole of my life. But the violence of death is something entirely different. My war experiences proper were limited to one day, for a Boche plane dropped a stray bomb while we were going up into the line, and I stopped a 'blighty' which ended my war service.

I had found it possible to kill Brandt because my hate drove me on. But a murder does not end with the killing; the greatest strain for the murderer comes after.

I forced myself to go back towards the house, but knew that I could not face Blake in Brandt's study. I sent up a message to say that I was going home, and asked Blake to keep Firth posted as a favour to me. But I did not drive straight back to Baker Street. There was only one person living who could steady my nerves and give me the courage to go on, so I drove out of London until I came to a large house standing by itself in large grounds beyond the village of Crowthorne, in Berkshire.

Many of the local residents consider this place an eyesore, and write to the papers about it. It resembles a barracks, and was once one of H.M.'s prisons. It is huge and gaunt and ugly, built of glaring red brick which shows no intention of ever toning down to a respectable colour, and stood empty for a long time before the doctor decided that it would just suit his purpose.

There were lights in some of the windows as I approached, and two men were on duty at the studded door in the thick, high wall—protected along the top with glass and iron spikes—which surrounds the house.

The men were sharp-eyed and strongly built, and the one who came to meet me held a heavy stick in one muscular hand, and a lamp in the other.

'What d'you want?' he asked suspiciously, peering at me as he held the lamp so that its light clearly illuminated my face.

'I must speak to the doctor,' I replied, trying to conceal my agitation. 'You recognise me? I've been to see him before.'

The man studied me, and shook his head.

'Maybe I recognise you,' he replied. 'Maybe I don't. But it's long past midnight.'

'I know that; but I must see him,' I insisted.

The man hesitated, his hand noticeably tensing on his stick. Then his mate called to him, and they conferred together.

'You can talk to him on the phone in the lodge,' I was told a few moments later. 'But make it short.'

I took up the receiver eagerly, and heard the cold, passionless voice which belonged to the man on whom depended so much.

'What is it?' he demanded icily. 'What do you want here?'

'I just want to know—' I began to stammer.

'I've no time for people who just "want to know" at this time of night!' came the angry reply. 'Listen, King—I've told you before that you must not come here unless you want to spoil all chance of success! I don't hold myself responsible for what happens, if you won't obey my rules. I know you're worried. Go away, and stay away—get some sleep—and leave the rest to me.'

The phone went abruptly silent as the receiver was put up at the other end. I hesitated; but knew that to try to force my way in to see him would merely wreck every hope that I had. So I returned to the car, and began to drive away.

'Good-evening, Mr King—or should I say "morning"?' murmured a quiet voice from behind me. 'No, don't stop, and don't look back. You're surprised to find that you haf a passenger in your car now, but I must ask you to drive me where I tell you to go.'

'I don't understand,' I protested. 'Who are you? What are you doing in my car?'

'That's of no importance at the moment,' was the reply. 'I am just a friend to you—at present! I haf the pleasure of taking you to see some lost property of yours.'

'Lost property?'

'Yes, Mr King—just a leedle box that you haf left in Brandt's garden when you went there to murder him!'

The gasp that came to my lips was stifled, but I know I must have jerked at the wheel.

'You're crazy,' I accused. 'I grant you you've got my name right, but otherwise I haven't the vaguest what you're talking about. In fact'—I rammed on the brakes and drew up at the roadside—'it's my turn to ask a question—how do you know that Brandt's dead?'

I reached into the pocket on the door for the gun that I kept there.

'I haf your gun, Mr King; I borrowed him from the pocket,' was the calm statement of my mysterious passenger. 'What were you about to do with it?'

'Capture you, you crazy lunatic,' I replied, with a harsh laugh, 'and take you to the police to explain how you come to know that Brandt is dead.'

'That would be very interesting, my friendt—for the police, but very painful for you,' was the cool retort. 'For I would haf to tell them that I witnessed the murder from the moment that the murderer climbed the wall into the garden, Mr King.'

'And what were you doing in Brandt's garden?'

'Waiting to haf the chance to kill him, Mr King—but I would not tell that to the police!'

I had turned round in the seat to face him, and as he spoke I flipped on the dashboard light, and the reflection showed me a long, pale face, almost expressionless, inexpressibly grim and cruel. The faint light was also reflected on the metal of the gun.

'Don't you think it dangerous to make a confession like that to me?' I asked.

'No—not to you, Mr King. I haf to congratulate you on the ingenuity of your methods. Mine would have been more ordinary.'

I turned back to the wheel, deliberately ignoring the gun, for I realised that this man was not depending on that weapon, except for defence should I make an attack on him.

'I'm going to drive to Brandt's house,' I announced, 'and we'll see what Mr Sexton Blake has to say about you.'

The laugh that came from behind me was full of real enjoyment.

'I haf always heard that you are a grand poker player, Mr King,' chuckled the voice, 'but we do not play poker now, so we will forget the bluff, if you please. I would not carry out your threat, if I were you, because your life should be a long and happy one if you only play your cards well now. But you are not an experienced player at this new game, which is harder than poker, and you will haf much difficulty if you try to depend only upon bluff. You need to haf good cards in your hand, and I fear that you haf too few of them at present. I haf the aces, and I fear that Sexton Blake is collecting the kings—'

There was a pause, while I thought rapidly. Once again I realised the truth that one killing breeds many.

'You led well,' continued the suave, soft voice, distorted by the foreign accent, 'but you need experience, for I haf killed many men. My methods haf not been so ingenious as yours, but I haf never been brought so close to the hangman's noose as you are drawing now, my friendt. I am offering you myself as a partner, because no one must know *why* Brandt died!'

I swung round, my foot once more hard on the brake.

'And you know?' I asked.

'Yes, of course.'

His reply convinced me of the truth, so that now there were two reasons why this man must follow Brandt. But first I must use him, for he spoke the truth when he said that I lacked experience in the playing of my hand. Blake still had to be disposed of. This man, with his boasted experience, might be able to do that job for me—then I could attend to him, as I had to Brandt.

'What's your name?' I asked curtly.

'Stein,' he replied. 'At your service, Mr King.'

'Good! Well, I'm forgetting the bluff, Stein!' I snapped. 'I have already misplayed my hand. I deliberately brought Sexton Blake in on this case, and—to use your words—he has already started to collect kings. Do you know Blake?'

'I do—too well! And I haf a great hate for him.'

'Splendid! Now we will be able to attend to him. Tell me where to drive to, so that we can talk.'

*　　*　　*

171

'So Blake has already trumped your first cards, and spoiled all your ingenious arrangements, Mr King? Belief me when I say that that is very, very unfortunate.'

We were in a bed-sitting-room at a Bloomsbury lodging-house, and Stein had been restlessly pacing the faded linoleum while I described what Blake had already done on the Brandt case. The box that I had left in the garden was standing on the table, where Stein had placed it for me to see.

Viewed in the light, the man looked like a seedy professor of languages at some small school. He was the typical down-at-heel foreign teacher in his rusty black suit and dubious linen. But the drinks and smokes that he gave me were of quality only found in the homes of the wealthy, or the spend-thrift, and the exquisite glasses that we drank from would have graced a collector's cabinet. Undoubtedly a man of mystery. Besides, a teacher of languages does not usually have a submachine-gun and ammunition in a suitcase in his cupboard.

'We must dispose of Blake,' he continued abruptly. 'It is the first thing we haf to do. To bring him against us was a very foolish mistake, my friendt, for you have over-estimated your own powers, and sadly under-estimated his, which is fatal. This is where you need me, with the perfect organisation that I haf formed to deal with such matters.'

He went out into the hall of the boarding-house and telephoned to a friend, whom he called Carl.

'I haf a friend mit me in my room,' he announced loudly for the whole hotel to hear. 'He is such a one as it would afford pleasure to you to meet, and I wish him to meet some of my young country-men, for he is a journalist for the English journals. Yes, bring Max mit you, Carl, and we can play a little game of cards while we haf our talk. It will be very, very interesting for all of us.'

He came back to where I waited in the room, and I helped him to open up a folding card-table, and to place the cards and ash-trays in readiness. The reason for this preparation was evident when a knock on the door heralded the appearance of the landlady herself, admitting Stein's guests in person, that she might satisfy her curiosity.

Stein was fulsomely, Continentally polite, and introduced me by a name that wasn't my own, as a representative of a paper that I would have scorned to be connected with. I could not help being amused at the play-acting, even though I knew the motives behind it to be so desperate. I found it hard to persuade myself that I was not living through a crazy nightmare, for anything less like desperate criminals than this untidy, effusive little professor, and the two gawky, grinning foreign students, Carl and Max, would have been hard to find. They were large youths in the early twenties, with close-cropped hair, square heads, and strong, youthful hands. Only their eyes betrayed them, after the landlady had gone, for they were the eyes of hard and desperate men, watchful and bitter.

Stein seated himself at the table, and began to deal the cards. Watching his facile fingers, and the way the cards slipped through them, I decided that I would hate to play a game with him for any stake. He wasted no time on explanations, but launched straight into his plans, speaking briskly and brusquely, and not waiting for comments. He was evidently the leader, and a clever one, which made it all the more necessary for me to send him shortly to follow Brandt.

'Our friendt here,' he rapped curtly, pointing to me, 'has Sexton Blake's confidence. He will be with Blake at Tonio's within two hours from now. Tonio's never closes before seven o'clock in the morning, so we haf plenty of time. When our friendt'—another nod in my direction—'drops his pipe, you, Carl, will start something over by the orchestra—a fight, a row, a commotion; I leave the detail to you. You will arrange it that the fight spreads while you, Max, will extinguish the light from the main switch, and call "Police!". The rest you may leave to me, but I can promise that when the light is switched on again, both Blake and our friendt will haf gone from sight at Tonio's! Is that clear to you?'

Carl and Max threw down their cards that they had taken up, and rose silently to take their departure. But Stein repeated his orders with fuller details to each separately, while I sat and watched. During the entire interview I never opened my mouth once the introductions were ended; nor did Carl and Max. Stein did the talking; the others were to do the work.

'Now for you, King,' he said sharply, the moment that the door had closed behind the other two. 'The next move is yours. I have the story that you must tell to Blake, so that you may bring him quick to Tonio's, where we can deal with him.'

He laughed as he filled our glasses again.

'Blake's hours are numbered!' he boasted; and I kept my eyes on my glass, for fear that they would betray to him my determination that he himself must immediately follow Blake.

*　　*　　*

'Is that you, Blake?'

I was relieved when I heard the familiar voice reply in the affirmative, for I had scarcely expected to find him at Baker Street.

'I'm speaking from a call-box at Victoria,' I went on. 'After leaving you I did some sleuthing on my own. I didn't mean to—I'd had enough before I left the house!—but the job was forced on me. I was driving away in my car when I almost ran down a man who plunged recklessly across the road immediately in front of me. He didn't even stop to curse me, which was queer enough. But that isn't all; I saw him clearly in the light from my headlamps, and I was startled to recognise that fellow Adams—Brandt's butler!

'And yet, on rapidly thinking it over,' I went on, 'I was convinced that this could not be Adams, for I had left him in the hall only a moment before, still dressed in his butler's kit, and more than a little blotto. This fellow was wearing a grey suit, and wouldn't have been able to avoid my wheels if he hadn't had all his wits about him.'

'What did you do?' interrupted Blake's voice.

'Followed him,' I replied. 'You can call it journalistic instinct, or just plain curiosity, but I scented something unusual. Here was this chap, the dead spit of Brandt's butler, right outside the house in which Brandt had been killed.

'Adams' story had not rung true to my ears,' I continued rashly. 'He had seemed to hesitate too much. Besides—that point about the violin, Blake—Adams was the first to find the body, and it struck me when I saw this man so like Adams, that the butler may have had some reason to take that violin up after finding the body, and then deny having done so. I can't explain what I mean—it's just a hunch.'

'What about this man you followed, Matt?' broke in Blake.

'I managed to trail him down this way,' I replied, 'and I'm on a hot trail. He's in a night club in Milk Street, near here, a doubtful sort of place called Tonio's. With him are a couple of tough-looking customers, and they are taking exceptional pains to talk without being overheard. Seen closer, my quarry looks like some race tout, but the resemblance to Adams is there—a striking resemblance. I may be making a fool mistake, Blake, but I don't think so. I believe I'm on to a valuable clue for you.'

'Tonio's night club in Milk Street, S.W.1?' rapped Blake's eager voice. 'Hang on there, Matt, and I'll be right along. I know Tonio's, and will meet you just inside the door to the dance-room. If your man leaves before I come, follow him, and get in touch with me again later at Scotland Yard, for I'll go straight on there if I don't find you at Tonio's. And, Matt—watch your step! Tonio's is a bad dive, and you're playing a dangerous game.'

'I'll be all right,' I protested.

'Probably,' came the curt reply; 'but I know Tonio's, and the people who run it, I'd rather go unarmed against a herd of African cannibals than say, or do, the wrong thing in Tonio's. The etiquette is very strict; and, Matt'—again Blake's voice prevented me from putting up the receiver—'look out for a little man with a bald head, very white face, thick glasses. He's the power behind Tonio. His name's Stein, and he's as deadly as a snake.'

I hung up the receiver, and turned to where Stein was waiting by the door of the call-box.

'Well?' he asked.

'OK! He'll be there,' I replied shortly. 'You'd better take me to Tonio's at once.'

*　　*　　*

Milk Street, Pimlico, is a blot on London's reputation. In the spacious days of the past century it was a select residential street, where solidly respectable families stayed while in town. There is a mews at the back where they kept their horses and carriages, and which is now turned into flats by people of distinctly doubtful reputations, many of whom are of foreign extraction and would hide a fugitive from justice for the simple principle of defying all law and order.

Numbers of night clubs have sprung up in London since the days of the War; their numbers fluctuate, and some of them are as respectable as a vestry meeting; but the dives down Milk Street are not classed as night clubs by the authorities—they are better known as plague-spots, the haunts of the worst of London's life

175

after dark.

Tonio's is the only elaborate place in the street. It is the only one to have the name in electric lights over the door and a uniformed commissionaire. This commissionaire knows most of the detectives at Scotland Yard by their Christian names, and has also an intimate knowledge of the cells of a number of H.M. prisons. What I did not discover until later is that he is on the payroll of Scotland Yard, where he is rated as a detective-sergeant (special service branch), and was formerly a prison warder.

He studied me curiously when I reached the entrance, but Stein had telephoned a few words to the right quarter, and I was admitted immediately.

'There's a rough bunch in there, Mr King,' murmured the commissionaire, to my surprise. 'Sure, I know yer; I reads yer stuff. If you've come to see a scrap down this way, the boys won't disappoint yer—they're spoiling for a dust-up, or I don't know nothing. You'll see some pretty fighting. You jus' watch young 'Arry Greene, the 'ead barman, lay about 'im wiv a bottle—pretty work that!'

'I won't be here long,' I explained. 'Just popped in to collect a friend.'

'O' course! I remember now as I saw 'im go in,' was the startling reply. ''Oi, Bill! Go 'nd tell young Mr Mason as 'is nurse 'as come for 'im.'

Before I could interfere, the man addressed disappeared through the door, to return a moment later with Dicky Mason, of the 'Telegram', the youngster that I had left to cover the Jacobs-Bates fight for me, and about the last man that I wanted to see. He was decidedly dishevelled, and distinctly 'happy'.

'What are you doing here, Dicky?' I demanded, while he gratefully shook hands with the commissionaire and the man called Bill.

'Fight over,' he replied briefly. 'Exit Bates, third round—knock-out. Pubs shut. Thirst. Evil companions suggest Tonio's. Dicky falls. Comes to see wicked criminal in his native haunts, and, behold, he finds Matt King—shocking!'

'Who else is here?' I insisted.

'Nobody,' declared Dicky, 'except McCall, of the "Meteor", who brought me here, and Jones, and Wilkes, and Poole, and

Riley, and—'

'Half the Fleet Street crowd,' I concluded for him. 'What's brought them here?'

'Thirst,' was the laconic reply. 'Same as has brought you, I take it.'

'You're a poor liar, Dicky,' I retorted. 'What are you holding out on me? After me giving you your big chance tonight, too—'

'Joke ruined,' decided Dicky sadly. 'Better nature prevails. If you want to know, you big fish, this place is going to be raided tonight—the biggest raid in the history of London after dark—and I wanted to see you nabbed and taken before the beak!'

'What time is this raid due?' I cut in fiercely, realising how it interfered with my plans.

'The Home Secretary was not communicative,' replied Dicky. 'He said, said he: "After I have made you Commissioner of Police, Mr Mason, I may take you fully into my confidence. Until then, there's the door—use it!" '

A thought evidently struck Dicky, for he eyed me suspiciously.

'What are you doing here, anyway?' he demanded. 'I thought you were spending a night with the nobs. What did you and Blake leave the fight for?'

'Work,' I retorted. 'Connected with murders—nasty things that you must never get mixed up with, my lad.'

'I still don't understand,' he protested. 'Who've you been murdering?'

'Brandt.'

'What! The Happidol millionaire? Goo' lord, who killed him?'

'I've just told you—I did.'

'Funny, aren't you?' snorted Dicky. 'What are you doing at Tonio's, anyway?'

'I've come to split up with my confederates,' I told him cheerfully. 'Here comes one of 'em now.'

'My hat, it's Blake!' exclaimed Dicky. 'This is where I beat it. But I wish I knew what was happening.'

'Read the "Telegram",' I called after him. 'And, Dicky, do Blake and me a favour—get the other blokes away on some false scent. The game Blake and I are sitting into is not for publication!'

As I turned to meet Blake I caught a fleeting glimpse of Carl by the orchestra, and Dicky Mason almost cannoned into Max.

Blake had pulled a heavy coat over his evening kit, but was otherwise just as I had left him at Brandt's. He made no effort to remove his hat, but stepped on to the dance floor, with his hands deep in his overcoat pockets. Dancing had been in full swing up to that moment, but it seemed to waver as many recognised the detective. I was amused to note a number of girls left in the middle of the floor, while their partners sought more secluded places.

'What's Blake want here?' growled a man not far from me. 'Just like his cheek to come walking in alone with his hands in his pockets! He'll get what he asks for one day.'

'He always does,' retorted another, 'and those who try to interfere with him get more than they want! But there's no one here tonight—'

The voice trailed off, as Blake began to walk slowly across the dance floor. I followed him, close to his heels.

'Where's this man of yours, Matt?' he asked abruptly, in a whisper that reached no further than my ears.'

'Over there,' I began, making a natural gesture with my pipe. But I was clumsy, and the pipe dropped from my fingers to fall to the floor.

'Don't point! It's dangerous in a place like this,' cautioned Blake.

But I was not attending to him. I was watching Carl.

Stein's men acted well. They did not immediately start their business, which might have betrayed the signal to so acute an observer as Blake. Quite an appreciable minute was allowed to pass between the clatter of my pipe on the floor and the start of the commotion in a distant corner.

Then, out of the corner of my eye, I saw Carl lurch against a gaudily dressed girl, who promptly responded by slapping his face hard. Carl so far forgot himself as to push the lady against the leader of the orchestra, whereupon a tall man seized hold of Carl and threw him into the drum.

This was the signal for the room to divide itself into two camps, supporters of Carl flinging themselves at the followers of the tall man. Dicky Mason had not done what I asked, for I caught sight of him in the middle of the fight, together with a number of other reporters, thoroughly enjoying the scrap.

'This is a put-up job—this scrap—' began Blake's voice close to me. 'Watch out, Matt!'

Even as he spoke every light in the room was abruptly extinguished, while the uproar rose to a crescendo effort.

'Stay by me! I think they're after us,' cautioned Blake's voice.

He started to say something else, but the words were cut off short. I forgot at that moment the part that I was playing, and began to lay viciously about me, one blow landing squarely home, and being rewarded by a grunt of pain.

'Help!' I bellowed at the full force of my lungs, suddenly realising how the presence of the Fleet Street men was going to help my plans. 'Help! Dicky! McCall! Poole! Riley! Help!'

'What-ho!' came Dicky's voice in reply, followed by another rush of scampering feet.

A thud caught me on the back of the head, and I decided to sink down under it.

A moment later the lights went on again, and I heard Carl's voice shouting for order.

'Hurt, Matt?' asked Dicky Mason, appearing at my side with the leg of a chair gripped in his hand.

'No,' I replied: 'nothing much. But—Blake? Where's Blake? He was alongside me—'

The struggle in the dark had left a good many figures spread out on the floor, and we turned each over in turn. But there was no sign of Blake. Then the same girl as the one involved in the start of the row gave a sudden scream, and pointed towards the orchestra.

The figure of a man lay there, flat on his back, with an ugly red stain spread over his white shirt-front. Dicky Mason and I reached him together, and one glance told us that he was dead.

'Blake,' I began—'Blake killed—like that! I can't stand more of this—'

I swung round towards the door to go out into the air, and I must have echoed Dicky's startled gasp—Blake was standing in the doorway, with Detective-Inspector Coutts beside him!

I looked back to the body.

'I'm afraid they got Sergeant Fellowes, Coutts,' interposed Blake's quiet, grave voice. 'I'm sorry I allowed him to impersonate me.'

*   *   *

179

With the realisation that I must act quickly, I crossed the floor at a run, and gripped Blake's hand.

'I thought it was you!' I stammered.

'You were meant to,' was the quiet reply; 'and, if I'd dreamed that they dare go so far as murder, it would have been me. Sergeant Fellowes is a married man.'

'Poor devil!' I muttered, joining Blake beside the victim. 'And I led him here, Blake—if it hadn't been for my hunch—'

'We'd never have got anything on Tonio's,' interposed Coutts' gruff voice. 'You don't want to feel too badly about it, King. I've lost a good man and a grand friend, but I intend that his death will not prove to have been in vain.'

He swung round and issued orders that no living person was to leave the hall.

'We know every exit—even your most secret ones—and I've men watching them,' he announced harshly. 'Someone is going to pay for this bit of work. Get against the walls; well away from that orchestra. Now, King'—he turned to me again—'let's hear how it started.'

I hesitated, trying to sort out a line of action, wondering how much I dare tell.

'Matt and this fellow, who we thought was Blake, were crossing the floor together,' interposed Dicky Mason rapidly, 'when a row started over by the band. One bloke lurched into another bloke's girl—there they are, over there—those are the two men, and the girl. The row started with them, and spread like wildfire until we were all in it. Of course, I realise now that it was staged.

'Anyway,' he went on, 'the lights went out next, and I heard Matt shouting for help, so I struggled over this way. When the lights went up Matt immediately began to hunt for Blake, and found—that!'

'And the man you brought me here to see, Matt,' interposed Blake's voice, with no trace of feeling in it. 'The man who so closely resembled Adams, Brandt's butler—where is he?'

I felt his eyes on me, and something warned me that he was suspicious.

'He was in here when the lights went out,' I replied. 'I—we were crossing towards him when the fight started.' I hesitated, scarcely able to believe my eyes as I looked towards the door. 'Why, there he is—by the door!' I cried.

'Why so surprised at seeing him here, Matt?' continued Blake coldly. 'Though, as a matter of fact, you're wrong—that man by the door is Adams himself. We brought him along to meet the commissionaire, who declares that he has never seen him before in his life, and swears that no man remotely resembling him has ever entered this club.

'Adams, come here a minute, will you?' added Blake, calling to the butler.

I watched like a man in a daze as Blake led the butler round in front of the startled crowd.

'None of you ever seen anyone resembling him?' he repeated, as they all shook their heads. 'Of course, I know that most of you lie from habit, but we won't quarrel over that now. Where's Adam's twin brother in the grey suit, Matt?'

'He must have got out, Blake.'

'He can't have got far, for we have every exit guarded.'

'Well, then,' an inspiration came to save me—'he might have altered his appearance.'

'That's what I think; that's what must have happened,' agreed Coutts.

'Possible,' agreed Blake, his eyes making me hate him as they bored into me. I knew that, for some reason, he had begun to doubt me, and that it must now be a fight to the finish between us.

'Fellowes was stabbed with a long-bladed knife,' went on Blake. 'Whoever stabbed him must have got some blood on their hands. We'll go round and look for ourselves.'

I followed the two detectives along the line of sullen, angry people.

'What's that red on your cuff?' Blake stopped before Carl and pointed.

'Blood—his,' was the curt reply, and Carl indicated the tall man, whose nose showed ample evidence of having bled profusely.

'Really? Give me that cuff,' ordered the detective. 'And, Coutts, on Mason's evidence, you can hold these two, and the girl, for starting the disturbance in here.'

Carl protested, but was led aside by Scotland Yard men, one of whom coolly cut the blood-stained cuff from his coat with a pen-knife. Carl scowled at me, and I realised that he was blaming me for the fatal mistake that had been made.

'I don't seem to be very popular,' I told Coutts, who was beside me. 'I suppose they realise that it was me who brought you here.'

'Good work,' replied the inspector. 'We've long wanted an excuse to clean this place up. My only regret is that we haven't got Stein; but he never shows up.'

'Who is Stein?' I asked. 'Blake mentioned him over the phone.'

'Nominal boss of the worst dope gang we've had operating here for years,' was the reply. 'We don't know much about them yet; we can't trace the man behind Stein, the source of the dope, or the way they distribute it; but we'll clean 'em up yet. Rumour has it that a woman is the moving force.'

'Why don't you arrest Stein?'

'The usual reason—he'd simply be replaced. It's the man who can't be replaced, the brain behind the organisation, that we're waiting for. Besides, he's too cute to have given us a shred of proof—yet.'

It was broad daylight before Blake and Coutts finished at Tonio's. They examined, and cross-examined, everybody, and searched the building over and over again. Then they held a council-of-war.

'What's the connection between this murder and the killing of Brandt?' asked Coutts. 'Is there one?'

'There is,' replied Blake. 'There's Matt King's quarry—Adams' double, whom King trailed here. That brought us here, and caused Fellowes' death. Matt, let's have your story over again.'

I repeated what I had said over the phone, choosing each word with care, aware all the time that two of the acutest brains in England were weighing it up.

'Was he hard to trail?' asked Coutts.

'Not very,' I risked. 'He had a car round the corner, not far from Brandt's place, into which he got, and I trailed the car down to here.'

'What was the number?'

'It was obscured.'

'And he got across London with an obscured number-plate? H'm!' Coutts made a note in his book, and underlined it.

'Was he alone in the car?' he continued.

'No; there was someone else at the wheel,' I replied, forcing myself to appear unmoved under Blake's unwinking stare.

'Did they come into Tonio's with him?'

'No; they just dropped him and drove away. I followed my man in here.'

'Past the commissionaire?' interjected Blake.

'No; now that I come to think of it, he was not at the door at that moment,' I declared. 'I didn't see the commissionaire until I came back, after telephoning to you, Blake.'

'Whom did you see? Who admitted you to the club?'

I pointed to Max, whom I understood to be the secretary, and he confirmed what I had said. But the commissionaire remained rock-like in his assertion that he had never left his post, and had never seen a man resembling Adams. It was at that moment that Blake quietly told me that the commissionaire was a detective-sergeant from Scotland Yard.

'You might drive me home, Matt,' suggested Blake, when he at last left Tonio's. 'I'm still without my car.'

This time I had no wish to have him with me, but I could not refuse him. I wanted to get away somewhere, to try to get into touch with Stein, to consider my next move. My nerves were shredded by repeated shocks and the need for sleep. A journey with Blake beside me in the car, watching me, asking his deadly questions, must be the last, ghastly ordeal to round off the night.

'Well, what do you think of your first active contact with murder?' he asked abruptly, as I turned out of Milk Street.

'Ghastly!' I replied truthfully. 'I wish I'd remained in my seat at the ISC.'

'Why didn't you?'

'Curiosity,' I replied. 'Call it a hunch.'

'And another hunch persuaded you to follow the man you saw near Brandt's,' he continued inexorably. 'Tell me when you feel another hunch coming, and I'll put on my bullet-proof waistcoat.'

'What actually do you mean by that, Blake?' I demanded irritably.

'A joke,' he answered. But I turned towards him and saw that there was no smile in evidence.

'After all, if everything had gone according to plan, Matt, I should have been doing this journey in a hearse, and I reason that that hearse is still waiting for me.'

'You think they'll try to get you again?' I asked.

'You know they will,' he replied shortly. 'Anyone who is not a fool must realise that,' he added.

'What made you send Fellowes to keep the appointment with me?' I asked.

'A hunch.' Blake laughed curtly as he replied. 'You're not the only one who gets hunches, Matt. Besides, I make it a rule to seldom do what is expected of me—I prolong my life that way! Tonight I was expected to turn up at Tonio's and meet you. Instead, I turned up at Tonio's to witness "my" meeting with you. Maybe I had a hunch, Matt, that it was a little too much of a coincidence that you should find a man resembling Adams waiting outside the house to lead you to Brandt's; I don't like coincidences, they look too much like prearranged trails. But I wish my hunch had warned me of the extent to which the enemy were going to go. As it is, I feel responsible for Fellowes' death.'

'Tell me when you feel another hunch coming, Blake,' I interrupted sharply, repeating his own words to me, and adding: 'If I'd known that you had a hunch there was something crooked about the trail that took me to Tonio's, we might have saved Fellowes' life. And, look here, I seem to be in this game fully now, and I want to stay in—to work with you—for I, also, feel responsible for that man's death, and must do my bit to avenge it.'

'Quite so,' agreed Blake. 'You were responsible, though you never intended Fellowes' (to my ears there was a hint of emphasis on the name) 'to die. I'm going to keep in touch with you until this case is ended. One more question I want to ask you. Exactly what route did your quarry's car take from Brandt's to Tonio's?'

I told him, choosing the route that I myself would have taken in similar circumstances.

'And did you happen to notice, Matt'—Blake's voice was very soft, and sleepy—'whether they still had part of Calvin Hill Road up?'

I hesitated, for I had not been along Calvin Hill Road for weeks.

'I can't say that I exactly noticed,' I replied, fearing a trap and yet knowing that I must risk a direct reply. 'No; I don't think they did. I don't remember seeing any red lights, or anything like that.'

'Ah! Goodnight, Matt,' was all that Blake said, as he climbed out at his chambers. 'Get some sleep now.'

But I did not go straight home. That last question troubled me, so I drove first to Calvin Hill Road. To my relief I saw that there were no traces of the road being up, but, as I was turning back, a taxi slowed up beside me, and Blake's head appeared in the window.

'You were quite correct, Matt,' he called; 'but I advised you to get some sleep!'

*　　*　　*

I went to my flat, but knew that I could not sleep. I must get in touch with Stein first. Every minute, every fresh happening, made it the more necessary for Blake to be put where he could do no harm. But he mustn't be killed. There had been enough killings—one too many!—as it was. There was only to be one more murder—Stein! And that not until Blake had been put where he could do no harm until my work was ended.

I was considering how to get in touch with Stein when the front door bell rang. I remembered that my man was out marketing, for I was usually at work at this time of day, so I went to the door myself. Whoever it was must be put off quickly, for I must go to the Bloomsbury lodging-house myself to find Stein.

'Hallo, Mr King! Still up? The guv'nor sent me over to keep an eye on you. I've brought my pyjamas and toothbrush, as he thinks I'd better camp in the house.'

I stared at Tinker, seeing nothing of his radiantly healthy young face, his broad, friendly smile, or the vivid pyjamas that he was gaily waving under my nose. I only saw him as a menace—something watchful and quick-eared, come to be always near me—a spy to wreck my plans!

'I don't understand what you mean,' I said harshly. 'Why should your master send you to watch me? What have I done?'

'Gosh! The old nerves aren't too good, are they?' he exclaimed, his eyes on the cigarette quivering between my fingers. 'Of course, a chap would be touchy after all that happened to you last night—two murders, and all that! Buck up, Mr King; I'm here to help you! You see, the guv'nor's worried about you. You made bad enemies at Tonio's by getting the police in, and—well, he thinks it will be just as well for you and me to become the Siamese twins for a bit.'

He worked his way in through the door and threw his pyjamas on to the first chair.

'If you ask me, it's going to be a colossal lark,' he declared. 'Next to my own job, I'd like to be a newspaperman, and the guv'nor says you want to take a hand at our game, so I'll pop round on your stories with you, and you can pop round on my business for the guv'nor with me.'

'And I'll tell you something else—' As he talked, he began to make himself at home, inspecting the contents of the sideboard, and hanging up his coat and hat. 'I've always wanted to have a scrap with you, and we might improve our early mornings—when we aren't on all-night jobs—putting on the gloves. What say, Mr King?'

I struggled for control, aware that nothing but some diabolical inspiration could help me in the playing of my cards now. I saw the challenge that Blake was throwing out to me, and could not help admiring the way in which Tinker played his part. If Blake suspected the real truth, this lad must know that he had been sent to live with a murderer—a man who already had two deaths on his guilty conscience. If I refused to have Tinker in the house, Blake would want to know why. That question would lead to others, and an increase of suspicion.

'It's absurd, Tinker,' I found myself saying. 'Blake's an old grandmother! Hang it, young 'un, I can take care of myself. Why should all your normal way of living be messed up? Mine's not the sort of house for a guest—I'm hardly ever home.'

'Suits me fine, Mr King,' interrupted Tinker cheerfully. 'I'm all for a roving life. Where do we go now?'

Our glances met, and I sampled the steel behind the mask of boyish high-spirits. Tinker knew all that Blake had suspected, and would not let me out of his sight.

'I suppose I'd better have a sleep; I need it badly,' I declared. 'You make yourself comfortable in here. Afterwards, we'll go over and have a word with Blake, and make him realise that your time ought to be more valuable to him.'

'Sleep's the stunt for you,' agreed Tinker; 'but what a chance for any revengeful blokes to get at you! You go and have your snooze, and I'll get a book and sit in a corner of the bedroom. I'm a quiet reader; I'll not disturb you, Mr King.'

There's no doubt about it. Luck, or Fate—call it what you like—does take a part in everything. I was wondering desperately how I could get rid of Tinker, and get in touch with Stein, when Jennings returned from his shopping. He showed no surprise at finding me there, or at my visitor. I have never known Jennings show surprise at anything. His face is the placid mask of the perfect servant, and I have sometimes doubted if he has any private thoughts of his own.

'Good-morning, sir!' he welcomed me quietly. 'There was one phone message at nine o'clock this morning. The doctor rang up, sir.'

'The doctor!' I forgot Tinker's presence. 'What did he have to say?'

'Nothing, sir; not to me, sir; but he wants you to telephone him.'

'Wants me?'

I hesitated; then I saw my road clear.

'I must phone at once,' I told Tinker, who was watching me curiously. 'My wife is in hospital, and is not yet out of danger.'

'Your wife? Gosh, Mr King, I didn't know you were married!'

'Very few people do,' I replied quietly.

As I gave a number on the Museum exchange, I was well aware that Tinker was listening to me, and feeling very uncomfortable and hating himself for doing so. Both Blake and Tinker drew a rigid line between crime detection and the sort of petty spying out of which so many so-called private detectives make their livings; and Tinker has won world-wide popularity among all the varied types that his work has brought him in contact with because he is such a thorough-going, clean-living young sportsman. I could see that he detested the thought of spying on me while I inquired about my wife.

'Is Dr Schwarz in?' I asked. 'This is Mr King. Can I speak to Dr Schwarz now?'

'Oh, you mean the professor!' corrected a woman's voice from the other end. 'Hold on, and I'll call him.'

'Professor!'

A moment later, Stein's calm voice came to me. I was glad that Tinker's diffidence kept him at the other end of the room.

'What iss it, my friendt?' Stein asked. 'I regret that I can gif no more classes this week.'

'My wife?' I asked sharply. 'How is she? You said that you wanted me to phone you.'

We allowed a few moments to pass; then I spoke again.

'I'm glad,' I said. 'Though I wish you could be more definite. And, doctor, do something special for me—tell her not to fret about me. I know she's worrying about me being alone here. Tell her I'm not alone. By a strange chance, I have a friend staying in the flat with me; he's going to sleep here, not leave me at all; so she hasn't to worry about me being alone. She knows him by sight, I believe—Tinker, Mr Sexton Blake's assistant. Will you tell her that he's staying here with me?'

I heard Stein's startled exclamation before I turned from the phone. My hand was trembling, and there was a line of sweat along my forehead, for it had been a strain.

'Here, drink this, Mr King!' Tinker approached with a stiff whisky that he had mixed. 'It's rotten to have someone in hospital,' he added, 'and I hope everything turns out all right. I couldn't help hearing what you said, and—as Mrs King is worrying—I'm jolly glad the guv'nor did send me over here.'

I hated his saying that, because it made me realise the despicable hypocrite that I had been forced by circumstances to become.

'I'm going to have that snooze now,' I decided, forcing my mind to concentrate on my plans. 'Help yourself to a book. I'm not going to worry about bed; that couch looks good enough.'

Every minute that followed seemed an eternity. I lay with eyes half-closed, making a pretence of sleep, while I watched Tinker, who sat bowed over his book. What would Stein do? How would he work the game now? It was up to him; there was nothing more that I could do. I was dog-weary, physically and mentally, and—despite all my worries—must have dropped asleep.

I awoke to the knowledge that Tinker had moved. The book lay on the floor, where he had dropped it, and he was over by the door leading to the bedroom. He crouched rigid; his young face set in a grim mask; one hand in his jacket pocket. There was no hint of indecision, or nervousness, as he suddenly reached for the handle, and flung the door open.

'Got you, you beauty!' he cried exultantly, as he flung himself through the doorway.

I swung myself off the couch, as I heard two bodies crash to the floor together in the adjoining room. As I did so, the other door opened, and Jennings came running in.

'Jennings!' I called. 'Come here!'

'Yes, sir; but what—what's happening in the bedroom?'

He drew close to where I stood, his face for once showing agitation. I think some instinct warned him, for he hesitated when close to me.

'Mr King!'

I shall never be able to forget his white face, his horrified, startled eyes, the moment before I hit him; then my fist connected with his jaw, backed by all my experience, and he crumpled up at my feet.

'A beautiful blow, my friendt!' praised Stein's cold voice, and I turned to see him framed in the doorway of the bedroom, a gun in his hand. 'But who iss this man?'

'The best servant, and one of the best friends that any man could wish to have!' I replied hysterically. 'I thought that perhaps you were alone in there, and that he was better out of things before he intruded.'

'Perhaps you were right,' agreed Stein; 'and now we must take him away with the young one, or else he may say who haf hit him.'

'You got Tinker?'

'Of course, my friendt. But he was a fury,' snarled Stein. 'It is no young boy, that one; it is a demon, and a giant, who haf the strength of a hondred! He haf broken one man's jaw, and it haf taken three strong men to put him quiet. But now he iss quiet, and—we go. You play your part carefully this time, and we get Blake.'

I watched them go from the room, carrying Tinker and Jennings.

'There's a servants' staircase, and a way out the back,' I suggested.

'I know—I haf found it. And I haf a big laundry basket waiting, and a van. Always I play my hands well, to the last detail. You do the same this time, my friendt.'

As he spoke he placed a small white capsule beside the glass in which Tinker had given me that whisky.

I took another drink, and dissolved the capsule in it. Stein certainly knew his job, for I barely had time to get back on to the couch before I seemed to drop into a black pit, soundless except for a regular throbbing, like the beat of a ship's engines, which experience of anaesthetics told me was the beating of my own heart. Then even that sound ceased as I passed into absolute unconsciousness.

Blake found me. I don't know how long he was in the room before I recovered; I never learnt what brought him there, except, perhaps, some failure on Tinker's part to report; but he was shaking me when I at last came out of the mists that had closed me in.

'Don't look so surprised, Matt,' he said, in his quiet, level tones. 'You've been drugged. Here's the glass on the floor, where I saw it when I first came into the room. Whisky, by the smell, and a little analysis will soon tell us what knock-out drops were added to it. Who mixed the drinks for you?'

'Tinker.'

'Are you quite sure? He never mixes them that way for me! Where is Tinker?'

'Why, reading a book—'

'Really? Where? And how do you know he's reading a book, when he's nowhere in sight?'

I forced myself to sit up and to look wildly about me. Blake worried me, for there was a note of steel behind the almost jocular tone of his voice, and I could not understand the grim smile at the corners of his mouth.

'Tinker was here a minute ago,' I insisted. 'He took a book; was sitting there reading when I went to sleep.'

'Do you remember going to sleep?' pressed Blake.

'Why, yes—of course.'

'What did you do?'

I stared at him, dreading the trap, yet powerless to avoid it.

'Just spread myself out, of course, and—er—went to sleep,' I said slowly.

'And the glass—did you throw that on the floor when you "just spread yourself out and—er—went to sleep"?'

'No, of course not. I put it on the table—over there.'

'Empty?'

Before answering, I tried to see the glass, but Blake's knee was in the way.

'No,' I risked; 'I left some in it. Someone must have knocked it off the table on to the floor.'

'Quite so,' agreed Blake; 'and emptied it on the way, for there's not a drop stained the carpet. There was nothing in that glass when it reached the floor, Matt!'

Curse the man! Nothing but an abnormal brain could cope with each small yet deadly point that he registered so easily, and I realised that he must be counting up his score. I told him that I must have been mistaken; that I must have emptied the glass before putting it down; that my head was muzzy as a result of the drug.

'Where's Tinker?' I repeated.

'There's been a fight in your bedroom,' he replied; 'and that must be when they got Tinker. You weren't mixed up in the fight, were you, Matt?'

'No; it must have happened while I was asleep,' I replied.

'Quite so,' agreed Blake again; 'and you must fight in your sleep, Matt.'

In the same quiet way, he pointed to my newly scraped knuckles, where they had connected with Jennings' chin. I knew that it would be no use telling him that the mark was a memory of the fight at Tonio's, because he had been with me after that scrap, and his eyes undoubtedly missed nothing.

* * *

Blake went through my flat with a speed and thoroughness that left me breathless as I trailed after him. Into such details as the angle at which a chair had fallen in the bedroom, almost invisible marks on the window-sill, and on the sill of an adjoining room, which opened into the back corridor, he read deep meanings, tracing the route that the raiders had come by, and much of their actions on arrival in the room.

'Tinker probably heard them moving. He's a reckless youngster at times,' he explained, 'and must have decided to tackle them single-handed. He got one of them down there—broke that chair in the effort. There must have been more than two of them, and one onlooker.'

'One onlooker?' I asked.

'Yes—a man who needs everlasting cigarettes to steady his nerves, and who sprinkled a neat pile of ash on the carpet by the bed while he stood there to watch how the fight was going to go.'

I remembered that Stein had smoked during most of our meeting the previous night, lighting one expensive cigarette from the stub of the last, but was startled when Blake continued:

'Stein always has smoked too many cigarettes. It'll be the death of him—a nasty death at the end of a rope—if he leaves ash about like this. Stein's a nasty customer, Matt,' he went on coolly. 'I heard Coutts telling you something about him. The trouble is that I know all about Stein—and have for a long time—but can prove nothing.'

'Coutts said he was mixed up with some dope-smuggling,' I risked.

'Yes, some big organisation spreading a new and deadly drug. I've been after them for a long time, and—I'm very near the truth, Matt.'

'Coutts mentioned a woman—'

'He was right. The power behind this gang is either a woman, or'—it seemed to my strained nerves that he hesitated, and that his eyes were not so steely as they studied me—'works through some unfortunate woman.'

It was my turn to hesitate, and Blake gave me plenty of time; but I turned to the door.

'My servant, Jennings, should be in the flat somewhere,' I said. 'Surely he must have heard something of this fight?'

'Perhaps he did,' assented Blake; 'and either ran away or tried to butt in, and was put to join Tinker. That depends on what sort of a man he is! What I want to know is what they've done with Tinker? And why?'

He began to search again, trying to discover the methods used by the raiders to remove Tinker. An examination of the windows again evidently convinced him that they had not gone that way.

'There are some back stairs, leading into a yard,' I suggested, and had to almost run to keep up with him as he burst from the flat. In the yard, immediately outside the back door, a man in blue overalls was meddling with the cover over a watermain. (Stein is undoubtedly a miracle at putting a job over to the last detail!)

'Seen anybody come out of this door recently?' asked Blake.

'Yes, mister—t'ousands of folks. The steps is quite wore away wiv the passage of countless feet throughout the ages.'

'I said "recently",' reminded Blake.

'To them wot reads 'istory as much as I do a fousand years is recent,' was the astonishing reply. 'King 'Enery the Eighth might 'ave come through that there door if it 'adn't been for the fact as this building ain't been up more'n five years, and King 'Enery's been dead five 'undred! If you means this morning, the only blokes wot as used that door since I been 'ere was the laundrymen.'

'With a very big laundry basket? Very heavy, so that it needed more than one man to carry it?' suggested Blake.

'Why ask me when you knows already?'

'I didn't know, but great minds are startingly unoriginal,' replied the detective. 'What was the laundry?'

The man hesitated, and I have seldom seen a man look so obviously guilty while thinking up a lie.

'The Whiterway,' he said at last.

Blake studied him; then turned abruptly on his heel. I followed him back to the flat, to find him at the phone. He was speaking to someone at Scotland Yard. With a grim frown, he finished his conversation, and then went down to the porter in the main hall.

'A laundry van, sir?' exclaimed the porter. 'Why, of course, they came this morning and took some washing from Mr King's.'

'Did you see the van? What laundry was it?'

'The Quickwash, sir. I saw the van when it passed—'

Blake spun on his heel again.

'Scotland Yard told me that a Quickwash Laundry van was stolen this morning,' he snapped. 'Our friends organise things well, Matt; but now I want to know why that man out in the yard chose to lie to me.'

'Perhaps he's one of them—one of the gang, Blake, put there to spoil the trail for us,' I suggested. 'And, Blake, wouldn't it be a good idea to watch him? He might return to the gang to report.'

I was startled to hear Blake laugh.

'Very well, Matt,' he chuckled, 'we'll let him lead us! If he hasn't gone already. But—mark this—there's going to be big trouble for someone if any real harm has come to Tinker!'

The man had not gone, and I was faced with the problem of signalling to him to carry on. He was still meddling with the cover

193

over the drain. In desperation I suggested to Blake that we walk past him to give the impression that we were going to seek the trail of the laundry van.

'You're wasted as a sporting correspondent,' was Blake's reply. 'Lead on!'

We concealed ourselves in a doorway, which gave a good view of the exit from the yard, and were shortly rewarded by the sight of the man coming out and climbing on to a motor cycle combination, which was waiting for him.

Blake looked round quickly, but there was no taxi in sight. There was a tradesman's covered van, however, belonging to 'J. Wotherspoon, Baker,' the driver of which was nowhere in sight.

Before I could say anything, Blake had gripped my arm and hurried me to this van.

'Rather a noticeable vehicle to trail anyone in,' he grumbled, 'but it'll have to do. Sit still, Matt, and try to look like a baker's express-delivery man—very express, for I'm going to have to "step on it" to keep that motor cycle in sight!'

The van was a large one, but Blake took it through the traffic in a manner that made me hold by breath. The motor cycle had a long start and might slip out of sight at any minute, but Blake closed up the gap by an exhibition of inspired driving. We seemed to scrape the wings of other vehicles, and to slide through gaps that scarcely looked wide enough for a baby car. I had heard much of Blake's powers as a driver under unusual conditions, and he proved them to me then, while I was also struck by his aptitude for sinking his personality into any character.

The angle of his hat, his attitude over the wheel, the expression of his face, made him no longer Sexton Blake, but a superior member of the trading community driving a delivery van with the ease of long habit. A taxi-driver swore at us as we scraped past him, and Blake's reply was precisely what J. Wotherspoon would have said himself in the circumstances, action, gesture, words, all true to the character.

This drive was the first occasion to sort out my thoughts that I had had since the latest development. Of one thing I was determined—there was to be no more question of killing Blake. I was leading him into a trap again; once more I was playing a traitor to as staunch a friend as any man could wish for; but there must be no more murder—except Stein's, and I did not think of that as murder.

Stein must hold Blake and Tinker until my arrangements were complete, and I could slip away to a life of quiet happiness in a place where no one could find me, where I could forget this nightmare. My last move before going would be to kill Stein, which would free Blake—I laughed exultantly at the thought.

'Joke, Matt?' He looked at me quickly, only taking his eyes from his quarry for the barest instant.

'Only wondering what Cannan would say about the prestige of the "Telegram" if he could see me,' I improvised rapidly.

He made no reply, but his face was stern as he bent over the wheel. The hard smile that I had noticed before was no longer in evidence, and it struck me that he looked worried and tired; not physically tired—Blake is too finely trained to show fatigue until the last gasp—but he looked heart-weary and bitter. I thought of our long friendship, and how little we really knew one another. I had seen an unguessed-at Blake in the last eighteen hours, the man-tracking machine that his personal friends seldom came in contact with.

'There's going to be real trouble if any harm comes to Tinker,' he repeated abruptly; 'but I don't think they'd dare. It's me they want out of the way.'

'But it's Tinker they've taken,' I pointed out.

'As bait with which to get me,' was the curt reply.

'But, Blake, you don't mean—'

'I mean, Matt, that I've got a hunch—and, this time, I'm sending no impersonator to take the medicine.'

I stared at him. He knew, then, that he was going into a trap; and yet the grim smile was showing again at the corners of his mouth!

The motor cycle combination in front had increased speed slightly, and Blake also accelerated. Traffic was thinning, for we were leaving London behind us, but our quarry made no attempt to throw off pursuit, for which bit of carelessness I cursed him. Had Stein himself been piloting that machine he would have taken elaborate precautions, thrown out the screen of bluff at which he was such an adept. Once again Blake seemed to read my thoughts.

'He doesn't seem to mind being followed, does he?' he said quietly. 'Either he's perfectly innocent—just a workman going home to his wife—or—' He shrugged expressively.

'You think we're on a wild-goose chase?' I suggested.

'No,' he replied. 'Do you?'

'I hope not,' I confessed. 'I'm worried about Tinker.'

The suburbs gave place to the real country, and still the trail went on. The motor cycle led us from the main road down narrow, twisting lanes.

'The man's crazy,' began Blake; then his foot went down hard on the brake, and he wrenched the wheel over to stop with the wings against the hedge. We had swung round a sharp bend in a narrow lane, to find the motor cycle combination standing in the middle of the road and blocking the way. The man still sat in the saddle, but had turned to face us.

'What's the game, mates?' he called. 'Just follering me for fun, eh?'

I stared at him, scarcely able to believe my ears. What did this mean? I had understood—Blake suddenly slithered to the floor on top of the pedals, while, at the same moment, the windscreen was shattered.

I heard the unmistakable whine of a bullet past my head, and the thud of it against the van. Paralysed, I sat there. Men had appeared by the hedge—many men— and I saw the sun glint on gun-barrels.

I thought for a moment that Blake was dead, then felt him moving by my feet. Hatred of Stein and his methods filled me with sudden loathing. This was worse than murder—I remembered that I had a gun in my pocket, and dropped to the floor by Blake.

'What is it?' he whispered.

'Gunmen along the hedge. A hold-up.'

'My hunch!' he reminded. 'What are you going to do, Matt?'

'Fight back!' I snarled. 'I've got a gun. Listen, they're coming!'

'They'll come to the door my side,' he reasoned rapidly. 'We've got to get out by the other; get over that hedge; and shoot—keep on shooting—raise even this quiet countryside!'

I felt for the handle of the door. The men were drawing near. I had no time to consider what I was doing. My mind was filled with blind hatred of Stein.

I flung the door open at a whispered word from Blake, and hurled myself out. Blake arrived at my heels. I swung round, ready to shoot. Blake was already in action. Guns has appeared in both his hands, and two men lay in the road.

'Hold your fire! Over the hedge! Shoot from there—cover me!' he called.

I tore my way recklessly through the hedge; then turned to see that Blake was still in the road. His face was like chalk, horrible in its mask of white anger. This was still another Blake; one that few men ever saw—Blake roused to fury.

Stein had made up his mind to be sure of Blake this time, for there cannot have been less than ten men against us. Four were sprawled in the road, where Blake's bullets had put them; the others were still behind the hedge.

I saw that Blake was swaying slightly, and realised that he was hit. I had a seven-chambered revolver, and every bullet must count, for there were no more. I began to pick off my men with careful deliberation.

'Don't shoot to kill, Matt—just disable them!' Blake had found cover behind the van, and was speaking quietly from there. 'Maybe they've had enough already.' He turned to shout: 'Listen, if you throw your guns down in the road, we'll hold our fire!'

'Very nice, Mr Blake; very nice!' murmured Stein's voice from directly behind me. 'But I have a machine-gun here, and you are too wise a man to argue with that.'

I swung round, and saw that the words were true. Stein was there, looking the simple-seeming professor, as usual, but with the tommy-gun held professionally. Both Blake and I were covered, and Stein's eyes were deadly.

'Let him shoot—' I began recklessly; but Blake threw his gun down.

'Life is too precious, Matt,' he said quietly. 'We've both got too much yet to do.'

*　　*　　*

'Face to face at last, Blake,' said Stein simply, as his men closed round the detective.

'A pleasure I've long waited for,' retorted Blake. 'I take it that you are Stein? I know all about you, but I've never seen your face.'

'So you know all about me?' Stein laughed. 'But for your cursed quickness a moment back all that knowledge would not haf helped you much! I've a mind to—'

197

I was hidden from Blake's sight by the hedge, for I had stooped down, and my expression managed to convey the threat to Stein. He looked startled, puzzled, for a moment; then he smiled.

'I will be kind to you, Blake,' he declared. 'I haf not the wicked hard heart that you think, as I will prove for you. You may die with Tinker. You haf worked together for so long that it iss not for me to separate you in death. Come, I take you to him, and we must go quick, for it may be that the shots are bringing many people here to discover their cause.'

They bundled us into a couple of cars that were hidden around the next bend in the road, and we were driven rapidly away, followed by our van, driven now by one of Stein's men. The wounded were put in the cars with us, so that the only traces of the skirmish left in the road were a few nasty-looking pools of blood.

I saw nothing of the route that the cars took, for I was on the floor of the car, with a pair of heavy feet to keep me down. By the time the journey took, however, we must have travelled a great distance, turning frequently and meeting little traffic. I wondered what Stein intended to do, and what he would say about my having wounded some of his men.

I realised that I was being rushed to the point where I must settle with him conclusively.

The cars stopped after a sharp right-hand turn, and I found, as the men scrambled out, that we were outside a porched doorway. I managed to look quickly about me, and saw signs of neglect everywhere. The rambling old house had curtainless windows; the drive was weed-grown; the gardens a ruin. Blake and I were hustled through the door into a dusty, unfurnished hall; through another door (with shreds of green baize still clinging to it) and down a long, dark passage. A man appeared in the passage ahead of us, a gun in his hand, but lowered the weapon when he recognised Stein.

'Back again?' I heard him say. 'And you, Blake! Gosh, you're a sure worker, boss!'

'What about the others?' demanded Stein. 'You haf them safe?'

For answer, the man led the way back along the passage and into a little room (formerly a pantry of some sort, by the shelves along the walls), where we found Tinker and Jennings. They were spread out on the broad shelves, about six feet from the floor, their ankles and wrists roped together, and a gag across their mouths.

'That iss very good, Sam,' decided Stein. 'Very good, indeed! And now we haf others to put with them, which is even better, my friendt.'

'Both of 'em?' asked Sam, taking up a coil of stout cord.

'Both,' replied Stein. For an instant, Stein's eyes met mine. 'And, Sam, gag them both now—for I do not wish what I haf to say to suffer interruptions.'

Blake and I both struggled. At first mine was only pretence, for I thought that Stein was bluffing. But he drew close to me, and looked into my face, and the diabolical glare that I saw in his eyes warned me that this was no pretence.

The gag that Sam's expert fingers clamped across my mouth prevented me from calling out, and Stein stood and watched my struggles, and laughed, because he had jumped one move ahead of me.

'This house haf been deserted for many years now,' he explained, when Blake and I were bound and on corresponding shelves to the one occupied by Tinker. 'It iss an old house, but it does not completely lack the modern improvements. No, my friendts, there iss gas! And, because I always choose the clever men to work for me, that gas iss now available in this room. And look, both of you, this room haf no window, and my clever men haf padded the door with rubber, and filled up every so-little crack everywhere.'

He chuckled and drew close to Blake. I was turned slightly on my side, so that I could see the detective's defiant eyes over the top of the gag.

'Death by gas-poisoning iss not a terrible thing,' went on Stein. 'Many choose it for themselves, so I am being kind to you, perhaps—'

Again he chuckled.

'The gas will escape into the room very, very slowly, for I haf arranged it that way,' he continued. 'It would take it a long time to kill you, for you are high from the floor. But I haf not the wish for you to die from the gas that you will take into your lungs, so my clever friendts haf made me a little machine. See, he stands there in the corner, this little machine. Before I go, I will set it, and, later, at a time known only to me—a short time; maybe a long time—a match will ignite itself, and there will be a so-small flash of flame. Just a small flash—but the room will have plenty of gas by that time, and—poof!—in the explosion which follows death will not be so pleasant! But it will be a fitting death for such a four as you.'

I struggled to speak, wrestling with the gag. Stein must not wreck my plans! It wasn't so much that I feared death, but I had just paid so dearly for the chance of enjoying the happiness of the years to come.

Stein laughed; stooped over his machine; and then ordered his men from the room.

'I haff already smelt the gas a little bit, for it iss turned on,' he told us, before he followed his men, and closed the door behind him.

Impossible to set down now the thoughts I experienced during the time which followed. They were too mixed; too horrible. I was trussed in a position which caused the utmost discomfort, my wrists and ankles being tied together behind my back, while a cord round my neck, like a tight collar, bound me to a staple in the wall, so that I could not roll from the shelf without hanging myself.

I watched Blake, bound in a similar position opposite to me. His eyes betrayed no apprehension, and I got the impression that he and Tinker were signalling to one another in some private way. The lad was on the shelf below me, and Blake kept looking down towards him.

The smell of gas shortly became oppressive, and I found myself hoping that he had miscalculated, and that the gas would do its work, quietly and peacefully, before his machine provided a spark. I could just see the black box in the corner, fronted by a white dial, and could hear the steady ticking of the clock that worked the time adjustment. That made me think of another time adjustment, a clock that had been ticking while I was at the Bates-Jacobs fight, ticking up my alibi. I even wondered if Stein had stolen my clock to make this machine—crazy thoughts! Random and horrible!

I remembered abruptly that, owing to the necessity of getting in touch with Stein, I never phoned the doctor.

Blake looked up towards me, and our eyes met. There was a strained look in his, and it seemed to me that he was listening; waiting—possibly, he also was listening to the ticking of that clock, waiting for a louder 'tick' than the others, which would be followed by a flash of light!

I wondered how Tinker was reacting to the strain. He and his master had probably been in similar predicaments before, and had learnt to wait with philosophic calm. Besides, they only had their lives at stake.

Abruptly, the strained look went out of Blake's eyes, and, at the same moment, I heard a steady drumming noise. It took me some little time to realise that he and Tinker were making the sounds by drumming on the shelves with their ankles and wrists. I began to copy them.

I could not see the use of what we were doing, but anything was better than just lying and listening. A sort of frenzy took possession of me, and I bruised my wrists with the force of my efforts.

The smell of gas began to be overpowering. Reason insisted that, if Stein really intended his machine to act before the gas put us out, the end must come almost immediately.

I stopped beating suddenly, pausing tensely. It seemed to me that my ears must be playing tricks with me. Blake and Tinker were also quiet, listening; and there could be no doubt about it—the thudding sound now came from outside our room, and it was the stamp of heavy feet on uncarpeted floors.

'Blake, where are you? Blake!'

A voice came to us faintly.

A sharp click from the direction of Stein's machine came at the same time as a sound from the direction of the door. With the frenzy of desperation, we all began to hammer with our ankles and wrists again. I found it hard to move, for a feeling of lassitude was creeping over me. It seemed that nothing could matter, except a quiet sleep.

Then there was a thud against the door. Anxious voices sounded outside. As though in a dream, I saw the door flung open and Coutts framed there. With him were other men.

'Here they are! Untie them!' ordered Coutts.

His men jumped forward, and eager hands soon had us down from the shelves and were tearing the gags from our mouths.

'Get 'em outside—gas escaping!' panted Coutts.

'Hurry!' commanded Blake, the instant that he could speak.

'Get out, everybody—before the gas ignites!'

Two Scotland Yard detectives snatched me up between them, and ran into the corridor. Ahead of me, others were carrying Blake, Tinker, and Jennings, while Coutts galloped behind, urging them. We had just reached the hall when there was a dull boom behind us, and a wave of hot air seemed to blow us forward. One of the men carrying me stumbled, but the other managed to drag us through the front door, as the whole world seemed to come crushing about us in one terrific roar of sound and blazing heat. At that moment, consciousness left me.

*   *   *

'No one hurt!' Blake's voice came to me as I revived. 'That's luck! But we've not got Stein. He didn't depend on gas alone for that explosion. That machine of his must have been a powerful incendiary bomb. Part of the house was destroyed by the explosion; the rest is blazing now. Sergeant Lear, I've got to thank you for saving us!'

I looked towards the man he was addressing, and saw a short, burly individual, with an ugly wound across his rugged face.

'How did he get Coutts here in time, Blake?' I asked, sitting up.

'My hunch, Matt,' was the quiet reply. 'I told you that I knew Tinker was only a decoy, so when I followed the trail that was laid to lead me into the trap, I used a van instead of a car.'

'We had to take the van because there was no other car handy,' I protested.

'That wasn't my reason for taking it,' retorted Blake. 'I took it because I knew that it had been chosen as a vantage point from which Sergeant Lear could watch the building. I knew that he was concealed inside.'

'I couldn't join you in that scrap you had with gunmen, Mr Blake,' interposed the detective-sergeant, 'because the first shot that was fired pierced the van and grazed my head, putting me out of action for a bit. I revived to find myself still in the van, round the back of this house, so I found a telephone and got a call through to the Yard.'

I didn't listen to the rest of his explanation, but lay back again. I realised bitterly what a poor chance of success any man has when he tries to pit his wits against an organisation that always seems to think two moves ahead, and to be prepared for anything.

*　　*　　*

'Matt, I want you to come along with us.'

Blake was addressing me, and for an instant I was seized with cold terror. But he continued quietly:

'We're going to Brandt's place, where I want to carry on my investigations, and conduct an experiment,' he explained. 'I feel confident that I can prove the actual time of Brandt's death, and how the murder was committed. You've been in this case from the beginning, and I want you there for the finish.'

I hesitated, wondering what excuse I could make, for there were other things that I had to do, which must be done without delay. But Blake took my acceptance for granted, and I had to follow him into one of the Scotland Yard cars. As we drove back to London, Tinker described how he came to be captured, and explained that he had been unconscious from the time he left my flat until he found himself on that shelf. Coutts left men by the house to search for traces of Stein and his gang, but did not seem to be very sanguine of results.

We stopped at only one place on the way to Hampstead, and that was the office of a large publishing house, where Blake left us for a short while and returned with a copy of a popular periodical under his arm. I noticed that he studied it during the rest of the drive.

Adams admitted us to Brandt's place, and I saw that there were two policemen in the hall, while other men in plain clothes were moving about the gardens. The body had been moved from the study, but otherwise the room was unchanged. Everything in the same position as at the time of the murder; the Happidols still leering from the walls. The violin and bow had been placed on the desk alongside the five snapshots, which still lay there.

'Close the door, Adams,' ordered Blake, as we filed into the room. 'We are going to need your services in this room.'

The butler obeyed, and I quickly surveyed the assembled company—Blake, Tinker, Coutts, Adams, and the two men from the Yard. The official detectives and Adams were looking puzzled; Tinker was quietly watching his master; while Blake looked pale and bedraggled as a result of the fight in the road. I could see that the feeling of an approaching climax had communicated itself to all of them, so that they waited eagerly for what Blake was about to say, or do.

For the first few moments he pottered about the room, seeming to be wasting time, but my eyes followed him, and it seemed that all my control must break as I followed his movements.

'All that we know at present,' he began abruptly, 'is that Brandt was murdered in this room by a blow over the heart, and that he cannot have been killed by the original of those photographs, because Bud Callaghan has been dead for some time. Beyond that, we can reason that there must be some connection between this murder and Stein, on account of Stein's recent activities against us; but the real question that I want to solve now is—when did Brandt die?'

'Nine twenty-seven exactly, when the music stopped,' announced Coutts, looking up from his notebook.

'I don't agree,' replied Blake. 'I have already tried to show you, Coutts, that Brandt cannot have been playing the violin he was holding at the time of his death. Now I am going to show you something else.'

My mouth seemed to go dry, as I watched him turn to Adams. What fresh diabolical reasoning was going to wreck my plans?

'As a keen musician, Adams,' went on Blake, 'you probably can recognise a number of pieces of music when you hear them played. Now, I want you to think back to when your master started his playing last night, for I want to know exactly what he played.

Blake turned to the music-stand and considered the music on it.

'Why, that is simple, sir,' declared Adams, stepping close to him and pointing at the music. 'Mr Brandt was always a gentleman of orderly habits, and here is his music arranged in the order in which it is played. Before starting, he always arranges it like that in a pile. As he finishes each piece he moves it to the left of the stand, alongside the other music.'

'Then,' interrupted Blake, 'it would seem that Mr Brandt only played these three pieces last night—"Arlequin", by Popper, Massenet's "Meditation", and Dvorak's 'Humoresque'. Only three pieces have been moved over to the left, and "Humoresque" is the last. Would you recognise "Humoresque" if you heard it played, Adams?'

'Of course, sir?'

'How does it go? Whistle some part of it, man!' commanded

Blake.

Adams flushed, and looked round self-consciously, then pursed up his lips and proved that he knew the piece.

'And was Mr Brandt playing that at 9.27, when you stood outside his door?' pressed Blake.

'At 9.27? No, sir, most certainly not,' replied the butler. 'He was playing a very modern piece, sir—"Tell Me Tonight" is its title, sir. Mr Brandt had very wide tastes in music; he could appreciate both classic and ordinary music, sir. As for "Humoresque", he played that much earlier, sir, while I was still in the dining-room.'

'And what time would that be?' rapped Blake.

'Before half-past seven, sir.'

'Take this pencil and paper,' went on Blake, 'and sit at that desk, Adams. I am going to read you out the names of a number of violin solos, and similar pieces of music. I will give each one an index number, and I want you to put down the number of every piece that you remember Mr Brandt playing last night. Are you ready?'

Blake opened up the blue-covered periodical that he had brought with him, and began to read. At first Adams remained still; then he began to jot down numbers. At last he interrupted, with a puzzled look on his face.

'But, Mr Blake, sir,' he protested, 'those are the identical pieces that Mr Brandt played! You have just mentioned "Tell Me Tonight"; immediately before that was "Melody", by Gluck, arranged by Kreisler—I have told you that it gives me great pleasure to listen to Mr Brandt when he is playing, and I can hear plainly during most of the evening, so that I miss little of his concerts, sir. You have brought it back to me vividly! Before the "Melody" he played another piece arranged by Kreisler—"Tambourin"—it is here on your list, sir, in its right order! This is magic, sir—this is Mr Brandt's programme!'

'You're wrong there, Adams,' said Blake quietly, while I seemed to stop breathing; 'it is Fritz Helman's programme, playing in a studio in Brussels! This paper is "Universal Radio", with full programmes of foreign stations, and Helman gave a recital in Brussels last night.'

'But I don't understand, sir—' began the butler. But was interrupted by Coutts, who demanded an explanation. Blake pointed to the wireless loudspeaker in a corner of the room.

'The music that Adams heard at 9.27 came from there,' he said quietly. 'Brandt was dead long before that. This is my theory of this part of the murder, Coutts. The killer killed Brandt the moment that he had finished playing one tune, and switched on the wireless in time for the beginning of Helman's next tune. He must have had his times arranged to the last second, and I admire his thoroughness, for he must have counted on a fact that is mentioned in this paper—Helman is temperamental, and will have no announcing between his pieces, simply commencing a fresh piece as he finishes the last—'

'But the wireless—who turned it off?' I broke in, determined to find out how much Blake knew.

Had he found out in some uncanny way about that portable wireless in the garden, with the wires that I attached to Brandt's loudspeaker? Did he know of my time-stop, which stopped the wireless sharp at 9.27 (a time when I was with Blake), and which also released the spring to pull the wires back and wind them on their spool, tearing the ends from the terminals on the loud-speakers?

'I don't know yet,' he confessed frankly, 'but in one of the terminals of that loudspeaker, Matt, is a broken fragment of wire, which seems to suggest that another connection was made there and then wrenched off. That suggests a theory, which I have still to consider in detail.

'But to return to Brandt,' he continued. 'I am now convinced that he was killed long before 9.27. Adams has just told us that "Humoresque" was played before 7.30, and it would seem that "Humoresque" was the last piece that he actually played. I am not going to ask you to accept Adams' word alone for the time that Brandt finished playing "Humoresque", Coutts. I am going to check it.'

I watched fascinated as Blake took out his watch.

'I will restring and tune this violin,' he explained, 'then I shall set my watch to seven o'clock and play each of the pieces on the left-hand side here—the pieces that Brandt played. We will see what time I reach, and finish, "Humoresque".'

He strung and tuned the violin, and then followed as strange a concert as could be conceived. Detectives, a dead man's servant, and a murderer sat in silence, listening to the beautiful strains of a violin superbly played. I had heard before that the violin was one of Blake's recreations; he could justifiably have made it his profession. I think that some of the others forgot what had brought us there, as they listened to the beauty of that music. Blake stood by the music-stand, much as Brandt had stood before I killed him, but there was no affectation about Blake's playing. Gracefully he brought "Humoresque" to its close.

'Well?' he asked, as the last lovely note died away.

Coutts started, as though he had been asleep, and glanced hurriedly at the watch.

'Seven-sixteen,' he said brusquely.

'Then we can take it,' declared Blake, 'that—leaving a margin— Brandt finished playing and died somewhere between 7.10 and 7.25? Two hours earlier than the murderer wished us to believe the crime to have been committed!

'And, Coutts, why should he wish us to have the time wrong?' demanded Blake, and answered his own question: 'Because he was arranging an alibi! When we find this murderer we will find a man whose time can be accounted for from 7.30 on—'

Blake broke off again, and suddenly lunged towards me. I saw his clenched fist smashing for my heart, recognised the blow, and parried it. Then I saw my final mistake! The parry was as unusual and secret as the death-blow; the man who knew one must know the other!

For an instant Blake and I faced one another with all pretence thrown aside; then I flung myself through the window.

It was not luck that got me away from Brandt's. It was the power that rules men's lives, for I still had work to do. I ran for a long way, and then took a taxi, making no attempt to hide my trail; and yet I reached the lodging-house in Bloomsbury unmolested.

The professor was in. He was in bed ill, they told me, and I forced my way past them, to be face to face with Stein again.

I shut the door behind me and turned the key in the lock. He was lying on the bed, fully dressed, and watched me coolly; but there was fear in his eyes and the tremor of a nerve in his cheek.

'You know why I've come,' I began, the words coming to my lips without effort. 'The game is ended, and I am sending you to join your leader—to join Brandt. Don't say anything—lies won't help now! I know why the Happidols sell; I know how the most deadly, insidious, and fiendish of drugs is spread—inside certain of those Happidols! I killed Brandt because of the evil that he has done. You know why I had to do this myself—why I couldn't go to the police—even to Blake—so we won't go into that.

'You've evaded the police for a long time, Stein. They know that you are mixed up with dope-peddling, but they have been trying to find the man above you—they never suspected Brandt and his Happidols. You're going to evade the police even longer, Stein! You're going to evade them for ever, as Brandt has done!'

'You can't kill me!' Stein was trembling, his face paler than ever, haggard and hideous now that the mask had gone. 'I almost saved you the task of killing Brandt. That night I haf gone to his garden to kill him, because he say that I am no good, that he will expose me to the police to haf done with me. Had I been earlier, you would not haf had to kill him, my friendt—I am your friendt—'

I killed him even as I had killed Brandt, but he was a stronger man and had time to scream.

Panting, with my face covered in sweat like a cellophane mask, I reached the doctor's place near Crowthorne. In my hurry I had crashed the car that I stole in London, and had had to run the last bit.

The same attendants met me at the gate, but they had orders to admit me at once.

The doctor met me in the great bare entrance-hall, and his stern, fierce face was strangely softened and kindly.

'You did not phone, Mr King,' he accused. 'You should have. But I see you have heard the worst. Just when I thought that we were winning—that we would cure her—her strength proved unequal to the great strain of the fight, and she died—this morning.'

I must have swayed, for his hand gripped my arm. He turned me slightly, so that I saw Blake at the moment that he entered after me.

'She's dead,' I found myself muttering to him. 'After all that I have done—Claire's dead! It's not fair! It's not right!'

Blake caught the doctor's eye.

'His wife,' the doctor explained quietly. 'Very young and very beautiful, but—like all my patients in this lonely, hidden hospital—a dangerous drug addict.'

'He's right!' I snarled, turning on Blake. 'A dangerous drug addict—started on the ghastly game by Brandt—"Happy" Brandt, the man who spread happiness!—the man who spread deadly drugs to addicts, hidden inside his Happidols! And, Blake—listen to this!—she was the woman you were after—the woman behind Stein—Brandt's lieutenant!'

Blake's hand closed on my arm, and I was startled to see that the ruthless set of his face was softened by that look that I had noticed before.

'I guessed something like that, Matt,' he confessed quietly. 'Let's go somewhere and talk—before Coutts comes.'

The doctor put a room at our disposal, and I told Blake the truth. I told him how I met Claire Duggan on the Continent, and at last persuaded her to marry me, though she insisted on the wedding remaining a secret. We were happy until I discovered the reason for her many strange moods. I realised that she had become addicted to drugs, and I used all my patience to discover the source from which she got her supply. This led me to the truth about the Happidols; but I could not go to the police, because I learnt at the same time that the drugs had placed her entirely in Brandt's power, and exposure of the gang would convict her as a ringleader.

So I set out to kill Brandt, while placing Claire in that hidden hospital where Dr Allardyce was fighting against the effects of this new drug that was causing havoc throughout the world. It was my plan to kill Brandt and smash his organisation; and then to take Claire away somewhere, where we could live in peace and forget the past.

I told Blake how I had staged the murder, and of what followed.

'I put the five photographs and the message "Refer to Blake" into the desk to start a false trail,' I explained. 'I wanted you called in that night, because I was fool enough to think that I could bluff you, and you were to be my alibi if suspicion ever pointed my way.'

'You made too many mistakes,' he said quietly; 'and I am afraid, Matt, that I suspected you of being in dangerous trouble even before the night of the fight. It is part of my job to study men, and I obviously begin with my friends. I wish I could have persuaded you to confide in me before you allowed an overload of terrible worry to drive you to acts of madness. As for suspecting you—the breakdown of my car at the fight; your insistence on going to Brandt's with me—there were too many simple clues waiting to be picked up. But I had to find *why* you had done it, and *how* you had done it.'

Coutts arrived to interrupt us, but Blake insisted on driving me back to London. Coutts and two detectives sat in the back of the car as tokens of my arrest for muder.

Blake is phenomenally quick, both in thought and action, and yet he was too slow to grab me that day as I sprang from the seat beside him.

We were in a welter of traffic, with a London bus hurtling its massive way along towards us. I heard startled shouts; the shriek of brakes; and a woman's scream. I caught a distorted glimpse of the bus as it seemed to hurl itself at me. I even seemed to feel the heat of the boiling radiator. Then followed blackness, so profound that it seemed to engulf everything, including pain.

And now, after what seems an eternity of nightmare situations, of tautened nerves and emotional strain, I feel at rest. No longer has my weary brain to grapple with the details of my 'perfect' crime; no longer have I to match my all too feeble subterfuges against the logic and keenness of a mind like Blake's.

The names of Stein and Brandt cannot rouse me now to that fierce, burning hatred which impelled me to my crimes.

I know the end is not far off. By my side these last days has sat a police-constable, and in his eyes I have read that he knows, too. Perhaps he thinks me fortunate to be escaping a fate I certainly deserve.

Fate, which has treated me so cruelly, spares me the last trick.

To Sexton Blake, the greetings of one who esteemed his honour, both as a friend and foe. To the memory of Claire, my dear wife . . .

*   *   *

Appended note by Horace Clegg, Esq., Solicitor, of 18, Scrivener's Walk, Lincoln's Inn:

'*This is to certify that the foregoing is a true transcription of the material dictated in my presence, by Matthew King, and taken down by a shorthand writer.*

'*At the point where the dictation abruptly finishes, the said Matthew King was overcome by a fainting fit caused, in my opinion, by undue exertion and anxiety to conclude his narrative. This fainting fit merged into a coma, during which, after half an hour's unconsciousness, he died from cerebral haemorrhage.*

'*This full confession of the said Matthew King, together with the death certificate and other relevant papers, are being lodged with Mr Sexton Blake, of Baker Street, London, W., in accordance with the verbally expressed instructions of the deceased.*'

THE GREEN JESTER
Donald Stuart

It is said that Donald Stuart (r.n. Gerald Verner, 1897–1980) wrote his first Sexton Blake novel on scraps of paper while roughing it on the Embankment. This, like a good many stories about Stuart (mostly emanating from the man himself), is wholly untrue, although his early life did have a certain nomadic tinge to it and his subsequent writing career was far from sedentary. He wrote in all 38 stories for the Sexton Blake Library, most of which he de-Blakeanised and had published in hardback under his real name. Much taken with the theatre, Stuart wrote the 1930/31 success Sexton Blake *(in which the decidedly Holmesian Arthur Wontner took the leading role, and Pedro the blood-hound constantly misbehaved himself on stage), and later adapted novels by Agatha Christie and Peter Cheyney for the West End. His style was heavily influenced by that of Edgar Wallace (at times it is difficult to tell one from the other) and, like Wallace, he had a weakness for the villain-as-least-likely-suspect. He was also, perhaps, overfond of the 'Suddenly—a shot/scream rang out' chapter-ending, which certainly gave his plots a breathless, headlong quality, although at times the pace was so hectic that even Stuart lost his grip on events. This didn't matter. His stories careered along, were immensely readable, and the piling of thrill upon thrill, sensation upon sensation (with a frequent hint of the supernatural for added measure), ensured him a devoted following both amongst Blake readers and in the mainstream hardback market. (The Duke of Windsor was an avid fan, although this probably says more about him than about Stuart's writings.) This particular story is vintage Stuart, and vintage Blake.*

When Sexton Blake first heard of the Green Jester, he laughed— and not without reason, for certainly the card, with its grotesque portrait of a jester, in emerald costume, complete with cap and

211

bells, one finger pointing derisively at the beholder, was conducive to mirth.

Mr Hamilton Lorne, who received it by post one morning, and later showed it to the detective at the club of which they were both members, laughed also, particularly at the doggerel rhyme scrawled across the back, for it ran:

> *My dear Mr Hamilton Lorne,*
> *You really should not have been born,*
> *But to remedy this,*
> *And take heed, I shan't miss,*
> *You will die—just an hour before dawn.*

Both Blake and Mr Lorne, an elderly retired stockbroker, came to the natural conclusion that it was a practical joke, rather feeble perhaps, and a trifle lacking in good taste, but a joke nevertheless, and so they laughed and the recipient crumpled up the card and dropped it into the wastepaper-basket.

Neither the Baker Street detective nor Mr Lorne were laughing at nine o'clock on the following morning; Blake because of the telephone message he had just received from Scotland Yard and the stockbroker because he was dead! He had been found stabbed to the heart in his bed by the maid whose duty it was to provide him each morning with a cup of tea, and the divisional surgeon who made the examination asserted that death must have taken place— about an hour before dawn!

It was obviously a case of murder, but neither Detective-Inspector Coutts nor Sexton Blake, who accompanied the Scotland Yard man to the scene of the crime, could find a single clue that offered a solution to the mystery. Whoever had killed Mr Lorne had certainly entered by the bedroom window, for a light ladder, usually used by the gardener, was found leaning against the sill, and on the gravel path beneath were a few confused traces of blurred footprints.

But that was all, and three weeks' patient inquiry failed to elicit anything further. The dead man had apparently possessed few friends and no enemies. His only relative was a distant cousin, who ran a sheep-farm in Canada and who, since there was no will, eventually inherited Mr Lorne's comfortable fortune.

The newspapers, after making a great stir about the affair and featuring the mysterious card with its grim prophecy, turned to other and more recent sensations, so that in an incredibly short space of time the whole thing was forgotten except by certain men in a large building facing the Thames Embankment, and by Sexton Blake himself.

Then, at the expiration of four months, an agitated man arrived at Scotland Yard and banged in front of Inspector Coutts a square card which he had received by the morning's post. It bore the figure of the Jester, and on the back:

> *My dear Mr Percival Haynes,*
> *What a pity blood flows in your veins,*
> *You'll forgive me, I hope,*
> *If I stop this with rope*
> *And release you from life's earthly pains.*

The terrified Mr Haynes, who lived at Sydenham and remembered the fate of the unfortunate stockbroker, raved and threatened and implored and, eventually being reduced to something like coherence, answered the numerous questions fired at him by the burly inspector. The card had arrived in a plain envelope, the name and address being printed in capital letters. He had brought the envelope with him, and the postmark showed that it had been posted in the West End of London in time for the last collection on the previous night. Coutts sent it and the card through to the fingerprint department, but though there were several prints on the envelope, the card revealed nothing except some excellent reproductions of Mr Haynes' own finger-tips.

The architect—for that was his profession—was so nervous that it was a long time before they could persuade him to leave Scotland Yard, and it was only after he had been assured that a detective would shadow him night and day and that his house should be subjected to police surveillance that he consented to go at all.

Three days passed, and Mr Haynes never went abroad without a faithful trailer at his heels, and slept in the comfortable knowledge that a plain-clothes man was somewhere close at hand, watching for any danger that might threaten him.

In spite of these precautions, however, on the evening of the fourth day he walked into his garden after dinner to smoke a cigar and never came back! A frightened servant who went to look for him an hour later found him hanging from the lower branch of a big oak-tree that grew at the foot of the lawn. He was stone dead, and the watchful detective who was keeping the house under observation had been neatly chloroformed and was lying unconscious in the adjoining shrubbery.

Inspector Coutts rubbed his bristly hair frantically when he heard the news and went round to consult Sexton Blake, but, although the detective did his best, as in the case of Mr Hamilton Lorne, there was not the ghost of a clue or the slightest shadow of a motive. The only solution that seemed at all probable was that the crimes were the work of a homicidal maniac, and this belief was strengthened when six weeks after the death of Percival Haynes a third murder was blazoned forth on the front pages of the morning dailies, the victim this time being an elderly spinster who lived alone in a tiny cottage on the Horsham road.

The discovery was made by the milkman, who, finding the previous day's supply of milk still on the step and receiving no reply to his repeated assaults on the little knocker, called assistance. The door was broken in under the authority of the local police, and in the dingy sitting-room they found all that was left of Miss Julia Rothe. Her head had been battered, and the bent and stained poker that lay by the body left no room for doubt regarding the weapon that had been used. On a little, old-fashioned bureau was the now familiar card, and on the back, in the same sprawling writing as the others, the following limerick:

> *Believe me, my charming Miss Rothe,*
> *To end your long life I am loath,*
> *But a blow with the poker*
> *In the hand of this joker*
> *Will be best, I am sure, for us both.*

That was all, but it was sufficient, taken in conjunction with the other two murders, to spread something like a panic. A wave of terror swept over the country following this latest atrocious and apparently meaningless crime. The perverted sense of humour shown by the rhymed warnings that the unknown murderer sent to his intended victims, and the utter wantonness of the killings, surrounded the shadowy personality responsible with an atmosphere of horror that no amount of sheer brutality could have done.

It was the very callousness, the joking way of treating carefully-planned, cold-blooded murder that seized on the public's imagination and caused even strong-minded men to open their morning mail with quickened heartbeats and a creeping of the flesh lest among the letters should appear one containing the fatal picture of the laughing fool, his raised hand pointing a menacing finger at them.

Scotland Yard was at its wits' end, but was helpless, for no amount of patient sifting, no amount of delving into the past lives of the three victims brought any result. The Green Jester, as the newspapers named him, had appeared from nowhere, struck swiftly and surely, and drawn back into the mists from whence he came without leaving a single trace of his identity behind him.

And so the situation remained when Detective-Inspector Coutts dropped in early one summer morning to see Sexton Blake at the latter's chambers in Baker Street.

He found the detective at breakfast clad in the acid-stained, almost colourless dressing-gown which was Blake's habitual garment during his leisure hours.

'You're an early visitor, my dear Coutts,' he remarked, glancing at the clock and waving the burly inspector to a chair. 'What is it—business or just a friendly chat?'

'Both!' jerked the Scotland Yard man, removing his bowler hat and running a stubby hand through his short, bristly hair. 'I'm getting into the deuce of a row at the Yard—the road to favour is paved with good convictions, Blake, and I've fallen down badly over this Green Jester business.'

The smile left Sexton Blake's keen, clear-cut face and became replaced by a grave expression that was almost grim.

'I fail to see what more you can do,' he said, 'or what more anyone can do, for that matter.'

'I know,' grunted Coutts. 'But because I've done my best doesn't cut any ice with the powers that be. They want results.'

He took the cup of coffee that the detective held out to him, and gulped down the steaming fluid noisily.

'It's these infernal newspapers that are the cause of the trouble,' he grumbled lugubriously. 'They stir up the Home Office with their rubbish about the incompetency of the police, and the Home

Office retaliates by going for the Chief Commissioner, and he takes it out of me!'

He set down his empty cup and tugged savagely at the tooth-brush moustache that adorned his upper lip.

'Yes, it's a difficult proposition, Coutts, old man,' murmured Sexton Blake, rising and crossing to the mantelpiece. 'Knowing what they're like at the Yard, you have my sympathy, but I really don't see what can be done at present.'

Searching in the pockets of his tattered dressing-gown, he found his pipe and began to fill it leisurely from the big china tobacco jar.

'It's not as if it were an ordinary case,' he continued thoughtfully. 'It's so extraordinary that it almost touches on the bizarre. If we could only discover some clue that would even suggest a motive for these crimes, it would give us something to go on. It's the absolute senselessness of the whole thing that makes it so impossible.'

Coutts gave a grunt which he intended to signify his entire agreement.

'It's my opinion that these murders are the work of a lunatic,' he declared. 'No sane man could be guilty of such utter nonsense as those absurd limericks.'

'But they were not absurd,' objected the detective, lighting his pipe deliberately and tossing the dead match in the fireplace. 'They were very much to the point. So much so, in fact, that in every instance their prediction was carried out—to the letter.'

'That doesn't alter my conviction that this Green Jester fellow, whoever he is, is mad,' answered the burly inspector stubbornly. 'It's obvious. Look at the people he's chosen for his victims—a retired stockbroker, an architect, and an elderly spinster.' He ticked them off on the fingers of his left hand. 'People leading ordinary, colourless lives, and without the slightest connection between them.'

'That last statement is not quite correct,' remarked Sexton Blake, blowing a cloud of smoke ceilingwards and watching it float away.

'Eh?' Coutts jerked his head round sharply and shot him a swift, inquiring glance. 'What do you mean?'

'I've spent a lot of thought on this business,' replied the detective slowly, 'and I've made one or two inquiries on my own account.

The results, I must admit, haven't been startling, but I learnt one thing which seems to me to be distinctly peculiar.'

'What's that?' jerked the Scotland Yard man eagerly, as he paused.

'Merely this,' answered Blake. 'You said just now that there was no connection between the three victims of the Green Jester. You're wrong—there *is* a connection.'

'Well, if there is, I haven't been able to find it,' growled Coutts, 'and, naturally, it was the first thing I looked for. As far as I can make out, they were all strangers to each other.'

'They were,' agreed the detective, with a nod; 'but one thing was common to them all.'

'What?' inquired the puzzled inspector.

'None of them possessed a single living relative,' said Blake impressively.

Coutts looked at him for a moment in silence and frowned.

'Are you sure of this?' he asked at length.

'Quite. I took particular pains to find out, and the only one of the three who can be said to have had a relation of any sort was Lorne, and his Canadian cousin is so many times removed as scarcely to warrant the description.'

The Scotland Yard man wrinkled his forehead and rubbed the top of his head vigorously with a podgy hand.

'H'm!' he grunted. 'It's certainly strange, but I don't see how it's going to help us much.'

'Neither do I—at the moment,' answered Sexton Blake. 'I'm merely stating a fact which it may be as well to remember for future reference.'

'Unless it's only a coincidence.' The inspector pursed his lips doubtfully. 'In that case, it would mean nothing.'

'Of course, there's always that possibility,' agreed the detective, but his voice lacked conviction. 'I'm inclined to think, though, that it's *more* than an accidental choice on the part of our humorous assassin.'

'Then you must have got some theory to account for it?' Coutts eyed his friend questioningly, but Blake shook his head and smiled.

'I haven't,' he declared. 'I'm only giving you my own private opinion. You can call it a hunch if you like, but I'm convinced that when we do reach the solution of the mystery we shall find that the whole thing hinges on the fact that these people had no near relations.'

'If we ever do,' corrected Coutts pessimistically.

'We shall—eventually,' said the detective confidently. 'At present we are passing through a period of quiescence, but I very much doubt if we have heard the last of the Green Jester. Our joking friend will break out again, and if I was a betting man I'd wager that the next person to receive one of those poetic effusions will be someone without living kith or kin.'

Blake had barely finished the sentence when the telephone bell rang shrilly—an abrupt, startling summons that made Coutts jump at the sound.

With a muttered word of apology, Blake crossed to the instrument and took the receiver from its hook.

'Hallo!' he called. 'Yes, this is Sexton Blake speaking.' There was a long pause while the detective listened to someone at the other end of the wire.

Suddenly Coutts saw his face change. His mouth set more firmly and his eyes narrowed, sure signs that something had awakened in Blake the keenest excitement.

'When did it arrive?' he asked crisply, and then, after a short interval, evidently in answer to the other's reply: 'All right, I'll come down at once. Inspector Coutts, who is officially in charge of the case, is here with me now. I'll bring him, too. In the meanwhile, don't leave the house under any pretext whatever, and keep someone whom you can trust with you until we arrive.'

He hung up the black cylinder and swung round, facing the burly inspector with a hard glitter in his grey eyes.

'That message was from Dr Roon!' he snapped grimly. 'The Green Jester has turned up again sooner than I expected. The doctor received a card by this morning's post, and, according to the usual stanza on the back, the time of his death has been fixed for twelve o'clock—midday!'

*   *   *

A jagged ribbon of blue light flickered across the horizon to the south, and was followed a few seconds later by a reverberating crash of thunder.

Sexton Blake glanced anxiously at the lowering, black storm-clouds that had so swiftly obscured the blue of the sky, and pressed his foot a little harder on the accelerator.

'I think we can just about make it,' he murmured to his companion; and Coutts grunted.

'How much farther have we got to go?' he asked, clutching desperately at his hat as an unexpected burst of wind came sweeping across the open country and threatened to tear it from his head.

'About five miles—maybe a trifle less,' replied Blake, his eyes fixed on the road ahead. 'Roon lives just on the other side of Dorking.'

A second peal of thunder, louder than the first, drowned the end of the sentence, and a large spot of rain splashed the windscreen, followed by another, and another. It had been a bright, sunny morning when they had left Baker Street in Blake's big, open Rolls, but the clouds had gathered with incredible rapidity, and, almost before they had reached the outskirts of London, the sky became overcast, and that eerie stillness and peculiar copper-coloured twilight that presages a thunderstorm overtook them.

As a matter of fact they must have run into it, for the rain was pelting down, and the rolling roar of the thunder almost incessant as, with the screen-wiper working madly, they tore through the narrow streets of Dorking.

Partly accountable to the weather, and partly due to the nature of the business that had brought him out on this journey, Sexton Blake felt a sudden and unusual fit of depression steal over him when, leaving the old town behind them, they once more found themselves on the open high road. It was as though a gigantic hand had attached a heavy weight to his heart, and, try as he would, he couldn't shake the unpleasant feeling off.

The shining surface of the road rendered driving difficult, and the big car slithered and skidded as Blake sent it forward at the utmost speed he dared. They were running now between straggling hedges, each leaf a miniature cataract, behind which lay dripping fields of vegetables and bedraggled corn, lit up clearly every few seconds by the almost continuous flicker of the lightning.

Passing a plantation of wheat, in the middle of which stood a melancholy and forlorn-looking scarecrow, its tattered garments rain-soaked and flapping dismally in the gusts of wind, they presently came to the red-brick pillars giving entrance to a drive.

'Here we are,' muttered Sexton Blake, skilfully swinging the car into the broad, gravelled way that lay beyond. 'This is the place.'

'Just the sort of day the Green Jester would choose,' growled Coutts, as Blake pressed the polished brass bell at the side of the door, and, removing his hat, shook it savagely.

They waited, and after a slight interval the double doors were opened noiselessly by a black-clad servant, obviously the butler.

'Your master is expecting us,' said Blake, withdrawing a square of paste-board from his pocket, and handing it to the man. 'Will you take him my card?'

The butler, a stout, sleek-looking individual, with jet-black hair, immaculately plastered down on either side of a central parting, took the extended card, glanced at it, and then regarded the detective with a look of puzzled astonishment.

'Dr Roon certainly was expecting you, sir,' he said civilly, but markedly stressing the 'was'. 'I understood, however, that he had gone into Dorking to meet you.'

'Do you mean he is out?' asked Sexton Blake sharply, his eyes narrowing.

'Yes, sir,' replied the man; and the expression of his face was even more puzzled. 'He went out about half an hour ago—directly after you telephoned.'

'I never telephoned at all!' snapped Blake.

And the sense of foreboding that he had experienced before increased.

'You—you didn't, sir!' At any other time the detective would have smiled at the almost comic dismay in the tone. 'I don't quite understand. There must be some mistake. Perhaps you had better see Dr Roon's secretary, sir. She took the message.'

'I think I had,' said Blake, grimly, stepping into the comfortably-furnished hall as the butler stood aside.

'Will you come this way, sir?' invited the man, closing the door, and led them across the polished floor to a tiny smoking-room on the left. Having ushered them in, he bowed and withdrew.

As soon as they were alone, Coutts turned to his friend with a look of alarm on his face which he made no attempt to conceal.

'I don't like it, Blake,' he jerked, shaking his bullet head. 'I don't like it at all.'

'Neither do I, Coutts,' said the Baker Street detective gravely. 'I certainly sent no telephone message, as you know, and it looks to me as though the Green Jester got to hear that we were coming and lured Roon out with a false call. If that's the case—'

He broke off, and, going over to the window, stared out with unseeing eyes at a mass of rain-soaked shrubbery, but his silence was more ominous than if he had completed the sentence.

Coutts felt a little icy shiver creep up his spine, and it was not due to his wet clothing.

'Twelve o'clock was the time, wasn't it?' he whispered huskily.

'So Roon told me,' replied Blake, and glanced at his watch. 'It's barely eleven yet, so—'

The sound of a light step outside made him pause, and a moment later the door opened and a girl entered.

She was tall and slim, and in spite of the efficient horn-rimmed glasses she wore was remarkably beautiful, with the flawless skin that sometimes goes with auburn hair, and large violet-blue eyes that the slight distortion of the lens failed entirely to spoil.

Standing on the threshold, she looked quickly from one to the other and instinctively picked out Sexton Blake.

'Will you come into the library, Mr Blake?' she said, and her voice was in complete harmony with the rest of her appearance, for it was low and sweet—a well-bred voice as the detective mentally noted. 'It is more comfortable there.'

Without waiting for a reply, she led the way up the broad staircase, talking as she went.

'I can't make out how there could have been any misunderstanding,' she said, opening a door on the first landing and admitting them into a large, book-lined room, furnished heavily but comfortably with deep, leather covered chairs and lounges, 'for I myself took the telephone message calling Dr Roon out.'

'Did the caller mention my name?' inquired Sexton Blake, seating himself in front of a glowing electric radiator and stretching out his numbed hands to the warmth.

The girl nodded.

'Yes,' she answered, 'otherwise the doctor would not have gone out.'

'Well, I can assure you the message never came from me,' declared the detective. 'What was the gist of it?'

'It was quite plausible,' she said: 'and neither Dr Roon nor I

221

doubted for a moment that it was correct. It was a man who telephoned. He said that he was Detective-Inspector Coutts'— Coutts gave a little snort—'and that Mr Sexton Blake had asked him to ring up because they had got so far as Dorking but couldn't get any farther owing to a puncture. He said they had put the car in the garage of the White Hart Hotel, and could Dr Roon meet them there immediately as the storm was so bad. I asked the doctor what I should say, and he replied: 'Tell the inspector I will leave at once.'

Sexton Blake's firm mouth compressed until the lips were only a thin line. The cleverness of the thing lay in its very simplicity—it was just what might easily have happened.

'Was that all?' he asked, and was surprised when the girl shook her head.

'No, there was one other thing,' she answered, and for the first time her cool, level voice shook slightly. 'The man who rang up particularly requested that Dr Roon should bring with him the card he received this morning.'

'And of course he took it,' muttered the detective. 'Tell me, Miss—er—' He paused and looked at her inquiringly.

'Grayson,' she murmured.

'Tell me, Miss Grayson,' he continued swiftly, 'did Dr Roon leave here on foot?'

'No, he went in the car,' she answered.

'Alone?' asked Blake eagerly.

'Yes, he always drove himself—a small two-seater coupé.' And then noticing the frown on the detective's brow: 'Do you think anything can have happened to him, Mr Blake? He told me about the card, and—' Her voice trailed away incoherently.

'I'm afraid the worst has happened,' answered Blake grimly. 'There is just a chance that the car may have saved him. If he'd been on foot, it would have been hopeless, but the Green Jester may not have been prepared for a car.'

He rose to his feet.

'Is there any other means of getting from here to Dorking except by the main road?' he inquired quickly.

She shook her head.

'Then he certainly never went there,' snapped the detective, 'or we should have passed him, and we passed nothing.'

'Unless,' put in Coutts, up to now a silent listener, 'he reached the White Hart before we passed through the town.'

'There's a faint possibility he may have,' agreed Blake, but his tone was doubtful. 'However, we can soon see. Would you mind ringing up the White Hart and asking if Dr Roon has been there, Miss Grayson?'

She went over to the instrument, which stood on a large roll-top desk in the centre of the room, and consulting a directory, gave a number.

During the ensuing conversation, Sexton Blake gazed moodily at the electric fire, his brows drawn together, and the long, slim fingers of his right hand caressing his chin.

In a few seconds the girl turned from the telephone.

'They have seen nothing of Dr Roon at the White Hart,' she announced in a low voice which trembled in spite of her efforts to keep it steady.

Blake swung round at her words, and his face was set and tense—a hard, determined mask.

'I never expected they would,' he said harshly. 'Somewhere between here and Dorking the Green Jester was waiting for him; and he's got him.' His hands clenched until the knuckles stood out white against the bronzed skin, and abruptly he strode over to the door. 'Come on, Coutts!' he said, with his hand on the knob. 'We've got to find Roon. I'm afraid we are too late to save him, but we've got to find him—alive or otherwise.'

He half opened the door, and at that instant the telephone bell whirred insistently. With a little exclamation that showed how strained her nerves were, the girl turned to the instrument.

'Perhaps that is Dr Roon,' she suggested, as she picked up the receiver.

But they knew she only said it as a forlorn hope, knew that she would be surprised if she were right.

'Yes?' she called into the vulcanite mouthpiece. 'Yes, this is the Larches.' A pause followed, and Blake saw a peculiar expression cross the girl's face—an expression in which wonder and fear were curiously mingled. 'Yes, he's here now,' she continued, still with that odd look on her face. 'Who is speaking?' Again there was a pause, while she listened to the reply, and then: 'Very well, I'll tell him,' she said, and, glancing up at the detective, who was standing by her side, held out the receiver. 'Someone wants to speak to you,

Mr Blake—a man. He wouldn't give his name.'

With a sudden, unaccountable quickening of his pulses, the detective placed the black cylinder to his ear.

'Who is that?' he asked sharply; and over the wire floated a little babbling laugh.

'That Mr Blake?' inquired a high, squeaky voice. 'Thought I might catch you—he, he, he!—even if you can't catch me! He, he, he!'

Blake felt his flesh creep as he heard the little trilling peals of laughter that interspersed the staccato sentences. There was something horrible and sinister about that inane chuckling.

'I had to ring you up,' the toneless voice continued. 'Too good a joke to keep all to myself. He, he, he! Do you want to laugh, Blake—eh! If you do, go and look for Roon. He, he, he!'

'Who are you?' demanded the detective, as the other broke off to laugh breathlessly.

'Wouldn't you like to know!' came the reply. 'But you never will. He, he, he! That's what makes it all so amusing. The newspapers call me the Green Jester. It's a good name, only I'm not "green". He, he, he! Go and look for Roon, Blake—and take Coutts with you. You'll laugh till you cry when you find him. He looks so funny.'

There was a final chuckle and a click as the unknown rang off.

*   *   *

'Who was it—that horrible voice?' asked the girl with a shiver, her face white to the lips.

'The Green Jester,' answered Blake curtly, his finger tapping frantically at the hook of the telephone.

And Inspector Coutts gave a gasp.

'Who?' he cried, his eyes round with amazement. 'Why did he phone? What did he want?'

His questions, however, fell on deaf ears, for Sexton Blake was already talking to the exchange.

'Hallo!' he said. 'That call that came through just now. Will you tell me where it originated? Yes, I know all about your rules, but this is police business. Be quick, please!'

He waited impatiently, his fingers strumming on the top of the desk, his narrowed eyes staring fixedly before him at a blank space on the opposite wall.

The burly inspector was bursting with curiosity, but knowing Blake, he wisely refrained from plying him with any further questions at the moment.

An age seemed to pass—in reality it was less than a minute—before the detective got his answer.

'Your call came from a public box in the post office, High Street, Dorking,' said the emotionless voice of the telephone operator.

And, with a word of thanks, Blake hung up the receiver.

Turning to Coutts and the girl he rapidly gave them the gist of the unknown's message.

'Roon's somewhere in the vicinity of this house,' he concluded. 'I am certain of that. And the first thing we've got to do is to find him. I should say he's at some point between here and Dorking—or rather, his body is,' he added bitterly. 'We were too late to save him. The only thing we can hope for now is that we shall discover some clue that will give us the identity of his murderer.'

He was at the door before he had finished speaking, and, with Coutts and the girl at his heels, began hurriedly to descend the stairs. In the hall he paused and shot a question at the agitated secretary.

'How long have you been in Dr Roon's employ?' he asked sharply.

She hesitated, evidently disconcerted at the abruptness of the remark.

'About—about five years,' she stammered at length.

'H'm!' The detective walked to the front door and opened it. 'I suppose you're fairly well acquainted with his family history?' he went on. 'Has he any relations—living?'

'I think he has a brother,' she answered, raising her eyebrows slightly in surprise. 'Yes, I'm sure he has. I've never seen him, because I don't think he lives in England, but the doctor has mentioned him several times.'

Sexton Blake frowned. The answer was not the one he had expected.

'Any other relatives beside this brother you speak of?' he inquired.

She shook her head.

'I have never heard of any,' she replied.

The detective bit his lower lip, seemed about to put another question, and then, apparently thinking better of it, refrained.

'You—you will let me know if—if you find anything, won't you?' said the girl, as he began to descend the steps.

'Of course! I shall come back here, in any case,' answered Sexton Blake absently. 'There are several other questions I should like to ask you.'

The storm had passed over, although there was a faint muttering of thunder in the distance, but the rain was still falling heavily. Sexton Blake, except for mechanically turning up the collar of his coat, seemed unconscious of this as he took his place behind the wheel and pressed on the self-starter. There was an introspective, thoughtful expression in his eye as the powerful engine started into life, and he waited for the stout figure of the Scotland Yard man to clamber clumsily into the vacant seat beside him.

'Where do we go first?' grunted Coutts, as the car shot forward with a jerk. 'This is like looking for a needle in a haystack.'

'We are going slowly along the road in the direction of the town—the way we came,' answered Blake, 'and we're going to keep a sharp look-out for any traces of Roon or his car, or both. If you take the left-hand side of the road I'll take the right.'

There was no need to look far, as it happened, for as they came out of the drive the burly inspector gave a loud exclamation and pointed ahead.

'Look! There, Blake!' he yelled excitedly, clutching at the detective's arm.

And Sexton Blake nodded, for he had already seen the object that had attracted the Scotland Yard man's attention.

Close to the plantation of wheat, its bonnet half buried in the ditch at the side of the road, was a small two-seater coupé.

'That wasn't there when we arrived,' said Coutts, breathing hard. 'It must have been put there while we were actually in the house.'

The detective nodded again, but made no other reply, and in a few seconds they drew abreast of the small car and came to a halt. Getting down, Blake stood for a moment gazing at the wet, slushy surface of the road. The tracks of the two-seater were plainly visible for apparently no other traffic had passed that way since it had been ditched, and the detective could see the high ridges of mud that the wheels had thrown up when it had swerved suddenly. With a word of warning to the burly inspector to be careful not to obliterate the marks, Sexton Blake walked a few yards back the way they had come, and presently stopped, bending slightly forward. The wheel tracks at this point were appreciably deeper, and between them was a tiny pool of black oil.

'Here is the place where Roon was held up,' he said, pointing this out to Coutts. 'It's obvious that the car stopped here for several minutes.'

The Scotland Yard man nodded.

'The Green Jester must have moved pretty quickly,' he grunted. 'Allowing that it took a quarter of an hour after the bogus telephone message for Roon to get out his car and reach this spot—I don't see how the Green Jester could have got here from Dorking in the time.'

'He couldn't,' declared the Baker Street detective, 'unless he's got wings. Even in a car he couldn't do it with the roads in this state, and there are no signs of any other car having been in the vicinity, except our own.'

'The only alternative is that it was an accomplice who did the phoning,' said Coutts, tugging viciously at his bristling moustache.

'If the call came from Dorking, yes,' agreed Sexton Blake, with wrinkled brows. 'But we've no evidence that it did.'

'I doubt if there's another call office nearer,' said the inspector, 'and he must have used a call office, unless—'

He broke off and looked at Blake as the significance of the alternative suddenly dawned on him.

'Unless he used a private phone,' finished the detective quietly. 'Which means he must live somewhere in the immediate neighbourhood. Yes, I'd thought of that.'

'We can easily put it to the test,' said Coutts excitedly. 'It shouldn't be difficult to find out from the exchange where that phone call came from.'

'H'm, perhaps!' Blake pursed his pips and rubbed his chin. 'He would have realised that, so I'm very much afraid that, even if we did trace the call, it would only lead to a dead end. However, there's no harm in trying when we go back to the house. In the meanwhile, we'd better have a look at that car.'

He turned and walked back to the capsized coupé. It lay half on the side-walk and half in the broad ditch that bordered the road, reared up at a drunken angle.

Wondering what horror he was going to find, Blake pulled open the door and looked inside. It was with a little shock of surprise that he saw it was empty, for he had expected to find the body of Roon.

Ample traces of a tragedy having taken place were there, however, for the light upholstery of the seats was dappled with great splashes of blood that glistened in the light from the door, and when the detective touched one of these with his finger he found it was still wet.

'Good heavens! It's like a slaughter-house!' ejaculated Coutts, peering in over Blake's shoulder.

'A very apt description,' murmured the detective, 'for undoubtedly that is the use to which it has been put. The question *is*—where is the body?'

He straightened up and looked about him, but there was no sign of the missing doctor, either dead or alive. The frown between Blake's eyes deepened. Had the Green Jester carried off the body of his unfortunate victim, and if so for what conceivable purpose?

The detective had no doubt whatever that Roon was dead. No man could have been wounded sufficiently to have caused all that blood and still remain alive. Besides, that jeering message from the unknown murderer was enough proof. He would never have phoned unless he had already carried out his threat. But why hadn't he left the body in the car?'

Blake shook his head in answer to his own unspoken question and then swung round sharply as Inspector Coutts' voice called out to him.

The Scotland Yard man had been searching round the derelict coupé, and was now standing on the other side of the ditch, pointing to a ragged break in the hedge that divided the wheat field from the road.

'Come here, Blake!' he jerked. 'Somebody has been through here! The wheat's all trampled down, and there's more blood.'

Sexton Blake sprang lightly across the ditch and joined him. The field was a morass of half liquid mud into which he sank up to his ankles. But he was too interested in the discovery the inspector had made to heed. The wheat was crushed and broken, as though by the passage of some heavy object, and the green of it stained here and there an ugly red—sinister marks that left little room for doubt as to what it was that had been dragged across that place.

'Obviously he came this way,' said Sexton Blake. 'But why did he bother to take so much trouble? I can't understand—'

And then, looking ahead, he suddenly realised the reason for the Green Jester's action, and into his mind flashed one sentence spoken in that high-pitched, squeaky voice:

'He looks so funny!'

'Good heavens, Coutts!' he cried—and there was a note of positive horror in his voice. 'The scarecrow!'

And, careless of the mud that splashed him from head to foot, he went racing in the direction of the forlorn, bedraggled dummy that he knew was not a dummy but a lifeless thing that had once been a living, breathing man!

There it was, the supreme joke of this perverted joker, hanging limply from the supports that had formed the framework of the original—a horrible, faceless travesty of a human being that made even the hardened Coutts go white as he looked at it.

Pinned to the tattered coat was a stained and crumpled card, and the grinning figure of the emerald-garbed fool seemed to be pointing mockingly at Blake as he detached the sodden pasteboard and read the doggerel verse scrawled on the other side:

> '*I don't like your face, Dr Roon,*
> *It is white, round, and flat like a moon,*
> *It annoys me to know*
> *That you're living, and so*
> *I shall take steps to kill you—by noon!*'

Silently, for he felt momentarily bereft of words, Sexton Blake handed the card to Coutts, and as he did so a church clock somewhere in the vicinity chimed the hour of twelve!

*   *   *

'Good heavens, it's horrible!' whispered Coutts huskily. 'Horrible, Blake! I've experienced some ghastly things in my time, but nothing to equal this.'

Sexton Blake, his face stern and set, nodded grimly as he bent over the body that they had succeeded in cutting loose from the frame of the scarecrow.

'The man who did this must be a fiend incarnate,' he muttered, gently covering the head with his handkerchief. 'Except for the clothes and the contents of the pockets, I doubt if anyone would be able to identify him.'

'I can understand murder up to a point,' remarked the inspector, with a shiver. 'Given no conscience and a distorted sense of values, anybody might become a murderer, but this is sheer wanton brutality.'

'It appears so,' murmured the detective, busily examining a little pile of odds and ends that he had removed from the dead man's pockets and placed on a second handkerchief borrowed from Coutts for the purpose. 'And yet—I don't know—something seems to tell me that there's a purpose behind it all—and a pretty strong purpose, too.'

The Scotland Yard man snorted—a habit of his when he disagreed strongly with anyone's ideas.

'You're always trying to find an obscure reason when one doesn't exist,' he grunted. 'I've said from the beginning—and you mark my words, for you'll find I'm right—this Green Jester fellow's a maniac—stark raving mad—and that's why we've never been able to catch him, because there's no motive, except the lust of killing, to give us a lead.'

'You may be right,' assented the detective a trifle absently.

He was looking through the contents of a leather wallet, and had come upon a five-pound note, which seemed to be taking up all his attention.

'Right—of course I'm right,' said Coutts decisively. 'Even your theory that all the dead people were without relations has been disproved. Dr Roon has a brother, and—what's that you've found?'

'Only a banknote,' replied Blake—'and it's rather curious.'

'Why?' jerked the burly inspector. 'Roon appears to have been quite well off; I don't see anything curious in his having a five-pound note on him.'

'So far as that goes, neither do I,' said the detective quietly. 'But when I find the name "Julia Rothe, Maytree Cottage, Horsham", written on the back, it strikes me as curious.'

'What?' Coutts almost shouted the word, and, stumbling over to Blake's side, bent down. 'By the Lord Harry,' he ejaculated, as he saw the faint pencil writing, 'what do you make of that?'

'Nothing,' answered Sexton Blake, 'except that it's a very extraordinary thing. Julia Rothe was killed by the Green Jester five weeks ago in her sitting-room at Horsham. In the pocket of the Green Jester's latest victim we discover a five-pound note that at one time obviously belonged to the murdered woman—a strange coincidence.'

'If it is a coincidence,' said Coutts, puckering his forehead. 'I should think it was far more likely to have been put there by the Green Jester himself—one of his distorted ideas of a joke, perhaps.'

'Probably.' Blake folded the note and put it back in the wallet. 'It would interest me to know, however, how he got hold of it in the first place.'

'Stole it—when he killed the poor woman,' said the Scotland Yard man, but the detective shook his head.

'It wouldn't have been in her possession,' he replied. 'It was changed somewhere—at a shop, most likely, where they didn't know her. That's why she wrote her name and address on the back.'

'H'm, it's certainly strange!' mused Coutts thoughtfully. 'However, we can discuss it later, in more pleasant surroundings,' he added, shivering. 'At present all I want is to get out of this infernal wet.'

'Then the best thing I can do is to notify the local police about this'—Blake jerked his hand towards the body—'and get them to send an ambulance. Go back to the house in the car and phone from there, while I have a last look round.'

'I will,' said Coutts, nodding, 'and I'll take those things with me, if you've done looking them over.'

He pointed to the small pile of personal belongings on the handkerchief.

'Yes, do. I've finished with them for the moment,' answered Sexton Blake, and turned his attention to the body, while Coutts wrapped up the contents of the pockets and stuffed them into his pocket.

'I won't be long!' he called over his shoulder as he squelched through the mud towards the gap in the hedge by which he had gained admittance to the field. But the detective only grunted in reply, being engaged in making a close examination of the dead man's shoes.

The inspector was saved a journey, however, for as he emerged into the road he saw a cyclist patrol plodding steadily towards him. Waiting until he came abreast, Coutts stopped the man, and, revealing his identity, told him, in a few brief sentences, what had occurred.

'Murdered?' exclaimed the policeman incredulously. 'Dr Roon?'

He stared stupidly, mouth agape.

'Yes,' snapped Coutts irritably, for the wet condition of his clothes had made him bad-tempered. 'I said so, didn't I? Hurry back to your station and tell them to send an ambulance and the divisional surgeon. Tell the inspector in charge to come along, too.'

The dazed constable saluted, and remounting his machine, went pedalling off swiftly in the direction he had come.

Retracing his steps, Coutts made his way back to Blake and explained his lucky meeting with the constable.

'Good!' said Blake. 'The sooner they send that ambulance the better. There's nothing more to be learned here, and I'm rather anxious to get back to the house.'

He searched in his pocket and produced a cigarette-case. Offering a cigarette to the burly inspector, he lit one himself and slowly inhaled the smoke, staring thoughtfully and silently at the sky line.

It seemed an eternity, waiting in that sodden field, before a jangling bell announced the arrival of the ambulance, and with it an inspector of police and a tall, grave-faced man, who proved to be the police surgeon for the district.

The brief preliminary introductions were soon got over, and after Coutts had given a short, concise account of what had occurred, Dr Partridge and the local inspector went over to the still form lying beneath the skeleton framework of the scarecrow.

Bending down, the divisional surgeon gently lifted the handkerchief with which Blake had covered the head. Drawing in his breath with a sharp hiss as he saw the injuries, he turned to Coutts and the detective.

'Good heavens!' he ejaculated in wonder and horror. 'This is bad! It looks as though some heavy instrument, such as a hammer or similar object, had been used.'

'Was that, in your opinion, the actual cause of death?' inquired Sexton Blake, coming over to his side.

'Most certainly!' replied the doctor, looking up. 'Any one of these injuries would have proved fatal, but I should say that the man who committed this crime was in such a paroxysm of fury that he continued to rain blow after blow long after life had ceased to exist.'

The detective nodded, but whether in agreement with the other's theory or at some private idea of his own it would have been difficult to judge.

The doctor finished his brief examination and began talking to Blake, while Detective-Inspector Coutts was issuing a few final instructions to the local police officer.

'Poor Roon!' he said, in a slightly-hushed voice. 'I knew him quite well. It's dreadful he should have died like this.'

'Was he in practice?' asked the detective, and the other shook his head.

'No, I think he gave up the medical profession a long time ago,' he replied. 'Anyway, before he came here, and he's lived in this neighbourhood for—let me see'—he screwed up his eyes in an effort of concentration—'just over six years.'

'What sort of a man was he?' queried Blake interestedly.

'Quite a decent fellow,' said Dr Partridge. 'A bit moody and taciturn at times, but on the whole quite a good sort. Of course, I've read about this Green Jester, as they call him,' he went on. 'And it seems inexplicable to me that anybody except a madman could be guilty of such appalling crimes, particularly as there appears to be no motive attached to them.'

'Everybody seems to think that the Green Jester's a maniac,' remarked the detective, smiling.

'Of course, it's the only feasible explanation,' rejoined the doctor emphatically. 'No sane man would make a joke of murder.'

'He's sufficiently sane, at any rate, to avoid capture,' retorted Blake; and then, changing the subject: 'Tell me! Did Dr Roon ever mention his brother to you?'

'Yes.' The divisional surgeon looked rather surprised at the question. 'Several times. He used to go and stay with him every now and again.'

'His brother lived somewhere abroad, didn't he?' inquired the detective; and Partridge nodded.

'In Paris, I believe,' he answered. 'I don't know much about it. It was only during the last two years that Roon spoke of him. They had a quarrel or something before that. Excuse me,' he added, turning as the local inspector called him, and, leaving Blake, went over to see what the man wanted.

The detective strolled back to the car while the body was being placed in the ambulance for conveyance to the mortuary, and presently, when it had driven off with the inspector and the divisional surgeon, Coutts joined him.

'Thank Heaven that's over!' growled the Scotland Yard man, huddling himself into the wet seat and rubbing his hands vigorously to try to warm them. 'What I want more than anything else at the moment is a hot bath and a change of clothes.'

'I'm afraid it will be some little time before you can get either,' said Blake, starting the car. 'We've got to go back and acquaint the household with the news.'

'I don't mind that so much,' said Coutts bitterly. 'It's when the news reaches the papers that's worrying me. The fourth murder, and we're no nearer catching this Green Jester than we ever were.'

'No, but we're very near catching a cold,' answered the detective dryly, as Coutts ended with a prodigious sneeze, and the inspector grunted.

A patch of blue had appeared in the sky, and the rain had almost ceased by the time they drew up in front of the covered porch and were greeted by the anxious face of the girl, who was standing in the doorway.

'Have you found anything?' she asked; and then, as Sexton Blake nodded gravely: 'Not—not what you feared.'

'Worse than we feared,' answered the detective shortly.

She gave a low exclamation, and her face went colourless.

'What—' she began tremulously; but he interrupted her.

'Let us go into the library,' he suggested, and glanced at the figure of the butler, who was lurking in a doorway near at hand.

The girl inclined her head, and in silence led the way up the staircase, followed by Blake and Coutts. In the big room she faced them, her back to the desk.

'Now, tell me!' Her voice was the merest whisper, and without waste of time the detective gave her a brief outline of the tragedy. 'Horrible!' She shuddered and looked at the vacant chair before the open desk. 'Why, a few hours ago he was sitting there, and now—'

'I know,' said Blake gently, as she turned away and sank into a chair by the fireplace. 'It's a dreadful occurrence, and the fact that we were all more or less prepared for it makes it no less of a shock. Under the circumstances I am sorry to have to worry you with questions, but since we were too late to save Dr Roon, the next best thing we can do is to try to find his murderer.'

The girl nodded.

'I'll help you all I can,' she murmured, 'though I don't quite see in what way.'

'Well, for one thing, I should like the address of his bankers,' said the detective, 'and also the firm of solicitors who had charge of his affairs.'

'I can give you those.' She pulled herself together with an obvious effort, and, rising, went over to the desk. 'Dr Roon banked with the Southern Union, Piccadilly branch,' she said, writing it down on a slip of paper, 'And his lawyers were Sneed, Soanes, & Sneed, of Bedford Row.'

She handed the paper to Blake.

'You mentioned that he had a brother,' he said, folding it and putting it in his pocket. 'Can you give me his address?'

'I'm afraid I can't,' she answered, shaking her head. 'I think he lives somewhere in Paris. Dr Roon used to receive letters from there, and he told me they were from his brother.'

'You never saw any of them?' asked Blake quickly; and again she shook her head.

'No, he used to destroy them as soon as he had read them,' she replied.

'I see!' The detective paused, as though he were listening, and then continued: 'How long has he been receiving these letters from Paris?'

The girl thought for a moment and Coutts frowned impatiently. Why was Blake wasting time with these futile questions? What did it matter how long Roon had been hearing from his brother?

'For some time,' she replied, at length. 'About two years.'

'Not before?' There was a little gleam of interest in Blake's eyes as he put the question.

'No! I think he had quarrelled with his brother and they only made it up two years ago.'

'Did Doctor Roon ever tell you what the quarrel was about?' asked Blake.

'No,' answered the girl again, and the detective nodded, as though he had expected her to make that reply.

'He was in the habit of making periodical visits to see his brother, wasn't he?' he went on.

She answered in the affirmative, looking a trifle surprised at his knowledge of the doctor's habits, as did Coutts, for neither of them knew of the conversation Blake had had with the divisional surgeon.

'How often did he go,' was Sexton Blake's next question.

'Once a month regularly,' she replied.

'And was he away for long?'

The detective was pacing up and down thoughtfully while putting his questions, and now he paused by the door.

'Sometimes a week, sometimes a fortnight, but more often only a week,' said the girl.

'H'm! His brother never visited him, I suppose?' Although he spoke to the girl, his half-closed eyes were fixed on the door.

'No, never,' she answered. 'I used to wonder—'

'Excuse me, Miss Grayson,' interrupted Blake. With a sudden spring he gripped the handle and wrenched the door open.

'You will hear better inside,' he remarked quietly, as the sleek, black-haired butler overbalanced and fell into the room.

*　　*　　*

Dusk was falling and a pale sliver of moon hung in the darkening sky when a man walked rapidly down New Bond Street, swung sharply into a side turning, and entered the vestibule of a large block of mansion flats.

He stepped into the waiting automatic lift with an assured air and, pressing a button, was carried noiselessly to the fourth floor. Leaving the lift, he crossed the carpeted corridor and, pausing outside a polished rosewood door, raised his hand and gave a gentle and peculiar tap on the small, grotesquely-patterned bronze knocker.

'Is Oswald in?' he asked, smiling pleasantly at the neatly-dressed maid who opened the door.

'I don't know! I'll see!' Her hard face remained expressionless except for the habitual scowl that marred the smoothness of her brow.

'You may see, but you know,' said the visitor, and, seeing her frown deepen, added: 'Why don't you cultivate a sense of humour, Alice? It is tragic to see a girl with your surpassing loveliness without a sense of humour.'

'You're too fresh, Slade,' she snapped, her black eyes blazing with anger.

'I've come straight off the ice,' he retorted, and chuckled as she flounced away, and was still chuckling when, after a short interval, she returned and held open the door.

'Mr Kyne will see you,' she said ungraciously.

'He undoubtedly will, unless he's gone blind,' said Slade, stepping across the threshold. 'Thank you, Alice, for your kindness in acting as an ambassador, or whatever is the female equivalent.'

She took no notice of his chaff, but led the way to a half-closed door that opened on the left of the spacious lobby. Pushing it wider, she stood aside and glared at him as he slipped past her and entered the room, shutting the door with a vicious slam when he was inside.

It was a large and luxuriously-furnished room, half-study, half-office, the walls panelled with expensive woods, and the chairs and lounges upholstered in costly brocades. At a rather ornate Empire writing-table, a man was seated, scanning a legal-looking document, which he laid aside at the noise of the slamming door, and raised his head.

'Good-evening, Slade! I expected you,' he greeted briefly, and waved a fat hand towards a chair facing him.

Mr Oswald Kyne was a smooth man in every sense of the word. Smooth was his thin, greying hair brushed back from his high forehead, smooth were his plump white hands glittering with too many rings, and smooth was his heavy-jowled, clean-shaven face.

Oily would perhaps have described him better, but the expression would have shocked Mr Kyne's sensitive nature. A money-lender by profession, a 'fence' and blackmailer by inclination and because nature had supplied him with a criminal brain, Mr Kyne had only one illusion left in the world—that he was a gentleman.

'Sit down,' he said, in a deep rolling voice, which sounded as though he mentally smacked his lips at every word. 'How did you manage to get away?'

'Told the girl I had to meet a relative who was coming from the North,' answered Slade, lighting a cigar which he took without permission from a box on the table. 'I suppose you saw an account of the affair in the papers?'

The smooth man nodded.

'Yes, the evening editions are 'umming—er—humming with it,' he said. 'Directly I read of the murder I guessed you'd be up. We seem to have had all our trouble for nothing.'

'I think we should have done that in any case,' said the late Dr Roon's butler bitterly. 'There was nothing in the house worth taking away.'

'H'm!' Mr Kyne frowned and pursed his fat lips. 'I was told that Roon was a rich man. I thought it was a cert to plant you there as butler.'

'Whoever told you Roon was rich is a bigger liar than you are!' said Slade coolly. 'And that's saying a lot. Roon was on the verge of bankruptcy. I reckon the Green Jester did him a good turn when he popped him off.'

He expelled a cloud of blue smoke towards the gilded ceiling.

'Well, I suppose it can't be helped!' sighed Mr Kyne resignedly. 'We made a mistake, that's all. I certainly thought we should be able to clear a nice little profit—with your skill as a draughtsman and access to his cheque-book. However, let's forget it.' He laid his fat hands on the blotting-pad. 'The Duchess of Lamport is looking for a new footman,' he went on quickly, 'and the Lamport diamonds are bee-utiful!' He spread his hands expressively and winked, 'I've got all the references you'll want, and you can leave your present job at once. Give the murder as an excuse—'

'Not so fast,' interrupted Slade. 'I'll leave my present job as soon as you like, and I'm doing no more lackey work yet awhile.'

'But my dear fellow,' protested Mr Kyne, 'this is a cinch—a certainty.'

'It may be, but I've got something better,' retorted the butler.

'Better than the Lamport diamonds!' said the fat man, in a hushed voice, as though his visitor had said something blasphemous.

'Yes.' Slade pulled his chair closer and leaned across the writing-table. 'Suppose I tell you that I know who the Green Jester is?' he said impressively.

Mr Kyne stared at him, his jaw dropped, his mouth an O of startled surprise.

'You know who the Green Jester is?' he repeated slowly, after a long silence.

The sleek-haired butler nodded.

'I do,' he replied, and, dropping his voice to a whisper: 'I saw the murder committed, Kyne!'

'Good heavens!' The moneylender lay back limply in his chair, and his forehead glistened in the light.

'The police haven't the ghost of a clue yet,' Slade continued. 'Nor has that interfering "busy", Sexton Blake. I was listening at the door of the library while they were talking to the Grayson girl until that cursed private detective caught me. I pretended to be very confused—admitted that I was anxious to hear if they had found the master!' He laughed harshly. 'I wasn't supposed to know anything about the murder then. I think they believed me.'

'Who—who do you think the Green Jester is?' muttered Mr Kyne, passing his tongue over his lips that had suddenly gone dry.

'I don't think—I know!' snapped the butler. 'And he's got to pay me a pretty big sum to keep my knowledge to myself. The Green Jester is—'

He whispered a name, and the stout man's flaccid face flushed until the veins stood out at his temples with some suppressed emotion.

For nearly a minute he looked at Slade in silence—a silence broken only by the ticking of the little silver clock that stood beside the blotting-pad. Then he rose unsteadily to his feet, and, going over to the door, he locked it.

'We've got to talk this thing over,' he said softly, returning to the table; and for close on an hour they remained whispering together, their heads almost touching.

Eleven was striking when Slade emerged from the entrance to

the block of flats, and he was smiling as though well satisfied with his evening's work.

Had he seen the figure that appeared from the shadow of the next doorway, as he set off up the street, he would not have felt so pleased, for the trailer had been at his heels when he entered Mr Oswald's Kyne's sumptuous abode, had waited patiently for him to come out, and now followed cautiously in his wake as he turned the corner!

*   *   *

Sexton Blake pushed aside a pile of papers and documents that he had been examining, and rose from his desk with a faint sigh of weariness. Crossing over to the mantelpiece, he filled and lit his old briar, and, dropping into an easy-chair, began to smoke reflectively.

The hands of the clock were approaching the hour of seven, and it was the evening of the day following the murder of Dr Roon.

During the intervening period the detective had been a very busy man indeed. He had visited the dead man's bankers, and also Messrs. Sneed, Soanes, & Sneed, of Bedford Row, and the net result of his labours had given him much food for thought.

The doctor's affairs were in a decidedly chaotic state. There was very little balance at his bank, and, according to Mr Harold Sneed, an elderly, rusty man, and the senior partner of his firm of lawyers, writs were out against him everywhere, and bankruptcy proceedings were imminent.

Roon had been quite well off—a rich man, in fact—less than two years previously, but an unfortunate speculation on the Stock Exchange, which should have brought him a huge fortune, went wrong and swallowed up nearly the whole of his capital. He had left a will, which was in the possession of the solicitors, in which he appointed his brother sole executor and residuary legatee, but it didn't appear as if the brother—whose name was James Roon and who lived in a small flat in the Rue Douane, Paris—was likely to benefit at all, for the dead man's debts amounted to over sixty thousand pounds, and his total assets were not a tenth of that sum.

Mr Sneed had wired acquainting James Roon of his brother's tragic death, and had received in reply a telegram from his housekeeper. It appeared that her employer was away on a tour with some friends, but that as soon as he returned, which she expected would be in about a week's time, he would communicate with the lawyers.

She stated that she couldn't get in touch with him sooner because he was on a walking tour, and she had no knowledge of his whereabouts. So much had Blake gleaned from his inquiries, and interesting as it was, it brought him no nearer to solving the mystery of the Green Jester, or helped him at all in discovering the identity of that grim and mysterious joker.

The slight piece of evidence he had picked up in that field of death, and which he had so far kept to himself, seemed to point to only one conclusion, and at the time he had been convinced that it was the right one. But his efforts to find some substantiating facts had so far met with failure. And not only that—the few facts he had found definitely clashed with his shadowy preconceived theory.

Passing his hand with a tired gesture across his brow, Blake knocked the ashes from his pipe and was in the act of refilling it when Mrs Bardell entered to announce the arrival of Detective-Inspector Coutts.

The Scotland Yard man looked worried and haggard as he came in, panting from his quick ascent of the stairs, and the dark circles round his rather prominent eyes testified to lack of sleep.

'Any news, Blake?' he greeted, throwing his hat on the couch and sinking into a chair.

The detective shook his head.

'None,' he replied. 'I was hoping that an inquiry into Roon's private affairs might supply us with some sort of motive, but it hasn't. This crime appears as senseless as the others.'

'Yes, you'll have to come round to my way of thinking in the end,' said the inspector. 'These murders are the work of a madman without a doubt.'

'I'm almost beginning to believe you,' said Blake. 'And yet—'

He shrugged his shoulders, leaving the sentence unfinished.

'And yet you don't really think anything of the kind,' grunted Coutts. 'Well, anyway, I'm working on those lines. I've had a long talk with the Chief, and he agrees with me.' He helped himself to a cigar from the box on the table at his elbow and bit off the end. 'I suppose nothing's happened with regard to that butler fellow, Slade?'

'I've had Tinker trailing him since yesterday afternoon,' answered the detective. 'He picked him up at Roon's house in the evening, and followed him up to town. The man's undoubtedly a crook. At nine o'clock last night he paid Mr Oswald Kyne a visit. The gentle Oswald only has two kinds of visitors, and Slade certainly isn't one of his victims.'

Coutts laughed.

'He may be a crook,' he said, 'but I don't think he's mixed up in this Green Jester business.'

'Well, anyway, Tinker's still sticking to him like grim death,' answered Blake. 'It may lead to nothing, but we can't afford to take any chances.'

'I'm afraid he's only wasting his time,' declared the burly inspector, shaking his close-cropped head.

But in this he was wrong, for Fate so arranged it that the humble Slade was destined to lead them to the heart of the mystery, and in doing so save the lives of at least two innocent actors in the sinister drama, the final scene of which was at that instant being set.

'It seems to me,' began Sexton Blake, 'that if there is a reason— Come in!'

He broke off as there came a tap at the door.

A moment later Mrs Bardell appeared in answer to his curt invitation.

'There's a young lady to see you, Mr B,' she announced breathlessly—'a Miss Grayson.'

A gleam of interest flashed into Blake's eyes.

'Ask her to come up,' he said; and Coutts rose to his feet excitedly.

'What do you think she wants?' he asked, as the housekeeper departed. 'Why has she come all the way from Dorking?'

'My dear Coutts, how should I know?' replied the detective, a trifle impatiently. 'I haven't yet achieved the art of telepathy. I've no doubt she will tell us herself, since that is obviously what she has come for.'

He greeted the girl with a smile as she entered a little nervously, and pushed forward a chair.

'I hope I'm not bothering you,' she said, sitting down, 'but I had to come to London this evening, and today, while I was looking through Dr Roon's desk, I found something which I'm sure you ought to see.'

She took off her gloves and fumbled in her bag.

'It's very good of you to have taken the trouble, Miss Grayson,' replied the detective, while Coutts watched the girl eagerly. 'What is it you found?'

'This,' she answered, and held out a folded paper. 'It was caught at the back of one of the drawers.'

Sexton Blake took the slip from her and opened it. It was a cutting from the newspaper, yellow with age, and as his eye fell upon a name printed on it he gave a sudden exclamation.

'What is it, Blake?'

Coutts came quickly to his side, and glanced over his shoulder.

'It appears to be the account of a fire at the Ritz Carlton Hotel, Brighton,' said Sexton Blake, and his voice vibrated with suppressed excitement.

The burly inspector grunted disappointedly.

'Then it can't be of any interest to us,' he grunted. 'I happen to remember that fire. It was about fifteen years ago, at the time when—'

'All the same, it is of immense interest to us,' retorted the detective quickly. 'Listen to this!'

Slowly and distinctly he read a portion of the notice:

'Among the few people saved from the burning building was Mr Austin Ballard, the well-known tobacco millionaire. He was occupying a suite on the third floor, and, being a martyr to insomnia, had taken a sleeping draught before retiring. The drug was evidently a strong one, for the fire failed to wake him, and but for the heroic efforts of two fellow-guests, Mr Hamilton Lorne and Mr Percival Haynes, he would have undoubtedly perished in the flames. As it was, he suffered a severe shock and several bad burns, and had to be rushed to the nearest hospital.'

Blake stopped reading and looked at the astonished face of Coutts.

'What do you think of that?' he said softly.

'Think!' The Scotland Yard man's voice almost rose to a shout. 'I don't know what to think. It seems that at last we have established a connection between the first two victims of the Green Jester.'

'We have done more than that,' answered Sexton Blake quietly. 'We have established a connection between the first two and the last. Otherwise, what was this cutting doing in Dr Roon's desk?'

'Yes, you're right,' agreed Coutts with a nod. 'But even now it hasn't got us much farther.'

'Hasn't it?' Blake's eyes were glittering as he spoke. 'I think it has supplied us with a clue to the whole of this mystery.'

He laid down the cutting and crossed over to a row of bookshelves that housed the famous 'Index'. While the inspector and the girl stared at him in silence he ran his finger along the series of volumes until he came to one which he pulled out. Rapidly turning the pages, he presently paused, and then came back to the table with the open book in his hand.

'Read that,' he said, and pointed to a two-column news item that had been clipped from a paper.

Coutts leaned forward, and his eyes nearly started from his head as he saw the heavy lead type headlines:

MYSTERY OF A MILLIONAIRE!
Mr Austin Ballard Goes Out and Never Comes Back!

Mystery surrounds the strange disappearance of Mr Austin Ballard, the tobacco magnate, who left his house at Esher yesterday morning with the intention of going for his usual walk, which he invariably took at ten o'clock.

He never returned, and although the police were informed and search-parties have been scouring the neighbourhood, no trace has yet been found of the missing man. Foul play is suspected since Mr Ballard was in the best of health when he left home.

'Great Caesar!' exclaimed the Scotland Yard man. 'I remember this case, all right. I knew Ballard's name was familiar when you read that fire account, but for the moment couldn't place it. He disappeared—let me see—'

He frowned.

'Just two weeks before the Green Jester killed Hamilton Lorne,' remarked Sexton Blake impressively, and pointed to a date on top of the page.

'So he did!' Coutts' face expressed absolute bewilderment. 'But what in thunder is the connection?'

Blake shook his head.

'That's what we have to find out,' he answered, 'and when we've found it we shall have learnt the secret of the Green Jester!'

A silence fell, during which Sexton Blake stared unseeingly at the open book on the table. From its white pages seemed to rise a faint mist, which took the form of a terrifying green figure— terrifying because it was faceless, and had neither shape nor substance. And somewhere in the back of his mind hovered four shapes, even less tangible—a stockbroker, an architect, a doctor and an elderly spinster, who had been sacrificed to satisfy the perverted humour of the Green Jester!

*   *   *

The chief reason that had brought Muriel Grayson from Dorking that evening was a certain fair-haired young man, in whom she was more than ordinarily interested.

After taking leave of Sexton Blake the girl hurried to the appointed meeting place, realising, with a sense of dismay, that she was already more than a little late.

However, since time and women have nothing in common, she consoled herself with the thought that he would undoubtedly wait, and having settled down in the corner of a bus that would take her within three minutes' walk of the little restaurant where at that moment her patient swain was trying to interest himself in an evening paper, she dismissed the matter from her mind and allowed her thoughts to dwell upon the tragedy that had so suddenly burst into the comparative calmness of her life.

She found it difficult to realise that Dr Roon was dead, and that shortly she would have to look for fresh work—still more that his death had been a violent one at the hands of the mysterious individual whose ghastly crimes she had followed with interest in the papers and speculated as to the motive behind them.

Dr Roon had held a theory, which he had often asserted, that they were the work of a maniac, and she gave a little shudder as it flashed through her brain that he must have proved or disproved this idea of his when he had met, face to face, the man who had killed him.

For no reason at all she found herself thinking of Slade. She had been the least surprised of them all when Blake had discovered him listening at the door, for she had suspected him of the habit for a long time.

There was something furtive and unpleasant about the man which had caused her to dislike him from the first, and she had often wondered since the murder of the doctor whether the sleek-haired butler knew more about it than he had said.

She was still thinking about him when the bus set her down at Piccadilly Circus. Her quickest way to reach her destination was by taking a short cut through a labyrinth of side streets, and so she set off, walking hurriedly.

By one of those peculiar coincidences which are more common in fact than in fiction, she suddenly saw the man who was occupying her thoughts. He appeared from the confusion of a traffic block, and was crossing the road swiftly, making for the very street that she was herself heading for. It was only a momentary glimpse, for, as he reached the pavement and disappeared down the narrow turning, the string of waiting vehicles moved forward, and she lost sight of him. By the time she entered the street herself there was no sign of him.

A little way down, drawn up by the side of the kerb, was a large limousine car, but the girl took no notice of it, and was passing it almost at a run when a spark of light from the interior attracted her attention, and she turned her head.

A man seated in the driving seat was in the act of lighting a cigar, and as the yellow flame of the match illumined his face, she stopped dead and stared.

The light from a near-by standard fell full on her, and he recognised her at the same instant. With a muttered exclamation of alarm, he jerked open the door and sprang out. Two strides and he was by her side, gripping her arm.

'Don't make a sound,' he whispered warningly. 'Come into the car. I want to talk to you.'

Almost before she realised what he was doing, the dazed girl found herself pushed into the dark interior of the limousine.

'I don't understand,' she began huskily. 'What are you—'

The sentence faded to a choking murmur as a heavy hand was clapped over her mouth and nostrils. In a panic of fear she struggled desperately to free herself from that strangling grasp.

But the man's strength was abnormal. She felt herself forced back on the cushions of the seat, and his other hand found her throat.

She tried to breathe; to shout for help. But the grip tightened, and presently, with a last convulsive movement, her senses left her, and she lay still.

*　　*　　*

The soft lapping sound of water washing against the wooden side of the boat woke the man who lay on a narrow pallet in the tiny cabin.

He stirred uneasily, opening his eyes and staring into the pitch, inky blackness that surrounded him. The noise of the water was a familiar one, for it had been his constant companion for longer than he cared to think. Turning with difficulty, because of the manacies that confined his wrists and ankles, he lay on his back, moving his jaws as best he could to try and ease the ache and stiffness caused by the gag that was securely tied about his mouth.

Although the darkness was intense, and by that, and that alone, he knew that night had fallen, he could picture every article of furniture in that small room, knew every crack in the walls and ceiling, and every mark on the threadbare, stained carpet, even down to the number of threads in its ravelled edge—for that had been his sole means of amusement during the hundred and five days he had been kept a prisoner in this place.

A hundred and five days! It seemed like as many years since he, Austin Ballard, had set out from his luxurious home for that morning walk, and had been accosted by the bearded man in the limousine car, who had inquired the way to town.

The car had overtaken him on a deserted strip of country road, and he had approached the driver to give him the required directions, when something had sprayed in his face, and he remembered no more until he had recovered consciousness, to find himself in his present surroundings.

The lapping water and the gentle swaying motion had told him that he was on board some kind of boat. That it was moored somewhere was equally evident, since there was never any propulsive motion. But whose boat, and where it was, he hadn't the remotest idea.

That was the most extraordinary thing about the whole business. The reason why he had been kidnapped, and the identity of his abductor, was a profound mystery, and, rack his tired brain as he might, he could find no solution. At first he had concluded that the usual ransom was at the bottom of it, but the green-masked man, who had brought him food and stood over him with a loaded pistol while he ate, said nothing to confirm this idea.

In fact, he had never spoken at all, remaining deaf to his prisoner's questions and threats until Austin Ballard had given up trying to gather any information from him.

For a long time he lay looking up into the darkness, and then, just as his weary eyes were closing, and he was almost dropping off into a doze again, he heard the sound of a step outside. The boat rocked as someone came on board, and he heard the noise of heavy breathing. Presently there came the grating of a key in a lock and a current of fresh, cool air blew on his face. Someone stumbled into the tiny cabin, panting. After a pause there was the scratch of a match.

As the yellow flame flickered to life Ballard made out the dim form of his captor. He recognised him by the long, black coat he wore, and the familiar baglike mask that enveloped his head.

The newcomer came over to the table that stood in the centre of the floor, and, shielding the match from the draught of the open door, bent down and lit an oil lamp. It gave very little more light than the match, for the chimney was dirty, but it was sufficient for the millionaire to make out a huddled figure that was lying just inside the entrance, and which had evidently been brought by the unknown.

Having lighted the lamp, the man in the green mask locked the door, took some cord from a cupboard, and, going over to the limp form, began to busy himself binding the ankles and wrists. When this was completed, he straightened up with a sigh of relief, and, producing a packet of sandwiches and a thermos flask from the voluminous pockets of his coat, laid them on the table. Again diving into his pockets, he took out an automatic pistol and a bunch of keys and approached the man on the narrow mattress.

Holding the pistol in his right hand, he stooped, unlocked the handcuffs round Ballard's wrists, and motioned to him to untie the gag.

This was the usual procedure, to which use had now accustomed the millionaire. In complete silence the unknown backed to the table, keeping Ballard covered all the while with the pistol, and picking up the flask and the sandwiches, returned and laid them by his side. He watched while his prisoner struggled to a sitting posture, and ate and drank greedily, for this was his one meal of the day, and when he had finished, replaced the handcuffs and snapped them shut. Before he could readjust the gag, Ballard spoke.

'Who's that you've brought with you?' he asked.

The man in the green mask remained dumb.

'How long are you going to keep me here?' continued the millionaire. But he might as well have been speaking to himself, for the other made no reply, but carefully strapped the gag in place, testing it to see that it was secure.

Slipping the automatic back into his pocket, he went over to a long, shallow chest, and, lifting the lid, took out a heap of folded rugs, which he proceeded to spread on the floor against the wall. When he had done this to his satisfaction, he crossed to the bound figure by the door, and, picking it up, carried it over to the rough bed he had prepared.

Ballard, watching, saw to his surprise that it was a woman.

He was puzzling his brains to account for this new arrival, and wondering who she was, when the green man straightened up, and, turning, regarded him steadily through the slits in his mask. And then suddenly for the first time he spoke—a high-pitched squeak that shook slightly as though with suppressed laughter. It was the voice more than the words he uttered that sent a little icy shiver down Ballard's spine.

'You want to know how long you're going to be here?' said the Green Jester, and chuckled shrilly. 'Well, I'll tell you—he, he, he! One more night and one more day. Make the most of your time, Austin Ballard, for it is very short. Tomorrow night at twelve you die!'

He chuckled again and blew out the lamp.

*   *   *

'But what the deuce could have happened to the girl?' said Inspector Coutts irritably, chewing the end of his pen-holder. 'There have been no reports of a street accident in which a woman was involved. I've explored that line of inquiry—so where can she have got to?'

Sexton Blake regarded him gravely from the other side of the desk.

'If my conclusions are correct,' he answered, 'she is in the hands of the Green Jester.'

He and the detective-inspector were seated in the latter's bare room at Scotland Yard, whence a telephone message had brought Blake post-haste.

At eight o'clock that morning a distracted young man, giving his name as Frank Guildford, had arrived at the big building on the Thames Embankment and told an incoherent story of the total disappearance of Muriel Grayson on the previous night. He had awaited at the appointed meeting-place from eight o'clock until half-past nine, but there had been no sign of the girl, and he had at last rung up the house at Dorking, thinking something had prevented her getting up to town.

He learnt, however, that she had left several hours before. At intervals of half-an-hour he had continued to ring up until nearly two o'clock in the morning, but she had not returned. Neither was there any news of her, when, after a sleepless night, he had tried again at seven-thirty, and he had immediately come round to the Yard. Inspector Coutts heard about the matter at nine, and instantly got on the phone to Sexton Blake, but the detective had already gone out, and it was not until twelve that the Yard man was able to get in touch with him.

Coutts flung down the pen and rubbed the back of his thick neck despairingly.

'The Green Jester,' he grunted. 'What the dickens would he want with the girl!'

'I think that he's got an excellent reason for wanting her out of the way,' said Blake. 'Listen, Coutts, I've been busy on this case all the morning and I've made one or two rather peculiar discoveries.'

'Everything about it's peculiar,' retorted the disgruntled Coutts savagely. 'What fresh enigma have you unearthed?'

'I've been down to the "Radio" offices, reading up an account of that fire in their back files,' answered the detective; 'and I've found out the names of the doctor and the nurse who attended to Austin

250

Ballard after he had been rescued by Lorne and Haynes and taken to hospital.

'Well,' growled the Scotland Yard man, 'what about it? It doesn't seem to be important.'

'You won't say that when I tell you that the doctor was John Roon,' said Sexton Blake quietly; 'and the nurse was Julia Rothe.'

'Good lor'!' Coutts almost overturned his chair as he leapt to his feet and began pacing up and down the large room. 'What on earth does it all mean?'

'It means,' answered the Baker Street detective grimly, 'that that fire which destroyed the Ritz-Carlton Hotel at Brighton also gave birth to the Green Jester.'

The inspector stopped with a jerk and glared at his friend.

'I wish you wouldn't talk in riddles!' he snapped. 'I've got enough to contend with as it is. What exactly are you getting at?'

'That something that occurred either during or after that fire,' said Blake, 'was the starting-point—the motive behind all these apparently meaningless murders.'

'But the fire happened fifteen years ago,' protested the inspector.

Blake nodded.

'I know,' he said; 'but, all the same, it's at the bottom of the whole business. I don't profess to know how or why, but it's obvious. It's the one point of contact which connects all the victims of the perverted humorist we call the Green Jester.'

Coutts frowned heavily.

'Well, it beats me!' he declared. 'It seems utterly mad!'

'But the man responsible is by no means mad,' replied Sexton Blake decisively. 'I should say he was the nearest approach to the perfect criminal that we are ever likely to find.'

'We haven't found him yet,' muttered the inspector pessimistically; 'and I disagree with you about him not being mad. I'm still of the opinion that the Green Jester is a homicidal lunatic.'

'In that you are no doubt with the majority,' retorted the detective. 'But has it ever struck you that that is just the impression he is trying to create?'

The burly inspector started.

'By Jove, Blake,' he cried, banging his fist on the desk, 'that's a new idea! I hadn't thought of that.'

Sexton Blake smiled.

'I thought of it from the first,' he said. 'The theatrical warnings with the figure of the laughing fool; the unnecessary rhymes, blatantly ridiculous, and pointing conclusively to a distorted brain; and, when he rang me up, the obviously disguised voice interspersed with those little cackling chuckles, all carefully calculated to give us the impression that we were dealing with a maniac.' He shook his head slowly. 'No, Coutts; the Green Jester is a clever man, with a grim purpose hiding behind the sinister nonsense and buffoonery with which he has tried to throw dust in the eyes of the police and the public.'

'I'm inclined to believe that you're right when you put it like that,' said the Scotland Yard man thoughtfully. 'But we still don't know what the purpose is, or the identity of the Green Jester.'

'I certainly don't know what the purpose is,' replied Sexton Blake; 'but somehow I feel certain of the identity of the Green Jester!'

'What!'

It was a morning of shocks for Coutts.

'Then who the deuce is he?' he demanded, recovering from his surprise.

Sexton Blake looked at him for a second in silence.

'I said I feel certain,' he remarked slowly. 'But at this stage I shouldn't like to say I am certain. At best it's a guess, and it would be a great injustice to name a man now and find myself wrong afterwards.'

'Huh!' grunted Coutts.

'I can see you are rather sceptical,' said Blake; 'but I'm afraid I must continue to risk your disbelief until I have something more like proof.'

It was nearly two o'clock when Sexton Blake got back to his chambers in Baker Street. There he found a note from Tinker conspicuously propped up against the clock on the consulting-room mantelpiece. He opened it and read, with a smile of satisfaction, the hastily scrawled message:

Slade is back again. Am keeping watch on movements and will report developments.

TINKER.

Tearing up the slip of paper, which had been delivered by special messenger, the detective dropped the pieces into the wastepaper-basket. The sleek-haired butler had given the lad the slip on the previous night, but was back attending to his duties at Dorking as usual, apparently, that morning; for Tinker had gone down there early to pick up the trail again.

Slipping into his dressing-gown, Sexton Blake consulted the 'Telephone Directory', and a few seconds later was talking to the senior partner of a firm of solicitors who guarded the interests of the vanished Austin Ballard. The result of his long conversation was obviously satisfactory, for there was a gleam of triumph in his eyes as he hung up the receiver after making an appointment for half-past three that afternoon.

Mrs Bardell announced lunch, and the detective was half-way through a leisurely meal when he heard the rat-tat of the postman, and presently the housekeeper brought him a little pile of letters.

He glanced through them quickly, but there was nothing of interest until he came to a large square envelope addressed in a sprawling, childish writing, and his pulses beat a trifle quicker.

Ripping open the flap, he withdrew a card bearing on it the familiar green-clad fool with the pointing index finger.

Blake smiled grimly as he turned it over, for he had been expecting that sign manual of the Green Jester ever since the disappearance of Muriel Grayson.

On the back was the usual doggerel verse and, reading it, the detective's lips compressed.

> *You are clever, I know, Sexton Blake,*
> *But you'll find you have made a mistake.*
> *If you don't give up prying,*
>   *And searching and spying,*
> *Then I fear it's your life I shall take.*

The postmark showed that the letter had been posted that morning in the W.C. district. Blake laid the card beside his plate and calmly went on with his lunch.

When he had finished, he rose, and, carrying the warning and the envelope into the consulting-room, he locked it in a drawer of his desk. Dismissing the matter from his mind, he filled in the half-hour before it was time for him to start to keep his appointment with the lawyers by writing some letters which he had neglected that morning. Sealing and stamping them, he took off his dressing-gown, struggled into an overcoat and descended to the street door.

He was closing it gently behind him when his hat was jerked from his head and something thudded into the woodwork behind him. There was no sound of an explosion, but he felt the wind of the second bullet as it flew past his ear, and the third drew a red line across the back of his hand as he involuntarily put it up to his face.

A stream of traffic was passing, and the shots might have come from one of the half-dozen cars that were in sight. There were no more, however, and, stooping, the detective picked up his hat. The Green Jester had followed his warning with action—but for once he had failed!

*   *   *

The sleek-haired Mr Slade, waiting on Dorking Station for the train that was to carry him townwards, felt remarkably good-tempered and at peace with the world. The reason for his amiability of temperament was due to the telephone message he had received that morning from his friend and partner, Mr Oswald Kyne. Mr Kyne had given him a piece of news that filled the soul of the butler with rapturous dreams of wealth.

Over and over again he congratulated himself upon the foresight that had made him follow Doctor Roon when he had left the house that fatal morning in response to the Green Jester's fake telephone call, for but for that piece of luck, he would never have witnessed the crime and thus held its perpetrator in the hollow of his hand. For, and Mr Slade chuckled as he always did when he thought of it, the murder had already been committed when Sexton Blake and the Scotland Yard detective had arrived at the house, and it was only by a matter of seconds that he had himself returned in time to admit them.

He was still chuckling when he got into a third-class compartment and the train left the station, but it was doubtful if he would have felt so extremely pleased with himself if he had been aware of the identity of the ragged youth who was travelling in the next compartment. But the butler was not aware of this, and, therefore, his pleasure at his own ruse was unspoilt.

Oh, undoubtedly he was clever, he thought complacently. His handling of the whole affair had been remarkably smart. The Green Jester was clever, too, but he, Slade, was cleverer. He had seized a chance that was going to make him independent for the rest of his life.

His mind was still filled with rose-coloured plans for the future when, at his journey's end, he raised his hand and gave his peculiar knock on Mr Kyne's bronze knocker.

This time it was the stout money-lender himself who opened the door and ushered his visitor into the large, ornately furnished room. There was an air of excitement and nervousness about that man that he could not conceal, and his fat, smooth face glistened with little beads of perspiration.

'Well,' said the butler, smacking him on the back heartily. 'Everything seems to be going fine.'

'I'm glad you think so,' retorted Mr Kyne gloomily.

'Don't you?' asked Slade, in surprise. 'Why, what's the matter with you? A cool two hundred thousand pounds as easy as kiss your hand and no trouble. It sounds fine to me.'

The fat man shook his head.

'It sounds a bit too easy to me,' he grunted. 'And I don't like the way that girl disappeared. It's been worrying me.'

'Oh, confound the girl!' snarled Slade callously. 'You know what happened to her, and why!'

'Yes, that's what's making me nervous,' answered the other, pouring himself out a drink and gulping down the neat spirit. 'Why shouldn't the same thing happen to us?'

The butler laughed harshly.

'Nonsense!' he exclaimed. 'He daren't try any funny business. He wouldn't have written to you making the appointment if he was going to try to double-cross us. Neither you nor I could have found him after I missed him last night, and if that girl hadn't come along I should have seen him, but he knew he'd have to make another appointment or we should split to the police. I tell you there's nothing to worry about.'

Mr Kyne wiped his shining face.

'Well, I hope you're right,' he said, and, opening a drawer in the writing-table, he took out a sheet of paper and passed it over to Slade. 'There's the letter,' he went on. 'He wants you to meet him at twelve o'clock tonight at Marlow—on an old houseboat moored to the river bank. There are full directions for finding it.'

'I can read that for myself,' snarled Slade; and Mr Kyne lapsed into silence.

The butler read the letter twice, and then, folding it, put it in his pocket.

'You'd better take me within walking distance of the place in your car,' he said, 'and then wait to bring me back. I shan't be more than an hour at the outside. If I'm not back by that time you can go to the nearest police station and tell all you know,' he added grimly.

They sat talking until the chiming of Mr Kyne's clock warned them that it was time to be moving, and the money-lender went out into the hall and struggled into his coat.

His car was garaged less than a hundred yards from the flat in which he lived, and in a few seconds they were speeding in the big limousine en route for Marlow.

Once clear of the traffic Kyne let the car out, and in an incredibly short space of time they were on the Bath road and running towards Slough. It was barely twenty minutes to ten when they passed through Maidenhead and swung to the right and on up the hill leading to Quarry Wood and Marlow, and although they didn't know it, behind them followed a second car, keeping at a discreet distance but never losing sight of them for a single instant.

They ran on, catching occasional glimpses of the sheen of the river, and presently, at the edge of a meadow, Kyne brought the car to a halt.

'This is the place,' muttered Slade, as he got out and peered through a tangle of trees towards the river bank. 'The houseboat lies a few hundred yards upstream.'

It was quite dark, and evidently gathering up for rain, for the pale moon that had been in evidence when they left the West End was no longer visible.

Leaving Kyne in the car the butler hurried across a strip of grass and plunged among the trees. It was a lonely spot, and there was no sound to break the silence save the gentle lapping of the river as it flowed against the bank.

The trees gradually became more numerous, and presently Slade found himself in the depths of a miniature wood. He had gone a considerable distance, and was beginning to wonder if he had made a mistake, when he saw a shadowy bulk loom out of the darkness, and, drawing nearer, discovered that it was the house-boat he was seeking.

For the first time he experienced a little qualm of fear. Suppos-ing the Green Jester should serve him as he had served his other victims? He shivered, and then the thought of the stout Mr Kyne waiting close at hand gave him courage.

The Green Jester for his own sake dare not harm him, for he knew that the moneylender shared his secret, and that if anything happened to Slade he would instantly communicate with the police. His fears left him, and he was quite calm and confident as he stepped from the bank on to the little deck of the houseboat and tapped at the door.

There was the sound of a shuffling movement inside, the scraping of a key in the lock, and then the door opened an inch.

'Is that Slade?' asked a voice softly; and the butler saw a figure partly obliterating the dim crack of light.

'That's me,' he answered; and the door was opened wider.

'Come in,' said the Green Jester, and when Slade had crossed the threshold, shut and relocked the door. 'Now let us get to business as quickly as possible, for at midnight tonight I am leaving England for good.'

*   *   *

Slade looked curiously round the dimly-lighted interior of the houseboat. His eyes stared with wonder as he caught sight of the manacled figure of the millionaire lying on the pallet bed. The girl he passed by indifferently—he had expected to see her there—but the first captive puzzled him.

'Who is that?' he asked, and seeing the surprise in his face the man in the green mask chuckled.

'That is Mr Austin Ballard,' he replied in his high, thin, squeaky voice—'a most important gentleman.'

'The—the millionaire?' gasped the butler, for he had read of the disappearance of the tobacco magnate and, like the rest of the world, had wondered. 'What's he doing here?'

'He is here for a purpose,' answered the Green Jester, 'and that purpose reaches its maturity at twelve o'clock tonight.' He chuckled. 'It is lucky that Mr Ballard is an orphan, and has no encumbrances such as a wife or children, for at that hour he is going on a long journey—and it would be a pity if there was anyone who would miss him.'

His meaning was unmistakable, and Slade shivered.

'You mean you're going to croak him?' he whispered huskily.

'A vulgar word,' said the other distastefully, 'but expressive. Yes, that is my intention. That is the reason why I have been keeping him here for so long.'

'But why have you waited?' demanded the astonished butler. 'If you wanted to kill him, why didn't you do so before? You've run an enormous risk keeping—'

'I know; but the time was not ripe,' interrupted the Green Jester. 'Tomorrow the papers will come out with the news that the body of Mr Austin Ballard has been found on the Bath road—er—stabbed to the heart, and there will be a lot of speculation as to how he got there, and the reason for his death. But I doubt very much if anyone will hit on the true solution to the mystery.'

He paused and looked across at the millionaire.

'I don't think even Mr Ballard himself knows that,' he continued. 'But since he will shortly be in the only condition in which a human being should be trusted with a secret, we might, I think, satisfy his curiosity.'

Again he paused and chuckled.

'Fifteen years ago, Mr Ballard,' he said, addressing the helpless man, 'you were rescued from a fire at the Ritz-Carlton Hotel, Brighton, by a Mr Hamilton Lorne and a Mr Percival Haynes. At great personal risk to themselves they got you out of the burning building just before it collapsed.

'During the process, however, you were so badly burned, and suffered such a severe shock, that, although you were rushed to the nearest hospital, your life was despaired of. For days you lay in a critical condition, but owing to the skill of Dr Roon and the untiring attention of Miss Julia Rothe, the nurse who looked after you, you were slowly dragged from the shadow of death. You never expected to see the world again, and during your convalescence, in gratitude to the people who had saved your life, you made a will.'

A flash of understanding lit the steady eyes of the millionaire, and the Green Jester nodded as he saw it.

'I see that you have guessed the rest,' he said. 'You had no living kith or kin, and you left your entire fortune to be equally divided between the four people whose efforts were the direct cause of your being alive, and you further stipulated that should any of them die before your own decease, the remaining ones should benefit pro rata, so that if only one remained alive at the time of your death he or she would receive the entire amount of which you died possessed. It was a generous scheme, for I have made inquiries, and I find that the sum involved is just over a million and a quarter pounds.'

Slade's eyes glittered avariciously as the Green Jester finished.

'And this comes—to you?' he asked huskily.

'It comes to me indirectly,' assented the other, 'after'—he paused significantly—'the death of Mr Austin Ballard has been proved.'

The butler's mind was working busily. He had had no idea that such a vast sum was at stake, and mentally he cursed himself for having put his own demands so low. However—he brightened as the thought entered his head—it could be treated, after all, as a first instalment. There would be larger pickings later.

The Green Jester seemed to have read his thoughts, to a certain extent, for he said, after a brief pause:

'You want two hundred thousand, don't you, as the price of your silence?'

Slade looked at him cunningly.

'Five,' he murmured gently.

'You said two,' snapped the man in the green mask sharply.

The sleek-haired butler smiled apologetically.

'Did I?' he answered. 'It must have been a slip. I meant five.'

The Green Jester leaned forward threateningly.

'Don't you try any tricks with me,' he hissed. 'You said two hundred thousand, and two hundred thousand is all you'll get!'

'We'll see about that,' retorted Slade, 'and don't use that tone with me. One word from me and you'll never touch a penny— you'll hang instead! And I dare say Mr Ballard would be willing to pay me what I'm asking you to save his life.'

For a moment the other was incapable of speech, so great was the rage that mastered him, but with a supreme effort he choked it down, and when he spoke, except for a slight tremble in the tone, it was the same high, squeaky voice as heretofore.

'All right,' he said, 'I'll make it five hundred thousand—but you won't get a penny more! You understand? And you won't get that for several weeks.'

'Oh, I don't mind waiting,' answered Slade complacently, 'so long as I get what I want in the end.'

'You'll get that,' said the Green Jester.

'Right! And I shall expect it the day after you draw your own money,' said the butler. 'And I warn you, if it doesn't arrive on that date, I shall inform the police who you really are.'

He crossed over to the door.

'I'd better be getting back to Kyne now,' he continued, 'otherwise he'll think something has happened, and carry out the programme we arranged before I came here.'

'Where is Kyne?' asked the man in the mask casually as he unlocked the door.

'Waiting by the edge of the field,' replied Slade, stepping through the opening on to the little deck.

They were the last words he ever uttered, for the other drove the knife he had slipped from his pocket sharply upwards, and with a choking cry the butler fell on his knees and collapsed in a heap!

The Green Jester bent down, made sure he was dead, and toppled the body gently into the swiftly-running river.

Mr Oswald Kyne, dozing in the car, looked up as he saw the shadowy figure approaching. It paused a few yards away and beckoned hurriedly.

'What the deuce do you want, Slade?' called the fat money-lender, with a muttered oath, as he got out of the car and walked towards the other.

'I want you!' hissed the squeaky voice, and, too late, Kyne realised that it was not the butler who had beckoned him.

Two strong hands leapt to his throat and buried themselves in the rolls of flesh. With the cry strangled in his mouth, Kyne bent backwards, struggling desperately to free himself from that choking grip. Tighter and tighter it grew, until his tongue protruded and his eyes bulged. Flashes of crimson shot across the blackness that was enveloping him. He felt his senses swimming and an indescribable languor stealing over him, and then—

'Put up your hands!' rapped a stern, cold voice, and out of the night sprang a bright beam of light!

The Green Jester released his hold of the moneylender and looked up as the torch focused on him—looked into the face of Sexton Blake!

*　　*　　*

'I want you, my joking friend,' said the detective quietly, and advanced towards the green-masked, crouching figure, a long-barrelled automatic held unwaveringly in front of him. He had barely taken three strides, however, when, by one of those freaks of chance that sometimes seem to play into the hands of the evil-doer, his foot caught in a rut and he stumbled.

Quick as a flash, the Green Jester took advantage of the accident. Jerking the semi-conscious body of the stout Mr Kyne up by the collar, he flung him at Sexton Blake, so that he struck against the detective's ankles even as Blake was recovering from that fatal stumble. The result was disastrous. Losing his balance completely, Blake went sprawling at full-length, his pistol flying from his hand as he did so.

The green man turned swiftly at the same moment, and went racing towards Kyne's car, and hurling himself into the driving-seat, thrust frantically at the self-starter.

'Coutts, here! Coutts—quickly!' yelled the detective, as he struggled to his feet and tried to run towards the throbbing car.

But he had wrenched his ankle in his fall, and could do no more than hobble, and even as the burly inspector loomed out of the darkness the limousine jerked forward and went tearing down the road.

'Quick!' panted Blake, pointing to the rapidly vanishing car. 'Get Tinker and follow him. Pick me up as you go by—I can't walk. Hurry, or we shall lose him, after all.'

'All right, Blake—you wait here!' grunted the Scotland Yard man, and disappeared into the darkness again at a run.

It seemed an age to Sexton Blake before the blazing headlights of his own car swept towards him and stopped with a grinding of brakes, but in reality barely fifty seconds elapsed between the time of the Green Jester's escape and their own start in pursuit. Coutts' strong arm pulled the detective on board, Tinker slipped in the clutch, and with scarcely a pause the powerful car bounded forward and went rushing off in the wake of its quarry.

'There he is!' grunted Coutts.

And Blake nodded.

It was going like the wind, and even as they looked, vanished into a patch of dense shadow cast by some over-hanging trees.

On and on they went, the miles reeling behind them. Suddenly Blake gave a triumphant exclamation.

'We're gaining, Coutts!' he cried exultantly. 'Go on, young 'un! Let her rip!'

And he was right. The distance between pursuer and pursued had appreciably lessened.

There was a sharp curve in the road in front, and round this the fugitive car skidded almost on two wheels, and they lost sight of it. Taking the bend themselves at full speed, Coutts gave a warning shout, for the Green Jester had pulled the limousine up and left it broadside in their path!

The road was narrow, and the big car blocked it effectually from side to side. Tinker saw the danger, and realised that it was impossible to pull up in time.

He applied the brakes, and jerked frantically at the wheel. With screaming brake-drums the huge machine swerved, bumped dizzily over the uneven clumps of turf that bordered the road, and crashed into a straggling hedge.

The windscreen shivered to fragments, and the occupants were almost jerked from their seats at the shock of the impact. Fortunately, beyond a few bruises, no one was hurt, and as they scrambled out, Blake caught sight of a flying figure against the greeny-blue of the skyline.

'There he is!' he shouted. 'After him, young 'un! I'm useless because of my ankle, but you and Coutts can get him.'

The Green Jester heard his voice and looked back, panting, as he stumbled over the rough ground. With a bit of luck he ought to get away—the country here was wild, the ground studded with gorse-bushes, and ahead the fringe of a thick wood.

If he could only reach the shelter of that there was a chance for him. He heard the thud of pursuing feet, and redoubled his speed, but he was out of condition, and the pace was too hot to keep up. There came a sharp, stabbing pain in his side and his breath became laboured, whistling through his throat in great gasps.

The gorse-bushes were growing more thickly now, so that he had to force his way through them, tearing his hands and face on the sharp spines. Suddenly, to his horror, he saw the reflection of a light strike the leaves in front of him. One of his pursuers had produced an electric torch, and was fanning it across the common. Capture seemed inevitable. The muscles of his legs ached and his feet were heavy, as though encased in leaden shoes.

Desperately he clenched his teeth and ran on, doubling from side to side in the hope of outwitting them; but the approaching steps drew steadily nearer. All at once the ground began to slope sharply, giving an additional speed.

But it was too late! He heard a shout close behind him, heard the hiss of panting breath, and as an outstretched hand reached forward to grasp his shoulder, gave one last leap to escape those clutching fingers.

He landed on something that crumbled beneath him, tried vainly to recover his balance, and found himself falling—falling— He struck a sharp object, and the impact made him shriek aloud with pain.

His wild hands grasped despairingly at tree and shrub and grass, slipped, and again he was falling—down—down—down——

The grey of dawn was breaking in the east when they found him, lying huddled up at the bottom of the sheer drop that led down into the valley—a twisted, sprawling figure, with neck awry, the face stamped with the fear of that last moment.

'A terrible end, but he deserved it,' said Sexton Blake gravely, looking down at all that remained of the Green Jester. 'Dr Roon was a clever man—almost a perfect criminal—but his last joke recoiled against himself.'

Coutts nodded.

'I'll go and phone for an ambulance,' he said.

* * *

'It was you who were really to blame for the Green Jester,' said Sexton Blake, some hours later, looking across the consulting-room at Baker Street, with a twinkle in his eyes, to where Mr Austin Ballard sat at his ease, smoking one of the detective's cigars with obvious enjoyment.

'Yes, I'm afraid it was,' agreed the millionaire, 'and it shows that even gratitude has a nasty habit of stinging at times.'

He looked haggard and ill, but the meal he had recently consumed—the first decent ones for weeks—had done much to restore him to something like his normal spirits.

Coutts, Tinker, and Blake, after attending to the details, made necessary by the tragic death of the Green Jester, had returned to the houseboat and released Ballard and the girl.

She was still under the influence of the drug that had been administered to her when they found her; but some strong coffee had proved an effective antidote, and now, sitting on the settee by the side of the millionaire, she was little the worse for her terrifying ordeal beyond a headache and a rather pronounced pallor.

'I'm still a bit puzzled as to the meaning of it all,' remarked Inspector Coutts, passing a stubby hand over his close-cropped head. 'What did Roon hope to gain by all these crimes?'

'A million and a quarter pounds,' answered Sexton Blake sharply. 'Quite a nice little round sum of money. Men have killed more people than Roon did for less than half that amount!'

He paused and blew a cloud of smoke from his lips.

'It was not until he lost his money by a disastrous deal on the Stock Exchange,' he continued, 'and was racking his brains to find some means of replenishing his exchequer, that he remembered the fire at Brighton, and the will that Ballard had caused to be drawn up in gratitude to the people who had rescued him.

'Then, thinking it over, he remembered the actual terms of the will. He was present, I think, when it was made?'

Ballard nodded.

'Quite right, he was,' he said, a little grimly.

'There took form in his brain,' Blake went on—'and I'm sure that the worry he was passing through must have affected his sanity and caused him to lose sight of values—the idea which later bore fruit in the birth of the will—I have seen a copy at the solicitor's— are to the effect that your entire fortune, in the event of your death'—Blake addressed his remarks to Ballard, but all were listening intently—'was to be equally divided between the four people who had been the cause of saving your life during the fire at the Ritz-Carlton. Namely, Lorne, Haynes, Miss Rothe, and Dr Roon himself. In the event of any of these people dying before you, their share was to go to the nearest living relative, and if there was no relative living, to be added to the amount for distribution among those of the four who remained alive.'

'The Green Jester would never have come into existence at all if Roon hadn't discovered, on making inquiries, that the people who stood in his way from receiving the full amount of your fortune were without kith or kin. It was this fact which must have first suggested the plan of campaign which he ultimately carried out. His first proceeding—and I am now no longer conjecturing, but stating what actually occurred—was to establish the fact that he possessed a brother.

'He mentioned him to several of his acquaintances, including his secretary. Then he went over to Paris, took a flat in the name of James Roon, in which he installed a housekeeper, giving out to her that he travelled a lot, and would only be there now and again at irregular intervals. The letters he received from his supposed brother he wrote himself, leaving them with this woman to post at stated intervals. When he used to go on the visits to his supposed brother, he was in reality becoming that very brother, just returned from one of his trips, and for this purpose he appeared in Paris disguised in a slight beard.

'Having prepared the way for the last act in the drama he contemplated, he proceeded to stage the first and kidnapped Mr Ballard. Taking him to the houseboat, which he had bought in another name, he kept him a prisoner there, ready to be killed when the moment was ripe.

'And here the undoubted cleverness of the man is made evident. He realised that if Lorne, Haynes, and Julia Rothe were murdered in the ordinary way, someone might discover the true motive, so he conceived the mysterious personality of the Green Jester, and devised the card and the rhyming warning to make it appear that the crimes were the work of a homicidal maniac.'

'He jolly well succeded, too,' interrupted Coutts, with a grunt. 'I, for one, was convinced they were.'

'Allowing a fairly long lapse of time to take place between each murder, so that no one should suspect any possible connection between the victims,' Sexton Blake continued, without pausing, 'he succeeded in getting rid of the three people who stood in his way, and then put into practice the tour de force that was to eliminate all chance of suspicion falling on himself—as it might have done when the will was read, and it was found that he inherited Austin Ballard's fortune. He sent himself one of the Green Jester's cards, and rang me up to say that he had received it. It was a stroke of genius.'

'Who—who was it, then, who was killed?' asked the girl in a low voice, during the short silence that ensued.

'The man whom the doctor had engaged to put through the false telephone call purporting to come from Inspector Coutts,' answered Blake grimly. 'It was the first time he had used a confederate, and he took good care that his accomplice shouldn't have the chance of squealing. Everything was planned carefully.

'The man was dressed as a telephone inspector, and the call was put through from a house less than two hundred yards from Roon's own. He called with the plausible excuse of testing the telephone, contrived to be alone, and phoned the message which took Roon out. Roon left in his car, but instead of going towards Dorking, he ran the car into a little lane in the opposite direction, where he had already arranged to meet his assistant, and there he brutally killed him and changed his clothes. Unfortunately for him, Slade—who I have since found was a crook—had followed him and witnessed the murder. He threatened to give Roon away unless he paid him to keep silent, and the doctor had to promise to keep in touch with him to save his whole scheme tumbling to the ground.'

'I'm surprised he didn't murder Slade as well,' said the burly inspector.

'Undoubtedly he would have done,' replied the detective; 'but Kyne tells me that Slade carried a gun, and kept him at arm's length.'

'Then it was Dr Roon himself who telephoned to you about—about the—' The girl hesitated, leaving the sentence unfinished.

'Yes,' said Blake. 'He must have waited until he saw us arrive, placed the body in the wheat field as we found it, adopted some sort of disguise, and, leaving the car by the side of the road, walked into Dorking and sent that message.'

'Why did he keep Mr Ballard a prisoner?' asked Tinker. 'Why

266

didn't he kill him at once?'

'Because he had no intention of killing him until all the others—including himself—had met their deaths,' responded the detective. 'Otherwise, the will would have come to light. His plan was to keep Ballard locked up in the houseboat where he could find him exactly when he wanted to, and when he had completed the rest of his ghastly scheme, murder him, and leave him somewhere where his body would be found and identified. Roon would then have gone off to Paris, and, after a lapse of a week or so, during which his beard would have grown, he would have turned up at his flat in the Rue Douane as his brother.'

'To find himself the inheritor of one million and a quarter pounds,' finished Austin Ballard.

'Exactly!' assented Sexton Blake. 'For by the terms of your will, Roon's brother, being next of kin, would have got the lot.'

Muriel Grayson shuddered.

'I shall never forget the shock I had when I recognised him in that car,' she said. 'I thought I had seen a ghost.'

'It must have been a pretty big shock for him, too,' said the detective, 'for he must have realised the danger of his whole carefully-planned structure falling to pieces. That was the night, Kyne tells me, that he had arranged to meet Slade, and was waiting for him, when you appeared unexpectedly on the scene. You can thank your stars, young lady, that you're still alive.'

He knocked out the ashes of his pipe, and there was a long silence, broken at last by Coutts.

'How did that note get in the pocket of the dead man?' he asked thoughtfully.

Blake shook his head.

'We enter into the realm of conjecture there,' he replied. 'But I should think the most possible explanation is that while Roon was spying out the land before killing Julia Rothe, he had occasion to buy something at Horsham, and received the five-pound note in change. Obviously, he never noticed her name and address on the back, or he wouldn't have left it in his notecase.'

'When did you first become suspicious that Roon was the Green Jester?'

Coutts helped himself to a cigar and bit off the end as he put the question and Blake smiled.

'When I examined the dead man's shoes,' he answered. 'They were size tens, and obviously much too big for the feet on which they were placed. The inference was conclusive.'

'Well, Mr Blake,' remarked Austin Ballard, rising to his feet, 'you've worked it out most clearly.' He looked at his watch. 'I'm going along to my solicitor's to destroy that will,' he said, with a chuckle.

'And if you make another,' said Sexton Blake, as he escorted him to the door and shook hands, 'leave your money to the Society for the Prevention of Nicotine Poisoning. You'll find it much safer.'

THE SECRET AMULET
Anthony Parsons

Although Anthony Parsons (1893–1963) spent no more than half a
dozen years in India (as an officer in the Indian Army and later the
RFC during the First World War) the country entranced him. Its sights,
sounds and smells stayed with him for the rest of his life and he was never
better than when weaving one of his typically complex and skilfully
plotted Blake stories against its rich alien backcloth. From India he was
drafted to Egypt (another country that captivated him) and then, after
demobilisation, spent most of the 1920s as a white hunter in Central
Africa, mainly with his brother-in-law (who died of blackwater fever in
1932). When Parsons came home in the late 1920s he began selling
articles and stories to magazines such as Blackwood's, Wide World,
and the Strand. *His first book,* Bush Gypsies—*an autobiographical,*
though fictionalised, volume of stories in the vein of Dornford Yates and
Sapper (though without the snobbery of the former or the thuggishness of
the latter)—had some critical success but didn't noticeably fatten his bank
balance, and he soon began pounding out better-paying fiction for the
thriller-oriented papers of the Amalgamated Press. When he started
writing Blakes in 1937, it was at once clear he'd found his natural
niche: subsequently, he wrote 99 full-length novels over a period of 19
years. He brought to the saga the authentic flavour of foreign parts, a
love of the 'impossible' crime, and a breezy and colloquial style that
perfectly suited the times and mirrored his own immense enthusiasm for
the task.

Colonel North, CIE, CBE, Chief Political Agent to the Government of India, banged down the desk telephone with an oath and
leapt to his feet.

'Anderson?' he shouted to his ADC in the next room.

'Sir—'

'They've got E22! He's lying at the Taj, with his throat cut from ear to ear. Worse still, the amulet's gone!'

'What—'

'Stolen, I tell you—together with the ten thousand rupees we gave him this morning for Major Loring. They've cleaned him of everything, the swine! He's been dead for hours. Come on!'

Snatching up his helmet he led the way outside to his car. It was like entering a baker's oven to enter a Bombay street at that hour of the afternoon, but neither of them noticed it; they were inured to heat, anyway.

'I wondered why he was late,' the Colonel said as they drove away. 'That's why I rang him; I thought he might have forgotten. But instead of him answering, Inspector Williams answered! By gad, it was a shock!'

'Who found him, sir?'

'One of the hotel boys, apparently. Went in to tidy up the room and found him lying there stiff. He fetched the manager, and the manager phoned the police—but according to what Williams says, he's been dead since one o'clock. One o'clock, mind you—and now it's close on five. In another six hours the Frontier Mail pulls out, and once that amulet leaves Bombay we're done!'

'You're sure it was the amulet they were after, sir?'

'What else could it have been? Nobody knew he had the money on him—couldn't have known. And even if they had, and they'd killed him for it, would they be likely to rob him of his miserable little amulet? Not on your life, Anderson! That's why we chose it for the "sign"—because nobody would ever bother to rob a man of his amulet. No, sir! Whoever's got that amulet now has got it because he knows what it means. And that's why he took it from E22's neck!'

They had reached the famous Apollo Bund by now, that beautiful boulevard which stretches between Bombay and the blue waters of the Indian Ocean, and presently they pulled up beneath the glass portico of Bombay's most cosmopolitan hotel. Leaving the sparkling sea behind them, they entered the crowded lounge and took the lift to the second floor.

'Room 121,' said the Colonel. 'Here we are!'

He knocked, and at once they were admitted by Inspector

Williams of the Indian Police—a tall, thin-faced, rather peevish-looking man.

'They've made a mess of him for you!' he said without any attempt at preamble, pointing to where all that was mortal of Agent E22—Mahomet Ali of the Political Department—lay stretched flat on his back upon the gaudy Mirzapur carpet. 'You can identify him for me, I suppose?'

The Colonel nodded. One glance at the dead face was enough to assure him that the man was indeed E22—but it was upon the disarrangement of the collar and tie that his eyes lingered longest, for it was about his neck that E22 had been wearing the precious amulet.

'No accident about that!' he said to Captain Anderson. 'It was the amulet they wanted, you see—and they knew where he kept it, too.' He turned to the Inspector. 'Have you made inquiries about Yakub the Afghan?' he asked.

'Yes, and he can be washed out, Colonel—he couldn't have done it. At the moment when this fellow was being killed, Yakub the Afghan was stuffing his fat face with chapattis a couple of miles away at the other end of the bazaar. And what's more, a couple of my policemen were with him. So that lets him out. Have you any other suspects?'

'No—have you?'

'Not a sausage! There isn't a clue in the place, Colonel—not one! No weapon, no letters on the body, no friends we can interrogate—nothing! And you know what this place is when it comes to checking up on anybody's movements or on the movements of strangers—you might as well be working on Victoria Station on August Bank Holiday. Anybody could have strolled in and slit his throat—anybody at all!'

'Save that anybody didn't!' retorted the Colonel acidly. 'I've told you already, Inspector, that whoever killed Mahomet Ali killed him for one thing only—the amulet he was wearing round his neck. And that's what we've got to recover before the Frontier Mail pulls out at eleven o'clock tonight.'

'Well, I don't know where we're going to start looking for it,' Williams said with a short laugh. 'There's something like a million people in Bombay, and it seems to me—for all the clues I can see in

271

this room—that any one of 'em might have the thing.'

Colonel North stood glowering for a moment, his eyes on the dead man's face. Suddenly he picked up his helmet.

'All right!' he said. 'Come on, Anderson!' He hurried out to the lift. 'There's a man staying at the Queen's—if he hasn't gone home yet—who'll knock spots off Williams,' he said as they went down to the street. 'A man who'll walk into that room and reel off a description of the murderer inside a quarter of an hour. I don't know why I didn't think of him at first—I must be crazy. You know who I mean?—the man the Government got out to handle that Maynard Case just recently, and who made mincemeat of our best officers.'

'Sexton Blake, sir?' whispered Captain Anderson.

'Of Baker Street, London, my lad! That's the fellow!'

Sexton Blake was in the middle of packing for home when one of the hotel 'boys' brought him the Colonel's card. '*Please see me,*' he read the pencilled note aloud. '*My business is very urgent.*'

'Yes, and so's ours!' Tinker grinned from the other side of the room. 'A date with a sixteen thousand-ton liner sailing for England, coolness, and a blessed spot of rain! Tell him we've gone, guv'nor. We shall be gone by tomorrow, anyhow.'

Blake stared at the card doubtfully. They had been six weeks in Bombay in the worst of the hot weather, and his sole idea now was to get back to Baker Street as soon as possible. He did not want to see the Colonel—or anyone else for that matter. But before he could say as much, the door opened quietly and there on the threshold stood the Colonel himself.

'Forgive this unwarrantable intrusion—please!' he said as Blake leapt to his feet. 'I must see you. My business is more than urgent—it's desperate. The life of the best man England's ever had along the "Bloody Border" depends solely and entirely upon you helping me now. More!—the safety of our entire Secret Service organisation depends upon you helping me, Mr Blake!'

The Baker Street specialist stared at him blankly.

'Are you sure that's all?' he asked at last. 'There is nothing you've forgotten, Colonel?'

'Listen, Mr Blake!' In a single movement, or so at least it seemed, their visitor had waved the hotel 'boy' from the room, banged the door shut behind him, advanced to where Sexton Blake

272

was sitting on his bed, and begun a graphic story of everything that had happened in the last hour. He spoke vividly and well. So much so, indeed, that long before he was finished he had both Blake and his assistant literally hanging upon his words.

'But what is the precise significance of this amulet?' Blake asked at the end of it all. 'Is there anything of value in it?'

'No. It's just a "sign".' Colonel North glanced behind him at the closed door and subconsciously lowered his voice. 'The head of our Secret Service in Afghanistan is a certain Major Loring,' he explained, 'who, under the name of Sher Khan and in the guise of a camel dealer, travels all over the country collecting information for us touching German activities in the Near East, Iraq, and Afghanistan. He has been up there ever since the war broke out, and his work is priceless. I've no need to tell you that it's also extremely dangerous. If ever he were discovered he would be crucified—just that!'

'Go on!' said Sexton Blake.

'Well, you will understand that Loring's work renders his movements very uncertain, and our first task was to devise some means whereby we could contact him at any time with a minimum of delay. To that end we established a kind of "go-between"—a man who, while himself staying put in Kabul City, could always tell us exactly where Loring had gone and how best he could be found. And so that that man might be assured of the identity and genuineness of anyone who comes inquiring for Loring, it was arranged that every messenger travelling from me to him should invariably wear about his neck a certain amulet.'

'And that's the one that's been stolen now, I take it?' asked Sexton Blake, beginning to see daylight for the first time.

'Exactly. I gave that amulet, this morning, to a new man—an agent named Mahomet Ali—together with ten thousand rupees which Loring had sent for to use as palm-oil among the tribesmen. Both are gone!'

'Why a new man, Colonel?'

'Because the old one is dead! He was killed in a traffic accident, last week, in Hornby Road. That's where Yakub the Afghan comes in. Three weeks ago, when that agent returned from Afghanistan, he had a hunch that he'd been followed all the way down from the border by a raking, roaring, hell-fire Afghan horse-dealer by the

name of Yakub. At least, he thought he had been followed by him.
And to be on the safe side I had Yakub shadowed by the police,
who reported that there was nothing wrong with him. However,
when the same agent was killed in the street, even though all the
evidence went to show that it was his own fault entirely, nevertheless I couldn't help wondering. And when the man is murdered
whom I appoint in his place—to do exactly the same job of work—
well, then, I'm definitely suspicious!'

'Has he been questioned at all—this Yakub the Afghan?'

'There's no need for it; he's got a perfect alibi.'

'Perfect alibis are frequently the first refuge of the guilty,' Blake
murmured a mite sententiously, but the Colonel shook his head.

'Unfortunately, this is a police alibi. The police were actually
with him at the time Mahomet Ali was killed—so that it couldn't
have been Yakub the Afghan who killed him, could it?'

'I don't know,' Blake glanced at his assistant, who hunched his
shoulders. He would need to look closer into that before offering a
definite pronouncement. It wouldn't be the first 'perfect alibi' he
had known to break down under pressure. At the same time he
quite appreciated that it would be fatal to allow Yakub to know
himself suspected—if indeed he had the amulet—because then he
would pass it on to someone else and all trace of it would be lost for
ever. The only thing to do with him was to make absolutely certain
that he had the amulet, and then grab him like lightning before he
had time to drop it. 'At what time did you say the Frontier Mail
pulls out tonight?' he asked suddenly.

'At twenty-three hours. Eleven o'clock, that is.'

'Then the sooner we get going, the better—if we're to catch our
boat in the morning! Come on, old son; you and I have got to work
fast,' he told Tinker as he jumped to his feet.

There was no time for thanks. With a brief handshake the
Colonel turned and led the way out to his car. Captain Anderson
had disappeared, so he took the wheel himself; but half-way along
Hornby Road he stopped.

'We're being followed!' he snapped.

'Gent in white coat and green hat?' Tinker asked without turning.

'That's the man. He's on a bicycle.'

'Drive on, then, Colonel—that's Blood-Alley, the boy I can't lose. He haunts me!'

'Blood-Alley—?'

'A chap named Ali Blud whose life my assistant saved during a scrimmage in the Maynard operations,' Blake explained for the Colonel's benefit. 'He follows us everywhere. In fact,' he added as they reached the Taj Hotel, 'I'm dreadfully afraid we shall find him a stowaway in our boat when we go home!'

It was obvious from the start that Inspector Williams resented the private practitioner's intrusion into the affair. He was not definitely obstructive, but on the other hand he was not helpful.

'This Yakub talk's all baloney!' he said at once. 'Yakub was stuffin' his face with chapattis from twenty past twelve this mornin' until sixteen minutes past two, and my men were there with him. And since Mahomet Ali was murdered between one and half past one, accordin' to the medical evidence—'

'Quite!' Blake soothed him, glancing at the body. 'Have you got the weapon, Inspector?'

'Not on your life, Mr Blake! If you'd been out here as long as I have you'd know that no Indian thug ever leaves his knife behind!' He followed the detective across the room, and stood by with a supercilious smile on his face, while the Baker Street specialist examined the body.

The dead man was a bearded Moslem of thirty-eight or so, a stoutish, well-built man, dressed in a European suit of cream tussore, white shoes, and gaily figured socks. He was lying flat on his back, with glassy eyes staring up at the ceiling, mouth open, and—half hidden by his beard—a sickening gash which extended almost from ear to ear across his brown, muscular throat. Death must have been instantaneous, it seemed. His head was bare, although when Blake glanced round the room in search of either helmet or hat there was no sign of either.

'He was wearing a white puggaree when he left my office this morning,' the Colonel said as though reading his thoughts. 'That's another thing that seems to be missing, now you mention it. You see where the murderer tore the amulet from his neck?'

Blake nodded. The dead man's neckwear had been wrenched open with extraordinary violence. The stud-holes in both collar and shirtband had been ripped clean out, while the tie itself was in two parts.

'A violent man in a violent hurry,' Blake mused as he considered the phenomenon. 'Where was he carrying the ten thousand rupees you mentioned, Colonel?'

'In his breast pocket when he left my office.'

'But he wasn't going up to Afghanistan in these clothes?'

'Oh no! He told me he was going up as a grain merchant.'

Once again Blake glanced round the room as though expecting to find some evidence of that fact—but, as was the case with the white puggaree, there was none. Indeed, the only thing in the room— apart from the body itself—was an empty suitcase lying open beneath the bed.

'Enter the bloodhound!' Inspector Williams commented sarcastically when a moment later Blake went over there and sniffed at the thing, but the detective said nothing. From the smell magnificent which assailed his nostrils—wood-smoke, dung-smoke, hookah-smoke, and sour mutton fat combined—it was plain that the suitcase had very recently contained native clothes. Possibly, he thought, the kit of the grain merchant in which the dead man had intended making the journey to Afghanistan.

It was Tinker who broke the momentary silence. He had been examing the dead man's clothes, and now he called Blake's attention to a 'U'-shaped mark which appeared on the left breast of the tussore jacket.

'Looks like a heel-mark to me,' he said.

It was a heel-mark, Blake thought. Kneeling beside the body he took out a small steel rule and made various calculations concerning it—the Colonel looking on breathlessly the while. Then he got up and commenced a tour of the place.

Room 121 was just an ordinary Indian hotel-suite of bedroom and bathroom combined. The door through which they had entered was on one side of the room, and on the other a second door led into the bathroom. From that, a third door gave access to the service stairs which, as in all Indian houses and hotels, ran up the back of the building for the use of scavengers, water-carriers, and the visitors' personal servants generally. Each of those doors, and door-handles, the detective examined with considerable care. In addition, after considering it for some time through his glass, he actually withdrew the key of the outer door from its lock and slipped it into his pocket.

'Well?' Inspector Williams challenged him when finally he came back to the body, but Blake made no reply. He was still searching for something. Presently he stooped and picked up a needle, and after a further search—during which the Inspector made a second *sotto voce* reference to bloodhounds—he stood up again with what he had found. It consisted of seven short lengths of thread—three of them white, and four black—which he laid carefully upon the table, together with the needle he had found.

'Well?' demanded the Inspector again, his voice midway between curiosity and irritation.

'Well, Inspector,' Blake said then, 'here is my own reading of the affair. In the first place, the murderer entered by the service stairs. He came in through the bathroom, killed Mahomet Ali with a knife of the kukri variety, crossed over and locked that outer door against the chance of surprise from the hotel, and then set about robbing him. He was a man of five feet nine or over, of powerful physique, and although I can't suggest what clothes he was dressed in, I can say that he was wearing a pair of European shoes, size ten. Furthermore, since it's obvious that his entry caused Mahomet Ali no sort of alarm, I should say that he was most probably a servant.'

'That he wasn't!' Williams stated flatly after a moment of complete silence. 'If he was wearing anything at all on his feet he couldn't have been a servant, because all servants in this country go bare-foot. And even men who aren't servants would leave their shoes outside another man's house.'

'Then, by heavens!—he was a European!' cried Colonel North.

'No, he wasn't!' Williams retorted grimly. 'Not if he used that service staircase at the back, Colonel. No European on earth could do that, in broad daylight, without being seen and remarked by half a hundred servants in the compound. You know that as well as I do.'

'What about Yakub?' Tinker suggested.

'Yakub's a hillman, young man. He wears chaplis—sandals, to you. Yakub never wore a pair of shoes in his life, and couldn't even if he wanted to. I don't suppose you've ever seen a real hillman's feet, young man?' The Inspector turned to Sexton Blake, who was watching him thoughtfully. 'Why did you take the key out of that door just now?' he asked.

'There are bloodstains on it,' Blake said. 'Proving that the murderer locked it after he had slit Mahomet Ali's throat.'

'Yet the door wasn't locked when the hotel-boy came in at four o'clock to discover the body!'

'I dare say he unlocked it again, before he went. I expect he did, so as not to throw undue suspicion on the service entrance. If that outer door had been found locked, you would at once have known that the murderer had escaped by the service stairs and was therefore a servant.'

'But on the evidence of those shoes of yours, no servant was involved!' the Inspector shot back with his widest grin. 'And another thing, if there was blood on the murderer's hands when he touched that key, don't you think they'd have left some mark on Mahomet Ali's white suit when he delved into his pockets to take the money?'

'No, I don't! Because he didn't touch Mahomet Ali's pockets, Inspector.'

'Just whistled the money out, I suppose?'

'Not even that. Because you see, Inspector, the money wasn't in Mahomet Ali's pocket—not then!'

'What d'you mean?'

'I'll show you.' Blake waved towards those bits of thread he had picked up from the carpet. 'The missing puggaree and that empty suitcase were the clues,' he said, 'and those bits of thread and the needle, the proof of it. Mahomet Ali had already stitched the money into his clothes—those clothes in which he intended journeying to Afghanistan, and which, incidentally, he had brought into the room in that suitcase over there. Some of the notes he had stitched into his white puggaree—as witness those snippings of white thread—while the rest he had stitched into the darker material of his posteen coat—as witness the snippings of black thread. The murderer, therefore, did not touch Mahomet Ali's pockets; he simply snatched up the clothes in which he knew that the money was hidden. And that explains why they are not here now!'

There was a moment of startled silence: it was Inspector Williams who broke it. With a totally unexpected movement, he thrust out his hand and caught Blake's in a grip of friendship.

'Salute to genius, Mr Blake!' he cried, his hard-bitten face alight with admiration. 'I'm just a boob; I ought to be back on the beat.

By jimmy, I've never—'

'Hey, guv'nor!' Tinker cried suddenly from the window. Looking out, something had caught his eye on the other side of the hotel courtyard—something that moved. Not twenty yards away, set high in the blank wall which formed the back of the servants' quarters, was a solitary window-hole which looked directly into the room where he was standing. 'Somebody was up there, watching us!' he told the others breathlessly when they joined him. 'He bobbed down when he saw me, but—there he is again!' He broke off as a man's head appeared for a fraction of a second above the sill. 'That's him, look!' But then he gaped. For a long minute he remained staring; then, with a helpless little shrug, he turned away. 'All right, gents!' he said. 'Wash it out. It's Blood-Alley again!'

'Wait!' Blake's voice drove through his assistant's like a rapier. Now he had it! A lightning glance back into the room had shown him the answer to everything. In his mind's eye he could see Mahomet Ali laboriously sewing Treasury notes to the value of ten thousand rupees into the folds of his puggaree and into the padding of his posteen coat. While upon the other side of the courtyard, with his face glued to that window-hole, some avaricious-eyed servant—

'Wait!' he shouted again, dashing into the bathroom and out down the service stairs at the back. He was gone for quite a time, but when presently they saw him returning across the courtyard he was carrying a bundle under his arm.

'By jimmy!—he's found the clothes!' exclaimed Inspector Williams, but that was not quite right. It was not Mahomet Ali's stolen clothes that Blake opened out for their inspection a few minutes later. They were the murderer's own!

'I found them rolled into a ball and thrust out of sight behind a heap of old boxes!' he told them breathlessly. 'That place seems to be a rubbish room of sorts—no, I didn't catch Blood-Alley, he'd gone when I got there. He'd told them he was Tinker sahib's servant, that's how he wangled his way in . . . but you see the meaning of these things, don't you?' he raced on, pointing to the baggy trousers and dirty shirt, both of which were horribly bespattered with blood. 'The murderer daren't try to get away in those, and he hadn't time to unstitch all those notes from Mahomet Ali's garments—so he did the only thing possible. He stripped off his own clothes, bundled them out of sight behind those cases, dressed himself in the clothes he'd stolen from Mahomet Ali—the ones containing the money—and calmly walked out.'

'With the amulet as well?' Colonel North asked quickly.

'No! He never had the amulet—that's where we've gone wrong! The Inspector here was perfectly correct when he said that it was a barndoor dacoity—it was a barndoor dacoity so far as the murder and the theft of the money is concerned. But that's only half the trouble. There are two of them in this business—one who came for the money, and a second who came for the amulet. And it was the second of the pair who wore shoes!'

'But hell's bells, Blake!' gasped the Inspector when at last he could speak at all. 'How in the world do you get at that?'

'Because it's the only solution that fits the facts, Inspector. Whoever wrenched open Mahomet Ali's collar like that put his foot on the body to get the necessary purchase—and he was wearing shoes. Must have been, in order to leave that heel-mark. In my opinion, Mahomet Ali was then already dead, because if—'

Blake stopped, every muscle tensed, his eyes keen as a hawk's. Suddenly he snapped his fingers.

'Wait!' he said softly, stooping and pulling open the dead man's shirt. 'As I thought!' he whispered. 'There were two of them, and the second was at least two hours after the first. See how that heel has impressed itself into the flesh? See how the mark remains there, as though made in putty? That's because the flesh was already dead when Number Two put his foot on the body and wrenched open that collar and tie.

'And now we see the reason for the violence and fury with which the collar and tie were torn,' he continued. 'I have already said that the wearer of those shoes was a powerful man, and it is easy to imagine his amazement when he opened that door and saw Mahomet Ali lying already dead. It is easy to imagine the fury that would assail him when he realised that someone had been there before him; someone who had pipped him on the post. He would leap forward with a snarl of rage, clamp his foot on the body, seize collar and tie and shirtband in one furious fist—and heave!'

'But you think that the amulet was still there?' Colonel North asked quickly.

'Undoubtedly, Colonel. The other man wasn't interested in amulets; all he wanted was the fortune he had watched Mahomet Ali stitching into those garments.'

'Then who's got the amulet?'

'That's the problem,' Blake admitted. 'Judging by the state of that heel-mark on the body, I should estimate that it was made somewhere around two hours after death—about half past three that would be. How does Yakub the Afghan's alibi stand him for half past three, Inspector?'

'I'll make inquiries.' The Inspector went out to use the phone and was gone for some time. When at last he did come back he was not alone. He had brought the hotel lift-boy with him, and from the expression on his face it was plain that something unexpected had turned up.

'Yakub the Afghan is reported as having been asleep in his lodgings all the afternoon,' he said as he closed the door behind him. 'But I've had an extraordinary tale from this lift-boy. He says that at about half past three he brought a man up to this floor; but he'd scarcely got back to the street level when the bell rang and there was the same man waiting to be brought down again. He didn't say anything to him, but all the way down in the lift—and across the hall—he was blowing his nose and holding a handkerchief over his face—'

'Yakub?' Blake snapped.

'No! He was a European. A "German" according to the boy—but he means a German type, a square-head. I expect he means a Swiss, really; there's a lot of Swiss in the city.'

'A Swiss—?' gaped the Colonel. Suddenly he caught his breath. 'Then, by heavens, I was right!' he cried in a great voice. 'It's the amulet they've been after all the time!' He swung round on the gaping lift-boy. 'What kind of sahib was this that you brought up here at half-past three this afternoon?' he demanded in Hindustani. 'Was he tall, short, fat, thin—what?'

'A big sahib, *huzoor*,' the boy said, a bit breathlessly. He described a circle with his hands to indicate just how big. 'And tall as that sahib,' he added, pointing to Sexton Blake. 'But his face was shaped like this'—forming a square with his hands. 'And his beard was like this'—chopping the air in a big 'V'.

'What was he wearing?'

'A white suit like yours, sahib, and a white topee. Also he wore dark glasses so that I could not see his eyes. His shoes were white, like his clothes, but on the toe of this one'—he pointed to his own left foot—'there was a black grease-mark; I saw it when he stepped into the lift. "That will be much trouble for the sahib's boy!" I thought to myself.'

The Colonel stopped him with a gesture.

'Just one thing more, and you may go,' he said. 'You say that you watched the sahib walk through the hall towards the street? How did he walk? Show me.'

The boy thought for a moment; then he grinned.

'Like this, sahib,' he said. And putting his right hand to his nose, in imitation of a man holding a handkerchief, he walked across the room with a peculiar swing—almost a sailor's 'roll'.

'Gustav Grabow!' whispered the Colonel. 'Grabow beyond a doubt!' He gave the boy a rupee and sent him packing, but the moment the door was closed behind his grinning face: 'The same man who knocked down and killed my agent in Hornby Road, Blake!' he burst out. 'The one I told you about. It wasn't an accident after all; it was murder! It was a deliberate attempt to get the amulet—the first attempt. This attack on Mahomet Ali is the second. He evidently thought it would be round G78's neck when he knocked him down, but it wasn't. It was in my safe. It always is in my safe except when it's in actual use, but evidently Grabow didn't know that. And having failed in that first attempt, he tries again on the man he knows I have appointed in G78's place. And this time he has succeeded.'

'Who is Gustav Grabow?' Blake asked swiftly.

'A Swiss. At least, that's what he says he is; but in view of this, I wouldn't be surprised to learn that he's a German. A German-Swiss, anyhow! He's a watchmaker, with a shop in the Sudda Bazaar. He told me he had another business in Peshawar, and in view of what we know now, I shouldn't be at all surprised. It'ud be excellent cover for him, wouldn't it?—right on the border.'

'You think he's a spy, then—for Germany?'

'Yes. By some means or other they've got wise to the fact that Major Loring is up there. They must have been watching Hussein's shop—he is the go-between I told you about—and they've tumbled to the significance of the amulet. They've realised that, given that,

Loring will be at their mercy. So they're determined to get it.'

'But why not have waited until Mahomet Ali was safely across the border and in their own country?' Blake asked doubtfully. 'That's the point that puzzles me. Why risk murdering him here?—because that Swiss came prepared to murder him, you know!—why risk murdering him here, with the almost certain risk of capture and discovery?'

'Because here they were certain of the man they wanted, while up there they wouldn't be. Mahomet Ali might have adopted any one of a hundred different guises. He would have got on to the train as a Muslim gentleman, and alighted as a purdah woman—or even a policeman! They had to get hold of him while they could see him and be sure of his identity—that's why they tackled him here.'

'Then we'd better get after Gustav Grabow!'

'At once, Blake! At once! He may pass on the amulet to someone else, don't you see? Someone of whom we have no knowledge, and therefore no suspicion.'

'Or someone with a perfect alibi!' Sexton Blake laughed softly, for the first time grasping in its entirety the whole ingenious plot.

It was already dusk when the famous Baker Street combination left the Taj Hotel on their mission; and—with the suddenness of which the tropics are noted—by the time they reached Sudda Bazaar night had drawn her dark head over the sun-baked city and the stars were hanging like great golden lamps in the soft velvet of the sky.

The two detectives walked warily along the dusty road, for of pavement there is none in Sudda Bazzar. Nor is there any form of public street lighting other than that obtaining from various oil lamps set in the open-fronted booths, and here and there, from the flickering tallow dips of the street vendors. After sunset, India prefers its age-old darkness—if only as a relief from the day-long glare of the sun. Down Sudda Bazaar way, perhaps, they had other and less healthy reasons for preferring the dark!

The shop of Gustav Grabow was situated at the far end, and, unlike the majority, its window was glazed. To the right of it was a native furniture shop, and to the left a melon-seller squatted silent and inscrutable as a crow beside his wares. Everywhere the thick dust permeated the atmosphere and lay like a blanket over man, beast, and food—but no one cared. No one even appeared to notice it. The melon-seller sat staring into vacancy as though unaware that the day had passed and night was at hand—as indeed he was unaware, for what was Time to him?

'Time,' says the East, 'is not money. Time is naught.'

'Looks as though our bird isn't at home, guv'nor,' Tinker whispered as they stood surveying Gustav's shop from the opposite side of the road.

'Wait here a moment, I'll see.' Blake walked along and crossed the road out of range of the melon-seller's candle; then he came back on the other side and stopped at the watchmaker's shop. He tried the crudely carved door. It was locked. He knocked, loudly, and waited. Then he knocked again.

Presently, as he had expected, the melon-seller woke up from his vision of Nirvana and shook himself free of his dreams. He peered round the corner post of his shop, and observing that a stranger was trying to gain admission to the shop next door, he spat the dust from his throat and spoke.

'He who knocks upon a locked door, knocks long, brother,' he observed sapiently. 'The feringhee is away.'

'But I want my watch,' Blake said.

The old man picked up his candle and held it forward that he might better see who spoke. Observing an Englishman, he touched his turban in salaam.

'Your pardon, Protector of the Poor,' he apologised. 'In the darkness I did not see your face. Yet it is truth that I speak, sahib—the *mistri* is indeed away. His shop has remained closed this many a day—eh, for a moon or more.'

'You're sure of that, Old Man?' Blake asked after a moment's silence.

'As Allah sees me, sahib! I sit here every day, but always the *mistri*'s shop remains closed. It is often so. It is said that he has other shops in other places, for myself I do not know. Soon, doubtless, he will return again.'

'But I saw him only a week ago, Old Man—in a motor car, along Hornby Road!'

The melon-seller sat silent for a time; and if he heard scratching and scrapings against the woodwork near where the sahib was standing, who in Sudda Bazaar took notice of rats? Finally, having duly cogitated that conundrum, he shrugged his shoulders.

'Doubtless it is as the sahib says,' he agreed. 'For myself, I am an old man—and foolish. I can but speak of what my eyes see and my heart knows. The *mistri* comes: the *mistri* goes. Only the all-seeing eye of Allah can follow the flight of a bird, sahib.'

'You're right!' Blake tossed him eight annas, and gave up his quest. 'I will return another day,' he promised. 'Allah keep you, Old Man!'

'And thou, too, sahib—who has the face of the West yet who speaks with the tongue of Islam.'

Blake went back by the way he had come, recrossed the road, and found Tinker waiting where he had left him.

'You were right,' he said succinctly. 'Gustav isn't at home—and according to that old man over there, who ought to know, he hasn't been home for a month or more. We'll go inside and have a look round.'

'Can we get in?'

'I picked the lock while I was talking to the melon-seller: the door's open now. Go softly!'

They recrossed the road, and moving silently as shadows along the wall, slipped through the half-open door without the ancient melon-seller seeing or hearing a thing. In any event he, poor soul, was wrapped in dreams of the wealth that had dropped so unexpectedly into his lap from the sahib's hand. Eight annas! A shilling! A fortune to one such as he. Allah was indeed compassionate! Truly did he hold all things in the hollow of his hand!

Meanwhile, inside the shop of Gustav Grabow, Blake was feeling his way cautiously through the hot darkness towards the living-room which he knew would be behind it. Everything he touched was gritty and smothered with dust. When presently he found the thick, unplaned door for which he was seeking, the handle of that, too, was thick with dust.

He pulled it open and passed through into the Stygian blackness beyond, treading warily on the beaten mud floor. He waited until Tinker followed him, and then closed the door and felt for his matches, listening intently the while.

Finally he drew a deep breath.

'There's no one here,' he whispered.

'And hasn't been for some time, judging by the dust on everything, guv'nor,' Tinker whispered back. 'Can we have a light?'

Blake struck a match, shielding it carefully from the door through which they had just entered—in case a chink of light might show through into the street. The room was empty—swept, garnished, but empty. No one had lived in it for some time, that was obvious. So far as he could see in the feeble light it appeared to be more a store-room than anything else, with a flight of bare wooden steps leading up from one corner to the rooms above.

He went over there, and, pausing, struck another match.

'Guv'nor!' Tinker whispered on the instant.

Blake looked where he was pointing—and smiled. He had made no mistake! There on the tread of the bottom stair was the plain imprint of a shoe, showing that someone had only very recently ascended those stairs. And alongside it—on top of them on some of the other stairs, he noticed—was the imprint of another shoe but in the reverse direction, indicating where someone had only very recently descended those stairs.

'He's been and gone again,' Tinker whispered.

'And not in the same footwear,' Blake said softly. 'Let's go up!'

Nineteen steps carried them to a landing from which three doors opened, and since there was a carpet on the floor he had to pick up the footprints again on the bare boards beyond. They led to the door on the right—into a room overlooking the street, he calculated—and before he dare strike a match he felt his way across the floor to where he judged the window would be. It was curtained.

Then he struck a match and looked about him.

Hangings from Kashmir and Persia! Silks from the south, and rugs from Bokhara! Carved lattice-work! Low-hanging lamps of silver and brass! Blake caught his breath. It was like entering Aladdin's Cave. A silver-inlaid charpoy stood at the side furthest from the window, and a magnificently carved cedar-wood chest—Indian equivalent to a wardrobe—flanked the wall immediately opposite. But here, too, on brass and silver and silk alike, lay the all-pervading dust.

Swiftly Blake crossed to the cedar-wood chest—there were fingermarks on it! Someone had opened that within the past few hours. Blake lifted the lid and peeped inside.

'Got him!' he exclaimed triumphantly as he lifted out a pair of white European shoes. He pointed to a spot of black grease which disfigured the toecap of the left of the pair. 'Remember?' he whispered.

'Gustav Grabow!' Tinker nodded, his eyes shining in the flickering light. 'The shoes the lift-boy noticed; it's him all right, guv'nor! It's him, all right—whatever the old melon-seller may say. He must be getting in and out through the back—but what's his game?'

Blake thrust the marked shoe into his pocket and turned to go back down the stairs.

'Something more lucrative than watchmaking, at all events, judging by the stuff in that room!' he said dryly. 'Let's look round the back of the place.'

There was a second door in the store-room which, upon investigation, was found to give access to what was undoubtedly the kitchen. Here the floor was of beaten earth, so that there were no footprints visible, but in one corner of the place—where a string bed had been pulled aside—a small trap-door stood revealed.

Blake looked at that in silence for a moment, conscious of the fact that it had neither lock nor bolt to secure it. It could, therefore, be pushed open from below—at any time—as readily as it could be lifted open from above.

'Where does that lead?' Tinker whispered.

'We'll have a look.'

Stooping, the detective poked his fingers through the hole provided and cautiously lifted the door. A square of pitch-darkness was all that rewarded his effort.

'But there's a ladder—look!' Tinker pointed out a moment later, indicating the tops of two stout bamboo poles which reached to within a few inches of the trap-door.

Blake struck a match and dropped it down the hole; it went out. He tried again, but that, too, went out. Finally, he set fire to a piece of paper and dropped that down—and that time suceeded in seeing what was below.

'Packing-cases,' he said. 'Cardboard cartons, and the like. I'm going down!'

'Why? Do you think you can get out that way?'

'I don't think, old son—I know!' Blake retorted cheerfully. 'It's in my mind that this house connects with another house somewhere—must do, or how can Gustav pass to and fro without being spotted? It isn't as though he were a native, remember. He's a European, and therefore—to a certain extent, at any rate—remarkable. Yet he can move about as easily in broad daylight as at night, and that suggests something underground, don't you think? Wait here a minute.'

He swung himself over the hole, felt around with his feet for the first rungs of the ladder, found them, and descended carefully to the bottom. He found himself on a boarded floor; and a moment later, when he struck a match, realised that the walls were match-boarded, too.

'All right?' Tinker called softly from above.

'Yes. You can come down yourself, now.'

Half a minute later the young detective was standing beside his chief in an underground chamber of perhaps eight feet square. As Blake had already observed, both floor and walls were match-boarded—presumably to keep the damp from ruining the alarm clocks and cheap watches which, if the labels spoke correctly, formed the contents of the bulk of the cartons with which the cellar was stocked. To all appearances, that was the sole purpose of the place; but in view of the priceless treasures lying about uncared for and unguarded in that upstairs room they had just left, neither Blake nor his assistant was deceived.

'Eyewash!' Blake shrugged. 'And this matchboarding is merely a blind to cover the entrance to a tunnel of some kind—or I'm a Dutchman. Some part of it must move sideways, or swing in-wards,' he added as he started tapping along the wall. 'Question is: which piece?'

Tinker tore up one of the cardboard cartons and made a torch, so that presently they were working in a better light. For a time they tapped and thrust and sounded in silence. Then Tinker caught his breath.

'Here we are!' he whispered exultantly. He had been working along that wall which would face the back of the house, and now he was pointing to a certain knot which had moved under his fingers. 'This is something to do with it, guv'nor!'

It was! Few men living today have a better or wider knowledge of secret hiding-places—their constructions and concealment—than Sexton Blake, and within a very few minutes of examining that loose knot, he knew the system upon which it was constructed. As a craftsman, the Swiss watchmaker had elected to use what is known as the 'Bernardi Cross-lock', and admittedly he had made a fine job of it. But he could not beat Sexton Blake.

Within ten minutes of getting to work, the private practitioner had discovered the particular 'cross' Gustav had used, and in a breathless silence a square yard of the panelling fell noiselessly inwards to reveal a gaping hole in the wall.

'As I thought!' With a grim little smile on his lean, hawk-like face, Blake peered into the darkness of the tunnel and sniffed. The air was bad, but quite safe. 'I'll see where it goes to,' he said as he made himself another torch from a carton. 'You wait here and watch this end, while I'm gone.'

He stepped through the panelling into the tunnel proper, holding the torch well in front of him, and marvelling at the amount of work Grabow must have put in before he was through with such a job. It must have taken him years, he thought, unless he had had help—and he could scarcely have had that if he wished to keep its existence a secret.

Blake pressed on slowly, keeping a sharp eye ahead of him and frequently stopping to listen for the least sign of alarm. The tunnel was some six feet high, in the main, and about four feet wide. Fortunately it was bone dry, and because of that few roof props had been necessary.

He counted his steps as he went. Thirty-one, thirty-two . . . of course they were not yard steps, but even so the length of the place must be considerable. Forty-six, forty-seven . . .

Suddenly he stopped, every muscle tensed, his eyes on a line of sacks he had just seen stacked against the wall of the tunnel some three or four yards ahead. For a moment he thought he had reached the end of the workings—for now he saw a shovel there, and a pick. But nothing stirred. Nothing moved. And after a brief hesitation he went on again when he perceived that the tunnel itself went on.

But when a few seconds later he reached those sacks he paused again. Something—some strange inner prescience—was warning him of impending danger: though how, or from what direction, he could not say. He listened intently, but not a sound broke the deathly silence. He even put his torch behind him so that its light might not blind his eyes as he peered into the darkness of the tunnel ahead, but he could see nothing. He was utterly and entirely alone in the place—or was he?

Suddenly he caught his breath. In bringing his torch to the front again the light had flickered for a second on something white lying immediately beyond the last of those eight sacks that were stood against the side of the tunnel. He leaned forward, and saw for the first time that the side of the tunnel had been excavated there—a deep niche had been cut and filled up with some white stuff that—

His thoughts stopped abruptly. For a moment he stood motionless, staring, while beads of perspiration ran down his cheeks and dropped unheeded off the end of his chin. But it was not the heat that was responsible: it was shock. For now he saw that the white stuff was quicklime, and that the thing he had noticed on the floor was a whitened skull.

The tunnel was not only a secret passage—it was a graveyard! Worse than that—it was a secret graveyard. A graveyard for murdered men!

So much the detective understood instinctively as he gazed at that dreadful niche. Nor did the exact significance of those sacks of lime which were yet to be used escape him. It was plain that the man Grabow was quite ready for other victims. Nay, more—he was expecting them!

Blake swallowed hard, and his jaw tightened. By heavens!—it was time that monster was laid by the heels. With cold rage at his heart the detective turned to continue his way along the tunnel—started violently, then halted.

Someone was standing there, blocking his way!

For the space of a split-second that seemed a year, Blake remained motionless, staring. Past the smoke from his dying torch he was aware in a vague kind of way of a man of enormous size—of a red beard, of eyes that were still and hard as pebbles. Then he saw the revolver, and knew that it was going to fire.

He flung himself forward in a flat dive, throwing the torch in front of him and aiming to get under that spitting gun, but he was a fraction of a section too soon. The other saw him coming, and instead of firing simply whipped up his gun and cracked it down hard on the back of Blake's head.

Blake saw stars. A vicious blue flame tore across his vision. In a whirling kaleidoscope, wherein sacks of quicklime, red beard, staring eyes, whitened skulls, and Tinker's freckled face were inextricably mixed, the detective crashed heavily to the floor.

He awoke to a sense of suffocation and dreadful nausea. For a long time he lay helpless in the impenetrable darkness, unable to think or to reason. But bit by bit his senses returned and presently—as at the turn of a switch—he blossomed into full consciousness of everything that had befallen him.

He tried to get up, but he was held fast to the ground. He tried to shout, but the gag in his mouth blocked all sound. Frantically he strove with his bonds, but as well try to snap steel chains as the raw-hide thongs with which he was pegged out to the floor of the tunnel.

Realising his impotence he gave up for a while until he was rested. Or until Tinker should come along, looking for him, he thought, with a swift rush of hope. Of course!—he had forgotten Tinker. He almost laughed aloud in his relief. He had left Tinker at the other end of the tunnel, in the cellar—but he would not stay in the cellar for ever!

He wondered how long he had been lying there. It couldn't be very long, or Tinker would surely have come to investigate before now. He fell to listening for his approaching footsteps. Once or twice he fancied he heard something—a faint rustling sort of sound. But when he listened again, it was never there.

Hallucination, he supposed. The silence was so profound that he was actually hearing it—or was he, he asked himself a moment later when another rustle sounded scarcely a foot from his ear? The next second all doubt as to his hearing was shattered for ever, for from right beside him came an unmistakable groan.

Tinker! He knew the truth in a flash, and his heart sank. They'd got Tinker, too! Caught him in the cellar, he supposed, and dragged him along here to suffer with his master.

Once again he struggled with his bonds—desperately, now urgently. For of a sudden he had remembered those sacks of quicklime; the spade and the pick, laid out in readiness. Exerting his strength to the utmost, he writhed and tore at the cords which held him. Useless! He tried cunning, expanding and relaxing his muscles—but he had been tied up at a moment when his muscles were already relaxed. That was useless, too.

With the perspiration dripping from every pore of him, he lay still for a moment, calming himself. And it was then, beyond the shadow of a doubt, that he heard naked feet creeping cautiously towards him along the tunnel.

'Grabow!' he thought instantly. 'Grabow—the butcher!' The monster was coming to do his foul work. To slit their throats, preparatory to burying them in that niche under his quicklime where they would never be found.

Violently he strove to get his hands free. He tried to shout out, but only the most inhuman sounds seeped through his gag. He had the fancy that Tinker was trying to shout, too—and then a light flashed on, blinding him.

'Sahib!' a thin voice called in Hindustani. 'Tinker, sahib! Tinker, sahib—?'

Blake caught his breath. Was he mad, or dreaming? Something leapt past him; native clothes brushed his face. There was the sound of cutting. Of spluttering.

'Blood-Alley—you old swab!' gasped a voice that could only be Tinker's. 'By golly, Blood-Alley!—for once in a way you've come at the right time! Gimme that knife!' In a moment Blake's own bonds were being severed—by Tinker on the one side and a grinning, beaming native boy on the other.

'You all right, guv'nor?' Tinker asked as he sat up.

Blake shook himself. By heavens, that had been a close call! For weeks past they had cursed Blood-Alley for his insistence upon following them everywhere they went. Now—?

'How did you get here?' he asked him.

Tinker spoke first. He had heard Blake—as he thought—returning down the tunnel, and had called out: 'Is that you, guv'nor?' A muffled voice had answered: 'Yes!'—and that was about all he knew. He had turned to get another carton to make a torch when something had whanged down on his head and he had known no more until he had awakened in the tunnel.

'I saw that badmarsh hit you, sahib!' Ali Blud broke in gleefully. 'I had followed you into the shop—because you are my father and mother and no harm must befall you—and I was watching you through the trap-door. I saw that badmarsh spring from the tunnel and hit you. And I saw him come up through the trap-door and return with a small box from his shop. Then he picked you up, carried you into the tunnel—and lo! the hole in the wall closed behind him again so that I could not find it.'

'How did you get in, then?' Blake asked him.

'*Huzoor*, I tried for a little time to find it, and failed. I became frightened for my master. I ran outside to the police-station at the bottom of Sudda Bazaar, and I told the police sahib there all about it. He called me "badmarsh", sahib. He did not believe me. But I told him to use the stretched wire to speak to Colonel North sahib, your friend, and to tell him to come quick-quick with the soldiers and the stutter guns—and then I ran back to the cellar. And that time I found the magic which worked the door, sahib. I had seen that badmarsh close it after he had hit Tinker sahib, and open it again before he carried him into the tunnel. And I did the same— and lo! the wall opened for me even as it had for him.'

'Blood-Alley, I will make it my business to see that you get your chance in the great Indian Police!' Blake told him fervently. 'For, by Allah, you're a man!' He swung round to a rush of feet in the tunnel. Men, and lights.

'Blake?' a voice called desperately. 'Blake?'

It was Colonel North himself, followed by the local police sergeant and half a dozen men. He had a drawn revolver in his hand. His face was white in the light from the torches.

'My God! What's going on here?' he gasped.

With a grim smile on his blood-smeared face, Blake told him.

'Your Gustav Grabow is a proper Jekyll and Hyde!' he said. 'What time is it?'

'Just ten. The Frontier Mail pulls out in an hour's time. Have you got the amulet?'

'No. Yakub the Afghan's got it. Let the police follow us to the end of this tunnel, and we'll grab it before he has time to start. Give me that torch, Sergeant.'

The torch came over, and, turning swiftly, Blake led the way forward along the tunnel. At the further end he paused. 'Lend me your revolver, Colonel,' he whispered, pointing to the door which blocked the mouth of the tunnel. 'Take the torch, old son, while I work the secret lock.'

That was the work of two minutes only. Just before the door swung outwards and downwards, Blake thrust forward his revolver, prepared to shoot it out with whoever should be upon the further side—but no one was there. This end of the passage opened directly into a furnished sleeping room in which a solitary oil lamp was burning.

'Yakub the Aghan!' gasped Colonel North, pointing to a lavishly embroidered posteen coat which lay across a roll of bedding all ready to be taken away to the train. 'That's his! I've seen him wearing it.' Suddenly he caught his breath. 'You mean that—that Yakub the Afghan and Gustav Grabow are in this together, Blake?'

'Closer than brothers, Colonel—as you can see for yourself!' Blake smiled. He held up his hand for silence. 'Quick! He's coming back, I think!' he whispered. 'Here's your revolver, Colonel; get over in the angle of the wall there and hold him up as he enters! Ask him for the amulet. Close that secret door, Sergeant, and remain immediately behind it ready to dash out if I call. That's right! Over here, Tinker!'

Now they were all set. Outside, someone was coming down the passage in chaplis—you could hear them dragging along the ground from their wearer's heels. Someone's hand touched the door-knob, and a man's deep bass voice broke out into a ribald song of the border. The door opened abruptly.

'Stick 'em up, Yakub!' flashed the Colonel, jambing his gun into the Afghan's ribs.

Yakub the Afghan came to an abrupt halt. He stood very still. So far, he had not seen Blake and Tinker standing behind the open door, but they could see him, and both noticed how his eyes shot instantly to the secret door leading into the tunnel. Not until then did he turn to the Colonel.

'Allah, sahib!' he complained. 'Since when have the Sirkar's officers taken to dacoity?'

'Where's that amulet?' snapped the Colonel.

'Amulet, sahib—?'

'That Gustav Grabow stole from Mahomet Ali this afternoon!'

The Afghan shook his head. His self-possession was astounding. He even contrived a weary little smile.

'It pleases the sahib to jest,' he said. 'For myself, I do not wear amulets. Nor do I know this Gustav Grabow.'

'Then make his acquaintance now!' Blake stepped abruptly round the door, and even as the startled man's jaw sagged at sight of him, he held up a mirror to his eyes. 'Take a good look at him, Yakub . . . or wait!' he added, when the Afghan continued to stand utterly paralysed now that he appreciated the immensity of the disaster that had overtaken him. 'Wait!' Blake said again. With a lightning sweep of his free hand he swept off the heavy turban and pulled down the ragged beard to a smooth 'V'. 'There!' he cried. 'Recognise him now?'

It was the Colonel who spoke.

'My God!' he gasped. 'Why, he—he is Grabow! He's Gustav Grabow, himself!'

'I warned you that Yakub and he were closer than brothers!'

The spell snapped. With a roar of concentrated fury, the spy hurled himself at Blake's throat. Once again the detective caught a vision of glaring eyes, red beard, and lips drawn back in a wolfish snarl—but this time it was light and he could see what he was doing. Side-stepping the broad-bladed knife which streaked upwards in line with his stomach, he came over with a swinging right that rocked the spy to his heels. But before he could follow it up with his favourite straight left, the Colonel sailed in with his revolver-butt, and the fight was over.

It was Blake's fingers that tore away the unconscious man's shirt, but the Colonel who grabbed the greasy bit of leather they found hanging upon a silver chain around his neck.

'Is that all we've been looking for?' Tinker asked into the dead silence, staring askance at the dirty little bag of tricks lying so incongruously in the Colonel's palm.

'That's all,' Colonel North said softly. 'Worth about eight annas in cash, but in the lives of men—?'

Suddenly he held out his hand to Sexton Blake.

'On behalf of those men, Mr Blake—'

'Nonsense!' smiled the detective. 'Blood-Alley is the man who made our success possible, you know!'

They caught their boat the next morning, Blake and his young assistant, but they had scarcely reached their cabins when Inspector Williams came aboard inquiring for them.

'I've got him!' he cried the instant he saw them. 'Snaffled him early this morning, fifty miles away, with the posteen coat and the white puggaree still in his possession and the money intact, just as Mahomet Ali stitched it in.'

'A servant?' Blake asked curiously.

'Yes, a servant—just as you said he'd be. In fact, it all fell out exactly as you said it would. He did see Mahomet Ali through the baggage-room window, and he did enter by the service staircase and do him in exactly as you described. Funny how one crime cut across the other, without in any way being connected—but it was surely Mahomet Ali's Friday the Thirteenth! If the servant hadn't have got him, Grabow would! Between the two, as things fell out, he hadn't a blessed chance, had he?'

Blake shook his head.

'I say—why was it necessary for Gustav Grabow to play about like that, Blake? The Jekyll and Hyde business, I mean?'

'Well, Inspector, in the beginning I don't think he intended to, frankly. I think he intended to scupper the Colonel's agent, and secure the amulet, all in the person of Yakub the Afghan. But when that other agent suspected him, and Colonel North asked you fellows to keep tail on him, you pinned him down, don't you see? Yakub the Afghan couldn't move; and so it became necessary for Gustav Grabow himself to do the work and take the chance, leaving Yakub the Afghan with the "perfect alibi" that originally he'd intended to keep in his own person. Of course, Yakub the Afghan was only one of the "alibis" he's been playing up between those two houses. He must have been at it for years.'

The ship's siren sounded for the third time, and with a quick handshake the Inspector hurried ashore.

'Tinker, sahib!' shrilled a voice from the quay.

'I'm watching you,' Tinker shouted back, his eyes on Blood-Alley, whom Blake had carefully placed in charge of a dock police-man.

'I'm going to save up and come to England on the next boat! And I shall bring you a fat buffalo.'

'Blimey!' gasped Tinker. 'Now what d'you think Mrs Bardell'll say to a fat buffalo hangin' around the place?'

THE BOX OF HO SEN
Anthony Skene

Anthony Skene (r.n. George Norman Philips, 1884–1972) was unique in that, although he was one of the major Blake authors of the Golden Age—racking up 39 full-length novels as well as nearly 90 novelettes, plus numerous non-Blake shorts, serials, articles and four mainstream thrillers—he was only a part-time writer. While his peers set to at the typewriter five or six days a week, Skene travelled the country as a quantity surveyor for the Office of Public Works, dictating stories to his secretary on coaches and trains. He usually reckoned on one week to finish a 25,000-word Union Jack, *three or four to see off a 60,000-word* Sexton Blake Library. *His classic contribution to the saga was Zenith the Albino, a wonderfully original creation and a perfect example of the pulp-writer's ability often to transmute dull or seedy reality into pure gold. Skene bumped into a real albino in London's West End: 'a man of about fifty-five . . . a slovenly fellow: fingers stained with tobacco, clothes soiled by dropped food. Yet he was dressed expensively, and had about him a look of adequacy.' Out of this chance encounter emerged the far from slovenly Monsieur Zenith, with his snow-white hair, leprous skin, pink-irised eyes; his opium-soaked cigarettes, ivory-headed swordstick, melancholy disposition (in this, not unlike his creator), and the bizarre habit (considering he was an eternal fugitive from the police) of wearing, even in broad daylight, immaculate evening dress. Blake's many duels with Zenith, written in a prose-style that was a captivating mixture of the mandarin and the hard-boiled, are highly enjoyable and characterised by a good deal of casual violence. Not a few of Skene's stories end up with more corpses scattered about than the final moments of a Jacobean tragedy.*

Upon a couch in a room of black and silver a figure of white marble came to life.

A bell rang; and a Japanese pushed the curtains aside to stand down in front of the couch.

'You rang, excellency.'

The figure of white marble opened crimson-irised eyes. Instantly his strange exotic charm became apparent; the debonair recklessness of his face; the fact that he was a true albino.

'Put out some clothes, Oyani.'

'His excellency will dine at home?'

The eyes of the albino turned towards a yen-hok, the pipe in which opium is smoked.

'I have dined already; I am going out. I have had sad dreams, Oyani. I need to amuse myself.'

The servant bowed and withdrew. Although, like everybody else who came in contact with Zenith the Albino, he had a deep affection for the strange character who was his master, he knew better than to expostulate. It was no use saying to Monsieur Zenith: 'You have had neither breakfast nor lunch. Would it not be wise to eat before the evening begins?' Because Monsieur Zenith suffered no sort of dictation from anybody on earth. He was a law unto himself. What he desired, that was all that mattered; and tonight he desired to go out and, as he called it, amuse himself.

The servant brought clothes and a porcelain cup filled to the brim with Turkish coffee.

The albino bathed and dressed. In his evening clothes, with white vest and tails, the white camellia in his buttonhole, and his crisp white hair brushed back from his almost colourless face, he looked startlingly perfect, like a piece of sculpture endowed with life. With his long legs and small waist and his broad shoulders, he wore his clothes to perfection.

He took his silk hat from the Japanese and allowed the yellow man to place a cloak around his shoulders. Gloves and an ebony stick, and Monsieur Zenith was ready to amuse himself.

The irony of that phrase might well have brought to his lips that melancholy smile of his. To be amused! To forget—that was another matter. By risking his life in some crack-brained scheme, which only his genius could make plausible, that was the only pleasure which the albino knew.

Tonight he was wilfully encountering a terrible danger because it gave him distraction; because it enabled him to forget for a little while that he was a monstrosity, as abnormal as a white crow or a five-legged sheep.

He strolled down the broad staircase to the expensive West End house which he was renting, knowing that his car with its Japanese chauffeur would be at the door. Monsieur Zenith expected perfect service, and he obtained it. Perfect loyalty was always accorded to him by his servants, and if Monsieur Zenith said: 'I am satisfied with you,' it was high praise. The man who heard the words was sufficiently repaid for any self-sacrifice which he might have devoted to the service of his master.

Zenith entered the car and gave an address.

'Tottenham Court Road—the Eclipse.'

He had adopted nothing in the way of disguise, despite the fact that every policeman in London had noted his description, and knew that he was wanted for more crimes than there was room upon a charge sheet to tabulate. It amused him to take the risk of passing through the streets with the light in the roof of his black Daimler shining down upon his extraordinary personality, making it easy for anybody to identify him at a single glance. He simply did not care.

Sooner or later someone, whether it might be a police constable on the beat or his arch enemy, Sexton Blake, the private detective of Baker Street, would succeed in arresting him and conducting him towards a police station. Then he would simply smoke one of the tiny opium cigarettes which he carried in a platinum case within his waistcoat pocket. Nobody smoked those cigarettes save himself, and one of them was marked by a crimson ring. That was death; and if all else failed and he saw that he was doomed to imprisonment, there was always that cigarette which he might smoke and thus obtain release. What did it matter? Only those who enjoy life fear death; and to Zenith life was a constant reminder of his abnormality.

At the Eclipse, in Tottenham Court Road, he got out and dismissed the car.

'I may walk back,' he said. 'I may come back in a taxi. I may not come back at all!'

He pushed his way into folding doors and descended a staircase. His entrance in the crowded room in the basement of the Eclipse public-house was the sign for a sudden silence. There were those there who knew him, and many who knew him not; but his appearance was sufficiently arresting to attract the attention of all.

He sat down and called for brandy. He had chosen the one empty table which the place contained, seating himself with his back to the wall, but otherwise taking no precaution to protect himself against the dangers which the place presented. There he was safe from police interference in the basement of the Eclipse. They did not care about police any more than he did.

If he was safe from police, however, he was safe from nothing else. The place was the rendezvous of a gang who hated him with a deadly hatred, and he had come down there for the express purpose of persuading that gang that they would do well to let him alone.

The proprietor brought him a single portion of brandy, and the albino waved it aside.

'That is no use to me. Bring me a bottle.'

The bottle was brought and he filled a tumbler to the brim. Brandy would have no more effect upon his physical and mental powers than would a glass of milk.

He drank deeply, looking around him. Then he lighted one of those opium-soaked cigarettes, and began to enjoy the situation. He was the only man in the whole place who wore evening clothes, the only one who had any pretensions to call himself a gentleman. His albinism and his bearing gave him a distinction which pleased his fancy for the theatrical.

A tremendous man with a debased face and a shock of coal-black hair came across and seated himself at Zenith's table.

The albino smiled. The thing, then, was beginning. Another joined the first—a thin man, short, stocky, quick in his movements. Then another—a yellow-haired Scandinavian.

Monsieur Zenith looked at them over the brim of his glass and smiled his glittering smile. He was their intended victim, and he knew it. He had been marked down for a bashing. If the intention of their hirers came to anything he would be found, an hour or so later, half-dead—lying in the gutter with concussion, a broken rib or so, and everything of value stripped from his person.

He knew this, and it gave him just that thrill which suffices to make life worth living. He continued to enjoy himself. At the same time, although he did not appear so, he was watchful. He knew exactly whence would come the signal to start the attack upon himself.

Two or three tables away from him there was a yellow man, not a Japanese this time, but a pure-blooded Chinese. His name was Ho Sen. Zenith knew him well; but the other did not suspect it. Zenith had chosen a chair from which he could watch Ho Sen, because he knew that the gang of toughs who were about to attack him were working under Ho Sen's direction and hire.

He drank his brandy and smoked. The others ordered drinks of different kinds and consumed them. The black-haired man was staring insolently at the albino, mistaking Monsieur Zenith's slender proportions for weakness. He was evidently saying to himself: 'Why do I want these other men, when all that I have to do is to smash up this albino fellow and leave him for dead? It's easy—it's a shame to take the money.'

After a while the game began to pall. Monsieur Zenith had finished one tumbler full of brandy, and filled another. Still the attack had not materialised.

He turned to the Chinaman, raising his hat, which he still wore, and smiling pleasantly.

'Why the delay, Ho Sen?'

Something like apprehension glittered in the Chinaman's eyes.

'Monsieur Zenith knows me?' he breathed.

Zenith smiled.

'Why, yes, Ho Sen. I have known you for a long time. You are in the opium racket. Making some money, I fancy; but, unfortunately for you, not intelligently. I am afraid that you will find Inspector Coutts knows about those barges upon the Lower Pool. The River Police have been talking to him.'

Ho Sen's face was bland, but his hands opened and closed nervously. He had not supposed that anybody on earth knew of his association with those barges in the Pool.

He said that he did not know what Monsieur Zenith was referring to, at which Zenith only smiled.

'I know other things,' he said, 'equally interesting. I know about the Box!'

To the Europeans around him his remark meant nothing, but to Ho Sen it seemed to mean a lot. The Chinaman blinked his eyes

301

and made nervous movements which were obvious to everybody.

He said:

'My friend knows a great deal.'

Zenith yawned.

'Much too much, shall we say, to live?'

Ho Sen half bowed.

'The river,' he said, 'comes to the sea.'

'And the fever of living to a sleep,' supplemented Zenith, thus completing the proverb from Confucius which the Chinaman had begun.

'It's a pity,' said the Oriental sententiously, 'that one who knows how to live should die!'

'It would be a pity,' corrected Zenith, 'if the one of whom you speak were to die. But what are dogs that they should pull the tiger down?'

The Chinaman turned away, and, with a sort of shame, gave a signal.

Zenith saw the signal and knew exactly what was coming. The black-haired man who sat opposite to the albino flashed a knife which he had been concealing in his sleeve. The small man brought out a length of lead piping from inside his vest. The Scandinavian swung a chair.

Zenith bent quickly, seized the legs of the small table and thrust it into their faces. Then he stepped backwards. His single pace brought him into the corner. He was holding the half-filled brandy bottle in his right hand.

The dark-haired man rushed, to be clubbed into insensibility by the bottle.

Zenith was not excited, not even breathing quickly. His expression was still bored. The perfection of his dress had not been affected by his rapid movements.

The other two, the small man and the Scandinavian, had been driven backwards by the weight of the table. The small man dropped to hands and knees and crawled forward, hoping to strike with his leaden cosh at Zenith's ankles. The Scandinavian was swinging the chair again.

Zenith kicked the crawling man in the face. He brushed the swinging chair aside, so that the Scandinavian blundered forward under the weight of his own effort.

The bottle arrived beside his ear; and this time it shattered, becoming a far more terrible weapon if Zenith had chosen to use it. He refrained from using it, not because he would have had any compunction about cutting the face of the Scandinavian to ribbons on the broken glass, but for the peculiar reason that if he did so his linen might have been stained by the blood of the other.

The little man had rolled over after receiving Zenith's kick; and now he staggered to his feet, blood coming from his split lips and lacerated gums where his teeth had been knocked out, his face white, and his expression foolish. He was able to stand, but quite unable to defend himself.

The albino dropped the bottle and whipped his lightning right to the point of the little man's jaw. Then he set the table back upon its feet and dropped back into his chair.

The inhabitants of that London speak-easy had drawn away from the struggle, anxious not to be involved, yet hoping and expecting that Zenith would get the worst of it. Now they cowered before his contemptuous smile.

He picked on the waiter who had attended him before, and crooked his finger in the man's direction.

'Bring me more brandy.'

The waiter said 'Yes, sir!' and disappeared to fulfil Zenith's order. The others remained standing at a respectful distance, but Zenith ignored their murmured remarks, whether of admiration or hatred, just as he ignored their stares of curiosity.

Next to Zenith himself, the least perturbed person in that place was Ho Sen, the Chinaman. He alone had remained at his table, giving the struggle only half his attention, although probably it meant more to him than to anybody else.

Zenith turned in his direction.

'Is this the best you can do, Ho Sen? I heard that you were out to bash me, and I came down here to give you a chance; but, upon my word, this is poor stuff.'

He waved his hand towards the three insensible men who lay upon the floor on the other side of his table.

'If you can't get better stuff than these thugs,' he continued, 'you had better get more of them. Possibly, however, you underrated my own abilities in looking after myself?'

Ho Sen responded to Zenith's wintry smile. There was a certain similarity between the two men. To each of them human life counted as nothing; and both were unemotional, cold as ice.

The Chinaman rose and bowed.

'Possibly,' he said, 'his excellency would honour me?'

He waved his hand towards the chair opposite to his own in an invitation that Zenith should take it. He gave the albino the title 'excellency' in imitation, perhaps, of the form used by Zenith's own Japanese servants. Whether the albino was in any way entitled to the rank implied by the term excellency it is impossible to say—he may have been. For in his time the albino, prince of crooks, had served and had the friendship of important people. In the lapel of his coat, just under the white camellia which he wore, was the ribbon of a foreign order. The insignia of another such distinction depended from his neck upon a ribbon, and was visible just beneath his white bow. Some said that he had royal blood in his veins, but it is doubtful whether anybody really knew anything. It is a matter about which Zenith himself would not have spoken.

He crossed the floor now, conscious of the honour which he was bestowing, and dropped into the chair opposite Ho Sen. He did it because he was in search of diversion; and because, in the circumstances Ho Sen was the most dangerous table companion that he could find.

The waiter transferred Zenith's bottle of brandy from one table to the other; and, with a curious gesture, Zenith filled Ho Sen's glass.

'I am afraid,' he said with his golden, effortless voice, 'that I cannot suggest a toast acceptable to both of us.'

'Why not, excellency?' returned the other. 'We are enemies, I grant. I admit that we cannot, with propriety, drink confusion to each other; but we have a common enemy—the one man whom we both fear. The only man in the world who is likely to frustrate our plans. I refer, of course, to the private detective, Sexton Blake, who lives in Baker Street.'

He raised his glass.

'I give you "Death to Sexton Blake." '

A strange expression had come into the face of the albino. He had half raised his tumbler, but now he put it back on the table.

'Some day,' he said, 'Mr Blake and myself will meet on equal terms for the last time. Which of us will survive I cannot say. But if it should be myself, I should take off my hat at the passing of an enemy whom I respect. I will not drink that toast with you, Ho Sen, because you are not a worthy adversary for Sexton Blake. You know that a gentleman does not lose honour by refusing to fight with *canaille*. Therefore the idea of a duel between Mr Blake and yourself is unthinkable. Mr Blake has done me the honour to cross swords with me, and I hope he will do so again. That is another matter. Frankly, if I saw the detective in danger of a knife in the back from such as you, I would step between him and it. We have a code, Ho Sen, which you would not understand.'

Ho Sen breathed a proverb about the equality of men who are soon to die. He had remained impervious to Zenith's criticism and contempt. That did not matter to him. He was a crook Chinese. He did not know the meaning of the word honour; and a sense of humour had been denied him.

'You came here, perhaps,' he went on, resuming their conversation as if Zenith had never snubbed him, 'in the hope of finding something out.'

Zenith's lips curled.

'No; only in the hope of amusing myself a little with your clumsy jackals. I did not succeed in amusing myself, even a little.'

'Perhaps,' said the other, 'I could take his excellency somewhere where there would be more—er—amusement?'

Zenith raised his glass.

'We will finish the brandy, then we will go.

'But I warn you,' he continued, 'that I am not sanguine that your efforts to entertain me will be a success, having been so often disappointed.'

They went out, side by side.

Ho Sen wore a neat lounge suit. On top of this he had an overcoat and a bowler hat. He carried gloves. Despite Zenith's rebuff when he had proposed to drink death to Sexton Blake, the yellow man talked in perfect English, and with a considerable knowledge of the world.

For some reason best known to himself, Monsieur Zenith was almost happy. The two men, so utterly different, and yet, in a subtle way, so much alike, walked into Tottenham Court Road and called a taxi.

Ho Sen gave the address to which he had invited Zenith, an

address in Soho. Ho Sen stopped the taxi fifty yards short of his destination, and walked the remainder of the distance.

Zenith smiled in comprehension. If the body of an albino were found tomorrow morning in a river, or upon a railway line, Ho Sen did not want a taxi-driver to give evidence that he had driven the albino in company with a Chinaman to such-and-such an address.

Ho Sen pushed open a plain door, sandwiched between two shops, and, with apologies for preceding Zenith, climbed a steep flight of stairs. The stairs were almost devoid of paint, and the treads covered by cheap oilcloth, worn threadbare about the middle. The landing was similarly unattractive.

Ho Sen opened another door upon the landing itself, crossed a kind of lobby, and emerged into a room of incredible luxury. It seemed impossible that so mean a staircase should give access to so luxurious a room. The floor, where it showed, was of teak. Objects of teak and sandalwood and bronze were everywhere. The walls were almost covered by tapestry, and the ceiling a tented expanse of highly coloured brocade.

The barbaric beauty of the large room was enhanced by shaded electric lights. Along the wall at intervals were suits of armour, some black and some of a copperish colour. In the middle of the magnificent carpet were heaps of cushions and dwarf tables, such as are used by Orientals for the purpose of taking a meal.

At the back of the room was a kind of dais surmounted by a brocaded canopy and containing a heavy chair made of blackwood and literally encrusted with jewels.

Ho Sen and Zenith were carrying their hats in their hands. Zenith looked around him with indifference. To him one room was very much like another, only parts of the prison which men call life.

'You will observe,' said Ho Sen, with a wave of the hand, 'that the door by which we have entered has disappeared. I assure you that you would have the greatest difficulty in discovering it again.'

Zenith hardly troubled to turn his head in that direction.

'Why trouble to find the door,' he said, 'when you are here to do it for me?'

'That is very true,' he said—'very true, excellency.'

A gong sounded from somewhere behind the dais.

Ho Sen said:

'Excellency will excuse?' And disappeared in that direction.

*   *   *

Monsieur Zenith crossed the floor so rapidly that he was almost treading upon the heels of Ho Sen; yet so silently that the China-man was unaware of it.

Ho Sen went out by a second door behind the dais. According to his calculations this second door should have clicked into place and become invisible just as the first had done; but the toe of a patent leather boot was thrust into the opening, and the door did not close.

The albino waited for perhaps twenty seconds, looking, not at the door, but at the room behind him. Then the lights went out, and a faint sizzling sound came to his ears.

The albino nodded, as if in confirmation of a suspicion, and thrust at the door.

It opened silently, and he passed through, again into darkness, allowing the door to close behind him, easing it back into position so that there was no tell-tale click of the lock mechanism to betray what he had done.

Ho Sen's ear had failed to detect the absence of that click when he had passed out. Nevertheless, the faint sound might have been heard by others; and Monsieur Zenith knew pretty well the danger of his situation.

If he could have been seen there in the darkness, immaculate in his evening clothes, his silk hat back on his head, his cloak over one arm, and his ebony cane in the hand of the other, it would have been observed that the expression of his face was almost happy. Danger gave him a thrill which he failed to obtain even from opium.

He raised the point of his walking-stick, and moved it slowly around himself.

It touched nothing.

His eyes were becoming accustomed by now to the darkness in the passage in which he was standing. He began to make out a heavily curtained window at one end of it.

For fear that he should be silhouetted against the window, he moved nearer to the wall and walked towards the darker end of the corridor.

A little way beyond the limits of the room which he had just left his elbow came in contact with a protuberance upon the wall against which he was moving, and, feeling around this protuberance with his fingers, he discovered it to be the moulded architrave of a small door.

He pushed gently upon the door where he imagined that it opened, and found that it moved silently inwards, revealing a rectangle of comparative brightness.

The albino passed in, taking such pains to move silently that each short stride took many seconds to accomplish.

He found himself in a square lobby, from which a step-ladder went upwards through curtains.

He allowed the door to move back into its place; then ascended the ladder.

Half-way up he was stopped by the curtains, and put his eye to the division between them. The thing which he saw caused him to draw a deep breath of astonishment.

The passage at the level of his eyes was a long, bare, box-like apartment. A red lamp filled it with weak light. Against the red lamp was visible the bulk of a man. The man's head was of elephantine proportions, and instead of a nose it was equipped with a slender trunk which seemed to be folded in at his breast like a proboscis.

He was handling a length of rubber hosepipe, coiling it up, compressing it into a space between his feet.

A pencil of red light from the chink in the curtains inscribed itself upon Zenith's white shirt-front and upon his white, sensitive face. A smile came to his lips as he recognised the smell of bitter almonds.

He understood.

So this was how it had been intended that he should die. This strange creature at whom he was looking was his intended executioner. That huge head which had amazed him was only a gas-mask. The object which the man was packing away was a kind of hose which he had been thrusting through some aperture into the room of the dais. He wore the gas-mask to prevent his becoming asphyxiated by the poisonous liquid which he had been projecting into the air around where he assumed Zenith to be.

Presently the man picked up some heavy apparatus from the

floor and moved towards the curtain.

Zenith stepped back quietly to the foot of the staircase and moved sideways, waiting.

The man came downwards, grunting at the weight of the box which he was carrying.

Zenith flung back the folds of his cloak for freedom; then raised his stick. He lunged in the fashion of a swordsman. The ferrule of his stick struck the other in the pit of the stomach.

Zenith caught the heavy box adroitly as it fell from the stricken man's nerveless fingers. The man had vocalised a groan as the breath was driven out of his body. Save for that, he made no sound.

He lurched forward, and Zenith lowered the box in time to straighten and drive his right fist at the point of the falling man's chin. The blow connected through the material of the mask, and the weight of the man's body, which had already descended upon Zenith's shoulders, became limp and dead.

Zenith lowered the man, carefully stripped off the gas-mask, and hit again in cold blood, driving the other still further into insensibility by a half-arm jab at the point of the jaw.

His attacker was, of course, a Chinese—he had expected that—a big fellow, the weight of whose frame was accentuated by a tendency to fatness. The man was breathing so heavily that the albino feared lest those long, painful gasps should give the alarm.

He lifted the heavy man with an astonishing absence of effort, and carried him up the stairs; then he returned for his overcoat and for the vaporising apparatus in its brass-bound box. These, also, he carried up to the platform.

He had only just reached there when the light went out. What did this mean? Had he accidentally touched a switch which extinguished it? He thought not.

Did it mean that somebody outside had guessed what had happened there, and had put out the light as a preliminary to attack? Again he thought not.

The light came on again, but this time from three equi-distant narrow apertures just below the level of his eyes.

He bent down and looked through one of these apertures, understanding at once what had happened.

The light in the room with the dais, and the red lamp in the raised corridor outside it, were controlled by the same switch, and that switch had been used now. When one set of lights were on the other light was off, and the other way about.

Zenith realised at once that this would be a necessary precaution, considering that the purpose of the passage was to give observation of the room.

It would not do for the red light to shine inwards to the room when the room was dark. When the room was lighted the passage, also, would be lighted indirectly by means of those wall holes, and the red lamp would then no longer be necessary.

He saw a man in a gas-mask come into the room below. The man looked about him, stood still for a moment or so, as if in doubt, then threw back tapestry-covered panels, which revealed a window.

He opened the window widely, exposing brickwork beyond; then depressed a switch which started powerful electric fans.

The room was being cleared of the vaporised prussic acid which had been injected into it.

The man's pause of doubt had been caused by his surprise at finding the room empty. He had expected to discover the resplendent figure of the albino spreadeagled in death upon the floor. He had found merely an empty room.

Presently he would return to Ho Sen, and perhaps others, with the information that Zenith had escaped. There would be a search. Sooner or later they would come to that raised platform where he waited.

Zenith smiled again.

Here were the gas-mask and the vaporising apparatus. He had only to assume the gas-mask and get the apparatus to work to form around himself an impenetrable zone of poisonous gas; but this did not promise to get him anywhere. Instead, he went with silent quickness back to the door at the foot of the stairs. He opened it for half an inch, stood watching, listening, trying to work out in advance exactly what was going to happen.

There was a light now in the corridor outside. He heard a door open, and guessed that it was the door of the room with the dais. It would be the man in the gas-mask coming out.

He closed his own door for a couple of seconds until footsteps had gone past it; then opened the door again and stepped out.

Within a few yards of him was the receding figure of the man whom he had already seen.

Zenith walked after him.

The heavy carpet obliterated all sound. The man in the gas-mask was totally unaware that Monsieur Zenith, whom he had expected to find dead, was following him to the sanctum of his master.

The man whom Zenith was following continued along the corridor, which was now lighted, and revealed as being thickly carpeted and panelled in hardwood; then turned into another passage at right angles thereto.

Zenith was following him at a distance of only a few feet; but the albino moved as silently as a shadow, and the other had no suspicion of his presence.

The second passage was a short one and terminated in heavy folding doors. Against these closed doors the Chinaman hesitated; then stripped his gas-mask from his head and rapped upon the panels.

Perhaps he was bidden to enter, or perhaps he took permission for granted. Anyhow, he went in with Zenith immediately behind him.

The room beyond was less luxurious than the room of the dais; but still decorated and furnished in Chinese fashion, its only furniture being a central group of chairs and cushions assembled under a heavy lantern. The doors, like the other doors in that place which Zenith had so far encountered, closed of themselves with a gentle click on ingenious and well-oiled springs.

The man in front of Zenith had still failed to observe the albino's presence. He made an obeisance and spoke a sentence in the Chinese language.

Zenith watched him, smiling. He had stepped sideways, so that every inch of him, from his patent shoes to the silk hat which he wore upon his head, was revealed to the astonished group gathered under the lantern.

Firstly there was a mandarin—a fat man, wearing the purple, and having his fingernails sheathed in the ancient fashion. This man was standing with his hands folded upon his breast.

Behind his shoulder stood Ho Sen, with his bowler hat in his hand; and, close to Ho Sen a pallid and pot-bellied man of middle age, dressed in soiled morning clothes. He was hatless and coatless. He had the air of being an adviser; and, from his appearance, one might have assumed that his advice would not be disinterested. He had bloodshot, rheumy eyes, and lank, dark hair brushed over his brow in a vain attempt to disguise his baldness.

Those were the three who mattered.

In addition, there were two Chinamen of the servant class who stood behind the mandarin in the position of a bodyguard.

All of them stared at Zenith as if he were a ghost.

The mandarin was the first to regain his self-possession. He bowed slightly and murmured that the unexpected visitor is the most welcome—a compliment which Zenith did not take seriously. Nevertheless, he returned the bow and responded to the other's salutation, which had been spoken in English.

'I am disappointed,' he said, 'because the thrill which I was promised has not materialised.'

Ho Sen spoke rapidly in Chinese, and the mandarin bowed again towards Zenith.

'There has been a clumsiness,' he admitted.

Zenith waved his hand in grandiloquent fashion.

'Your apology is accepted; you did your best.'

'Perhaps, my son,' said the mandarin, 'it would be well for us to speak together?'

Zenith looked at Ho Sen.

'Possibly you will present me?'

Ho Sen stepped forward.

'Permit,' he said, bowing deeply, 'that I present his excellency, Monsieur Zenith.'

He turned and bowed again.

'His Serenity, Wa Ho, Mandarin of the Imperial Purple, Brother of the Dragon, and Companion of the Yellow Snake.'

The pallid man in morning clothes, who had stood beside Ho Sen, listened to these flowery formalities with a smirk.

'This man is dangerous,' he said, indicating Zenith.

The mandarin smiled and murmured further proverbs. The gist of them was that conversation is of mutual advantage. He waved Monsieur Zenith to one of the teakwood chairs under the lantern; and the albino accepted the chair without hesitation. He sensed that while in that room he would not be molested. Such an act would be regarded as a violation of hospitality. The fact that he had been presented to Wa Ho meant that he was accepted, for the time being, as a guest, and that for the moment he would be treated on that basis.

The mandarin lowered himself into a second chair. And bowls of China tea, without either milk or sugar, were brought in by one of his retainers.

Zenith raised a cup to his lips out of politeness; then waited for what Wa Ho had to say.

'You have acquired knowledge, my son, and of a kind which is dangerous.'

'Knowledge, you mean, relating to a certain box?'

'It is so.'

'You are afraid that I should make use of that knowledge?'

The mandarin bowed.

'Your knowledge,' he said, 'is power—power such as never was in the world before; but it is also danger. Between those of noble birth a word is a bond. Suppose that there should be the matter of a gift? Much money? Might it then be forgotten, this matter of the box?'

Wa Ho spoke in perfect English. His nationality was betrayed only by an upward inflection at the end of his sentences. What it amounted to was, that he was offering Zenith a bribe to keep out of things. This was tactless. He had taken the wrong line. His mention of danger had given Zenith an incentive to keep on. His reference to world power, although Zenith knew of it already, was another incentive. The money mattered nothing. Zenith would rather have fought for five shillings than have been donated five thousand pounds.

Wa Ho did not appreciate this; but Zenith returned Wa Ho's frankness without hesitation.

'The gift of which you speak,' he said, 'is nothing to me. The power of which you speak is a great deal. As for the danger, that, if anything, attracts me.'

The mandarin's face expressed no emotion.

'You are a strange man, my son.'

All this had been heard by the pot-bellied man with bewilderment. This disinterested frankness was a thing which he simply did not understand. It must have appeared to him that something extremely subtle was going forward; but, for once, he was wrong.

Monsieur Zenith and his Serenity, Wa Ho, were alike great enough to be honest one with the other.

'It is a pity,' said Wa Ho, 'because there might have been a matter of friendship.'

He arose, bowing, to show that the audience was finished.

Ho Sen said something in Chinese, and one of the guards went out of the room.

Zenith, whose politeness was never at fault, had risen at the same moment as Wa Ho, and had returned the obeisance with which Wa Ho had favoured him.

'It means,' he said, 'that we are beginning exactly where we left off.

'We will now take leave of you,' he added.

'We!' It was Ho Sen who echoed the word.

'Yes'—Zenith pointed towards the other European in the room—'this gentlemen will accompany me.'

The other now spoke to Zenith for the first time.

'You're making a mistake,' he said. 'I am staying here. I have got business to do.'

Zenith smiled his glittering smile.

'On the contrary,' he said, 'you are coming with me.'

Then, when the other man did not move, he crossed the distance between them with extraordinary speed. He stared into the face of the other man.

'It would be better if you did as I suggest.'

'I prefer not.'

Zenith was still smiling.

'Possibly,' he said—'possibly, Mr Simpson Stead, you would prefer that I should continue my conversation with his Serenity, Wa Ho, telling him of a certain Indian prince to whom you gave advice. And how much money it cost that individual to get free of you; and of the treachery.'

The other held up a hand.

'I spoke hastily,' he declared. 'There's no need for us to quarrel, Monsieur Zenith. I suppose we can be friends?'

Zenith's eyes flashed. He seemed to increase in height. The expression in his face was so terrible that the other recoiled as if he had received a blow.

'Did you say friends?' hissed the albino, with deadly deliberation. 'Did you say *friends*?'

'A figure of speech,' faltered the other. 'Just a figure of speech, my dear sir.'

Zenith did not relax. He still appeared tensed for a blow as rapid and almost as deadly as that of a striking rattlesnake.

'You will not address me as "My dear sir". You will apologise.'

The other apologised hastily.

'And now,' continued the albino, 'we will go out together.'

Wa Ho had been listening to every word of this conversation. Probably he approved of Zenith's attitude; it was one which he understood. To a Chinaman caste has an importance which Europeans often fail to appreciate. It was to Wa Ho as if one of his own coolies had seated himself in the presence of the mandarin.

Wa Ho made a sign, and one of his servants brought hat and coat to the man whose company Zenith had decided upon.

Zenith moved towards the door by which he had come in.

'We will go out this way,' he said; 'and directly we are outside the door we will change hats. I want to see what is going to happen to a man in a silk hat.'

He bowed ceremoniously to the mandarin.

Wa Ho said that parting was as a little death.

Zenith said nothing.

The servant, who had preceded them, threw the teak doors wide open. The passage outside appeared to be empty. Immediately inside the doorway was an electric light switch.

Zenith pushed it up, and the huge lantern went out.

In front of Zenith was the one lamp which lighted the corridor.

The albino shook his sleeve, and a tiny plated revolver, which had been accommodated in a wrist holster, came down into his hand.

He fired without taking aim; and the one lamp in the corridor expired also, leaving black darkness both inside and outside Wa Ho's room.

With an unerring instinct for direction, the albino recrossed the floor in the darkness, went past where Wa Ho was still standing, and succeeded in opening the rear door which had been used by the servants.

Outside was a rectangular lobby. He crossed this, opened

another door at random, and found himself again on an ordinary staircase. He went upwards.

On the landing above was a window opening on to a flat roof.

Zenith raised the sash, stepped through; went along the roof until he came to a dividing wall; vaulted this, and gained another roof on a slightly lower level.

Here there were two windows, one brightly lighted, and the other in darkness. He crashed his elbow through the glass of the darkened window, undid the fastening, and stepped through into the room beyond.

The electrics snapped up, and he found himself looking at a frightened but angry man.

'What's this, eh?' said the man. 'What's this?'

Zenith removed his hat.

'Pardon this interruption, sir, but I have—er—fallen among thieves, and this seemed to be my best means of escape.'

'What do you mean?' gasped the man. 'Where do you come from?'

Zenith pointed vaguely in the direction of Wa Ho's premises.

'I come from over there,' he said.

He opened a notecase and brought out a banknote, which rustled agreeably.

'If,' he said, 'a matter of ten pounds—'

The man held out his hand. He was one of those to whom money spoke louder than words.'

'Well,' he said, 'if that's how you put it.'

He held the banknote up to the light.

'It's a perfectly good one,' Zenith said, with a smile.

The other man grinned, opened his door.

'Well,' he said, 'you gents will have your little game. This way, sir, if you don't mind.'

* * *

'Simpson Stead is murdered!'

Inspector Coutts of the CID exploded these words at Sexton Blake, the celebrated private detective of Baker Street, at the moment when he entered Blake's consulting-room. It was ten o'clock at night; but Inspector Coutts cared nothing for hours when he was working on a case, and he knew that in this respect Sexton Blake resembled himself.

Both Blake and Tinker, the detective's assistant, showed interest at the police officer's statement. They both knew Simpson Stead by sight. Indeed, there were not many people interested in criminology who did not know the face of that unmitigated rascal.

Simpson Stead had been a crook lawyer, who specialised in international affairs. It must be said in Stead's defence that he never pretended to be anything but what he was—a man who could be hired to take up any point of view, and who knew no scruples in defending it. The fact which Simpson Stead tried studiously to conceal—that he could also be bought over to double-cross a client; and, indeed, frequently was so bought over—was also known to the detectives. They heard of his murder without either sorrow or surprise.

'He had that coming to him,' said Sexton Blake; and then a question: 'Who did it?'

The fat, red face of Inspector Coutts expressed perplexity. He gesticulated.

'If I knew that, I shouldn't be here.'

Sexton Blake smiled.

'Quite so, my dear Coutts.'

He took his briar pipe from the pipe-rack and began to fill it.

'What are the circumstances?'

Inspector Coutts took off his bowler hat and put it on again. There was a legend that he slept in his bowler hat but this was not generally believed. It was however, unquestionable that he was seldom seen without it. It might have been expected that, on entering Blake's consulting-room, he would have removed his bowler as a token of respect; but after pointed hints to this end, which the inspector had never appeared to understand, Blake had accepted this eccentricity as part of the man's character.

Inspector Coutts said:

'There aren't any circumstances.

'Someone,' he went on—'someone stuck a knife in Stead's back. Neighbourhood of Greek Street, Soho. Man was found running down the street. How he lived with the wound which he received is a miracle. He died in the gutter. One of our men, who got there before he passed out, has noted that he said "Wa Ho" several times, whatever that may mean; and, in addition, another word, undoubtedly a name, which will interest you considerably—the word "Zenith". I've got a theory about this, Blake.'

Sexton Blake was puffing away at his briar, while he scribbled aimlessly upon his blotting-pad. He did not appear to be very interested in the inspector's remarks; but Coutts and Tinker knew him well enough to understand that, if necessary, he would be able to repeat the whole of the inspector's communication word for word days, or even weeks, afterwards.

'What's the theory?' he murmured.

Inspector Coutts always had a theory of some sort. Nine times out of ten it was wrong. Sometimes it was even childish; but the tenth time the burly inspector would hit the nail on the head. The other nine times Blake would come to his assistance; and Inspector Coutts always found it convenient to forget that it was Blake who put him upon the right track when, but for the famous private detective, he would have gone from blunder to blunder.

'Well,' said the inspector, trying to look intelligent, 'you know what I am, Blake—hard-headed and matter-of-fact. As a rule I don't go in for scientific deductions and reasoning, and all that kind of hookum; but this time I've got a hunch. I don't mind admitting that it isn't backed by evidence, not at present; but I've got a kind of what's-its-name intuition that the Chinks are involved.'

Blake jerked up his head and looked at his official friend with almost startled interest.

'That's a queer idea, Coutts.'

The inspector looked almost uncomfortable.

'Yes, I know it is; but the fact is, Blake, there is something queer going on among the Chinks everywhere. We've had trouble in Newcastle and Cardiff. There's been a spot of bother Limehouse way. Of course, the reason doesn't come out. You can't make 'em talk; and I dare say there's a killing occasionally that we don't get to know about; then, as you know, Simpson Stead had already specialised in the foreign element. I agree that he might just as well have been running with Frenchmen or Italians as with the Chinks. Frenchmen use the knife, so do Italians. But, there you are—I've got this idea in my mind, and I can't shake it. I should like to know what you think. If you tell me I'm wrong, I'll believe you.'

Sexton Blake shook his head very slowly.

'I don't think that you are wrong. There has been trouble between the Chinese—always is, of course—but lately it has been accentuated. I've known about it. Tried to get to the bottom of the thing, but failed. It might be a tong war; but somehow I don't think it is. If Simpson Stead got himself involved in whatever is happening, that might easily account for his murder.'

Blake got up and walked about the room.

'I'm glad you brought this to me, Coutts, especially since Zenith has been mentioned. It didn't occur to you, by the way, to suspect that Zenith was Simpson Stead's murderer?'

Coutts rubbed his chin.

'No, it didn't, Blake. I could easily imagine that Zenith had murdered Simpson Stead; but not that he had used a knife. A knife isn't quite the weapon which Zenith would use, if you know what I mean.'

'I entirely agree with you,' said the detective.

He jerked out questions.

'What have you done about it? How does the thing stand now?'

'We have taken Stead's body to a mortuary,' said Coutts. 'Thought you might like to have a look at him. He's not pretty, Blake. You know what Simpson Stead was like when he was alive. He's even less pleasant now that he's dead; but that won't affect you one way or the other.'

'Anything in his pockets, Coutts?'

'Letters, papers, keys, cash—all the usual stuff.'

'Discover anything from the papers?'

'Nothing much. Most of them bills. A note or two from business connections. Not interesting. Got his address, if that's any use to you.'

Blake nodded in satisfaction.

'Ha! Somewhere in Bloomsbury, wasn't it?'

'Yes, Goldwyn Square. Behind the British Museum. Bachelor establishment, I should imagine. Sort of office and residence rolled into one.'

Blake reached for his hat and overcoat.

'We will go there,' he said.

Tinker look at his guv'nor expectantly.

'Am I in this?'

Blake said:

'If you like.' And then: 'Get us a taxi.'

Within ten minutes their cab had pulled up outside an old-fashioned house with a stone front and steps up to the door.

Inspector Coutts rang the bell, and his summons was answered almost immediately by an anaemic-looking youth, who opened his mouth widely in astonishment when he realised the identity of the callers.

'Nothing wrong, I hope?' he quavered.

Inspector Coutts asked the youth who he was.

'Me? I'm only Mr Stead's clerk, gentlemen.'

'We want to come in,' said the inspector. 'We want to have a look at your master's rooms.'

The young man appeared about to close the door.

'I couldn't permit that, gentlemen; I couldn't, really. I have very strict instructions.'

'The circumstances are unusual,' Inspector Coutts told him. 'Mr Stead has been murdered, and we want to look for a clue to his murderers.'

The young man looked as though he would faint away.

'I don't think that I quite caught what you said, sir. Mr Stead murdered?'

'Yes; he was killed in Soho earlier this evening.'

'Dear me, that's dreadful! Very disturbing, indeed! Who killed him, if I may ask?'

'If we knew that,' returned Inspector Coutts heavily, 'we shouldn't be here at the present moment.'

'Ah, no, of course not! And you want to come in—to search the place, I think you said.'

'That's what we want.'

'Well, in the circumstances, really I don't see—'

Inspector Coutts pushed his way in.

'That's all right, my lad; we're police. You give us all the help in your power. That's the best thing that you can do.'

Blake and Tinker followed Inspector Coutts into the narrow hall, and Stead's clerk closed the door behind them.

'To start with,' said the inspector, 'do you know anybody who might have desired your employer's death?'

He did not get a straight answer to this.

'Well, sir, you see, my master's business was very funny. He dealt with all kinds of people, if you understand me. Some of them were rather—well—'

Inspector Coutts bit off a laugh.

'Say that he had business with crooks, and that he double-crossed some of them.'

The youth tittered.

'Well, you know, that's rather unkind, isn't it?'

Inspector Coutts went on with his questioning.

'Did he have any business with foreigners that you know of?'

'Mr Stead's business was all with foreigners.'

'What kind of foreigners? Did he have any business, for instance, with Chinese?'

'Yes, he did, sir. He certainly did. There was one called here only yesterday.'

'What about?'

'I don't know, sir. I know very little about my master's business. I am really only here to take messages, answer the telephone, and that sort of thing while he is away from home. Was, I should say.'

Inspector Coutts was going on to ask another question, when there came a loud bang with a crash of broken glass from somewhere in the rear of the premises.

Simpson Stead's clerk jumped.

'Goodness me! What was that?'

'Are you alone in this house?' snapped Sexton Blake.

'Yes, sir, I—'

Blake pushed past him and dashed along in the direction from which the sound had seemed to come.

When Inspector Coutts and Tinker had followed him more slowly they found a large room with a shattered window. The window was up, and the room was empty.

Empty as the room was, it provided considerable interest, for it had been completely wrecked by someone who had been searching for something. Drawers with deed-boxes had been emptied upon the floor, and left lying there. Their contents had been spread over almost every inch of the threadbare carpet. The lock of a press had been forced, and the coats and hats from a wardrobe cupboard had been dumped in an untidy heap just beyond it.

While the detectives were still looking in astonished silence at this spectacle, the window clattered down again, and more glass crashed down into the area beyond.

The youth, who was with them, turned with a sickly smile.

'That window never would keep up. I think that the sashcord is broken.'

Inspector Coutts turned to Tinker.

'You can see what's happened, my lad. Someone has been in this room. When he closed the window on going out it came down quicker than he had bargained for, and the glass shattered. That's the noise which we heard. Blake must have opened the window again and followed him.'

Tinker narrowly inspected the window-sill.

'That's quite right,' he agreed. 'There are footmarks on this sill. The man who got out of the window must have stepped from the sill to the top of the area railings, and then jumped down to the surface of the yard. No doubt my guv'nor followed in the same way.'

Inspector Coutts was starting to make some remark when, from the alley which passed across the rear of Simpson Stead's house, there came the repeated explosion of a pistol.

Bang, bang! Two shots very close together.

Tinker raised the window again, and climbed out on to the sill.

'The guv'nor may want help,' he explained; then stepped out on to the top of the area railing and jumped.

Inspector Coutts followed more sedately by means of the back entrance. He came out into the alley which ran along the back of the house, to meet Sexton Blake and Tinker returning, and, with them, a smallish man, whom Sexton Blake was holding by the coat-collar.

The small man was expostulating that Blake had no right to treat him so roughly.

Inspector Coutts said: 'Hallo, what's this?' in his best official manner; and Blake replied that he was bringing along a man who might probably be made to answer a few questions.

They went back into the house of Simpson Stead, and into the room which had been ransacked before they came to it.

Blake's prisoner went on complaining about his treatment. Blake asked him if he imagined he could fire revolvers at people in this country without getting into trouble.

Blake's prisoner was a Chinaman. He was dressed in European clothes, and his English was perfectly good. He instantly replied that he had not fired a revolver at anybody.

Inspector Coutts ran his hands expertly over the man's clothes.

'Hasn't got a gun here, Blake,' he said.

Sexton Blake laughed shortly.

'No; he probably chucked it over a fence when he saw that I had him. We could find it, if we wanted to.'

The inspector turned on Blake's prisoner with the deliberate intention of intimidating the man.

'This is a serious matter,' he said. 'Shooting with intent will get you five years.'

He turned to Sexton Blake.

'Do you wish to charge this man?'

'That depends,' returned the detective, 'on his willingness to talk.'

He began to question the Chinaman on his own account.

'Did you find what you wanted?' he asked, indicating the disorder of the room.

'I don't know what you mean,' was the reply.

'I mean that you searched this room. You came here for the purpose of searching this room.'

The face of the yellow man betrayed nothing.

'I haven't been here before,' he said. 'I come here to see a friend of mine.'

'What friend?'

It was Inspector Coutts who snapped in with this question.

'I do not think I can be made to answer.'

'Oh, yes, you can! Mr Blake will charge you with the shooting; then you will be searched and asked to account for your movements. We shall find your pistol with your fingerprints on it, and you will go to prison.'

'I did not shoot. I hear a pistol fired; but I know nothing about it. I come here to see my friend. You mistake me for someone else.'

Inspector Coutts drew Sexton Blake aside.

'I think we shall have to charge him,' he muttered.

Blake shook his head.

'Not sure that we can, Coutts. I am not prepared to say that he fired the shots. He may be innocent. I admit that he doesn't look like it; but we don't want to put ourselves in the wrong.'

The yellow man was smiling when they turned. Possibly he had detected the purport of Blake's remarks.

'Is it permitted that I go?' he asked in his stilted fashion.

The inspector looked at Blake, and the private detective nodded almost imperceptibly.

The pallid youth, who had described himself as Simpson Stead's secretary, was hovering in the doorway, intensely interested, but too much in awe of the detectives to take part in the proceedings.

Blake turned to him with a question.

'Have you ever seen this gentleman before?'

The youth hesitated, and then shook his head, 'No.'

'Think again,' urged Blake. 'You have said that your master had Chinese visitors. What about this one?'

'No,' said the youth again, 'not this one. Never this one.'

He was so anxious to assert that he had never seen their prisoner before that the detectives came to the conclusion that he was lying. Nevertheless, they had to let their prisoner go.

'In that case,' said Blake, 'you had better show this gentleman out.'

*   *   *

The moment that the Chinaman had gone out through the door, Blake snapped his fingers to attract Tinker's attention, and pointed at the Chinaman's back.

Tinker knew exactly what he was intended to do; and, as the Chinaman left the front door, he himself emerged from the rear.

Blake and Coutts went on to discuss the events at the house in which they were.

'Rather a coincidence,' said Blake, 'that you should suspect Chinamen, and that we should find one in the neighbourhood of this place who cannot, or will not, account for his movements.'

'It's more than a coincidence,' said Coutts. 'There's no question, Blake, that that Chink was the man who broke into this room and did all the damage. Simpson Stead was killed because he had something which the Chinks wanted. It may be still here, or we may have lost it by letting that man go.'

'I have an impression,' said Sexton Blake, 'that the thing, whatever it is, is still here; or, at any rate, that it was not found by that man. If his search had been incomplete in any respect I might imagine that it had been succesful; but, as you see, he has turned the room upside-down. We have reason, moreover, to suppose that the object which he sought was not one which could conveniently be carried in his pockets.'

Inspector Coutts did not quite follow this. He said as much.

'Don't quite get you there, Blake. How on earth can you know anything about what the fellow was looking for?'

Blake pointed to one or two smaller drawers in a bureau which stood against the wall on one side.

He stepped across and attempted to pull the drawers out. They were fastened. Of the pedestal writing-desk, which stood in the centre of the room, all the deeper drawers had been wrenched open. The more shallow ones had been untouched.

'See what I mean, Coutts? Our man didn't examine those drawers. The reason must have been that he knew they were incapable of containing the thing which he was after. The fact gives us a very fair indication as to the size of the thing. We can say, for instance, that it is approximately four inches high or thick. Here are drawers three inches deep, which the searcher didn't consider it necessary to investigate. Here are other drawers five inches deep, which he has burst open.'

By this time Simpson Stead's secretary had returned. He may have noted Tinker's absence, but he made no comment thereon.

Blake asked further questions of him.

'How long were you in this place before we arrived?'

The youth looked astonished.

'I've been here all day,' he said.

'Do you sleep here?'

'No; I generally get here about nine in the morning, and stay till six, or thereabouts.'

'It's a long time after six now.'

'Yes; but Mr Simpson Stead used to like me to remain until he came in.'

'What about lunch?'

'I had lunch on the premises. We never knew when a call might come through which needed attention. Mr Stead liked me to be here.'

'So that you have been in this place all day long until the present moment?'

'Yes, sir.'

'Where were you?'

'Most of the time I was in the front room. This is only a kind of filing-room. The front room is Mr Simpson Stead's private office, where I work.'

'So you have been all day long in a room adjoining this one. You say that you didn't hear these drawers being forced open, and the rest of it? The man who wrecked this room must have made a lot of noise. Can you explain how you failed to hear him?'

The youth said that he could not explain it at all.

Blake stared at him in doubt for a long moment.

'I can explain it. You had been informed that Mr Simpson Stead was dead; and you had been offered fresh employment.'

The youth held up his hands in apparent horror.

'Oh, no, sir! Certainly not, sir!'

'I don't see why not,' persisted Blake. 'The man who searched this room hadn't been in it for more than half an hour. He came in from the street—by the front door, I mean.'

'Oh, no, sir! Excuse me, but you're wrong there.'

'How many visitors have you had today?'

'None whatever. You were the first visitors we had.'

Blake laughed.

'Look at this, Coutts.'

He raised the window belonging to the room. It crashed back almost immediately into place.

'Do you see that?' he said. 'I did my best to get that window to remain in position, but it wouldn't do so. If I had forced my way into this room by means of the rear window, do you think that I should be unaware of the fact that it wouldn't remain open? Yet the man who searched this room was unaware of the fact. That's why he let it crash. The obvious deduction is that he had never raised the window before; that, in other words, he came in by the door in the usual way.

'I'll tell you what happened,' Blake said, again addressing the youth. 'About half an hour before we arrived, that Chinaman, whom we have just seen, came to the front door and talked to you. You may have known him; or you may not. I am not sure about that. I am sure, however, that he told you of Simpson Stead's death, and asked you if you would be looking out for fresh employment. He promised you a more remunerative position. Either you know his address, or he gave you an address to apply to.'

Unexpectedly, the youth broke down and began to snivel.

'He didn't!' he exclaimed. 'I've never seen him before!'

Blake smiled.

'Oh, yes, he did!'

He held out his hand.

'I'll trouble you for that man's address.'

The youth repeated his previous story. He had never seen the man before, knew nothing about him, and had been completely unaware of his presence upon the premises.

Inspector Coutts stepped forward, and fixed the young man with a fierce stare.

'Listen,' he said. 'If you persist in your refusal to give evidence, you will be taken to the police station and searched. If we don't find an address among your belongings, we shall have a look at your private papers. If we don't find it there, we shall check up on Simpson Stead's address book.

'Let me tell you,' he added, in a terrible voice, 'you are making yourself an accessory after the fact. Don't forget, my boy, that this is a matter of murder.'

The youth had been better able to stand Sexton Blake's plain speaking than Inspector Coutts' bullying. His resistance crumpled up.

'I didn't mean any harm,' he said. 'I'll tell you the truth, gentlemen. Indeed, I will.'

He pointed at Sexton Blake.

'It's quite right what he said. The gentleman offered me a position. I didn't know that there was anything wrong in that. Mr Simpson Stead's business was rather—er—peculiar, and I didn't know where I should get another job. So, of course, I was very pleased. He asked me, the Chinese gentleman did, whether he might have a look at Mr Simpson Stead's papers, and I let him go into the back room. That's the truth, gentlemen. Every word of it is true. I didn't mean to tell you lies; but, naturally, I didn't want to lose my new job.'

Inspector Coutts held out his hand.

327

'What's the address?'

'I haven't got it, not in writing. I—er—know him.'

'I see. He was one of Simpson Stead's clients.'

'Yes, sir.'

'One of the Chinamen who called upon Simpson Stead.'

'Yes, sir. He was. His name is Ho Sen.'

'Where does he live?'

'At No 179b, Greek Street.'

'Greek Street!' Inspector Coutts turned and looked at Sexton Blake.'

'This thing is becoming a little easier to understand,' he said. 'I was right, Blake. My deductions are justified. I'll stake my seniority that Ho Sen is the murderer of Simpson Stead.

'And,' he added despondently, 'I have let the fellow go!'

'Why worry?' asked Blake. 'You have got his name and address.'

'He won't go there. I know what these Chinks are. He'll disappear.'

'He won't!' chuckled Blake. 'Not with Tinker tailing him!'

* * *

But here the detective was wrong. Tinker's attempt to trail Ho Sen had been defeated by the fact that the rear passage which he entered had no direct communication with the street in front. As Blake and Coutts left the house, Tinker rejoined them.

'Sorry, guv'nor,' he said. 'Couldn't make it!'

The lad was breathing heavily. He had twice run the full length of the rear passage before admitting to himself that he had failed to carry out Blake's instructions.

Blake patted the lad on the shoulder.

'Never mind, Tinker. You did your best. I'm sure of it.'

The building which had been used both as a residence and office by the late Simpson Stead, was situated in a quiet square, with a railed-off space containing shrubs and a grass-plot in the middle of it.

When the detectives descended the lawyer's steps, they were naturally talking about his tragic fate.

'I've put the fear of Heaven into that chap,' said Inspector Coutts, jerking his thumb over his shoulder to indicate the lad whom they had just left behind them.

The inspector's remark was justified.

Before leaving the youth who had been Simpson Stead's secretary, Inspector Coutts had continued to use the bullying tone which he had learned when a policeman on the beat, and had squeezed the youth dry of a lot of information. Some of that information was very interesting to Inspector Coutts as a police officer, but, unfortunately for the detective's investigations, very little of it bore upon the killing of Simpson Stead, or his association with Chinamen.

The detectives had travelled thither in a taxi-cab, and had instructed the driver to wait. To their surprise, he had disappeared.

As they stood looking about for him, the vehicle suddenly appeared a hundred yards along the road. It was coming towards them.

'Sorry, gents,' said the taxi-driver. 'Bloke wanted me to run him along the road, and as you was a long time—'

Blake chuckled.

'As we were a long time, you thought you would pick up a fare between whiles. That's the coolest piece of impudence that I've run against for a long time.'

The taxi-driver muttered again that he was sorry, and the detectives climbed into the cab.

Tinker, who had been the last to think about entering the vehicle, stood staring towards the railings on the other side of the road.

'Just a minute, guv'nor,' he said in a singular tone; then crossed to a spot beneath the shadow of overhanging trees.

Blake half opened the door of the cab on the offside.

'Looks to me, Coutts, as if Tinker has spotted someone lying on the pavement.'

He got out and followed his assistant.

Coutts himself descended from the cab and stood looking after them. The taxi-driver took no interest in the proceedings.

Blake found Tinker bending over the body of a man.

The lad switched on a flashlamp.

The man was Ho Sen. He appeared to be insensible. The bright light of the torch shining into his eyes seemed, however, to recall him to consciousness. His eyelids flickered, and he sat up, rubbing his jaw.

Blake seized him by the collar and lifted him on to his feet.

'Glad to see you again,' he said. 'We have just been coming to the conclusion that we let you go before we had quite done with you. Someone else appears to have done us the service of seeing that you didn't get clear away.'

Ho Sen blinked, and turned his head aside. The torch, shining into his face, revealed such expression as his countenance was capable of betraying.

'You can't arrest me,' he said definitely, 'just because I happen to have fallen down in the street.'

Blake spoke to Ho Sen sternly.

'You've got a bruise, Ho Sen, on the side of your jaw that looks to me like the imprint of knuckles. You have been knocked out. Who did it?'

'You are quite mistaken,' said Ho Sen. 'I fell over and knocked my chin on the base of the railings.'

Inspector Coutts had joined the group by this time. He took Ho Sen by the arm.

'I think you had better come with us,' he put in, 'instead of returning to Greek Street.'

The mention of Greek Street obviously worried Ho Sen a little.

He repeated the words. 'You can't arrest me,' but he did not seem so sure, as he had previously, that what he said was the truth.

Blake's foot touched something which lay upon the pavement.

It was a knife!

*   *   *

Instead of picking up the knife which he had found, Blake told his assistant to shine the torch upon it.

The knife had a pear-shaped blade, broadest towards the tip. The handle was of hard wood, which was very heavily carved, and inlaid with ivory.

Blake bent, placed his handkerchief around the hilt, and raised the weapon.

He had already observed that the blade was stained with blood.

Inspector Coutts, still holding the Chinaman by the arm, turned to find out why Blake did not follow.

'What have you got there?' he questioned.

Blake offered the weapon for his inspection.

'A knife, Coutts. Chinese, I think. Blood upon the blade.'

Coutts jerked round to face Ho Sen.

'Is that yours?'

Ho Sen shook his head slowly.

'Not mine.'

'Do you know anything about it?'

'No, nothing at all.'

'You observe that the blade is stained by blood?'

'Yes—no.'

'Do you mean yes, or no?'

'Yes, now that you ask me, I do see.'

Blake carefully wrapped the handkerchief round the hilt of the knife; then handed it to Inspector Coutts.

'I would suggest,' he said, 'that you take Ho Sen to Cannon Row, and see whether Records can bring up any fingerprints on it.'

He asked Ho Sen another question.

'That's not your blood—on that knife, I mean?'

Ho Sen said that it was not. He was looking somewhat frightened.

'Two hours ago,' said Inspector Coutts to the Chinaman, 'Simpson Stead was murdered in Soho. He was murdered by means of a knife. His assistant has just admitted that your address is in Soho, and we find you with a knife in your neighbourhood. On the knife is blood. That is good enough grounds for me to charge you. You will be brought up tomorrow, while your case is looked into. I should say that you are in a very nasty position.'

Ho Sen said nothing.

On the way from Bloomsbury to Cannon Row Police Station both Blake and Coutts addressed questions to the Chinaman; but he refused to say another word.

The detective remained at Cannon Row after Ho Sen had been charged to hear whether the experts attached to the Yard had been able to bring up fingerprints upon the hilt or blade of the knife.

They learned that the attempt had been unsuccessful. They were provided, however, with several particulars concerning the blood.

It was the blood of a middle-aged person who suffered from anaemia.

The description might have fitted Simpson Stead.

The detectives had returned to the taxi, which they had kept waiting, and were taken to Soho to the address which Stead's clerk had given them as Ho Sen's.

The number in Greek Street was a mean-looking door between two shops.

The detectives pushed the door open and started to ascend a staircase.

Half-way up they were met by a girl of about seventeen. In one hand she held a pail containing dirty water, and in the other a floorcloth. The stairs behind her were wet.

'What are you doing, my girl?' asked Sexton Blake.

'I should think you could see for yourself,' was the impudent reply. 'I'm doing these stairs.'

'Who told you to do these stairs?' persisted the detective.

'That's my business, Mr Man. I'm not bound to answer your questions.'

This was a situation which Inspector Coutts was fully competent to handle.

He stepped forward.

'I am a police officer,' he said. 'You had better keep a civil tongue in your head, miss, or else you will find yourself in Queer Street.'

The girl appeared frightened.

'I didn't know you was police,' she said. 'The other gentleman didn't say so. You can't expect me to answer questions to anybody as likes to come and ask 'em.'

The inspector threw out his chest.

Tinker grinned, knowing what was coming.

'I may as well tell you that I am Inspector Coutts, of the CID, Scotland Yard. This gentleman wishes to ask you some questions, and you will have to answer them.

'At the same time,' he added, addressing Sexton Blake, 'I really don't know, my dear Blake, what point there is in your questioning. I don't see why the girl shouldn't wash the steps down.'

'I can see why she should,' Sexton Blake told him.

'What do you mean, Blake?'

'Bloodstains.'

'Good heavens! Of course! I didn't think of that, Blake!'

The inspector became excited and energetic at once.

'Now, look here, my girl, who told you to wash these stairs at this time of night?'

'The man I work for—Mr Windross.'

'We will go and see Mr Windross.'

The girl's painted mouth twisted into a grin.

'You will have to go to Stoke Newington, then. That's where he lives.'

'When did he tell you to wash these stairs?'

'He didn't tell me. It was his manager.'

'Where's his manager, then?'

'Down below. First on right.'

'Do you mean in the next shop?'

'That's right. Windross and Company. That's where I work.'

'And what were you doing there at this time of night?'

The girl looked sulky.

'Mr Shutz had better tell you that. He's the manager.'

Inspector Coutts turned to descend again.

'You had better come with me,' he said over his shoulder.

As Blake and Tinker were following, there was a crash behind them, and dirty water came flowing down the stairs to where they were. The pail clattered after it.

Inspector Coutts turned with offended dignity.

'Did she do that purposely?'

'Of course she did it purposely,' said Blake. 'She knew what she was swabbing those stairs for; but she has told us something, all the same.'

He turned, and ran up the stairs past the girl to the first floor; then, almost immediately, he came down again.

'All right, Coutts. Carry on!'

The shop on the right was a narrow-fronted place, devoted to the sale of foreign newspapers, picture postcards, and erotic literature. An envelope, stuck by its gummed flap to the wall, advertised '*Letters may be addressed here*'.

The man Shutz was smoking in the shop parlour. He was a bald man, with a deeply lined and very knowing face. His flannel shirt was of a striking check pattern. He was coatless.

On seeing the detectives, he stood up, and came forward. His glance was apprehensive. He moved reluctantly, as if anxious to keep open an avenue of escape. If ever a man looked guilty, he did.

Blake said: 'Let me handle this,' quietly to Coutts. He saw that the one chance they had of getting information was to frighten Shutz badly; and, somehow, he did not think that Inspector Coutts' browbeating tactics were going to be useful here.

To the bald man, he said:

'Your name is Shutz? We are detectives. Scotland Yard. We want you as an accessory to the murder, just after nine o'clock this evening, of Simpson Stead.'

The bald man was obviously panic-stricken. His mouth opened, and remained open. He made one or two attempts to speak, but failed to articulate.

Seeing the effect which Blake was striving after, Inspector Coutts produced a pair of handcuffs from his overcoat pocket.

Still the bald Shutz did not succeed in articulating a word.

The situation was almost comic.

Blake had intended to frighten the man, in order to extort a confession concerning the washing of the stairs, but he had succeeded too well. The man was so frightened that he could not speak.

Blake brought out his pocket-flask.

'Here, Shutz. We don't want to be too hard on you. Have a pull at this.'

Shutz stretched out a trembling hand, seized the flask, and drank greedily. The brandy gave him a little courage.

'I don't know anything about it,' he said.

He invoked a large number of saints to bear witness that he knew nothing about it.

Inspector Coutts gave him a broadside.

'Come, now, that won't do. We've got you taped, my lad. We know why you had the girl to wash the stairs down.'

'I didn't tell her,' protested the man wildly.

The girl, who was standing in the doorway over the shop, began to argue about this.

'Yes, you did, Mr Shutz. You know you did. You said: "Wash them stairs down!" I says: "Can't it wait until morning?" You says: "No; it's got to be done now!"'

But Shutz would not agree to this for a moment.

'It wasn't me who told you. It must have been someone else. I didn't know anything about it. What did you want to wash them for? They're not our stairs.'

'Whose stairs are they?' asked Sexton Blake quickly.

'They belong to a party next door; but I don't know anything about them.' This from the man Shutz.

Blake took a hand again.

'Look here, Shutz, you can't lie yourself out of this. You've got just one way of getting clear, and that is by telling the truth. Someone said to you: "I want those stairs washed down; and I want it done quickly!"'

Shutz began to say something, but Blake stopped him, with upraised hand.

'You're going to deny it, but it's no use. We know what we're talking about. Are you going to make a clean breast of it; or are you coming with us?'

'Well,' protested the man, 'what could I do? I'm in their hands, ain't I? I mean, they'd cut my throat.'

'Who would?'

'Them next door.'

'Who are they?'

'I don't know who they are. Chinks, mostly; but they're customers of mine, and I can't offend them.'

'Customers, eh?'

Sexton Blake seized the man Shutz by the wrist and ripped open the sleeve of his shirt. Upon the forearm there were two or three faint blue marks.

'Yes,' he said smoothly, 'and we know what they bought from you now. You use it yourself. You're getting deeper and deeper, my man. You'd be wanted under the Dangerous Drug Act, if you weren't wanted for murder.'

Murder—that word terrified their prisoner again beyond the power of speech.

The girl, who seemed more intelligent than her employer, evidently feared the extent to which she herself might be implicated.

'I don't know anything about drugs,' she hastened to put in.

Blake swung round on her.

'No; but you know why you were washing those stairs.'

'So help me, I—'

'You were washing those stairs in case there might be blood upon them.'

'I—'

'Why did you spill that pail? I'll tell you—because you had not finished the job; and you were afraid we might find blood on the stairs lower down. That was it, wasn't it? You had better own up. You can't get away with it.'

The girl was intimidated by the stern expression on Blake's face.

'Well, all right; I did, then; but I didn't know where the blood-stains came from, did I?'

'Do you mean that a murder occurred within twenty yards of this place, two hours ago, and you never connected it with bloodstains on these stairs?'

'I didn't know anything about it.'

'We shall call witnesses to prove that you did.'

'What do you mean? I'm only the shop-girl. I'm not told any-thing.'

'And you're paid not to see anything, eh?'

The girl looked sullen. She mumbled that it was better not to see too much in that place.

'Very well,' said Blake crisply. 'You will be arrested, and the man Shutz will be arrested with you. In the first case, the charge will be obstructing the police. Later, a more serious charge may be brought against you.'

Inspector Coutts looked astonished. He wondered if Blake had taken leave of his senses. He himself had no doubt that the girl and Shutz possessed guilty knowledge, but he could see clearly that there were no grounds for their arrest.

Blake took him by the sleeve and whispered a word:

'Bluff!'

'Then,' said Inspector Coutts, as if agreeing with every word that Blake had uttered, 'I had better get in touch with my men.'

He walked out, and Blake and Tinker went with him. They walked a few yards down Greek Street, then entered a shop where there was a telephone.

If they had been watched—which they probably were—it would appear that they went into that shop for the purpose of telephoning the police. This was the effect at which Blake was aiming.

He knew that he had succeeded in frightening Shutz, and that the man, not being of an independent nature, would immediately seek advice or assistance. He knew, also, that the person from whom Shutz would seek advice would be the person who had directed him to have the stairs washed down; or, in other words, an accomplice of Simpson Stead's murderer.

He stood just inside the shop door and managed to keep the street under observation.

He saw Shutz come out of his own shop, pass along to the door which belonged to the newly washed staircase, and disappear.

'Our decoy has just entered the trap,' he said. 'We will give him two minutes; then follow.'

Inspector Coutts looked doubtful.

'What's the idea, Blake? We've got Stead's murderer already, I reckon.'

Blake was looking at his wrist-watch.

'This,' he said absently, 'is not a one-man affair. It's deep and it's wide. I doubt if we know half of its implications. For instance, who is Wa Ho? Where is Zenith? We don't know, but we want to find out.'

*   *   *

Blake's taxi still remained beside the kerb. The chauffeur, swathed in his heavy overcoat, and with his peaked cap pulled down over his brows, appeared to be dozing.

This appearance, however, was not justified by fact. He was extremely wide awake. In proof of this, while the conversation between the detectives and Shutz was still going on, the taxi-driver had heard a faint sound in the interior of his vehicle. The sound coincided with the passing of a man.

The driver got down from his seat, rounded the cab on the off-side, and opened the door.

On the seat was an envelope. The envelope bore a message scrawled in pencil.

'The driver of your cab is Zenith the Albino.'

The man read this strange message, stuffed the envelope into his pocket, closed the door of the cab, and followed the man who had just passed.

The message had been perfectly correct. The driver was Zenith,

337

and he knew exactly what had happened. The confederates of Wa Ho were striking back at him, firstly with the object of making it impossible for him to interfere with their plans; and, secondly, to revenge themselves for the trouble to them which was following the killing of Simpson Stead.

Although Zenith himself had been guiltless of the actual killing, he knew well that Simpson Stead's death was due to his own action. He had insisted upon Stead's company, when he made his getaway from Wa Ho's place, for the very purpose of confusing those whom he foresaw were about to attack him. He had said something about changing hats; then he had shot the light out and left Simpson Stead in the darkened corridor.

The man had, perhaps, imagined that Zenith was still with him. The details of what had transpired were unknown to the albino; but the fact remained that Simpson Stead had lurched out into Greek Street with a fatal knife-wound in his back.

Zenith had strolled along to Simpson Stead's house in Bloomsbury, well knowing that things were about to happen there. He had seen Ho Sen enter, and, after that, had been a witness of Ho Sen's attempt to murder Sexton Blake.

Monsieur Zenith had avoided discovery with some skill, and had then waylaid Ho Sen, imagining that the yellow man might have found that box which had become an object of such tremendous importance.

At great risk to himself, he had previously found and taken away the knife by which Simpson Stead had been killed. He had found it, in fact, upon the stairs which led to Wa Ho's quarters.

The washing-down, which had aroused Blake's suspicions, had been ordered, not because of the chance that blood from Simpson Stead's wound might have dropped upon the linoleum, but because the knife was missing; and it was feared that it might have fallen upon the stairs, leaving traces of blood behind it—which, as it happened, was the case.

Zenith had the knife in his possession, carefully wrapped in his scarf and placed in his breast-pocket. When he had knocked out Ho Sen as the most convenient means of searching the man, it had occurred to him that to leave the knife in the neighbourhood of the insensible man would embarrass Wa Ho considerably. His calculations had been justified by the arrest of Ho Sen.

In order to watch what took place after that, he had bribed the driver of Blake's taxi, and had taken the man's place. It had been a reckless act; but, so far, the albino had remained undiscovered by Blake and Coutts.

When the detectives had left him, however, Zenith had not troubled to play a part any longer, and it was obvious that Wa Ho's spies had fathomed his identity and were trying to bring about his discovery.

The man who had just passed his taxi would be one of Wa Ho's people. Wa Ho was trying to do for him what he had already done for Ho Sen—to make him a subject of suspicions; even, if possible, to bring about his arrest.

The taxi-driver's heavy overcoat, which Zenith wore, with the licence plate hanging on to one of its buttons, and the man's greasy peaked cap pulled down well over his eyes, looked incongruous with the albino's evening trousers and patent shoes; but he did not worry about that. He had always sworn to die rather than suffer arrest; and that note, which had been thrown in at the cab window, might have been no less fatal than a knife or a bullet.

Monsieur Zenith was not one to turn the other cheek to the smiter. Far from it. Always he struck back with a minimum of delay.

He was about to strike now.

The man who had tossed the envelope through the door of the taxi had gone straight on without looking round; but Zenith had had a look at his back, and was able to pick him out again in less than a hundred yards.

The man turned into a small restaurant with Chinese lettering upon the plate-glass front, and lace curtains behind the glass which concealed all view of the interior.

The man whom he was following went straight on across the floor of the restaurant and through a door at the back.

Zenith followed him there, also, without hesitation.

The room beyond was in darkness. Zenith made a movement backwards towards the lighted restaurant, but he received the weight of a man's shoulder, which swung him sideways. The door clicked shut.

Then lights went on, and Zenith found himself in the service-room of the restaurant.

Three heavy men were facing him. One was a Chinaman. The other two Europeans. Each of them looked dangerous.

The biggest of the three, a man whose clean-shaven face looked as hard as granite, and whose eyes were small and brilliant as boot-buttons, held a heavy revolver against the albino's middle.

'Just wanted to make sure it was you,' he said. 'Now we know, we're going to put you where you belong. We're going to gun you out.'

Zenith raised his eyebrows with a smile. He knew that the threat was not an empty one. Here, in the service-room, they were well back from the street, and a report, even from the revolver, might not be heard that far. One or two people in the restaurant might hear it; but they were all Chinamen, and knew better than to talk.

To show fight was useless. These three who faced him were professional killers, and he knew it. The money which had been offered to him to drop out of the affair of the box had now been offered to them to see that he dropped out of everything. In other words, that he died.

He said, thinking of the only thing which could have delayed his execution, even for minutes:

'Then you won't get the box!'

The gunman's eyes flickered towards his Chinese confederate.

'What's he talking about?'

'Don't shoot,' said the other desperately.

He spoke to Zenith himself.

'You've got the box?'

It was a question. Zenith's life depended upon the answer.

'Naturally, I've got the box. When I want a thing I get it.'

'You have it here?'

Zenith smiled again.

'The object of which you speak is large enough to contain fifty cigars. As I haven't a parcel under my arm, it is clear that the box is not on my person.'

'Where is it?'

'It is in a safe place.'

'You will tell us where that place is.'

'I think not.'

The gunman spoke again.

'What's the use of talking to this guy? I wasn't told anything about no box. I got to bump him off.'

But at this the Chinaman was almost as excited as if it had been his own life which hung in the balance.

'No,' he said desperately, 'you must not shoot! I do not know much; but there is some talk of a box; and it is important. The master will never forgive!'

'You see,' said Zenith, with a shrug of the shoulders, 'that you are a little premature, my friend. Better put the artillery away!'

The gunman raised the revolver and brought the barrel down hard upon Zenith's cheekbone.

A bead of blood appeared on the albino's skin, in startling contrast to his colourless face. He rocked slightly upon his feet; but gave no other sign that the blow had taken effect. Only his eyes glinted dangerously. The smile upon his lips did not change for one moment.

'You must wait,' said the Chinaman to his confederates. 'On no account must you kill. Keep the honourable Zenith here, while I telephone.'

He went out of the room.

Zenith dug his forefinger and thumb into his waistcoat-pocket.

'Don't be frightened!' he said. 'I am only going to smoke a cigarette!'

The heavy gunman grinned offensively.

'What d'you take me for? One move from you that ain't right, and I'll let you have it where it hurts!'

Zenith lighted a cigarette, and blew the smoke into the other's face. He had calculated that the effect of this insult would be either a bullet in the middle, or another clout with the butt of the gun. He did not know which; but he was content to find out.

The man raised his heavy revolver to repeat his previous blow. It was the move for which Zenith had been waiting.

With the left hand, he caught the descending wrist of the other. With his right hand, he zipped across two terrific blows to the point of the gunman's jaw.

The other man sprang at him; but by now Zenith had possession of the revolver. He stabbed the barrel at the face of the advancing man.

The man groaned, and fell backwards. As he fell, he dragged a pistol from his own pocket.

Zenith ground the heel of his patent shoe into the man's wrist, then he used his own weapon as a cosh.

He opened the door of the kitchen, reversed the key, and locked the door behind him; then he went back through the restaurant, and into the street.

He was in a hurry to return to his seat upon the borrowed taxi.

It served no useful purpose, his thus riding with Blake and Coutts; but he did get a kick out of it. He was still hoping, moreover, that the fact of his being in the same place as the detectives might give him another chance to put a spoke in the wheel of Wa Ho.

There had been a certain respect between himself and Wa Ho. Nevertheless, they were at war.

Although the murder of Simpson Stead did not strike him as a matter which needed to be avenged, he could not forget that the knife which had been driven into the breast of Simpson Stead had been intended for Monsieur Zenith. If possible, he would take a keen delight in saddling Wa Ho with that killing, and seeing the mandarin brought to justice.

Before he had reached the cab, however, he was stopped by a man he failed to recognise for several moments.

The man was seemed extremely angry.

'Here, that's enough of this! Who d'you think you are?'

The man was easy enough to recognise in one respect, for, over a shabby blue serge suit, he was wearing a silk hat and evening cloak.

The silk hat and evening cloak were Zenith's own property. The man who now addressed him was the licensed driver of the taxicab which Zenith had been using.

When by certain arguments, in which Treasury notes played a prominent part, Zenith had borrowed the man's cab, his peaked cab, his overcoat, and licence plate, the man had grumbled that without cap and overcoat he would catch his death of cold. Zenith had responded to this objection by placing his own hat on the other's head, and draping his own cloak around the man's shoulders.

He surveyed the angry driver now with a very unusual amusement.

'Pardon me,' he said, in his wonderful voice. 'But you haven't got that hat at quite the right angle, my good man!'

He raised his hands and adjusted the topper upon the man's head, then stepped back to admire the result.

'That's better!' he said.

'And,' he went on, 'if I might suggest it, wear the cloak with a trifle of insouciance. H'm, not quite so good!'

The man had been literally petrified by rage, or he would not have allowed Zenith to get that far.

'Look here,' he almost shouted, 'I want my cab!'

Zenith held up a protesting hand.

'My dear good man, why didn't you say so before? Here is your cab, exactly as you left it.'

He stripped off the coat and the peaked cap, and took his own silk hat and cloak in return; then, dressed once more as he loved to be dressed, he walked back to the cab, holding the cabman affectionately by the arm.

The man was still growling with rage.

The albino's extraordinary audacity and impudence had been too much for his slow wits, and he had parted with his cab before he fully realised what was happening. When realisation had come to him, he had decided that the albino had wronged him.

The Treasury notes which Zenith had given him had formed an excuse for several drinks, and, with the drinks, his rage had increased. He had gone back to his favourite cab rank as miserable without his vehicle as a cavalryman without a charger, and one of his mates had thereupon informed him that his cab was standing in Greek Street.

He had said that he was going to give that 'pink-eyed fellow a slosh in the gob,' and had hurried to that place. On arrival, however, he had had the sense to realise that Monsieur Zenith could not be manhandled with impunity, and suffered himself to be led back to his cab without another word.

The albino, still in the same flippant mood, insisted upon tucking his rug under his legs. At the same moment, and unknown to the man, Zenith replaced that envelope upon the rear seat of the cab—the one which bore the message: '*The driver of your cab is Zenith the Albino.*' After that, he went away.

It occurred to him that he had been taking most extravagant risks in thus appearing undisguised in a place where Sexton Blake might appear at any moment, and, also, that this was an excellent opportunity to look for a certain box upon which turned the fate of nations, and, consequently, power. Power over millions of men. Over millions in money.

★   ★   ★

Strangely enough, Sexton Blake himself was at that moment thinking thoughts similar to the albino's own.

It is true that the box was somewhat more of a mystery to him than it was to Monsieur Zenith; but he, too, realised that Ho Sen's search of the house in Bloomsbury had been incomplete.

He had the best of reasons for knowing that Ho Sen had failed to discover the object which he sought. He had deduced merely the size of this object, but imagined that he had only to see it to realise its importance, which may have been true. Consequently, he had decided upon paying a visit on his own account to the house of Simpson Stead, and, as he realised that his visit might involve a trifle of housebreaking, it was his intention, as a preliminary, to shake off his company of Inspector Coutts.

After the detective had seen the man Shutz disappear up the staircase down which Simpson Stead had come in his last moments of life, they had passed along to the entrance and ascended after him as silently as possible.

This was the moment when Zenith had faced death in the kitchen of the Chinese restaurant.

Shutz had disappeared; but this fact did not present any difficulty to Sexton Blake.

He pointed to one of the doors upon the upper landing.

'That way,' he said softly.

'Eh! How do you know?'

There were several other doors upon the landing.

Inspector Coutts waved his hand towards them. He could not make out how Blake knew that Shutz had gone in by that one door.

The private detective smiled.

'The young woman who washed the stairs was good enough to mark the door for us,' he pointed out.

Coutts looked at the door with interest.

When the girl had washed the staircase, she had neglected to swab down the whole of the landing, and had been content to clean the space between just one door and the top of the stairs. The

implication was that she knew the purpose for the washing down—
that it was to prevent the discovery of bloodstains—and that she
knew that there would not be bloodstains anywhere else but outside that one door.

If Simpson Stead had come out from there, the chances were that
Shutz had gone in by the same means.

Blake took Inspector Coutts by the sleeve and led him towards
the head of the stairs.

'I think,' he whispered, 'that this is the time for us to make a
mistake. We can't force our way in on these people while they are
prepared and expecting us. I suggest that we knock on one of the
other doors, and appear to go away satisfied with what we can get.
We can come back later with more hope of discovering something.'

Inspector Coutts saw the force of this.

He said:

'Blow it, Blake, you're quite right!' and went up to one of the
other doors and banged on it heavily.

Minutes passed, and no one came in response to his knocking.

He tried the door-handle, and found that the door was open. It
led to a continuation of the staircase.

Blake whispered to Tinker to remain there upon the landing,
and himself accompanied the police officer to the floor above.

There, for the look of the thing, they created a considerable
disturbance knocking upon doors and asking questions; then they
went downstairs again, were joined by Tinker, and descended to
the street.

Blake looked at his wrist-watch. It was nearly one.

'Well, Coutts,' he said, 'I think we can call this a day.
Tomorrow, if you are agreeable, we will visit this neighbourhood
again.'

The inspector nodded agreement. He appeared to be thinking
deeply.

'So,' he said, 'you reckon that the explanation of Stead's murder
is behind that door there.'

'I reckon,' said Blake, 'that Simpson Stead was murdered
behind that door, and managed to get out into the street before he
died.'

'What about proof?'

Sexton Blake shrugged his shoulders.

'You've got the knife, if it is the knife. You may be able to get it identified. That ought to fix somebody.'

He was not tremendously interested in the murder of Simpson Stead, whom he knew to be a worthless character. His mind was deeply occupied by the mystery of some object which Simpson Stead appeared to have had in his possession.

They reached the taxicab, and Inspector Coutts threw the door open.

'Hallo!' he ejaculated. 'What's this?'

He picked up the envelope from the rear seat. On seeing what was written thereupon, he gasped with astonishment, and handed the envelope to his unofficial friend.

Blake walked quickly to the front of the cab. His hand had gone to the 'V' of his waistcoat and come out again, holding a pistol. He let the pistol drop into his jacket pocket at the moment when the driver turned. At the same instant, he realised that this was not the driver they had had before. The previous man had worn his cap over his eyes, and his coat collar turned up. This one wore his cap well back upon his head and his coat collar down.

'How long have you been on this cab?' asked Blake.

The driver pretended not to understand.

'Wotcher mean, sir?'

'How long have you been on that seat? Three minutes? Five minutes?'

The man had the sense to see that it was not going to be any use to tell lies to Sexton Blake. He started to tell the truth, after his own fashion.

'Well, you see, it was like this, sir—'

Blake smiled.

'I haven't time for all that, my man. Answer a question or two. How long have you been here?'

'About five minutes, sir. I—'

'Who was here before you?'

'Gentleman who took my cab down in Bloomsbury. Made me get out of it, sir. I—'

'What was the gent like?'

'Like, sir? Like nothing on this earth. He was—'

'What was the colour of his eyes?'

'Believe me, or believe me not, sir, they was pink.'

346

'I see. He took the cab over in Bloomsbury and left it here. Is that it?'

'Yes, sir. He—'

'That will do.'

Blake turned to his companions.

'Confound the man's audacity,' he said, laughing. 'Our chauffeur has been Zenith the Albino.'

At this, the taxi-driver became interested again.

'What?' he said. 'Zenith? Was that Zenith?'

'That's right,' said Blake. 'You've missed a chance to collect a handsome reward. How much is it, Coutts? Five thousand? Six thousand now, is it?'

'Yes; six thousand pounds.'

The man became incoherent with astonishment.

'Well, think of that, now! Fancy that, now! Zenith the Albino driving my cab!'

'But this envelope,' said Sexton Blake, 'remains very interesting.'

He turned again to the taxi-driver.

'Monsieur Zenith picked you up while you were outside the house in Bloomsbury?'

'That's right, sir. He came to the off-side of the cab and talked to me. He said he wanted a little fun with some friends.'

'Then he took your place; and you went away.'

'Yes, sir.'

'How far did you go? Did you see what happened?'

The man hesitated.

'Well, I had a look back, like. A fellow came out, shortish chap. "That's the bloke," I thinks, "what Pink Eyes is going to have a game with," but the shortish bloke goes past the cab and across the road. Pink Eyes goes after him. I thought there was going to be some dirty work; then I see Pink Eyes come back again to my cab, so I reckon that's all right, and I hops it.'

'There you are,' said Blake triumphantly to his companions. 'That all links up. I thought that man Ho Sen had been knocked out. He had been. It was Zenith who did it. We couldn't understand how a bloodstained knife should be found in this neighbourhood. We can understand it now. Zenith put it there. And you see this'—Blake held up the envelope on which the message was written—'that's a counterstroke. To suit his own purposes, Zenith had Ho Sen arrested. Other people, who appear to be connected with Ho Sen, since they apparently come from the same address, are doing their best to have Zenith arrested. This is very interesting, Coutts. There's a proverb which is rather apposite. I don't know whether it will apply in this connection, but I hope that it will. "When rogues fall out—" You know the rest of it.'

'Just a little war,' suggested Inspector Coutts. 'A case of dog eat dog. Eh, Blake?'

'More to it than that,' said the private detective. 'The pieces upon the board at present are: One, a certain object of extreme value. Two, Zenith the Albino, whom we find outside the house where that object is suspected to be. Three, a Chinaman, Ho Sen, who has searched Stead's house in the hope of finding that object; and, four, some unknown other, probably named Wa Ho, who is party to the murder of Simpson Stead, and the author of the attempt on Zenith's freedom represented by this piece of paper. It looks like the beginnings of a nice little problem, Coutts; but at present I suspect that we can see our way to take a hand in the game, we must place some more of them. Then we can make a move or so on our own account.'

'This object which you are seeking,' asked Coutts, 'do you reckon it is up there, at the top of that staircase?'

Blake shook his head.

'I don't think so. We have reason to believe that Ho Sen came from there immediately before he searched Simpson Stead's quarters. If I ventured upon a theory, I should say that Simpson Stead was murdered because he refused to give the object up, and that Ho Sen immediately rushed over to Stead's house to secure it.'

'Then,' suggested Coutts, 'our next move is to go back to Stead's house and search on our own account.'

'Not tonight,' said Sexton Blake promptly.

As the reader knows, he had already decided on doing exactly what Coutts had suggested, but he wanted to do it by himself.

'I would recommend,' he said, 'that you drop me and Tinker at Baker Street, and then go on to the Yard. You will be going back there?'

He knew that Coutts liked to go back to his office and clear up there before going home.

'Come for us in the morning,' he said; 'we will go into the whole thing together.'

Blake knew that this was a bait which might serve to satisfy the inspector.

Coutts had discovered that he usually had better results when working with Blake, and was always willing to await an opportunity of doing so; but Coutts agreed rather reluctantly on this occasion.

When Blake and Tinker stood upon the pavement outside Blake's room and watched the inspector's taxi disappear in the distance, the detective turned to his assistant with a perplexed smile.

'I don't understand Coutts tonight, my lad. He's up to something.'

Tinker chuckled.

'Bet you he's going back to Greek Street.'

Blake did not respond to Tinker's humour.

'I hope you're not right. For one thing, I don't want him to visit Greek Street again without me; and, for another—'

'What's the other reason, guv'nor?'

'Something nasty might happen to him. I can't get Inspector Coutts to realise that this is not an ordinary murder case, that the killing of Stead is nothing. I hope he will wait until morning. I may have proof by then.'

* * *

The house at Bloomsbury which had belonged to Simpson Stead was dark and silent, in common with most others in its respectable neighbourhood.

Blake reconnoitred it carefully from the other side of the square, fixed its position in his mind, then went out of the square again and made a detour so as to reach the passage which ran along the rear of the short gardens at the back.

Here he experienced the difficulty which Tinker had already discovered in finding communication between the front and rear of Stead's premises, other than by going through the house itself; but, having more time at his disposal than Tinker had had, he at length found a way through from a second street behind the square.

A break in the clouds, which allowed the moon to show for a few moments, helped him to pick out Stead's house by enabling him to see the shattered window out of which Ho Sen had escaped after making his own incomplete search of the place.

Blake had changed to rubber-soled shoes, and was wearing a dark blue raincoat strapped in at the waist. He passed along the garden, hugging the shadow of the high wall which bordered it, and brought up against railings which surrounded the area which gave light during the daytime to an underground kitchen.

By ascending steps towards the back door, he was able to get a foot on to the top of this railing; then stepped on to the window-sill, and got a hold upon the woodwork of the broken window.

He was moving very cautiously. For one thing, he was not sure that the house was uninhabited; and, for another thing, he was nervous lest he might be seen in the act of breaking into it, and be picked up by a watchful policeman.

When working upon a case, especially a case in which the issues appeared as important as now, Blake showed little respect for the law. If he were pulled in by the police, he had sufficient influence to get clear of any serious charge; but he did not wish to use this influence too often. He was particularly anxious to search Simpson Stead's house, but he was also anxious to do it without being detected in the act.

He raised the sash very carefully, inch by inch, and, when it was lifted far enough to give him admission, fixed it in place by means of a stick forced up between the sash and the frame. Then he climbed through, and just as carefully reversed his operations with the window until it was closed behind him.

He hesitated for a moment, and then pulled down a blind. The fact that the blind was now drawn, whereas it had not been so previously, might betray his presence to anybody who entered the room, or even inspected the house closely from outside. This, however, was a risk which he had to take.

After drawing the blind, he listened for several minutes, came to the conclusion that his entrance had not been discovered, and went to work, scrutinising the room by means of an electric torch. It was not a long scrutiny. He merely began where Ho Sen had left off.

After ten minutes he had investigated half a dozen possible hiding-places which Ho Sen had overlooked, and had assured himself that that room, at any rate, did not contain the object which the Chinaman had been seeking.

He extinguished his torch, and then raised the blind again, leaving the room exactly as it was when he first found it.

Then he went along the passage past the stairs, and into a large room in the front. This room was also an office, but it was better furnished and more comfortable. He had already learned from Stead's clerk that it had been the sanctum of the lawyer himself.

He wondered that Ho Sen had given so much time to the rear office, while this one remained unexamined. Then he remembered the clerk whom they had interrogated earlier in the evening. He had assumed that Simpson Stead's clerk had been bribed by Ho Sen—indeed, the youth had admitted as much. It was possible, however, that despite the influence over Stead's clerk, which he obtained by means of that bribe, Ho Sen had desired to keep his search as secret as possible, and had begun with the room least visible from the street.

Here the blinds of the bay window were drawn, and there were muslin curtains on the inside.

Blake immediately switched on the torch again and started his search by an examination of Simpson Stead's pedestal writing-table.

Sexton Blake was in the peculiar situation of not knowing exactly what he was looking for. He knew the size of the thing within limits, and hoped that, if he found it, he would be able to recognise its importance. The fact that his knowledge did not go beyond this point was a severe handicap. Nevertheless, the detective went to work in his usual painstaking manner to answer the question of whether Simpson Stead's room did or did not contain the object which Ho Sen had been seeking.

The drawers of the pedestal-table were locked. Some of them were obviously too shallow to be the repository of the mysterious object in question and these he left alone. The remainder he opened by means of a bunch of skeleton keys.

In one of the drawers which he did open he found a further bunch of keys, which simplified his search considerably.

Against the walls were two large presses and a bookcase. Embedded in the brickwork was a shallow wall-safe. The drawers of the presses and the drawers of the bookcase were all locked, and the locks were of an expensive type. To open them by means of his picklocks would have taken some hours, but the keys which he had discovered made everything easy for him.

He unlocked the presses and went through their contents methodically. Then he searched the deeper drawers in the bookcase. The keys which he had found even included one which opened the safe.

He was in the very act of swinging the safe door back when he thought that he heard a faint sound outside the room.

He clicked out his torch and stood silent. The hinges of the room door creaked ever so little, but enough to convince Blake that his suspicions had been justified.

Someone was coming in, and, to judge by the caution which the intruder was using, he had no more right there than Blake himself.

The detective slipped his right hand into the upper part of his waistcoat, and brought out a pistol from his shoulder-holster. He associated this nocturnal visitant to the house of Simpson Stead with the intrigues of the unknown desperadoes who had been represented by Ho Sen.

He had in mind his theory that they had murdered Stead himself for the sake of some object which that house contained. And further, that they had already half-searched the house without discovering that object. What more likely than that this newcomer was a confederate of Ho Sen, who had forced his way to the house for the purpose of continuing the search which Ho Sen had begun?

After the single movement occasioned by the act of drawing his pistol, Blake remained absolutely motionless and silent.

After a longish period—perhaps half a minute—hinges creaked again.

Blake realised that the intruder was now in the room, and had reclosed the door. He resisted an impulse to switch on his torch in the hope that this other would make some move to betray himself, or perhaps to throw further light upon the description of the object which he sought.

For many more seconds, however, nothing happened. There was no sound. One less watchful and cautious than the detective might indeed have been persuaded that he was alone; that that creak of the door hinges had been an effect only of the imagination. But Blake knew that it was not so. Somewhere within that room, less than half a dozen paces from himself, there was another human being.

Why did this other person do nothing—make no move, no sound? Was it possible that Blake's presence was known, and that the other was stalking him in the darkness?

Blake's finger found his trigger, otherwise he remained impassive.

From a distance the noise of a taxi-engine became audible. Someone returning from a late social or business appointment was being driven towards the house.

The taxi turned as it came into the square, and, for the moment, its headlights shone upon Stead's windows.

To Blake's eyes, accustomed to the darkness, the room became visible. He realised that he was standing within a few paces of his arch enemy, Monsieur Zenith—realised also that Zenith had seen him.

Blake saw the albino smile, and glimpsed the tiny plated revolver which appeared in the man's hand.

The automatic and the revolver exploded in the same moment.

It would be nice to narrate that Sexton Blake fired with the object of rendering Zenith incapable, with the object, say, of breaking the albino's arm. But the truth is that Blake simply did not dare to attempt any such thing. He knew that Zenith would shoot to kill, and that the range being what it was, his only chance of escape was to get his shot in first.

He had had perhaps a slight advantage because the light which had been coming through the windows had revealed Zenith a split second before it had swung round upon himself. Nevertheless, he was astonished to find himself unhurt.

After that single moment of faint radiance from the headlights, the taxi had passed the house, and the room was in darkness again.

The air was acrid with the reek of cordite. Blake had taken a single step sideways, and was now waiting, still with finger on trigger, for the albino to fire a second shot.

Nothing happened. If the reports of the automatic and the revolver, which had seemed to be of shattering loudness in the silence of the night, had been heard by any other person inside or outside the house, that person had taken no action to make the fact evident.

It seemed possible to the detective that Zenith was playing his own game and waiting for an opportunity to locate himself.

He dared neither to speak nor to move, because he feared that to do either might invite another shot from the revolver, and that he could not be lucky enough to be missed by the albino a second time.

Minutes passed. Blake could stand the suspense no longer. He slowly brought up the point of his torch, held it well away from his body, and switched on, sending the white beam in the direction where he had last seen Zenith.

The albino was huddled with his back against the wall. His silk hat lay on the floor beside him. From his temple there trickled a bead of blood.

Blake switched on the electrics. To his astonishment he found himself desperately sorry for what he had done. It was odd, because he well knew that Zenith would have killed him without compunction. If he had killed Zenith, surely no man on earth could suggest that he had not been fully justified. Nevertheless, when he came to examine the albino's wound more closely, and found that the man was still living, he sighed with relief.

Monsieur Zenith was merely unconscious. Blake's bullet had only creased him. It had robbed him of consciousness by striking him a glancing blow upon the side of the skull, with the effect of a stroke from an iron bar. The skin was broken, but the bullet had not penetrated Zenith's skull. In a short time, a few minutes perhaps, Monsieur Zenith would be again his debonair and dangerous self.

Blake picked up the plated pistol which had fallen from Zenith's nerveless fingers, and thrust it into his own pocket. Then, with a bit of tape from the desk, he tied the albino's thumbs together behind the man's back.

His previous remorse had now been replaced by triumph. He was making a capture which had been the ambition of his life. He promised himself that there should be no mistake about it this time.

While he was tying Zenith's wrists with a second length of tape, the man blinked his eyes, drew a deep breath, and struggled into a standing position. His vitality enabled him to recover completely in a matter of seconds.

On seeing Blake he smiled again—the same desperately sad

smile which had transfigured his face before at the moment of the shooting.

Zenith looked down at his hands ruefully.

'Tied me up, have you? Deuced inconvenient, Blake!'

Blake was not wasting time in sentiment. He said:

'I have got you, Zenith, and you are coming with me to a police station!'

Zenith nodded slowly.

'Yes; I was afraid that would be the programme.'

He seemed to ponder for a moment, then made a proposition which was in keeping with his reckless temperament.

'Look here, Blake! We've always had a certain respect for the rules of the game, haven't we? You know there are things which I have not done. Give me an "out", as they call it.'

He guessed at Blake's thoughts, and laughed.

'Oh, I am not asking you to let me go—I know you wouldn't do that—but, as you know, there is one cigarette in my case—which is in my waistcoat-pocket—that I have marked with a red circle. To smoke that cigarette is to finish. Well—let me smoke it!'

Sexton Blake shook his head. His face was stern.

'Not that way, Zenith!'

'Why not?' pleaded the albino. 'The only trouble between us is that the world isn't big enough for you and me at the same time. Why put society to the trouble of a trial, and put upon me the humiliation of a prison? You can attain your end just as surely—more surely, in fact, by allowing me just one whiff of perfumed smoke. Why not?'

Blake opened the door.

'Because that is not my way, Zenith!'

He was keeping Zenith covered. He did not dare to take any chances.

'This way,' he said. 'We will go out by the front door and walk until we find a taxi. If you try to escape, I shall shoot you down!'

Zenith shrugged his shoulders, and laughed.

'I should hope,' he said, 'that in that case I should be lucky enough to get your bullet through the head instead of across it!'

* * *

The electrics were still on in Simpson Stead's room. Blake was not worrying now about his presence being observed. He had no fear of being picked up by an unusually alert policeman; on the contrary, it would have suited his plans very well indeed. The resourcefulness of Monsieur Zenith had saved him more than once, when arrest seemed as certain even as it did now, and Blake was tensed to meet emergencies. He would have been glad of any help that he could get.

As he followed the albino through the door of the room, he had his pistol-barrel against Zenith's back. He fully expected that, despite the threat of the pistol, the albino would make a dive for freedom. In that case, he would aim at the man's legs. He felt that he would not like to remember in days to come that he was the killer of Zenith.

Despite the crimes of the albino, Blake could not resist a measure of liking for the man. He was doing his duty in handing Monsieur Zenith over to the police, but it was a disagreeable duty. He wanted to put it through and be done with it as soon as possible.

As Zenith emerged through the doorway, something happened. Powerful arms clutched him around the middle and jerked him sideways.

On impulse, Blake stepped forward. A big man hurled himself at Blake's pistol-hand. The detective jammed the muzzle of the pistol into his attacker's face.

Another man jumped from behind on to the breadth of the detective's shoulders. Hands seemed to be clutching him everywhere. He had a momentary glimpse of the albino, bound as he was, struggling vainly in the grasp of a dozen men.

Then he himself was fully bound, his pistol torn from his fingers, and a gag thrust into his mouth. He saw that the men who had attacked himself and Zenith were all Chinese. There must have been over a dozen of them. He recognised that they were not men of the coolie class, but educated Chinamen, students probably. He knew, from that, that this was no ordinary matter of revenge or robbery, but something political.

He found himself bound hand and foot by cords, which the men seemed to have ready for the purpose. Then he was carried into Stead's room and laid upon the floor. The albino was laid behind him.

A big man entered. He was covered from head to foot in a closely buttoned raincoat; a soft felt hat was upon his head. He peeled off these garments, and stood revealed as a mandarin in full dress.

Blake recognised one of the orders which he wore. He was evidently a person of some importance. A Brother of the Dragon.

The man said something in Chinese; and those who had attacked Blake and Zenith went away. They went so silently that Blake, although he listened, could not tell whether they departed from the back or front of the premises.

The mandarin recited something with folded hands. It appeared to be a prayer. Then he went to the safe and opened it. Out of the safe he took a box about as large as one used for containing fifty cigars. He touched the box to his forehead, and placed it upon Simpson Stead's table.

After that, he spoke in English for the first time.

'To his excellency Monsieur Zenith, and to Mr Sexton Blake, I offer regrets. They have discovered more than it is safe for men to know, and they must not live.'

Rather surprisingly, Zenith spoke now. Their captors had omitted to gag Zenith, possibly because they realised that, to serve his own purposes, he would refrain from giving the alarm.

He said:

'So, Wa Ho, Simpson Stead had the box after all?'

'It should have been discovered before,' said the mandarin. 'Ho Sen was here. Why did he waste time in searching tables, when he might have gone to the safe?'

The mandarin turned towards where Blake was lying.

'Perhaps this matter is still a mystery to honourable Mr Blake. I should explain. Tibet is a country of great importance to my people. The Thanai, the Priest-King of Tibet, has deserted his country—Mr Blake will have read of it in the papers. He brought with him the diadem, which, of itself, confers sovereignty upon its possessor. The man who possesses this diadem'—and here the mandarin laid his hand upon the box—'is, by that alone, ruler of Tibet and its people. The Llamas will obey the diadem, whether he who wears it be of their own race, or Chinese, or even an Englishman. Therefore, we have fought to secure it.

'It was stolen from the Thanai, and we took the advice of Simpson Stead as to the best means to secure it for ourselves and our country.

'Simpson Stead was a traitor. He secured the diadem and kept it for himself. What use he would have made of it, I don't know. Possibly, dog that he was, he would have sold it to the highest bidder.

'We suspected that, even before Stead was killed in mistake for his excellency Monsieur Zenith. We discovered it for certain almost immediately afterwards. We suspected, then, that the diadem was here in this place. We sent Ho Sen to search for it, but he bungled. He will perhaps pay the penalty. It is of no consequence. Even I, Wa Ho, Mandarin of the Imperial Purple, Brother of the Dragon, and Companion of the Yellow Snake, am of no consequence beside what this means to my country!

'You, honourable excellency Zenith, and you, honourable Sexton Blake, are witnesses of Wa Ho's triumph. It is unfortunate that you shall not live to talk of it. You will pardon, and you will understand.'

The mandarin picked up two broad-bladed knives, which had been left by his people upon the table. He approached Zenith, raised one of the knives to his forehead with a deep obeisance, and laid it at the feet of the albino. Then he repeated the operation again with the other knife, this time placing it beside Sexton Blake.

'It is fitting,' the mandarin intoned, 'that men of noble blood should die by their own hands, but this country has strange manners. The word is not enough. Therefore, my friends, you will be honoured to die by the hand of Wa Ho himself.'

'It is an honour,' acknowledged Monsieur Zenith.

'Perhaps,' he went on, 'it will be permitted us first to see the diadem?'

The mandarin bowed his head in thought.

'What you ask is reasonable,' he said. 'You shall look upon the diadem in the same moment as Wa Ho himself. Then the diadem, and the power which it means, shall be given to my country.'

He raised the box, and carried it across the floor to a spot where both Zenith and Blake could observe his movement.

'Behold,' he said, 'I open the box, and—'

As he spoke, he had pressed his thumb to the curious wrought-iron catch which held the lid of the box in place. His words faltered, and then ceased.

The box dropped from his hands to the floor—

The mandarin stood looking stupidly at a bead of blood upon his thumb.

He stood so for what seemed to be a long time—it might have been half a minute. Then his legs gave way as if they had been made of wet cardboard. He collapsed amid his flowing silken robes, and rolled over. A rattling sound came from his throat. He twitched and lay still.

For a second or two there was silence. Then the albino spoke.

'The catch of the box,' he said unemotionally, 'contains a spring which actuates a needle. The needle contains the deadliest poison known to mankind. A secret, in fact, of the Llamas themselves. One who sought to open the box without knowing its secret would inevitably be inoculated with the poison. I'm surprised that our friend didn't know it.'

He laughed a little.

'This is a strange situation, my dear Blake,' he went on. 'Although I am bound, I have the use of my hands. I cannot get at my own bonds to unfasten them, but I can get at yours. We have perhaps five minutes to consider the matter. After that, it is probable that Wa Ho's auxiliaries will have returned. In which case, naturally, the knife—for you and for me. I will free you as the price of my freedom. I shall take the gag out of your mouth, when you can tell me whether you agree, or do not agree. I am indifferent. It may amuse you to know that I should consider it not unbecoming to die in your company. I feel, too, that it is fitting for us to die on equal terms.'

Having said these words without any trace of haste or excitement, the albino rolled over and contrived to place himself across Blake's body, so that his hands could work upon the gag which had been placed in the detective's mouth. He pulled the gag out, and rolled clear.

'Now, Blake,' he said, 'you have not long to think the thing over. Will you give me my freedom as the price of your own? Or will you wait and die beside me?'

Blake did not hesitate. Directly he had learned that the box had been the treasured property of the fugitive ruler of Tibet, he knew its importance. To the Government of Great Britain it would probably be worth millions of pounds; or, for that matter, to any of the half-dozen nations who were struggling for the strategic mastery of Northern India.

He said quickly:

'I agree, Zenith, on condition that I have the box.'

Zenith rolled back again into his previous position. His fingers plucked at the knots which held Blake's ropes in place. The untying of those knots took the albino a long time. They had been expertly tied, and he had only his fingers to work with.

At last, however, Blake felt the knots loosening, and spread his powerful shoulders to ease the ropes. His arms became free, and he snatched at one of the knifes to sever the ropes which bound his feet.

Then he crossed to the door, turned the key in the lock, and hurled a book through Stead's window. The window burst like a bomb. He knew that it might bring the yellow men to them; but it was also certain to bring police.

He went back to cut Zenith's lashings.

Zenith held out his hand, with a smile.

'And may I have my little pistol?'

Blake handed him the weapon, without the formality of removing the cartridges. He knew Zenith. The man's code would not allow him to use the weapon against Blake at that moment. Later on, it might be another story. But now the man's personal honour was involved. And Zenith's honour, which would allow him to steal, or even, upon occasion, to kill, would not permit of treachery.

He smiled as he thrust the weapon back into his wrist-holster.

'How did you know,' asked Blake, 'of that poisoned needle?'

'Wa Ho,' said Zenith, 'is not the first man who has tried to open that box in my presence. It was I who stole it. A man who served me was too curious to know why this uninteresting-looking box should be so important. He was'—and Zenith waved his hand towards the heap of embroideries and silks upon the floor—'as Wa Ho now is!'

'Perhaps,' suggested Blake, 'you will show me how to open the box?'

Zenith bowed.

'Certainly, my dear Blake, with pleasure! You squeeze it thus, farthest from the fastening. The lid flies back, and there you are.'

Blake found himself looking at an article like the crown of a prince, but light in weight and unjewelled. The thing was made of a spongey white material. When he raised it, it was lighter even than aluminium.

'The sacred metal of Tibet,' exclaimed Zenith. 'Neither platinum nor aluminium nor pewter. The metal which men have forgotten how to make. That is why there can never be a duplicate.'

He placed it upon his own brow.

'It fits,' he said, 'but not quite so much to my liking as the silk hat, which I usually affect.'

There was a heavy knocking upon the outside door as he handed back the crown.

'That will be police,' said Zenith. 'You will forgive me if I leave you?'

He walked to the door, opened it, and turned round.

'Permit me to wish you au revoir.'

Blake grinned.

'Au revoir, Zenith,' he said grimly.

The albino went out; passed along the passage towards the rear.

Blake waited for a moment, allowed the police to knock for a second time, and then threw the front door wide open.

*   *   *

At 3 a.m. Sexton Blake and Inspector Coutts entered the office of the Minister for Foreign Affairs. He had been telephoned at his home, and had motored to Downing Street in order to receive the detective.

He was already there, and, beside him, a short dark-skinned man, to whom Sexton Blake was immediately presented, but whose royal identity he had already recognised.

'I understand,' said the Foreign Minister, 'that you have an important communication to make?'

Sexton Blake placed the box which contained the diadem upon the table in front of the official.

'Inspector Coutts,' he said, indicating his companion, 'became alarmed at unrest among the Chinese population of London, and called upon me to aid him in finding out its cause. Its cause is here.'

The Foreign Minister stretched out his hand for the box, but Blake prevented his touching it.

'I should warn you,' he said, 'that to open the box by the obvious means is certain death. You will permit me.'

He pressed the heavy spring, and the lid flew open.

The dark-skinned man uttered a cry of relief.

'The diadem,' said Blake, 'of the Priest-Kings of Tibet. That is the object, sir, which, with my help, Inspector Coutts has been able to place in your possession.'

The minister rose, to grip first Blake, and then Coutts, by the hand.

'I need not tell you, Mr Blake,' he said, 'that you two gentlemen have performed a public service of inestimable value. It will be possible for us to reward Inspector Coutts in a fitting manner, but as regards yourself—'

Blake shrugged his shoulders.

'I need no reward,' he declared.

The dark-skinned man put in a word.

'Perhaps it may be left to me.'

He took from his fingers a ring which scintillated in the light of the electrics.

'If Mr Blake would deign to accept?'

He spoke the strange English words with difficulty, but he had perhaps had occasion to use them before.

Blake bowed.

'I thank your Highness.'

The minister rang his bell.

'You will excuse my sending you gentlemen away in this peremptory fashion,' he said to the detectives, 'but your discovery has altered the whole trend of foreign affairs. I must get to work at once.'

As Blake and Coutts walked away along the echoing corridor, following the night commissionaire who had admitted them, Coutts turned to Blake with a question.

'My men have got an idea, Blake, that when they found you in Simpson Stead's house after Wa Ho died you were not alone. They had got hold of a story that a man in a silk hat was seen leaving the premises at the rear. Could that be Zenith?'

Sexton Blake smiled.

'It might have been.'

'You haven't any idea?'

'No idea whatever.'

'You say that you were tied up by Wa Ho's people. How did you get free?'

Blake placed his hand upon the shoulder of the inspector.

'Look here, Coutts, you haven't done too badly over this matter of the Thanai's box?'

'No, Blake, I haven't. I am tremendously obliged to you, old man!'

Blake laughed; smacked the inspector upon the shoulder.

'Then don't ask so many questions!'

THE FOUR GUESTS MYSTERY
Robert Murray

Robert Murray (r.n. Robert Murray Graydon, 1890–1937) was the son of William Murray Graydon, an expatriate American who settled in England in the 1890s and became one of the most prolific suppliers of serials to the Amalgamated Press, as well as a notable Blake author. Robert Murray himself started writing at an early age (his first published story was written while still at school), and like his father he wrote quantities of fiction of all kinds. He had a fondness for the fantastic (his character Captain Justice—a cross between Cutcliffe Hyne's Captain Kettle and Sidney Drew's Ferrers Lord—was forever discovering lost civilisations beyond the Arctic ice or battling monster robots on South Sea isles in the pages of Modern Boy*), but it is as a Blake writer that he will best be remembered. His major contribution to the mythos was Detective Inspector George Coutts, the gruff and grizzled Scotland Yard man whose qualities of honesty, loyalty and tenacity were allied to a dependence upon Blake's aid and advice whenever the CID were in a jam (pretty often) and a sly appreciation of the private detective's choice Partagas; all so finely characterised that he became a permanent member of the cast, to be used by other authors at will. Like most pulp-writers, Murray was never happier than when he had a regular series running, and his mainstay from 1918 to 1926 was Blake's on–off battle with the Criminals' Confederation, a monstrous conspiracy masterminded by the malevolent Mr Reece. There was a touch of old-fashioned melodrama about Murray's style (no bad thing in itself), but he could on occasion come up with a story that, for its time, was bang up to date—such as this thoroughly entertaining tale from detective fiction's Golden Age: a classic locked-room murder in a country house.*

It was one of the most peculiar letters Sexton Blake had ever read. He set it down beside his empty coffee-cup while he proceeded to fill his pipe, frowning blackly as he tamped the tobacco down in the charred bowl.

Tinker looked slightly guilty as he noticed the expression on the detective's lean face.

'I suppose that's a bill from the garage, guv'nor?' he said, with the humility of an uneasy conscience. 'It wasn't altogether my fault. The other fellow was partly to blame, and I didn't do any more than smash his windscreen, buckle a wheel, and crumple one of his mudguards.'

Sexton Blake stared blankly.

'What in the name of sense are you gibbering about?' he asked.

'Oh, I had a bit of a smash-up with the car yesterday!' confessed Tinker sheepishly. 'Skidded and smashed into another car in Oxford Street. I thought that was a letter from the garage—'

To his surprise and relief, Blake made no further comment. His thoughts were otherwise engaged as he turned his attentions to the letter he had just opened. He shook his head in puzzlement as he read it for a second time.

'What do you make of that?' he queried, tossing the missive across to his assistant. 'Is it genuine, or the work of a practical joker?'

The letter was written on expensive paper. The address was: 'Droon House, Mayes, Middlesex.'

Dear Mr Blake' (it said),—*I have reason to believe that I shall be a dead man within the next twenty-four hours. One of four persons will be guilty of my murder!*

In order that the innocent shall not suffer, and that the crime may be brought home to the right individual, I ask you to favour me with a personal visit as soon as possible.

The letter was signed: *Lucien Ashby Droon.*

'It's certainly a rum sort of letter,' agreed Tinker, with a bewildered shake of his head. 'Yet it has a genuine ring about it. Have you any idea who is this fellow Droon?'

'Not the slightest,' admitted Blake. 'Never heard the name before. If the letter is genuine, why the dickens couldn't the man be more explicit?'

'By the way he writes, he evidently expects to be murdered whether you visit him or not,' remarked Tinker. 'He must have a heap of dangerous enemies if he suspects four persons of being anxious and ready to bump him off. What do you intend doing about it, guv'nor?'

Blake hesitated. The letter had piqued his curiosity, but he wasn't in the habit of rushing off on possible wild-goose chases on the strength of a few written lines from an unknown man.

Mr Lucien Droon might be a harmless, weak-minded old gentleman who imagined himself to be in danger of meeting with a violent death. On the other hand, he might be a perfectly normal individual who had good reason for what he wrote.

In addition to the address, the note-heading bore a telephone number. Blake reached for the instrument, and called the number of his mysterious correspondent.

'This is Lucien Droon speaking,' answered a deep, masculine voice. 'You have received my letter, Mr Blake. I regret I can add nothing to its contents, except through the medium of a personal interview.'

'That can be arranged,' remarked Blake. 'You know where I live.'

'Mr Blake, you don't understand!' There was a strained note in the man's voice. 'It is impossible for me to leave here, and even more impossible for me to fully explain matters. At the present time there are four persons in this house, any one of whom would not hesitate to take my life at the first opportunity that occurred!'

'Get rid of them, or send for the police,' suggested Blake impatiently.

'They are friends of mine,' was Lucien Droon's amazing reply. 'Though I suspect all four, it is just possible that only one is guilty of any intent to commit murder. Which one I cannot determine. That is where I require your assistance. I can assure you that a visit to Droon Hall will leave you with no regrets, Mr Blake.

'I will put it in this way. I am giving a house-party at Droon House. I shall be honoured if you will be my guest over the weekend. Bring your assistant with you. I can promise you an entertaining time.'

The man laughed in a queer way; the strained laugh of one whose nerve was on the point of cracking.

'Shall we say seven o'clock this evening, Mr Blake?' he urged anxiously. 'I am not asking you to investigate a crime, but to prevent one. I will have a conveyance meet you at the station.'

'Quite unnecessary,' said Blake, prompted to acceptance by sheer curiosity, and a professional interest in Lucien Droon's unexplained premonitions of violent death. 'I shall drive down in my own car. But I can stay only till tomorrow morning. I have other calls on my time.'

'You will stay longer than that!' assured Lucien Droon confidently.

'So you are going to Droon House?' asked Tinker, as the detective rang off.

'We are both going,' corrected Blake, turning methodically to the remainder of his morning correspondence. 'Mr Droon has been kind enough to invite us to join the house-party he is holding over the weekend. Mayes is about an hour's run. If the Grey Panther is still serviceable after your recent escapade, please have it outside the house at six o'clock this evening.'

Sexton Blake never tackled a prospective case blindfolded. He preferred to be equipped with a certain amount of groundwork. But from the many sources of information at his disposal he was able to learn nothing definite regarding the man who sought his advice and assistance.

Lucien Ashby Droon's name figured in both the Post Office and the Telephone Directories. There was no doubt that he existed as the legitimate owner of an estate in rural Middlesex that was known as Droon House.

'Strikes me we're going to be mixed up in a rum sort of house-party,' remarked Tinker thoughtfully. 'According to Droon, there'll be at least four potential murderers in the bunch.'

'A most intriguing outlook,' commented Blake. 'But nothing out of the ordinary. One never knows when one may be in the company of a potential murderer. They don't wear their heartlessness on their sleeves.'

The telephone bell rang many times during the course of the day. Most of the calls were of no importance. It was late in the afternoon when the clear, but slightly agitated, voice of a woman gave Sexton Blake a mild thrill of surprise.

'Is that Mr Sexton Blake?' she asked hurriedly. 'Please take my advice, and don't go to Droon House.'

At once the speaker rang off.

'The mystery deepens!' mused the detective, with a smile. 'As usual, there is a woman in the case. Whether her message is intended as a threat, or a friendly warning, remains to be seen.'

The strange incident was the one thing calculated to cement his determination to adhere to his acceptance of Lucien Droon's invitation. He traced the call, to learn that it had come from a public telephone-box at Mayes Railway Station.

On one point Blake was certain. He would remember the woman's voice, should ever he hear it again.

Taking no more luggage than a couple of light suitcases, the detective and his assistant left Baker Street shortly after six o'clock. The Grey Panther behaved admirably, despite Tinker's recent encounter in it with a burly Benz in Oxford Street.

Mayes was no more than a village, nestling in heavily-wooded country. Droon House was part of an estate that any man would have been proud to own. Lights blazed in the windows of the low-built, rambling manor as Blake drove through spacious, well-kept grounds, where deer roamed among the trees, in peaceful company with strutting partridges, pheasants, and other game birds.

'There's one thing about it, this fellow Droon must have pots of money to keep up a place like this,' remarked Tinker enviously. 'See, there's a private swimming-pool over there, and a golf course just beyond.'

The visitors were evidently expected. A chauffeur was waiting to take their car to the garage, while a majestic, grey-haired butler greeted them in the oak-panelled hall, and took possession of their suitcases.

It was not until he had conducted them to a big, handsomely furnished room on the first floor that the man tendered Blake a sealed envelope.

'Mr Droon instructed me to give you this as soon as you arrived, sir,' he informed stolidly. 'If there is anything else you require, please ring.'

The door closed behind him. Tinker glanced approvingly at the apartment that had been placed at their disposal. A log fire crackled cheerfully in the grate, casting a ruddy glow on the two oak beds and massive, old-fashioned furniture.

Blake slit the envelope, to read the note Lucien Droon had sent him. It was brief, but definite in its wording:

Dear Mr Blake,—Considering the circumstances—which will be fully explained to you before the evening is out—I think it advisable that your true identity be kept secret from other guests in the house.

'*You and your assistant will be introduced as Mr Blakely, and his nephew Mr Curtin. Dinner will be served at seven forty-five, when I shall have the pleasure of making your acquaintance. Don't be surprised at anything that happens.*

LUCIEN DROON

'Huh! That's a good start off! Means we've got to watch our step!' observed Tinker, as he read the missive. 'One slip of the tongue, and you'll spill the beans. Grub's at a quarter to eight. That's the most welcome and definite piece of information Droon's given us as yet.'

There was nothing in the atmosphere of Droon House to invite a suggestion of impending tragedy.

'So far we have seen none of the guests nor even Droon himself,' remarked Blake, as he proceeded to shave and change. 'The man may have some good reason for preserving this atmosphere of secrecy and mystery, but it's none the less strange.'

'The whole thing may be a colossal practical joke, arranged by some of our bright friends,' suggested Tinker, struggling desperately with a highly starched collar. 'One of these potty murder games you read about in the papers, with a dummy dead body, false clues, and all that sort of thing.'

'If that is the case,' said Blake grimly, 'there will be real bloodshed before the night is out. I don't like practical jokes, especially on the subject of murder.'

It was twenty minutes to eight when the sonorous note of a bronze gong boomed through the house. Side by side Blake and Tinker descended the wide sweep of stairs.

The butler was waiting to conduct them to a room at the farther end of the spacious hall.

'Mr Blakely and Mr Curtin,' he announced as he flung open the door.

'Now to meet the four murderers and their victim!' breathed Tinker, as he and the detective stepped over the threshold.

*   *   *

The room was an ante-chamber, with a curtained doorway leading to the brightly lit dining-hall, where a table was laid with snowy napery and gleaming silverware.

It was occupied by four persons—three men and one woman. They were distributed about the room in a distrait, awkward manner, and, of course, in evening clothes.

Sexton Blake surveyed them one by one, in what seemed but a single, swift glance. All were strangers to him.

The woman was strikingly beautiful, and he immediately labelled her as 'dangerous'. Auburn-haired, violet-eyed, and perfect in form and complexion, she stood regally by the fireplace, smoking a cigarette and toying with an empty cocktail glass. Her impersonal gaze was tinged with sudden interest as she studied Sexton Blake's tall, commanding figure.

Near her stood a lithe, handsome, dark-haired man, with hard, black eyes and a neatly trimmed black moustache. Blake decided at once that he was either an Army officer or a professional card-sharper.

Wedged in a chair sat an enormously fat man, with a round, pink, benevolent face, a bald head, and a large, greedy mouth. He smiled in bland appreciation as he sipped a glass of pale sherry.

The third man was almost insignificant in appearance: frail in build, pale of face, and retiring in manner. He occupied a seat in a far corner of the room, clutching his knees with thin, white hands, his eyes blinking nervously behind horn-rimmed spectacles.

'Droon certainly has a varied choice of friends,' thought Blake.

By the silence that greeted his entry he guessed that their host had not, as yet, put in an appearance.

Introductions were out of the question. His polite bow was acknowledged in a like manner. The situation was strained and vaguely apprehensive.

Mechanically Blake accepted an appetiser, tendered to him on a silver tray. Somewhat dubiously Tinker followed suit.

'Mr Droon will be here in a few moments, sir,' informed the butler, in a low voice.

'Queer-looking bunch!' muttered Tinker, under his breath. 'I don't think much of the men, but the woman's a stunner! Droon's a nice sort of host to leave us all parked here like this!'

'The situation is decidedly unusual and awkward,' agreed the detective, in an equally low tone. 'It seems that we all are strangers to one another.'

'Nice, convivial sort of a house-party!' grunted Tinker. 'If there's any murdering to be done, I'd like to start on Droon right away!'

Several minutes passed. Even the butler was looking slightly ill at ease. The fat man finished his glass of sherry and glanced restlessly towards the laid table in the next room.

'Our host appears to be somewhat overdue,' he remarked to no one in particular. 'Does Mr Droon know we are waiting?' he asked, addressing the butler. 'Where is he?'

'Mr Droon is in his study,' answered the man. 'I knocked on the door five minutes ago to inform him that dinner was ready.'

'You'd better knock again,' suggested the tall, dark-haired man curtly, as he lounged against the mantelpiece, with his hands in his pockets, and a sullen look in his hard, black eyes. 'I haven't set eyes on him since I arrived here.'

It struck Blake that the statement was made with unnecessary deliberation. The man seemed anxious to make it known that he and Lucien Droon had not yet met.

The butler disappeared. It was quite five minutes before he came hurrying back, breathing heavily, with an anxious, bewildered look on his face, as he stood in the doorway, staring helplessly at the occupants of the room.

'I don't wish to give any cause for alarm,' he said apologetically. 'But I can't understand what has happened to Mr Droon. He is still in his room, with the door locked, and I can't get any reply.'

'Can't get any reply!' Sexton Blake turned like a flash, all his senses on the alert. 'How do you know Mr Droon is still in his room?'

'The door is locked on the inside, sir. The key is still in the lock.'

'Did he answer you when you knocked before—about ten minutes ago?'

'Yes, sir. He called out, and said that he was coming at once.'

The fat man lifted his mountainous body out of the chair, a startled look in his small, blue eyes.

'Perhaps Mr Droon has been taken ill?' he suggested. 'It seems strange that he should keep us waiting all this while.'

Blake and Tinker glanced grimly at one another, reminded at

once of the true reason of their visit to Droon House.

'I don't like the sound of this, guv'nor,' said Tinker bluntly. 'Yet, in that note he wrote, Droon said: "Don't be surprised at anything that happens." '

The detective nodded, and threw a quick look at the four strangers.

Alarm and uneasiness were written on each face. The woman appeared to be the most composed, as she stood frowning and crumpling the end of her cigarette between her slim, white fingers.

Automatically Blake took control of the situation. The butler made no protest as he gripped him by the arm and urged him from the room.

'Which is Dr Droon's study?'

'At the far end of the hall, sir. The last door.'

Blake tried the handle. The door was securely locked, and the key was on the inner side. There was a light in the room; he could see it shining through the crack under the door.

The detective clenched his fist and beat hard against the stout panels. None but the deaf, or the dead, could have failed to hear the noise he made.

But there was no response—no sound of voice or movement on the other side of the barred door.

'What about the windows?' suggested Tinker. 'Can't we look into the room and see if Mr Droon is there?'

The butler shook his grey head.

'That's the first thing I thought of, sir. The window is fitted with steel shutters, and Mr Droon has always kept them closed and bolted during the past few days. They latch on the inside. It is impossible to open them from without.'

'Then there's only one thing to be done,' said Blake grimly. 'We'll have to break down the door.'

As he drew back, hunching his muscular shoulders and preparing to charge the massive oak barrier, a bell pealed hideously. The sound echoed alarmingly through the big, silent house.

At precisely the same moment, and mixed with the noise of the bell, came a determined rat-tat-tat on the knocker of the front door.

The butler turned whiter than ever as he stared hopelessly at Sexton Blake.

'See who it is,' jerked the detective. 'It may be Mr Droon himself.'

Momentarily the fierce hammering ceased. Over the sudden silence came the throbbing of an engine, a sound of gruff voices, and the rasp of booted feet on the entrance steps.

'Sounds like a police raid to me,' drawled the dark-haired man, as he stood in the hall.

It was a strange remark to make. Blake darted a sharp glance at the man, while the butler walked nervously along the hall to fling open the door.

Metal buttons glittered in the glare of the electric light. Several figures, some clad in familiar blue uniforms, tramped into the hall.

'By gosh, it *is* the police!' exploded Tinker.

The woman uttered a low cry of alarm—the first sound she had made.

Sexton Blake remained silent. He was staring in undisguised amazement at a thick-set, broad-shouldered man, who came strutting along the hall with a hard felt hat cocked aggressively over one eye, a pugnacious expression on his florid, red-moustached face.

Recognition was mutual.

Detective-Inspector Coutts, of the Criminal Investigation Department, New Scotland Yard, stopped dead, his eyes bulging in astonishment, as he glimpsed the tall figure of the Baker Street detective.

'How the blazes did you get here, Blake?' he exclaimed incredulously. 'Does nothing ever happen that you're not first on the scene?'

'First on the scene! What do you mean by that?'

Towering over Coutts, with a couple of constables pressing close on his heels, stood a hawk-nosed, hatchet-faced inspector of the local police.

'Let's hear all about it!' he demanded officiously, pushing his way farther into the hall. 'Where's the body? Who telephoned through to the police station and reported that Mr Lucien Droon had been murdered? Who's this man, Mr Coutts?'

'Sexton Blake,' answered Coutts promptly.

'That has properly spilled the beans!' muttered Tinker under his breath.

Blake glanced towards the people clustered in the doorway to the right of the hall. The auburn-haired woman had turned as white as death; the fat man seemed to have shrunken to half his size, like a punctured balloon, as he stared glassily at the Baker Street detective.

The insignificant individual with the spectacles had not left his seat. Only the dark-haired man retained any traces of composure.

Yet on every face was stamped an expression of fear.

*   *   *

The mystery of the locked room at the end of the hall now assumed a new and more sinister significance to Sexton Blake.

Drawing Coutts and the hawk-faced inspector to one side, he explained in brief sentences just how he came to be present at Droon House, and described all that had occurred since his arrival.

'It's by sheer chance that I happen to be here,' jerked Coutts excitedly. 'I came to Mayes this evening to consult with Inspector Rawson regarding the Lipping Green poisoning case. Not ten minutes ago an urgent telephone-call was put through to the police station.'

'It was a man speaking,' intervened Inspector Rawson, who had answered the telephone. 'He asked the police to come at once to Droon House, as Mr Lucien Droon had been found murdered. Do you mean to say there's no truth in it? That the whole thing's a spoof?'

Sexton Blake glanced grimly towards the locked door at the far end of the hall.

'There may be a lot of truth in it,' he said meaningly. 'But we shan't know for certain until we force a way into that room. But first of all—'

He murmured a suggestion to Inspector Rawson. The latter turned officiously to the four mysterious strangers who formed the remaining members of Lucien Droon's house-party.

'No one can be permitted to leave this house,' he said brusquely. 'You people will kindly go back into that room and remain there for the time being.'

The men made no protest; the woman threw a cold, scornful glance at the police as she obeyed the peremptory order.

'According to Blake's story, if anything has happened to Droon, one of those four knows all about it,' declared Coutts. 'Get one of your men to keep an eye on them, Rawson. Plant him in the same room and tell him to keep his ears open. Of course, the whole thing may be a spoof. The sooner we get into that room the better.'

In grim silence Blake and his companions approached the locked door. A burly, sixteen-stone constable tried it with his shoulder.

' 'Tis a mighty strong door,' he remarked, 'with a broth of a lock, and a bolt top and bottom. Whoever shut himself in there didn't intend to be disturbed.'

'He's going to be disturbed within the next few seconds,' grunted Rawson. 'Never mind damaging the door, O'Mally; go to it, man!'

O'Mally accepted the challenge. He drew back, charged like a bull, and planted the sole of a huge foot in the region of the lock. The door creaked and groaned, but stood firm. A second kick shattered one of the hinges. The third onslaught sent door and man toppling into the room beyond.

A blaze of light streamed through the aperture. Blake caught a glimpse of a lofty room, with bookshelves, handsome oil paintings, and numerous trophies of the chase—the snarling masks of tigers and lions, antlers of elk and deer, and the great grey head of an African elephant.

'By heavens!' exclaimed Coutts in an awed whisper.

Seated at a desk in the centre of the room was the motionless figure of a man in evening-dress. He had fallen forward in the chair with his iron-grey head pillowed on his arms.

He might have been asleep, but for the damning evidence of a brass-handled dagger that was buried to the hilt between his shoulders.

'It's the master—it's Mr Droon!' choked the butler, white-faced and trembling like a leaf.

Death had come to Lucien Droon with the swiftness of a thunderbolt. The merciless dagger-thrust had been instantaneous in its effect.

Blake's lips tightened as he crossed the room to the motionless figure at the big writing-table.

'Stabbed clean through the heart!' jerked Coutts in a hushed voice. 'Murderer must have crept up behind him and polished him off with one stroke.'

Blake nodded as he glanced at the brass-handled dagger, buried to the hilt beneath the man's left shoulder-blade. A great amount of force must have been used. The murder was particularly cold-blooded and deliberate. There was, of course, no question of suicide. Lucien Droon had been savagely done to death.

'Don't touch that dagger,' ordered Inspector Rawson, needlessly. 'There may be fingerprints on it.'

'I doubt it. Probably the murderer wore gloves,' remarked Blake. 'Droon has not been dead for more than half an hour, at the most.'

He shook his head puzzledly as his keen eyes swept every corner of the room.

'What I should like to know,' he said quietly, 'is how did the murderer make his escape? How did he get out of this room, with the door locked and bolted on the inside, and steel shutters fastened over the windows?'

Inspector Rawson rubbed his chin blankly as he digested the detective's comment. It seemed humanly impossible for Droon's murderer to have left the room. The steel shutters at the windows were latched on the inside, and it had taken several minutes to break open the massive oak door.

Coutts poked and probed into every corner of the room. There was no place where a dog could have lain concealed, let alone a human being. There were no cupboards. The recesses by the fireplace were filled with bookshelves. The floor was of parquet, and the walls as solid as marble.

No one could have left the apartment. Yet Lucien Droon had been stabbed through the heart within the past half-hour, and his murderer had disappeared into thin air!

It was certainly a mystery. Coutts stared helplessly at his companions. There was not the slightest clue to the manner in which Droon had been slain, alone in the room, with barred door and shuttered windows.

'It's uncanny!' said the CID man bluntly.

'Droon was a true prophet,' remarked Blake meaningly. 'He knew he was going to be murdered, yet he must have been taken completely by surprise when the fatal blow was struck.'

'It would seem that one of those four persons in the dining-room must be the murderer,' declared Inspector Rawson. He suddenly slapped his thigh in a gesture of tense excitement.

'What about the man who rang through to the police-station and announced that Droon had been murdered!' he barked. 'It must have been the murderer himself! Who else could have known that the man was dead!'

Blake nodded. He threw a sharp glance at the pallid-faced butler.

'According to this fellow, Droon was alive a quarter of an hour ago, when he knocked on the door to announce that dinner was served. And at that time Droon's four guests were gathered together in the same room. They were there when Tinker and I came downstairs.'

'That means they all have a cast-iron alibi,' exclaimed Coutts incredulously.

'Seems like it,' agreed Blake. 'Unless—' He turned again to the butler. 'Are you quite certain that Mr Droon answered you on the first occasion when you knocked at the door?'

'There's not the slightest doubt about it sir!' declared the man vigorously. 'Mr Droon called out, and said that he would be along in a couple of minutes.'

'Then he was alive at that time,' muttered Rawson perplexedly.

'It may have been the murderer who answered, and not Droon at all,' suggested Tinker.

'Then it could not have been any one of the four guests—the three men and the woman,' pointed out Blake. 'Yet we have the dead man's own word for it—reason enough to assume that one of them is the murderer.'

'The biggest mystery to me,' jerked Coutts, 'is, how did the guilty person get out of this room after he, or she, had stabbed Droon in the back?'

'It doesn't seem possible; but it must have happened,' averred Blake. 'There must be some other exit from this room which we have yet to discover. That can wait. Let us tackle one point at a time.

'The message to the police station was probably telephoned from this house. How many telephones are there here, and where are they situated?'

'There is only one telephone,' replied the butler definitely. 'And it is here in this room.'

He pointed to an instrument that stood on the writing-table

within a few inches of the dead man.

'Then the message came from here!' exclaimed Inspector Rawson. 'It must have been the murderer! Droon would scarcely ring through to announce his own death. He died instantly. Possibly he never saw the person that stabbed him.'

The inspector lifted the receiver and called the exchange.

'No doubt about it,' he declared, a few minutes later. 'The operator states that it was exactly half an hour ago when someone rang through from here, and asked to be connected with the police station. It was a man's voice.'

'That's one point in favour of the woman in the case,' said Blake. 'We can assume that Droon was already dead when the message was phoned. Yet the butler declares that Droon answered him when he knocked at the door.'

'It sounded like Mr Droon's voice,' assured the man.

'Ten to one it wasn't!' exclaimed Rawson. 'But why the dickens should the murderer go out of his way to send for the police?'

'A touch of bravado,' decided Blake. 'He must have been confident that there was little likelihood of his being suspected or arrested.'

'Maybe he's right!' muttered Coutts grimly. 'It strikes me we're going to have a dickens of a job to prove that any one of Droon's four guests could possibly have committed the murder.'

'Yet one of them must be the guilty person!' Inspector Rawson spoke positively, and added: 'Droon had good reason to know that his life was in danger, and he definitely informed Mr Blake that the potential killer was one of the four guests in his house.'

'That is so,' concurred the detective thoughtfully. 'We have four suspects. Possibly we shall learn more when we get them to give an account of themselves.'

By this time the police surgeon had arrived on the scene. So far the body of the murdered man had not been disturbed. It remained sprawled face-downwards across the writing-table, with the knife-handle glittering brightly in the glare of the electric light.

Lucien Droon was a well-built middle-aged man, with iron grey hair and moustache. He was immaculately garbed, in a dinner-jacket suit, spotless linen, and patent-leather shoes. The expression on his face conveyed nothing of the horrors of violent death.

'He died instantly,' was the surgeon's verdict, as he made his examination and carefully withdrew the dagger from the fatal wound. 'I doubt if he even felt that stab that killed him. Nasty-looking weapon, that ought to prove a useful clue, gentlemen.'

Blake examined the dagger with keen interest. It was an unusual type of weapon with a needle-point, six-inch steel blade and a smooth brass haft fashioned in the form of a cross; it was a solid affair and finely balanced. There was no inscription on the blade to give any clue as to where it had been made.

'Looks like a home-made knife,' jerked Coutts, looking in vain for any trace of fingerprints on the handle.

'Ever seen it before?'

He glared challengingly at the butler.

The man shook his head vigorously, shrinking back from the crimson-stained weapon.

'I've never seen it before,' he declared. 'I can assure you that Mr Droon never owned a knife like that.'

Sexton Blake surveyed the walls of the room. It struck him that there were plenty of weapons handy that the murderer might have used. Lucien Droon had been either a much-travelled man, or an inveterate collector of sporting trophies. Staring glassy-eyed down at him were the stuffed masks of many handsome specimens of big game, mixed with a variety of native swords, spears, shields, and other relics of foreign climes, including a few stiletto-type daggers.

From one wall glared a snarling tiger and a magnificent Nubian lion; on another hung the huge head of an African elephant with upturned trunk, gaping mouth, and bristling, ivory tusks.

'Blake, have a look at this! Here's something like a clue at last!'

Coutts' voice was sharp with excitement as he stood over the writing-table on which Droon's lifeless figure had sprawled. The body had now been lifted up in the chair, revealing the fact that the man had been engaged in the task of writing at the moment when a murderer's hand had struck him down.

A pen was still gripped in the fingers of one hand on the blotter, on which several lines of writing had been inscribed. They were the last words Lucien Droon would ever pen.

To Sexton Blake, he had written. *In the event of my death you will find hidden in this room evidence which will enable you to trace the hand that caused my end. One of four people gathered together in this house will be the guilty party.*

To find the necessary proofs, turn back—

The writing ended abruptly in a long ink smear caused by Droon having toppled forward on the blotter with an assassin's knife buried between his shoulders.

'That proves Droon was taken by surprise,' declared Coutts emphatically. 'He was in the act of writing that message.'

'Probably you're right,' agreed Blake cautiously. 'But it doesn't explain how the guilty party gained admittance to this room, or how he departed, leaving the door bolted and the windows shuttered and fastened on the inside.'

'Nab the murderer, and we'll soon find out all about it,' said Inspector Rawson grimly. 'It's one of the four people staying in this house. According to what Droon wrote, we'll find proofs of the killer's identity hidden in this room. See what it says. "To find the necessary proofs, turn back—" Turn back what?'

'The carpet, perhaps,' suggested Tinker.

But there was no carpet in the room. The polished parquet floor was dotted with a number of animal skins and costly Persian rugs. These Coutts kicked to one side and proceeded to examine every square inch of the neatly fitting wood blocks.

The search was fruitless. Blake was surprised to find that the drawers to the dead man's writing-table were empty—save for paper, envelopes, a stick of sealing-wax, and a railway guide. There was nothing in Droon's pockets beyond watch and keys.

The entire room was searched with meticulous care, even to the books on the shelves and the pictures on the walls. There was no hidden safe, or anything of that nature. Absolutely nothing was discovered that gave the slightest clue to the murderer of Lucien Droon. The room might, indeed, have been contrived for the effect of mystification it was now producing.

'Now, I wonder what the dickens the man was driving at when he wrote that letter?' muttered Coutts, with a puzzled shake of his head. 'Curse it! He seemed almost anxious to be murdered. It's a pity he didn't finish it. We don't know what kind of proofs to look for.'

'Papers, most likely,' decided Blake. 'Easy things to hide, and darned difficult to find.'

'It seems strange that the murderer left that message there, instead of destroying it,' remarked Tinker.

'I don't suppose he saw it,' grunted Coutts. 'It was hidden by Droon's body as he fell forward on the table.'

'On the other hand,' suggested Blake, 'he may have read the message, searched the room, and discovered the incriminating proofs we are unable to find.'

'Never thought of that.' Inspector Rawson scowled blackly. 'There's only one thing to be done!' he snapped. 'We'll have those four people in here one at a time and run the rule over them. Mebbe they'll come through with the truth when they learn that Droon accused them of being likely to make an attempt on his life.'

'Just what I was going to advise,' nodded Blake. 'Ladies first, Rawson—and be careful how you handle her. This thing is going to take a lot of solving.'

*   *   *

It was a grim and unpleasant task that Blake and his companions had to take in hand. A blanket was draped over the body of Lucien Droon, while Rawson departed to fetch the first of Droon's mysterious guests.

The pretty, auburn-haired woman seemed to be entirely unperturbed as she was ushered into the brightly lit room. She threw a quick glance at the shrouded figure of the murdered man and turned her violet eyes coolly on Blake's tall, stern form.

'Is it true that Mr Droon has been murdered?' she asked evenly.

'It is!' broke in Coutts bluntly. 'You must realise that everyone is under suspicion, and nobody will be permitted to leave this house until the murderer has been found.'

'A trifle compromising for me,' said the woman, with a shrug of her white shoulders. 'I am the only woman in the house, with the exception of Mr Droon's cook and housekeeper.'

'We'll soon find you a chaperon, if that's all that's worrying you,' assured Inspector Rawson. 'Have you any idea who killed Droon?'

'Not the slightest,' came the instant reply. 'Surely it is your duty to find that out.'

'We're going to do it!' snapped Rawson. 'We've already got a pretty good idea who sneaked in here and stuck a knife in Droon's back.'

'He was stabbed?' The woman expressed mild surprise as she threw another fleeting glance at the blanket-draped figure. 'I can't think of anyone who would have any reason for wishing to do Lucien Droon an injury.'

Coutts smiled knowingly at the thought of the statements Droon had made in the letter he had addressed to Sexton Blake.

'Mr Droon was a friend of yours?' suggested the Baker Street detective.

'Exactly—or I should not be here. I have known him for many years,' claimed the woman. Without waiting to be questioned she gave her name as Isabelle Page, and an address in Kensington. She was a widow of independent means.

'How does it come,' asked Blake politely, 'that you are a guest in this house?'

'Mr Droon wrote, inviting me to join his house-party. I arrived little more than an hour ago. I had not seen Mr Droon—until now!'

She winced slightly as her eyes glimpsed the dead man.

'Is there any particular reason *why* Mr Droon asked you to come here?' demanded Coutts.

'Not that I know of. He said nothing in his letter. You can read it for yourself.'

Isabelle Page extracted an envelope from the evening bag she carried. The writing was similar to the strange message Sexton Blake had received. The letter was brief and friendly in tone. Droon stated that he would be delighted if Mrs Page would join his party at Droon House over the weekend.

Coutts and Blake stared at one another. This did not seem to be a very promising start.

'Mrs Page,' said the detective suddenly, 'you know who I am?'

'Certainly,' smiled the woman. 'You are Sexton Blake. Apparently you were here in the house *before* Mr Droon was murdered. That leads me to believe that Mr Droon sent for you, possibly because he had an idea that his life was in danger.'

'Ah! So you know that, do you?' challenged Inspector Rawson suspiciously. 'And do you know that, before his death, Mr Droon informed Mr Blake that he had reason to believe that *you* might make an attempt on his life?'

Isabelle Page was either a magnificent actress, or absolutely innocent of any complicity in the crime. She stared incredulously

381

at the detectives, a blaze of indignation kindling in her eyes.

'That is an outrageous suggestion to make,' she said contemptuously. 'There is not the slightest reason why Lucien Droon should say such a thing. I make an attempt on his life? It is absurd!'

Sexton Blake frowned. Somehow he believed the woman's heated denial to be genuine.

'Droon made no direct accusation,' he said placatingly. 'There was no mention of names. But he did say that he went in fear of his life, and that if anything happened to him the guilty person would be one of the four guests in this house.'

'I suggest,' said the woman disdainfully, 'that you direct your suspicions at the other three. They are complete strangers to me. I have never seen the three men before, but they all claim to be old friends of Lucien Droon's.'

Blake raised his eyebrows in surprise. It seemed strange that Droon's house-party was comprised of four persons who, apparently, were unknown to one another. The circumstances had led him to look upon them as four possible conspirators.

The detective played his trump card.

'We shall soon know who the murderer is,' he said firmly. 'The proofs of the guilty party's identity are here in this room.'

He handed Isabelle Page the incompleted note the dead man had written. The woman never turned a hair as she read it through. If anything, her expression was one of relief.

'Then you have only to find these proofs to enable you to arrest the murderer?' she said, almost gladly. 'That at least will clear me of any suspicion.'

'Unfortunately we cannot find the proofs,' confessed Blake, ignoring an angry glare from Coutts. 'But we know they are hidden somewhere in this room. I don't think we need trouble Mrs Page any further. I suggest she goes straight to her room and remains there until the morning.'

Isabelle Page walked unhurriedly from the room, while Inspector Rawson departed in search of the next victim of their mild inquisition.

'Why the dickens did you tell that woman we hadn't found the proofs, Blake?' grumbled Coutts irascibly. 'It was a stupid sort of slip to make.'

'Nothing of the kind,' denied the detective calmly. 'I want all four suspects to know that the proofs have not been discovered, but are still hidden here in this room.'

Coutts rubbed his chin bewilderedly. Rawson returned, accompanied by the sleek, dark-haired man, with the restless black eyes.

The man was palpably ill at ease. His lips twitched nervously as he glanced at the blanket-covered body of Lucien Droon.

'Droon dead—murdered! I can't believe it,' he said unsteadily. 'Who killed him?'

'Perhaps you did?' suggested Coutts, without any beating about the bush.

'Me kill Droon? You must be crazy!' exploded the man, his voice shrill with alarm. 'I've known Droon for years, but I haven't set eyes on him since I entered this house at seven o'clock tonight.'

The man was subjected to a similar catechism to the one Isabelle Page had undergone. His explanation was almost the same as the woman's. His name was Philip Roe. He lived in chambers in Jermyn Street, and enjoyed a private income. He produced a brief, friendly note from the dead man, inviting him to spend the week at Droon House. It was the first time he had set eyes on Isabelle Page or the other two members of the party.

'Droon must have gone off his head,' he declared wildly. 'There's no earthly reason why he should suspect me of trying to kill him.'

Blake watched the man keenly as he handed him Droon's unfinished message. Roe's hands trembled, and he sucked in his breath nervously as he read the written words.

'You have found these proofs?' he jerked. 'Then—then you know who murdered Droon?'

'We do not. We have not yet found the proofs; but we know they are hidden somewhere in this room,' informed Blake. 'Tomorrow morning we intend instituting a thorough search. In the meantime, you had better go to your room and stay there, Mr Roe.'

'I'd sooner go home,' said Philip Roe, with a shudder. 'It's horrible to think of sleeping in the same house with a dead man—and his murderer.'

'You will be quite safe,' assured Blake dryly. He shook his head puzzledly as Roe left the room. 'Hang it all, Coutts, we're not getting any further at all. I don't believe that fellow is the guilty one, though the mention of hidden proofs seemed to shake his nerve a bit.'

'The murderer must be one of these four people,' vowed Inspector Rawson, combing his moustache with hard fingers. 'Either that, or Droon was out of his mind when he wrote those letters.'

'The fact remains that he was murdered,' remarked Blake, pointedly. 'His fear of a violent death, at least, was no delusion. Let's hear what the last two men have to say for themselves. It seems that one of them *must* be the killer!'

The fat, bald-headed man was the next to submit to interrogation. He was amazed, indignant, and confident by turns. He was a retired business man. His name was George Grubb, and he had known Lucien Droon for some years. He, too, produced a letter of invitation to the house, and had not the slightest idea who could have a motive for taking Droon's life.

Yet there was every evidence of uneasiness in his flabby face as he read the dead man's last written words, and asked haltingly if the proofs of the murderer's identity had been found.

Sexton Blake gave him the same answer as the other two had received. Mr Grubb was dispatched to his room, quaking like a jelly.

'That man has not got the pluck to commit a murder,' mused Blake. 'But I wouldn't trust him any farther than I could throw him. Fetch in our last hope, Rawson.'

There was nothing new to be learned from Mr Septimus Trull, the insignificant-looking little man, who described himself as an analytical chemist, who had known Lucien Droon for several years.

He was horrified to learn of his friend's terrible death. He could throw no light on the affair. Yet once again the reading of Droon's unfinished letter produced unmistakable signs of alarm and uneasiness that were compatible with a guilty conscience.

'Tomorrow we shall find the hidden proofs and be able to get a line on the murderer,' assured Blake.

Mr Trull was conducted to his room with instructions to remain there until the morning.

Sexton Blake lit a cigar and smiled grimly at sight of the perplexed, baffled expressions on the faces of his companions.

'There's only one thing to it,' declared Inspector Rawson, thumping the table with his fist. 'One of those four people was deliberately lying!'

'As a matter of fact, all four of them were deliberately lying,' corrected Blake. 'They are keeping something back. Yet they are strangers to one another, and it seems extremely probable that one of them is the murderer.'

'Yes. But which one?' growled Coutts, running his fingers through his stiff hair. 'I can't make anything of this case, Blake. If it comes to the point, each of those four can prove that they were together in a room with you and Tinker about the time Lucien Droon was killed, and I don't know what better alibi they could have than that.'

'We don't know for certain the time Droon was killed,' observed the detective. 'If it was the murderer that answered the butler's knock, imitating the victim's voice, then Droon may have been dead for some time before Tinker and I came downstairs.

'There's just one thing that's got me absolutely baffled,' continued the detective candidly. 'Droon was stabbed in this room, with the door bolted, and the windows fastened on the inside. How, in the name of all that's wonderful, did the murderer get out of this room?'

There was no answer to the question. It seemed utterly impossible that anyone could have left the room once the door had been bolted and the shutters latched.

Blake waited until the body of the murdered man had been removed to the police mortuary; then he and his companions, aided by a couple of constables, made another thorough search of the death-chamber.

Nothing was overlooked. Every square inch of walls, floors, and ceiling were tapped and found to be perfectly solid. There was no secret exit. The fireplace provided no way of escape from the room; the narrow chimney would not have admitted a cat. Windows and frames were immovable.

There was no trick in regard to the door that had been forced open. Blake himself sent for the necessary tools with which to repair the broken lock, hinges, and bolt.

'What's the idea in doing that now?' inquired Coutts, working on the fact that their second search of the room had failed to reveal any clue that might lead to the tracing of Lucien Droon's slayer. 'If there's anything hidden in this room we should have found it.'

Blake tolerantly reminded him that Messrs Roe, Grubb, and Trull, and Mrs Isabelle Page had been given the impression that any further search for the mysterious 'proofs' mentioned in Droon's incompleted letter would not be pursued until the morning.

'Meaning,' he remarked, 'that if the murderer is still in the house, and is fearful that evidence of his identity is still concealed here, he—or she—may attempt to institute a search of their own during the night.'

'I see,' ruminated the CID man. 'You mean to keep your ears and eyes open, building on the theory that anyone who attempts to enter this room before morning will be the guilty party?'

'Your perspicacity is dazzling,' smiled Blake. 'Joking apart, I mean exactly what you have suggested, but I am not anticipating that the hunch I am following will have any result.'

Inspector Rawson decided to withdraw his men and leave matters in the hands of Blake and Coutts. It was his intention to return to the house first thing in the morning to see if he could get any nearer solving the mystery of Lucien Droon's baffling murder.

'In the meantime,' he said heavily, 'I have given instructions that no one is to leave the premises. Any attempt to do so will be construed as a sign of guilt. That, of course, applies only to the four suspects, and the servants in the house. I shall leave one constable on patrol outside in case you may need him.'

Blake had no intention of returning to Baker Street that night. He sent for Bellamy, the butler, to ask him several pointed questions, by which he elicited the information that the rooms occupied by Roe, Grubb, Trull, and Mrs Page were all situated on the first floor.

Other apartments were readily placed at the disposal of the detective, his assistant, and the Scotland Yard man. Tinker was the first to take advantage of this accommodation. It was eleven o'clock when he went to bed. In the meantime Coutts had been busily engaged with the telephone, communicating with his immediate superiors at headquarters.

The house of death was wrapped in a fitting silence. Closing the door to Droon's den and extinguishing the lights, Blake and Coutts parked themselves in a room on the opposite side of the hall.

There was no attempt at conversation. Both were using all their mental powers in an effort to solve the riddle of the locked room in which the owner of Droon House had met his end.

For the hundredth time Blake reviewed all the possible suspects in the case. He was compelled to attach his suspicions to the persons Droon himself had designated as likely to attempt his life. The similarity of their stories pointed to collusion, yet each had claimed to be an absolute stranger to the others.

'The most likely party—on form, as a follower of the Turf would say,' decided Blake, shortly after a clock in the hall had struck twelve—'is Philip Roe. And yet there is not a shred of proof against him, no more than there is against Grubb, Trull, and the woman.

'All four came here at Droon's written invitation. Why should a man invite his potential murderers to be his guests? On his own admittance he suspected each of them, yet he displayed no haste to invite me into his confidence. Either he did not anticipate any immediate danger, or he wished to commit suicide by proxy.'

Another hour passed without any suspicious sound to disturb the silence of the sleeping house. At two o'clock Coutts woke up and decided it was time he went to bed. Blake remained seated just inside the partly closed door, with an empty pipe clamped between his teeth.

His lonely vigil promised to be a fruitless one. If the murderer was still on the premises he made no attempt to visit Droon's study in search of the evidence that would proclaim his guilt.

It was close on four when the detective concluded that he might just as well follow Coutts' example and turn in. He satisfied himself that the room opposite had not been visited before he ascended the stairs, and then entered his own apartment.

Tinker was sleeping soundly. Blake removed his coat, kicked off his shoes, and flung himself on the bed. Ten seconds later he was on his feet again, ears strained, every sense on the alert.

A board had creaked.

Someone had crept past the door and along the passage in the direction of the stairs.

Silent as a ghost the detective glided across the room and invaded the pitch-blackness that lay beyond. He could see nothing and hear nothing, save the pounding of his own heart. He knew that the rooms directly adjoining his own were occupied by George Grubb and Philip Roe. Grubb weighed close on twenty stone. It was unlikely that he could pass so stealthily along the corridor.

Inch by inch Blake sidled along the wall, fumbling until he found the newel-post at the head of the wide stairs. Immediately below he sensed sounds of movements—the click of a latch and the faint whine of a door being opened.

A thread of light split the darkness—the light, perhaps, from the broken and imperfectly fitting door. The prowler, whoever it was, had entered the room of mystery, closed the door behind him, and switched on the electric light.

Blake folded himself over the smooth banister to slide noiselessly to the foot of the stairs. He felt that he was on the verge of solving the mystery of Lucien Droon's unknown slayer. The murderer was revisiting the scene of his crime, intent on discovering and destroying the hidden evidence of his guilt.

The detective was unarmed, but the element of surprise was in his favour. He reached the door, sank to his knees, and applied an eye to the keyhole. He could see nothing but a narrow segment of the carpet. The key was in the lock on the inner side. But he heard certain sounds to convince him that someone was pulling open the drawers to the writing-table in the centre of the room.

Blake hesitated for no longer than a matter of seconds. The time for action had arrived. He received a jarring shock of disappointment as he clutched hold of the door-handle, turning it, while he pressed his shoulder against the panels.

The door was unyielding. Whoever had entered the room had shot the bolts and locked himself inside.

Blake suppressed a sound desire to kick himself. It was he who had been at such pains to repair the fastenings of the broken door earlier in the evening, with the result that he had given his quarry an unintended advantage.

The man was locked in, while he was locked out. By the time he forced a way into the room a lot of things might have happened. And already strange things were happening.

From the other side of the door came a rapid succession of sounds. The first was a dull, heavy thud, like the impact of a clenched fist against a padded seat.

Immediately after came a stifled gasp, a low groan of mortal agony, and the muffled crash of some heavy, inert object toppling to the floor.

Blake felt the hair bristling on his scalp as he stood close up against the door, with the beat of his pulse drumming in his ears. Something seemed to tell him that, for the second time that day, death had visited the locked room at Droon House!

Discarding all caution, he rattled the handle fiercely, and threw all his weight against the stout panels, setting up a din that echoed through the silent house.

'Who's inside there? Open this door before I break it down!'

There was no response, neither had he expected one. The door stood firm, challenging the swing of his shoulders and the combined force of weight and muscle.

Again and again the detective threw himself against the massive barrier of solid oak, realising painfully that he had made a good job of his recent efforts to repair the wrenched hinges and twisted bolts. The door itself was splintered along the edges of the stiles, but the fastenings held firm.

Click! The hall suddenly was flooded with light as someone pressed the electric switch. At the head of the wide stairs appeared the dishevelled, bewildered figure of Inspector Coutts, his hair standing straight on end, his sleep-heavy eyes bulging with alarm.

'Blake for the love of Heaven what's happening now?' he blurted, as he caught sight of the detective, crouched in the hall below.

'Guv'nor, where are you?' It was Tinker's voice, sharp with anxiety as the lad came hurrying along the passage to Coutts' side.

'Give me a hand with this infernal door!' panted Blake, rubbing his bruised shoulder, and regretting the fact that he wore no shoes. 'There's a man locked inside this room!'

'What's that? A man inside—'

Coutts and Tinker descended the stairs like a human avalanche. Close behind them came the white-faced, trembling butler, a heavy poker clutched in one hand.

Alarmed voices rang through the house. The next to appear at the head of the stairs was the huge, quaking figure of Mr George Grubb, enveloped in a flamboyant dressing-gown.

Blake snatched the poker from the butler's hand, thrust it into the narrow crevice between door and jamb.

'Something queer's been happening inside this room!' he jerked, levering the stout metal bar amid a harsh splintering of rending woodwork. 'I don't know who's inside; but we'll soon find out. Bellamy, run outside and see if you can find that constable who was left on guard. Tell him to keep an eye on the windows at the back of the house, in case anyone tries to escape.'

The butler hastened to obey. Blake's eyes were fierce with excitement and determination as he wielded the poker, wrenching and battering at the bolted door.

'Who is the man?' queried Coutts, as he added his weight to the crashing onslaught.

'I don't know. I didn't see him!' panted the detective. 'But he came from one of the rooms on the first floor.'

'Then it can't be Grubb,' declared Tinker. 'There he is at the top of the stairs, scared stiff with fright. It must be either Roe or Trull.'

'Or the Page woman,' suggested Coutts, drawing back for a final charge. 'Both together, Blake!'

The door quivered, sagged, and with a last rending crash, swung back on its hinges.

Blake was first across the threshold, brandishing the twisted poker recklessly in one hand. One glance at the interior of the room wrenched a gasp of amazement and horror from his lips. The scene was entirely different from what he had been led to expect.

Sprawled face-downward on the floor, just behind the late Lucien Droon's writing-table, was the motionless figure of a man. His face was hidden, but no one could help seeing the brass-handled dagger that was buried to the hilt in his back, two inches below the left shoulder-blade!

The room was exactly as Blake had last seen it, except that the drawers to the writing-table had been wrenched open, and their contents scattered on the floor. The windows were closed, and steel shutters securely fastened.

'By thunder, the man's dead!' exclaimed Coutts huskily. 'Murdered in exactly the same way as Lucien Droon!'

'And with exactly the same type of weapon!' jerked Blake.

He stepped forward, his hands trembling slightly as he lifted the dead man's limp, lolling head and turned it sideways.

The face revealed was that of Philip Roe, his eyes wide open in an expression of blank surprise.

The detectives stared aghast at one another. Mystery was piled on mystery—murder on murder! First Lucien Droon, and now the man Blake had strongly suspected of being the original slayer!

Roe's alibi was tragically complete. He was the second victim of Lucien Droon's mysterious, phantom killer. Yet he, obviously, was the man who had crept down in the night, to lock himself in the death-chamber and search for proofs of the murderer's identity.

*　　*　　*

'Murder in duplicate!' were the words that flashed through Sexton Blake's mind as he surveyed the grim scene, so similar in almost every aspect to the one that had greeted his eyes on the first occasion they had invaded the death-chamber.

The circumstances were exactly the same, with the exception that Philip Roe was clad in dressing-gown and pyjamas, and lay sprawled on the floor behind the writing-table, instead of huddled in a chair, as Lucien Droon had been.

The lights were full on, the windows closed, and the steel shutters latched. The door had been locked and bolted on the inner side.

The man had been stabbed in the back within the last five minutes, yet there was no sign of the murderer.

Tinker shivered. The whole thing was too uncanny for words. He was not superstitious, but he failed to see how any human being, of ordinary flesh and blood, could have escaped from the room after the crime had been committed.

It seemed more like the fell work of a ghoul, or some other world, beyond earthly conception.

'By thunder, it's Philip Roe, sure enough!' exclaimed Coutts, in a strained voice. 'Stabbed—just as Droon was stabbed! And with the same type of dagger! No question about it—the murderer is still in the house!'

Blake nodded as he bent to examine the weapon that was embedded beneath the dead man's left shoulder-blade. Terrible force had been used by the hand that had struck the fatal blow. Yet there were no sign of fingerprints on the brass cruciform haft.

He went over it minutely with a powerful pocket lense. There were no tiny scraps of lint to indicate that it had been wiped with a cloth, after use. The metal was scrupulously clean and brightly polished.

'This clears Roe of any suspicion of Droon's death,' jerked

Coutts. 'That leaves the woman and the two other men.'

'I hope you do not include me in that statement,' protested George Grubb, trembling and white-faced with horror, as he surveyed the corpse of Philip Roe. 'I have not left my room until just now, when I was disturbed by the clamour. Bellamy, the butler, can prove that I was just opening the door as he came past.'

'That's quite true, gentlemen,' substantiated the butler. 'Mr Grubb was in his room when Mr Blake first gave the alarm.'

'Shut up!' snapped Coutts, for no other reason save that the obese Grubb seemed to be on the verge of another outburst of indignant protestations. 'No one's accused you of anything—as yet! What about it, Blake? Where's Trull and the Page woman?'

Blake straightened his back and turned towards the door.

'I'll attend to them,' he said shortly. 'In the meantime, telephone to Inspector Rawson—tell him to hurry along with the police surgeon.'

The detective went up the stairs three treads at a time, switching on each light he came to. The door to Isabelle Page's room was the first along the right-hand passage. He rapped sharply with bunched knuckles.

'Come in!' was the instant response.

Blake was disconcerted to find the woman lying in bed, smoking a cigarette, with her glorious hair spread like a crimson halo on the white pillow. She surveyed him coolly, with a hint of amusement in her eyes at sight of the confused expression on his flushed face.

'Philip Roe has been murdered,' remarked Blake deliberately. 'Have you been here all time?'

'Certainly. I was instructed not to leave my room,' answered Isabelle Page, flicking the ash from her cigarette with a sweep of one bare, white arm. 'So that is what all the disturbance is about? Mr Roe has been murdered? What might *you* have been doing at the time?' she asked mockingly. 'Really, Mr Blake, your presence in the house seems a distinct incitement to crime! I begin to fear for my own safety.

'I am not conventional,' she added, sitting up and clasping her knees with her arms. 'If you would care to take a chair and tell me all about this latest tragedy—'

Sexton Blake closed the door with a bang. It was difficult to deal with a woman in a négligé, especially a woman so attractive and so self-composed as Isabelle Page, murderess though she might be.

His temper was on edge as he stalked along the passage and beat a thunderous tattoo on the door of Septimus Trull's apartment.

There was a slight delay before the latch clicked and the door swung open.

Trull stood on the threshold, a dazed, bewildered expression on his pale, bespectacled face. In one hand he held a brass-hafted dagger—an exact replica of the one that had been found embedded in Philip Roe's back!

Blake's eyes narrowed. His shoulders hunched in a defensive attitude.

'All ready for your next victim, Trull?' he snapped grimly.

The man blinked his eyes uneasily and made a helpless little gesture.

'Really, Mr Blake, I don't know what you are talking about,' he said weakly. 'Your suspicions are most unjust.'

Blake stared hard at the incriminating dagger.

'A most extraordinary thing has happened,' continued Trull, with almost pathetic emphasis. 'Awakened by a sudden commotion, I reached beneath the pillow for my watch to see what the time was. This is what I found—hidden under the bolster!'

He held out the dagger, with its slender, wicked-looking blade and its brass handle. He made no attempt to prevent the detective taking it from his fingers.

'I don't know how it came to be there—I have never seen it before. Did—did I understand you to say that Mr Roe had been murdered?'

Blake stared sharply at the shrinking, inoffensive-looking little man.

'Trull, you're either a cunning scoundrel and an infernal liar, or an innocent man!' he said coldly. 'That remains to be seen. What are you doing fully dressed?'

'I laid myself on the bed without troubling to remove my clothes,' explained Trull apologetically. 'I feared I should be unable to sleep, but I must have dozed off.'

Blake grabbed the man by the arm and urged him towards the stairs. Without coming to any fixed conclusion he realised that Septimus Trull was the logical suspect in the double murder mystery. He was one of the four potential killers nominated by

Lucien Droon. Roe was dead, and so far as his murder was concerned both George Grubb and Isabelle Page seemed to have a
clean-cut alibi. The process of elimination left Trull clearly
revealed as the most likely culprit.

'Rawson's on his way,' announced Coutts.

His face crimsoned with excitement as Blake detailed the latest
development in the case. Fierce-eyed, he glared at the quaking,
agitated figure of Septimus Trull.

'By glory, Trull's our man—there's no doubt about it!' he
declared confidently, producing a pair of gleaming handcuffs and
placing them meaningly on the table. 'Better come through with
the truth, Trull! The yarn of finding that dagger under your pillow
won't wash at all!'

For several moments Septimus Trull seemed not to have heard.
He remained staring in fascinated silence at the motionless figure
on the floor. Suddenly he drew himself up to the full extent of his
meagre stature, a spot of crimson flaming in his pale cheeks, his
eyes flashing behind his spectacles.

'You are accusing me of having murdered Lucien Droon and
Philip Roe! I deny it most emphatically!' he cried excitedly. 'I
know nothing of these crimes. I had not left my room from the time
I entered it, when Mr Blake knocked at the door!'

'You were fully dressed, and you had that dagger in your hand!'
challenged Coutts harshly.

'I have already explained both those points,' pointed out the
little man, with a certain amount of dignity. 'Were I guilty, and my
story untrue, why should I have faced Mr Blake with the dagger,
when I had ample time in which to conceal it?'

'You were taken by surprise when Blake knocked!' snapped the
inspector. 'You forgot you had the knife in your hand.'

But Blake shook his head.

'The man who so shrewdly, cunningly and deliberately planned
and executed these murders could not be guilty of such a foolish
slip,' he said quietly. 'That is why I am inclined to accept Trull's
explanation.'

'Accept my foot!' growled Coutts, stubborn as a bulldog once it
had its jaws clamped on an adversary. 'This fellow's as guilty as
Judas! Who else could have stabbed Roe? Your own evidence

clears Grubb, and you found the Page woman in bed with nothing on except a—'

'Grubb certainly seems to have a clear alibi,' interrupted Blake hastily. 'But it won't hold water if we can find a secret exit from this room. There must be some way by which the murderer made his escape, unless—'

'Unless what?'

'Unless the murderer was not actually in the room when the crime was committed.'

Coutts stared blankly at the detective.

'What the dickens do you mean?' he exploded. 'How the devil could anyone have stabbed Roe unless they were inside the room? You yourself heard the sound of the blow and Roe's dying groan as the dagger penetrated his back.'

Blake shrugged his shoulders evasively, an action which Coutts misconstrued as an admitted inability to argue the point.

'The fact remains,' remarked the Baker Street detective quietly, 'that neither you nor I have the remotest idea how the murderer did leave this room.'

'As a suspected person, may I be allowed to make a few remarks?' asked Septimus Trull, his meekness tinctured with irony. 'What was Philip Roe doing in this room? I suggest he came here in search of the proofs of the identity of Lucien Droon's killer, which you said were hidden here. And I submit that that is a proof of Roe's own guilt. The discovery of the proofs would have named him as the murderer.'

'Yes, we got all that worked out a couple of years ago,' sneered Coutts. 'Got any more brainwaves? Answer this question. If Roe murdered Droon, then who, in Hades, murdered Roe?'

Trull looked startled and vaguely uneasy.

'I see your point,' he conceded. 'The similarity of the murders leads you to the conclusion that both were committed by the same person? And the murderer is still in the house?'

'Here in this room!' snapped Coutts, looking him straight in the eyes.

Within a few minutes the CID man had found someone to share his suspicions and to support his conviction that Septimus Trull was the guilty party.

Inspector Rawson arrived, greedily swallowed every detail of the amazing and mystifying happening that had occurred during his absence, and immediately jumped to the conclusion that they need search no farther for the murderer of Lucien Droon and Philip Roe.

'Trull's our man!' he declared, glaring accusingly at the person named. 'If only we can discover the way he got in and out of this room, it'll be all over bar the hanging.'

'How about the motive?' suggested Blake mildly.

Rawson made an impatient gesture.

'We'll get to the bottom of that before long,' he said cock-suredly. 'It's my contention that Trull murdered Droon, and Roe suspected that he was the guilty party. He sneaked down here and found the proofs. Trull caught him in the act, and killed him in the same cold-blooded way he did Droon.'

'Darned good reasoning!' agreed Coutts. 'Just what I thought!'

'Trull apparently walks about bristling with daggers,' remarked Blake dryly.

'I shouldn't be surprised at that!' snapped Rawson, missing the gentle sarcasm in the detective's tone. 'We've found three daggers all of the same type up to now. Possibly we'll discover more if we search the man's room and luggage.'

'One dagger would have sufficed to kill Droon,' said Blake. 'Your own theory doesn't include the possibility that Trull came here intending to claim more than one victim.'

'My theories are designed to include every possibility!' declared Rawson recklessly.

Septimus Trull was left in the charge of two police officers, while the remainder of the party searched the room he had occupied. The contents of his weekend suitcase were of the most innocent description. Nothing in the slightest degree suspicious was found until Rawson poked his hawk-like nose into the empty fireplace and produced a handful of charred flakes of paper, which he placed carefully in an empty envelope.

'Trull burned a paper of some kind,' he contended. 'Ten to one it was the evidence Droon had left hidden in his study. Roe discovered it, and was murdered for his pains. Trull destroyed the incriminating paper as soon as he got safely back to his room.'

There was a certain soundness about the inspector's reasoning.

Unquestionably he was building up a strong theoretical case against Trull, but with all the fundamental points missing. There was not a shred of actual proof that would justify the man's arrest on anything so serious as a murder charge.

Sexton Blake crossed to the bed to pull aside the pillow and the heavy bolster. He saw something more than the thin gold watch that lay ticking there; clearly marked in the soft overlay was a shallow, cross-shaped imprint.

It was the exact size and shape of the brass-handled dagger he had taken from Septimus Trull. It offered dumb proof of the truth of one of his statements, at any rate.

Inspector Rawson grinned contemptuously.

'Proof be hanged!' he derided. 'It merely proves that Trull himself hid the dagger under his pillow. I shall arrest him for the murder of both Droon and Roe.'

'Please yourself,' said Blake gravely. 'But you have yet to prove why—and how—he committed the crimes.'

White and shaken, Septimus Trull continued to protest his innocence with a fervour that impressed Coutts to such an extent that he was reluctant to offer any further definite comment. He was quite content to allow Rawson to handle the case in his own way and on his own responsibility.

'You don't believe in Trull's guilt?' he asked Blake, tugging uneasily at his moustache.

'He is the most likely suspect,' answered the detective cautiously. 'If you can discover any way in which he can have left this room after stabbing Roe, it will considerably strengthen the case against him. Or,' he added, 'if you can discover any way by which Roe could have been stabbed without the murderer entering the room.'

Blake balanced one of the brass-hafted daggers in the palm of his hand.

'This is actually a throwing-knife,' he declared. 'The blade is heavier than the handle.'

'What difference does that make?' demanded Coutts helplessly. 'The knife couldn't have been thrown from outside this room unless the windows were open. And we know well—darned well—they weren't!'

For the third time, Lucien Droon's study was thoroughly

searched. Again no trace was found of any secret door or opening in walls, floor, or ceiling—no possible way by which the slayer could have left the room, or even hurled the dagger with deadly aim and effect from some point beyond its confines.

It was an old and well-built house. The walls were eighteen inches thick. The bookshelves and glass-fronted curio cabinets were solid, immovable fixtures. The stuffed elephant, tiger, and deer heads were held in place with heavy screws that had not been turned for many a long year; in some cases the rust had almost eaten away the slots of the screw-heads.

The whole room seemed as solid as a bank vault. The door and windows offered the only way of exit and entrance. Yet the murderer could have used neither.

His coming and going were wrapped in an impenetrable cloak of mystery that defied solution.

*   *   *

Septimus Trull remained deaf to all further questions. He seemed to realise the strength of his position, and displayed a close and apparently genuine interest in all attempts to solve the problem of the manner in which Lucien Droon and Philip Roe had been done to death in a locked room.

Inspector Rawson questioned the constable he had left on guard outside the house. The man had neither heard nor seen anything of a suspicious nature. He was positive that no one could possibly have left the house without attracting his attention.

'The murderer is still on the premises,' declared Rawson, glowering meaningly at Septimus Trull. 'We have searched the premises from top to bottom, and we can lay our hands on every possible suspect.'

He paused, wilting, as if something had gone out of his nature.

'Have you any further suggestion to make, Mr Blake?'

The question was sincere. It was a lame admission of uncertainty. The inspector was in a quandary. He had come to realise that he would be taking a serious step in arresting Trull on a murder charge, considering the purely speculative nature of the case against him. Even Rawson, anxious as he was for the glory of a murder arrest, had to recognise that much when he looked at the thing impartially.

Somehow, in such grave moments of indecision, Sexton Blake was always the dominant personality; people looked to him to accept responsibility.

'Yes, I have a suggestion to make,' said Blake, with one of those rare, fleeting smiles that gave no man reason to sense inferiority. 'In fact, I was about to invite your approval of an idea I have in mind, Rawson. Two heads are better than one, you know.'

'Three are better than two,' grunted Coutts jealously, yet knowing that his co-operation in any future move was unquestionable.

Blake beckoned them into the next room, leaving Trull in the charge of his guards. The detective passed his cigar-case, with affirmative results, and propped his back against the mantelpiece.

'Here's my idea,' he said briskly. 'I will admit, in the face of such meagre evidence as we have, that Trull comes under grave suspicion of being the guilty party in this case. If that is so he alone can supply the answer to the riddle which we, so far, are unable to solve.'

'There are so many riddles,' admitted Rawson. 'Which particular one do you mean?'

'The chief one. How did the man who did these murders escape from a room that was locked and shuttered on the inside without leaving any clue to the manner of his departure? We will give Trull an opportunity to prove whether he is guilty or innocent.'

'Darned if I can see what you're driving at, Blake!' said Coutts bluntly.

The detective explained in a few explicit sentences.

'We'll take a risk with Trull. We'll apply a certain test to him. We'll lock him in a room where Droon and Roe were murdered, and leave him alone until morning!'

'What the blazes for?' exploded Rawson blankly.

'If Trull is guilty,' said Blake impressively, 'he will not be in the room when we open the door in the morning. He will take advantage of the opportunity to escape, and disappear in the same mysterious way as he did on two previous occasions. You can reduce that possibility by having your men patrolling all parts of the house. In the meanwhile, we will keep guard outside the room.

'If Trull is innocent,' he finished up, 'we will find him where we left him.'

'By James, that's an idea, Mr Blake!' exclaimed Rawson admiringly. 'But if Trull is the man we're after, he may smell a rat and act accordingly.'

Blake was prepared for all emergencies. He explained his plan in further detail. Five minutes later the three detectives returned to the room where Septimus Trull sat huddled in a chair, staring dully at the spot where Lucien Droon and Philip Roe had been struck down with a knife in the back.

Rawson made an elaborate ritual of glancing at his watch.

'Only two hours till daylight,' he remarked. 'Hardly worth going back to the police station until then. Benson, you and Forbes can clear off home and get some sleep.'

'What about our prisoner, sir?' asked one of the two constables who had been guarding Trull.

'I shan't charge him until the morning. In the meantime, he will be safe enough locked in this room, while Mr Coutts and I make a further search of the house.'

Blake was watching Trull keenly out of the corners of his eyes, to see how he reacted to the inspector's words. The result was scarcely what he had expected. The man was either as cunning as a weasel, or the prospect of being locked alone in the room was genuinely displeasing to him.

His jaw sagged, and a look of consternation and dismay flashed across his face.

'Do you mean to say you intend imprisoning me in the room where they were murdered?' he exclaimed shrilly. 'No—no! I protest! I refuse to be left alone in here!'

'Guilty conscience, eh?' snapped Rawson grimly. 'Afraid your victims will return to haunt you at the scene of your crimes?'

Trull's lips tightened. He threw a bitter look at the inspector, and shrugged his narrow shoulders.

'If that's what you think, by all means lock me in here!' he said scornfully. 'I have nothing to fear, even were it possible for Droon and Roe to return from the dead!'

'The fellow's a darned good actor!' muttered Coutts. 'He was only pretending to be scared. I've an idea your scheme's going to succeed, Blake.'

Rawson tested the steel shutters that covered the windows to the study. He had long since taken possession of the key that locked them.

As if to prove his defiance of fear, Septimus Trull deliberately seated himself in the handsome, carved chair, in which Lucien Droon had been found dead. He was still seated there, pale and composed, in the glare of the electric light, as the three detectives withdrew, closing the door, and fastening it with a padlock and chain, drawn through two strong staples.

Rawson posted four of his men in various parts of the house, one on the first floor, where the apartments occupied by George Grubb and Isabelle Page were situated.

A fifth constable was instructed to cover the outside of the house. Nothing was left to chance. Even if he managed to escape from the locked room, Trull would not get much farther.

Blake and his companions seated themselves in a room directly opposite the one occupied by their prisoner. For a time they sat in silence, waiting for the first signs of dawn to flush the dark sky. Tinker stretched himself on a couch and fell asleep.

'Even if Trull is the murderer, this case is a long way from ended,' remarked Coutts at length. 'We don't know why Droon was killed, or why he should have fastened suspicion to each of the four guests in his house.'

'It is one of those cases which refuse to be completely solved by direct methods,' said Blake quietly. 'Droon carried his secret to the grave. It may require a confession on the part of the murderer to clear up the loose ends. Our chief concern at the moment is to find out, not why Droon was stabbed, but—how.'

'We know nothing of Droon, except that he was ostensibly a wealthy man,' ruminated Coutts. 'There must be someone who can tell us—'

Blake suddenly went to the door and called to the butler, who was seated in a big chair at the far end of the hall.

'Bellamy, how long have you been in Mr Doon's service?'

'Four years, sir.'

'Then you must know something of his private affairs?' suggested the detective.

'I am afraid not, sir. It is scarcely customary for an employer to take one of his servants into his confidence,' returned Bellamy, a trifle pompously.

'Had Mr Droon no relations?' pursued Blake.

'I have heard him speak of an elder brother, but I have never seen him. Possibly Mr Sutton, the lawyer, could give you further information.'

Blake snapped his thigh, his eyes sparkling.

'Mr Droon had a lawyer! Why didn't we think of that before? He is the very man we want to see. Do you know Mr Sutton's address? What's his full name?'

'Mr Sugden Sutton, sir. I have often telephoned to him for Mr Droon. He has an office in Cliffords Inn, and a private house at Ealing.'

Blake glanced at his watch.

'Wait until eight o'clock, and then telephone to Mr Sutton. Inform him that Mr Droon is dead, and request him to come here quickly as he can.'

'We might have known Droon would have a lawyer,' grunted Coutts, stretching his short, thick legs. 'He should be in a position to tell us all about his client's private affairs, and perhaps give us a hint as to why Droon went in fear of his life. Trull's keeping mighty quiet.'

For the past hour not a sound had come from the locked room on the opposite side of the hall. A streak of light shone steadily from the gap at the side of the splintered door.

'Wonder if he's still there!' muttered Inspector Rawson, tugging impatiently at his moustache. 'Gad, I shall be glad when this waiting is over! It seems a couple of centuries ago since Coutts and I first came here. Two murders in ten hours is a record for this area!'

Another hour dragged by. A pile of white ash and cigar-ends adorned the brass tray at Blake's elbow. He rose to his feet as the first glow of daylight crept between the drawn curtains.

'Seven o'clock,' he announced. 'We've given Trull plenty of time to make a move if our suspicions are correct.'

Coutts' sleep-heavy eyes brightened with excitement and anticipation as they moved across the hall to the locked room. He rapped on the door with his knuckles while Rawson fumbled for the key to the padlock.

There was no reply, no sound of any kind from the other side of the stout panels. Rawson slid the chain through the staples turned the handle, and flung the door open.

'By James, he's still here!' exclaimed Coutts, his voice sharp with disappointment, as if he regretted the fact that their prisoner had not disappeared in thin air.

'Not only here, but asleep!' said Rawson jingling the length of chain in his hand. 'What a nerve he's got!'

Septimus Trull was still seated in the low-backed, carved chair, behind the big writing-table. His attitude was one of deep slumber. He had slumped forward across the leather-covered top of the desk, with his head resting on his folded arms and his horn-rimmed spectacles hanging from one ear. A bald patch on the top of his skull gleamed pinky-white.

Blake looked at him sharply. It seemed to him that there was something unnatural about the man's posture—something not quite in keeping with ordinary, sound sleep.

'Wake up, Trull!' barked Inspector Rawson gruffly. 'It's seven o'clock and I'm going to take you along to the police station.'

But Trull made no movement or response. A louder command failed to stir his senses. Almost fiercely Sexton Blake shouldered his companions out of the way, to make several quick strides across the room.

A gasp of horror escaped him as he reached the man's side. Septimus Trull would never move or speak again! Buried to the hilt between his shoulders was a brass-handled dagger similar to those that had ended the lives of both Lucien Droon and Philip Roe!

The mystery murderer of Droon House had claimed a third victim!

* * *

'My heavens! This—this is a terrible affair!'

Inspector Rawson scarcely recognised his own voice. His hand was white and damp with perspiration as he goggled down at the lifeless body of Septimus Trull sprawled across the desk in almost identically the same attitude as Lucien Droon had been found the previous night.

The same room! The same circumstances! The same type of weapon! A locked door, shuttered windows, and the three detectives seated wide-awake in a room less than ten yards from the scene of the crime!

The killer had come and gone like a wraith, leaving no visible trace behind him save the remains of his latest victim and the weapon he had employed.

'This is a knock-out!' muttered Coutts huskily. He took off the hard, felt hat that seldom left his bullet head and ran his fingers distractedly through his stiff, red hair. 'If this sort of thing goes on much longer there won't be anyone left alive in this infernal house! Trull's gone the same way as the other two.'

He turned to glance meaningly at his companions.

'I guess we were all wrong in our suspicions of Trull, Blake. The little fellow was speaking the truth. He didn't have a darn thing to do with the murder of Droon, or Roe, either.'

'I never thought he had,' answered Blake swiftly. His lean jaw was set, his eyes as hard as flint. 'My chief idea in submitting Trull to this test was to try and convince Rawson that he would not be justified in making an arrest.

'And now'—the detective shook his head regretfully as he surveyed the hunched figure at the big desk—'I almost feel that I sent Trull to his death. I never dreamed the murderer would strike again.'

'The murderer!' exclaimed Rawson, in hollow tones. 'Who the blazes is the murderer? Roe is dead! Trull is dead! There are only Grubb and the Page woman left.'

The words had scarcely left the inspector's lips when the silence of the sleeping house was suddenly torn asunder by a piercing scream of terror. They listened for one startled moment, then—the crack of a revolver and the tinkle of broken glass!

'That was Isabelle Page's voice!'

Blake turned like a flash, streaking through the door and bounding up the stairs, with his alarmed companions behind him like hounds in full cry.

The lights were burning. On the first landing he blundered headlong into one of the men Rawson had instructed to patrol the house during the remaining hours of darkness.

'Hear that, sir?' gulped the detective. 'It was a woman's voice, and came somewhere along this corridor.'

A door opened. George Grubb's round head came cautiously into view, like a penny balloon, with a grotesque, terror-stricken face painted on it.

'Merciful Heaven, what's happening now?' quavered the man,

his small eyes bulging from their sockets like those of a lobster. 'Who fired that shot? I demand to be allowed to leave this house at once. I won't submit to this outrageous treatment a moment longer! I shall complain to the Police Commissioner—'

Sexton Blake placed a hand beneath Grubb's three quivering chins, shot him backwards into the room, and closed the door with a bang.

Without standing on ceremony he opened the next door, and stepped quickly into the apartment occupied by Isabelle Page.

The woman stood in the centre of the room, clad in a vivid red-and-yellow kimono and scarlet mules. In one hand she clutched a tiny silver-plated revolver. Her violet eyes, wide with alarm, were fixed on the window. The curtains were half drawn.

The glass in the lower frame was shattered to fragments, littering the floor like hoar frost. Through the aperture streamed the faint, grey light of early dawn.

Isabelle Page drew a shaky breath; a slight smile of relief twitched her red lips as she turned her head to meet Blake's stern, searching gaze.

'Too late, as usual, Mr Blake! He's gone!'

'Gone! Who's gone?' snapped the detective brusquely.

'I don't know who it was,' answered the woman, tossing her revolver carelessly on the bed. 'I woke up and saw a man's head and shoulders outlined against the window. It was too dark for me to distinguish his face. Knowing that two persons had already been murdered in this house tonight, I was determined not to be the third victim.'

'She does not know that Trull is dead,' was the lightning thought that flashed through Blake's mind. 'Either that, or she is bluffing!'

'I think I must have screamed,' went on the woman, wrinkling her straight nose, as if disgusted at her own weakness. 'I had a revolver under the pillow. I fired one shot; but the man had already vanished.'

'Is it your custom to carry a revolver?' demanded Coutts, from the doorway.

'Always—when I am sleeping in a strange house,' answered Isabelle Page coolly. 'And I happen to possess a Police Firearms Licence, if that's what you're driving at!'

Sexton Blake strode across the room, flung up the shattered

window frame, and stuck out his head. The rear wall of Droon House was entirely covered with a green mantle of tangled, thick-growing creeper, strong enough to support the weight of a dozen men, let alone one.

Peering downwards, the detective glimpsed a shadowy figure, standing in the shrubbery several yards away from the house.

The man spoke, revealing himself as the constable who had been keeping watch on the exterior of the house.

'That you, Peebles?' barked Rawson, peering over Blake's shoulder. 'How long have you been there? Seen anything of a man trying to climb in this window?'

'Haven't seen a living soul, sir,' answered the constable emphatically. 'I was round the other side of the house when I heard a woman scream, and then the sound of a shot. Did it come from this side?'

Rawson's eyes probed the spacious grounds stretching far and wide before him.

'Blake, I believe that woman's lying,' he whispered. 'Probably she fired that shot to distract our attention and give the murderer a chance to get away. Either that, or it's a bluff to cover her own guilt.'

'Mustn't jump to conclusions,' said Blake quietly. 'The way matters are developing I shouldn't be surprised to find that the murderer is someone entirely apart from the four people Droon named.

'Two of them are dead—murdered in the same manner as Droon. That clears them of suspicion. It is not unreasonable to assume that George Grubb and Isabelle Page are marked down for the same fate?'

The detective peered down at the thick, tough branches of the tangled creeper that covered the rear of the house.

'Easy enough for a man to climb up to this window, or even to have been hiding in the creeper when Peebles passed this way on his beat.'

In proof of his statement Blake swung his legs over the window-sill, and easily lowered himself to the ground below.

Daylight came as the sun pierced the grey mists of dawn and flooded the scene with golden light.

Somehow, the atmosphere of murder and mystery was immediately dispelled. It was difficult to conceive the grim tragedies that had descended on Droon House during the hours of the night.

Yet two corpses were stretched stark in the police mortuary at Mayes. A third victim sprawled lifeless across the writing-table in Lucien Droon's study.

Blake, on the garden path, stood sweeping his gaze to right and left. Directly beneath the windows at the back of the house was a broad bed of soft earth, that stretched from corner to corner of the building. It was bounded by a path of reddish sand, damp with the heavy dew that had fallen during the night.

No person could have passed over or along the flower-bed without leaving clear impressions of his footprints in the soft soil. Yet there was none.

Blake examined every inch of the ground before turning his attentions to the path.

Here a beaten trail of bootmarks described a complete circuit of the house. They were repeated over and over again, one on top of the other, and all had been made by the same person—a heavily built man, wearing rubber soles of a distinctive pattern.

'Those are my marks, Mr Blake,' volunteered Peebles, the constable, holding up an outsized foot in proof of his statement. 'I must have walked round the house fifty times since I came on duty.'

'And you saw or heard nothing during the past two or three hours?'

'Not a thing, sir—not a sound, until the scream and the pistol-shot.'

Blake shook his head puzzledly as he fumbled for a cigar. No one could possibly have approached or left the house without leaving visible traces of his coming and going in the damp, soft earth.

What had become of the man she had seen peering through her window—provided that Isabelle Page's story was true?

'Either he climbed straight up to the roof, or entered one of the adjoining windows,' decided the detective swiftly.

He turned to Coutts and Rawson, who had joined him by the safer route of descending the stairs.

'Get your men to make another search of the house, Rawson,' he instructed; 'particularly the attics and the roof itself.'

The inspector obeyed without question.

'I've interrogated the constable I left patrolling the corridor of the first floor,' he remarked heavily. 'He declares that neither George Grubb or Mrs Page could possibly have left their rooms without him seeing them.'

'Unless they went out of the window,' remarked Blake quietly. 'Grubb weighs close on twenty stone. I can't imagine his clambering up and down that creeper without making enough noise to disturb everyone in the house.'

'Leaving the woman as the only suspect?'

The detective shook his head. He held out his hands, blackened and scored by the tough, dirt-encrusted branches of the dense veil of creeper. His clothes were in no better state—covered with dust, dead leaves, and twigs.

Isabelle Page had appeared as clean and fresh as a flower when they had entered her room, and the inference was obvious.

'It proves nothing,' grunted Rawson, 'except that the woman is lying. There was no man at her window.'

Blake shrugged his shoulders.

'We have got to look at the murders from a fresh angle,' he said firmly. 'For the time being we will eliminate Grubb and Mrs Page as suspects. Yet the guilty party is still in the house. He, or she, can't have left it!'

'There's only the housekeeper, the two maids, and the butler,' recited Coutts. 'Take your choice. The butler was seated in the hall, within full view of us during the whole time Trull was locked in the study.'

'You can't consider the maids—they are no more than girls,' declared Rawson. 'And the housekeeper is a most estimable woman, who has lived in Mayes all her life. She can carve a chicken, but I'm darned if she'd stick a knife in a man!'

'Doesn't follow,' jerked Coutts. 'I've known women who'd faint at sight of a drop of blood poison a whole family without turning a hair. Vice versus.'

'Versus what?' inquired the inspector innocently.

'I was quoting Latin,' informed Coutts with dignity. 'Vice versus—that means—er—"the other way round." '

'Plain English is good enough for me,' said Rawson. 'Latin's a dead language.'

Coutts was not to be beaten.

'We're dealing with dead bodies, aren't we? Maybe you've never heard of corpus *delicti?*'

'The name's familiar,' admitted Rawson gravely. 'But I don't think I've met the fellow!'

Blake walked to the verge of the stretch of lawn, a dozen yards away, and propped himself against the back of a rustic garden-seat. From there he had an unobstructed view of the rear wall of Droon House, and could see the two constables crawling about amid the towering chimney-stacks on the flat roof.

A plan of the entire interior of the house was stamped clearly in the detective's mental vision. On the ground floor, at the rear of the premises, was the kitchen, the butler's pantry, and Lucien Droon's study, with the steel shutters securely fastened over the windows.

They alone seemed to offer dumb testimony to the fact that the owner of Droon House had gone in fear of his life.

There were four windows on the next floor. The first from the left marked the room that had been placed at the disposal of Blake and his assistant. Next to it was Isabelle Page's apartment, with the shattered pane of glass.

The adjoining room was directly over Droon's study, and Blake knew it to be unoccupied. The fourth and last room was tenanted by George Grubb.

Both Philip Roe and Septimus Trull had been accommodated in an angle of the corridor on the east side of the house. On the top floor were the servants' quarters.

Blake's face was grave. He was struck by the magnitude and complexity of the mystery he was called upon to solve. It was surely the most baffling case of its kind he had ever known. Three men had been deliberately and callously murdered in circumstances that defied solution.

Each had been dispatched in the same manner—stabbed in the back in a locked room from which there was no possible way of escape.

The motive in each case was entirely obscured by the variance of facts. Lucien Droon alone had any premonition of a violent end. He had nominated the four members of his house party as those likely to attempt his life. Two of them had since suffered the same fate as himself, which suggested that Droon had been entirely wrong in his suspicions.

'There's no help for it,' said Blake, after a long silence. 'We've got to switch back to the theory that the murderer was not inside the room when he did his work—it is humanly impossible that he could have been. Therefore, the daggers must have been thrown, or propelled in some way, with considerable force and deadly accuracy.'

Coutts jammed his hat further over his eyes.

'How the blazes could anyone fling a dagger through an eighteen-inch wall?' he asked ironically. 'With the door locked and the windows shuttered that room's as near airtight as a vacuum-chamber. We've examined every square inch of the walls, floor, and ceiling. There's not a crack or a crevice through which anyone could insert a pea-shooter, let alone a nine-inch dagger with a four-inch cross-hilt. There's not even a ventilator, or a gas-pipe in the ceiling.'

'Which all goes to prove,' remarked Blake, 'that the murderer could not have been inside the room else he could not have got out again. You can't dispute the fact that Trull was absolutely alone when we locked him in.'

Inspector Rawson nodded and tugged moodily at his moustache.

'Whether the murderer was inside or outside the room, we're getting no nearer to the bottom of this mystery,' he complained. 'We've made no progress at all.'

'On the contrary, we have made considerable progress,' denied Blake quietly. 'We have narrowed our field of investigation, and eliminated several of the suspects—or, rather, events have tragically eliminated them.'

'Oh, yeah!' snorted Coutts. 'And all we've got to do now is to find out how the murders were committed, why they were committed, and who committed them.'

Inspector Rawson hurried away to consult with the police surgeon, who, for the third time within twelve hours, had been summoned to Droon House to certify death in its most violent form.

Blake entered the house and ascended the stairs. George Grubb and Isabelle Page were still locked in their rooms, with a plain-clothes detective keeping an observant eye on the two doors. The detective advised him not to relax his vigilance.

'You don't think they'll try to escape?' scoffed Coutts.

'By no means,' was Blake's bland response. 'I want to make certain that someone is close at hand in case either Grubb or Mrs Page should find it necessary to require immediate assistance.'

The unoccupied room directly over Lucien Droon's study was locked on the outside. It was unoccupied for the tragic reason that its late owner had no further use for it. It was Lucien Droon's bedroom. Blake had already thoroughly searched it on two occasions. For the third time he turned the key and stepped inside, followed by Coutts.

The thick curtains, suspended from a brass pole, were drawn across the window. Droon had evidently been something of an ascetic. The room was plainly, almost austerely, furnished. The fittings were of the most ordinary description, with one exception.

The fireplace had been entirely removed, and the recess it had previously occupied was now filled with a massive steel safe that must have weighed over a ton.

For what purpose Droon had had the safe installed in his bed chamber it was impossible to conjecture. It offered no more protection to valuables than a tin biscuit-box. The lock had been removed, and the door gaped open on its hinges. In the circumstances it was not surprising that the steel strong-box was empty.

According to Bellamy, the butler, it had been in the same condition ever since he had come to Droon House.

The safe puzzled Blake. The room itself puzzled him. It didn't seem in harmony with the rest of the house. He couldn't understand why it was that he should have right at the back of his mind, a vague, disquieting idea that the solution to the mystery of Droon's death was to be found somewhere in this simply furnished, almost empty apartment.

There was nothing to support such a theory. He and his companions had already searched every corner of the room, including the clothes in the wardrobe, without finding papers, letters, or anything in the nature of a clue.

Mechanically, Blake examined the window. It was closed and securely latched. Still unsatisfied, he allowed his gaze to rove over every article in the room. Suddenly his hand darted to a bronze ash-bowl that stood on a small table by the bed.

'What's that you've found? Huh, nothing but a cigarette-end!' grunted Coutts, with a shrug of disappointment.

'Exactly. A half-smoked cigarette,' agreed Blake, rolling the charred stump between his fingers, while a gleam of interest kindled in his eyes. 'The point is that the tip is still moist! Someone has been inside this room, smoking, within the past twenty minutes.'

He called to the detective on duty in the corridor. The man shook his head positively.

'I'm certain that no one's entered this room, sir,' he declared. 'They couldn't have done so, without me seeing them.'

'Not even yourself!' snapped Blake. 'Do you smoke?'

'Only a pipe, sir. And I can assure you I haven't been within twelve feet of this door.'

The clamour of an electric bell suddenly rang through the house. Sexton Blake placed the cigarette-end carefully in an envelope, and walked to the landing at the end of the passage.

Bellamy, the butler, was already half-way up the stairs.

'Mr Sugden Sutton, the lawyer, has arrived, sir,' he announced. 'I have shown him into the study.'

'Ah, now we may get some real information,' muttered Coutts, rubbing his hands together.

Midway down the stairs Blake shot a curt question at the butler.

'Bellamy, do you know anyone who smokes Pyramid cigarettes?'

'Mr Droon smoked nothing else, sir,' answered the man promptly. 'He was seldom without one in his lips. You'll find a box in nearly every room in the house.'

'Meaning,' mused Blake ruefully, 'that anyone might have helped himself to a cigarette, and left it unfinished in Droon's bedroom?'

'Some clue!' grinned Coutts.

*　　*　　*

Mr Sudgen Sutton outraged all popular conceptions of a lawyer. He was short, tubby, pink-faced, and a bit of a dandy in his attire. His tail-coat fitted him like a glove. He wore white spats, and a double-breasted white waistcoat.

He turned from conversation with Inspector Rawson, to extend a plump hand to the Baker Street detective.

'A real pleasure to meet you, Mr Blake, though the circumstances are somewhat unfortunate,' he greeted briskly. 'This has come as a big shock to me. Your telephone message was on the vague side. I had no idea until I arrived here that Mr Droon had met with a violent end.'

'You had no reason to foresee the possibility that he might be murdered?' asked Blake bluntly.

Mr Sutton looked shocked.

'Not the slightest!' he declared. 'Such an idea has never entered my head. In fact, I doubt if I can be of very much assistance to you in this terrible affair.'

The atmosphere of the room was close and depressing, despite the fact that the body of Septimus Trull was no longer in evidence.

At Blake's suggestion, Inspector Rawson unlocked the steel shutters, and flung the window wide open, allowing the fresh air and morning sunshine to brighten and purify the chamber of death.

Mr Sutton listened in growing horror and amazement to the sensational story that was briefly but graphically related to him.

'Terrible—terrible—terrible!' he repeated, shaking his round head from side to side. 'Three murders in one night! And the criminal still at large!'

'Still in the house!' said Blake, smiling grimly as the lawyer started half-out of his chair. 'Did Mr Droon never hint to you that he feared an attempt on his life?'

'Never!' declared Sutton emphatically. 'Our dealings were of a most ordinary nature.'

'Do you know anything of his four guests—Isabelle Page, Philip Roe, Septimus Trull, and George Grubb?'

'Never heard of them,' came the instant reply. 'I knew none of Mr Droon's friends. In fact, Mr Droon has been a client of mine for no longer than eighteen months. He was a very reserved man—'

Inspector Rawson frowned as a sound of raised voices came discordantly from the hall. Conspicuous were the shrill, indignant tones of George Grubb.

Sergeant Kedward rapped, and thrust a red face around the door.

'Having a bit of trouble with this fellow, Grubb, sir,' he said apologetically. 'He refuses to stay in his room any longer. Says he suffers from asthma, and demands to be allowed to go outside for a bit of fresh air.'

'Curse his asthma!' growled Rawson.

'I am not a prisoner! I insist on my rights!' wheezed Grubb, stamping up and down the hall like an enraged elephant. 'Send for my lawyer—let me telephone Scotland Yard, or the Home Office! I must have air! The atmosphere of this terrible house is killing me!'

'Let him have some more atmosphere,' suggested Coutts unkindly.

'Unless you intend charging the man, I suggest you handle him tactfully,' said Mr Sutton gravely, as befitting one of his profession. 'His request is not unreasonable.'

Blake nodded, and pointed through the open windows which gave on to the expanse of lawn at the back of the house. Less than twenty yards away, in full view of all of them, was the rustic garden-seat, facing the lawn, and the wide vista of grounds beyond.

'Take Grubb out there, and let him sit down for half an hour, until we decide what to do with him. Tell him not to move without permission. We can keep an eye on him from here.'

His suggestion was adopted. Mr Grubb waddled past the windows, still proclaiming his grievances to the world at large. His gross bulk almost filled the wide seat from end to end. He relaxed and spread, like a stranded jelly-fish.

'He's safe enough there,' grunted Coutts. 'If he tried to run away he'd shake himself to pieces.'

'Now, Mr Sutton, tell us all you know about Mr Droon and his affairs,' continued Blake. 'Surely you have some information that may throw light on this mystery?'

The lawyer made a helpless gesture.

'I wish I could help you,' he said sincerely. 'But my dealings with Mr Droon were purely legal and financial.'

'He was a wealthy man?' said Coutts.

'He *was* a wealthy man,' said Sutton, laying particular stress on the past tense. 'Eighteen months ago Mr Droon came to me and entrusted me with the investment of eighty thousand pounds. I bought certain stocks and shares that brought him in an assured income of just over three thousand pounds per annum. Per annum,' he repeated, as if relishing the words.

The lawyer suddenly leaned forward, with a puzzled frown on his pink face.

'Here is a peculiar point that may interest you,' he said eagerly. 'Mr Droon told me that he was a man of modest tastes, and that it was his intention to live quietly on the interest of his capital.

'Yet within six months he sent for me, and instructed me to sell twenty thousand pounds' worth of stock.' Mr Sutton paused impressively. 'Three months later,' he went on, 'Mr Droon again sent for me, and requested me to sell another thirty thousand pounds' worth of stock.'

'So he realised fifty thousand pounds' worth of his capital in eight months?' exclaimed Blake. 'Did he tell you why he wanted all that money?'

'He told me nothing,' declared the lawyer, 'but he appeared to be very worried and distraught. It was not my business to question him regarding the expenditure of his money, though I expressed a hope that he was not indulging in rash speculation on his own account.

'He assured me that this was not the case. Yet'—Sutton made a vague gesture with his plump hands—'two months ago Mr Droon came to my office and commanded me to sell another twenty-five thousand pounds' worth of securities. All that now remains in my hands, out of a fortune of eighty thousand pounds, is four thousand five hundred pounds. Approximately,' he added, blowing his nose vigorously. 'There have been one or two odd payments.'

Coutts and Inspector Rawson stared bewilderedly at one another. Both were wondering how on earth Mr Lucien Droon could have managed to fritter away seventy-five thousand pounds in little over a year.

He had been a bachelor. According to Bellamy, the butler, he was a man of simple tastes who seldom left his home, except on very infrequent trips to town.

'The man must have been a gambler on a large scale?' suggested Rawson. 'Probably plunged on the Stock Exchange, and lost all he had.'

'Seventy-five thousand pounds takes a lot of spending,' agreed

Coutts, thinking of his own modest pittance.

Sexton Blake suddenly sat erect in his chair, a hard gleam of excitement in his eyes.

'I think I shall be nearer the mark,' he said slowly, 'if I suggest that Lucien Droon was being blackmailed!'

'Blackmail!'

Coutts jerked himself erect, a startled look in his eyes.

Sutton nodded his head gravely as he digested the idea.

'By James, I believe you've hit the right nail on the head, Mr Blake!' he exclaimed. 'Blackmail would certainly account for the big sums of money Droon frittered away during the past year.'

'But who the dickens could have been blackmailing him?' asked Inspector Rawson.

'That's easily answered,' declared Coutts, pounding the table excitedly with his clenched fist. 'It was either Isabelle Page, Philip Roe, Septimus Trull, or George Grubb.'

'Or the whole bunch of them,' ventured Tinker.

'Not unlikely,' agreed Blake, leaning back in his chair and watching the blue smoke from his cigar drift and swirl through the open windows. 'But it doesn't explain why Droon was murdered. It makes his death all the more inexplicable. Why should a blackmailer dispose of his victim?'

'Sounds like killing the goose that laid the golden eggs,' concurred Sugden Sutton, fondling his smooth-shaven chin.

'On the other hand,' continued Blake, retaining the close attention of his companions, 'assuming that Droon was being systematically blackmailed, it is not unlikely that he was driven to desperation, and decided to take action against his persecutors.'

'Even a worm will turn,' remarked Rawson tritely. 'I think you're getting nearer the mark, Blake. Bled white of nearly every penny he possessed, and faced with complete ruin, Droon refused to submit to any further extortion.

'He laid his plans accordingly. He invited Roe, Trull, Grubb, and the Page woman to the house, and then sent for Mr Blake, intending to make a clean breast of everything.

'Faced with exposure, and possibly imprisonment, one of the blackmailers murdered Droon in order to close his mouth for ever. How does that sound?'

Blake shook his head:

'Your theory certainly supplies a motive for Droon's death,' he said slowly, 'but how about Trull and Roe? Why were they murdered? How were they murdered? And who is the murderer?'

'Either George Grubb or Isabelle Page,' declared Rawson. 'It must be one of the two. Possibly Trull and Roe knew that either Grubb, or the woman, had stabbed Droon. It was necessary that their mouths should be closed as well. Having committed one murder, the culprit did not hesitate at two more.'

'Very plausible,' said Blake. 'But there is not a shred of evidence to support your theory. It is humanly impossible that either Grubb or Isabelle Page could have entered this locked room and stabbed Trull in the back. They have a water-tight alibi.'

'Blake's right,' agreed Coutts gloomily. 'Both Grubb and the Page woman were locked in their rooms on the next floor at the time Trull was killed.'

'We shall never find the murderer,' said Blake, 'until we discover how the crimes were committed. Grubb and Isabelle Page are still under suspicion. But if each is innocent, in which direction are we going to seek for the guilty party?'

There was a long silence. Rawson scowled, and tugged helplessly at his moustache. Blake lit a fresh cigar, and gazed through the window to where George Grubb sat huddled in the garden-seat, glowering across the peaceful grounds of Droon House.

Sugden Sutton coughed, and opened the leather attaché-case he had brought with him. He sorted through a number of legal-looking documents.

'It may interest you to know,' he said quietly, 'that though Lucien Droon's private fortune had been reduced to less than five thousand pounds, his life was heavily insured.'

Blake was on the alert at once.

'What do you mean by heavily insured?'

'Droon was insured against death to the extent of fifty thousand pounds,' informed the lawyer. 'The premiums were regularly paid, and the policy is absolutely sound.'

Blake's lips tightened. A hard gleam of interest crept into his eyes as he gazed searchingly at the man.

'Why didn't you tell us this before?' he snapped. 'The fact that Droon was worth ten times more dead than alive is a most important point. It may contribute the motive of his murder!'

'By James, you're right!' jerked Coutts excitedly. 'Did Droon leave a will?'

'I have it here,' said Sutton apologetically. 'I drew it up, and Mr Droon signed it just a week ago.'

'Who benefits by Droon's death?' The words left Blake's lips like whip-cracks.

'His elder brother—Marcus Droon,' answered the lawyer, promptly. 'He is Lucien Droon's sole heir. This house, and every penny he possessed, before and after death, are willed entirely to Marcus Droon!'

'By James, I believe we're getting on the right track at last!' exclaimed Coutts. 'It's not easy to imagine a man murdering his own brother for the sake of fifty thousand pounds insurance money; but such things have happened.'

'We can't neglect a single possible clue,' agreed Blake. 'This is one of the most baffling cases I have ever tackled, and I am determined to get to the bottom of it. What do you know of this Marcus Droon? When did you last see him? Where does he live?'

'I knew little of him. I have never set eyes on the man,' declared Sutton. 'All I can tell you is that he lives at Porthcawl, in Cornwall. I sent him a telegram, notifying him of his brother's death, so soon as I received your telephone message this morning. He can't possibly arrive here until late tonight.'

'Providing he is at Porthcawl!' remarked Coutts meaningly. 'I hope Mr Marcus Droon will be able to prove his whereabouts during the past twelve hours.'

'In a case like this it is foolish to jump to conclusions,' said Blake cautiously. 'I have never known of such mystifying and meaningless murders. It is impossible to definitely point the finger of suspicion to any particular person.

'There are so many opposing theories. Lucien Droon may have been murdered for his insurance money. We can't eliminate that possibility. On the other hand, I am almost entirely convinced that he was the victim of ruthless blackmail.'

'Droon knew he was going to be murdered,' reminded Coutts. 'Obviously, he didn't suspect his brother. He deliberately directed suspicion to Philip Roe, George Grubb, Septimus Trull, and Isabelle Page.'

'One of them must be the guilty person,' declared Inspector

Rawson, for the second time. 'I've got an idea it's the woman. How about sending for Grubb, and asking him point-blank why he was blackmailing Lucien Droon? We may startle him into making a confession.'

'It's worth trying,' agreed Blake, somewhat reluctantly. 'If Grubb is the murderer he must be one of the most cunning and diabolical scoundrels in the history of crime. But I don't think he is.'

Rawson walked to the open window.

'Mr Grubb—come along in here,' he shouted gruffly. 'We want to talk with you for a few minutes.'

George Grubb made no reply. He sat grossly in the rustic garden bench, with his arms folded, and his head nodding on his chest.

'The fellow's fallen asleep.' Rawson shouted a second time in a voice that could have been heard half a mile away. Again there was no response. The fat man remained still and silent, his bald head gleaming in the rays of the sun.

There was something about the man's inert, flaccid attitude that brought Sexton Blake to his feet. He clambered through the window and walked the few yards that separated him from the apparently slumbering man.

'Grubb—wake up, man! We want to—'

The sentence was unfinished. Blake's hand remained poised in midair, in the act of descending on George Grubb's shoulder.

The man would never speak or move again! Death had struck him down like a thunderbolt. He was stone dead, with a brass-handled dagger buried to the hilt in his broad back!

The mystery murderer had struck again, claiming a fourth victim in broad daylight, under the very eyes of Sexton Blake and his companions!

*   *   *

White-faced and shaken, the little party stared incredulously at one another. George Grubb had gone the same way as Lucien Droon, Philip Roe, and Septimus Trull. Another suspect had been ruthlessly eliminated.

Of the original four visitors to Droon House, only one remained—Isabelle Page!

It seemed impossible that the man could have been murdered,

seated there in the bright sunshine, never for one moment obscured from the gaze of Sexton Blake and his companions.

Death had been instantaneous. The body was still limp and warm. The man had been alive within the past ten minutes. An unseen hand had struck him down with murderous, malevolent force.

'By gosh, this is enough to give a fellow the creeps!' exclaimed Inspector Rawson huskily. 'I'll swear no one could possibly have approached Grubb without our seeing them. Why, I watched him lighting a cigarette no more than five minutes ago!'

Blake nodded. The cigarette, still smouldering, lay on the path just as it had dropped from the dead man's fingers. The detective's eyes blazed with excitement as he straightened his lean figure and pointed meaningly to the embedded brass-handled dagger.

'This proves that I was correct in my original decision,' he said with quiet firmness. 'That dagger was thrown or projected in some way. The death blow was not delivered by hand. No one has been anywhere within a dozen yards of Grubb since he walked to his bench and sat down.'

'Thrown? Yes, I guess you're right,' admitted Coutts. 'But it must have been thrown with terrific force and accuracy. Grubb presented a pretty big target, but—'

The CID man shook his head bewilderedly as he stepped back to survey the scene of the crime. The dead man was seated with his back to the rear wall of the house, and the room in which the detectives had been seated. There was a clear open space of at least a dozen yards between the heavy bench and the house itself.

'The dagger came from the direction of the house,' declared Blake, running his gaze keenly along the array of windows he had subjected to such a close scrutiny earlier in the day.

'Then it must have been thrown from one of those windows on the first floor,' snapped Rawson. 'The rooms are all empty at present, except for the one occupied by Isabelle Page. By thunder, I said all along that woman was the most likely suspect!'

Blake shrugged his shoulders. The window of Isabelle Page's apartment was closed, and the blinds drawn. He knew that a constable was posted outside her door to guard against any suspicious move on her part.

'I can't imagine a woman having the strength and skill to throw a knife from that distance,' said Tinker bluntly. 'I don't believe it could be done.'

'You can't be certain what to believe where women are concerned,' remarked Rawson. 'The dagger might have been propelled through the air by some kind of a catapult. She killed Grubb in the same way she did the other three men.'

'The circumstances are not exactly the same,' reminded Blake. 'Grubb was stabbed in the open air. Droon, Roe, and Trull were seated alone in a locked room, with the windows closed and shuttered.'

'I'm going to question Isabelle Page, and search her room,' declared Rawson doggedly. 'I'm betting she's the only person who could have thrown that knife!'

Within the next few minutes the inspector's dogmatic ideas received a crushing rebuff. The door of Isabelle Page's room was wide open. The woman herself stood on the threshold smoking a cigarette and addressing a very uncomfortable-looking young constable.

'The lady wants to go downstairs, sir,' explained the policeman. 'But I told her she couldn't be allowed to leave her room without your permission.'

'I refuse to be kept a prisoner any longer!' cried Isabelle Page, her eyes flashing angrily. 'You have no right to subject me to this treatment.'

'You're lucky compared to some!' snapped Rawson, glowering suspiciously at the pretty woman. 'George Grubb refused to be kept prisoner, and now he's dead! Stabbed through the heart with a dagger—right outside your window!'

'Dead! Another one murdered!' Isabelle Page shrank back. There was no mistaking the expression of horror and dismay in her eyes.

'Yes, right underneath your window,' repeated Rawson. 'Looks to me as if the dagger was thrown from this room within the past twenty minutes!'

'Excuse me, sir, but that isn't possible,' interrupted the young constable stoutly. 'The door to this room has been open all the time, and I've been talking to the lady for well over half an hour—ever since Mr Grubb went downstairs with the sergeant.'

Rawson's face fell. Isabelle Page's innocence was unquestionable in face of such an alibi. It was impossible for her to have opened the window without the policeman seeing her.

But the inspector was still unconvinced. He was not satisfied until the woman's room and her suitcase had been once more searched with scrupulous thoroughness. Nothing was found—not a shred of evidence to convict Isabelle Page of any complicity in the mysterious murder of George Grubb.

In turn each room along the corridor was searched, and those on the top floor facing the rear of the house. The constables on guard were positive that no one had entered or left any of the apartments.

'Yet the dagger must have come from the direction of the house,' declared Blake, with a baffled shrug of the shoulders. 'And by that I mean that the murderer is still under this roof.'

The problem was no nearer a solution. The grim, uncanny mystery of Droon House seemed to be absolutely unfathomable. It defied elucidation. Four men had been murdered, each with the same type of weapon—a needle-pointed, brass-handled dagger.

There was no direct clue to the murderer. It was not even possible to determine how the series of crimes had been committed. Death had reduced the number of possible suspects to less than half a dozen.

There were only Isabelle Page, Bellamy, the butler, the housekeeper, and the two maids. Yet Blake suspected none of them. At the same time he could not rid himself of the impression that the actual murderer was still in the house, lurking in safe hiding, probably planning a fresh outbreak of crime.

Who would be the next victim? Of the original four visitors to the house only Isabelle Page was left. Of the other three, each in turn had met the same fate as Lucien Droon.

Each suspect, one after the other, had become a victim of the mystery murderer, thus proving their innocence in respect to Droon's death.

'Isabelle Page must be closely guarded for her own sake,' advised Blake, as he sat in the study half an hour later. 'We have got to prepare against the possibility that she is in grave danger of her life.'

Coutts made a helpless gesture. His face was grey and lined with worry. The complexities of the case had filled his brain with a churning mass of illogical facts that did not contribute one direct clue to the unknown killer.

Isabelle Page had not yet been tackled with the suggestion of blackmail. Blake preferred to keep that theory to himself for the time being.

'Hanged if I can see a glimmer of daylight anywhere!' said Coutts wearily. 'In the first place it seemed to be a straightforward, open-and-shut case. Droon knew that he was in danger of being murdered, and he stated quite definitely that either Roe, Trull, Grubb, or the woman were likely to attempt his life.

'Now three of the four are dead—killed in the same way. And we haven't discovered a trace of the evidence nominating the guilty party which Droon declared was hidden in this room.'

'Perhaps there is no such evidence,' said Blake enigmatically, as he examined, for probably the twentieth time, the four brass-handled daggers. 'If we could fathom the state of Droon's mind when he sent for me and wrote that last unfinished message we might be able to tackle this case from an entirely fresh angle.'

'What do you mean by that, Mr Blake?' inquired Inspector Rawson puzzledly. 'You're not suggesting that Droon had gone off his head?'

'He might have been rendered desperate by incessant blackmail and deliberately designed a scheme of revenge directed at his persecutors,' explained the detective. 'He may have contemplated suicide in such a manner that either Roe, Trull, Grubb, or Miss Page—or all four of them—would be suspected of having murdered him.'

'Great snakes, that's a pretty wild theory,' grunted Coutts. 'There's no question of suicide. Droon was murdered, so was Roe, and Trull, and Grubb. If Droon wasn't dead I should have been more inclined to suspect him of having murdered the other three, especially if they'd bled him white with blackmailing demands for money.'

Blake raised his head and stared admiringly at the inspector.

'I was thinking the same thing only a few minutes ago,' he said thoughtfully. 'I can easily imagine a victim of blackmail planning a wholesale extermination of his persecutors. Unfortunately, Droon was the first to be wiped out. That shatters that theory, unless—'

He paused, narrowing his eyes, a strange expression on his lean face as he bent his eyes on the sinister-looking, cross-shaped dagger he had been turning over and over in his hands.

'Coutts, look here!' he jerked, a note of excitement in his voice. 'This dagger appears to be quite plain and perfectly rigid. I have already pointed out to you that the blade is heavier than the handle, adapting it to the purpose of being thrown, point first. The cross-part of the handle seems to be made in one piece.'

'Sure thing,' agreed the inspector. 'But what about it?'

'Just this—look!'

Blake grasped the dagger in his two hands and pressed the round, brass knob at the top of the haft. At the same time he applied steady pressure to the metal cross-piece. Each section folded back, lying snugly and neatly along the smooth, round handle. The hinge, or, rather, the pin, was so well made as to be practically invisible, and the depressions into which the cross-pieces fitted seemed to be merely part of the design of the handle, for they were duplicated by others on either side of the haft, which latter were, of course, dummies.

The weapon was now one straight, rigid bar of steel and brass. As Blake released his hold the cross-shaped guard clicked back to its original position.

'You see the idea? The handle is made to fold back into one straight piece,' explained Blake keenly. 'All four daggers are the same. I'm willing to bet ten pounds to a pinch of salt that each was ejected from some kind of a powerful spring gun. Hence the accuracy and the tremendous force that enabled the blade to embed itself to the hilt in each victim's back from a distance of a dozen yards or more!'

'By gosh! I see what you're driving at!' exclaimed Coutts enthusiastically. 'With the cross-piece folded flat against the handle the whole dagger can be slipped into a spring-gun with a barrel of little more than an inch and a half in diameter. As the dagger leaves the barrel the cross-hilt automatically springs into position.'

'What a devilish contraption,' muttered Inspector Rawson disgustedly. 'It explains how Grubb was probably murdered, but I'm hanged if I can see how Droon, Roe, and Trull were killed in this room, with the door locked and the windows shuttered.'

Blake jumped to his feet, his eyes bright with excitement.

'The first thing to be done is to find the weapon from which these daggers were discharged,' he declared. 'It must be hidden somewhere in this house, or in the grounds. It is probably a heavy metal affair, with a barrel at least five feet in length to ensure any sort of accuracy.'

Inspector Rawson sent for half a dozen extra men to augment the search. Once again every square inch of Droon House was examined from cellars to roof-trees. The collection of obsolete firearms hanging in the study and the lofty hall were taken down and subjected to close investigation.

Nothing escaped attention, including beds and mattresses, and every article that might possibly conceal the presence of anything in the nature of a spring-gun.

The result was negative. The search yielded absolutely nothing. The mystery of the death-dealing daggers remained unsolved, even after the grounds, the garage, the greenhouses, and the gardener's sheds had been scrupulously investigated.

Nothing in any way resembling a spring-gun was to be found.

For over an hour Sexton Blake paced thoughtfully up and down the terrace outside the house, passing and repassing the spot where George Grubb had been found dead.

'The only way to solve this mystery,' he decided finally, 'is to study it from an absolutely new angle—the more abnormal and seemingly preposterous the better. The solution is here, right in the house if only I can find it.'

A germ of inspiration suddenly incubated in the detective's toiling brain. He entered the house eventually to discover Bellamy, the manservant, seated in the butler's pantry reflectively sipping a glass of beer.

'Bellamy,' said Blake confidingly, 'do you think you could find me some personal article belonging to the late Mr Droon which he, and he alone, handled just prior to his death and which has not since been handled by anyone else?'

The butler looked mildly surprised at the strange request.

'Why, that shouldn't be very difficult, sir,' he answered, after a moment's thought. 'Mr Droon must have brushed his hair when he dressed for dinner. There's a pair of silver-backed brushes in his dressing-room that no one is likely to have used since. Would you like me to get them for you?'

Blake fetched the brushes himself, handling them with great care, for each was marked with an excellent set of fingerprints that must have been left by Lucien Droon.

'There is a million-to-one chance,' mused the detective hopefully, 'that Droon may have committed some indiscretion in his younger days that brought him within reach of the law. In that case, his fingerprints would be filed at Scotland Yard. Obviously, there is some secret in Droon's life which might give me a line on the possibilities of his having been a victim of blackmail.'

With his usual thoroughness Blake did not immediately send the brushes to Scotland Yard for purposes of comparison. Instead, he wrapped them carefully in tissue-paper and drove to the local mortuary, where the bodies of Lucien Droon and his fellow-victims of a cold-blooded murderer were ranged in mournful state.

To take an impression of the dead man's fingerprints was not a pleasant task, but it proved well worth the effort. A quick comparison showed at once to Blake's expert eyes that the prints on the silver-backed brushes were *not* those of Lucien Droon.

It was an astonishing discovery, for there were no other prints on the brushes. It was quite clear that some other person than Droon had made use of the brushes on the night of the murder!

Were they the murderer's fingerprints? Blake easily satisfied himself that the brushes had not been used by either Roe, Trull, or Grubb. Later Blake was able to include Bellamy, the butler, in the same category.

Within twenty minutes Tinker was on his way to Scotland Yard, carrying the silver-backed brushes and a sealed envelope addressed to the Commissioner of Police himself.

He returned to Droon House later in the day. The result of his mission had provided Blake with a staggering surprise.

Of the two sets of fingerprints he had sent to Scotland Yard, one had been definitely identified. The other set was not known to the police; it held no place in the files of the Fingerprint Department. And it was the set from the dead hands of Lucien Droon!

It was only left to assume that the prints on the hair-brushes were those of the mysterious murderer.

For the time being, the detective decided to keep his amazing discovery to himself. He felt that the key to the mystery was in his grasp. But he had yet to decide whether Lucien Droon had been a blackmailer, or the victim of blackmail.

'Also,' he mused, as he went in search of his companions, 'I must definitely ascertain the manner in which the murders were committed. That will pave the way for a final show-down.'

Coutts and Rawson were seated in Lucien Droon's study. The death-chamber had a strange fascination for them. With commendable diligence and patience they were still endeavouring to elucidate the problem as to how three men had been brutally stabbed to death in a locked room—spring-gun or no spring-gun.

Coutts glanced up as Blake entered, nodded, and tossed a telegram towards him.

The wire was from Marcus Droon, and had been handed in at Porthcawl, in Cornwall, that day. It baldly announced that the dead man's brother would arrive at Droon House at the earliest possible moment, and expressed a hope that the police had succeeded in apprehending the murderer.

'That will be done within the next twelve hours,' said Blake casually.

'Eh? What will be done within the next twelve hours?' growled Inspector Rawson.

'Everything,' assured the detective. 'The mystery will be solved; the murderer arrested, and the case closed.'

Coutts glanced sharply at his friend.

'You're holding something back, Blake,' he challenged. 'You've got something up your sleeve, and I suppose you'll keep it there until you feel like taking us into your confidence. Confound you for a human oyster! Where's that fellow Bellamy? I want a drink—and want it bad!'

'We differ, as usual,' smiled Blake. 'I want a drink—and want it good.'

Rawson tugged helplessly at his moustache.

'Marcus Droon seems to have a clear alibi,' he said slowly. 'That telegram was dispatched about the time Grubb was murdered.'

'If Droon himself sent the wire!' snapped Blake promptly. 'I'm going to try an experiment tonight,' he went on, suddenly switching the subject. 'I am hoping to stage a demonstration of the manner in which Lucien Droon was murdered, with Mrs Page as the potential victim.'

Coutts was the first to catch the gist of his words.

'You're going to get the woman to spend a night in the room where Droon was killed?'

'I am going to have a few words with Mrs Page,' replied Blake evasively, jumping briskly to his feet. 'Come to my room in half an hour's time, and I'll explain exactly what I intend doing tonight.'

* * *

Droon House was wrapped in silence and darkness, save for a solitary bulb that was glowing in the hall, and a narrow streak of light that gleamed beneath the locked door to the room in which Lucien Droon, Philip Roe, and Septimus Trull had been mysteriously stabbed to death.

Inspector Rawson and Coutts sat side by side in the wide, gloomy hall, sucking moodily at their pipes, and listening to the methodical ticking of the grandfather clock at the head of the stairs.

Their straining ears caught only those vague sounds audible in the dark hours of the night; the creak of joists and beams; the rattle of loose plaster in the walls; the squeaking of mice, and the sighing of wind in the ventilators.

On the floor above, a constable was posted outside Isabelle Page's bedroom. Occasionally he paced up and down, making certain that the doors to the other apartments along the passage were locked on the outside.

Two men patrolled the grounds, shivering in the cold night air, and grumbling that there was as yet no moon to lighten their task of keeping observation on the exterior of the big house.

Coutts stirred restlessly and uneasily in his chair. The uncanny nature of the series of murders had got on his nerves. He was indulging in wild fancies, visualising an eventual opening of the study door, to find Sexton Blake stretched on the floor, with a brass-handled dagger embedded in his back!

Another hour passed.

In the dark room, directly above the death-chamber where Sexton Blake was keeping his lonely vigil, a faint sound suddenly broke the heavy silence. It was the comfortless, plainly furnished room where Lucien Droon had slept previous to his death.

The noise was repeated—a slick click, too faint to reach the ears of the constable patrolling the corridor outside.

The pale beam of a flashlight stabbed the darkness of the room. It shone from within the massive, steel safe planted immovably against one wall.

Then the light was extinguished. The murderer of Droon House had crept stealthily from his strange hiding-place. His rubber-soled shoes made no sound as he glided across the floor to bolt the door that was already locked on the outer side.

Breathing evenly, he made for the window, reached up and lifted down the hollow, brass curtain-pole. He unscrewed the brass knobs at each end of the rod, and slipped a needle-pointed bar of steel into the hollow interior.

Resting the curtain-pole against the wall, he opened the window, knelt on the ledge, and fumbled beneath the canopy of the rolled sunblind overhead, drawing out, yard by yard, the snaking length of a light, silk rope-ladder.

The man was dressed entirely in black. He wore black gloves on his hands, and a black hood over his head. He was utterly invisible against the side of the house as he hung the metal curtain-pole round his neck by a loop of string which he tied to it, and lowered himself carefully down the dangling ladder.

*   *   *

Sexton Blake yawned, and stretched his cramped limbs. It was oppressively close behind the heavy curtain screening the deep alcove to one side of the fireplace in Lucien Droon's study.

A glance at the luminous dial of his watch showed him that he had been standing there for over two hours. Nothing had happened in the dimly lighted room, with its locked door and tightly shuttered windows—just as it had been when Lucien Droon had been struck down.

Blake kept his eyes glued to the two holes he had cut in the curtain. He was directly facing the massive writing-table at which was seated a realistic dummy figure made up to resemble Isabelle Page, who was sleeping safely in her room overhead. A dressmaker's dummy, a flaxen wig, and one of Miss Page's gowns—these were the raw materials of the deception which, viewed from the rear, was perfectly convincing in the light of the shaded lamp.

Only the shaded table-lamp was burning. Most of the room was in shadow; but Blake's eyes had grown accustomed to the subdued light. For the twentieth time he swept his gaze over the opposite wall, with its array of hunting trophies, native weapons, and snarling masks of long-dead wild beasts.

There was the mask of a tiger, that looked uncannily lifelike, also the grey head of an enormous African elephant, with upcurled trunk, yawning, red mouth, and gleaming ivory tusks.

Blake found something attractive in the big elephant's head. It was a remarkably fine specimen, and with its bristling tusks must have weighed a tidy few pounds.

'Darned thing must be fastened to the wall with eight-inch screw bolts,' mused the detective idly. 'Take a lot of shifting if anyone wanted to move it. Those tusks must be worth—'

Blake's muscles suddenly tautened. He rubbed his eyes and stared again. Was it only his imagination, or had he observed some sort of a movement right at the back of the elephant's gaping jaws?

His heart commenced to beat like a drum, and cold beads of perspiration broke out on his forehead. He was not mistaken—something queer was happening in the black recesses of the elephant's throat!

It was almost as if the dead brute's tongue was slowly poking into view. But it wasn't anything like a tongue. It more closely resembled the circular muzzle of a single-barrelled shotgun.

Blake was rigid and quivering with excitement. His throat was dry; his clutching hands threatened to rip the hanging curtain from its fastenings.

Click! Something flashed from the elephant's jaws and sped across the room like a streak of light. There was a dull thud, and a louder, heavier impact as the dummy figure in the guise of Isabelle Page lurched forward and sprawled across the surface of the writing-table.

The light from the table-lamp gleamed brightly on a brass-handled dagger buried to the hilt between the dummy's shoulders!

For the life of him Sexton Blake could never clearly remember exactly what happened during the next few minutes. He had a vague idea that he let rip a terrific roar of excitement as he sprang from his hiding-place to switch on all the lights and unlock the door, at which Rawson and Coutts were already wildly pounding.

Even as the detectives tumbled headlong into the room he darted across to the window, to unfasten the shutters and leap forth into the darkness.

He could hear a pounding of feet, a crashing of undergrowth, and the lusty voices of the two constables bawling excitedly to one another.

'There he goes! Head him off, Wilson!'

'Watch your step! He's doubled back again!'

'Careful, you darned fool! He's making for the other end of the garden!'

There was a splintering crash, and a volley of violent oaths as one of the constables tripped and tumbled headlong into a cucumber-frame.

'What in the devil's name is happening?' bellowed Coutts, as he soared ungracefully through the open window to immediately find himself entangled in the tenuous coils of some object that was dangling against the wall of the house.

Blake switched on his electric flashlight.

'A rope-ladder!' he gasped, as he concentrated the silvery beam on the silken coils that were wound around the inspector's head and shoulders. 'He came from the room overhead—Lucien Droon's bedroom!'

'Who?' spluttered Coutts, providentially saved from slow strangulation.

'The murderer!' snapped Blake. 'What's that you've found, Rawson?'

'Hanged if I know!' blurted the inspector, holding up a five-foot length of hollow metal. 'Looks like a curtain-pole to me.'

'It is, and it isn't!' exclaimed Blake triumphantly, after a hasty examination. 'It's the spring-gun we've been looking for!'

A dejected-looking constable, minus his helmet, and covered from head to foot with mud, brambles, and tree-mould, loomed out of the darkness.

'The fellow got clean away, sir!' he panted ruefully. 'Not a bit of good trying to find him in this infernal darkness!'

'Who was it?' barked Coutts.

'Dunno, sir. Only caught a glimpse of him dangling against the side of the house as Mr Blake opened the shutters. He was all in black, with a black mask over his face.'

Sexton Blake made a peculiar observation.

'Never mind,' he said casually. 'He'll come back later on. We can nab him then.'

Flashlight in hand, the detective scrambled actively up the slender rope-ladder. He had no difficulty in finding what he sought. In the wall of the house, half-screened by creepers, was an oblong aperture, where one of the bricks had been removed.

Another brick, slightly below the first, had been removed from the inner side of the hollow wall, directly behind the elephant's head that hung in Lucien Droon's study.

Blake found himself gazing through the mouth of the elephant, straight into the room beyond, and directly in line with the massive writing-table in the centre of the floor.

The mystery of the locked room was a mystery no longer. Here was the manner in which the murderous spring-gun had sent Droon, Philip Roe, and Septimus Trull to their deaths!

* * *

'All we've got to do now is to catch the murderer,' remarked Inspector Rawson, with a distinct note of sarcasm in his voice. 'I suppose you've got that already arranged, Mr Blake.'

It was half an hour later. The room above Lucien Droon's study had yielded its secrets—the dummy curtain-pole coiled in the sun blind, and the safe with the false back, beyond which was the secret chamber where the mysterious murderer of Droon House had lain in hiding.

It was no more than three yards square, and contained nothing save a mattress and blankets, a supply of food and water, two more of the cunningly devised, spring-handled daggers, and a pair of earphones, complete with batteries, which were connected with a dictaphone, cleverly concealed in a hanging lamp in the room below.

Everything pointed to a carefully planned murder plot, devised by a man who was both a mechanical and a criminal genius.

Blake glanced up from a close examination of sundry finger-prints he had discovered on a water-jug in the secret chamber.

'The same!' he exclaimed triumphantly. 'That clinches it! What was that you were saying, Rawson? Who is the murderer? Why—'

A bell pealed noisily through the house. They listened quietly as Bellamy went to open the door. The manservant uttered a startled exclamation that came clearly to the detective's ears.

'You—you gave me quite a shock, sir!' he was heard to say. 'Why, I thought at first that—'

A sharp rap, and the door opened.

'Mr Marcus Droon, gentlemen!' announced Bellamy.

The first thing that struck Blake—not unexpectedly—was the remarkable resemblance between the murdered man and his brother.

But Marcus Droon looked considerably older. His shoulders were stooped, his eyes sunken, and his hair almost white. In addition, he lacked his brother's careful consideration of attire and well-groomed appearance.

He wore a battered felt hat, a grey flannel shirt, baggy, shapeless tweeds, and clumsy brown brogues, thick with dried mud.

'Well, gentlemen, I hope you have caught the murderer,' was Marcus Droon's first remark.

'We have caught him,' said Sexton Blake simply. 'Close the door, Bellamy.'

Rawson and Coutts stared blankly at one another.

'You came by road, Mr Droon,' observed Blake pleasantly.

'I drove up in my own car,' admitted the man coolly.

'I know Porthcawl well,' smiled Blake. 'It possesses a distinctive clayish soil, which I notice you have recently trodden. A very clever touch, that.'

Blake made a sudden, lightning movement. There was a flash of steel and a metallic click. Marcus Droon staggered back, glaring fiercely at the handcuffs that encircled his wrists.

'There's your man, Rawson,' said Blake quietly. 'Watch him carefully. A cleverer criminal I have never come across—nor a more determined one.'

Rawson sprang to his feet, with a roar of excitement.

'I told you all along Marcus Droon was our man!' he declared triumphantly.

'You're wrong,' said Blake. 'Marcus Droon is dead—murdered by his own brother. Your prisoner is Lucien Droon.'

'*Lucien* Droon!' exploded Rawson and Coutts together.

'Exactly,' said Blake briskly. 'His real name is Rufus Carter. He is an escaped convict who has been at liberty for several years.

'Here are the bald facts. Ten years ago Rufus Carter was a big man in the engineering world, and trusted partner in a well-known firm of contractors. There was considerable sensation when he was arrested on a charge of embezzling many thousands of pounds. He was tried, found guilty, and sentenced to several years' penal servitude. The stolen money was never recovered. Carter had served only a few years of his sentence, when he managed to stage a successful escape from Parkmoor. He was never recaptured.'

'I remember the case,' muttered Coutts, rubbing his chin

thoughtfully. 'But what is all this leading to, Blake? Where do the murders come in? How did you learn?'

'One thing at a time,' interrupted Blake, staring grimly at the prisoner, who had sunk dejectedly into a chair, with his head resting in his manacled hands. 'I am going to assume that, after his escape from Parkmoor, Carter recovered the money he was supposed to have embezzled, went abroad for several years, and returned to this country in the name of Lucien Droon. He bought this estate through Sugden Sutton, the lawyer, and prepared to settle down in comfort and security for the remaining years of his existence.'

Blake paused.

'Then there came into Carter's life,' he said impressively, 'the menace of blackmail. His secret was known to several people. Separately and individually, they proceeded to bleed him of every penny he possessed, until, rendered desperate by these merciless extortions, Carter deliberately planned the series of murders that have been engaging our attention.'

Rufus Carter, alias Lucien Droon, suddenly straightened his back; as if throwing a great weight off his shoulders. His face was composed; the fires of defiance and desperation had died in his eyes.

'I give you best, Mr Blake,' he said resignedly. 'By heavens, I never dreamed you would discover the truth. By inviting you here I thought I was taking a step that would absolutely assure the success of my plan.

'You are absolutely correct in your details,' he went on, the others listening with rapt attention. 'I am Rufus Carter. After escaping from Parkmoor I went to America with the stolen money I had hidden. I made a small fortune in speculation on Wall Street, and returned to this country in the name of Lucien Droon.

'Certain people discovered my secret. How, it is not necessary to explain. You know their names. Septimus Trull was my valet in the old days. George Grubb was a client of mine, and Philip Roe a clerk in the office where I worked.'

'And Isabelle Page?' asked Blake.

'An adventuress, who was once known to me,' admitted Carter candidly. 'In less than a year I had been blackmailed of practically every penny I possessed. I was faced with ruin. In a moment of desperation I planned to exterminate the whole gang like a brood of vipers, after placing them under suspicion of causing my own death. My brother was necessary to that plan. It was essential that I should assume his identity in order to claim the insurance money, payable on my own demise.'

Coutts glared incredulously at the man.

'You cold-blooded devil!' he jerked. 'You deliberately killed your own brother because of the close resemblance between the two of you?'

Rufus Carter laughed shortly.

'My brother Marcus was the cold-blooded devil,' he corrected. 'He deserved to die. He was the biggest blackmailer of the lot. I had no compunction in killing him. I played on his sense of greed. I told him that Roe, Grubb, and the others were blackmailing me as well: thus preventing me from paying him what he demanded.

'I hinted that I had a plan that would enable me to turn the tables on them. He readily consented to help me, and without suspecting the truth, came up from Porthcawl prepared to assume my identity for a few hours.

'Like a fool he followed my instructions to the letter, locked himself in my study, and couldn't fail to discover the written message I had left lying on the desk. While he was reading it I thrust the spring-gun through the hole at the back of the elephant's head and killed him like the dog he was.'

Carter's eyes blazed in memory of the mental torture he had suffered.

'I killed Trull, and Philip Roe, in the same way,' he admitted quietly.

'George Grubb I shot from the window of my room, and I was only waiting my chance to dispose of Isabelle Page in the same manner.'

Never had the three detectives listened to such a cool, cold-blooded confession of wholesale, premeditated murder.

'May I smoke,' asked Carter. With his manacled hands he took a cigarette from his waistcoat pocket and placed it between his lips. Mechanically, Coutts gave him a light.

'Why did you leave that written message, hinting that proofs of your murderer's identity would be found in the room?' asked Inspector Rawson.

'To throw a scare into the four of them,' answered the prisoner promptly. 'I guessed that they would attempt to search the room, thinking that I had left evidence of the manner in which they had been blackmailing me. It was successful. It enabled me to use the spring-gun on Roe and Trull.'

'But confound it all,' exploded Coutts, 'how could you be in two places at once? You have just come up from Porthcawl by road. You sent a wire from there. The mud on your boots, that Mr Blake pointed out just now—'

'There is only one answer to that question,' enlightened Sexton Blake. 'Carter has an accomplice, who sent the wire from Porthcawl, and came up by car, bringing those clothes and the muddy boots with him. Carter met him on his arrival, changed, dismissed his accomplice, and came straight here, as if he had just arrived from Porthcawl.'

Rufus Carter nodded.

'Nothing escapes you, Mr Blake,' he said admiringly. 'I had an accomplice—a man I met in prison. He shall remain nameless. It was arranged that he should go to my brother's cottage at Porthcawl, as soon as my brother came to Droon House. He knew exactly what to do. My programme was scheduled almost to the minute; but I had expected to dispose of Isabelle Page several hours earlier. It is your turn, Mr Blake. How did you get on the right track?'

'Fingerprints,' said Blake briefly. 'After that, largely obvious deductions. From fingerprints on your hair-brushes I discovered that the Lucien Droon, who had used the brushes was actually Rufus Carter, an escaped convict. In that fact was the ostensible motive for blackmail.

'Then I was surprised to find that the fingerprints of the Lucien Droon who was dead—were not the same. The whole plot was clear to me from that moment.'

There was a long silence.

Rufus Carter smiled crookedly. There was a slight click as his teeth snapped down on the tiny capsule that was concealed in the end of the cigarette. Blake leapt towards him, grabbed him, and forced it open. But he was too late. The capsule had been swallowed, and the deadly cyanide did its work at once.

The murderer of Droon House had gone to join his victims.

'The case is closed,' said Sexton Blake quietly. 'Perhaps it's better it happened this way.'

SEXTON BLAKE SOLVES IT
Pierre Quiroule

Pierre Quiroule (r.n. Walter William Sayer, 1892–1982) was working as a counter-clerk in the Fleet Street branch of the Midland Bank just prior to the First World War, when he became aware that certain writers working in the popular fiction field were depositing, every month, nearly as much money as he was earning in a year. Sayer tried his hand and discovered that he could deliver what editors wanted. Not unnaturally, he left the Midland Bank. After the war he set up shop in an office in Fleet Street and began writing Blakes, mainly for the Sexton Blake Library. *The 60,000-worder suited him; it gave him the freedom to indulge himself in the kind of expansive plots featuring espionage and international intrigue—invariably starring his character 'Granite' Grant of the Secret Service, sometimes aided (often impeded) by the beautiful French spy Mme Julie—at which he undoubtedly excelled. It also gave full rein to his descriptive powers in the evoking of far-flung lands and exotic climes (usually mugged up in the St Bride's Library). Unlike his fellow toilers in the Blake field, he deliberately widened his sights, wrote newspaper features, scripted films for the Quota, and kept his eye constantly open for new markets to crack, although he did have a habit of rubbing employers up the wrong way. During the 1930s Dorothy L. Sayers, something of a Blake champion, was supervising the* Evening Standard *short story slot and Quiroule sold her the idea for a special Blake tale. The Amalgamated Press, as copyright holder, was not amused. But all was resolved, and here is that tale—the only Blake story to appear outside the Blake fold.*

As a rule Sexton Blake did not receive clients at Baker Street so early as half-past eight in the morning. Yet it was 8.30 to the minute on this particular morning when Brambleby arrived.

An altercation on the stairs, in which the voice of his devoted housekeeper Mrs Bardell, predominated, first attracted Blake's attention. He glanced up from his correspondence as the door flew open and his visitor precipitated himself into the room.

'Reckon that fe-male 'd take the bun an' all the currants in the chin-wagging stakes!' he announced gustily, and fell to puffing and blowing with noisy vehemence.

That 'fe-male' stood at the door with arms akimbo, horrific in her indignant disapproval.

'All right, Mrs Bardell,' said Blake in conciliatory tones. 'Please shut the door, Tinker. Thank you.'

His visitor ceased his boisterous respirations and eyed the criminologist with frank curiosity.

'Say, you're a tonic!' he observed appraisingly. 'Don't mind me—I'm a bit flustered. And these elderly fe-males always get my goat somehow. Guess you're this detective gink they call Sexton Blake?'

'You've guessed right, my dear sir.'

'And you're a feller of in-ter-national repute, as these writer guys put it?'

'Now you flatter me.'

'Reckon I don't. And I'm not trying. I like the cut of your phiz—it's sure good. Guess he'd be a soft clam who'd try to pull the wool over your eyes. Hiram Brambleby's not competing.'

'Then I'm to understand I'm addressing Mr Hiram Brambleby?'

'Sure thing—Hiram K. Brambleby, of Chicago. Reckon that address'll always find me. Waal, I'm honoured to meet a feller of in-ter-national repute. Shake?'

Sexton Blake gravely took the extended hand. 'A mutual privilage, Mr Brambleby,' he said, 'since by the brevity of your address your reputation must be at least as broadcast as my own.'

Hiram K. Brambleby tipped up his suitcase and firmly planted himself upon it.

'Waal, reckon they know the name of Hiram K. Brambleby in li'l ol' Chi,' he modestly admitted, then, glancing at his watch, added hastily: 'But there's no time to pass further compliments. Reckon I'll have to hustle some to catch that boat-train, and the taxi guy's ticking up the dollars outside.'

'Then I'm entirely at your service. Pray proceed.'

'Yep, I'm going to. Just a li'l question, mister—before I start. Have you seen the papers this morning?'

'I have,' nodded Blake.

'Lamp that li'l paragraph about a feller being stabbed to death in Sir John Pallyster's house last night?'

'I spotted it.'

'Good. That clears the line. Now listen, mister, and don't jam my transmission; there ain't time for us both to talk. Reckon it happened a couple o' weeks ago now. I was on the train coming through to Brussels—just having a li'l smoke in the corridor at the time—when I heard two ginks having a sort of argument in the carriage behind me. The door was partly open, so I couldn't help hearing something of it, not having my ears plugged with cotton-wool. Waal, I don't rightly know what the rumpus was about, but I remember hearing Sir John Pallyster's name mentioned, and the bone of contention appeared to be concerned with some letters written by a guy they called Captain Pallyster, whom I took to be some sort of relation of Sir John's. T'any rate, one of the ginks was contending that he hadn't had a square deal, and he was getting quite snuffy about it when the other suddenly closed the door and cut off my reception.'

Hiram K. Brambleby ceased abruptly, glanced at his watch, then jumped up and grabbed his suitcase.

'Reckon that's all,' he announced decisively. 'I'd forgot all about the matter until I lamped that li'l paragraph in the paper ten minutes ago. I was in the cab at the time, and I leaned forward and tapped on the window. "D'you know a detective gink who happens to be domiciled in these parts?" I asked. "Not 'arf I don't," ses the guy at the wheel. "Watcha call him?" I countered. "Sexton Blake's his monicker," he winks. "Sexton Blake it is," ses I, "and in double quick time." And—waal, reckon you've got the whole story now. And, having eased my conscience, so to speak, I guess I'll make a beeline for that boat-train.'

'Wait!' cried Sexton Blake, rising hurriedly from his chair.

But Brambleby did not wait. Already he was half through the door. He turned to make a final pronouncement.

'Hiram K. Brambleby of li'l ol' Chi, that's my address,' he declared. 'Reckon a postcard 'll always find me. So long, mister.'

And the door closed on him.

Blake turned and met an amused glance from his youthful assistant.

'Guess he's blown across from li'l ole 'Murrica right enough!' Tinker chuckled.

'Yes, a breezy character,' Blake remarked, and picked up the morning paper.

The tragedy to which Brambleby had referred was briefly reported as follows:

'Late last night a man named William Smith was stabbed to death in the library of Rookwood, the Sussex home of Sir John Pallyster, Bart. The circumstances of the crime, which is engaging the attention of the police, are entirely mystifying. It appears that the unknown assassin concealed himself in the library, and afterwards escaped without revealing a clue as to his identity.

'Sir John Pallyster has served a distinguished career in the diplomatic service. His only son, Captain Denvers Pallyster, was killed in the war, and the present Lady Pallyster is his second wife, whom he married a few years ago.'

'Not much to be got from that,' Blake observed. 'Get me the noon editions of the evenings directly they're out.'

'D'you think our American friend's story's got anything to do with the crime, guv'nor?' Tinker asked inquisitively.

'Haven't thought about it yet,' Blake answered shortly, and turned his attention to the interrupted correspondence.

The noon editions all splashed the 'Sensational Sussex Crime'. Blake took one of the papers that Tinker had just brought in and spread it open on his desk.

'Well, what d'you make of it, guv'nor?' asked Tinker, when Blake had carefully perused the double-columned report.

'Things appear to look a bit black against Sir John,' said Blake.

'That's what I thought, guv'nor. Seems to be in a very sticky position. Going to do anything about it?'

Blake struck a match and sucked in his cheeks. 'I think,' he observed inconsequentially, 'that this is precisely the opportunity to get in a round of golf. Yes,' he added, getting up, 'and we'll take Pedro with us—he can hunt for your lost balls!'

It was about an hour later that the Grey Panther purred up to the lodge-gates of Rookwood and Sexton Blake, in tweeds, alighted.

'Just run her on to the grass verge and wait there,' he told Tinker. And, approaching the gates, he pulled at the bell-handle.

Barker, the lodgekeeper, answered the summons.

'Sir John at home?' Blake inquired.

'He's up at the house, sir; but he ain't seeing nobody—not after what occurred last night.'

'I think he'll see me.'

'I think he won't, sir. Nobody to be admitted on any account, unless it's the police. Them's my orders.'

'Um-m!' murmured Blake, and abruptly observed: 'I notice you're limping.'

The lodgekeeper appeared momentarily startled. 'What d'you mean?' he demanded almost fiercely. 'I ain't limping, sir.'

'My mistake,' said Blake airily. 'Well, how long are you going to keep me waiting here?'

'I tell you,' began Barker, when the clatter of hoofs caused him to glance hurriedly over his shoulder. 'Here comes Sir John,' he muttered. 'Better stand out of the way, sir.' So saying he withdrew the heavy bolts and flung open the gates just as the two horsemen appeared round the bend in the drive.

Sir John Pallyster was a man of some three score years, erect of figure and with iron-grey hair and lean aristocratic face. He looked pale and careworn, and little pouches hung beneath his sombre eyes. Behind him, on a grey filly, rode his groom.

The baronet's gaze was fixed ahead as he rode through the gates. He would have passed Blake unheeded had not the latter deliberately placed himself in his path. With an angry exclamation the groom spurred forward to urge the intruder out of the way, but Blake was too quick for him. Grasping the stirrup iron, he stared up into Sir John's face.

'Sir John,' he said softly, 'I am interested in the letters of your son, the late Captain Denvers Pallyster.'

A sudden rush of colour mounted the baronet's face and as quickly faded away. He reined in his horse, flung himself from the saddle, and, throwing the reins to the surprised groom, stood eyeing his accoster with tightened lips and bleak, arrogant face.

'Shall we walk back, Sir John?' suggested Blake politely.

Without a word the baronet turned, and the two of them passed back through the entrance gates. The lodgekeeper had been a silent

441

witness of this puzzling encounter. As Blake passed him he muttered confidentially: 'Better nurse that foot, you know!'

Barker started violently, changed colour, and stood there staring after Blake in obvious perturbation.

Sir John strode on stiffly erect. After a brief silence Blake asked casually: 'How far are the links, Sir John? Hope to get in a little golf while I'm down here.'

The baronet stopped abruptly. 'Who are you?' he demanded, eyeing his companion with sombre, hostile eyes.

'Blake—just Mr Blake, at your service.'

'I don't know you, and I don't require your services. What d'you want?'

'The privilege of your hospitality for a few days, Sir John. Perhaps even one night would be enough for my purposes.'

The cool request caused a shade of doubt to cross Sir John's face. He stole a measuring glance at his companion.

'For your purposes!' he echoed. 'And pray what are your purposes? If you have come to blackmail me . . .'

'Don't mention that word,' sharply interrupted Blake. 'None must know. The crime that occurred last night in your library—it must be handled delicately. The police must not discover too much. Isn't that the position?'

Sir John swallowed and made an effort to preserve his composure.

'What exactly do you mean?' he demanded a trifle hoarsely. 'What business is it of yours?'

'I will be frank, Sir John. The letters written by your dead son must not become known. We must arrive at the ends of justice without dragging their contents into the glaring light of publicity. Tell me if I have divined your thoughts.'

As he heard these words Sir John seemed to waver. A gleam of hope sprang into his sombre eyes, but quickly faded.

'It is impossible,' he muttered. 'I don't know who you are, why you are here and what your motive is, but I say again it is impossible. You apparently know something, but you don't know all. And you must rely on no assistance from me. I cannot account for what occurred last night. The police must solve the mystery.'

'But they must not know anything about your dead son's letters, Sir John.'

'I tell you everything must come out in the end,' reiterated Sir John impatiently. 'How you discovered your information I don't know, but it is of no use to you now. You are only wasting my time.'

'Then let us waste no more time,' suggested Sexton Blake. 'Come, this is the way to the house I presume. You will surely not refuse to extend to me your hospitality for a night or so.'

For a moment Sir John hesitated, then with a shrug he strode on again.

Rookwood faced south-east and was invisible from the drive until one was almost upon it, for the wide avenue of elms swept in a complete half-circle from the lodge-gates to the house.

As the two came in sight of the imposing frontage, with its colonnaded terrace and facade of windows, Chief Inspector Bexley came hastening down the entrance steps. He saluted Sir John, cast a casual glance at his companion and jumped into the waiting car, which immediately drove off.

Ascending the broad flight of steps, Blake followed Sir John into the main hall, with its famous ceiling adorned with rich arabesque ornamentation. Outside a door over towards the right a sergeant and a couple of constables were hovering. They became immediately alert at Sir John's entry and subjected his companion to a covert scrutiny.

'Send Mr Lynton to me,' said Sir John to one of the footmen.

The butler came quickly in answer to the summons, and met his master with a glance of anxious inquiry.

'Mr Blake is staying here for a few days, Lynton,' said Sir John in cold, indifferent tones. 'See that he has every attention.'

'Very good, sir,' replied old Lynton, and, addressing himself to Blake, added: 'If you will come this way, sir.'

Sir John had turned abruptly away. Blake followed the butler up the wide curving staircase.

On the first floor landing he paused to glance out of the window—across the herbaceous borders and beautifully-kept lawns. A little to the left, rising among the trees, was the roof of a small outbuilding.

'What building is that?' he asked of Lynton.

'That's the pavilion, sir.'

'Anyone occupying it?'

'Oh no, sir. Very seldom used.'

'Then that'll suit me better, Lynton. We'll get along there right away.'

'But, sir,' the butler began to remonstrate, when Blake gave his arm a friendly squeeze.

'Got to get Sir John out of this little trouble somehow, eh?' he whispered confidingly.

Old Lynton's face was a study in conflicting emotions. He met Blake's steadfast gaze, hesitated, then muttered with suppressed excitement: 'He couldn't have done it, sir. It's a lie—an infernal lie!'

'Knew I could trust you, Lynton,' said Blake. 'Sure of it directly I saw your face. Bet we'll both make it our business to look after Sir John's interests. Let's get along to the pavilion, eh?'

'Certainly, sir, if you wish it. Anything you want, sir—just let me know.'

'I will. Relying on you, you know. Just one or two little questions. Did you see Mr William Smith last night?'

'I admitted him, sir.'

'Ever seen him before?'

'Not to my knowledge, sir.'

'Um-m! Can't tell me anything then? No little confidences to make, eh?'

The butler met Blake's questioning eyes and wavered irresolutely. Then suddenly he clapped his hands to his bald head with a distracted gesture.

'I can tell you nothing, sir,' he said desperately. 'My mind's all at sixes and sevens. I feel I shall go crazy.'

'No you won't,' Blake assured him. 'Must keep a cool head you know, to look after Sir John's interests. Relying on you.'

'I'll try to face it out, sir,' Old Lynton muttered.

'Of course you will.'

They had now reached the foot of the staircase.

'I'll have fires lit in the pavilion at once, sir,' the butler said. 'If you'll come along with me, sir, I'll . . .'

Blake laid a detaining hand on his arm.

'Leave you to attend to the pavilion,' he said. 'What time is the inquest?'

'At three o'clock, sir.'

'Huh! Have to hustle. Where's the body?'

'In the conservatory, sir. I'll show you the way.'

'Don't bother— I can find my way about. And the library— I know where that is. Got to get past that police barrage over there, eh? Right—you just attend to the pavilion.'

'I'll see to it now, sir.'

'And—I was forgetting—my car's just outside the gates, Lynton. Got a young friend in it. Also a dog—big fellow, but perfectly matey. Tinker's his name—the young chap I mean. Might just tell him I'll find him at the pavilion later.'

'I'll send word by the footman at once, sir.'

'Thanks. Well, I'll just toddle off to the conservatory—along the corridor there, eh? I'll be seeing you again.'

Old Lynton lingered momentarily to gaze after him.

'Don't I know a toff when I see one?' he told himself, and smoothed his bald head with the same nervous gesture.

The inquest was held in the billiard room at Rookwood. At five minutes to three that afternoon, Sexton Blake happened to be crossing the hall just as Sir John was passing.

'Pardon me, Sir John,' he said confidingly, 'but if you take my advice you'll say as little as possible at the inquest this afternoon. Thought I'd just mention it.' And, oblivious of the baronet's glassy stare, Blake continued his way to where the butler was hovering.

'Where's the billiard room, Lynton?' he asked.

'This way, sir.'

When they had gone a few yards along the corridor Blake stopped.

'That's all right,' he said. 'Just wanted to ask you a question or two. You remember admitting William Smith last night?'

'Yes, sir.'

'D'you remember his handing you his hat?'

'Yes, sir; it's in the conservatory.'

'I've seen it—hard black felt hat, eh?'

'That's right, sir.'

'And his gloves?'

'They're also in the conservatory, sir.'

'I've seen them, too. And his—well, what about his umbrella?'

'Didn't have an umbrella, sir. Carried a walking-stick. That's also in the conservatory.'

'Is it? Don't remember seeing it.'

The butler gave a slight start and thoughtfully rubbed his nose.

'Now you mention it, sir,' he said slowly, 'I recollect that I didn't take his stick. He wouldn't let me have it for some reason. Had it tucked under his arm when he entered the library.'

'H'm! Valuable stick evidently,' murmured Blake. 'Wouldn't let it go out of his hands. Thin sort of stick, Lynton—crooked handle with knobs on, eh?'

'No, sir; can't say it was. Thickish sort of handle and perfectly straight, as far as I can remember. Sure it hadn't any knobs on it.'

'Um-m! thickish sort of handle, was it! Made of ebony, eh?'

'Don't think it was made of ebony, sir. Seemed more like cane.'

'Rather a stout cane, Lynton—perfectly round and smooth?'

'Yes, that's how I should describe it, sir.'

'And he took it into the library with him?'

'Yes, sir.'

'H'm! It's not in the library now. Did the police find it?'

'I'm sure they didn't, sir. But it's funny it should have disappeared.'

'Very odd,' agreed Blake. 'Might have a search for it—not now, after the inquest. One other question. That bowler hat—quite sure it was the one you took from Mr Smith?'

'Positive, sir.'

'Huh! Well, we'd better be toddling along to the billiard-room. One little word of advice. Don't let 'em rattle you, Lynton. Just answer yes or no. A wise head keepeth a still tongue, eh?'

'I understand, sir.'

'You understand everything, Lynton.'

The jury was already assembled in the billiard room—local tradespeople mostly, with a goodly sprinkling of villagers: all as much impressed at seeing the interior of the great house for the first time as by the gravity of the occasion.

The coroner entered at that moment and took his seat. After him came Chief Inspector Bexley and other police officers, followed a moment later by Sir John Pallyster, whose pale aristocratic face was sphinx-like in its fixity of expression.

After the usual preliminaries the coroner opened the proceedings and the room hushed into silence. In a few formal words he outlined the nature of the inquiry, then the jury, with solemn faces, filed out to view the body. On its return Sir John Pallyster was called on to give evidence.

'Mr Smith,' he said, 'came to see me last night at nine o'clock about a private business matter. During the course of our conversation I had occasion to leave him to go into the study adjoining the library. That must have been a little before half-past nine. When I came out a few moments later I found Mr Smith lying on the floor dead. I immediately telephoned the doctor and the police.'

The baronet ceased his brief recital and there followed a momentary silence. Then the coroner asked:

'You can give us no further information, Sir John?'

'I have no further statement to make,' replied the baronet in cold tones.

'You cannot tell us anything more about the dead man?' the coroner insisted.

'Only that he introduced himself to me as Mr William Smith,' said Sir John, and sat down.

The coroner appeared a trifle disconcerted, then with a shrug nodded to Dr Talgath. The latter stated briefly that there was no doubt of the cause of death. The deceased had been stabbed twice with a sharp-pointed weapon and the second blow had penetrated the heart, causing death instantly.

After that Sergeant Coleman described the finding of the body on the floor of the library, and his evidence was supported by Constable Derne. It was then that Chief Inspector Bexley warmed up the inquiry. Carefully removing from a piece of paper a jewelled-hafted dagger, he held it up for inspection and, turning to the coroner, said quietly:

'This, sir, was the weapon with which the crime was committed. With your permission, sir. I will call upon Mr Lynton, the butler, to answer a few questions.'

The coroner nodded and Bexley proceeded.

'Do you recognise this dagger, Mr Lynton?' he asked.

The butler's face was drained of colour. It was evident that he was bracing himself to face a dreadful ordeal. And while he hesitated, trembling with indecision, Sir John broke in harshly.

'I use it as a paper-knife,' he said. 'It was given me by a distinguished Italian nobleman.'

The silence that followed this utterance was broken by the

remonstrative voice of the coroner.

'I must ask you please not to interrupt the witness, Sir John,' he said, and nodded to Bexley to continue.

'When did you last see this dagger, Mr Lynton?' asked the inspector.

'Last night,' muttered Lynton, almost inaudibly.

'And was it then thrust in the body of the dead man?'

'Yes.'

'Is this knife generally lying on the escritoire in the library?'

'Yes.'

'Was it lying there yesterday?'

'Yes.'

'And did you see this dagger, when you entered the library at nine o'clock last night to announce Mr William Smith?'

'Yes.'

'Was the knife lying on the escritoire then?'

Old Lynton hesitated. He seemed like a hunted animal brought to bay.

'Was this dagger lying on the escritoire when you entered the library at nine o'clock last night?' insisted the inspector.

'No—not exactly,' muttered Lynton.

'Not exactly! Then where precisely was it?'

A long pause followed before the butler muttered in a hoarse, gasping voice: 'Sir John had it in his hand.' And with that old Lynton uttered a sob of anguish and collapsed in his seat.

An intense silence followed this dramatic disclosure, and all eyes strayed towards Sir John. The latter's face, however, remained utterly immobile as if chiselled in stone.

'I should like to call one more witness, sir, if I may,' said Bexley. 'I should like to ask Lady Pallyster a question.'

Sir John sprang to his feet, his eyes suddenly blazing with anger. 'What is this?' he demanded. 'What has my wife to do with the matter?'

The coroner raised a remonstrative voice. 'I must ask you to keep silent, please, Sir John.' He glanced around, and asked: 'Where is Lady Pallyster? Someone please fetch her.'

Presently Lady Pallyster came into the room—a slim, girlish figure, her sleek raven head accentuating the strange pallor of her face. From the dark rings under her eyes it was evident that she had spent a sleepless night.

After she had been sworn, Chief-inspector Bexley continued his evidence. Taking out a white silk pocket-handkerchief, he displayed on it a number of obvious bloodstains.

'I would like to ask Lady Pallyster,' he said, 'if she remembers embroidering these initials in the corner here?'

Lady Pallyster's hand fluttered to her heart. She answered in the affirmative with an almost imperceptible nod.

'And will your ladyship please say whose initials they are?' asked Bexley.

'My husband's,' came the trembling reply, and with a little hysterical cry Lady Pallyster fainted away.

When Lady Pallyster had been supported from the room and order had been restored, Bexley continued.

'I will explain the circumstances in which this handkerchief came into my possession, sir. At the moment that William Smith was stabbed last night it appears that the library door and all the windows were fastened on the inside. The casement window of the little study adjoining the library, however, I found unfastened, and on the stone path immediately below that window I found a spot of blood. Further along, at the door leading to the servants' quarters, I found another spot of blood, and I found a third bloodspot on the landing of the stairs leading up from that doorway. Close by stood the linen basket, inside which I discovered this bloodstained handkerchief.'

Bexley paused to let this significant statement sink in before adding: 'The evidence of those bloodspots seems to suggest that the person who left them behind last night climbed out of the study window walked along the stone path to the servants' entrance, went up the stairs and wiped his hands on this soiled handkerchief in the linen basket. With your permission, sir, I will ask Sir John Pallyster how the cuff of his shirt came to be smeared with blood last night?'

Even the coroner gasped at this question. In the stilly silence that followed Sir John was heard to mutter: 'I refuse to answer the question.'

Chief Inspector Bexley nodded noncommittally and sat down

amid a breathless silence. The drift of his damning evidence had been only too apparent. The coroner shifted uneasily, seeming at a loss how to proceed, his respect and regard for the baronet making his task all the more irksome to him. And at this juncture Sexton Blake rose from his seat.

'Have I your permission, sir,' he asked, 'to put a question to the previous witness?'

The coroner turned to him with obvious relief, glad at this unexpected refuge from his embarrassment.

'What is your name?' he asked.

'Sexton Blake, sir.'

'Proceed then, Mr Blake.'

'Did the deceased man leave a hat behind him, inspector?' asked Blake.

'Yes,' nodded Bexley.

'Was it a hard black felt hat?'

'Yes—a black bowler hat. Here it is,' Bexley held it up.

'What size is that hat?' asked Blake.

'Six and seven-eighths.'

'And what size in hats did the dead man take?'

'Six and seven-eighths.'

'You have measured his head?'

'I have.'

'No doubt then about that bowler hat having belonged to the dead man?'

'He left it behind him—what doubt can there be?'

'I'm asking you. However, d'you think that's a new hat?'

'I don't. Seen a bit of wear—but it's good quality.'

'Just so. It's evidently been worn a long time, and therefore has settled down to the shape of the wearer's head. From its shape could you say whether the wearer was brachycephalic or dolichocephalic?'

'What?' queried the inspector.

'Perhaps the doctor can help us?' suggested Blake.

'You mean whether he was short-headed or long-headed?' said Doctor Talgath.

'That's it,' nodded Blake.

The doctor took the hat and examined it. 'I should say the wearer

450

was rather inclined to be dolichocephalic, that is, long-headed,' he murmured at length.

'So should I,' agreed Blake, and asked of Bexley: 'Then how d'you account for the fact that the dead man in the billiards-room is brachycephalic or short-headed?'

Bexley remained silent, frowning with some perplexity. Blake turned again to the doctor.

'One other question,' he said. 'If a man were stabbed twice, doctor, could you tell merely from the wounds whether the same weapon had been used on both occasions?'

'Of course,' assented the doctor.

'Then how is it,' asked Sexton Blake with slow emphasis, 'that you've omitted to mention the fact that the first blow struck at that dead man was not delivered with the Italian dagger which Sir John uses as a paper-knife?'

Blake sat down amid a silence in which the proverbial pin might have been heard to drop. Then someone clapped his hands in sheer nervous tension, and immediately there came a swelling murmur of applause. The coroner strove vainly to assert his authority, then took the opportunity to adjourn the inquest for further medical evidence.

In the hubbub and confusion that followed, Sir John Pallyster, with that same sphinx-like expression on his face, walked swiftly from the room. Blake was following after him when his arm was grasped from behind. It was his assitant, Tinker.

'A great performance, guv'nor!' he muttered. 'Got 'em completely stumped.'

'Bit stumped myself at the moment,' Blake admitted, and glanced at his watch. 'Be outside the study window with Pedro at six o'clock,' he said, and Tinker left him with a nod.

Along the corridor Blake found the butler hovering in wait. The old servant's eyes were suspiciously moist. Blake dropped a friendly arm on his shoulder. 'Bet we'll get him out of this mess somehow, eh?' he muttered confidingly.

Old Lynton was almost too affected to speak. 'If you'd only make use of me, sir,' he choked, 'let me help in some way . . .'

'So we will, Lynton. Let's get out of the way of the traffic. This'll do. That walking-stick—had a look for it in the library?'

'Not yet, sir. I was just going . . .'

'Right. Don't suppose you'll find it there. But if you do, just hand it to me and say nothing. Understand?'

'I understand, sir.'

'Good.' Blake nodded and sauntered off. The butler stood gazing after him with his face transfigured with hero-worship.

The french windows of the library were in the centre of the north-east wing of Rookwood, with the casement window of the study further along at the north-west extremity. At six o'clock Blake found Tinker waiting there with Pedro. On the stone path beneath the study window stood an upturned flower-pot, placed there by the police. Blake lifted it aside, revealing a brown splotch of blood. He took the lead from Tinker's hand.

'What's this, boy?' he whispered. 'Good fellow—have it then!'

The bloodhound bristled excitedly, snuffed at the brown stain, circled round for a moment, then moved off the stone path on to a gravel walk that ran away from the house.

'Won't do, boy,' muttered Blake, and he dragged the reluctant animal round the corner to the rear door that led to the servants' quarters. A second upturned flowerpot stood there, and beneath it another of those brown splotches. The bloodhound suddenly ceased to hold back. This time he required only a momentary snuff at the spot to pick up the scent. It took him through the door and up the narrow stairs, which they ascended step by step.

They reached the landing above, with Pedro still hot on the scent. In the corner stood the linen basket and close by it a third upturned flower-pot at which Pedro snuffed momentarily, then, ignoring the linen basket, made for a second flight of stairs.

'Um-m! New departure' muttered Blake to Tinker.

At the head of the second flight of stairs Pedro, still snuffing eagerly, entered a wide corridor joining with the main staircase and dragged Blake along it. Presently he paused, snuffed about the carpet, came back a few paces snuffed to right and left then pawed excitedly at a closed door.

Blake dragged the dog away just as the door opened and a woman peered anxiously out. It was Lady Pallyster. A little cry escaped her as she half recoiled and a pink envelope fluttered from her hand to the floor. Blake stooped and picked it up, glancing momentarily at the address.

'I beg your pardon, Lady Pallyster,' he said, handing it back to her. 'Pray don't be alarmed—there's nothing to fear.'

He turned away without further remark, dragging Pedro with him. At the head of the stairs Blake thrust the lead into Tinker's hand.

'Take him down again,' he said. 'I'll join you in a few moments outside the study windows.'

Blake met the butler as he was descending the main staircase, and drew him aside.

'Looking for you,' he said. 'Just a little personal question. Shan't mind if you don't answer. Her ladyship happy—on good terms with Sir John? You know—domestic bliss?'

The butler remained silent.

'Just so,' murmured Blake. 'I understand. Another little question: ever heard of Major Christopher Waddon?'

'He's Lord Mordon's nephew, sir. Lives at the Manor about a mile distant.'

'Often round here, Lynton?'

'Not so much of late, sir.'

'Just so. Dashing young fellow I suppose, Lynton? Rather a kill with the ladies, eh?'

Again the butler maintained a significant silence.

'Just so,' nodded Blake. 'That's all for the present, Lynton.'

Outside on the path below the study window Blake rejoined Tinker and Pedro.

'He still wants to go off there along that gravel walk, guv'nor,' said Tinker.

'Huh! That makes two coincidences,' Blake grunted. 'So neither the study window nor the linen basket have much bearing on the mystery. Appearances are certainly deceptive.'

'What d'you mean?' Tinker questioned.

'Ask Pedro,' said Blake. 'He's itching to tell us. Give me the lead. Now, off we go.'

The gravel walk slanted away almost at right angles from the stone path bordering the house. It led them straight on through a gap in the shrubbery, past flower beds and herbaceous borders, to enter presently a thick clump of acacias, where it was almost lost. But Pedro seemed quite sure of the scent. It was evident that he was picking up those spots of blood at frequent intervals.

On emerging the path widened again and ran across the open park until it reached the lake, shimmering like burnished steel in

453

the gathering darkness. The lake narrowed in the centre, where it was spanned by a wooden bridge, to which the path they were following led directly. Suddenly Blake stopped, dragging back Pedro.

'So that's it!' he exclaimed. 'Look, Tinker—straight ahead beyond the lake. They're the entrance gates, with the elm-lined avenue sweeping away on our right in a half-circle. D'you get the idea? This path we've been following is a short cut from the house to the lodge-gates—saves going all the way round by the main drive.'

'So it does,' Tinker agreed. 'But what does it signify?'

'Why, that the fellow who dropped those spots of blood must have been taking this short cut from the house to the lodge-gates. However, we'll see what more Pedro can tell us. Off you go, boy!'

Eagerly straining on the lead Pedro made for the bridge, pulled Blake half-way across it, and there suddenly seemed to get fuddled, for he snuffed about him in evident anxiety and doubt, then decided to go back. Blake, however, dragged the hound across the bridge, hoping that he would pick up the scent on the other side. But it was no use, Pedro was obviously stumped. He pulled back on to the bridge, and there again found the scent.

'Funny thing,' Blake remarked, 'those spots of blood either started or ended on the bridge here according to Pedro. Hullo! handrail broken away.' He stopped to make a closer scrutiny, and added: 'And quite recently, too—curious!'

For a moment he stood meditating. 'Pity it's dark,' he muttered. 'However, let's see what we can find. Just take hold of Pedro.'

Blake came off the bridge, stooped to the soft earth at its immediate foot, and proceeded to search about with the aid of his torch.

'Plenty of imprints of iron-studded boots,' he ruminated. 'Coming and going, too. They're obviously Barker's. Ah! What's this? A more elegant footprint—see, Tinker! And coming from the house only. Wait here a moment.'

Tinker watched his master hasten across the bridge, saw him stooping about on the other side, searching with his torch. Presently he came back.

'None over there,' he said shortly. 'The owner of those elegant boots seems to have come as far as the bridge and no further. He was in the deuce of a hurry, too, by the shape of them. We're getting on, Tinker, my lad. Take Pedro back to the pavilion—he can't help us any more—and join me outside the french windows of the library. That's where we've got to have another look for those elegant footprints.'

Tinker obeyed—and asked no questions. He couldn't quite see how Blake was 'getting at it', but was prepared to take his word for it.

Rapidly retracing his steps, Blake presently arrived at the spot where the gravel walk joined the stone path surrounding the house. And at that moment Barker came round the corner from the servants' entrance and almost collided with him. So startled was the lodgekeeper that he stood gaping at Blake.

'Better get a move on, with that little pink missive,' Blake advised him. 'Her ladyship'll be wanting an answer.'

Furtively Barker slipped the envelope out of sight and sidled past.

'Stop!' said Blake. 'There's a shorter cut to the lodge gates than by going down the drive. This way—along this little gravel walk and across the lake.'

Barker drew back; a hunted look sprang into his eyes. 'Curse you! I won't go that way,' he snarled. 'It was an accident—he stuck me in the foot and I hit out at him.'

'Enough!' Blake interrupted him. 'You keep a still tongue, my son. I'll call on you when I want your evidence. Now, just toddle off with that letter.'

Barker slunk off without another word.

When Tinker joined his master a few moments later, Blake was groping about behind the shrubbery that fronted the french windows of the library.

'Found 'em,' he muttered, thrusting the torch back into his pocket. 'Nothing more to be done tonight, my lad.'

'You've found what?' Tinker asked.

'The imprints of Mr Elegant Boots,' said Blake.

'And what's the next move?'

'Probably a very early morning dip in the lake,' was Blake's cryptic reply.

A pale, insipid dawn was breaking as the leaking derelict of a punt pushed out across the waters of the lake. Slowly it approached the wooden bridge with its broken handrail, crept into its shadow and hovered there beneath. Blake leaned on the long pole, glancing around.

'There's Mr Elegant Boots,' he muttered suddenly, and eased his ancient craft a little further along.

The body was scarcely visible—sunk in a rank growth of weed and wedged against the sheet of wire netting through which the water was draining.

'Catch hold of him,' Blake muttered to Tinker, and still looked about him. 'Ah, here's our missing walking-stick,' he said a moment later, and reached for it.

From the stout cane there protruded at the ferrule a thin stiletto blade. Blake pressed the catch in the handle and the blade slipped back into its cane sheath.

'Hold on to him tightly,' he warned Tinker, and pushed gently on the pole.

They dragged the swollen body on to the bank, and Blake dropped on his knees beside the drowned man. In one of the pockets he found a little packet of sodden letters still tied with a pink ribbon. He seized them eagerly, glanced briefly through them and climbed to his feet.

'Leave him there, Tinker,' he said. 'The police can take care of him. I have an urgent appointment with Sir John. You go and get some breakfast.'

Entering the hall of Rookwood some few minutes later, Blake encountered old Lynton. 'Afraid it's a bit early to bother Sir John,' he observed, 'but if you'd be good enough to announce me I'd like a word with him.'

'This way, sir,' said the butler.

They found Sir John Pallyster sitting huddled in his own apartment at the end of the corridor. He had evidently not slept in his bed. Blake carefully closed the door on old Lynton.

'Sorry to trouble you at this early hour, Sir John,' he said, 'but I thought you'd like to have this little packet of letters. Apart from you, there's only myself who knows of their existence—the other two fellows are dead. And you can rely on me to forget all about them.'

Sir John took one brief glance at the letters and, with a stifled sob, rose tremblingly to his feet.

Sexton Blake hastily opened the door. 'Perhaps if you can spare a moment to come down in the library after breakfast,' he added, 'you'll be interested to know just what happened there the night before last.' And he closed the door behind him.

Pedro came fawning on his master as the latter entered the pavilion. Blake stroked the dog's ears. 'Coffee,' he sniffed. 'Smells good, Tinker!' He thoughtfully filled his pipe. 'The problem is,' he ruminated, 'to reveal to the police the truth by suppressing a part of it.'

'Don't follow your meaning, guv'nor,' said Tinker.

'What! Haven't you got it yet?' Blake asked.

'I'm blowed if I have!'

'Then let's go over it,' suggested Blake, dropping into the camp-chair. 'Our American friend, Brambleby, was right, of course—it was blackmail. Sir John confirmed that on my first encounter with him. That, of course, gave me an advantage over the police.'

'Don't see it,' declared Tinker. 'They didn't tumble to the evidence of that bowler hat, nor that William Smith wasn't stabbed the first time with the Italian dagger.'

'William Smith wasn't stabbed, he was drowned,' corrected Blake, and as Tinker stared his surprise he added: 'But we'll start at the beginning. At nine o'clock on Tuesday night William Smith, whose real name is probably not quite so English, is shown into the library. He has left his hat and gloves behind with the butler, but has clung tightly to his walking-stick. He gets down to business with Sir John at once, and shows him the letters written by his dead son.

'Sir John agrees to pay him his price, and goes into the study adjoining to write out a cheque. While he is in there William Smith hears someone prowling outside, unlocks the french windows and comes face to face with Mr Short-Head—the fellow who was quarrelling with him on the train, who hasn't had a square deal according to Brambleby's story, and who has followed him down to Rookwood.

'What does William Smith do? Instinctively he presses the catch of his sword-stick and impulsively sticks Mr Short-Head in the stomach. Short-Head collapses, and Long-Head—alias William Smith—snatches the Italian dagger from the escritoire and finishes him off with it, then beats it through the french windows, which lock automatically on the inside as he closes them behind him.

'Sir John then appears from the study—probably having heard some noise, but not knowing what has happened. On the floor lies Mr Short-Head with the dagger stuck in his breast. Sir John's first thought is for his dead son's letters. He feels in the dead man's pockets for them, getting that smear of blood on his shirt cuff, but can't find them. They have mysteriously vanished. Sir John is puzzled. Even if he recognises that the dead man is not William Smith, he can't account for it. And still clinging to the hope that he can recover those letters, he keeps silent.

'Meanwhile William Smith has plunged across the flower-beds, where I found his elegant footprints, and emerged on the gravel walk, making a beeline for the lodge-gates. On the bridge across the lake he collides with Barker, and in the mêlée his sword-stick, which he has forgotten to sheathe, gets stuck in Barker's foot. Barker doesn't like it and cracks him over the head with his cudgel. William Smith topples over into the lake, breaking the handrail.

'Barker is carrying a letter from Major Waddon to Lady Pallyster. He feels a bit panicky and limps off to the house, dropping spots of blood on the way, goes straight up to Lady Pallyster's room, still leaving spots of blood behind him, and tells her his incoherent story. She implores his silence—afraid that her little flirtation with Waddon will be discovered. She binds up Barker's foot, carelessly using one of her husband's handkerchiefs to staunch the blood. That bloodstained handkerchief Barker just as carelessly drops in the linen basket as he passes it on his way down.'

Blake paused in his recital to suck reflectively at his pipe before adding: 'And that's about all, Tinker. As I said, we've now got to reveal the truth by suppressing a part of it.'

'What part of it, guv'nor?' Tinker asked.

'Lady Pallyster's little flirtation with the dashing Major Christopher Waddon,' said Blake, 'and also any reference to those letters written by the late Captain Denvers Pallyster to the beautiful Mme Sylvestre.'

'Who the dickens is she?'

'The fascinating Mme Sylvestre,' replied Sexton Blake, 'was shot by the French during the war as a spy. Those letters reveal that she had got Sir John's son in her toils; that in his infatuation he disclosed to her information that would have branded him as a traitor to his country. However, you can straightaway forget all about that, my lad. Just pass me the coffee-pot!'

SELECT BIBLIOGRAPHY

The stories in this volume were originally published as follows:

Union Jack

1110 *The Treasure of Tortoise Island*, 17 January, 1925
1379 *The Green Jester*, 22 March, 1930
1512 *The Four Guests Mystery*, 8 October, 1932

Detective Weekly

8 *The Box of Ho Sen*, 15 April, 1933
20 *The Man I Killed*, 8 July, 1933
51 *The House of the Hanging Sword*, 10 February, 1934

Sexton Blake Annual

The Secret Amulet, 1940
Under Sexton Blake's Orders, 1941

Evening Standard

Sexton Blake Solves It, 23 November, 1936

Those who wish to relive their youth and those who'd like to know more about not only the *Union Jack* and the *Sexton Blake Library* but also the *Magnet, Gem, Nelson Lee* and other papers of 50 or 60 years ago, may be interested in *Collectors' Digest*—edited by Eric Fayne, Excelsior House, 113 Crookham Road, Crookham, Near Aldershot, Hampshire GU13 ONH—which is issued monthly and deals with the world of Sexton Blake, Greyfriars, Billy Bunter, Cliff House, St Frank's, Morcove, Nelson Lee, St Jim's, Rookwood and a multitude of other nostalgic delights.

ACKNOWLEDGEMENTS

My thanks to the following for their help, at one time or another, and enthusiasm: Derek Adley, Bill Bradford, John Bridgwater, Mary Cadogan, Chris Harper, Bill Lofts, Horace Owen, the late Josie Packman, Dr Malcolm Scott, the late Geoffrey Wilde, and Norman Shaw, doyen of dealers, who's pushed more than a few choice items my way over the years.

J.A.